THE COMPLETE MIDNIGHT HARBOR SERIES

SECRETS DRENCHED IN BLOOD

USA TODAY BESTSELLING AUTHOR

NIKKI ST. CROWE

Cover Design by Opulent Designs
Proofreading by Jane Beyer

Content Warning

Some of the content in this book may be triggering for some readers.

Graphic rough sex, graphic violence, graphic language, bondage, submission, blood play/blood drinking, spanking/punishment, control/obedience, death of parents (off page)

Please visit Nikki's website for a full list of content warnings in all of her work.

https://www.nikkistcrowe.com/content-warnings

Author Note

SECRETS DRENCHED IN BLOOD is a complete collection of books 1 - 5 of the MIDNIGHT HARBOR SERIES (aka *HOT VAMPIRE NEXT DOOR*)

This omnibus collection includes the following books:

- Hot Vampire Next Door: Book One
- Hot Vampire Next Door: Book Two
- Hot Vampire Next Door: Book Three
- Hot Vampire Next Door: Book Four
- Hot Vampire Next Door: Book Five

BOOK ONE

ONE

I was two years old the first time I had dinner with a vampire.

My mother loved to tell the story of how I threw mashed potatoes on the crisp black button-up shirt of Julian Locke.

"I was embarrassed at first," Mom would say, "but then, when that man took his shirt off to soak the buttery stain, oh boy." At this point, Mom loved to fan herself for dramatic effect. "I was grateful to you, Jessie-girl. So damn grateful."

Every family member that's come before me has bound themselves to the Locke Vampire House since the early 1800s when the treaty between mortals and supernaturals was signed. By binding ourselves to them, once we're of age, our veins are like a 24-hour juice bar.

There are rules, of course.

1. A vampire shall not pierce the flesh of a mortal without their permission.

2. A vampire shall not enter the dwelling of a bound mortal without their permission.

3. A vampire shall not drain a mortal's veins.

No one wants an empty 24-hour juice bar, so it's really in everyone's best interest that they only take what they need.

I've lived in Midnight Harbor my entire life, so I've always been surrounded by the things that go bump in the night.

Though supernatural creatures coexist in Midnight, it's not without its drama.

The vampires hate the wolves *obviously*.

The witches are extremely protective of their virgins, but the vampires love to sink their teeth into an innocent every now and then.

And the shifters will throw an absolute tantrum if the witches cast spells near their territory. Apparently, witch magic to a shifter nose can stink up a house for a week.

And the fae just want to go back to the faerie realm but can't, so they're disgruntled about being permanently displaced and cut off from their family and their courts.

The humans are split on their opinions of the supernaturals. Except for me. My opinion is very clear. I plan to leave Midnight Harbor to escape the supernatural world.

When you turn twenty-one, you're legally required to pledge yourself to a House, and my birthday is right around the corner. It's expected that I'll pledge to the Lockes, but I don't want to be a blood bag.

Not that I want to be some shifter's mate. And I certainly don't want to be a virgin for the rest of my life. Though I'm not even sure I'd qualify at this point. I know how to take care of my own pleasure, and I have the toy collection to prove it.

What I *want* is a normal life. Somewhere out in the world where I'm not required to tap a vein like a juice box.

"Jessie," my boss says. "Did you hear me?"

"Huh?"

Rita frowns at me. Her dark braids are wound up in a knot on top of her head. Giant emeralds hang from her earlobes. Perfect winged eyeliner accentuates her big almond eyes. She smells like spices and incense.

Rita is a witch and a powerful one at that. She owns the Magic Coffee Shop and was kind enough to give me a job last year when I begged and pleaded.

"I said I'm leaving for the day, but if you need anything, holler. I'm just gonna be home working on spells."

"Okay, have fun. Don't sacrifice too many virgins!"

She chortles as she pushes through the front door. "Oh darling," she says over her shoulder, "everyone knows sacrificing a virgin is bad luck!"

After Rita's gone, and with the place empty, I busy myself with cleaning and restocking. I may not be the most proficient barista, but what I lack in coffee-making skills, I more than make up for in organization. There's just something about matching labels and boxes lined up on shelves and full canisters that makes my heart sing. Sometimes I can't relax until a place is cleaned and organized.

Rita had me help her move some boxes in her house last month, and when I saw her apothecary room, I almost keeled over. It was like a pack of rabid dogs ran through there. Spoiled toad's stool and blackening mugroot. Peeling labels and empty containers.

My fingers itched just looking at that room.

"Don't judge me on my messes," Rita said when she caught me wide-eyed in the doorway. "Every Hallow's Eve, I make a vow to be cleaner and more organized, and every year I break it."

"Then let me help you straighten up," I said. "Please dear god."

She agreed, though I've yet to get an invitation back.

The bell above the door jingles, and I call out from the stock room. "Be right out!"

I set aside the box of coffee filters and smooth down my Magic Coffee apron before heading out to the front.

When I see who's at the counter, the air freezes in my throat.

Bran Duval.

Black sheep of the Duval vampire family.

And also my neighbor.

Blood floods my face when he turns his heavy gaze on me. He's caught me peeping in his windows more than once. I can't help it if my second-story bedroom window looks in on his bedroom window. And he never shuts his blinds.

I saw him naked just last night and part of me wonders if he lingered in the square of his window just to give me a show.

He drives me mad.

I've had more than one hate-sex dream about him.

In fact, I'm having one right now.

Crap.

Gelatin cake.

Gelatin cake.

You don't grow up in a town of supernaturals without learning the lesson of guarding your scent, especially when you're feeling horny.

My best friend Sam and I decided early on that in order to stop lusting after the supernaturals, we'd think of gelatin cake. The old-fashioned kind, shaped like a loaf with the gross meat pieces suspended inside.

I get sick to my stomach just thinking about it. And as soon as I have that image firmly burned in my mind, I feel my body unwind and settle.

I can totally do this.

Be cool. Be cool.

"Hey," I say as I come behind the counter.

Bran's black hair is messy and wet like he just got out of the shower. He's wearing his usual: black t-shirt and jeans, black boots. Everything about Bran is dark and a little dangerous. Even in a town of supernaturals, he's not the type you'd want to bring home to Mom.

"That boy is trouble," my sister said when she watched him move in next door. "If I had a choice and the means, we'd be moving right now."

"Did you call him a boy?" I'd said. "He's several hundred years old."

"Well, he looks like a boy, so that's what I'm calling him. It makes me feel better."

Bran was turned into a vampire when he was twenty-ish years old. He may be one of the oldest in town, but he's one of the youngest in appearance. It somehow makes him more menacing. Like a wolf in sheep's clothing.

"I think this is the first time I've ever seen you in here," I say to him, now trying to act casual when I am freaking the fuck out. "I never took you for a coffee connoisseur."

"And I never took you for a peeping Tom, and yet here we are."

Fucking hell.

Shame flares in my face, and I'm sure it's making my freckles stand out even more. With my pale Irish skin, it makes it impossible to hide my embarrassment.

Bran stares at me, blank-faced. Vampires, on the other hand, have always been very, very good at hiding their emotions.

I lick my lips and decide to ignore that accusation since it's technically true. "What can I get for you?"

"Care to tap a vein?" he asks.

Now I'm starting to sweat. I need to get him out of here.

I smile tightly at him. "We're not allowed to tap a vein in a witch-owned property. But you know that."

He smiles back, but it's the coldest smile I've ever seen. "I suppose I did."

"Now, coffee. What can I get started for you?"

"I didn't come here for coffee."

I take a step back. I'm not exactly sure what he's jiving toward, but better to be prepared than sorry. There hasn't been a nonconsensual vampire attack in over a hundred years, but if someone broke that law, I'm pretty sure it would be Bran.

He's not only arrogant and rebellious, but insufferably difficult. I mean, he lives in suburbia next door to me when he could live in the Duval Mansion outside of town. I don't know why he moved out of the mansion, but rumor has it that he got into a big argument with his older brother and got kicked out.

"What did you come for then?" I ask carefully.

His bright amber eyes seem to glow in the dim lighting as he says, "I came to warn you, little mouse."

Two

I don't like that Bran Duval, second in line in the Duval Vampire House, is insinuating that I'm a rodent, but that's not the most shocking part of that sentence, so I let it go.

"Warn me about what?" I ask.

"Your Pledging," he says. "I thought you might want to know that the Duval House plans to put a bid on you."

"They what?!"

He *tsks* like he's annoyed with my reaction, as if it's an *overreaction*. IT'S NOT.

Most families have been established so long, the Pledge is more of a formality than anything. If I actually planned to stay in Midnight, everyone would expect me to pledge myself to Locke House as a blood donor, since that's who my family has been with for nearly two hundred years.

Never in my wildest dreams would I have expected a rival vampire family to bid for me.

"Why would they do that?" I ask. "That doesn't make any sense."

"I agree. I told my brother he was out of his fucking mind."

I snort. "You don't have to be an ass."

"I know a difficult blood bag when I see one."

My eyes widen. "Excuse me? You don't even know me!"

He taps at his ear. "Vampire hearing, remember? I've been listening to you whine and complain for months."

By the time this night is over, I think I will have filled my embarrassment quota for a lifetime. And I might also be wanted for staking a vampire.

"You've been *listening* to me?"

"It's not as if I enjoy it."

My mind flips through all of the possible things he's heard me say and do. So many embarrassing and—

Oh god.

Has he heard me getting myself off?

I am so ready to leave Midnight Harbor. I hate this place. I hate supernaturals!

"I need you to leave," I say. "Before I call the Guard."

"Now why would you do that?" he challenges.

I grab a bamboo straw from the canister on the counter and brandish it like a knife. "Because I'm about to murder a vampire."

His eyes flare bright gold. In a flash, he's disappeared from my line of sight.

I stumble back, because I know what it means when a vampire disappears. They're using their supernatural speed, and who the hell knows where they'll pop back up.

As I reach for one of the knives in the block on the counter, Bran slams into me, his hand around my throat. The air rushes out of me.

I stab blindly, first with the knife, because let's be honest, I don't want to kill him. I'm not the killing type.

The knife lands with a sickening *shwump* in his chest. He looks down at the hilt protruding from his flesh as I let out a little yip of shock.

The air takes on the tangy scent of his blood.

He breathes fast through his nose as his eyes turn molten.

The first lesson my mother taught me as a child of Midnight Harbor was that when a vampire's eyes change color or glow, don't run, *walk* away. Slowly, carefully. It was one of those lessons passed down from mother to daughter from a time when the lessons were hard won.

I haven't had to worry about tangling with a pissed off, hungry vampire.

They've all minded their manners.

Until now.

Bran pulls the blade out of his chest and, with a quick flick of his wrist, lodges the blade in the hardwood floor. I wind back with the bamboo straw, ready to strike again, but Bran catches me before I can get close. He yanks the straw from my grasp and snaps it in two with one hand.

Teeth gritted, he forces me back against the wall and presses into me.

"I don't want to fight you," he says. His breath fans down my neck. A new kind of thrill races across my shoulders.

I'm suddenly so turned on, I want to melt into a puddle and disappear through the floor boards. Never in my life has my body ever been such a fucking traitor.

Bran scents the air, and his eyes flash again. His mouth comes to my ear, and he whispers, "Naughty girl."

I buck beneath him. He pushes more of his weight into me and laughs, low and beneath his breath.

"Get off me," I say and throw a punch at him. He catches my fist. Before I can comprehend what he's doing, he has both my hands trapped above my head. My back arches automatically; my chest pushes out, and the V-neck of my t-shirt pops open. Bran's eyes sink to my cleavage.

"There are rules," I say through clenched teeth.

He inhales. "And?"

"And if you don't follow them—"

"If I don't follow them," he says, "there's no one to stop me."

"Rita would gut you."

He pulls back and laughs. "Rita won't stand against a Duval, and certainly not me."

Though it's been a while since I kept up on town gossip and the shifting alliances, I think Bran might have a good point. I'm just a mortal, not even a bound one yet. I wouldn't be worth starting a war with the vampires.

And though I don't exactly know what drove Bran out of Duval

House, I do know that no one messes with him. He's the kind of vampire that parts a crowd.

"Fine. Go on then," I challenge. "Bite me. Let's get this over with. I have shit to do."

He laughs again, lets me go, and disappears from sight.

I hear the bell clang before I catch sight of him again. He stops in the open doorway.

I pick up a piece of the bamboo straw. With its uneven break, it's even more of a weapon now. And I'm not pulling my punches.

Bran says, "One more thing you should know."

I make a stabbing motion with the straw. "Oh yeah?"

"It was your sister that encouraged the Duval bid."

I suck in a sharp breath, and by the time I exhale again, Bran is gone.

THREE

When I get home after closing the coffee shop, I find my sister on the couch, watching *Real Housewives*, a glass of wine in hand.

Though every donor family receives a stipend from their vampires, Kelly works full-time at the city clerk office. I don't exactly know what she does, but it often leads to her downing a bottle of wine every night.

There's already an empty bottle on the kitchen counter.

"Hey," I call.

"Hey. How was work?"

I look at Bran's house through the kitchen window. I think his house is a mirror of ours. His kitchen looks at our kitchen, which would mean his dining room was opposite ours, and his living room is in the front of the house.

There's a light on in the dining room, but I don't catch any movement.

Maybe he's watching me from the shadows and will use this against me in the future.

I turn away.

I will be extremely happy when I move from this place.

"The shop was slow tonight," I answer Kelly and plop down on the other side of the couch.

"Mmmmm," she says as she sips at her wine, her attention more on the TV than on me.

"I have a question for you," I say.

One of the women on the TV shouts at another. Kelly waves at me and says, "Hold on just a sec."

On the show, more women join in until the whole room is screaming at one another.

While I cleaned up the coffee shop, my mind wandered over the possible reasons my sister could have to encourage Duval House to bid on me over the Locke House.

Maybe the Lockes haven't been treating her well? After our parents died, Kelly and I would have dinner with Julian Locke at least twice a month. I thought he was going to ask Kelly to be his blood mate, but his visits stopped all of a sudden.

I just assumed she'd turned him down.

The Duvals have more money than the Lockes, so maybe my sister just wants to think of my future?

Or maybe there's a reason that I'm not even thinking of.

"Kels," I try again.

"Can this wait? You know this is my favorite show."

If I wait another hour to talk to her, she's going to be drunk and passed out. I have to catch her after work and before wine.

With a sigh, I stand up. "Sure."

"Thanks, Jess," she says before taking another sip. She's drinking red tonight, which usually means she had a really, *really* shitty day.

There's another reason Kelly might encourage a Duval bid—maybe she wants to get rid of me.

Humans pledged to different vampire Houses can't live together. When a vampire drinks from you, their scent is all over you. Humans co-habiting share scents, too. Vampires, much like the shifters, are a territorial lot.

Kelly did take on a lot of responsibility after our mom died. Kelly was only twenty-six at the time. I was seventeen. She sold her condo on the river and moved back home so I didn't have to disrupt my life.

I was so deep in the grief that I never did thank her for it.

And maybe now she's ready to move on from the responsibility.

"Kel?" I say.

"Hmmm?"

"Love you."

She finally looks over at me and smiles. "Love you too, you nerd. Now go."

I grab my bag from the counter and disappear upstairs. In my room, I collapse on my bed and check my phone to find a text from my best friend, Samantha.

Party at the Harbor tomorrow night, the text reads. *You game?*

I call her because I have so much to tell her, and it's too much to type.

"Say yes," Sam says by way of a greeting.

"The party? Sure I guess."

"Yay."

"So, I have a super weird story."

"Oh do tell."

I roll over on my belly and hold myself up on my elbows. I can just see a sliver of Bran's bedroom window. The room is dark. He can probably hear me talking, but I don't care.

I relay the coffeeshop story to Sam.

Being my best friend, she responds accordingly with, "What. The. Fuck."

"I know. You think Bran's lying?"

I can just picture him hearing this and rolling his eyes in a very smarmy vampire way.

"As much as I want to say yes, why would he? Has he ever even talked to you before?"

"You know how to make a girl feel so damn cool."

Oh shit, shouldn't have said that. Now Bran's gonna think that I've been wanting him to talk to me and that him talking to me somehow makes me feel better about myself.

Or maybe I'm reading way too much into Bran and his feelings, or lack thereof.

Sam munches on something on the other end. "I'm just saying, why would he come to the coffee shop of all places to tell you something completely out of left field?"

"Maybe he's just trying to get beneath my skin? I think I annoy him."

"Did you ask Kelly?"

"Not yet. I tried. She shooed me away."

"Oh yeah. Real Housewives night."

I stretch just a little when I see a light flick on in Bran's bedroom. I'm half hanging off the bed at this point. I catch sight of him in the window frame, and then he's gone again. My heart skitters in my chest.

"So why don't you go next door and ask him?"

Bran comes back into view of my window and looks across the valley between our houses. I let out a yelp, and in my haste to duck out of sight, I end up falling off the bed and landing with a thud on the floor.

"I can't do that," I say to Sam, my face mashed into the rug.

"Yes you can."

I didn't tell her he attacked me at the coffee shop. Technically, it was in response to me threatening to murder him, but those are minor details.

"Just go knock on his front door and ask him what he knows," Sam says like Bran is any old neighbor and my request is for a cup of sugar and not secret details about his family asking for my blood pact.

"Just don't go inside the house. Stay on the front porch. There's no telling what someone like Bran Duval would do to a poor innocent virgin like yourself."

"Sam!"

He probably heard that. Not that I necessarily care if he knows I'm a virgin. In a town like this, it's practically stamped on our driver's license.

"Go over there," she coaxes. "Then tell me what he says. This is kind of a big deal. When's the last time a rival vamp family bid for someone's expected blood bag?"

"A long time."

"Exactly. And if he came to warn you, I'd think that meant he cared to some degree."

I sit up. "I highly doubt that."

"Go on. Go."

"Okay fine. I'm going."

"Atta girl."

We say goodbye, and I slip my phone into the back pocket of my jeans. If Bran attacks me again, I want a lifeline.

When I go back downstairs, my sister is still fully invested in her TV show and barely notices me leave through the back door. I make my way around the house and go up the few steps to Bran's wide front porch. The sun has already set, and the street lights glow golden along the curb, but Bran's porch is dark.

I reach out and knock on his door.

Immediately, my heart rams into my throat.

What the hell am I doing?

Did he not just have me around the throat in the coffee shop?

I'll just stay on the front porch like Sam suggested. I'll keep my distance.

When Bran doesn't answer, I sigh and turn away—

And nearly run right into him.

Four

I yelp and lurch back like the scared human I am.

Bran is leaning against one of the porch columns, arms crossed over his chest.

"What the hell!" I yell and clutch at my chest. "I think I'm having a heart attack."

"You're not having a heart attack."

"How would you know?"

"I can hear your heart. It's fine. Now what do you want?"

After I catch my breath, I level my shoulders and say, "Don't pretend like you weren't just listening to my phone conversation."

"Contrary to what you might think, little mouse, my world does not revolve around you."

I huff. "Okay. Well…you must know why your brother would agree to bid on me, and I'd like to know what you know."

"I must, mustn't I?"

"Don't do that. Don't be all vampire-y. Just tell me."

He pushes away from the porch column. I step back.

At his front door, hand on the doorknob, he says, "Come inside, and I'll tell you."

Oh, he was definitely listening to my phone conversation.

"I'm not doing that," I answer.

"Why, little mouse?" His voice lowers an octave, and his eyes flare briefly. "Are you afraid?"

"I'm not a mouse," I say through clenched teeth. "And no, I'm not afraid."

He pushes the door in and disappears into the shadows. "Then what are you waiting for?"

The door hangs open. I peer inside, trying to gauge the level of shit I'd be stepping into if I walked over the threshold.

I was right, his house does seem to be a mirror of ours. I can just make out the outline of a sectional couch in the living room and a coffee table in front of it. There's a table in the dining room and beyond that, the kitchen. There's still only the one light on in the dining room.

Now that I'm standing at his front door, I'm starting to doubt my actual reasons for being here. I think it might have less to do with my upcoming birthday and Duval House and more to do with my fascination with Bran.

But I'm never going to tell him that.

Or anyone.

I step inside.

The door shuts behind me, and I find Bran standing behind it, his eyes glowing in the darkness.

"You're a liar," he says.

"No, I'm not. About what?"

"About being afraid."

Goosebumps lift on my arms. The hair rises on the back of my neck. All of my mom's old warnings run through my head. And some of Sam's too.

Don't go inside, she said.

So what do I do?

I've always been a glutton for punishment. And the truth is, I really wanted to see inside the house of the infamous Bran Duval. It doesn't look like a murder den, so that's definitely good.

There are framed black and white pictures on the angled wall beneath the staircase. The images are grainy like they were taken with a very old camera. Beneath the framed art is a skinny hall table with a stack of history books on top.

Despite the murky lighting, I can tell the house is extremely clean and clutter-free.

I immediately like it.

Kelly has always been a hard worker, but when it comes to our house, she's thrown all effort out the window. I know she's busy and tries to provide for us, but sometimes the clutter drives me bananas.

"So little mouse," Bran says as he walks around me to the kitchen, "what is it you want to know?" He flicks on a hanging light over the kitchen island. There are no dishes on his counter, no stacked coffee cups in the sink. There's a top-of-the-line espresso maker on the counter, but it looks untouched. Which is in stark contrast to the many liquor decanters on the old cabinet between the kitchen and dining room.

Some of the decanters are half empty, some full.

"You said my sister encouraged the Duval bid. How do you know?"

He goes to the cabinet and pulls out the cut crystal top from one of the decanters. The cork makes a loud *fwop*.

Bran fills a tumbler and takes a long swig. "She met my brother two nights ago," he says. "You want a drink?"

"Sure. You got any whiskey?"

Bran fills a second glass. I take it when he offers it and swallow back a gulp. When the alcohol burns down my throat and settles some of my nerves, I feel infinitely better.

"Your sister met with Damien," Bran goes on, "and told him that if he bid for you next week, she'd give him something he's been wanting for a very long time."

"And what's that?"

"I don't know." He slings back the rest of his liquor and sets the glass down.

"You don't have any idea at all?"

Bran just stares at me, face blank.

I narrow my eyes. "You *do* know."

"I have my suspicions."

"So tell me."

"That's not my business to tell, little mouse."

"Stop calling me that."

He smirks.

I knock back the rest of my drink too and put the glass in the sink. I might like his exceptionally clean house, but dirtying it up gives me a smug thrill.

"Thanks for nothing then," I say.

"You could just turn it down," he says.

I stop just out of the reach of the kitchen light, but with his vampire sight, I know he can probably see every hair on my head. "I'm leaving Midnight Harbor the first chance I get, so I'm not accepting any bid."

This is the first time I've admitted this to anyone, and it shocks me that it's Bran I'm telling.

I've made comments in passing to Sam, that someday I might want to move away, but I've never outright told her I'm doing it and probably soon.

She'll be crushed, but I have to do what's right for me, and I don't fit in Midnight Harbor. I've always felt that way.

Bran comes forward. He's still wearing the black t-shirt I stabbed him in, so there's a fresh hole in the chest. I'm proud of that hole. "Fleeing the nest, are you?"

I nod. "Just think, you won't have to listen to my whining and complaining anymore."

"I'll look forward to it."

"Well okay then." I start for the door, silently cursing myself for listening to Sam. I didn't exactly get anywhere with Bran.

Just as I reach out for the doorknob, Bran appears in front of me. All of the amusement is gone from his face. He's serious and distant again. I'm not sure which Bran I like more. Or hate less.

"Ask your sister about the day you were born," he says. "That might be a good place to start." Then he opens the door and shoves me out. I stumble into the twilight and then hurry down the steps.

As I cross back into my yard, Bran calls out, "Hey little mouse?"

I stop and look back.

He's leaning against the open door as he says, "You don't want to know what I'd do to poor innocent virgins like you."

My mouth drops open. "How dare you—"

He slams the door shut, leaving me standing there between our houses, fuming and suddenly throbbing between my legs.

Because the truth is, I do want to know.

Five

"Here you go," Rita says to me and hands me two blended coffees. Whenever I come to Magic Coffee Shop outside of my work schedule, I always insist on making my own drinks, and Rita always insists that I not.

I throw a five-dollar bill in the tip jar, and Rita plucks it out and crams it in my hand. "You keep your money. I know you have dreams." She winks at me and busies herself with the steamer.

Knowing it's pointless to fight a witch, I pocket the money. "Thanks, Rita. I'll see you later."

I join Sam outside on the sidewalk. It's just a little after ten in the morning, so Sam has been up for about ten minutes, tops. I couldn't sleep last night and rolled out of bed, exhausted and frustrated at eight a.m.

Sam takes the frozen coffee from my hand. "The suspense is killing me. You have to tell me about last night. You never called me back."

We walk west down River Street. Since only the oldest vampires can walk in the daylight, and even then, only early morning and late afternoon, and the shifters have a shopping center in their territory, Sam and I pass mostly witches and humans as we head toward River Street Bridge.

Finally, I can talk without having to worry about extraordinary hearing.

I fill Sam in on the very little info Bran gave me.

"So he said to ask Kelly about the day you were born?" Sam says as she fishes out a heaping scoop of whipped cream from her drink with her straw. "And did you ask Kelly about your birthday?"

We stop at an intersection as traffic rolls through beneath a green light.

"Not yet. She was up early and off to work before I had the chance."

"Has she said anything to you about the Pledge coming up?"

I shake my head. "She hasn't even asked me about the party afterward. And you know how much—"

"—Kelly loves planning a party."

"Exactly."

When the light switches, we cross. Already the patio at Silver Garden is full of brunchers, and the din of conversation rises over the faint rushing of the river down below the street.

A few witches we know call out hello as we pass the restaurant's back deck.

Since the bridge will take us to the shifter side of town, Sam and I take the stone steps down to the river walk and follow it north.

A jogger runs past, her ponytail swinging behind her. Up ahead, a mother wipes the face of a toddler while a baby wails in a stroller. When the wind shifts, I catch the faint sugary scent of their fae magic.

I set my drink down on a nearby bench and approach the stroller. There's an adorable little girl nestled in a thin blanket with two pointy ears sticking out around a bowed headband. Her face is red from crying so hard.

"Hey little one," I say. "It's okay."

The mom exhales. "I knew getting ice cream so early was a mistake," she says as she tries to wipe a glob of chocolate from the toddler's face.

"I can try to settle her while you finish up with the little guy," I say.

"Oh you would be a life saver, thank you."

I unclip the stroller straps and hoist the baby out. As soon as she's upright and blinking in the sunshine, she settles, fat tears streaming down her face. I bounce her on my hip and coo at her.

Sam hangs her elbows over the walkway railing and scrolls through her phone. She has six little brothers and sisters. She has more experience with children than most mothers, but she really, really dislikes children.

I used to babysit for a fae family a few years back and have some experience with the finicky fae babies. I heard that being born on the mortal side and being unable to travel back to their realm causes colic in a lot of little ones. The baby I watched wouldn't ever let me put him down. He was permanently attached to my hip while I was there.

By the time the mom finishes cleaning up the toddler, the baby is smiling at me, tears dried up.

"You are amazing," the mom says. "She's been in a mood for days."

"I think we all have been." I boop the baby's nose, and she giggles.

"Come on, Mommy!" the toddler shouts. "I wanna see the fish!"

"Thanks again." I hand the baby back, and the mom settles her on her hip before pushing the stroller away.

"Ew, babies," Sam says when we start walking again.

"What? She was adorable."

Sam slides her phone back into her pocket. "I'm never having kids. That will be part of my Pledge requirement. If the Mulligan witches want me, they'll have to give me a lifetime supply of witch birth control."

I twirl my straw around my drink. If ever there was a time to tell Sam I plan on moving, it would be now.

I think I want kids someday. Maybe? I don't know, honestly. I've always craved something else other than being a blood bag, but I guess I never really sat down to figure out what that was.

If I told Sam that I want to leave Midnight for something normal, I know she'd remind me of her older sister who tried to leave and go to college and eventually found her way back home. She's now married to a witch.

Knowing that Sam will just try to talk me out of it, I decide to hold on to the secret a while longer.

I'll tell her eventually.

We hang out for the rest of the morning, walking down the river walk before heading to Whimsy Books at noon. Sam works there most afternoons. It certainly pays better than babysitting her siblings.

I say goodbye to her after my coffee is gone and head home. I had plans of cleaning my room, but now that I'm sitting on my bed, I can't stop staring at Bran's house.

It's still mid-afternoon, so he's probably sleeping. Bran uses blackout shades in his bedroom, but the rest of his windows are unprotected.

As I stare at the window, I can't help but picture him in a king-sized bed, tangled in black silk sheets. He probably sleeps naked.

And thinking about Bran naked brings to mind the image of him standing in his window two nights ago completely bare.

Am I hoping for a repeat?

No.

This is my bedroom goddammit. And this is my comfy window seat. I lived here first. I can sit wherever I want.

Gods, I hate him.

I can't figure him out.

I want to know why he cares what happens to me, why he would go out of his way to warn me.

He left Duval House. Technically, leaving means he's a sovereign entity. He could start his own house if he wanted to. So even if I accepted a bid from Duval, Bran wouldn't have to see me. If I annoy him as much as he says, if I accepted a Duval bid, Bran would probably see me less than he does now because I'd have to move.

It doesn't make any sense. And it'd have helped if I'd actually paid attention in school when they taught us lowly mortals about the different Vampire Houses and the relationships between members.

There was a whole semester dedicated to it. I didn't pay attention because 1) I was already planning on leaving Midnight by then, and 2) even if I hadn't been, I'd be pledged to the Locke House.

The little I know about the Duvals is that Bran and his older brother Damien are Turned brothers, *and* blood brothers, born to the same parents. They were turned by Vincent Montenaro in the 1700s somewhere in Europe. They came to America at the turn of the century (the 19th to be more specific) and were original founders of Midnight Harbor.

I know that Damien is considered the charismatic brother, the nicer brother, though there have been whispers that he's just really good at hiding his darker side while Bran doesn't bother.

Of the five vampire families in Midnight, the Duvals are equally loved and hated. They wield a lot of power and money and influence. If you want something, whether you're human or witch or something else, you'll acquire that thing much easier if you have the support of the Duvals.

So why did Bran leave his house?

I really want to know now that he's warned me about the possible bid.

Did he leave because of something sinister?

I mean, I can't imagine what could possibly ruffle Bran's feathers enough to get him to abandon his house and his brother.

At a little after three in the afternoon, after I've sat in my window seat so long my butt has gone numb, Bran's blackout shade snaps upward. The movement catches my attention and without thinking about *why*, my gaze immediately goes to his window.

He stands in front of the glass, his arm propped on the window frame as he leans into it, just as casual as can be.

And yep, he's naked.

Six

I can't stop staring at him. I can't tear my eyes away.

Bran is ridiculously manscaped.

Well, not ridiculously.

Expertly.

Perfectly.

And what he has below that manscaping is—

It's at this moment that I realize I've been staring at his crotch for far too long, and I drag my eyes up to meet his.

There's a smile on his face that I can only label as *self-important.*

I scowl at him and though my window is shut, I yell, "You're doing that on purpose. Now who's the perv?"

He raises a dark brow, and his lips move in reply.

I think he says, "You were waiting for me."

So I say, "No, I wasn't."

Ahem, I think 'Yes, I was.'

I definitely was.

I look away for just a second, and when I look back, he's gone and I spend the rest of the afternoon avoiding my bedroom even though I really want to catch sight of him again.

I can't help but wonder what he's doing, what he's thinking. Why is he torturing me? He probably gets a rise out of making me blush.

And it infuriates me even more.

When Kelly comes home from work, she's got two bags of groceries in her arms. I take one and start unpacking it.

"I am so glad it's the weekend," Kelly says as she drops her bag on the counter. "This has been an extremely long week."

I put away a block of cheese and a tub of yogurt in the fridge. "What happened?"

She slides onto one of the bar stools at the island and scrubs at her face. "The shifters are trying to slip out of paying their share of the summer taxes, and the witches have had it *up to here* with the vampires because one of the Rowan vamps stole one of the Mulligan virgins and debased her."

I put the bread in the cupboard and the box of cheese crackers in the pantry as Kelly goes on.

"But let me tell you, that virgin was not going to stay a virgin much longer. I saw her flirting with the grocery store clerk a week ago. I'm surprised she didn't jump his bones right there! I don't get paid enough to deal with this."

"What's the shifters' excuse for not paying taxes?" I ask not because I care but because I know Kelly needs to vent, and the quicker I let her do that, the quicker I can ask her about this Duval nonsense.

"They're trying to say their land is smaller than the vampires' land, so their share should be smaller, which I don't exactly disagree with, but these things were agreed upon over a century ago. If they want to change it, they have to go about it the fair and legal way, instead of just *not* paying taxes. Don't they understand that that money helps fund the schools?"

"Lots going on then," I say.

She blows out a breath. "You have no idea."

For the first time, I notice the heavy bags beneath Kelly's eyes. She might be a disaster in organization and house chores, but she's extremely particular about her facial care and spends an insane amount of money on it every month. She usually treats her eyes with patches at least twice a week.

With all of the groceries put away, I cross my arms over my chest and lean into the island. "So...my Pledge is coming up, and I was wondering..."

Kelly sighs again. "Right. I know." She gets up and pulls the corkscrew from the drawer. "That snuck up on us, didn't it?" She tears off the foil from the bottle of wine she bought and then turns the corkscrew into the cork.

"Yeah definitely snuck up on us."

I don't know how to slide into this conversation without being obvious. Kelly instigated the Duval bid, though I'm only getting that from Bran. Sam had a good point—why would Bran come to me with something so outlandish if it wasn't true? But then again, who do I trust more? My sister or the annoyingly hot vampire next door?

Maybe I should just come right out and ask her.

"Speaking of birthdays," I start.

Kelly yanks out the cork with a loud pop.

"What was it like for you when Mom brought me home?" I ask.

My dad died before I was even born, so I know everything surrounding my birth was chaotic and traumatic and a complete blur.

Kelly's back is to me, so I can't see her face, but the way she tenses up and goes still leads me to believe I've hit on something.

"Why do you ask?" she says carefully.

"I don't know. I was just thinking...like it must have been weird for you because you were older and you were used to being an only child and then this wailing baby comes home and disrupts everything."

Kelly pulls a wine glass from the shelf. "I never thought that. You were cute and chubby, and you smelled like sugar and heather and thistle." The wine glug-glugs into the glass. "I used to rock you to sleep sometimes because you would cry and cry some nights. When I'd finally get you to calm down, you'd suck your thumb in the most adorable way. Like the poster child for all babies in the world."

I laugh. "You never told me that."

She grabs the glass around the stem and turns to me, one arm folded over her middle. "I took the role of big sister seriously."

"You definitely did. You even became my guardian after Mom died. Not every sister would do that."

She nods. "We're a team. You and I. I wouldn't have left you to the wolves."

In Midnight Harbor, that phrase is almost literal.

Kelly comes over and gives my shoulder a squeeze. Her dark brown hair is wound up into a perfect bun on top of her head. Several wispy strands hang around her thin face. The older she gets, the more she looks like our mother. She got Mom's nose and Mom's thin lips, and sometimes when she wrinkles her nose at something annoying or disgusting, it's like déjà vu.

"About my Pledge," I start, "is there anything—"

Kelly's phone rings in her bag. She breaks away to dig for it. When she pulls it out and reads the screen, her mouth screws up in a grimace. "Shit."

"What is it?"

"Julian. He wants me to come to the house." She looks forlornly at her wine. "Goddammit." She puts the glass into the fridge and picks up her bag again. "I'll be back later, okay?"

"Sure."

She plants a quick kiss on my cheek before hurrying out the door, leaving me to stew longer in my unanswered questions.

Sam texts me a little after seven to remind me of the Harbor Party. *I'll swing by to pick you up in a little over an hour.*

Sounds good, I type back and then hurry into the shower.

Harbor parties are always a mixed bag, so I'm not planning to try too hard. As I flip through my closet, my phone rings. I don't recognize the number, but it's local. I slide to answer it and say distantly, "Hello?"

"Are you going to the Harbor party tonight?"

The voice is hoarse and sensuously rich, and the sound of it in my ear is like silk dragging over my skin.

My reflection in the mirror shivers.

"Why do you care?" I ask Bran and put the phone on speaker. If he keeps talking directly in my ear, I might spontaneously combust.

"My brother might be there," he says.

"So?"

"What will you wear?" he asks, dodging the question.

I come out of the bathroom and go to my bedroom window, phone in hand. I'm not surprised to find him at his bedroom window too. At least this time he's fully clothed in a black t-shirt and jeans. The shirt is loose around the collar, and even from across the space between our houses, I can tell the material is thin. His dark hair is wet, and several chunks stick up at his forehead like he just raked his fingers through it.

Bran is the type of vampire that makes careless look sexy as hell, and it makes me angry.

I'm still in a bath towel, and when he sees me, his eyes ignite.

I know that look. I've been around enough vampires to know when one is hungry for a bite.

"Will you be there?" I ask.

He leans into the window frame. "Maybe," he says into the phone.

"Then you'll see what I'm wearing when I get there."

"Perhaps I want a sneak peek." He levels his gaze at me.

He's baiting me, and I think I'm about to bite.

I don't know why.

I'm not exactly sure what makes Bran so irritating and tempting at the same time.

"Fine." I turn away and disappear back into my bathroom and into my closet. Up until this point, I'd planned to wear jeans and a baggy sweatshirt, but if I put that on for Bran, he's going to—

I was about to say *be disappointed*.

Why the fuck do I care?

I shake my head and pull out the jeans and my tie-dye sweatshirt. After setting them out on the table, I open the drawer for a pair of panties and hear Bran tsk-tsk through the phone.

"What?" I ask.

"No panties."

"Hey! How the—"

He knows the sound of my panty drawer opening?

I stand frozen in the middle of my closet, my core clenched tight. I'm suddenly flush all over and so fucking turned on, I want to scream at him.

No panties.

No panties?!

The thought makes me wet.

I'm tingling between my legs like a live wire has been jacked into me.

Shit.

Murdering Bran is looking more and more likely.

Except...a little part of me wants to do as Bran says if only to show him how much I don't care. The no panties thing feels like a dare, and I'm not about to chicken out.

Seven

I decide against the jeans and pull out a short black bodycon skirt and an oversized vintage white tee. I put the clothes on and tuck the shirt into the skirt.

Back at my bedroom window, hand curled around my hip, I raise a brow and say to the phone, "Well?"

Bran's eyes flash again, and my chest flutters with butterflies. He says nothing, and I get the question in his gaze.

I turn sideways so as not to give him a show and lift the hem of my skirt, baring my thigh all the way up to my hip.

"Good girl," he says. "Behave yourself tonight."

"I don't plan on it," I say back.

He smirks at me and ends the call. We stare at each other across the expanse between our houses.

It's at this moment I realize he told me Damien would be at the party. Is Bran warning me again? Should I be worried?

I'll be with Sam, and Harbor parties are notoriously packed. And I'll be wearing the protection rune Mom gave me before I was old enough to know what it was.

It hasn't failed me yet.

I turn away from the window, but I can feel Bran's eyes on me until I disappear inside the bathroom again.

Once I'm safely out of sight, I press into the wall and suck in a deep breath. A voice in the back of my mind says I shouldn't be playing these games with a vampire like Bran Duval.

But I can't seem to help myself.

I never understood the adrenaline junkies I've seen on TV. Jump out of an airplane? No, thank you. Careen down a steep mountainside on nothing but two skis? Nope.

Tempt a vampire?

The rush is downright intoxicating.

Downstairs, I pour a glass of Kelly's wine while I wait for Sam. My glass is empty by the time she shows up. As usual, she's ten minutes late. We drive downtown, and Sam parks on a side street since all the good spots are taken.

By the time we walk down the slope to the water, the party is already well underway.

The Harbor sits at the end of the river where the freshwater meets the salty ocean. The building was built in 1901 and was originally the Guards' water rescue station. They rebuilt on the north side of the river about ten years ago, so the original building was converted into a community space.

Mostly, it's for weekend parties and Pledges now.

It's a two-story building, clad in white cedar shake shingles. The window casings are painted hunter green, with the hardware and gutters pained black.

The front entrance is a thick, arched door.

Music wends out the open windows, and voices carry from the deck on the water.

Sam and I go in the front, and I tug down the hem of my skirt as some of the witches call out hello.

"Why do you keep fidgeting with your skirt?" Sam asks me as the witches come over.

I am, in no way, going to tell her I'm going commando because Bran Duval told me to. Just thinking about that confession brings heat to my face.

"It's itchy," I say instead. "I think Kelly forgot to use fabric softener."

Bianca is the first witch to reach us and air kisses our cheeks. "Evening, dolls," she says.

For most of my life, I've wanted to hate Bianca Mulligan. She's tall, thin, blonde, rich, and extremely powerful. Everything about her screams mean girl, but while she knows she wields power and influence, she's never acted like it matters to her.

She's always been kind to me and to all the humans in Midnight. There's just something about her that radiates warmth and charisma.

Bianca hooks her arm in mine. She towers over me by several inches despite the fact that she's wearing flat heeled boots and I'm wearing chunky sneakers. "Jessie," she says as she steers me to the bar. "Are you getting nervous yet for your Pledging?"

When we come up to the bar, the bartender is immediately at our call. That's what hanging with Bianca will get you. "Jack and Coke," Bianca says.

"Whiskey sour," I say.

The bartender gets to work, and Bianca turns her attention to me.

This is the other thing I love about her. Though people are always vying for her attention, when Bianca is engaged in a conversation with someone, her focus is solely on that person. She knows how to make someone feel valued and important.

I've always wondered if that's something she was taught or if it just comes naturally. I think in the long run, giving someone her full attention wins her more than her looks.

Except right now I want to squirm beneath her big green eyes.

When will I tell people I plan on leaving? I don't know when the right time is.

I should probably say something before my Pledging. It's scheduled for Tuesday night, the night of my birthday. But every time I think about telling someone, it makes my heart race and my hands clammy.

Everyone except for Bran, apparently. Somehow telling him a secret no one else knows feels like a token of intimacy.

"I'll pledge to the Locke family," I say. "Nothing really to be nervous about."

"Hmm," Bianca says as she rests an elbow on the bar top. "Is that what you want?"

"I don't know. It's what's expected."

She cants her head and frowns at me. "But not what you want."

It isn't a question, but I still don't know how to answer her.

I'm saved by Sam. "What did you order?" she asks when she sidles up.

"Whiskey sour."

"Caleb!" she calls to the bartender. "Can you add one more whiskey sour?"

"You got it," he calls back.

The rest of the witches join us. There's Gwen, Rita's niece, and Lannie Lo.

Lannie nods at my bottom half. "I love the skirt."

This reminds me that there's nothing beneath that skirt, and my throat thickens around a reply. There's a little part of me that feels...well, *improper* for going without panties, and I think that's exactly what Bran intended.

Without thinking about it, I scan the crowd for him.

The sun has already set below the tree horizon, so the younger vampires have joined the party. Usually, you can tell when a Duval vampire is afoot because they'll be surrounded by people who hang on their every word.

Those people are usually humans, and we call them the Besotted.

Not every human family in Midnight is Pledged to the super elite, but there are a lot who wished they were. There's the power that comes with favor, and the money.

"Who are you looking for?" Sam asks as the bartender sets our drinks on the bar top.

"Oh, no one." I grab my whiskey and drink it back. The alcohol burns down my throat and hits my bloodstream. I was already feeling a little warm with the wine, and now I'm downright fuzzy.

"Come on," Bianca says and coaxes us out to the back deck.

Beneath the pergola, mixed groups have already claimed several tables beneath the twinkling string lights suspended from the rafters.

Along the water, there are three separate sitting areas, the chairs situated around raised fire pits.

Fire crackles in all three pits, and we go to the gathering space on the far left.

"Bianca!" everyone calls out.

There are a few shifters—wolves, to be more specific—and two humans. One of them is a virgin. Tessa, I think her name is.

Sam and I go to the railing and lean against it. We're quickly swept up into a debate about whether or not a virgin should be paid more for her blood the older she gets.

"Like a vintage wine," Tessa says. "If I'm going to be a virgin for the rest of my life, I should get paid for my sexual frustration."

Everyone laughs. My glass is nearly empty, and the alcohol is definitely going to my head. Everything is funny, especially this.

"I can't imagine being a virgin forever," I say.

Evan hangs back over his chair, and I can feel his eyes drinking me in. "That would be a travesty, Jess. A damn travesty."

I warm beneath his gaze, and he scents the air, catching my faint interest.

Evan hasn't taken a mate yet, and I gotta say, he's looking sexy as hell in his navy-blue tank. I know he's wearing that particular outfit so he can show off the heavy lifting he's been doing, but I don't care. His hard work is paying off.

As the night goes on, and the drinks keep flowing, and the twilight glows brighter, I find myself drifting toward Evan. Soon I'm sitting on his lap, my arm draped casually over his shoulders, his arms wrapped around me. His hand is on my bare leg, and I'm distantly aware that there's not much material between his fingers and my core.

If he just inched up his hand…

He inhales again, and his gaze turns heavy. "Jess," he purrs and readjusts us. I can feel him growing hard beneath me.

"Yes?" I say back as my drink sloshes over the rim of the glass and wets my t-shirt. Evan laughs. I laugh. "Dammit! That was gonna be a good sip."

"I'll get you another soon." He pushes a lock of my hair behind my ear. "How come we've never hooked up?" he asks.

Voices rise in the distance, but I've got more important things to pay attention to.

"Because you're a wolf," I say.

"So?"

"So...my mom warned me about wolves."

He laughs, his eyes catching a glint of the string lights. "I'm sure she didn't mean *me*."

"Oh no?"

"No." He leans in, his hand cupping the side of my face. I go in to meet his mouth when a strong arm wraps around my waist and hauls me back.

I'm just about to fight the person when his scent fills my nose.

Amber and musk and something deeper.

By now, I know who that scent belongs to, and my body, being the traitor that it is, knows too.

Bran Duval.

Eight

"Let me go." I try to wiggle out of Bran's grip, but he has my back crushed against his chest, his arm still locked around my waist. It's like fighting the wind—pointless.

Evan lurches to his feet. "The fuck, Duval?"

"The little mouse has had enough for one night," Bran says. "She's leaving."

"Quit calling me that! And I am *not* leaving."

I was just starting to have fun.

"You don't control her," Evan argues. "She isn't even from a Duval family, for Christ's sake."

"And she's not wolf bait either," Bran says.

"And *she* is standing right here," I say.

Bianca appears in my line of sight, but her gaze is firmly on Bran. I think they might be close to the same height, so being stuck between them, I really do feel like a mouse.

"Bran," Bianca says. "What are you doing?" Her voice is level. There's no snark, no accusatory bend to her question. It's just a question. And the way she delivers it begs it to be answered.

"Yeah," I say. "What are you doing?" As if she needs my drunken help.

Bran pushes me behind him, but he keeps one hand wrapped around my wrist. He takes a step toward Bianca, proving that he does have a few inches on her. She folds her arms over her chest.

Get him, Bianca! Curse him!

But then she frowns and steps back, and I realize that here, Bran is the oldest by several centuries. He out ranks us all. Even in Midnight, where different factions operate by their own code, Bran is clearly at the top of the unspoken hierarchy.

No one messes with Bran Duval.

I know that.

I've always known that.

Sam steps forward. She's been downing drinks just as quickly as I have, so she's got the courage of alcohol and the fierceness of a best friend at her back. "I would like it very much if you got your hands off my best friend." Sam sways as she delivers this request.

"Who here is sober?" Bran asks the crowd.

Adam, the other wolf, raises his hand.

"Take that one home," Bran says when he points a finger at Sam.

Adam nods and hurries to Sam's side.

"Jess?" Sam says.

I scowl up at Bran. He looks down at me, and I catch a glint of fangs.

"I'll be okay," I tell Sam. "I brought my backup stake."

Bran snorts.

"You sure?" Sam's expression hardens. "I could call the Guard."

Bran rolls his eyes.

"I'm sure."

Adam puts his hand gently at Sam's lower back and motions her toward the parking lot.

Bran tucks me in beneath his arm, his hand on my hip, and using his vampire speed, tears us away from the Harbor.

———

The first time I was introduced to vampire speed, I was five.

Julian Locke and several other Locke vampires came over for a BBQ.

One of the female Lockes, Sasha, threw me onto her back, told me to hold on tight, and carried me away into the night.

It was like riding a roller coaster. That was what I told my mom later when Sasha deposited me, starry-eyed and breathless, by the bonfire.

"She was so fast!" I shouted and everyone laughed.

Being carried off by Bran is nothing like that.

It's like being caught in a tornado.

His speed is ten times faster than Sasha's.

And when he stops and rights me in the middle of Midnight Cemetery, it takes the world about another full minute to catch up to me.

Bran puts his hands on my shoulders, keeping me upright.

When I finally have my bearings, I curl my hand into a fist and punch Bran.

Except I'm a human, and he's a vampire, and he catches my punch easily.

"No," he says. That's it. Just *no*.

I fight to get my hand back, but he won't let me go, and worse, he doesn't budge an inch as I flail in his grip.

"Why are...you—" I yank harder "—being such...an...asshole?!"

He lets me go abruptly, and I stumble back.

He turns away and stalks toward the cemetery fountain. I can hear the water splashing into the pool, but it's too dark to make out the bronzed shape of the intertwined lovers at the fountain's center.

"Running with the dogs?" Bran says to the darkness. "Beneath you, little mouse."

I let out a growl of frustration and charge at him and leap on his back.

He deftly swings me around, and in a blink, he has me pressed against the trunk of an old oak tree.

The air leaves my lungs in a useless gasp.

"You're playing a dangerous game, mouse."

"Stop fucking calling me that."

His eyes flash in the darkness, and the prey in me shrinks beneath his stare. My skin erupts in goosebumps.

"This is your fault, you know," I say, and as the words come out, I know I've just set my own trap.

Bran laughs, low and beneath his breath. "My fault? How so?"

"You told me not to wear panties, so by the time I got to the Harbor, I was horny as hell."

What I don't say is that I thought he was going to come to the party for me, but I think he knows that.

His gaze levels, dangerous and dark. "So you threw yourself to the wolves?"

"He was willing."

I lick my lips, and Bran watches my tongue dart out. I feel him grow hard against my thigh, and that burns away the last of the alcohol in my bloodstream. It yanks me back into reality.

He's hard.

Because of me.

A thrill builds in my belly.

Bran's hand comes to my face. His fingertips press hard at my jaw, but his thumb is gentle as he wipes the wetness from my lips.

"And now?" he asks. "Are you horny now?"

"Nope."

He leans in and puts his mouth at my ear. "Liar."

With no fabric to shield me, my wetness is coating my inner thighs. I knew he'd know that, but I like watching how he reacts to my defiance.

"Why did you bait me anyway? Tell me to go commando?" I squirm beneath his weight, but he just presses closer. "Was this your plan all along? Get me riled up and see what I'd do about it? Then show up at the Harbor at the last minute just to humiliate me?"

He laughs. "No. I did it to test your obedience."

My eyes widen, and I grit my teeth and start swinging, but he dodges me easily and then catches both wrists, pinning them above my head.

I don't know how I keep ending up in this position with him, but I both like and hate it.

Bran drops his free hand down to the hem of my skirt, fingers trailing along the press of my thighs.

A thrill races up to my core.

"If you want my help mouse," he says, "then you need to listen to me."

My eyes flutter closed as his fingers slip beneath my skirt. "I don't need your help."

"No?"

My entire body tenses up like a flower curling beneath the heat of a wild flame.

I'm going to get burned, but there's nothing I've ever wanted more than what I want in this moment.

I want him to touch me. Hell, I've fantasized about this so many times, I have to wonder if this is a dream.

His fingers coax my legs open, and I readjust, opening my thighs for him.

"Do you really plan to leave Midnight without knowing why your sister is pawning you off?"

I can feel the heat of his touch just inches from my wet center. He's so close. So impossibly close.

A moan escapes me, and I squirm in his grip.

"Mouse?"

"Huh?"

"Look at me."

I open my eyes to find his glowing impossibly gold. It's the flame all over again, burning bright in the dark.

"Look at me when I touch you."

And then he sinks two fingers inside of me, and my world comes undone.

NINE

I moan as Bran fills me up, and his thumb flicks at my clit. He drops my wrists, and I have to put my hands on his shoulders just to stay upright. My knees are shaking, thighs quivering. I want more of him. I want him to throw me on the mossy ground and fuck me until I can't—

"Mouse."

My eyes are closed again. I widen them, my vision a little blurry and distant.

He strokes my clit, and pleasure builds at my center. I feel like a firecracker ready to explode.

"Why were you throwing yourself to the wolves?"

I pant as he slowly enters me again and curls his fingers deep inside of me.

"I...because...you..."

"Yes?"

I think a little part of me wanted to make him jealous. But I can't tell him that. He strums at my clit again, and a shiver races through me. "Oh god." I arch my back again, and he presses closer, his cock digging into me. He's so fucking hard. Does he actually want me or is this just a vampire power play? Some kind of game of lust and dominance?

Maybe I don't care.

The crescendo gets closer. My wick has been lit.

He's going to make me come.

Bran Duval is going to make me come in the middle of Midnight Cemetery.

And just as I toe the edge, he pulls out of me.

I blink stupidly at him as the thrum of the orgasm slips away. "What are you doing?" I say a little breathless.

"The wolves are not allowed to touch you."

"What?" I lean heavily against the tree, the bark biting into my back.

"If I see that fucking dog touching you again, I'll neuter him."

I swallow hard, trying to catch my breath. My clit is still throbbing, and I can feel my juices coating my inner thighs. "I don't care about the wolves," I say because I think I might say anything just to get his nimble fingers on me again.

"If you want my help, mouse," he says, "do as I say. Stay away from the wolves."

"What—" I push away from the tree to argue, but I take one step, and suddenly, he's gone.

I turn a circle. The moonlight has found a pocket between the trees, and it shines through the cemetary now. I don't catch any movement. "Hey! Don't just leave me here!" I shout.

The crickets go quiet at my outburst. I hold my breath to listen.

Nothing.

He really fucking left me?

I clench my hands and let out a long, drawn out growl.

"I'm going to murder you, Bran!"

———

The cemetary is on the northeast side of town, and I live on the southeast side. It takes me nearly a half hour to walk home, and by the time I come through the front door, my buzz is definitely gone and has been replaced with rage.

I am seething.

Bran has been messing with my head and my body, and all I want to do is jam a stake through his heart.

No, you don't. You want to screw him, a voice says in the back of my head. *Let him be the first.*

Well maybe I can sleep with him and then murder him.

How dare he tease me, order me to stay away from the wolves, and then leave me!

The house is dark save for the light over the kitchen sink. I go there and fill a glass of water and drink it down. My throat is raw, and my head is starting to pound. I grab some aspirin from the cupboard and down two.

As I'm standing at the window, plotting all the ways I might be able to murder Bran, I catch movement in his house.

It's Damien Duval.

Damien is about the same height as Bran, but his build is stockier, his black hair close-cropped.

I remember Bran warning me that Damien would be at the Harbor, but I never did see him. Was he planning to go to see me?

I can't wrap my head around Damien wanting me in his house. Blood is blood. There are no special humans, no special blood to covet.

Why the hell would Damien risk peace to bid for a human destined for the Locke vampires?

Bran says something to Damien, and I can see the irritation plainly on Bran's face as he points his finger at his brother's chest.

Damien throws his hand up, exasperated, and Bran shakes his head and turns away.

What I wouldn't give for vampire hearing right now.

Dare I sneak outside and listen in?

I feel like this is the least of what Bran deserves. I might not have the strength or the speed to match him in a physical fight, but vampires aren't granted supernatural intelligence when they're turned. One thing I can fight with is my brain.

Except one might argue that eavesdropping on two extremely old, extremely powerful vampires is a very, very stupid idea.

As I make my way for the back door, I talk myself through a list of possible excuses should I get caught. I was stargazing. Watering the grass. Taking out the trash. Chasing a raccoon.

The possibilities really are endless.

I quietly shut the door behind me and make my way across the deck and realize my shoes are clunky and loud. I shuck them off and put bare feet to the wood. Much better.

On the grass, I tiptoe across the yard that separates our house from Bran's.

The closer I get, the louder their voices are until I'm right below one of the cracked kitchen windows.

"You're going to start a fucking war," Bran says.

Damien grumbles. "They're keeping secrets, Bran. Something is going on here."

Who are they talking about?

I dare a peek through the window. Bran is standing in the center of the kitchen, his arms crossed over his chest. Damien is pacing.

"This isn't the way to do this," Bran says.

Damien stops. "I need to do something. You know I must. The Lockes need to be put in their place anyway. They've been shifting their weight around. Have you not felt it?"

Bran frowns like he doesn't want to agree with his brother, but gives a quick nod just the same. "I still don't think this is the way to manage this. If there is something special about the girl, they're not going to just give her up."

I clamp my hand over my mouth to stop a startled gasp from escaping.

They're talking about me.

Something special? What does that mean?

Bran goes on, "This kind of war would be bloody and violent. There are better ways. More discreet ways."

"Like what?" Damien asks. "We're running out of time."

"Her Pledge is still a few days away." Bran shoves away from the counter. "Give me at least that before you do or say something. All right?"

Damien runs his hand over his close-cropped hair. "Fine. Fine."

Bran picks up a glass of liquor and slings it back. He gives an almost imperceptible wince. Damien grabs a glass out of sight and empties his too, then he sets it down with a thud. "Keep me updated."

"Of course."

Damien nods. He gives Bran a pat on the back and then makes his way for the door.

I hear it open and shut a second later.

I stay still outside the window and watch Bran from the darkness outside the house. His arms are crossed over his chest again, and he stands there in the kitchen, unblinking, unmoving like he's trapped in a deep thought.

The wind shifts, and a chill shoots down my spine. I exhale, and Bran's eyes dart to me.

At the last second, I duck out of sight and crouch in the grass, my back pressed against the side of his house. If he comes out to look, I am so dead.

I stay there for what feels like an hour but might actually be ten minutes. When I think the coast is clear, I scamper across the yard, slink up the steps to my back deck and then slowly, carefully open and shut the back door.

Once I'm inside, I let out a relieved breath. I don't know if he saw me. I think if he did, he would have come out to confront me. Peeping Tom and an eavesdropper now. He'd never let me live that one down.

I go upstairs to my bedroom and find his bedroom shade already drawn even though it's barely after midnight.

I yank my curtains closed to send the same message.

Now more than ever I need to talk to my sister. I need to know what the hell is going on. Clearly, she's telling the Duvals something that isn't true, but why?

Not wanting to miss her again, I grab my pillow and my phone and make a bed on the couch downstairs. I set my alarm for an hour before she usually gets up.

Except, I'm startled awake before sunrise and yelp when I see Kelly standing over me.

It takes me a second to blink away the sleepiness, and when my eyes finally focus, I lurch to my feet.

Blood is pouring down my sister's neck from a massive torn wound. "Help me," she says right before she collapses in my arms.

TEN

"Kelly! Oh my god. Kelly!"

The blood pouring from my sister's neck soaks the front of me when I catch her as she falls. Her eyes flutter. Her skin is clammy and pale. I grab my pillow from my makeshift bed on the couch and yank off the pillowcase, pressing it into her neck.

"Help! Someone help!" I scream.

Where's my phone? I know I brought it downstairs with me before I curled up on the couch, but—

The back door slams open and bangs loudly against the wall. I let out a startled yelp.

"What is—" Bran stands in the rectangle of early morning light. When he scents the blood, his eyes flash amber. "Mouse, are you hurt?" he asks, his voice dropping an octave.

"It's my sister." I hoist her up. She's almost dead weight in my arms.

"Invite me in," he says.

I lick my lips, swallow hard. What was Bran just saying to his brother earlier?

This kind of war would be bloody and violent. There are better ways. More discreet ways.

I look down at my sister. Did Bran do this? Is this some kind of twisted game to get invited into our house?

I try to sort out all of the reasons he might want to be invited in, but the panic has my thoughts jumbled.

"Mouse," he says again, more sharply this time.

"I'm not inviting you in."

"She'll die then."

I curse beneath my breath. I could call the Guard, but they're human. They travel on four wheels, not two legs. Kelly's already lost a lot of blood...

Goddammit.

Winding my arm around her waist, I drag Kelly to the back door. She's not completely unconscious, and her legs mostly stay beneath her.

"This is ridiculous," Bran grumbles. "Invite me in."

"I'm not inviting you in!"

I get to the kitchen, past the island, and Kelly's legs buckle beneath her. I catch her before she goes down and switch tactics by hooking my hands beneath her arms and dragging her backwards. When I get her shoulders out through the door, Bran pushes me aside and grabs her, yanking her the rest of the way out of the house.

There's blood everywhere. I'm covered in it. My hands are soaked in it. I can't decide if I want to sob or scream.

She's going to be okay. She has to be okay.

We live in a town of supernaturals. People don't just die.

Bran puts his wrist to his mouth, eyes flashing as he bites into his arm. I've grown up around vampires, but I'll never get used to the sound of teeth piercing flesh, the skin ripping open, the blood rushing out.

I step back, arms crossed over my middle as Bran positions his bleeding wrist over my sister's mouth. "Drink, Kelly," he orders, and my sister's eyes flutter, her lips moving as the blood drips down her throat.

It only takes a few seconds for her to swim back to consciousness, and then she grabs Bran's arm and brings it to her mouth, taking in a long drink.

I've never had vampire blood before, but I've heard that when you're ill or wounded, the blood is like a drug. It takes the pain away, eases out the knots in your muscles, the ache in your bones.

"All right," Bran says and yanks his arm back. "That's enough."

Kelly collapses to the deck, panting at the brightening sky, Bran's blood coating her mouth.

"Kelly?" I scurry to her side. "Are you okay?"

She runs her tongue over her teeth. "I... think so?"

"Do you remember what happened?"

Still covered in blood, she sits upright and smooths over her disheveled hair, painting her blond highlights in streaks of red. The wound in her neck is gone. "I'm not exactly sure what happened," she answers as I help her to her feet. When she spots Bran, she scowls. "What is he doing here?"

"*He* saved you," Bran says.

Kelly scoffs.

"You don't remember?" I frown. "You were bitten."

Her gaze goes distant.

"She's been compelled," Bran says.

"No, I haven't," she argues.

"Then where were you thirty minutes ago?"

"I was—" She cuts herself off and blinks several times. "I was...some-where...and..."

"Did you do this to her?" I ask Bran.

He scowls at me. "Why would I?"

I want to throw his words back at him—*There are better ways. More discreet ways*—but what would it prove other than my eavesdropping? Besides, I have a very distinct feeling in my gut that Bran wasn't responsible for this. Now that I'm out here, now that he's saved her... I mean, I suppose saving her could also be a way to get beneath my skin, but we've already established that he is very, very much beneath my skin already.

"She was called to the Lockes earlier," I tell Bran.

"Did you see her when you got home?"

"You mean after you abandoned me in the cemetery?"

"He abandoned you in the cemetery?" Kelly asks.

"Focus, mouse," Bran says. "Did you see her afterward?"

When I came home, I automatically assumed Kelly was already in bed, but I never bothered to check.

"I'm not sure," I admit. "She might have been gone."

Bran's expression softens, and he puts his hands gently on Kelly's shoulders, forcing her to look at him. "How are you feeling?"

"I'm fine," she says. "Just...jittery."

"That's the blood," he tells her. "Go inside and take a shower, then lie down. Okay?"

She gives a reluctant nod before turning and disappearing into the house.

Bran looks over at me. "She could have died."

"But she didn't."

"Why didn't you invite me in? It's not against the rules. You were risking nothing by doing it."

"Risking my innocence maybe."

He makes a PAH sound before pulling off his white t-shirt. I've seen him naked half a dozen times, but the sight of him shirtless, the shadowed lines between his taut abs, the swell of his biceps—it catches me off guard every single time. Like you know the sun is going to set every day, but every day, when it burns at the horizon, when it paints the sky in jeweled shades of red and pink and orange, you can't help but admire it.

Bran catches me staring and smirks. I curl my upper lip at him until he comes over and takes my hand in his and swipes away the blood with his balled-up t-shirt.

"What are you doing? You're going to stain your shirt—"

"Will you stop fighting me?" His eyes light up in the silvery early morning light. "You are infuriating."

"You're a menace."

A hint of a smile pulls at the corner of his mouth. When my hands are as clean as they're going to get, he steps closer and threads his hand through my hair, fingertips pressing against the back of my skull as he forces me to tilt my head up to him.

The shiver that takes over me is involuntary. Primitive.

He draws the shirt over the line of my jaw. The sweep of it, the pressure of his caress, forces my lips to part, and Bran's gaze sinks to my mouth.

A few hours ago, his fingers were inside of me, but somehow, the thought of his mouth on me is more illicit.

And then I blink back to reality and remember my sister was just attacked and Bran gave her his blood and he's plotting something that has to do with me and my Pledge.

I bat his hand away. "I'm fine. Thank you."

"Are you?"

"Yes. Goodnight." I start for the door when he grabs my wrist and yanks me back.

"No," he says.

He seems to like that word.

"No what?"

"Your sister was just attacked. You really think I'm going to let you stay in that house when I can't get inside?"

My mouth drops open. "What? But...why the hell do you even care?"

"I gave you my word I'd help you, mouse, and I always keep my promises. Until we know who attacked your sister, you'll stay at my house."

And then he pulls me down the deck and across our yards and into his house.

Eleven

As the sky turns pink and the birds start singing, Bran pushes in his back door with a kick of his boot. The door wasn't latched to begin with, just slightly ajar. An indication of how fast he left his house when I started screaming in mine.

That knowledge warms my gut, and the warmth runs over my body, and I can't help but wonder why he would even care. I know he's sticking to his word or whatever, but why does he want to help? There's more to his motivation than what he's telling me, which isn't much at all. I just need to figure out what game he's playing and keep playing it in the meantime.

When he shuts the door behind us, he looks me up and down, his eyes flashing in the murky morning light.

I'm covered in blood. He's covered in blood.

I catch a glint of fangs.

He dragged me over here under the guise of protecting me, but I'm suddenly questioning just how safe I am in his house, covered in blood.

I take in a breath. "I need to go. I shouldn't be here." I turn back for the door, but he's suddenly in front of me, his arm barring me from leaving.

"I won't hurt you," he says quietly with a low rumble in his chest.

I roll my eyes and try to play it off like that's the last thing I was worried about. "My sister was literally just attacked. I'm not leaving her alone."

"I'll call the Guard and the Lockes," he says and shoves away from the wall. "Julian will put someone on the house. Unless he was the one responsible for tearing up her throat."

I follow him across the kitchen to the wet bar. "That's unlikely. My sister is one of Julian's favorites. In fact, I heard he asked her to be his blood mate, and she turned him down."

Bran gives me a look.

"What?"

"Have you ever been bitten by a Locke?"

I'm not sure why that's relevant. "No."

"Why?"

"I'm not pledged yet."

He scoffs. "A Pledging is just a formality. And anyone over eighteen can give consent to being bitten. Has a Locke ever asked you?"

"Well...no."

Pulling a tumbler out of the bar's cabinet, Bran pops the top off a decanter and pours himself a jigger's worth of scotch. "And why do you think that is?"

"I don't know. I never thought about it, I guess."

"I'll tell you why." He slings the drink back and empties the glass in one gulp. He barely winces when he swallows it. "Your sister didn't turn Julian down. She agreed to be his blood mate if he promised that you would remain untouched until your Pledging."

"That's ridiculous. And how would you even know that?"

"I know a lot of things."

I snatch the glass from him and hold it out for a pour. He furrows his brow at me but finally gives in and lets a splash of amber liquid fill the bottom. He watches me as I drink it back. The liquor is smokey but smooth, and it immediately makes everything feel better. I'm exhausted and keyed up and anxious and confused. I need something. Something to take the edge off.

"Another," I say.

He frowns at me and doesn't move to refill my glass.

I cock out my hip. "Really?" I reach for the decanter, and in a blur, he moves it out of my reach. "I'm not a fucking child."

"Compared to me, you're just a baby."

"So what does that make you? A cradle robber?"

He snorts. "I haven't fucked you yet, mouse."

Hearing him say that out loud makes my face immediately heat up. I definitely, *definitely* like it when he talks like that, but really, *really* wish I didn't.

Setting the glass down with a thud, I take a step closer to him. My heart is beating harder, and my belly is soaring as I repeat, "*Yet*?"

His eyes glint again in the early morning light. The air grows charged between us. I'm daring him even though I'm not entirely sure I'm prepared to be fucked by Bran Duval. I'm not afraid of having sex. And I'm not really worried about my first time, considering I've got plenty of toys at home. But the thought of losing my virginity to someone like him makes everything clench up tight.

It's like taking your driving test in a Lamborghini.

Nothing afterward will ever compare, and I'm not sure I want to be chasing that high for the rest of my life.

Oh yes you do. Chase that dragon, girl.

I swallow hard, feeling a flush of heat sinking lower in my belly.

Bran's nostrils flare.

"Mouse," he says in a purr.

"Yes?"

His eyes burn brightly now, like two candle flames lighting up the dark.

"You should take a shower," he says.

I blink. "What?"

"You're covered in blood, and my control is growing weak."

"I thought you said you wouldn't hurt me."

The corner of his mouth lifts in a smirk. "Oh, mouse, I promise it wouldn't hurt."

I huff and turn for the door again, but Bran snatches my arm in his grip and pulls me into him so close, I can feel the tickle of his breath on my neck.

There's nothing quite like a vampire's mouth being close to your throat. It's like reaching your hand out to pet a feral dog. The thrill is exhilarating. The fear almost tangible.

"Am I not free to go?" I challenge.

The line of his Adam's apple sinks low in his throat right before his tongue darts out and wets the swell of his lips. His glowing eyes are firmly locked on the beating pulse of my heart in my neck.

I suddenly don't care what his answer is because the devil on my shoulder is saying, *Feel those teeth sink into your throat and his cock inside of you. Why not take the risk now before you leave town? When you can do it and get away with it?*

I was never one to sow my wild oats. I'm not a huge risk-taker. Leaving Midnight is the biggest leap I've ever thought about taking. And even then...a little part of me has been wondering if leaving town is a coward's way out. That in reality, I'm afraid that if I stay, I might actually like being pulled deeper into the world of the supernatural. That I might like toeing that dark line.

Bran takes a step back and holds his arm out with a flourish. "If you want to leave..."

Fear is telling me to *go, go.*

But everything else is saying: *stay, stay.*

And not just in Midnight, but here, now, in Bran's house.

I want to sink into his wickedness and let him do wicked things to me.

"I don't have clean clothes," I say because that's the only logical thing that comes to mind.

"Guess you'll have to go without."

With a smirk, he turns for the stairs.

I go to the staircase and peer up. He's already out of sight, but I can hear him opening a door somewhere in the recess of the second floor. Do I dare go up? It's suddenly dawning on me that I'm alone again in Bran Duval's house. I can't shake the feeling that I've crossed over some threshold that I can't return from.

Screw it.

Hand on the banister, I go up.

Twelve

As I go up the stairs to the second floor of Bran Duval's house, it feels like my heart is lodged in my throat. I'm sure he can hear my rapid pulse. I'm sure he thinks it's hilarious.

I keep going.

When I reach the second-floor landing, I follow the sound of running water and end up in Bran's bedroom. There's a rectangle of light stretching across the dark hardwood floor as the sun rises outside.

Bran should be in bed soon. He might not burst into flames if he's caught in daylight in his own house, but I've heard the effects can feel like the flu to a vampire. I don't want to be the cause of that. I'd never hear the end of it.

I take a tentative step inside.

I've fantasized about being in this bedroom. And I often wondered what it would look like from this side of the window.

The bed is king-sized with a headboard done in rich brown leather. The dark charcoal duvet looks like expensive linen, the kind that when rubbed between your fingers summons images of rainy afternoons in bed, a cup of hot tea in hand, steam rising around your face.

The room smells like Bran, like amber and leather and musk.

It makes my head swim.

Iron tables sit on either side of the bed with emerald green sconces hanging from the wall.

The bed is made, the corners tucked in neatly.

It's all a goddamn delight.

His neatness makes my nerdy side damn near glow.

In the attached bathroom, the shower turns on.

I turn around the room, trying to drink in all the details before he comes out. There are more black and white photographs framed on the wall above the six-drawer dresser. From afar, they look like landscape photographs, but when I get in close, I can just make out the silhouette of someone in the background.

"My self-portrait phase," he says, suddenly beside me, and I step back, feeling like I got caught snooping.

"That's you?" I ask and nod at the center image. The camera is facing the edge of a cliff and a cloudy valley down below. The figure stands at the cliff's edge, facing a darkening, stormy sky.

Bran nods and leans a shoulder against the bathroom's doorframe. "Taken in the 1950s."

The other two images are taken on a bridge and in an underpass.

"They're incredible."

"Thank you."

I shift my gaze to him, looking for sarcasm and finding none.

"Shower is ready," he says. "I have to go to bed."

"I really can go home. I don't have to keep you—"

"Don't," he says.

"Don't what?"

"You're not going home. You're staying here. End of discussion."

I'm not sure why when he talks to me like that, my panties practically turn into a puddle. I usually hate being talked down to. It's why Kelly and I used to fight so much when I was a kid.

With Bran though, it's not an older sister trying to boss me around. It's...almost like he's protecting me.

But from what?

He stares at me a moment longer, then blinks and shifts away. "Don't open the blinds. Come to bed when you're done."

"You want me to sleep with you?"

"My bed is the safest place for you." He darts to the nearest window and pulls down the dark blind.

"I'm not sure I believe that."

"I'll behave." He's a blur as he crosses the room and pulls down the second blind plunging us into mostly darkness. "For now."

The shiver that hits me morphs into a blazing heat that sinks to my pussy.

Bran tsk-tsks.

I roll my eyes in the dark and follow the bleed of light from the bathroom.

If I survive this night, or rather *day*, I might start to believe in miracles.

———

I shut the bathroom door but don't lock it. What's the point? Bran could smash through it with nothing but the power of his pinky finger.

His bathroom is as dark and rich as his bedroom with white subway tile done with black grout in the shower stall and around the double vanity. The counter is spotless. There's nothing on it except for a glass bottle of hand soap.

What a dream.

I tear off my bloody clothes and toss them into the garbage can. No sense trying to scrub the stains out.

When I pull open the glass door on the shower, steam spills out. I duck inside and test the water. It's scalding hot. I dial down the heat and then get in beneath the stream.

I breathe out. There is nothing like the power of a hot shower when you're feeling filthy and out of sorts. The water immediately sooths some of my earlier anxiety and fear.

Beneath the showerhead, everything feels like it could be okay.

I soak my hair then use Bran's shampoo. The bottles on the tiled shelf are black, the writing in French. The soap is pearly white and smells like the woods.

It's as I'm rinsing the suds from my hair that I hear the shower's glass door click open and feel a blast of cold air on my backside.

I know it's Bran before I turn around. "I didn't invite you," I say, feeling the distant stir of a thrill at my core, the rapid thump of my heart in my chest.

"It's my shower," he says at my ear.

The air is hot, but my skin is cold as his hands trail down my arms and lift goosebumps.

My inner walls clench up as my clit throbs.

"Bran," I start, not exactly sure where I'm going, but feeling like I need to go *somewhere*.

His hand follows the flat plane of my stomach, then dips down, down.

I moan. I can't help it.

It's the promise of his touch. The feel of him hard at my back.

He cups my mound, and I wiggle against him, trying to rock to leverage some friction. But he tightens his hold on me and presses me against the cool shower wall.

"Needy little mouse," he says at my ear, his voice rough like rock salt.

I think I knew that if I let him drag me home, that if I stayed here and went up those stairs, we'd end up exactly right here.

I think I knew it, and that's why I stayed.

I'm not sure what's going on between us, or if this really is just some ploy to gain my trust, or break me in some other inconceivable way, but I think I'm too far gone to stop it.

I think maybe I want to give in to it regardless of the consequences.

He flicks a finger over my clit, and I tremble beneath him.

"Why are we doing this?" I say to the tiled wall, panting hard now.

"Because it's fun?" His fingers curl, sliding between my wet folds.

"I think you like torturing me."

"You might be right." His hand disappears, and I moan in disappointment. But he spins me around to face him.

Water droplets glisten on his face and in his raven hair. He's so devastatingly hot that it almost makes me angry.

"Is this part of the game then?" I ask, feeling bold and a little drunk on the moment.

He leans in, his mouth just an inch from mine. "Oh mouse, everything is a game." And then he kisses me, hard and fast.

I'm suddenly ravenous and blind with the need for him.

This feeling burning through my veins is like shouting at the moon, like running through empty streets after midnight, like stepping on the gas pedal and blasting through a red light.

The thrill is intoxicating.

I don't care if we don't like each other.

I don't care if I'm supposed to pledge myself to the Locke vampires.

Or that I plan on leaving Midnight.

Or that Bran might be twisting me for his own ends.

I just fucking want him. Just flesh and bones and fucking and kissing and—

He pulls away from me and sinks to his knees. I look down to find his eyes glowing that vampire fire.

Fangs protrude from his mouth.

His earlier warning comes back to me, *"...my control is growing weak."*

I'm tempting him, and I want to be tempted too.

The thought of him biting me—

"Tell me to stop," he purrs.

I hang my head back, let the water spray across my body. I'm burning hot and I think a little delirious.

"Not a chance."

He lifts my leg, draping it over his shoulder, baring me to him and then he sinks his fangs into my inner thigh.

I can't help it—I hang my head back and cry out in ecstasy.

Thirteen

I've kept myself in neat and tidy little boxes my entire life. Be the dutiful daughter. The quiet little sister who never rocks the boat. Those neat and tidy little boxes spill over into my life with my clothes organized by color and type, my desk clean, everything in its place.

I like the control. The order. I like that labels spell things out, cut and dry, no question.

Being bitten by Bran Duval in his shower is the most chaos I've ever invited into my life.

And I'm surprised at how good it feels.

If this is what it's like being bitten, why haven't I tried it yet?

The euphoria washes over me like a break of warm sunlight.

Bran sucks at my thigh while his fingers slid inside of me. I moan and grip at his shoulder to keep myself upright.

The pain of the bite, the pleasure of his fingers, it's damn near delirious.

He twists his hand so he can slide his thumb up to my needy clit. He flicks at me, causing me to jolt and then he goes still.

With heavy lids, I look at him as he straightens in front of me.

Fangs sharp and protruding from his mouth, he's covered in my blood, eyes glowing such a bright amber, I swear they're phosphorescent.

He runs his tongue over his lips, lapping up the last drops.

"You taste just as fucking sweet as I thought you would," he says, and I pant out a breath as my pussy clenches up again.

I want more of him.

I can't believe this is happening, and I don't want it to stop.

"Fuck me," I say.

"No," he says.

I whine. "Please."

He gets in close to me, the spray of the shower bouncing off his broad shoulder, wetting my eyelashes.

"I'll fuck you when I'm good and ready," he says, but while his words show restraint, I can feel the head of his cock prodding at me. I shift, rising on my tip toes and rocking my hips so his shaft slides between my legs.

He growls, his hand coming to my chin, fingers pressing hard against my jaw. "You don't control this."

I arch my back, rubbing against him. I'm nearly blind with the desire for him.

"I don't see you pulling away," I say.

He laughs through his nose, eyes still molten metal. "Watch me."

And then he's gone, the shower door softly clicking closed behind him.

"What the hell?" I shout.

I'm breathing heavy, and my clit is buzzing.

"I'll just finish myself then." I lean against the shower stall and reach down, but Bran is suddenly there again tsk-tsking at me.

"No." He takes my arm and pins it against the wall. "You don't get to come until I say so."

I scowl at him. "Why not?"

He leans in at my ear and whispers, "Because deep down, you like me telling you what to do."

I buck against him. He laughs.

I want to prove to him just how wrong he is, but the truth is, I like control, but I also like being controlled by him.

Apparently, Bran Duval knows just how to press my buttons, because while I'm horny as hell and near delirious with wanting to come, doing it myself now doesn't hold the same thrill.

What does make me buzzy is the thought of listening to him.

I go still against the wet shower wall. Bran's nostrils flare, and he arches a brow. He lets go of my arm, hands dipping to my hips. With his knee, he nudges my legs open just enough to open my thighs.

"Is this what you wanted, mouse?" he says, voice rumbly and hoarse as he slides his cock between my legs. The head of his shaft sends a shockwave of pleasure straight through me as it drags over my clit.

"Fuck. Yes."

He pumps his hips, pressing me against the wall with his weight as he fucks my wet folds hitting that pleasure zone again and again, building the buzz of an orgasm with barely any effort at all.

The spray of the water beads on my face. Bran's mouth comes to my jawline and kisses slowly as he switches his pace, teasing me more than fucking me.

"Bran." My voice is reedy and far away.

He kisses down my jaw, to the hollow behind my ear, then sinks to the pulse in my throat.

Razor sharp fangs graze at my flesh.

He keeps sliding that hard cock between my legs, every nerve ending firing like a wick.

"You want to come, mouse?" he asks and puts his mouth on the rapid beat of my heart.

"Yes."

"Say please."

I whimper when he stops entirely and drags the tip of his tongue over my throat.

My knees are shaking. My pussy is so tingly, it feels electric with the craving to come.

I know giving in to Bran's demand is the same as giving in to a monster, but goddammit, I think I might say or do anything right now.

"Please," I moan out.

Bran's grip tightens on my hips as he picks up the sliding tempo of his cock, fucking my clit as the pressure builds and builds.

"Go on then," he says at my ear, "let me hear you come, naughty little mouse."

That does it.

The dam breaks.

I grip at his shoulders, eyes clenched tight, starbursts behind my lids as the orgasm spills over me in a delicious wave of heat and pleasure.

I cry out, body quivering on Bran's thick shaft.

"Fuck, mouse," he says, and then he groans loudly, muscles coiling up tight as he comes. Cum spills all over my pussy and drips down my legs.

I collapse against him and breathe hard against the rise of his shoulder, holding on to him for dear life as the last of the orgasm fades out, leaving me spent and trembling in his arms.

"Oh my god," I say. "Oh my god."

He pulls away and looks down at me, lips swollen and wet, vampire eyes glowing amber.

I make a move to wash myself between my legs, but he snatches my wrist. "No," he says, and that's all he has to say now, because he and I both know I'm going to listen.

He helps me rinse out my hair and then shuts the shower off.

When I step out of the stall, he towels off the dampness, then tosses it to the corner, takes me by the hand, and leads me out into the pitch-black bedroom.

I can only hear the soft rasp of the sheets as he pulls them back, then his command: "Get in bed, mouse."

I slowly feel my way to the bed and climb in beneath the sheets. I'm immediately enveloped by the soft cotton and Bran's scent, like whiskey and oak.

It's the most delicious scent that immediately makes me want to sigh into the pillow as I lay my head down.

Bran slides into me and pulls me into his chest, arms wrapped around me.

"Good girl," he says, his voice hoarse and sleepy.

"Shut up," I mutter. He tightens his hold on me, tucks me into his side.

I lay there, blinking into the darkness, thinking there's no way I'm going to sleep in this situation, but before I know it, I'm out.

We wake to an incessant pounding noise.

Groggy, I moan and roll over. "What is that?"

Bran is already up and has flicked on a lamp on the bedside table. He pulls on a pair of jeans, no boxer briefs, I notice.

"Someone's at the front door," he answers and then disappears in a blur.

Oh god. What if something happened to Kelly while I was descending into horny madness?

I slip from the bed and then realize I'm still naked with no clothes to put on. I decide since part of the reason I'm here and naked is because of Bran, he owes me a shirt or two. I go to his walk-in closet and find rows and rows of clothing. Most of it is black, but I find a few flannel shirts that are big enough to be a dress on me.

Pulling one on, I'm filled with a tiny thrill that I'm in Bran Duval's house, dressing in his clothes.

Nothing like this would ever happen in the real world. Or rather, the world outside of Midnight Harbor where people think vampires and witches and fae are fiction.

Once the shirt is buttoned enough to cover the important bits, I follow the hallway then descend down the stairs. The circular window on the first landing shows dark, stormy clouds outside, making it seem later than it actually is.

"Where is she?" a familiar voice says at the front door.

Bran is standing in a rectangle of dusky light, the jeans hanging low on his naked hips. From my vantage point on the stairs, I can see every ridge of muscle in his back, every dimple. His hair is still mussed, but it looks more like sex hair than it does sleep hair.

"In my bed," comes Bran's reply.

A hand slaps hard against the door, but Bran has it firmly in his grip, and it doesn't budge.

"She may not be pledged to my house yet, but rest assured, Duval, she's mine. Now go fucking get her."

Julian Locke is here?

The shadowed lines of muscle between Bran's shoulder blades grows deeper as his body coils. The hair on my arms rises, goosebumps covering my skin.

"Say that again and find out how true it is," Bran says, almost a growl.

"I don't know what you're up to, but this won't end well. Jessie is ours."

I come down the rest of the steps, and the vampires cut themselves off, finally realizing that I'm there.

When I step around Bran, Julian looks me up and down in nothing but a buttoned flannel shirt and clamps his mouth shut.

Julian Locke appears to be at least ten years older than Bran, when in reality, in vampire years, he's nearly fifty years younger. It's easy to forget that when they're standing next to one another.

Where Bran's skin is flawless, smooth, without wrinkles or blemishes, Julian's got pronounced lines around his eyes and in his forehead. His dark hair is shaved close to the scalp while his face is covered in thick facial hair.

"What's going on?" I ask.

Julian licks his lips. "Your sister is worried about you."

"Me? She was the one who came home last night with her throat all torn to shreds."

Bran takes a step closer to me. "You wouldn't know anything about that, would you Julian?"

The way he goes pale, the flash of a blue glow in his eyes says that yes, he does know something about it.

"What happened to her?" I ask.

"I wasn't with her last night," he answers. "But if someone got rough with their bite, I'll see to it they're punished."

"It wasn't just the bite." Bran crosses his arms over his chest and takes another step my way, close enough that half his body shields me now. "Kelly was compelled."

Julian's nostrils flare. "Like I said, I'll look into it. In the meantime, it's time for Jessie to come home."

I've known Julian Locke my entire life, but while he's been a fixture in my world, I never exactly felt comfortable around him. There was always something about the way he looked at me, like I was a zoo animal, and everything I did was a performance for him.

I think deep down a little part of me wanted to leave Midnight Harbor because I didn't want to align the rest of my life with Julian and the Locke vampires.

"I appreciate your concern, Julian," I say, "but I'm just fine staying here."

I catch Bran's smug grin out of the corner of my eye.

"I would advise against that," Julian says.

"Why?"

Julian looks at Bran. Some unspoken language passes between them. The tension boils in the air, and instinctively, I take a step back, letting Bran act as my shield.

"You don't want to do this," Bran says.

Julian scowls, deepening the lines around his eyes. "You don't have the power of the Duval house at your back."

"Have you forgotten who I am, Julian?" Bran moves to the threshold. "I don't need it."

There's an obvious twitch to Julian's expression. Finally, he backs off, and the tension fades. Julian looks past Bran at me. "Just be careful, Jessie. I've known Bran for centuries. He's broken a lot of hearts in that time."

With that, he turns and disappears out of sight.

Bran gives the door a shove, and it slams closed.

"What was that all about?" I ask.

Bran stalks past me and goes upstairs. I follow and find him tugging on a black t-shirt in his bedroom, then boots. "Nice shirt," he says.

I frown and cross my arms over my chest. His flannel is easily three times as big as me, and it hangs off my body like a bedsheet on a clothesline.

"I like you in my clothes," he says. "I like thinking about you pantie-less in my clothes even more."

"Don't change the subject."

He stands and crosses the room to tower over me. "It's too bad we have somewhere to be. I can still taste your sweetness in the back of my throat, little mouse, and I'd very much like another bite."

Heat flames in my cheeks. "Well, you'll have to wait for another century to pass, because I've thankfully come to my senses."

He smirks at me, clearly reading my bluff. "Uh huh. Let's get you home and get dressed."

"Where are we going?"

He steers me out of the room and down the stairs. "I think it's time we go talk to your boss."

"What? Why?"

He nods at the protection rune hanging around my neck, the one my mom gave me when I was just a kid. "Because of that."

I lift the pendant by its clasp. The stone is black obsidian with the rune carved into its face. The rune itself always reminded me of an upside-down chicken leg. "What about it?"

"It was made by Rita."

"How do you know that?"

"Because, mouse, it smells like her. Now tell me, why would a witch give a mortal girl a protection amulet when she was just a child?"

A lump wedges itself in the column of my throat. That's a very good question. One I never looked at too closely. Witch charms are common in Midnight Harbor, obviously, but not usually protection charms, not when that mortal family has been pledged to a vampire house for decades.

But I barely knew Rita before she gave me a job at the coffee shop. She would have said something if she was the creator of the charm, wouldn't she?

Unless it was supposed to be a secret.

Fourteen

My house is empty when I go inside. I can feel it. All of Kelly's blood from the night before is gone, almost like it never happened.

Last night I was worried sick about my sister, but today, in the daylight, I'm more pissed than sympathetic.

Kelly is keeping secrets from me too, and I think she's been artfully dodging me this entire time, taking advantage of my willingness to let things slide so as not to create waves.

My sister knows me so damn well.

Upstairs, I unbutton Bran's flannel shirt. I consider folding it up to return it to him, and then decide against it. It smells like him. Just holding on to it gives me butterflies. He's screwing with my head, driving me mad. When I'm thinking outside of the lust, I feel silly for obeying him, even if it does send a fresh wave of desire straight down my belly.

I'm caught in the storm of Bran Duval, and I'm not sure how to find my way out, or even if I want to.

After pulling on jeans and a white V-neck t-shirt, I check my reflection in the bathroom mirror. Shadows from smudged mascara circle my eyes. My hair dried funny while I slept, so it's kinked on one side. I look disheveled and unhinged.

Bending over, I tie my hair into a messy bun, then run a wipe over my face. Starting with a somewhat clean slate, I put on a fresh coat of mascara and a run of rose-tinted lip balm on my lips.

"Better than nothing," I mutter and then grab my bag and hurry back downstairs to find Bran waiting on the front porch for me.

In the fading light, he's hot as sin, deadly as lightning, and when his eyes drag over my body, and the irises flicker with desire, I tense up as if anticipating a rumble of answering thunder. There's this wild roaring in my gut when he comes to stand beside me the second I cross over the threshold. I like that he stays near me as if he's telling the world I'm his, even though that makes little sense. Even though the very thought makes me feel like I've lost touch with gravity.

I don't know which way is up anymore. What happened between us early this morning has changed something, and I'm still spinning, wobbly on my axis.

I pull the door closed and start down the porch steps, Bran following behind.

"Are we driving or walking?" I ask.

"With your useless mortal legs?" I can practically hear the eye roll in his words. "Walking would take forever. We'll drive."

"You don't have a car," I point out. Most vampires in Midnight Harbor don't. They can get anywhere on foot much faster than a car could.

"No, but you do." He holds out his hand.

"You're not driving my car."

"Why not?"

"It's a classic 1995 BMW M3 Coupe." I'm not a car fanatic, but I know this one is a gem. My dad bought it brand new off the lot, and my mom babied it after he died. Kelly let me have it when my mom passed.

It's got a 5-speed manual transmission and original leather interior with hardly a crack.

I love that car.

"Do you even know how to drive?" I quip.

"I've been driving since cars were invented." He flicks his fingers at me, indicating I should hand over the keys.

A little flare of defiance ignites in my gut, and I cross my arms over my chest, my bag banging against my hip.

"Mouse," he says, a warning edge to his voice. In one fluid motion, he's suddenly inches away from me, towering over me. "Don't make me make you."

I think that's exactly what I wanted and just the barest promise of it has my insides clenching up. And he knows it too. He knows it so damn well.

With a sigh, I dig into my bag and produce the keys attached to the retro motel keychain I bought online. I drop it into his outstretched hand, and he turns over the plastic tag.

"*Dude, where's my car?*" he says, reading the cursive text on the keychain tag.

"What? I think it's hilarious."

"Please tell me you don't actually like that movie."

"It's a funny movie."

The grumble of revulsion rumbles in the back of his throat. "I suddenly think less of you."

Snorting, I follow him across the front yard. The BMW, shining candy red in the street lights, sits waiting on the blacktop.

"Okay then, tell me a better movie than *Dude, Where's My Car?*" I challenge.

"How about any?" He opens the driver's side door and looks at me across the roof. "Literally any other movie."

"Oh really? I take it you haven't seen *Transylmania* then."

He climbs into the car, his long legs scrunched up between the seat and the steering wheel. He adjusts it, and the seat slides back with a thunk.

"Christ, mouse, you're practically eating the dash in this thing."

"We can't all be six-five gods."

"Six-four," he corrects.

Shit, he's nearly a foot taller than I am. I mean, I know he's much bigger than I am, but putting it into actual numbers makes me feel even smaller.

Bran turns the engine over then wraps his hand around the stick shift.

I have this thing with guys driving stick-shifts. A fetish, maybe. Man and machine working in beautiful, quick unison. I once went on a date with a guy who drove a stick-shift, and I could barely hear a word he said. I was so focused on his hand moving through the gears as he sped down the freeway.

I think I fell more for his way with cars than I did for him. We only went on the one date.

The anticipation of seeing Bran drive my car suddenly overwhelms me. I think subconsciously my defiance on the keys wasn't because I was worried about the safety of the Bimmer, but what seeing Bran drive it might do to me.

He pushes in the clutch and shifts into reverse. The car has always been lithe and speedy, but with Bran behind the wheel, it feels like it's propelled by rocket fuel.

We're in the street and shooting through the night before I can settle into my seat.

"Slow down," I chide.

"I will not," he answers and shifts into second, his thigh working as he pushes at the clutch.

"So," I start, hand still griping at the door handle as the headlights cut through a dark section of road, "we're going to the coffeeshop to confront my boss about the necklace I've been wearing since I was a kid that apparently smells like witch?"

"Yes," Bran says, "exactly that."

"And what if she laughs at us? What if she shoves us out the door?"

Or worse—what if she fires me? I need the job to save up money to move out of Midnight Harbor, even though my Pledging and moving feels so far away.

"She'll answer me." Bran takes a sharp turn. The car hugs the shoulder, and the velocity forces me to the left, closer to Bran. "Rita owes me."

I can't help but laugh. "Seriously? For what?"

He looks at me briefly before turning back to the road, the car slipping through the night.

"What could you possibly have done for a witch?"

"The 'what' doesn't matter."

"Rita hates vampires. I know this as fact. She's probably going to toss you out the front door the second you walk over the threshold."

"I will enjoy the look on your face when you realize you're wrong." He slows for another sharp turn and downshifts.

I bury a happy little sigh watching him work at the clutch with confidence.

God, he's hot.

"Shall I pull over?" he asks, eyes on the road.

"For what?"

"You must be soaking wet," he says. "Judging by the scent on the air."

My mouth drops open, and then I stubbornly cross my legs as if doing so will hide the smell of my desire.

I hate vampires!

"Maybe I'll take you in the backseat," he says, eyes still on the road, hand loose on the steering wheel. "Maybe I'll bend you over the hood of the car and—"

A little moan escapes me, and I rub my thighs together without thinking.

He glances at me, smug as hell. "Over the hood it is." The car slows down.

"Stop that!" I say, groaning. "Like I said before, what happened in the shower was a momentary lap in judgment. It won't be happening again."

"Oh mouse." He downshifts again as the street spills into downtown Midnight Harbor. "It's cute that you think so."

Just the promise of more of him makes my pussy throb and my stomach clench up.

Fuck. I'm in trouble.

———

Bran parks right out front of the coffee shop. There's lots of foot traffic in this part of town, and heads turn our way when we climb out of the car, and people realize a MacMahon is with a Duval vampire.

There are no rules against our being together, but it's highly unusual for someone from a family typically pledged to the Lockes to be seen with a Duval.

In all of Midnight Harbor, the Lockes and the Duvals probably have the biggest rivalry. They're founding families, and its members, by their very nature of being immortal vampires, have been around the longest.

If anyone were to ask my opinion, I'd say the Duvals hold more power. Bran and his brother Damien are some of the oldest in Midnight Harbor, but more than that, they were turned by a Montenaro, which is one of the oldest vampire houses in the entire world.

I've never been one to care about power, but it's hard not to be swayed by the pull of it, especially with Bran.

Car keys jangling from his hand, Bran goes up on the sidewalk and rakes his eyes over the people staring. They quickly look away and hurry out of sight. It's like I've walked into the middle of town with a black panther at my hip. People give the Lockes a wide berth, but they don't part seas.

I meet Bran in front of the bay window of the coffee shop. Gold string lights glow from inside where my window display from last week shows off Rita's charms, apothecary jars (with my remade labels), and several different flavors of bagged ground coffee. I'm supposed to work tomorrow and redo the display, provided I can get past all the shit that's currently going wrong in my life.

Bran pulls the door open and holds it for me.

With a deep breath, I step inside.

Indie folk music plays alongside the hiss of the milk steamer and the grind of coffee beans. Rita stands at the end of the counter, looking over some paperwork, while Winnie, another witch from Rita's coven, mixes some drink orders.

The tables are nearly full, and the din of conversation fills the cozy space.

The decibel lowers when Bran walks in behind me, and it makes me want to address it to absolve myself of some of the guilt and shame I'm feeling. Not that I have any reason to feel either. I owe no one allegiance.

I'm promised to no house. And if my mom were alive, I know she'd support whatever decision I made. Even if she did have a massive crush on Julian Locke.

When I catch one of the shifters eyeing me up and down then Bran, I almost shout, "What? What are you staring at?" But then think better of it.

When Rita looks over at me, a smile spreads across her face until she realizes who stands beside me. Her smile quickly vanishes.

I hurry over and lower my voice. "Can we talk in the back?"

Her gaze goes to the space behind my shoulder, and while I didn't hear him move, I'm positive Bran is behind me already, probably looking like the bad decision he most definitely is.

"Sure," Rita says and scoops up her work. "He coming too?"

"Is that okay?"

"Don't ask for her permission," Bran says to me, even though he's staring at Rita while he says it. "Because I don't need it."

Rita huffs and turns for the swinging door to the back room. "Someday that mouth of yours is gonna get you in trouble."

"It hasn't yet."

I put my fist to my mouth, hiding a laugh.

Bran gives me a dead look.

"What? She's probably right."

I follow Rita through the swinging door, through the storage room, and into her office. There are no windows in the interior room, but Rita hired an artist to paint a trompe-l'œil painting that looks like a stone balcony overlooking a whimsical English garden. More string lights hang from the ceiling and are strung around the painting, giving it the look and feel of fireflies in the garden.

Rita dumps her work on her desk amongst several other piles then stands at its corner, one hand on her hip, the other splayed on the desk.

Being in her office always makes me itchy. It's a complete and utter mess. There are old sticky notes stuck to the filing cabinet that I'm absolutely sure hold no relevancy anymore.

Pencil nubs dot every surface along with several uncapped markers that are probably so dry, you could use them to whittle wood. On the opposite wall, three long shelves hold books, jars, and various other treasures, but there's no rhyme or reason to the display with jars stuck between books and books stacked on top of jars.

My gaze gets stuck on a jar with a peeling label that says *fae quarrel*. The inside is nearly empty save for one red flower. Despite the fact that the flower has been snipped from its stem, the petals are still vibrant with color and look velvety smooth.

"So what's this about?" Rita asks.

I lick my lips trying to figure out how to start the conversation. It's not every day you accuse your witch boss of making you a protection amulet that she and your mother have kept a secret.

"Well...so there's this thing...well, what I mean is...Bran was saying..."

Bran leans against one of the filing cabinets. "What the little mouse is trying to ask is, why did you make her a protection amulet?"

I send a withering glare his way. I've been letting him get away with the nickname in private, but calling me mouse in front of my boss is crossing the line. Except my anger does nothing to him. He isn't even looking at me. His attention is squarely on Rita.

I turn back to my boss to find her lips parted, ready to deny, but somehow locked in the second before the words can get past her lips.

Then she sighs and drops into her desk chair. "How did you know?"

"I can smell you on it," Bran replies.

The line of her dark brow sinks over her wide, brown eyes. "Truly? I made that thing over twenty years ago."

"I have a good sense of smell," Bran answers.

She scoffs and turns in the chair, the casters creaking beneath her weight. "Your mom asked me for it," she tells me.

"Why?" Bran pushes away from the cabinet and comes to stand beside me. I don't know if he's sensing the world is starting to shift for me, if Rita's admission has caught me off guard, or if he just wants to be near.

Either way, I'm grateful for him, even though I want to hate him, even though every rational thought in my head is telling me that falling for the devilish vampire is a mistake.

Am I though? Am I falling for him?

I look up at him beside me, at the strong line of his jaw, the straight slope of his nose, the swell of his lips, the way his hair runs back in thick, jet-black waves, and every detail about him, ever angle, every curve sends butterflies into a frenzy in my gut.

Oh shit.

I think I am falling for him.

He looks down at me, eyes narrowing as he tries to read my sudden panic.

This is clearly not the most important thing going on in this room!

I need to get my head together.

Rita props an elbow on a stack of pamphlets for the coven's annual fiscal report and scratches her nails through several of her tight braids. "I didn't ask the why," Rita says and exhales, long lashes fanning over her cheeks. "And it's not a protection amulet."

"Really? Are you serious?" I take a step toward her, the amulet now clutched in my hand. "Then what is it?"

Fifteen

The amulet swings from the end of the necklace. "Please tell me, Rita."

She takes a deep breath and then—"It's a binding amulet."

My heart squeezes in my chest. The world spins.

I drop into one of the vintage waiting room chairs that sits in front of her desk and bend over, head in my hands.

Nothing is making sense.

Rita must be lying.

But why would she? This isn't some kind of gotcha game. Rita would have no reason to lie.

I suck in several deep breaths. No one says anything as I try to get a handle on the swirling thoughts in my head.

"Jessie," Rita says. "I've wanted to tell you, but your sister asked to keep it between us for now and—"

I lurch upright. "Kelly knows it's a binding?"

Rita frowns. "I suspect your mother told her on her deathbed."

Of course. Of course! "What else don't I know?" On my feet, I put my hands on the mess on Rita's desk and lean into her with venom in my voice. "What else have you been keeping from me, Rita?"

The boldness comes out of nowhere, and guilt turns sour in my stomach at the surprise that registers on Rita's face.

This is so unlike me. I'm only bitchy with Bran because he's earned it.

"I'm so fucking tired of the secrets!" I yell.

A hand comes to the back of my neck, fingers gently pressing at the knotted muscle. The rich tenor of Bran's voice is at my ear. "Calm down, mouse."

Rita blinks in quick succession as the surprise morphs into agitation. I can see the regret pinched around her brown eyes. "I wanted to tell you. I really did, but it wasn't my place."

Bran pulls me back. "Do you know what was bound?" he asks her.

Rita shakes her head. "Bindings, for the most part, can be applied universally. I only ask the why if I suspect its being abused. In this case, it was a mother asking for her child."

"How do we undo it?" Bran asks. I'm glad he's thinking rationally, asking the right questions. I can't keep my thoughts straight. I just want to scream with rage. I can feel it burbling up at the base of my throat. But I clench my teeth together to keep my voice locked away.

"I need a new moon," Rita tells us.

I pick up the amulet again and turn it over in my hand.

Bran says, "When is that?"

Without looking at the calendar, Rita answers right away. Witches and shifters always know the cycle of the moons. I couldn't care less. *Usually*.

"This coming Thursday."

Two days *after* my Pledging.

Great.

"Will you do it?" Bran asks her.

"Of course."

"Do you need anything from us before then?"

I catch the thinly veiled contempt that comes across her face before she says, "Us? Is there an *us*, Mr. Duval?"

It's funny hearing Rita use the title considering that in appearances she's nearly thirty years older than he is.

It's a sign of respect, I realize, one you give to your elders.

And Bran is our elder by several hundred years.

"The only reason I'm here asking these questions is because Bran clued me in," I say. "He didn't have to, but he did. So yes, there is an *us*. For now, anyway."

"You're cute when you're defending me," Bran says.

I whack him in the abs, but he barely flinches. It's like hitting a wall of iron. "Stop doing that."

"Stop doing what?"

I wave in the air. "This. Being this way. Saying those things. Acting all—"

Annoyingly hot and stuff.

Bran is smug from his lofty height.

"Thank you for telling me now," I say to Rita, eager to get the hell out of here. "And I really appreciate you undoing the binding."

"It's your right to have it undone. I should have said something earlier." She takes a step toward me. "But Jessie, give some consideration to the consequences." Her gaze is heavy and intense as she adds, "We have no idea what we're unbinding. Just be prepared for that."

I give her a quick nod and shove Bran out the door.

———

I barely look up as we exit the coffee shop. I don't feel settled until we're back into the night, and Bran is behind the wheel of the Bimmer and I'm in the passenger seat. He turns the engine over and pulls out of the parking spot, making his way down River Street.

Pressure is building in my chest, making my ribs ache. What the hell is going on? Up until this moment, I'd wanted to think that Kelly pawning me off on the Duval House was just some kind of big sister I-know-better-than-you move. But now...now it's so much bigger than that and it's growing by the second and—

I have a sudden flash to the conversation I overheard between Bran and his brother Damien. In all of the chaos with Kelly, I completely forgot about it.

Turning in my seat, I regard Bran with suspicion.

He gives me a quick look before returning his eyes to the road. "Well spit it out."

"Everyone is keeping secrets from me, including you."

"Me?"

"I heard you talking to your brother. You said, 'If there is something special about the girl...' And now look, we find out I've been bound for some unknown reason. What did you mean by that? What do you know? What does Damien know?"

"I thought I smelled a mouse outside."

"Besides the point!"

Bran slows and downshifts to turn onto a side street, away from the main part of downtown. He licks his lips, teeth raking over his bottom lip. I see the moment he makes a decision.

"All right. Fine. Maybe I've kept some things from you too, but only because there are still a lot of unanswered questions, and if there's anything I've learned in my multitude of centuries, it's that making assumptions can cost you more than you're willing to pay."

"That sounds like a really fancy way of saying you've been lying to me."

"Lies are different than unspoken truths."

I grumble and face the road again. "I'm officially extremely excited about leaving this fucking town."

Bran shoots me a look. "You're still planning on leaving?"

"Of course. Even more so now. Because everyone is keeping shit from me."

"Don't you want to know why?"

"No."

"Now who's lying?"

I cross my arms over my chest and slump in the seat. Deep down, I do want to know, but I'm too afraid of what the truth might reveal.

Bran slams on the brakes and whips the wheel around. I brace myself with one hand on the door handle and the other on the dash. "What are you doing?"

"You're right. You deserve transparency." He takes us back the way we came. "I promised you I'd help you, so I will."

"And how do you plan to do that?"

We don't head downtown though. Bran takes the next left turn, and the headlights sweep over a roadside sign that reads *So Good Food— where you can fill up on so good food for just $10!*

That's a Locke House restaurant.

"Earlier you asked me how I knew certain details about the Locke house." Bran shifts and the car picks up speed again.

I'm momentarily distracted by the movements, but I shake myself out of the hypnosis. "Right. Yeah. I did say that."

Bran smiles at me, his face highlighted by the soft neon glow of the dash lights. "I know things because I have a spy in Locke House."

———

I have to say, I'm not surprised by this news. I'm gathering that Bran Duval deals in information. It's cleaner than fists and blood.

It makes me like him even more.

When So Good appears on the horizon, the back deck that sits over the river is lit up with big-bulbed string lights. Bran slows and pulls into the parking lot.

"Here?" I say and sit forward in the seat.

The parking lot is packed. It's a Saturday night, after all, so I'm not surprised. I am surprised, however, that a Duval vampire is totally casual about stepping foot inside.

"Your spy is here?"

"Yes, but maybe don't call them my spy when we walk in the door."

We climb out, and laughter and revelry filters out the open windows and from the deck. Bran leads us up the three wide steps to the wrap-around porch and then holds open the screen door for me.

I've been to So Good many times before but usually with Kelly, and sometimes with a Locke or two. Never with a Duval.

I'm braced for the same reaction that we got at the coffeeshop, but no one pays us much notice as we step inside.

I relax a little. Maybe this won't be as bad as I thought.

"This way, mouse," Bran says at my ear and then steers me toward the back with a hand at my hip.

We go down a hallway, bypassing the dining room all together.

When we come to a closed door with a metal placard labeled MANAGER, Bran knocks.

Within seconds, the door pulls open, and a woman peers out at us.

It's Runa, one of the higher-ranking Locke vampires. I've always thought of her as one of the cooler ones with her nose piercing and her full-sleeve tattoos. Her hair is dyed lavender and shaved on one side of her head, and long on the other. Today the long side is braided into a thick fish-tail braid.

Her bright blue gaze sweeps from Bran to me and then back to Bran. Her eyes narrow, and then she speaks to him in a language I don't recognize.

He replies immediately in the same language.

I think it might be Italian or Latin

Then she slams the door in our faces.

"What was that all about?" I ask.

"Come on." Bran guides me back through the restaurant, then out the front door and back into the car.

"What is happening? What did she say?"

Bran starts the car up and drives us a few miles down the road. "Runa just told me to go fuck myself."

"I thought she was your spy?"

"Oh she is."

"I'm so confused."

"We have a standing meeting every other week, but I needed her sooner than that. We can't use phones to communicate. Too obvious. So I asked her if she thought Julian would be pissed if I bit you in the restaurant, and Runa told me to—well, you know."

"Okay...so now what?"

"She'll meet us at our usual spot. We just have to give her a while." He sends a devilish look my way. "However will we pass the time?"

"Very funny."

Bran takes us to an upscale part of town where the river widens and spills into Midnight Lake. Here the houses are further apart, and each comes with its own dock and boathouse. They are as fancy as the people that inhabit them.

We turn down a winding driveway back through the trees and

finally come up on a modern house, constructed of black steel and glass and stone.

"Whoa." I duck down so I can see the house better through the windshield. "Whose place is this?"

"It's mine."

Car parked, he pulls up on the parking brake.

"Are you serious? Why would you live in suburbia next door to me if you have a place like this?"

"I have many places like this."

"That still doesn't answer the question."

He climbs out, so I'm forced to follow. At a large steel door on the lower level, Bran punches in a code into a keypad, and the deadbolt thunks open.

The interior is dark and cold. It smells like Bran but only vaguely, like it's been a few weeks since he inhabited the space.

He punches in a second code into a security system, shutting it down, then flicks on a light. The entire ground floor lights up with soft, inset lighting.

I don't wait for an invitation.

The main living space is massive and open-concept with a modern kitchen to the right and a living room and dining space to the left. In the far corner, floor-to-ceiling windows overlook Midnight Lake, and the dark, still water is dotted with the lights of the night, making it look like an impressionist painting.

The house is neat as a showroom, and it makes me fucking giddy. There are no empty wine bottles in the sink or stacks of random bills on the concrete counters. No shoes kicked off into a corner or sweaters hung over chairs.

"If this place were mine, I'd never leave it," I tell him.

He's at the built-in bar behind me pouring himself a drink. "It's a little cold for my taste."

"So why did you buy it?"

"I didn't buy it. I built it. And mostly to piss off Julian Locke."

Laughter spills out of me before I think better of it. "Why?"

"He wanted to buy this waterfront and put in a marina. So I bought up the waterfront instead."

I roll my eyes. "And then built a million-dollar house just to prove a point?"

Drink now in hand, he leans against the bar and meets my eyes. "Precisely."

"Why don't you like Julian?"

"That's a very long story."

"We've got time."

He slings back the drink. "We don't, actually."

The front door bangs open, and someone darts inside, a blur to my mortal eyes.

Runa grabs Bran by the throat and slams him against the wall. "You can't come into my bar demanding my attention. You're going to get us caught!"

I go still beside the leather sofa, trying not to be conspicuous.

Bran's eyes fire amber. The line of his jaw flexes as he grits his teeth.

I've yet to see someone get the best of Bran, and while I have no idea what the dynamic of this relationship is, there's a roiling trepidation in my gut that tells me it won't end well.

Bran grabs Runa by the arm, his hand circling her wrist. His gaze is pinned on her, face blank.

Then I hear a bone snap and Runa falters.

"You do not come into my house," Bran says after the second crunch of bone, "and threaten me."

Runa lets go of Bran's throat and cries out as her knees buckle.

"I don't work for you," Bran goes on, his fiery gaze following her as she crumples to the floor. "If I want your services, I'll get them however I wish. Do we understand one another?"

My heart is beating hard in my chest, and I bump into the sofa without realizing I've been backpedaling.

Sometimes, it's easy to forget the danger of a vampire.

Sometimes it's easy to forget just how insignificant we are in the eyes of an immortal.

"I can't hear you, Runa," Bran says even though she hasn't answered him. She's been too busy crying out in pain.

"Yes! All right! I hear you."

Bran lets her go, and her hand flops uselessly against her arm.

I slap a hand over my mouth as the urge to vomit sneaks up on me.

I guess I was wrong about Bran's currency. His investments are in information. But he deals in violence. And right now, he's spending what he's earned.

Bran steps around her and gathers his empty glass and a bottle of scotch. "Would you like a drink?" he asks as if he didn't just crush her arm.

Runa takes a hiccupping breath, arm held close to her chest. "Yes."

I may have been surrounded by vampires my entire life, but I've never witnessed the intimate inner workings of the power dynamic. Everyone behaved in the Locke circle. And if there were showdowns between houses, that happened outside the awareness of the mortals. Or at least *this* mortal.

It's unsettling how casual they are about this.

Bran dips down and offers Runa a glass. Her wrist is popping, her arm straightening out as her body heals the wound. She takes the glass with her good hand and slings back the dark caramel liquid, then huffs out a breath as the alcohol burns down her throat.

"Mouse?" He raises the bottle at me.

"Yes please." My voice comes out a little too breathy, and his gaze lingers on me as the fire dies out of his irises.

He pours as he walks to me then holds out the glass.

He doesn't speak, but I still hear him loud and clear. *She deserved it.*

Deep down, I know that the show of dominance is important in a world of dominant creatures, but damn if it isn't a little scary.

And if I'm honest, hot as hell.

Which must make me sick as hell, right?

Hand unsteady, I take a sip then pull the glass away, but Bran stops me and urges me to tip it all back.

Our eyes are locked on one another while I empty the drink, and as the rich, smokey liquor goes down, tears well up beneath my lids.

"You good?" he asks.

If I said no, what would he do?

A pinch appears between his dark brows.

"Yes," I answer. "I'm good."

He gives me a quick nod before turning away. "Get up," he tells

Runa, and she climbs to her feet as he deposits the liquor back on the bar. "What can you tell me about Jessie in relation to the Locke house."

Runa's attention wanders to me. She stretches out her arm, wiggles her fingers. There's a ring of bruising on her wrist, but at least her hand isn't flopping around like limp cheese.

"That's a broad question," she says.

"Julian showed up at my house earlier tonight trying to stake his claim." Bran is a blur as he crosses the room to stand just to the left of me. "Why would he go to all that trouble?"

"The MacMahon family has been pledged to the Lockes for decades. Of course he'd try to protect what he thinks is his."

"But I'm not his," I point out, my voice still a little shaky. "My Pledging is still a few days away."

"Look, I wish I could help on this." She tugs down the hem of her shirt after it rode up in the tussle. "But I'm rarely privy to Pledging details."

Bran paces away. "Think harder, Runa."

"I'm serious. I've got nothing."

Bran darts to the kitchen. I hear a drawer open, then something slice through the air.

A wooden stake lodges itself in Runa's right shoulder. This time, she bites back her cry as blood seeps from the wound.

"Try again." Bran pulls a second stake from the drawer and tosses it in the air, end over end, catching it again. "I'm waiting."

I've never seen a vampire staked before. I heard it's messy and that when the vampire dies, they burst into ash, permeating the air with the stench of burning hair and cinders.

I really don't want to witness that.

"Bran," I start. It's not that important. Not important enough to take a life.

But he cuts a withering glare my way, and I quickly clamp my mouth shut again.

"I don't know what you want from me," Runa says, voice wobbling on the pain. "I have—"

The second stake hits the air and whizzes past her head, sinking itself into the wall behind her.

"Okay! Fine!" She holds up a hand. "There is something. It was a long time ago."

"I'm listening." Bran pulls out a third stake.

She talks fast. "A bunch of the Lockes were at the MacMahon house for dinner. Jessie would have just been a kid at the time. One of the vamps, Sasha, took Jessie for a joy ride. Tossed her on her back and raced away. It was just for fun. We do it with the littles all of the time."

Runa looks at me guiltily. "Except when Sasha came back, she was acting strange."

I remember that night. I remember holding on to Sasha for dear life while I laughed and laughed as the world blurred past and then...nothing. There was a blank space in that memory. I could never remember the ride back.

"Go on," Bran says.

"The next day," Runa says, "Sasha was dead. Because Julian killed her."

Sixteen

Sasha is dead?

"No," I say and shake my head for emphasis. "I was told Sasha moved away. I specifically remember that."

With a grit of her teeth, Runa removes the stake from her shoulder. The one Bran threw at her with terrifying precision. The second stake missed, but I suspect that was on purpose.

"Julian can tell you whatever he wants you to hear," Runa says as she walks over to a nearby table and sets the bloody stake on top.

I'm suddenly itching for a rag so I can clean that mess up. I know it's just my brain looking for anything to distract me and stop the agonizing mental pain of my life going sideways.

Bran comes over to me, but he speaks to Runa. "What did Sasha do to earn that punishment?"

"That I don't know." Runa examines the new hole in her leather jacket where the stake pierced her flesh. She frowns at the mangled material. "There is a rumor, however, that a shifter witnessed whatever happened."

"Which one?" Bran asks.

Runa smirks. I sense a roadblock before she even answers.

"Cal."

I catch the barely perceptible flinch on Bran's face.

Callen Crawford. The Alpha of the Midnight pack.

Great.

Just fabulous.

"Well, I guess that's our dead end," I say.

Bran scowls at me. "If you think an alpha is going to stop me, you're sorely mistaken, mouse."

"Oh really? You're what, you're going to visit the Midnight Pack and demand to see the alpha and ask him what he maybe saw over ten years ago? Besides, don't you think that if he did witness Sasha doing something she shouldn't have, he would have reported it? Cal may be vicious, but he's always followed the rules."

Except...now that I think of it, Kelly was just complaining about the pack not wanting to pay their taxes. Something about land disputes.

Bran doesn't answer me. Instead, he goes to the table and retrieves the stake. Runa cringes. "I'm telling you what I know. I swear it."

"Go." He nods her toward the door.

"I expect payment for this."

"I'll have something for you by the end of next week."

With a quick nod, she's gone, and the front door clicks closed behind her.

"What do you pay her?"

Bran tosses the stake into the sink and taps on the faucet. "Information about her blood descendants."

"Really? She can't find out that information on her own?"

"There's this whole thing with a witch curse on her blood line and Julian forbidding her from contacting them because of it." He opens a cabinet to reveal a row of yellow tubs holding disinfecting wipes. He pulls one out. "I get an update on the family and I tell her what I know and she can carry on her immortal life, feeling cozy about her blood line."

"That's actually...kinda sweet."

The look he gives me could singe hair. "Don't try to paint me as a good guy. You'll be sorely disappointed." He says this as he wipes the blood from the table, scrubbing it clean.

"If you say so."

"Mouse." The word comes out throaty and vibrating with a warning.

But while I just witnessed him crush a vampire's arm and then stake her, there's this little voice in the back of my head that says I have nothing to fear from Bran Duval. Other than my heart getting broken.

Goddamn that heart anyway.

Best to protect it with everything I have.

"Yes, you're the bad guy. That's something we can both agree on. So now what?"

He tosses the bloody wipe and washes his hands. "Now we visit the Midnight Pack."

———

The shifters live on the north side of the river in a self-contained community surrounded by hardwoods and pine. I think I've crossed the river a total of one time in my life when we went on a field trip to the Guard station when I was a kid.

The Guard is Midnight Harbor's version of a police force, but in a town of supernatural creatures, their power is limited. They mostly deal with mortal disputes, but when their station was rebuilt on the north side of the river, on the edge of the shifter neighborhood, there was talk that they had an unspoken alliance with the shifters.

It was the squabbling and gossip that originally led me to want to leave Midnight. I hate politics. And politics with supernaturals is politics on steroids.

The second we take the Crawford Bridge across the river, I feel like we're being watched.

The tall pines loom over us as Bran drives the car around a sharp turn on the road. When we get near the shifter neighborhood, maple and oak trees start to take over the woods, and the headlights cut across several driftwood sculptures hanging from the lower branches.

They're called Valhalla ladders, and they're made from collected wood that's then strung up on twine and hung for protection. I know this because Sam's dad is primarily Norwegian and made a ladder with the kids one year to hang in their bay window.

While the Midnight Pack is diverse in its members, Cal is Scandinavian and the pack is steeped in Scandinavian culture because of it.

When we crest the next hill, old-fashioned lampposts appear along the side of the road and send soft golden light into the night.

I can't help but take it all in. I immediately like it. There's a quintessential small-town vibe to it with one block of shops, the buildings original to the early 1900s judging by their style.

Music filters out from a bar and grill where the front doors have been propped open by rusty milk cans. There's a sign hanging in the window, the curling neon tubes spelling out *Galloway's* in a bright orange glow.

"Do you know where you're going?" I ask Bran.

He's got one hand casually on the steering wheel, the other curled around the head of the stick shift.

"Of course I do." He nods to the end of the main street and to a massive estate house sitting like a lord at the top of the hill.

I've heard about the pack house, but it's even more formidable in person.

The light of the waning moon sends a soft glow around the many steepled roofs and jutting chimneys. Once we turn off the main street, Bran has to navigate to an unmarked road that is at an almost constant incline as it winds back through the pines.

Finally, the road cuts into the property and wraps around the house. There's a parking lot to the south with at least half the spots taken.

Bran parks and shuts the car off. The engine ticks in the quiet as it cools down.

"We're really doing this?" I ask.

With the car off and the dashboard dark, I can only see the barest hint of Bran's face. I can't read his expression, but there's a buzz of energy in the air like he's preparing for battle.

"You want answers, don't you?"

"I'm not sure what I want." I pick at the frayed hem of my t-shirt. "This still feels like a dream."

"Then let's wake you up."

I snort. "Easier said than done."

"You'll be glad you went this far when it's all over."

"But what is *it*, exactly? Aren't you a little worried? We can't stuff this goose back into the oven."

He laughs, his raspy voice filling the intimate interior of the car.

"I'm serious."

"I know you are." He reaches across the center counsel and takes my hand. The skin-on-skin contact sends an immediate, needy thrill between my legs even though there's nothing sexual about it. Even though there are much bigger things to be thinking about.

"I suggest you get that under control if we're walking into a pack house," he says.

I hang my head back against the headrest. "This is a horrible idea."

"You can't control yourself around me," he teases in that thick, horny voice of his. "I'm not surprised." He unlocks our hands and drags a soft touch across my palm. That needy thrill turns hot and buzzy.

Gelatin cake.

Gelatin cake.

It's not working!

His hand leaves mine and goes to my thigh. The curl of his fingers hit just a few inches from the seam of my thigh to my center, and I've never wished for a skirt more in my life.

Why did I have to wear pants?!

He grips me harder, hand trailing closer, and a gasp escapes me.

"If it'll help get you through this meeting," he says and leans across the center counsel, bringing his other hand to my jaw, tipping me toward him, "how about I give you something to look forward to?"

"And what's that?"

"I'll fuck you."

My clit throbs and my inner walls clench up at the scant promise of his cock inside of me. I've fucked myself with a dildo before, but something tells me fucking Bran will be a ride I won't soon forget.

"But..." I say and pant out a breath, my brain trying really hard to remind my mouth that I already told him I didn't want him.

"But what?" His mouth finds my throat and kisses then nips, and I shiver beneath his teeth.

I gulp down air. I don't know what my objection was going to be. It's gone now, lost to the wind.

"Fuck me now," I say.

"Needy little mouse."

"What's to stop us?"

"We're in a pack parking lot, and I don't relish the idea of getting staked with my cock buried in that tight little pussy."

"Oh fuck." I love it when he talks like that. "Then drive us away. We can come back."

His hand trails closer to my center. "No."

"Why?" I moan.

"Because I like seeing you desperate."

The noise that comes out of my throat can only be described as *sexually frustrated.*

He lets his finger graze the seam of my jeans, sending a buzz through me.

"If you don't fuck me soon, I might be the one staking you."

"You could try. You would fail." He laughs in the quiet cab of the car and then pulls away, leaving me panting and so fucking horny. He finds a pocket of moonlight, and in that silver glow, shoots me a devilish grin.

"I really do hate you." My eyes are heavy, and I'm sure I'm flushed.

"I know, mouse. You hate me so much, I bet your panties are fucking drenched."

He's not wrong.

———

It takes me a few seconds to get control of myself, and the walk from the parking lot to the front of the house in the cool night air helps unravel some of my arousal.

And thank god too because we're stopped before we even make it up the stone steps to the double front door, proving my earlier suspicion that we were being watched the second we crossed the bridge.

The shifter that meets us is the pack's beta, Fox, which is ironic, considering he's a wolf shifter. The story I heard from Sam was that his real name is Waagosh, which means "fox" in the Ojibwe language. Fox is half Ojibwe. I'm not sure how he found himself here in

Midnight Harbor, but from what I've heard, everyone loves him. Unless you've found yourself in the unfortunate position of being on his bad side. I guess you don't get to be beta without breaking some bones.

"Bran Duval," Fox says, his voice like sandpaper drawing over cut wood. "To what do we owe the pleasure?"

Bran is loose and casual, but I sense his energy, standing as near to him as I am. He's a master at appearing one way while being another. I admire the way he does this as if he's confident he can walk into any room and make friends, or enemies, and he's okay with either.

I've always wanted people to like me, and sometimes, I've gone overboard, trying to fit in or belong.

"I need to speak to Cal," Bran answers.

Fox leans his shoulder against one of the stone columns that runs three stories high to the roofline above us. He crosses his arms over his chest. "What for?"

"I have a question for him."

"Whatever you have to ask him you can ask me." Fox tilts his head, regarding us like we're peasants.

"All right." Bran steps forward. "I was wondering if Cal knew why Julian Locke might stake one of his own."

Fox goes still. Clearly that's not where he thought this conversation was going. He narrows his eyes. "Why would he know anything about that?"

"A little birdie told me."

"You and your birds." Fox grunts. "You always were too nosy for your own good."

"And you're too bold for your age."

"This is pack territory," Fox says. "I shouldn't have to remind you of that."

Bran clasps his hands behind his back. "Now that we've pissed around, can we get on with it then?"

The front door bursts open, and several younger pack members spill out. They see Fox and quickly bow their heads and dart away.

Fox catches the heavy door before it slips closed and holds it for us. "Come in and I'll see if Cal is about."

Bran takes my hand and drags me behind him. As we pass, he says to Fox, "As if you don't know where your alpha is at all times."

"As if I'm going to give you free access to him whenever you want."

"This is starting off great." I let out a nervous laugh, hoping to lighten the mood, but no light can penetrate the dark moods of these two men.

We enter into a foyer with a domed ceiling far above us with a wrought iron frame and stained class inlayed between. Hanging from its center is a chandelier that looks small in the cavernous space, but I bet it would easily be three times the size of me if I were standing next to it.

Fox takes us down the hall to the left. The pack house might be massive, but there's a comfortable din of conversation and laughter in the air like it's a house well-loved and inhabited by family.

I suppose being part of a pack gives you that, whether they're blood or not.

Being absorbed into the pack life was never even a consideration for me, but feeling the warmth of the house makes me wonder if I snubbed it for no good reason.

"She can wait here," Fox says as he stops at the open pocket doors.

"She comes with," Bran says.

"Yeah, this is technically about me," I point out.

"Humans don't get access to the alpha without being pack pledged." Fox almost sounds bored explaining this to me. I guess he probably has better things to do.

"I'm not going to leave the little mouse in a house full of dogs," Bran says.

Fox straightens, a rumble sounding in his chest.

"Take it back," I say out of the corner of my mouth.

Bran sighs. "Fine. Wolves. Better?"

Fox doesn't look like it's better.

"You'll have to excuse him," I say. "He's not used to civilized conversations." I end with clenched teeth and a frown at Bran. He just scoffs.

"Please," I beg, even though I'm aware that I didn't want to come here in the first place, and now I'm groveling to get Bran on the inside. He's really going to owe me, and thinking of him owing me...

Gelatin cake. Giggly gelatin cake!

"Fine." Fox turns away. "This way, Duval."

Bran gives me one lingering look. I can feel him hesitating, so I put my hands to his back and shove him away. "Go. Before he changes his mind."

"Behave," he says beneath his breath. "And don't let any of the mutts touch you."

I roll my eyes.

"Mouse."

"Yes. Fine. Now go."

He turns away and darts after Fox.

Of course, not even ten minutes later, I'm surrounded by wolves, with Evan and Adam at the head of the group.

"Jess!" Evan calls out and wraps his arm around my shoulders. "What are you doing here?"

"Bran," I say. "He had to talk to Cal."

Evan makes a snide comment that I don't hear, but that makes Adam and a few others laugh.

"That explains why you smell like him."

"I do?" I lift my shirt to sniff it and catch a lingering scent that reminds me of Bran. That rich amber smoke.

"Are you *with* Duval?" Evan steers me out of the room and down the hall, his arm still around me.

"Um...no. He's just helping me with something."

The others fall into step behind us and start discussing a movie they've all just watched.

"He seemed awfully possessive of you the other night at the Harbor," Evan points out.

"Yeah, well..." I trail off because I really have no explanation for it. He did seem possessive, and he seemed possessive ten minutes ago, and while it should piss me off, it just makes me fill up with butterflies.

Arm still around my shoulders, Evan guides me into a billiard room where five pool tables are set up in the center beneath stained-glass bar lights. There are three games in session, with the last two tables open.

"Want to play pool with us while you wait?" Evan smiles down at me with that dazzling smile of his. He really is handsome in that All-

American footballer kind of way. The cut of his bicep flexes against my shoulder as he deposits me at one of the tables.

"Sure, why not."

Playing a game of pool is innocent enough, right?

Except ten minutes later, we're in the middle of a game, and Evan plays one of the oldest tricks in the book.

"Here, let me show you how to get that shot." He slides in behind me, his groin suddenly at my ass.

Oh shit.

He wraps his arms around me and rests his hand over mine, the pool cue between us, his mouth at my ear.

And that's when Bran walks in the door, and his eyes light up with fiery rage.

Seventeen

I once heard my mom liken the rage of a vampire to a summer storm.

"It can come out of nowhere," she'd said. "Quiet one minute, roaring the next. And it will destroy everything around you before you even know what hit you."

When I spot Bran at the doorway, when I see his eyes light up fire orange, I know I'm standing at the edge of a storm.

The air freezes in my throat.

I swear the hair rises along my arms and along the length of my neck.

Don't let the mutts touch you.

Evan is draped over me, his arms around me one minute and the next he's flying across the room.

Everyone starts moving, but most wolves can't match the speed of a vampire the age of Bran Duval.

A split second before Evan crashes against the bar, Bran is there catching him with a fistful of his t-shirt. He slams him straight down to the floor.

The hardwood cracks, shards exploding in the air. The impact ripples out through the floor, and I feel the answering reverberation a half second later as it echoes up through the soles of my shoes.

I don't think I breathe. Not one breath.

And then Fox is sprinting across the room, fist cocked back, ready to strike.

"Bran!" I shout.

Bran doesn't turn, doesn't flinch, and yet he catches Fox's fist in the cup of his right hand.

The room goes still.

Fox grits his teeth, winds back with his left fist. Bran catches that one too.

"He knew what he was doing." Bran's voice is strangled and raw.

Fox curls his upper lip, strain appearing in the raised tendons in his neck. I don't think he's trying to punch now so much as he is trying to retreat. And Bran isn't letting him.

"He knew what he was doing," Bran goes on, "the second he smelled me on her."

Evan coughs from the floor, the sound wet and reedy.

Fox grunts.

A lock of my hair flutters in front of my face. I look to my left just in time to see a blur of muscle and plaid dart past.

Something cracks. More splinters hit the air.

When I turn to Bran, Cal Crawford, Alpha of the Midnight Pack, is at his back, the sharp end of a broken pool cue pressed between his shoulder blades, angled toward his heart.

"Let him go," Cal says.

The others shrink back, heads bowed.

The tension in the room is thick enough to choke on.

Bran's nostrils flare, his jaw flexing as he weighs his options.

Come on, Bran! Let him go!

"I know you, Duval," Cal says. "How much would it piss you off to die in pack territory?"

I think I know that answer.

Bran lets Fox go, and the shifter shakes out his hands as if he's trying to bring feeling back to his fingers.

Cal tosses the broken cue. "Outside. Now."

I'm frozen in place as the Midnight Pack's alpha stalks toward the door, right past me. I've seen Cal around, obviously, but I've also seen the sun in the sky. Doesn't mean I can handle standing right next to it.

Cal Crawford is large and impressive. I don't know his exact age—shifters live longer than mortals, but they aren't immortal. But if I didn't know any better, I'd think he just stepped out of a Viking saga.

His blond hair is shaved short on the sides, but left longer on top. There are black tattoos running back along the sides of his skull, down the back of his neck to disappear beneath the collar of his red and black flannel. A neatly trimmed goatee hides what I'm guessing is a sharp jawline, judging by the cut of his cheekbones.

When he passes me, he barely looks at me.

Talk about feeling insignificant.

Bran takes me by the hand and leads me out of the room and through the foyer and out the front door.

Cal waits for us in the dark in the middle of the gravel drive.

Fox trails behind us.

"Let's get this out of the way first," Cal says, the boom of his voice echoing around the open space. "One, you are hereby banned from shifter territory. If I catch you on our lands again, I'll tear out your heart with my bare hands."

Bran tightens his hold on me when I let out a little hiccup of fear.

"Two, the only reason you're leaving here on two legs is because I govern this pack with a very clear set of rules. Evan overstepped. He'll be dealt with." Cal's dark gaze cuts to me. I think I catch a flash of pity in his eyes. "Three...Jessie I've been waiting for you to come to me for a very long time. You want to know what I saw that night in the woods."

It's not a question.

I swallow around the lump forming in my throat.

"You were there?"

He nods.

"What did you see?"

His gaze slips to the house, then back to me. "Not here. Come. I'll tell you what I know, and then you'll be gone."

Bran and I have no choice but to follow.

―――――

Cal leads us along a dirt path that winds back through the pines to a cabin that overlooks the river. Fox stays at our backs, the two wolves boxing us in.

It makes my skin crawl. Bran seems totally fine even though he was threatened with imminent death if he so much as stepped out of line.

The windows of the cabin are lit up from within, but when we step inside, the place is empty. Though the fireplace is cold and dark, I catch the faintest scent of burning wood on the air. There's a coffee cup on the wooden table in the center of the main space, but I can't tell if the coffee inside is fresh or not.

"Sit," Cal orders.

I dutifully take a seat, but Bran stays standing and leans against the wall behind me.

Cal all but rolls his eyes.

Fox stays near the door.

"We're waiting," Bran says.

I send him a withering look over my shoulder, but he ignores me, his gaze fixed on Cal.

Cal goes to the vintage fridge and yanks on the metal handle. The glow of the fridge spills out around him as he ducks inside and pulls out a bottle of beer. He doesn't offer us one. Not that I'd take it.

With a twist of the cap, the beer hisses. He takes a swig then props a hand on the counter and leans a hip into it.

"You want to know what I saw in the woods," he states.

"Yes. We've established that," Bran answers.

Cal runs his tongue along the inside of his bottom lip as he stares at Bran.

"Please tell me." I wring my hands in my lap, knee bobbing beneath the table. If there's something to know, I need to know it now. I can't take this suspense anymore.

What happened with Sasha when I was a kid?

"I was running," Cal says. "I run in the woods at night. Always have. I stopped by the riverside to take a drink when I heard a child laughing."

Fear flutters in my chest.

"I went up the riverbank to see who it was, and that's when I spotted Sasha coming to a stop with Jessie on her back."

That I remember. I remember the world spinning to a halt.

"Sasha set Jessie down, and Jessie tripped over some exposed tree roots, and she went down in an instant."

His gaze lands on me. "You started crying, and you kept saying your necklace fell off. Sasha ducked down to help you, and I immediately smelled blood on the air. Sasha noticed too. I could see her eyes glowing across the clearing."

My heart beats a little harder.

"'It'll be okay,' Sasha said to you. 'Let me see.' You lifted your hand to her and there was a cut on your palm, blood running down your arm. At this point, I think Sasha was just panicking that you were hurt and then...then something changed."

I sense Bran moving closer to me.

"I've seen bloodlust in vampires plenty of times before, but this was different," Cal says. "This was almost...hypnotic."

My knee bobs faster.

"She was on you in a second, teeth sunk into your wrist. I raced out of the woods. By the time I reached you, she was backtracking and swaying on her feet. 'Oh shit,' she said. 'Something is wrong.' I tried grabbing you, but she snatched you away before I could and like that—" he snaps his fingers "—she was gone."

A cold sweat breaks out along the back of my neck.

"Why didn't you report it?" Bran asks.

"I don't get in the middle of vampire business. I did tell Jessie's mom though."

His voice is distant and muffled like I'm underwater. I swallow hard again, this time because I think I might be sick.

"What did she say?" Bran asks. "Her mother?"

"She made me a deal."

I lurch away from the table. Bran pulls me into him. "What kind of deal?"

"Keep my mouth shut, and she'd make sure the pack got what it needed. It's one of the reasons the Guard station was rebuilt on our side of the river."

"You asked for that?" Bran says.

I'm vaguely aware of Cal nodding. "Vampires hold too much power.

My opinion on that likely is no surprise to you. Controlling the Guard station gave me more sway."

"I think I'm going to be sick."

Bran ushers me out the door. I make it just in time to the side yard and collapse to my knees as the retching starts.

Nothing comes up.

Bran kneels beside me and holds my hair back as my stomach violently tries to deal with this information and finds it impossible to get anything out.

It's just me gagging in the dirt, eyes burning, tears streaming down my face. It's like I'm trying to purge my soul.

"Mouse," Bran whispers. "It's going to be all right."

"You...don't...know that."

"I do."

I can finally suck down a full breath. "What is happening?"

"I don't know."

Footsteps sound behind us. Bran looks up. "Is there more?"

"That's it," Cal answers.

"Then we'll be on our way." Bran puts his chest to my shoulder and then scoops me up in his arms effortlessly. I want to tell him to put me down, but I have no energy for it. And besides, the feel of his arms around me, holding me close...it's the only thing keeping me together.

"Thank you," he tells Cal.

"It's the last you'll get from me," Cal warns. "And mostly I did it for her."

"Then I thank you for her."

Arms tight around Bran's neck, I snuggle in close to him, feeling the burn of tears.

My mother betrayed me. My sister betrayed me.

And for what?

I don't know who to trust anymore, and the fucked-up thing? I think the only person I *can* trust is Bran Duval.

———

It takes Bran less than a minute to get us back to the Bimmer. He gently sets me in the passenger seat and then clips my seat belt around my body. I'm numb and so far away, I barely notice. I barely notice the car ride back to the house either. So when Bran guides me into his house, I don't protest.

He sits me at his table and pours me a tumbler of bourbon.

"Drink," he says.

It isn't until the alcohol is burning down my throat and warming my belly that I finally blink back to consciousness.

"How could they do this to me?" I blurt out.

He's sitting in the chair next to me, his long body stretched out. He's got his own tumbler of bourbon in hand, long, pale fingers curled around the glass.

"My guess? Your mom was protecting you. And your sister was passed the torch."

"That's far too nice of an explanation." I take another sip. "You bit me. Did you sense anything weird?"

"You were wearing your necklace," he points out. "Cal said that night you lost it when you fell."

"But Rita said in order to undo the binding, it has to be destroyed. So why would it matter if I was wearing it?"

"To undo it, sure. But when it comes off? That might distance the effects of the magic and let whatever it is they're trying to hide leak through."

Whatever they're trying to hide.

Something about me.

My mother and my sister have been hiding something about me. I don't understand why or how. I don't care in this moment.

I just want to know.

I sling back the rest of the drink and hiss at the burn. When I set the heavy glass down, it thuds in the quiet.

"Then let's find out what they're trying to hide."

Bran frowns at me.

I unhook the necklace and let the charm dangle in the air between us. We both watch it spin from the end of the chain.

"Bite me." I drop the necklace and hold out my wrist. His eyes sink to the blue veins running beneath my skin.

"Are you sure you want to do this?"

"Yes."

His pale fingers circle my wrist as he angles my arm up to him.

His irises flare, and my heart thuds against the back of my tongue as he licks his lips, fangs sharpening.

I think he wants to know as much as I do.

I think he's also just as afraid as I am.

He reaches beneath the table, and I hear a loud pop. When he brings his hand back, there's a sharpened stake in his grip. He gives it to me.

"If something happens," he says, "use it."

"I won't do—"

"Jessie."

It's the first time I've heard him use my name, and it kicks up a wave of fear in my gut.

"Promise me," he says.

I think I might promise him anything if it means getting some answers.

"Okay. I promise."

He gives me a quick nod and then sinks his teeth into my flesh.

Eighteen

Growing up with vampires, you hear stories about what it's like to be bitten.

A pinch. A pleasure. A heady mix of lust and fear.

But I'm realizing now that being bitten isn't a one-size-fits-all thing. It's like a sunrise.

Not a single one is the same.

When Bran sinks his teeth in my flesh, I gasp in surprise at the first pinch of pain. It sends a shockwave up my arm and instinct has me pulling away.

But Bran's grip is tight, his hunger stronger.

I feel the blood leave me as he sucks from my vein, a mild pressure, and then the pain is fading away, replaced with a buzzy warmth that runs through my body like honey.

It's over within seconds, and when he disengages from me, he collapses against the chair and slouches like he's drunk, head lulled back, blood dripping from his fangs.

"Anything?" I ask. I'm feeling a little swimmy and lightheaded.

Bran's bright amber eyes land on me, heavy and half-lidded. "It's sweeter than it was before."

He runs his tongue over his bottom lip, sucking back the last drops. His mouth is bright red, teeth stained with blood.

"Do you feel okay?" I ask.

"I feel horny."

I swallow hard, my gaze straying to his crotch and the considerable bulge of his cock.

"Besides that..."

He reaches across the table and grabs me by the arms, hauling me onto his lap so that I'm straddling him. He's so hard it almost hurts.

He grabs my ass, rocking me against him, and a fluttery breath escapes me. I wrap my arms around his neck, leaning into him, and he brings his mouth to the V of my shirt, kissing along the sensitive flesh just above my breast.

"Do you remember me making you a promise, mouse?" He tugs down the collar of my shirt, exposing the cup of my bra.

"Yes," I say, feeling the answering thrill of that promise between my legs.

He kisses along my bra, a tease of his lips on my skin.

"I always keep my promises," he says.

"I know but—"

"But what?"

"But...shouldn't we talk about this? When you bit me, could you tell if there was something wrong with me? Because—" his lips trail up the curve of my throat, closer to the rapid beat of my heart "—because I'm starting to worry and..."

He stops his pursuit of my pulse and looks up at me, eyes bright in the shadows. "There *was* something different," he admits, "but I don't know what."

"Okay. So?"

He grabs my wrist again and holds my arm out where blood is still beading in the puncture wound, droplets sliding down toward the crook of my elbow.

Bran drags his tongue from the end of the trail all the way up to the teeth marks. He draws from the wound again, and his eyes glow brighter.

"Bran," I moan. "Please. I don't know what's happening, and I feel out of control."

He pulls back and regards me with a look so hot, I'm nearly trembling beneath it. "Then bend to mine, mouse."

"What?"

"Bend to my control."

My clit pulses beneath his words.

I think he's trying to distract me. And it's working.

Whenever he gets me like this, I'm mindless. Just body and pleasure and the delirious need for him.

He slides his hand around to the back of my neck, fingers almost bruising as he grips me tightly and rocks his hips forward, grinding me on his cock. "Say yes, mouse."

Maybe he knows exactly what I need right now.

Maybe he knows better than I do.

I'm anxious and worried and...*afraid*. I'm afraid of what we're uncovering.

And right now, I just want to run away from it.

As my life burns down around me, the only thing that feels right is giving in to the pleasure of Bran Duval.

"Okay."

He stands in one swift motion, and I slid down the length of him. His grip still on my neck, he steers me into the living room. "Take off your clothes."

The pressure disappears, and when I turn around, I find him leaning against the back of the couch.

"All of them?"

He says nothing, just watches, waiting.

Hands shaking, I take up the hem of my shirt and slide it off. I let it drop to the floor and then move to the button of my jeans, taking down the zipper.

Pants off, I kick them aside and stand awkwardly in my panties and bra.

"Go on, mouse." He's stoic and distant, but there's a very clear bulge in his pants.

Reaching behind me, I unhook the bra, let the straps slide off my shoulders. Tossing it aside, my nipples immediately bud in the cool air.

"Pull your hair back," he tells me, so I do, sliding it behind my shoulders so there's nothing to shield me from his gaze.

With a deep intake of breath, I slip my panties off and stand there naked in front of him.

We were naked in the shower together, but somehow this is different.

I've never felt so vulnerable.

He's silent as he takes in the sight of me.

"Get in that chair," he orders and tips his head at the side chair behind me.

I make a move to sit, but he tsk-tsks. "No. Turn around. Knees on the seat."

Oh god.

I give him my back, and as instructed, kneel on it, hands propped on the chair's low back.

"Good girl," he says, coaxing a buzzy thrill from my pussy. "Legs spread."

I open as much as the chair will allow, bearing everything to him.

I can't catch my breath, and I'm shaking and wound up tight.

I don't know what he's planning to do, but I'm nearly faint with wanting.

Goosebumps travel down my spine as the air parts when he comes over. He grabs me by the neck again as his other hand trails up the back of my thigh.

"Mouse," he says, "you're already dripping down your legs."

I moan at the pressure of his grip and wiggle my hips as if I'm trying to tempt him to move faster.

And then he slaps my pussy with the flat side of his palm.

I let out a little yip and instinctively pull away, but he's still got me by the neck and holds me in place.

"Who's in control?" His mouth is suddenly at my ear.

"You are."

His fingers come to barely an inch from my pussy, and I'm sick with wanting him to touch me.

Blood rushes to my clit, pulsing through me. I want to shift to feel him but have to clamp down on the need. I think he'd leave me high and dry and not think twice about it.

Now that I'm in it, as the lust is pounding through me, I need this. I need him to fuck me and drive away the chaos.

I need to feel in control by Bran being in control.

"We need a safe word, mouse," he says, teasing his fingers closer to my wet slit. "Just in case I pound this little virgin pussy too hard."

"I'll be okay," I say.

He spanks me again, and I jolt from the sting and pleasure, his fingers just grazing my clit enough to send a bright flash of pleasure through me. I exhale in a delirious rush.

"Give me a word, mouse. It can be anything."

"Um…" I can't think straight. I don't want to delay it any longer. I blurt out the first thing that comes to mind. "Tomato."

There's a distant chuckle behind me. "Tomato," Bran says. "Promise me you'll use it if you need to."

"I promise."

"I'll behave, but I plan to fuck you hard and fast. I will not be gentle."

My chest tightens with the thrill of it. "Okay."

He inches closer to my opening, and I get just the barest sensation from his fingertip grazing my wet opening. A ripple of excitement courses over me.

"You want to be fucked, mouse?"

"Yes."

He finally drags his fingers over my wet center, and I moan into the back of the chair, arms shaking. He slips two fingers inside of me, but it's not enough. Not nearly enough.

"Go on then."

"What?" I squeak.

"Fuck yourself."

He's making *me* do it?

His grip on my neck squeezes just a fraction, coaxing me into action like I'm an animal. And maybe I am. I don't feel cognizant of anything except for the driving need between my legs.

I shift my hips, pushing my ass back, fucking myself on his fingers.

"That's a good girl," he says and applies more pressure to my neck, driving me faster on his fingers.

The pressure builds. My breathing quickens. My shoulders are like gelatin, arms trembling. My swollen pussy is so slick, I can hear the distinct wetness of it as Bran's fingers slide in and out.

I find a delicious rhythm chasing the orgasm, and then—

"Stop."

His voice rings out with command, and I come to a halt, his fingers still curled deep inside of me.

I let out a little mewl of frustration.

I'm so close. My nerves are blinking like pulsating stars.

I want to come. I've never wanted anything more than I've wanted this.

I pant against the chair's back, waiting and waiting.

"I can feel you clenching around me."

"When?" It's the only word I can get out.

When will you fuck me?

When will you end this torture?

How is he so in control?

The rasp of his zipper causes me to moan with anticipation.

"Get upstairs," he says.

He doesn't have to tell me twice. I climb off the chair and hurry up the stairs completely naked and dripping wet.

"Faster, mouse," he says on my heels.

I pick up the pace, the sensation of being chased sending a shiver down my spine.

I hurry down the hall and stumble into his bedroom.

Without warning, he's on me, tossing me onto the bed on my stomach. He forces my legs open, grabs me by the hips, and yanks my ass into him.

The hot throb of his cock is suddenly at my wet opening.

I quiver against the sheets.

He holds himself there, the head of his shaft pressing so close. So close.

I have to fight the instinct to push into him.

"Bran, please," I moan. "Please."

"Don't forget your safe word, mouse."

"I won't."

And then he pushes inside of me.

The feeling of him filling me up is a sensation I wasn't prepared for. And the hard drive of his hips, the pulse of his thickness, it makes white stars dance behind my eyes.

This is nothing like fucking myself with my toys.

This is raw and real and so fucking hot. I can't find my voice or my thoughts.

I've never been so inside my own body and flying all at the same time.

Bran's pace is brutal, punishing and not at all human.

I cry out, fingers clawed into the sheets.

The pain of being torn through for the first time ever is faint and faraway as the searing heat of him sheathed inside of me takes over, turning me mindless and blind.

There is only the pleasure and the descent into the madness of being steered into an orgasm by Bran and his commanding words.

I know in that moment I'm his.

I'll do anything he tells me to do if only to experience this feral bliss every fucking day.

He grows harder the faster he punishes my pussy and my own orgasm builds.

"Not yet, mouse," he says.

"I'm close."

"Not yet."

My inner walls clench up as if my pussy is willing him to let me let go.

In a blink, he pulls out of me, spins me around so I'm in his lap again, straddling him.

His hands at my hips, he guides me down the length of him.

"So fucking tight, mouse." He pumps into me. "I knew fucking this pussy would be good, but I wasn't prepared for how good."

"You've thought about this?"

"I thought about this pretty little pussy on my cock every fucking day."

Oh my god. Somehow this admission does more than the fucking. Pleasure is drumming through me now, threatening to spill over.

"Oh god," I say on an exhale. "I can't...anymore..."

"Go on," he orders. "Come on my cock."

That's all it takes.

The orgasm tears through me. I can't control the loud cry that comes out of my throat. Bran grips me tighter, holds me to him as my body quivers through the shock waves, curling into itself.

"Fuck, mouse." The head of his cock throbs at the center of me, and then his pumping cadence falters, muscle and tendons constricting along his chest and down his arms as he spurts cum inside of me, a growl of pleasure coming out through his gritted teeth.

I'm still burning through my own pleasure, but I have to see him.

I want to see what I can do to him.

He lets out a panting breath, eyes burning in the shadows. The pleasure is etched in his face, in the lines around his eyes and the flex of his jaw as he pumps another load into me.

We ride through the last ebb together and then collapse against one another, breathing hard. We stay like that for a long time before Bran finally pulls out of me.

"That was...intense," I admit with a laugh.

"Don't leave Midnight," he says suddenly.

"What?"

"Don't leave."

"Why?"

The glow in his eyes intensifies as he grits his teeth as if me making him elaborate is a discomfort he doesn't want to endure.

"Why Bran?"

"Because I don't want you to."

His admission burns through me, lights a fire in my chest.

I wish I could leave it at that, bask in the glow of it.

But I can feel there's more.

"And?"

"And," he says. "I did sense something in your blood."

"You did? What?"

He lifts me off of him and sets me on the edge of the bed.

"Bran."

In a blur of movement, he's gone. The tap in the bathroom turns on.

"Bran!"

I find him bent over the sink, water dripping from his face.

"Tell me."

He sighs. "Fae," he answers. "When I bit you without the necklace on, I could taste fae in your blood."

BOOK TWO

One

You tell yourself a story about who you are and who you're meant to be as you get older.

The story I told myself was that I would pledge to the Locke vampire house just like everyone in my family who had come before me, despite the fact that every time I thought about it, there was a strong hum of dissonance in my gut.

As I got closer to Pledge age, I decided that maybe what I really needed was to leave Midnight Harbor, that I didn't belong there, and no amount of faking it would make it better.

But Bran's words have changed everything I thought I knew about myself and yet...

It almost feels like I've sloughed off a coat that never fit.

Fae.

He tasted fae in my blood.

I'm still naked and dripping his cum down my legs, but my world is spinning and I don't know what to do first.

Clean up or scream.

Bran is beside me in an instant. "Come on." He brings me into the bathroom and wets a rag. "Open up, mouse," he says, nudging my knees apart. He cleans me up with a gentle hand and I'm so taken aback back by it, so grateful for him, that I'm suddenly teary-eyed.

A fat tear streams down my face and Bran reaches over, swiping it away with his thumb.

"I'm sorry," I say.

"Don't do that."

"What?"

"Don't apologize for your pain."

I nod and then put my face in my hands and suck in several deep breaths.

Bran lets me sit in the silence and the turmoil and it might be the kindest gift anyone has ever given me.

When I feel just slightly more together, I pull my hands away and shove the hair out of my face. He's in the doorway now, my clothes in his hand. I didn't even hear him leave.

"Thank you."

He leaves me to dress.

Once I'm clothed and after several more holy-shit-I-can't-breathe-this-is-insane moments, I leave the bathroom and find Bran at the window staring out into the night. I don't even know what time it is. Everything about my life is twisted and unfamiliar, including my sleep schedule.

"Now what?" I ask. "Where do I go from here?"

My stomach growls, clearly having an opinion on the matter.

Bran looks at me over his shoulder, his gaze on my midsection. "When's the last time you ate?"

I shrug. "I honestly couldn't tell you."

"Then the first thing we'll do is get you some food."

"What, now? I'm not hungry."

He gives me an admonishing glare. "You have to eat, mouse."

"Oh, do I? Oh, thank god you were here. I had no idea that was even a thing mortals did."

He saunters over.

I've always wondered if a vampire has to make considerable effort to walk the speed of us lowly humans, and if so...what does it mean that he's doing it now?

It makes me feel like stalked prey.

Which makes me think he's definitely doing it on purpose.

Using his height, he dominates my personal space so I backpedal, bumping into the wall. His hand comes to my jaw, forcing me to look up at him.

I exhale in a nervous little hiccup.

"You keep talking to me like that, I might have to punish this mouth later."

My tongue darts out, wetting my lips, and he watches the movement with hunger.

"I've only ever given one blow job before," I hear myself saying and then immediately turn red in the face. What the hell? He knew I was a virgin, to a certain degree, but this somehow is more embarrassing. Like I'm freely admitting my deficiencies in the bedroom.

"And?" he says.

"And...it was with Matt Thompson. He said I sucked at it. The pun unintended."

Bran's face darkens. "Matt Thompson is a fucking idiot."

"While I agree with that...I'm just saying...I don't really know what I'm doing in that department."

He dips down and kisses me gently, his mouth lingering on mine. "Don't worry, mouse," he says against my lips. "I'll teach you how."

"Another promise, is it?"

"Mmmm." He reaches up and rubs his thumb over my bottom lip. "I'll look forward to fucking that hole too."

His words send a pulse through my clit. I *am* inexperienced in the bedroom. I know my own pleasure, but I'm realizing there is power in giving pleasure to someone else too. And maybe that's why Bran loves to control mine. Maybe that's why I love it when he does.

And maybe that's why the thought of giving him something he can't get on his own sends a delicious thrill through my veins.

"Fuck," I say, drawing the word out into several long syllables.

He kisses me again and then he's gone and the air immediately cools with his absence.

"Come on, mouse. It's time to eat." He smirks at me from the door. "You'll need your stamina if you're going to keep up with me."

He doesn't mean in a foot race.

Like a dutiful little mouse, I follow him from the room, down the stairs and out the door.

————

Bran takes me to Crook & Pawn, one of the Duval restaurants. I've literally never stepped foot inside but I've always wanted to. Sam went once with Bianca and described it to me like a New England boarding school on crack.

I never thought I'd get to see it with my own eyes and never on the arm of Bran Duval.

He holds the door open for me and I step inside. There are inset lights in the short entrance hall, giving the space a hushed, soft golden glow. Dark wood covers the walls in the same deep, rich mahogany as the creaky old floor. Oil paintings in gilded frames depicting landscapes and birds and wild horses hang on the wall.

It's the kind of place that instantly brings to mind leather and tobacco and liquor and whispered gossip behind curls of smoke.

There isn't smoking inside, or at least none that I can smell, but I still get the feeling like there should be or there once was.

We leave the hall, Bran with his hand at the small of my back, me with my head slightly bowed as if I can hide the fact that I come from a Locke family and very much do not belong here.

But as soon as we step foot into the main room, the entire place goes silent save for the classical music playing through the embedded sound system.

Just when I think I understand the silence, that I'm getting used to the kind of attention Bran commands in Midnight, everyone rises from their tables in a cacophony of clattering dishes and chair legs scraping on the wood floor. And then every single person in the room bows their head to Bran.

I look over at him, mouth agape.

There's no emotion on his face. None of the cocky arrogance I'd expect.

Because clearly this happens every single time he steps foot inside the place, and clearly, he's very much used to it.

I know vampire houses and witch covens operate on their own rules, but I never stopped to think just how different one vampire house might be from another.

This level of veneration doesn't exist in the Locke House.

I always knew Bran had a certain level of respect in Midnight Harbor even outside of his house, but I'm not prepared for this. Not at all.

When the bowing and worshipping comes to an end, a hostess hurries over and gives another reverential nod. I can't remember the girl's name, but she's definitely mortal and not too much older than I am. Her attention darts from me to Bran and lingers on him in a way that makes my stomach twist. "Good evening, Mr. Duval. Your usual table?"

"Yes, Merra. Bottle of red too."

"Of course." She leads us through the dining room and all eyes track us. When we reach a back corner booth, Bran motions for me to slide into it. Merra hands me a menu fastened inside a thick leather cover. "I'll be back with the red." She scurries off.

"Mouse," Bran says, his eyes scanning the restaurant. "If you keep gaping at me like that, I might have to find something to put in that pretty mouth."

A shiver races through me and Bran grins.

"You're so funny."

"Yes, I get that a lot. 'You know that Bran Duval, he's such a funny guy.'"

I roll my eyes at him, then, "They're all acting like you're a king."

"I am."

"No, you're not."

"What is a king but a man who declares he's one?"

I frown at him. "That's not how that works."

"I hold the power. They know that."

There's so much about Bran that I've clearly missed over the years.

"And what do you do with all that power?"

He finally looks over at me, his hand finding my thigh beneath the table and squeezing. "I fuck innocent virgin neighbor girls."

I catch more than one person shooting their attention to us, probably eavesdropping on our conversation.

There's no such thing as a secret in a room full of vampires.

If this gets back to Julian...

Not that it should come as a surprise. He did find me half-dressed in Bran's house this afternoon, after all.

"You make it a habit of fucking innocent virgins, do you?" I challenge with a sharp edge of jealousy in my voice.

"Only the naughty ones."

My face flames and I shift on the leather of the booth, thighs rubbing together to ward off the sudden thrill between my legs.

Is it possible to keel over from being horny too often?

There's no such thing as a break when I'm with Bran.

Every touch is electric. Every word edged with innuendo.

Every look molten and ravenous.

We are two storm clouds always threatening to clash.

Merra returns with a wine bottle, but when she pops the cork out and fills a wine goblet, the dark red liquid looks too thick for wine.

Bran immediately drinks it back and runs his tongue over his sharpened fangs, a flare of light coming to his irises.

"What can I get for you?" Merra asks me.

"Oh. Sorry. I didn't even look at the menu." My eyes glaze over the words written in fancy script on the thick paper.

"She'll have a grilled cheese and French fries," Bran answers and takes the menu from me to hand it back. "With a root beer."

"What if I don't want that?"

Bran shoos Merra away with a curt flick of his hand.

"You have a grilled cheese at least three nights a week and always with French fries," he says.

"How would you—"

He taps his nose.

"Right. Of course."

He's not wrong. I do make a lot of grilled cheeses. Kelly doesn't love cooking and neither do I. And judging by the gnawing in my gut, my stomach is here for it.

Merra left the bottle of blood on the table and Bran reaches over to grab it by the neck. The thick liquid glug-glugs as it splashes into the goblet.

"Whose blood is that?" I ask.

He peruses the label. "Says it's Vintage Mitchell Smith, bottled in '79."

"Wait, really?"

I snatch the bottle from him only to find the label mostly blank. It just says, *Red—bottled in Serona with mortal consent.*

He's laughing at me.

"See. You are funny."

He brings the goblet to his lips and takes a tentative sip while his other arm winds behind me along the booth.

A few days ago, I thought he hated me. I thought he couldn't stand the sound of my voice. But now I don't know what to think.

We are inexplicably tangled in one another now, but there's a little voice in the back of my head that keeps reminding me this could all be some grand vampire game just to keep things entertaining in his long, long life.

It makes me want to know. It makes me want to put a magnifying glass to it and dissect it until I can label all its parts and put it in a neat little box.

"What are we doing, Bran?"

His eyes cut to me. "We're having dinner."

"No. I mean...you and me." I lower my voice. "What we just did—"

He cuts me off with his mouth on mine, his arm sliding off the booth, his hand threading through my hair pulling me into him. The kiss isn't long, but it is intimately deliberate.

It feels like a declaration to the entire room.

When he pulls away, my grilled cheese and fries are on the table and Merra is standing by awkwardly, her gaze downcast. "Was there anything else?"

"No," Bran answers. I notice he doesn't say thank you. I suppose the king isn't accustomed to thanking his peasants.

"Thanks, Merra," I say and she nods and darts off.

"Eat, mouse," he tells me, his hand still tangled in my hair but his eyes on the restaurant now. I get the distinct feeling he's waiting for something, biding his time.

Turns out I was right.

I'm nearly finished with my food when the front door bangs open and a figure darts into the restaurant and comes to a sudden stop at our table.

It takes my human eyes a second to focus on the vampire.

Hands on her hips, Sky Carter stands in front of us, boobs revolting against the tight V-neck of her shirt. My stomach sinks.

Sky Carter is fourth in line at the Duval House and worse—she's Bran's ex.

There is a very pointed look on her face. One that could pierce flesh if wielded properly.

"Sky," Bran says in a bored tone of voice.

"You have a taste for trash now, do you?" While she barely looks at me, we all know she's referring to me.

"What do you want?" he asks her.

Is he just going to ignore the fact that she called me trash?

"Damien has summoned you," she answers.

"Try again." His voice rings with authority.

With a sigh, she says, "Damien *asks* that you come to the house."

"Fine."

Sky relaxes. I don't. Bran's body is a hard line beside me, muscles tense.

He is the viper coiling to strike.

I feel the cold air in Bran's absence first. I hear the snap of a neck second.

Sky's eyes roll back in her head as her body thuds heavily to the floor.

I yelp in surprise and the sound rings out in the abrupt silence of the restaurant.

"Come on, mouse." Bran holds out his hand for me and I quickly take it, letting him guide me out of the booth.

As I step over the undead dead body of Sky Carter on the floor, my gut twists.

I will be paying for this later.

I can't get comfortable in the bucket seat of the Bimmer.

How could I when Bran is driving us to Duval House in my car where it'll surely get back to Julian Locke?

My Pledging is right around the corner. Instead of the distant annoyance I was feeling about it before, it's now hovering on the horizon like a storm cloud. What will Julian do?

Better yet, what the hell will I do?

Everything has become far more complicated.

"What do you think your brother wants?" I ask.

"With Damien, it's always hard to say." Bran is relaxed in the driver's seat, one hand on the leather steering wheel, the other wrapped around the stick shift.

"And Sky—" I start.

"Don't worry about Sky."

"Easy for you to say. She's not known for showing restraint. You just snapped her neck in the middle of the restaurant because, well…why? Because she called me trash? I'll admit I was really hoping you'd set her straight but—"

"No one is allowed to speak to you that way." His gaze cuts to me quickly before returning to the road. The leather steering wheel groans beneath his grip. "If someone does, you're to tell me."

A thrill blooms in my chest. Kelly has always looked out for me, but not in this live-or-die kind of way. The protection of an older sister is much different than the protection of a vampire like Bran.

"Sky will take it out on me," I say.

"I won't let that happen." He guides the Bimmer off the road and onto the black pavement of the Duval House driveway.

"As if you could stop it. Sky is like a trap-door spider just waiting for the perfect time to pounce."

He laughs.

"I'm serious!"

"I know you are." Another car passes us, the headlights sweeping over his face. "Sky won't hurt you. It wouldn't be worth the risk of my wrath. She knows that."

"Does she?" I ask, frowning at him. "Why would she know that?"

Bran and I have only been fucking around a few days. I don't know why Sky would know anything about me other than the fact that I'm Bran's neighbor and I might annoy him sometimes.

He doesn't look at me as he follows another curve in the driveway.

Duval House finally reveals itself nestled among the hardwoods at the back of a sprawling, well-manicured property.

It's seriously straight out of an English period drama.

Several spotlights are trained on the front of the estate, giving it an ominous feel. Matching flags with the Duval House crest fly from the twin towers on the north and south ends.

Almost every window is lit golden in the night.

Bran ignores the fork of the driveway where the pavement winds back to a parking lot and a six-stall carriage house. Instead, he turns us toward the house and drives beneath an attached porch.

"I wish I was fancy enough to have a drive-thru porch."

"It's called a *porte cochère*."

I like hearing his tongue roll over the French syllables.

I almost tell him to say it again but don't want to look like a simpering dork.

When Bran climbs out, someone is at the driver's side in an instant.

"Come, mouse," Bran calls.

The stranger climbs in behind the wheel and looks at me, waiting.

"What is happening?"

Bran ducks down into the open doorway. "This is Lance. Lance is going to park your car. You are going to get out of the car and follow me. Now, mouse."

Lance gives me an awkward look.

"Be gentle with her, Lance," I say.

He nods. "You have my word, Ms. MacMahon."

Lance knows who I am?

"*Mouse.*"

I scurry out of the car.

There's another guy at the massive double doors, holding one of them open for us.

"This is some white glove service," I mutter.

It makes me wonder again why Bran would ever leave Duval House. It never made any sense. It still doesn't.

The side entrance comes in on a sitting room that must be the size of my entire house. There are wingback chairs and red velvet settees and several leather side chairs positioned in front of a fireplace where a low fire crackles on the bricks.

The people in the room lurch to their feet and bow their heads as we breeze past, but Bran doesn't give them a second look.

We cross a foyer where the black and white marble floor gleams beneath two chandeliers. We pass a grand staircase that has a landing halfway up where the staircase branches off into opposite directions.

When you're a human living in suburbia, it's easy to forget the opulence and the elegance of the supernatural houses. I try not to gape around like a fish out of water as Bran guides me with his hand at the small of my back.

"Why did you leave here?" I blurt out. "This place is amazing."

"It's crowded," he answers distractedly.

"Do you still have a room here?"

"I have many, yes."

"Where?"

"Damien and I shared the north wing."

"The entire wing? How could that possibly get crowded? You probably had more room there than at your house and—"

Bran takes a fistful of my shirt and yanks me to a stop. I bounce off his chest from the sudden shift in momentum, so he hooks an arm around my waist, drawing me back in to keep me on my feet.

"Hey! What—"

Damien is suddenly in front of us.

Damien Duval is the type of man that if I didn't know about the things that go bump in the night and I passed him on a sidewalk, I might think he was a college student studying history or poli sci. He has that kind of air about him, just this side of arrogant and the kind of intelligence that makes most conversations with him hard to keep up with.

I immediately flash back to a few nights ago when I overhead Damien and Bran in Bran's kitchen. Damien was worried about the Lockes throwing their weight around, and thought I might somehow be significant. 'Special' was the word he used.

"Bran," Damien says and then his gaze trails me up and down.

I can't help but shiver beneath the weight of it. Bran yanks me behind him and says, "*No.*" Damien isn't the least bit put off by the threatening rumble in his brother's voice.

"We need to talk." Damien is heading in the opposite direction before I can blink. "Alone," he adds.

Bran sighs.

"What am I supposed to do while you're gone?" I ask and eye the people lingering in the foyer. We're a half-football-field away but I'm sure they can hear us. I don't know if I relish the idea of being alone in the Duval house.

"Jimmy," Bran calls.

A young woman is beside me in a second. "Jessie, hi," she says.

Jimmy, short for Jimena, is currently third in-line at Duval House. In chunky heeled combat boots, she stands several inches taller than me. She smells like rose oil and paint thinner and there is a rainbow of dried paint on her long, brown fingers.

"Look after my little mouse for me," Bran tells her.

"Of course." She smiles down at me with a warm gaze even though I'm absolutely certain she has better things to do.

Bran swivels around and is gone.

"Sorry," I say.

"For what?" Jimmy hooks her arm through mine and steers me away.

"I'm sure babysitting wasn't on your agenda for the night."

"And I'm sure being thrown into the lion's den wasn't on your agenda either." She says the latter with an aye, *aye-ther*. I've always thought people who pronounce it that way are too fancy for me.

"Everything about the last few days has been unexpected," I mutter.

"So I've heard."

"You have?" I gaze up at her. "What have you heard?"

She guides me through open pocket doors where stained glass is inlaid in the transom windows above. Classical music plays through a sound system while a coffee steamer hisses from the far side of the room.

It's a massive library with a full coffee bar and a winding iron staircase that goes up to the open second-story loft.

"Whoa."

It's so big, and the stacks so plentiful, you could easily get lost in them.

There are work tables set up equidistant from one another on my left. Matching library lamps with pull chains sit on each of the tables and cast golden light around the room. A plush red rug with the Duval crest runs down the center aisle. Six iron chandeliers hang from the vaulted ceiling. There are sitting areas with overstuffed leather chairs dotted around the room.

It's somehow cozy and huge all at the same time.

"Can I get you a coffee?" Jimmy asks. "We have anything you could possibly want."

I follow her to the bar where two humans mix drinks for a couple waiting at the far end.

It's late at night and if I drink coffee, I'll be up till the sun rises, but I guess that might just be my life now.

Though there is a distant nagging voice in the back of my head that reminds me I have a job and a shift to work tomorrow.

"How about tea?"

"Sure." Jimmy leans against the bar. "We have a passion fruit tea." She gives a chef's kiss. "It's excellent."

"I'll take that."

"Scott," she calls and the guy pouring foamed milk into a cup looks up. "Two passion fruit teas, iced, please."

"Coming right up," Scott says.

"So," I say, unsure of exactly *what* to say. I don't belong here and while no one stands and bows like they do when Bran's around, I still get the feeling everyone is whispering about me.

I trail off in a nervous laugh and Jimmy saves me.

"Is Bran being nice to you?" she asks.

I snort. "Does he know how to be nice?"

Jimmy laughs flashing gleaming white teeth. "One of the reasons I aligned myself with Bran and the Duval House when I came to America was because Bran can be both brutal and restrained. He's good at knowing when to push a button, when not to."

Oh, don't I fucking know it.

"Why did you leave your house overseas?" I ask, wanting desperately to move the conversation away from me and my *buttons*.

"Our matriarch died." Jimmy waves her hand dismissively. "It was a long, brutal feud over lovers and cattle, as most vampire wars are." She laughs again. "Anyway, the house started to fall apart afterward. New leadership took over but it wasn't the same. I had known Bran for decades at that point so I asked if he'd have me and he and Damien said yes." She holds her arms out like *voila*. "Here I am."

"Do you like Duval House?"

She scans the library, her long lashes nearly hitting the arched line of her brow. "I do. It's much more structured than the house I came from. More order. On the other hand, I'm a free bird. I don't like being tied down and Bran and Damien have always been good about letting me do my thing when I need to."

I nod at her paint-splattered hand. "Like art?"

She wiggles her fingers. "Art among other things." Her attention wanders to a pretty girl sitting on the arm of a velvet sofa. The girl smiles back. From my vantage point, I can't tell if she's human or vampire. I think human, if I'd have to guess, judging by the looseness to her posture. Vampires always have this edge of alertness to their bodies, as if they could attack at any moment. Or be attacked.

"Jimmy!" someone calls from the pocket doors.

"Stay here at the bar," Jimmy tells me. "This should just take a minute."

Jimmy darts away.

Scott is just scooping ice from a cooler into my cup when the air is disrupted beside me and I turn, thinking it's Jimmy or Bran.

A chill runs down my spine.

It's Sky.

Mother son of a bitch.

It's impossible to tell she was just lying dead on a restaurant floor not that long ago. She's obviously healed. There isn't a bruise anywhere on her skin. There is, however, a very clear thread of disdain on her face.

She reaches over the coffee bar and snatches a bottle of vodka. If I'd known you could get a spiked drink, I might have changed my order.

She twists off the cap and pours two sloshes into a white ceramic mug. She sips from it, keeping her gaze trained on me the entire time.

"Hi Sky," I say. "Nice to see you on your feet."

Internally I cringe. What the hell? Do I have a death wish?

I think having Bran's protection has embolden me, but where is Bran now? Not here. Not here to protect me.

Sky reaches across me and I shrink away like I'm afraid to get burned. She dips her hand inside a large glass canister and pulls out a bag of organic fruit snacks. Except on closer inspection, I see the label mentions they're "made from legally acquired blood."

Blood fruit snacks. I did not know that was a thing.

Sitting on one of the bar stools, Sky crosses one long leg over the other knee and leans back. She tears off a corner from the bag and plucks a bear-shaped gummy from inside, then puts it between her teeth and tears off its head.

The hair rises at the back of my neck.

"Did Bran ever tell you why he left Duval House?" she asks.

If words were ever used as a weapon, Sky has just racked a bullet in the chamber.

Scott sets my tea in front of me. "Enjoy," he says.

I pick it up, swirl the straw inside. The ice clinks together. "I don't think he did, no."

"Mmmm." Sky decimates another bear with the cut of her teeth. "I know why. Do you want to know why?"

Shit.

Yes, I do.

Very much so. It's a question that's plagued me ever since he moved in next door. But I thought the answer might be a bit of drama between him and his brother. Or maybe something political.

Now I have the very distinct impression the answer might gut me.

Sky leans over. Her breath smells like vodka and strawberries as she says, "He left Duval House because of you."

THREE

I am distantly aware that storming off in search of Bran in Duval House is more than a little reckless.

I am distantly aware that Sky's admission is as good as her striking a match and lighting the wick of a bomb.

And I'm the bomb.

But right now, I don't care about any of that. There's a knotting in my gut that feels a lot like betrayal.

"Bran!" I yell as I stalk down the hallway. All of the vampires and pledged humans give me a wide berth. "Bran Duval!"

"Jessie." Jimmy is suddenly beside me. "What's wrong?"

"I need to see Bran."

"Okay. But if you'll just—" She cuts herself off, her gaze going distant as if she's listening to something out of range of my hearing. "Bran said to follow me."

"Oh, he did, did he?" She guides me down the hall, then down another and finally shows me into an office where Bran is sitting on the edge of a giant desk. His brother is at the window, a glass of liquor in his hand.

"What's wrong, mouse?" Bran asks, only a slight edge of concern in his voice. "Did someone touch what's mine?"

He means me.

I come to a stop in front of him. Slouched as he is against the desk, we're nearly the same height and the intensity of his stare at eye level causes me to pull to a stop.

"Mouse," he coaxes.

I take in a breath. "Did you leave Duval House because of me?"

His gaze cuts over my shoulder to Jimmy and his face sharpens to a look of reproval.

"It wasn't me," Jimmy answers.

"It was Sky," I say. "And the fact that you're doing that thing with your face tells me all I need to know."

He pushes off the desk and rises to his full height. It makes me feel small and immediately I second guess myself. But no. *No.*

"Mouse," he says with warning.

"Why?" I shove a finger in his chest. "Why haven't you told me? And why would you do that? That doesn't make any sense."

"That's what I told him," Damien says to the window.

"Why, Bran?"

"That's a very long story." His voice is low and throaty.

"I have time."

"Mouse."

We face off silently and stoically for several long seconds. Bran is stubborn. But I can be too.

"You promised me you'd always tell me the truth. Last chance."

He still says nothing.

Decision made, I swivel on my heel and turn to Jimmy. "Could you please show me the way to my car?"

Her eyes dart to Bran and then, "Sure. Of course."

I can feel Bran's attention on me as I leave the room. He doesn't try to stop me. Good thing too, because I'm *this close* to punching a vampire in the face.

———

Jimmy walks me across the Duval property and shows me to my car. The keys are tucked in the visor—a very obvious place for keys to be. No one would dare steal a car from Duval property, though, so I suppose I'm not miffed about it.

"Thank you," I tell Jimmy as I slide in behind the wheel.

She comes into the open driver's side door and says, "Try not to be too hard on him. He often does what he does out of love."

I snort. "I think what you mean is he does it because he thinks he's better than everyone else and he thinks he can get away with doing whatever he wants."

She doesn't argue that. "Be careful, okay? Bran would lose his shit if something happened to you."

I roll my eyes. "I don't think that's true."

"Just...promise me, okay?"

"Fine. Sure. I will obey all traffic laws."

She steps back and I slam the door shut and crank the engine over, feeling just slightly guilty for taking out my annoyance on Jimmy.

I roll down the window and say, "Thank you."

She nods and, in an instant, she's gone.

———

I half expect to find Bran on my front porch when I get home, but he isn't there.

I park in the driveway and go inside. The house is dark and quiet. Kelly still isn't home? I go upstairs and find her bed made and unrumpled so I shoot her a quick text.

Where are you?

Locke House comes her quick reply.

Not that long ago, talking to my sister about my Pledging and my childhood seemed like the most important thing, but now? Shit is piling up and I don't even know where to start anymore.

Why the hell would Bran leave Duval House for me? Clearly Damien knew about it. Which explains why I heard the rumor they got into a fight over him leaving.

I decide the best thing to do is take a shower, scrub the night and Bran from my skin, and then try to sleep somewhat normal hours. But as I'm padding down to the kitchen for a bottle of water in nothing but my robe, I hear a knock on the back door.

I know who it is before I pull it open.

I find Bran with an arm propped on the door frame, leaning into the open doorway as much as the magic of invitations will allow.

I don't know what that strange magic is or what governs it, but it works better than any charm.

Bran will never be able to cross that threshold without being invited by myself or Kelly.

"What do you want?" I ask.

"I came to explain."

"I'm listening." I cross my arms over my chest and Bran watches as the silk material of my robe rides up on my bare thighs.

"If I tell you," he says, his gaze finally returning to my face, "it might change things between us."

"You not telling me has clearly changed things between us."

I can feel the power shifting. He's treating this whole thing like a scale of justice. One wrong move and the scales will tip. Right now what we have going on is a delicate balance of control, a synergy of give and take. If I'm being honest, I'm afraid of the scales shifting too, but I need to know.

"Invite me in," he says, "and I'll tell you."

I laugh, but it's more derision than humor. "I'm not doing that."

"Mouse."

"Tell me."

"I'm not telling you when I can't get to you."

"Why?" I cock out a hip. The robe slips again. "Because you know that if you can just touch me, tease me, *control* me, maybe the truth won't be so bad for me to hear?"

He doesn't answer, but the sharpened edge to his expression tells me I've nailed it.

I exhale, uncross my arms. He watches the robe again.

And an idea comes to me.

It's as much about me taking back some control as it is about getting revenge.

I go upstairs.

"Mouse!" he calls.

I come back a minute later with my favorite bunny vibrator. It's a deep violet shade made of silicone with an innie and an outie point of contact so I can fuck myself and hit my clit at the same time.

It's gotten me off more times than I can count.

Bran's gaze sinks to it in my hand and then he narrows his eyes.

"Mouse." His voice reverberates with warning.

"Last chance."

"I'm not playing games," he says.

Well, I am.

And I'm about to take this one home.

I settle myself into the doorway just this side of the threshold and prop my foot on the other side. The robe parts, exposing me, and Bran's nostrils flare.

I am a responsible owner of toys and always wash mine after use, so when I pop it in my mouth, I know it's nice and clean.

Bran growls in the back of his throat as I close my eyes and fuck my mouth with it, getting it nice and wet.

When I pull it out, I let my lips pop around it.

Bran's eyes are glowing now.

I readjust, hit the ON button and the toy vibrates in my hand.

Bran's breathing intensifies as I drag the toy over my pussy. I might have been anticipating the sensation, but the way Bran leans in, teeth gritted, makes the pleasure sink a little deeper.

I arch against the doorframe and slip the vibrator inside my slick channel.

"Oh fuck," I moan for dramatic effect but when I increase the pace and Bran puts his hands on his side of the door frame and the wood groans around his grip, the pleasure pounds through me like a summer storm.

I keep fucking myself, the soft nubby end hitting my clit with every thrust.

The tie on the robe slips open and my nipple hits the cool air, beading to a peak.

Bran bites at his bottom lip, drawing blood. His dark brow is sunk into a deep V as he mops up the blood with a swipe of his tongue.

I moan again.

"Mouse," he says, his voice low and throaty.

"I bet you wish it was you inside of me."

Whoa. Where did that come from?

But I immediately see the teasing has hit him exactly where I intended.

There's a very clear bulge at the front of his pants.

I fuck myself a little harder and hit the button for more intense vibration. The sensation pulses through me and there's a very distinct wet sound coming from my pussy now.

I groan and pant and groan again as the orgasm rises, rises, the nub hitting my throbbing clit just right.

"Oh...fuck..." I pant out and then capture my nipple between two fingers, rolling it for a stroke of pain.

As the orgasm takes hold and I cry out, the doorframe groans beneath Bran's grip and the wood cracks.

The pleasure roars through me like a forest fire, consuming my veins, pulsing and thrilling every hollow corner of my body. My thighs quiver and I arch, knees trembling as I hold the toy deep inside, the nub tight against my clit as several aftershocks pound through me.

When I come down and refocus, I find Bran staring at me with two eyes like embers.

I've never seen so much pain and anguish on his face before.

The doorframe groans again, his knuckles white.

I pull the vibrator out, and then drag my tongue over my juices glistening on the violet shaft.

"Mmmm," I say. "So sweet."

"You'll pay for this one, little mouse." The rumble is gone from his voice. Now he is cold and distant.

It sends a shiver down my spine and a new pulse through my pussy.

I know I will. But for right now, I'm high on the orgasm and the victory. I needed to take back some of my own power just to prove to him and myself that I could.

"Stop fucking keeping shit from me," I say, and grab hold of the back door, "and maybe next time you can join me."

Then I slam the door in his face.

Four

I just slammed the door in Bran's face.

He's going to get my ass for that one but for now I'm safe and sound in my own home and I'm gonna soar on this win for as long as I can. I fucking earned it.

Up in my bedroom, I hesitate just outside the square of moonlight pouring through my bedroom window. I haven't turned on the overhead light yet, so I can easily see across the valley between my house and Bran's.

His window is dark.

I quickly snap my curtains shut and then get ready for bed, thinking I'll sleep like a baby.

Wrong. I toss and turn all night with this constant nagging desire to go to my bedroom window and peek through the curtains to see if Bran is there, to see if his bedroom light is on.

Somehow, I manage to stay beneath my quilt until my phone tells me it's just after seven in the morning. I think I slept some, but not enough judging by the heaviness in my eyes and the ringing in my ears.

I pull on a pair of leggings and pass my bedroom window and find myself lingering in the slant of pale blue light stealing through the crack in the curtains.

I can't help myself. I reach out and pull one back a few inches.

My heart sinks. Bran's blinds are shut tight. Not that I should be surprised. It is morning, after all, and vampires hate mornings. He'll be sleeping for the rest of the day.

Which is just as well because I have a life to return to and a shift at the coffee shop to work. But I'd be lying if I said I wasn't excited about what might happen when day falls and night breaks.

Bran will come looking for me. Of that I'm absolutely sure.

Just thinking about his promise before I slammed the door in his face has my skin prickling and my nerves lighting up.

You'll pay for this one, little mouse.

Oh, the things Bran Duval promises to do to me in the dark. It's enough to keep that teasing flame at my clit flickering long after it should have died out.

I hate the way he can sway me like that, but damn if I don't love the rush it gives me.

I haven't felt this much *in my skin* in...well, ever.

In the kitchen, I get the coffee maker going and then return to my bathroom to scrub my face and throw on some makeup. I only bother with mascara, a brush of blush, and a swipe of tinted chapstick. With my freckles, I've always thought it was pointless to wear concealer or foundation. I like my freckles. Let them shine.

Returning to the kitchen, I find the coffee maker has done its job and steam is rising from the pot and curling in the sunlight shining through the kitchen window. I find my favorite travel mug in the dishwasher and fill it up, add some creamer, and screw on the top. I still have forty-five minutes before I'm supposed to be at work but if I stay here any longer, I'm worried about what I might do.

I could probably walk in Bran's front door and up to his bedroom and slip into his bed and—

Nope. Nope.

To work it is.

Climbing in behind the wheel of the Bimmer while the dew burns off of the grass feels familiar, and I take in a deep breath of the fresh morning air, then exhale.

Everything is going to be all right.

———

Rita is behind the counter when I walk into Magic Coffee Shop. She looks up when the bell dings, announcing my arrival. Her dark brow sinks over her brown eyes. "What are you doing here?"

"I'm scheduled to work today." I hang my bag on the hook in the back and then tie on one of the waist aprons with the Magic Coffee Shop logo embroidered in rainbow thread on the hip.

Rita's frown deepens.

"What?" I say.

"It's just..." She licks her lips and tucks her pen into her top knot of braids. "Why don't you take the day off? I know you have a lot going on and—"

"Rita, I want to be here." I sigh and scrub at my face. "No, I think what I mean is, I *need* to be here. Is that okay? I want to just work and clear my head and be normal for a second."

She purses her lips together and regards me with the warm, concerned look of a mother. Finally, she nods. "I was planning on being here for the morning anyway, so I'll catch up on some paperwork and maybe pop down to the supply store after the lunch rush."

"Sounds perfect."

As she passes me for her office in the back, she wraps her hand around my arm and squeezes. I catch the scent of her oil blend— patchouli and lemongrass and lavender. "If you need me, you just call for me, okay?"

"Sure. I'll be fine. I promise."

With a nod, she lets me go and disappears in back.

It isn't long before the shop is full and I'm so busy, I don't have a spare minute to dwell on all the shit going wrong in my life. It's absolute bliss.

Gwen, a witch barista who works at the shop, shows up for her afternoon shift a little after two, so when my best friend Sam walks in the door at half-past-three, I can take a little break to chat with her.

After a quick hug, she sits on a stool at the counter and grabs a honey stick from the display cup. "Where the hell have you been?" She reaches over the counter for the scissors and clips off the end of the stick. Honey oozes out the end and she licks it off.

"You won't believe me if I told you," I answer.

"Yes, I would. Because you don't lie."

I pull to a stop and frown at her.

"What?" she says.

Fae can't lie. I don't lie on principle, but I *have* lied in the past. Like that time Principal Manwell caught me skipping class and I told him my sister had an emergency which was totally not true.

But...how can that be? Fae can't lie. That's like written in the fae canon or whatever.

Maybe Bran was wrong. Thinking this, thinking I have an out, fills me with so much damn relief I nearly weep.

"Jess," Sam prods. "Why do you have that dumb look on your face?"

I arch a brow at her and she laughs.

"I just realized something is all. Anyway..." I fill one of the portafilters with freshly ground espresso and tamp it down. "I've been with Bran Duval."

Sam clamps her teeth on the honey stick as her eyes get big. "Okay. Okay. Definitely didn't expect that twist, but I'm here for it," she says. "Go on."

I twist the filter into the espresso machine and push the button to brew. The machine churns to life.

"It all started after Kelly showed up with this nasty bite on her neck," I say.

"I've clearly missed so much."

As I make Sam her favorite frappe, I fill her in on *most* of the details, but have to leave out a few key points considering anyone in the coffee shop could be listening in with their supernatural hearing.

I don't tell Sam about the mind-bending sex with the infamous Bran Duval. I can dish all those details later.

"Here's where things get a little wild," I tell her as I slide the frappe over the counter. "Are you ready for it?"

She upends the rest of the honey stick into the cup. "I've had the most boring twenty-four hours compared to yours, so yes. Mom sent me to Mulligan House for a celebration ritual that amounted to a turkey dinner and a bonfire for burning our fears." She rolls her eyes. "I don't know if I'm cut out for being bound to a witch house. I find all of the rituals and ceremonies"—she lowers her voice and leans in—"*insuffer-able. So go on, I could stand for some excitement even if it's not mine."

"Okay, well...Bran bit me and—"

"He what?!"

"And he said he tasted something different in my blood."

"He...*what?*"

I want to tell her exactly what he thinks he tasted in my blood but again...*ears.*

"And then I found out when I went to Duval House with him that he supposedly left the house because of me. And now he won't tell me why. How the hell does that make any sense?"

Sam puts her head in her hands. "I'm trying to compute all of this and it's not working."

"Welcome to my Shit Show, Sam. Pull up a chair and pour a stiff drink, because it's wild in here."

"You aren't kidding." She sits with the information for a second and then sips from her frappe. "Okay. So. First thing...he bit you. What did he taste?"

I scan the people in the shop. Most are absorbed in their own conversations, but a few people are alone with their devices.

"He has a theory, but...hold on." I pull out my cell phone and bring up the text window. I hit Sam's name and type up a message that says: *he thinks he tasted fae blood.*

My heart drums a little harder as my thumb hovers over the SEND button. Being with Bran and being inside his world sorta feels like a dark fairy tale. And in that dark fairy tale, it's not that big of a deal, the girl finding out she has fae blood running through her veins.

But out here in my normal life, telling Sam will somehow make it very, very real.

Sam widens her eyes at me, telling me to hurry up.

I send the message with a deep breath and Sam's phone pings a second later. When she opens and reads the message, she nearly falls off her stool. She grabs at the counter at the last second and the stool knocks back to the floor.

"WHAT?!" she says too loudly.

Several heads turn our way.

"Shhh!"

"WHAT?" she repeats, still clutching at the counter.

"I know it sounds crazy."

"Crazy? Ha. Ha!"

"Are you okay?"

She gives me a look. "After you dropped that asteroid? I mean! How...but...okay...*he...you*...do you believe him?"

I left out the part about Sasha and her bite because that's a giant secret that isn't entirely mine to tell.

The Sasha information is a thorn in my side that I can't seem to pluck out. The secret about her biting me and then "disappearing" didn't come from Bran. It came from Runa and Cal. It's much harder to ignore proof when it comes from multiple sources.

"I honestly don't know what to believe at this point," I tell Sam. "I suspect Kelly has been avoiding me and she's the only person who might be able to shed more light on it."

"Your Pledging is two days away," Sam points out.

I collapse against the back counter and let out a sigh that sends my bangs fluttering over my forehead. "I know."

"What if Damien bids on you? Are you going to accept it?"

If I joined Duval House, I'd have to leave my home and the only other place I could go would be Duval House, which would put me further away from Bran. Unless...would he come back?

Is that even what I want at this point?

Once you accept a bid and Pledge yourself to a House, there's no backsies. That's a decision you make for life. I have to be careful about what I do, if I do anything.

I could still leave Midnight.

But thinking about leaving immediately brings to mind Bran in his bed, pleading with me not to go.

And going doesn't hold the same allure it did.

One very hot, very annoying vampire has taken that place.

Everything about Bran is a whirlwind, a chaos storm, and I'm swept up inside of it.

I hate him and I'm pissed at him and yet...I can't get enough of him.

"Jessie!" Sam snaps her fingers in my face. "What are you going to do?"

"I—"

The bell above the door rings out. Instinctively, I turn to the customer to greet them, but the air gets lodged in my throat and no words can find their way out.

The one and only very hot, *very* annoying vampire is standing in a triangle of sunlight in the doorway. Smoke rises from his shoulders and curls in the light. Dark sunglasses shield his eyes, but I know he's looking right at me.

Vampires very rarely come out before five p.m. Too much UV light. Too much risk of spontaneously combusting.

But Bran isn't just any vampire. And he's not here for an afternoon jolt of caffeine.

"Get your keys," he tells me.

"I'm working."

"Get your keys and get in the car, mouse." His voice rumbles with authority.

Sam looks between me and Bran at the door. The rest of the coffee shop does the same. This is a reality TV show taking place right in front of their eyes.

What will the girl do?

I fold my arms over my chest. "And what if I don't?"

What I expect him to do is lay out some minor threat that could also be construed as a sexual punishment. I'm almost looking forward to it. I pretty much asked for this, didn't I? I'm the kid testing out the outlet with the pointy tines of a fork.

But what Bran says instead catches me off guard and makes my heart drop to my feet.

"If you don't, then I'll leave Midnight right now and never come back."

And here I thought I had the upper hand. I was wrong yet again. Bran isn't a storm I'm caught up in. He is the sun and I am involuntarily drawn to him, stuck in his gravitational pull.

I won't refuse him. I can't. I don't want to, knowing what the consequence will be.

And he knows it.

He's found my weakness and now he's making me admit to it. As much to him as to myself.

"Jess?" Sam says.

"Looks like I have to go." I untie my apron. "Gwen, are you good?"

The witch nods at the other end of the counter. "I'm good."

I grab my bag from the back and give Sam a quick hug. "I'll call you later?"

"You better." She eyes Bran over my shoulder. He's still smoking in the sunlight but he hasn't flinched.

How long before a vampire bursts into flames?

How long before I smolder in his wake?

When I reach him, I'm faced with my reflection in the lenses of his sunglasses. They're so dark, I can't see his eyes, but I can feel the weight of his stare.

"After you," he says.

I step out into the light and fish the keys from my bag. We cross the street together, leaving a trail of smoke behind us. Bran is oddly calm about the whole thing, considering he's walking tinder at this point.

At the Bimmer, Bran stops at the trunk. "Open it, mouse." I fumble with the keys and get the one I need trapped in the ring of my *Dude Where's My Car?* keyring. "Hurry, mouse."

I finally get it untangled and pop the trunk. Bran shoves aside my bag of jumper cables and bungee cords and climbs in.

"What are you doing?"

"Drive until sunset," he orders, a very clear thread of anger reverberating in his voice.

"Are you—"

He grabs the trunk and slams it closed, sealing him inside. Smoke wafts out in a plume, causing me to cough. You'd think it'd smell like burning flesh, but there's only the faintest hint of spice and ash.

"Okay then." I wave the smoke away and climb in behind the wheel.

———

I drive in circles for what feels like hours. I decide to take some of my favorite roads, the narrow lane that winds along Midnight Lake where the houses are practically built on top of each other, each vying for a view of the water.

I head north after that and pass a few of the farms on the outskirts of Midnight, where the farmers not only deal in eggs and beef, but also in blood for the few vampires in town who choose to go the animal route instead of the human one.

As the sun descends below the treetops, I'm way back in the woods on a dirt road.

It's here that my trunk pops open.

I glance at the rear-view mirror for only a second, but when I look back at the road, Bran is there in the weak beam of my headlights, his shirt charred at the shoulders.

"Christ!" I slam on the brakes. The tires skid over the gravel and I have to whip the wheel around just to stay on the road.

I finally come to a stop and throw the car into park.

"What the hell are you doing?" I yell. "I could have crashed my car!"

Bran stalks to the driver's side door and rips it open.

"Hey!"

He grabs me by the arm and yanks me out, spins me around and slams me over the hood. I huff out a breath, hands braced on the warm metal as the engine continues to run.

"What are you—"

There's a clank of metal, a snap of leather, and a second later, my arms are crossed over my back and tied at the wrists with Bran's leather belt.

He bends over me with all of his weight, his groin at the swell of my ass. "Are you listening now, mouse?"

My heart is slamming against my ear drums. "Yes."

I have a safe word. I could use it if I needed to.

"I have very little respect for human life," he admits. "And even less patience for games."

"I thought we were—"

His hand curls around my throat as his mouth comes to the curve of my ear. "Quiet, little mouse. It's my turn to speak."

I swallow hard. His grip tightens.

"I operate on a very thin line," he says. "With you, I try very, very hard to control myself." His voice rumbles. He's suddenly thick and hard at the seam of my ass. "But that control has its limits. If you want this, little mouse, you only get it one way. *My* way. Do you understand me?"

My pussy throbs. "Yes."

The pressure of his weight disappears and I'm just exhaling with relief when he yanks my pants down, baring me, and cracks me across the ass.

"Ouch! What the—" I wiggle against the car, but Bran presses his free hand at the small of my back, locking me in place. He spanks me again, hard, and a sharp thrill pulses through my pussy as the pain radiates across my cheek.

He takes up a length of my hair and wraps it around his hand, yanking my head back. "Will you obey me?"

I pant out a breath. I'm suddenly throbbing and wet.

Say what you want about Bran Duval, he knows all of the buttons to push.

I'm over here playing checkers and he's launching a fucking rocket ship.

"I will only ask you this once. Yes or no, mouse?" His other hand follows the curve of my ass, his fingers trailing devilishly close to my slick opening. Instinctively I push into him and he pulls my hair harder.

"Yes," I say.

"Yes what?"

Every day, you're faced with choices. Do you want almond milk or oatmilk? The red shoes or the black ones?

Sometimes the choices are life-altering, like this one.

Sometimes it'll change you irrevocably and your life will branch off in an entirely different direction.

This is that choice.

I can feel the tremor of it at the center of me. A seismic shift.

I will never be the same after Bran Duval.

I will never be the same after this choice. It's throwing everything I thought I knew about myself into question.

And yet...and yet...

There is now a spotlight on what I want and what I need and I know it includes Bran as much as he frustrates and annoys me.

I don't know why. I don't know what it says about me to like this so damn much, but if I don't look too closely at it, maybe I'll come out the other side unscathed.

"Yes," I say, "I'll obey you."

"Good girl." He spins me around. "Now get on your knees."

Five

I asked for this.

I said I would obey Bran because I want all the sinful things he's promised to do to me in the dark.

I want to feel the pleasure of his punishments and the pain of his control.

I want to feel the power that comes with all of it. The power of giving in to him and to the desires of my own damn body.

He watches me expectantly, waiting. His patience only goes so far.

I sink to the ground. Gravel bites at my knees. He reaches down and brushes the hair away from my face, then drags his thumb over my bottom lip.

With his other hand, he unzips his pants. My heart kicks up expectantly and my tongue flicks out, wetting my mouth.

His hardness bulges at his boxer briefs. If my hands weren't still tied behind my back, I might reach out to stroke it, feel him strain against the material.

He pulls the waistband down and his cock comes out, heavy and thick. He takes it in his hand and gives it several pumps.

I inhale deeply. I already admitted to him that I don't know how to give a good blow job. Last night I fucked myself with a vibrator right in front of him. I knew what I was doing last night, and I was soaring high on that confidence.

Now...I'm a little sick with nerves. What if I do it wrong? I've given so much of myself to him already, but I don't want to look like the inept mortal girl I know I am. Especially next to him.

The head of his cock swells in the cuff of his hand. "Open up, mouse," he orders.

I lick my lips again and swallow hard.

"I don't really know—"

He shoves his cock in, catching me off guard. There's no time to think about it now.

He pumps into me and I exhale roughly through my nose.

He's hard as a rock, filling my mouth. I flatten my tongue, trying to find room for him as the head of his cock throbs in the back of my throat.

Taking a length of my hair, winding it around his fist, he pulls my head back and his cock out.

"Breathe," he says and I gasp for air as tears well in my eyes. "Good girl." Then he shoves back in, pumps harder as he groans above me. There's a tortured thrill building between my legs, and butterflies in my belly as he uses me for his own pleasure.

The head of his shaft throbs on the back of my tongue as he pushes in further. I gag, but he continues his assault, growling around gnashed teeth.

"Fuck, your mouth feels so fucking good."

A warm flush comes to my cheeks. He's breathing harder now, and his grip on my hair tightens as he angles me up.

"Look at me, mouse. I want to see you when I come in your mouth."

When I meet his gaze, tears streaming down my face, his eyes glow amber in the semi-darkness and his fangs sharpen.

"Fuck," he grunts out. "You will be my undoing." He drives deeper as if punishing me for it. As if he can't get enough of me.

And just when I think I can't take much more, he growls loudly and spills his hot seed down my throat.

I'm not ready for it and I let out a strangled sound around his thickness.

His cum is coppery and salty and when he pulls out of me, I move to spit it out.

"No." He clamps his hand over my mouth. "Swallow it."

Several beads of cum sit on my tongue as his gaze burns into me.

Another order I can't refuse and the authority in his voice makes me burn hotter with need.

I swallow it back and the taste of him fills my mouth.

"Good girl," he says and then lifts me up, presses me against the car's front fender.

Please fuck me now, I think.

I'm mindless, spinning, buzzing with need. Being used is apparently another one of my kinks. My clit is throbbing, my nipples are tight, and I'm so wet, it's dripping down my inner thighs.

I'm burning and mascara is probably running down my face, but I need more of him.

I want all of him.

"You made me another promise," I say, voice thin, almost a whimper.

He once told me he'd bend me over the hood of my car.

I want that to happen right now.

Bran drags his thumb roughly over my bottom lip. "When I bend you over the hood, I won't be fucking this hole." Then his hand sinks between my legs where my panties are still askew. He slips his fingers down my wetness, then teases at my opening and I mewl at the pleasure, rocking my hips against him. "And I won't be fucking this hole."

My eyes shoot open. "What?"

"I'm going to fuck that tight ass and you're going to take it like a good girl."

"But—"

"Mouse."

There's a very clear ring of warning in his voice.

"Okay," I say a little breathy, even though I'm not absolutely sure what I'm agreeing to. In all my own pleasure, I've never gone down that road.

"That's the right answer." He zips up his pants and then reaches around me to unknot his belt from my wrists.

"Wait...but..."

"Get in the car." He goes to the driver's side door, the belt hanging from his grip.

"But I...you can't..." I'm still throbbing and soaked.

"You don't get to come," he tells me. "Not until I say you can. Now get in the car." He slides in behind the wheel and shuts the door.

Fuck. Fuck!

I breathe heavily, trying to think through my options. But of course, I don't have many.

"Mouse," he says. "I won't tell you again."

He'll probably leave me here. He already did it once in the cemetery and town is a lot farther away from here. I'd be walking all night.

I fix my pants and numbly walk around the car. Every step is torture as the friction from my panties hits just right at my swollen clit.

Goddamn him.

I carefully climb into the passenger seat, thighs pressed together, trying to stave off the needy heat between my legs.

I want to murder him.

"You're doing this just to torture me," I tell him.

He puts the car in gear and pulls away from the shoulder. "Do you remember what I told you the night you went to the Harbor party?"

I think I know what he's getting at.

When I don't answer, he goes on. "I told you not to wear panties and you didn't. I told you I did it to test your obedience. It wasn't to torture you, mouse." He glances at me briefly, his eyes catching the light from the dashboard. "I did it to teach you the lines not to cross. Disobeying me is one of them. And testing my patience is not something either of us wants."

My stomach dips. Am I flying too close to the sun?

Do I have no idea what I've gotten myself into?

"Should I be afraid of you?" I ask.

"Absolutely." He comes up to a stop sign and looks over at me again, his gaze lingering on me this time. "You can trust me to keep my word, however. So long as you keep yours."

He means as long as I obey him.

I already said I would. I don't plan on backtracking now. But there's clearly so much I have yet to learn. Every second of this relationship is a walk across a tightrope.

I had no idea that before Bran, I was just surviving.

Now I'm living.

The danger, the pleasure, the control, the thrill of it all, it is intoxicating and I'm officially addicted.

"What about my safe word?" I ask. "I can still use it at any time?"

"Yes, but don't think of it as a pause button. Think of it as a ripcord." He turns onto the next street and shifts through several gears as we hit a straightaway and the Bimmer picks up speed. The velocity presses me against the bucket seat.

"Are you saying that when I use the safe word, that's it? We're done?"

"I'm saying I won't know until you use it."

Well, goddammit. That makes me not want to use it. I'm glad I haven't yet.

Because the truth is, the thought of not having Bran anymore makes me feel hollow.

We are tangled in one another now and I think it's that way for him too, as much as it is for me. It's why he's working so damn hard to draw the lines and make sure I know where they are.

Through the control, he's revealing his deepest secret—he doesn't want this to end either.

Bran Duval likes me.

He might *more* than like me.

It might be immature to think about it that way, but it still sends butterflies flitting through my stomach, nonetheless.

The Infamous Bran Duval, a several-hundred-year-old vampire, likes me.

I smile to myself.

Bran says, "Why are you smiling?"

"No reason."

"Mouse."

Am I disobeying him by not telling him all of my inner thoughts? I have to leave some of the mystery.

"I was just thinking I like this song," I say as an 80s pop ballad plays through the radio.

"Liar."

I laugh to myself and then—

"Wait. You're right. I am lying. I forgot to tell you...I realized today that I can lie."

He frowns and downshifts as we reach our next turn. "That is...interesting."

"See! I knew it meant something. Fae can't lie."

He checks for traffic at the stop sign and then turns, the headlights sweeping across the front of Midnight Library and its dark stained-glass windows.

"Try it again," he says. "Tell me an obvious lie."

"I like you," I say with a sardonic grin.

He cuts a look to me. "Mouse."

"Okay. Okay." It wasn't a lie anyway. "It's morning." I spread my arms out. "See?"

His frown deepens. There's a special kind of satisfaction that comes with baffling Bran.

"I know what I tasted in your blood," he says. "I wasn't mistaken."

"You had to be."

"I suppose it's possible the binding amulet has muddled the taste of your blood."

The absolute relief I feel when he says as much is damn near orgasmic.

It's like everything has been put back in place. I don't have to doubt who I am.

"Maybe Sasha said she tasted fae blood too, but was mistaken just like you. Maybe Julian Locke thinks I'm fae, but I'm not."

"But why bind you then?" he points out. "What was your mother trying to hide?"

Okay, he has me there. "Well...I don't know."

"Exactly. I'll admit, the lying is a wild card I didn't consider until now. But it's not a nail in the coffin, so to speak." He's quiet for a second, then, as if making a decision, takes a sharp right turn.

"Where are you going?"

"We need to speak to your sister. Let's not delay it any longer. I want answers and she can give them to us."

"My house is the other way."

"She's not home."

"How do you know?"

"She called in sick today and I heard she's been staying at Locke House."

I swallow around a lump in my throat.

Bran takes the next left turn, ignoring the blinker. "I suspect Julian has been keeping Kelly from you ever since he found you with me."

I've been desperate to speak to my sister and now that I might actually get the chance? I'm afraid of what she might reveal.

I'm afraid of what the truth might be.

My mom did go to an awful lot of trouble to keep secrets about me hidden.

It's possible that I'm going to look back on this and realize that being fae was the least of my worries.

Six

Locke House is a bit of a misnomer, since the property isn't just one house but two. The Second Residence, as it's called, was added to the property in 1941 when Locke House took in several widows who lost their husbands to WWII.

My maternal great-grandmother was one of those women.

My mom used to brag about that fact to anyone who would listen, even though every citizen of Midnight Harbor already knew the story of the war widows.

Julian's decision to take in charity cases was looked upon with reverence and admiration.

I was never so sure. Sometimes I secretly thought Julian saw the war widows, my great-grandmother included, as easy prey.

Unlike my dad's family that had been bound to the Locke House for over two centuries, my mom's family were outsiders. Meaning they had no idea the supernatural world existed until they were brought into it.

The Second Residence had tried to match the original house's Italianate architecture but never came close enough. It's just a white box with some decorative black trim and a wide front porch with simple, straight columns.

The main house, however, was always supposed to be the center of attention.

It was constructed in the mid-1800s by some renowned architect that I can never remember the name of. The house is overly designed with decorative cornices and multiple towers and a front door so big you could drive a truck through it.

And it honest-to-god has a room called the belvedere because it overlooks the pond at the back of the Locke property.

Kelly and I used to joke that our dining room was the belvedere because it had a clear view of the other neighbor's trash cans.

"Dinner is ready!" she'd call up to me. "Meet me in the belvedere."

No matter how many times we used the joke, it was always funny.

The first edge of worry comes over me, thinking about Kelly. I've been so wrapped up in my own shit that I didn't take enough time to properly check in on my sister since the bite.

With the worry is guilt.

Bran parks the Bimmer in the lot behind the Second Residence. Unlike at Duval House, there's no Lance waiting beneath a *porte cochère* to valet my car for me.

Locke House might have a belvedere, but I'm beginning to realize most of what Julian does, he does for show. Duval House is bougie as fuck, but it's casual wealth. The Duvals don't show off. They just *are* rich and surrounded by luxury because it's who and what they are.

They don't even have to try.

When we walk out from the parking lot, there are several vampires and a few humans milling around the side garden that stretches between Second Residence and Locke House. Cody and François are the only two who come forward. They've been together since 1969 when François changed Cody at Woodstock.

François has his arm draped over Cody's shoulders. He's taller than Cody by several inches, though he's given an extra few for the height of his frohawk.

Cody is dressed in brown jeans and a short sleeve button-up shirt with pearl snaps. I don't think he ever left Woodstock. His feet are bare.

"Jessie," François says, giving me a friendly nod. "'Tis a brave move, bringing a Duval here."

Even though it's been several centuries since François left France, some of his accent still comes through.

"There's no rule against it, is there?" I ask.

"I suppose not."

"Is my sister here?"

"She is," François answers.

"In the main house," Cody adds.

I can't shake the feeling that they're hiding something from me.

"How has she been since that horrible bite the other night?"

Cody and François share a look. "We know nothing of a bite," François answers.

"Mmm. Well, Julian said he'd handle it so maybe he did. But Kelly came home the other night with her throat torn. Bran had to heal her."

Cody threads his fingers with François's hand that hangs over his shoulder. "We didn't know anything about that, Jess. Honestly."

I give them a nod. "Okay, well…we're going to head in then."

"I'd leave the Duval outside," François suggests.

Bran mimics François and hangs his arm casually over my shoulders. "*The Duval* will go where Jessie goes."

It's weird hearing him say my name.

I don't like it.

The guys regard me with an equal measure of worry and surprise.

"Your funeral," François says to Bran.

Bran says nothing.

We leave the guys and follow the paved walk from the Second Residence up the gentle hill to Locke House. Bran removes his arm from around me and I immediately miss the weight of his nearness.

I don't think he's doing it to be distant. I think he's doing it so his hands are free in case he has to fight.

While there has always been tension between the Duvals and the Lockes, there hasn't been outright fighting in a very long time. Longer than I've been alive.

After the fight at the Pack House, I know Bran can hold his own when surrounded by supernaturals, but the Lockes do have quite a few older vampires within their house. Vampires that would nearly match Bran in age and strength.

As we make our way up the curving front steps, I watch him out of the corner of my eye, trying to gauge how he's feeling. This was his idea. But is he worried?

His face is blank.

"We don't have to do this," I whisper beneath my breath.

"Yes, we do," he says evenly just as the double front doors crack open and light spills out.

———

"Jessie!" A curvy woman comes out of the house with her arms spread for a hug. Maggie is third in line at Locke House and everyone considers her the house's mother.

I let her envelop me and she squeezes just hard enough to make me grunt.

Bran clears his throat and Maggie steps back to give him a look. She clucks her tongue in a tsk-tsk.

"Bran Duval. Good evening. What brings you all the way over here to Locke House?"

While I haven't Pledged yet and certainly haven't aligned myself with the Lockes, I'm still more of a member here than Bran is and I think it might be best if I do most of the talking.

"I need to see Kelly. Where is she?"

Maggie keeps her eyes on Bran and Bran keeps his eyes on Maggie. "I think she's around here somewhere."

"Can you help me find her?"

Maggie tenses up and drags her teeth over her plump bottom lip in a half-wince.

Next to me, Bran goes rigid.

Locke House, like Duval House, is always busy. There are people hanging around in the background and a friendly game of poker going on in the next room over. So I don't notice until several seconds after the vampires that Julian Locke has arrived.

He comes into the square of light cast by the modern chandelier above us. He's wearing a loose-fitting shirt that hides the fact that he's cut like a Greek statue.

His piercing blue gaze sweeps from me to Bran.

"Bran," he says. "Nice of you to visit Locke House. And you brought our girl home." He smiles at me, dares me to contradict him.

I'm not here for conflict so I keep my mouth shut.

But Bran has other ideas.

"Don't provoke me," Bran says. "I know you can smell me on her."

Bran keeps using that fact as leverage against anyone that dares cross the line. I don't want to like it as much as I apparently do. It's a huge turn-on, knowing that every supernatural I cross paths with knows that I'm his.

Gelatin cake.

Gelatin cake.

Julian runs his tongue along the inside of his bottom lip. There's a hint of a disgusted scowl marring his face, but he catches it and widens into a smile instead. "Jessie is free to do as she pleases until her Pledging. If our girl wants to sow some wild oats, so be it."

Now I'm tempted to open my mouth.

Just who does he think he is, disrespecting me like that?

Bran puts his hand out, as if to stop me from jumping Julian. I'm not an idiot, but no one misses that he does it.

"We're just here to speak with Kelly," Bran says. "Can you show us to her?"

Maggie gives Julian a pointed look. The feeling I had with Cody and François comes back, like there's a secret here I'm not supposed to know.

"Maggie?" I say, because I feel more comfortable addressing her than Julian. And also, I trust her more. "Please get Kelly for me. I'm worried about her."

"Oh, don't be!" She squeezes my arm and Bran edges closer to me. "I'll go see if I can find her. How's that sound?"

"Bring her to my office," Julian says. "We'll wait there. Come." He waves us through the foyer. Bran doesn't hesitate and as he follows Julian across the marble floor, he threads his fingers with mine, tugging me close to his side.

I know where Julian's office is—the double doors at the very end of the main foyer hall—but I've never been inside. I've never had a reason to visit him, and I've definitely never been invited.

Once upon a time, when I was maybe thirteen or fourteen, I did have a crush on Julian. It's hard not to. There's something magnetic about him, something quietly intense too.

He's more handsome than gorgeous, more rugged than polished. I think at the time I thought that made him more human than the Duvals.

One look at Bran or Damien and you know they're something other than human.

With Julian, it's a little harder to spot on the first glance.

He opens one side of the double doors on his office and waves us in. The ceilings are soaring, the walls uneven plaster and lathe painted in an off-white paint that contrasts just slightly with the crisp white crown molding.

Bookshelves line the back wall with a marble fireplace in the middle. There's an overstated desk to my left that sits squarely in front of the windows and a sitting area to the right with heavy leather furniture.

"Have a seat," Julian says. "Bran, you want a drink?"

"No."

"Jessie?"

"Um...no thanks."

Julian goes to the bar just inside of the double doors and pours himself a few fingers of vodka. He drinks it straight. Ugh.

"So, Bran," Julian starts.

Bran slowly circles the room, getting extra nosy as he scans the objects in Julian's office. "So, Julian."

"What the fuck are you really doing here? And why are you dragging Jessie into this?"

Bran pauses at a marble bust that sits on one of the shelves. He pulls it off. "Did you know this was a fake?" He turns it over as if inspecting it and then the stone cracks in his grip, raining to the floor in a dozen pieces. "Oops."

Julian's upper lip curls. "You're playing with fire."

Bran dusts off his hands. "No, I'm trying to put one out. One that you started."

Julian's gaze sweeps to me, then he drains the rest of the liquor. "I don't know what you're talking about."

"Don't you?" Bran crosses back to me hovering near the door. "Why don't you tell Jessie why you killed Sasha the night she took Jessie for a ride."

Julian goes eerily still. I don't think he even takes a breath for several long seconds, then, "Sasha left town."

"We know the truth," I hear myself saying. "Please, just tell us the reason."

His nostrils flare with irritation. "Even you know, Duval, that the head vampire of a house can do as he pleases with the vampires bound to his house. It's written in the rules. I don't have to explain myself to either of you."

"That might be the case," I say, "but I'm asking you anyway. Please just tell me what happened."

He screws up his mouth, the glass still clutched in his hand. I swear I hear it crack. "All right. The truth is she bit you that night and so her death was her punishment."

"Even I know that's overkill. No pun intended," Bran says with a smirk.

"I deemed it necessary." Julian returns to the bar and pours a second round. His shirt slouches on his shoulders as he straightens his spine. "Now answer my question. Why the fuck are you toying with Jessie?"

"He's not toying with me," I say and Bran says, "Because I can."

The fuck. I scowl at him with enough venom to singe his eyebrows. If only I really was fae, one of the elementals I've heard about, the ones who can burn a place to the ground with nothing more than a look.

Bran would be tinder by now. Asshole.

Julian frowns at me with open sympathy like I'm just a brainless idiot that got trapped by the big, bad vampire.

"Please don't let him manipulate you any further," Julian says.

"Don't worry about me, okay? This isn't about me."

Or is it?

"I want to see my sister."

Both Bran and Julian's attention wanders beyond the office.

"I think Maggie has her," Bran tells me.

"And?" I coax.

There's a troubling look that comes across Bran's face. And Julian registers it at the same time I do.

The office doors bang open and slam against the wall.

Suddenly I'm alone in the office. "Bran!"

I race out after him. Where the hell did he go?

"Bran!"

I run down the hall and slam into a round table in the middle of the foyer when Kelly's voice causes me to shift directions at the last second.

"What's happening?" Kelly slurs.

I whirl around and see her clutched in Bran's grip, her legs buckling beneath her.

Several higher-ranking Locke vampires are in a loose circle around them.

"Kelly!" I shove in between the vampires to get to my sister's side. I don't see any bites, no trailing blood to explain why she's so pale and dazed.

"Kelly?" I put my hands on either side of her face. She's burning up and slick with sweat. She shakes in my grip. When I force her to look at me, her eyes find mine, bloodshot and glassy.

"Jessie?" Her voice is reedy and thin.

"What's wrong with her?"

Bran adjusts her in his grip. He answers me but looks at Julian as he does. "It's called compulsion fever. It can happen when a vampire compels a mortal too many times."

The rage that comes over me is nearly blinding.

I don't stop to think about the risks or the consequences.

I don't care about any of that.

I whirl around and charge Julian Locke.

Seven

I was eleven years old when my mother sat me down for The Talk.

Not the birds and the bees.

The vampires and the shifters. The witches and the moons. The magic and the fae.

That's a talk that every mortal child has to have when living in a place like Midnight Harbor. It's a rite of passage.

I can remember being on the playground the winter of fifth grade when Addison Marquor came over to the monkey bars where Sam was dangling from a cold bar and I was eating a sucker beneath her.

Shoulders back and her head held high, Addison proudly told us her mother sat her down at the kitchen table over the weekend and gave her The Talk.

Sam and I were desperate for the details but Addison had always been the type of girl who thought information was gold and anyone who didn't have it was meant to stay poor.

When I finally got to have The Talk, I felt like such an adult. I thought my mom was cracking open the universe and spilling all its secrets.

But it was just a bunch of dumb rules.

Don't go running through Pack territory, especially not close to the full moon when shifter magic is more potent and wolves more volatile.

Do not, under any circumstances, go near the pack alpha under a supermoon.

Don't insult a witch. At least not to her face.

Don't tell the fae "thank you" unless you want to be indebted to them.

Don't walk into a room of vampires and pretend you're anything other than food.

And definitely do not provoke a vampire.

Sorry, Mom. Looks like I'm breaking rules left and right these days.

I go straight for Julian's throat.

I don't have a plan. There is only the one blinding thought: to shred the skin from his bones.

He hurt my sister. He's *supposed* to protect my sister.

As I reach out, teeth gnashed, fingers curled like claws, Julian catches me at the wrists and whirls me around.

Stars blink in my field of vision when he throws me up against the wall and my skull cracks loudly against the plaster.

Suddenly I'm swimming and I can't see straight and a dull ache shoots through my head.

Stupid, Jessie. What were you thinking?!

Julian hoists my arms above my head, just one hand needed to capture my wrists beneath him. His fangs sharpen and his eyes glow bright blue.

"You may not be Pledged to my house—" he starts and then cuts himself off.

Bran is at his back, his eyes like fire, his fangs like razors. "Don't."

"You have no weapon," Julian points out.

"I can tear your heart out through your rib cage."

Julian glances to his right, maybe assessing his chances. There are several vampires inching closer and none of them are on Bran's side.

"If you hurt her," Bran says, his voice low and even, "I will destroy everything you've ever touched."

When Julian turns back to me, his fangs have retracted but the blue glow is still in his eyes. He scans my face, one long sweep of his gaze. "Just a toy, huh?"

Bran says nothing.

The Locke vampires edge closer.

"Bran," I say.

Kelly is slumped in Maggie's arms. Her eyes are drooping like she's high or dying.

I can't leave her here. I can't let Julian have her anymore. I don't know much about compulsion fever, but it looks like it's destroying her from the inside out.

I have to get her out of here.

I give Bran a pleading look. I'm powerless here. And I have nothing to give.

"Let us leave here unharmed," Bran says, "—all three of us," he clarifies. "And I'll give you my lakeside property."

Julian frowns, but he looks over his shoulder. "You think your garish modern house is worth more than—" He cuts himself off and frowns at himself.

"Go on," Bran coaxes. "Worth more than what?"

A door bangs shut somewhere deep in the house and Julian's thoughts wander. His dark brow sinks lower over his flashing blue eyes. Finally, he pulls away from me. "Go on. Take them both if you must. Just blood trash now, aren't they?"

"What did you say?" I yell.

"Mouse," Bran says.

"That was a low blow! He has to—"

"Mouse!" Bran's voice rings with command as he shoots me a castigating look. Even a few of the Locke vampires shrink back.

I shut my mouth. But inside I'm burning.

Bran scoops up Kelly in his arms and then gestures for me to follow him.

We make it out the door and across the front porch and down the front steps.

At the bottom I look back to the open door to see Julian framed in the golden light of the chandelier behind him, several of his Locke vampires flanking him like soldiers.

Bran might have threatened to destroy Julian, but I'm vowing here and now that when it comes to Julian's demise, it'll be me that wields the wooden stake.

———

Bran drives the Bimmer back to our quiet street. I sit in the back with Kelly's head in my lap, her arms curled into her chest, hands tucked beneath her chin like she's a child.

"I never should have left her after that bite," I say.

With no attention on his speed, Bran gets us across town in less than ten minutes. "Kelly is a big girl, mouse."

"We're all big girls, aren't we? Until we find ourselves in the clutches of a big, bad vampire."

"This isn't a fairytale."

Our houses come into view and I nearly weep at the familiar sight.

"No," I say, as Bran parks in his driveway. "I suppose it's not."

With the engine off, Bran comes around to the backdoor and reaches in for Kelly. She moans, her head lolling, until Bran gets her comfortably in his arms. He makes his way for his front door.

"What are you doing?"

"Julian hasn't been invited inside my house."

"Yeah, but it's owned by a vampire. I thought the magic of the invitation rule only applies to a mortal-owned house."

"I don't own the house," he says.

"Seriously? Who does?"

He doesn't answer me as he turns the door knob and then kicks the door in with the toe of his boot.

There are no lights on inside so I grope around until my eyes adjust to the darkness. I finally locate a light switch and flick it on, and the recessed lighting comes on in the entry hall.

"I'll put her in one of the spare bedrooms," Bran says when he's already halfway up the stairs.

I follow him. It's a three-bedroom house, and Bran picks the first bedroom on the left. There's a queen-sized bed against the wall and two black and white photographs framed in thick black frames that hang above the bed.

I know right away they're Bran's work. I can see his style now that I know what it is. High contrast, interesting subjects, haunting light.

Bran has the duvet pulled back and is depositing Kelly on the bed before I can help.

"What do we do for her?" I ask as I come around and slip off her leather booties. She's wearing her favorite socks, the ones with the pineapples wearing sunglasses. "Is compulsion fever dangerous?"

"Only if you keep doing it." He readjusts the pillow beneath Kelly's head. My heart thuds loudly in my chest seeing him take care of my sister like this.

I hear Julian's words echoing in my head—*just a toy, huh?*

Maybe the reason I didn't lose my mind in Julian's office when Bran insinuated that he was playing with me was because I knew he was bull-shitting.

Who was he trying to fool? Julian? Or himself?

"Does she need something while she heals? Like, is there some old witch's brew that's an antidote? Some ancient elixir? Or—"

"Rest," he tells me with a half-cocked grin on his face. "She'll be okay. I promise. But some pain meds will help break the fever."

"Do you have any?"

He gives me a look like I'm being ridiculous.

"Got it. We have some. I'll run over and get them."

"I'll come with you."

"It'll only take a second."

"Mouse."

"Okay. I guess you're coming with."

Outside, the streetlights cast wide circles of golden light on the pavement. Across the street, the front window on Mrs. Haraway's house is twinkling with golden string lights. She's the neighbor that has her Christmas tree up October to March. And the rest of the year, her house is always decked out in golden string lights.

Further down the block, Mr. Taylor is walking his golden lab.

It's all so normal.

And here I thought I wanted more normal than this.

Instead, I backtracked and descended into the very center of the world of the supernatural.

Even though I've lived in Midnight my entire life, I took this quiet, normal life I had for granted. I wanted to escape it.

Now I just want to come home after a long day working my normal job at the coffee shop and find my sister drinking a glass of wine on the sofa while binge-watching an old season of Real Housewives.

But I don't think I'll ever have that life back.

How could I after the last several days? After everything I've uncovered?

I go to the front door and unlock the deadbolt with my key. I step over the threshold.

I make a big show of turning to Bran and waving out my arm like I'm a showman at a circus. "Bran Duval, won't you please come in?"

He steps inside and comes over to me, wraps his hand around the back of my neck and brings his mouth to my ear. "Good girl," he says, causing a goddamn riot in my panties.

"Damn you," I mutter.

He smirks at me.

We always leave the light on above the stove, so there's a warm glow in the kitchen when I go there for the bottle of ibuprofen.

Bran looks around our living room. It's weird, him being in my space. I've given him more of myself than I've ever given anyone, but seeing him inspect my entire life in the pictures on the wall and the odds and ends on the bookshelves gives me a weird sort of glow. It's almost like he wants to know me better.

I find the pain meds shoved in the back of the vitamin and supplements cabinet.

Bran picks up my monthly copy of *Cosmopolitan*. "Really, mouse?"

There's a bold headline across the bottom that says *The Beginner's Guide to the G-Spot.*

I go over to him and snatch the magazine from his hand. "This is why I didn't want to invite you in."

"More lies." He moves to the built-in cabinets and scans the books on the shelves and pulls out a beloved copy of *Pride and Prejudice*. He holds it up. "Yours or Kelly's?"

"Who do you think?"

"Kelly."

"Yes."

"You're not a romantic at heart," he decides and puts the book back. He isn't wrong.

"Let me tell you a secret," he says.

"Go on."

"Mr. Darcy was based on my brother."

I burst out laughing. "Really?"

He nods and continues to scan our shelves. "Jane Austen met him at a ball and immediately hated him. And loved him too, I suppose."

I roll my eyes. "Damien seems like the type of guy to be loved and hated. Like his brother, *I suppose*."

Bran rewards me with another one of those lopsided grins. "We are very much alike, Damien and I."

"Oh really? Does he fuck his neighbor too and call her a toy?"

All of the humor is suddenly gone from Bran's face. "I didn't want Julian to know."

"Know what?"

I can't miss the way Bran's shoulders rise with a heavy breath, the way his chest expands and he closes his eyes.

He's reluctant to answer.

"Know what, Bran?"

"That the thought of him taking you away from me makes me want to murder things."

When he opens his eyes and looks at me, his irises are molten amber.

Warmth spreads through my chest. Of all the answers I thought he'd give me, that wasn't one of them.

I swallow hard and try to catch my breath.

"Really?" I squeak. "Is it because of the sex? Because you like controlling me? Because—"

"No."

"Then wh—"

"If I told you to hide something where you'd never look, where would that be?"

"That's a really weird question."

"Humor me."

I cross my arms over my chest as I think. Somewhere I'd never look? I never go into Kelly's room but I doubt I'd hide something in there. I'd never find it again. There are a few closets in our house that I don't go into often, but I do get an urge to reorganize them at least twice a year.

"Well," I start, "my first guess might be those drawers." I nod at the cabinets. "Kelly loves shoving shit inside of them. Like important documents and stuff so I never have a reason to go in there and if I opened them, and I saw the mess, I'd have to reorganize them and then Kelly would yell at me when she was looking for a thing from nine years ago that she needs *right this second*."

Bran opens one of the drawers in the cabinet and roots around inside.

"What are you looking for?"

He opens the next drawer.

"Bran?"

On the third one, he spots something that makes him pause and then he pulls it out to the light. The envelope has my handwriting on the front. It reads *Important Shit. Don't lose.*

I don't remember writing that. I don't even know what's inside the envelope.

"What is that?" I ask.

Bran is a blur as he crosses the room and comes to a stop in front of me. His speed kicks up a sharp breeze and it sends several loose strands of hair fluttering around my face.

"Open it." He hands it over.

A creeping shiver rolls down my spine. There's this shadow in the back of my mind like I should know this envelope. I should know what's inside.

I finally take it from him with shaking hands. The flap has been sealed, so I run my finger inside the fold and rip it back.

There's a piece of thick, folded paper inside. I pull it out and unfurl it, my fingers rubbing over the embossed symbol of a notary stamp on the bottom.

It's a deed to a house.

The address listed is Bran's house.

And the owner?

Is me.

Eight

"What is this?"

Bran moves around me and starts grabbing things from the kitchen. Bread. Butter. Slices of cheese.

"Bran. Hello?" I go over to him as he dumps everything in a bag. I wave the deed for his house in his face. "What is this?"

He holds out his hand for me to take. I look from it to his face.

"We're going to return to my house—" he says.

"*My* house, apparently."

"—and I'll make you a grilled cheese sandwich, pour you a drink, and tell you everything."

"Where have I heard that before?" I say with a bit more venomous sarcasm than I initially intended.

He doesn't move. Doesn't argue. Doesn't force. Bran Duval knows the art of patience and he knows exactly when to use it.

I huff out a breath and take his hand. He leads me out of the house and across our yards and inside his house. He dumps the ingredients on the kitchen counter, then fills a glass with water from the fridge and hands it to me.

"Go check on Kelly," he tells me. "While I heat up the pan."

I leave him in the kitchen and return to my sister upstairs. She's still sleeping soundly in Bran's spare bedroom despite the glow of the bedside lamp. There's just enough room on the bed beside her so I sit down on the edge and give her a soft nudge. "Kels?"

She stirs and her eyes flutter. "Jessie?"

"Hey."

"Where...*ughhh*." Hand to her forehead, she winces and then kneads at the space between her brows. "Wine headache. What time is it?"

"It's late."

She sits up and looks around. "Where am I?"

"We're at Bran's."

She frowns. "Our *neighbor*? Bran Duval?"

"The one and only."

I can just picture him down in the kitchen being all smug about that.

"Why are we here?"

"It's a really long story." I put my hand to her forehead. She's still hot to the touch. "Here." I shake out two pills and hand her the glass of water. "You have a fever and we need to bring it down."

"What? But—"

"Just trust me. Please take the medicine."

With another wince, she manages to sit upright to down the meds with a swig of water and then collapses back against the pillows. "I'm glad you're here." She smiles sleepily up at me as she drifts off again.

"Me too." I give her hand a squeeze and push the hair from her face. Now that she's with me and I know she's safe, I can feel a phantom knot releasing at the center of me. I hadn't realized until this moment just how important it was to have my sister at my side.

And maybe deep down I always knew she wasn't exactly safe at Julian's side.

When I'm sure Kelly is resting again, I make my way back downstairs. Bran is just tossing a butter-coated slice of bread into a hot cast iron pan. The butter sizzles. Despite the fact that he doesn't eat mortal food, he seems at ease in the kitchen.

I slide onto one of the stools at the counter. "Did you guys have grilled cheese sandwiches back before you were turned?"

"We definitely did not." He lays out two slices of cheese and then covers it with the second slice of buttered bread. "Grilled cheeses weren't mainstream until the 1920s when sliced bread was first invented."

"Is it weird that I feel sorry for you? Because you haven't eaten mortal food since the 1700s? I love food."

"I know you do. And yes, it is weird." He flips the sandwich.

"Grilled cheeses are the best. When the cheese gets all gooey and the bread crusty and—" Something occurs to me. "Hold on. Is that why you call me mouse?"

He glances at me over his shoulder. "I'm shocked it took you so long."

"Honestly, I am too."

A glob of cheese melts from between the slices and pops when it hits the hot pan.

"So," I start. "You were going to purge all of your secrets. How long do I have to wait?"

Bran slides the toasted sandwich onto a plate, then cuts it in half. The bread crunches loudly beneath the bite of the blade.

He puts the plate on the dining room table. "Come sit, mouse," he tells me and then goes to the bar and pours us each a drink.

I have the distinct impression he's taking extra steps to prepare for this conversation and it leaves an unsettled feeling in my stomach.

I know he's been keeping things from me and I know that even when I demanded his honesty, he was still reluctant to give it. I'd be an idiot to believe otherwise. But I'd be lying if I said it wasn't starting to weigh on me.

Bran sharing his collected information with me would be a sign that he trusts me. And I desperately want it.

I don't think Bran trusts very many people.

But beyond all that, these secrets...they're about me. And I deserve to have them.

I sit and he takes the chair across from me and leans back in it languidly, his tumbler of liquor clutched in his hand.

He looks relaxed. I know he's not.

He waits for me to take a bite.

"If you've never had a grilled cheese, then how do you know how to make them?"

"It's just buttered bread with cheese between it."

But when I take a bite, the bread is the right bit of crunch, the cheese the right bit of melted. I don't know if it tastes better because of the novelty of it being made by a vampire, but it's the best damn grilled cheese I've ever had.

"Mmmm," I say as a string of cheese stretches from my mouth to the sandwich. I break it with my fingers and then eat it like a length of spaghetti.

Bran watches me the entire time with the look of a starving man. He takes a long pull from his drink. "I need you to know something, mouse."

I suck the last of the cheese from my fingertip. "I'm listening."

He takes a deep breath. "There is nothing more valuable in this world—in *our* world—than secrets. There's always more money to make, but secrets are finite and they always retain their value so long as they remain a secret.

"Kingdoms have fallen because of secrets." He turns his glass on the table, his gaze on it instead of me. "I need you to know that when this began, I wanted the secrets and nothing more."

I hold the sandwich between my hands, suddenly not so hungry. "Okay."

"I need you to know that what this is now"—he gestures between us —"was not what I intended, but now that I—"

He frowns and takes another swig of the liquor and tries again. "I would die for two people in this world—Damien and Jimmy. I thought that would always remain to be true. Two people and no more. But lately, the way I've felt when you...when *someone*—"

I hold my breath.

He sighs and sits forward.

"When someone *what*?"

"If I found you the way we found Kelly?" There's a new heaviness to his expression, a new tightness around his mouth.

"I will do anything for you, mouse. That's what I need you to know." It looks like it pains him to say it. Like he'd rather be admitting anything else.

A lump wedges in my throat. I try to swallow it back, but tears burn in my sinuses, only making the lump bigger.

Is he saying...

Is Bran Duval saying he would die for me?

Tension comes to his jaw again. "I need you to know that how it began and how it is now are not the same."

I give him a quick nod. "Okay. I hear you."

He laughs, low and beneath his breath, takes another swig from the glass. "And now that you know that... I *have* been keeping a great many things from you, mouse. And now it's time I come clean."

———

My stomach churns. I can't eat now. How can I?

I wash down the taste of cheese with a swig of the bourbon. It burns down my throat and warms my belly. I think the alcohol hits my bloodstream immediately because I'm buzzy and hot.

"I'm ready," I say, a little breathless from the booze.

"Are you?"

I nod. "Yes."

"Promise me you won't run."

"I think that depends on what the secrets are."

"I didn't murder anyone."

I laugh nervously. "I guess that's a good sign."

"Promise me, mouse. Because I will chase you and it won't be fun for either of us when I catch you."

The buzziness in my stomach sinks between my thighs and I'm suddenly throbbing.

It might be fun.

I might want to tempt fate.

Bran frowns at me. "*Mouse.*"

"Okay, yes. I promise."

"Do you remember how I told you I bought that lakeside property just to spite Julian?"

"Yes."

"I don't like him. I've never liked him and I like doing things to spite him." He inhales through his nose then gets up to refill his glass. With his back to me, I notice the tension in his shoulder blades, the sweep of bone rising beneath the expensive material of his t-shirt.

"It's been well known in the vampire houses that you were not to be bitten."

"Why? Says who?"

"Julian." Drink poured, he turns back to me. "So to spite him, I bit you." And just so it's clear *when* he means, he adds, "*Last year.*"

I laugh. "No, you didn't."

"Yes, I did."

A creeping chill rolls down my spine. "No, you didn't," I repeat, but I'm less certain this time.

"Your birthday last year," he says and leans against the bar. "You wore a tight summer dress the color of deep forest ivy. You smelled like amber and roses. You looked like sin and regret."

My breathing quickens as my heart kicks up.

"I wanted to devour you the second I saw you. I couldn't explain it then and I still can't explain it now." His eyes flash briefly as his gaze goes distant and his memories return to that night.

It's a tradition in Midnight Harbor to throw a big birthday party the year before your Pledging. It's like your last hurrah before binding yourself to a house. Your year of going out.

I did wear a deep green dress. And the amber-rose scent was a perfume Sam bought me as a present.

All of this is true, but—

"I didn't see you there."

"I know," he says. "I wasn't planning on being there, but Damien and I are partial owners of the Harbor—"

"You are?"

"—and there was an issue with the boiler. Damien sent me because he had other things to attend to and I begrudgingly went."

He takes another sip. "I'll admit, I was in a foul mood. One, because I had to deal with something as mundane as a boiler and two, because I knew it was your party and the fact that Julian had a moratorium on you annoyed me.

"It was petty. I'll admit that much."

He smiles to himself as he raises his glass again. "I was coming up from the basement and you were stumbling out of the bathroom, drunk. You tripped. I caught you. It was a real cinematic moment, mouse." He drinks. Looks over at me.

My cheeks are burning red.

I don't remember any of this and yet, when he describes it, I sense shadows shifting on the walls, ghosts that I should know the shape of.

"'Bran Duval,' you said to me and laughed. Your lips were swollen like you'd been kissing someone and it immediately made me envious of whoever it was. 'Jessie MacMahon,' I said back and you smiled up at me. 'I like it when you say my name,' you said. 'It sounds hot on your hot face.'"

"Oh god."

He laughs. "You're cute when you're drunk."

"Shut up."

"'You should stop drinking,' I told you. 'Why?' you asked. 'Because of vampires like me,' I'd said. 'Someone might take advantage of you.'"

I have a feeling I know what drunk-me might have said.

"'So why don't you?' you said. 'I'm a tasty snack.'"

Yup. That sounds about right.

"'And you're also drunk,' I pointed out. 'So?'" He shakes his head. "Such a brave little mouse."

His gaze darts back to me, to my mouth. "I kissed you first, bit you second. Not my finest moment," he admits. "Immediately, I could tell there was something off about your blood. I couldn't put my finger on it at the time. It was something nagging me in the back of my head.

"'I'm going to tell everyone I just got bit by Bran Duval on my birthday,' you said to me. I couldn't let that happen. There was the taste of your blood and the smell of the witch amulet around your neck. One odd thing about a mortal girl could be brushed off as a coincidence. Two odd things smelled like a secret." He takes another pull from the glass and sets it down. "I compelled you that night. Made you forget."

Even though I knew that this would be the conclusion to the story, it still pains me to hear it. I think that's the worst part about living amongst vampires. At any moment, they can steal something from your head. Bottle it up and make you forget.

I want to punish him for it, but what would be the point?

"It wasn't long after my birthday party that you moved in next door."

He nods. "You asked me why I left Duval House. That's why. Because I knew there were more secrets to uncover and being closer to you would allow me to get them."

"And? Were there?"

Guilt hardens the sharp lines of his face. "Yes."

I inhale deeply, then chug back the rest of my drink. "Rip it off like a bandage. Go on."

"I started to wonder about your blood. Why it tasted off. You were presented as mortal, living with a mortal family. But Julien was trying to keep you from others. So I started to wonder about your origins. I started digging into your past."

I lick my lips.

"I went to the hospital and looked up your birth certificate."

My breathing quickens. "And?"

The fine lines around his eyes deepen as he frowns at me. "There's no record of you being born in Midnight Harbor."

Nine

"That can't be true," I say, but my voice comes out barely a whisper and it's rough, like sandpaper, like it hurts just to get the words out.

"I used a lot of favors to find out otherwise," Bran tells me.

I get up from his dining room table and pace.

Bran is on edge, watching me, ready to chase me if I bolt.

Am I on the verge of running?

Can I run far enough to escape this?

I feel like I've left my body. My feet are moving and my hands are shaking and my heart is beating hard in my chest, but this isn't my life.

It can't possibly be my life.

Just when I think there is an end in sight, another corner comes into view, another turn in the labyrinth.

I look back to Bran when I reach the edge of the living room where the large front window overlooks the darkened street. Before Bran, there were only humans and a few witches that lived in my neighborhood. Not many windows remain lit after midnight.

"If there's no record of me being born, how do you explain my mom being pregnant? There're pictures of her with her pregnant belly and Kelly standing beside her."

"That does seem to be true." Bran comes over to me. "But she disappeared just a month before her due date. Kelly stayed at Locke House until your mom returned."

I've never once heard Kelly talk about staying with the Locke vampires as a child. How could I have missed that detail? How could Kelly have never mentioned it?

Bran leans his shoulder against the window casing and the glow from the streetlight skims his face in a golden haze.

All of this feels like that, like a waking dream.

All of these secrets.

Him.

Me.

The fact that we've barely spent more than a few hours apart in the last handful of days. The fact that right now, as the ground shifts beneath me again, all I want to do is clutch to him. Fuck him. Lose myself in him.

Somehow, Bran Duval has become the only real thing in my life. The anchor that keeps me rooted to the earth.

He isn't the comforting type, but I can't think of anyone else I'd rather be with right now.

"Do you have a theory about my mom and my birth?" I ask him.

His gaze skips to the street where a cat crosses over the pavement and disappears into the shadows of an evergreen bush.

"I don't have all of the secrets you need," he admits. "There are the facts, though. Your mother disappeared right before you were born. She returned with a baby. Your blood tastes like the fae."

I frown up at him. "I can *lie*. I thought we agreed fae was out?"

He looks back to me. "We did no such thing."

"But—"

"You're forgetting something else, mouse."

I cross my arms. "Okay, what?"

"Once upon a time, we could easily travel between the mortal realm and the fae realm. But not long after you were born, the gate was sealed and all of the fae on this side were stuck here."

"What are you saying?"

"I'm saying, I don't believe in coincidences."

I snort. "Are you trying to tell me that the gate was sealed because of me? Or in relation to me?"

"That's exactly what I'm saying."

"No. That's ridiculous."

"Is it?"

"Yes!" I throw up my arms.

Bran scowls at me like I'm being overly sensitive.

"None of this makes sense." I scrub at my face.

"Have you considered that there's a very simple way of confirming whether or not you're fae? We could have the answer right now if we wanted it."

I go still.

Iron.

It hadn't occurred to me, no. Because I never wanted to believe I could be fae in the first place. And beyond that, iron is hard to come by in Midnight simply for the safety of the fae that do live here. You can't buy iron at the gas station, just like you can't buy a stake or a vial of shifter's bane.

"I don't have any iron sitting ar—"

Bran disappears in a blur, ruffling the hair around my face.

When he comes back and holds out his hand, there's a metal bar strung on a length of leather cord dandling from his grip.

"Shit. I was being sarcastic."

"I wasn't."

"Why do you have that?"

"For the fae, obviously."

"Do you have an entire closet somewhere full of weapons for every creature that lives in Midnight?"

He opens his mouth to answer but I hold up my hand. "Wait. Never mind. I don't want to know."

"Take it from me, mouse," he says.

I tuck my hands beneath my arms.

My heart is suddenly pounding against my eardrums and my mouth is dry.

I don't want to touch it.

Because I don't want to know.

"Mouse."

"Maybe I'll leave Midnight after all," I say eyeing the iron in his hand. "I don't have to do this. No one is making me. Are you going to make me?"

He frowns at me, but it's devoid of his usual edge of irritation.

If I didn't know any better, I'd almost think Bran feels sorry for me.

"You're not leaving," he says.

"If I touch that and—"

"I know."

Tears burn in my sinuses.

I don't want to appear weak in front of Bran, but I'm quickly losing my shit just thinking about the consequences of touching that piece of iron.

If I react to it, that's it.

Then I'll really know I'm fae and my entire life will have been a lie and my mom and sister have been keeping a very big secret from me for who knows what reason.

Bran reaches over and grabs me gently by the wrist. He guides my hand over his. My fingertips tremble over the bar of iron now lying flat in the palm of his hand.

Is it just me, or can I feel the heat already?

I try to yank my hand back, but you can't fight a vampire's grip and especially not one as old as Bran.

"Please," I say, bordering on a whine.

"Don't you want to know?"

Fuck.

No.

No, I do not.

But I have to know.

I exhale, shoulders deflating.

There's no way to move forward until I do this.

I let Bran lower my hand over his and the second my fingers brush the iron, white hot pain races through my skin.

I yank back with a high-pitched hiss as the pain sinks to bone and reverberates up my arm like someone whacked my funny bone with a baseball bat.

Smoke curls from my hand as a giant red welt blooms across my fingertips.

Tears stream down my face.

Bran tosses the iron aside and yanks me into him, his arms wrapping protectively around me.

Before I can get hold of myself, I'm sobbing into his chest.

Not from the pain.

From the sheer magnitude of the truth.

I cry and cry and cry, body shaking, barely able to catch my breath.

And Bran holds me close, surrounds me with his scent and his protection.

I'm so fucking relieved to have him that I cry harder.

I cry for who I was and who I no longer am.

I cry for the void at the center of me, where so many unknowns still lurk.

When the tears finally dry up and I can take a full breath without it catching on a sob, Bran blurs away and returns with a tissue.

I plop onto the couch and dry my face and tuck my hair behind my ears.

Am I surprised by this?

This isn't new information, only a confirmation.

It could be worse. I could have found out I was an honest-to-god mouse shifter.

Bran hands me my glass of liquor. I take a generous sip and let the alcohol warm my insides and drive away the tension building at my breastbone.

Everything is going to be okay.

I'm going to be fine.

I've got this. I can handle this. I can—

Bran looks over me at the stairs.

"What?" I ask.

"It's Kelly," he says. "She's up."

———

We wait for her to come downstairs on her own. It takes her a good twenty minutes and I pace the entire time.

When her footsteps finally hit the staircase, I hurry over to the bottom and peer up at her as she descends. Her eyes are heavy and circled in shadows, but some of the color has returned to her cheeks and she doesn't shine with sweat anymore.

"Jessie?" she says when she sees me standing beside Bran. "What is going on?"

"You had compulsion fever," I explain. "We brought you here to keep you safe."

She comes down the last few steps, her hand trailing on the banister. The black nail polish on her fingernails has started to chip away. Kelly never goes longer than a week without getting her nails done.

"Keep me safe from who?"

"Julian," Bran answers.

Kelly rakes her teeth over her bottom lip. The look she gives me next is haunted and hollow. It's the look of someone who knows they've been drowning.

Why didn't she tell me she was in trouble? We could have figured it out together.

"Kelly, I really, *really* need you to tell me everything," I say. "I know you've been keeping things from me. I can't take the mystery anymore."

My sister frowns at me and her gaze goes distant. "I..." She licks her lips and closes her eyes. "I don't know if I can."

"Why not?"

She leans her weight into the column at the base of the staircase banister. "It's...when I try..." She squints as if trying to make out the shape of the secrets from a distance.

"She's been compelled to forget," Bran says.

I go to my sister's side. "Try harder, Kels."

Her eyes turn watery as she taps at her forehead. "It's all a blank right here. And my head is still pounding and..." She trails off again. "Wait."

"What?"

"Mom!" Kelly clutches at my hand and squeezes. "Mom wrote you a letter. Julian didn't know about it so he couldn't compel me to forget."

"Where is this letter?" Bran asks.

"At the house. In our mother's bedroom."

"Come on." Bran darts for the door and yanks it open. "We'll go together."

———

When Mom died, after we picked out a funeral outfit, Kelly and I shut her bedroom door and pretty much sealed it off.

I've been in there twice since then and every time I get the creeps like I'm walking into a tomb.

As we step over the threshold now and Kelly flicks on the bedside lamp, a shiver crawls down my spine.

Mom's hairbrush is still on the dresser. Her earrings from when she last took them off rest beside the brush. The romantic comedy she was reading sits on the bedside table, her favorite bookmark still tucked inside the pages where she left off.

The bed is made, but it's full of ghosts.

The room still smells faintly of her perfume. The sweetness of jasmine and clary sage and vanilla.

It only takes one deep breath of the scent to immediately transport me to a time when Mom was alive and her life filled this room.

It makes me miss her all over again.

"Where's this letter?" Bran asks.

"Um..." Kelly turns a circle in the center of the room. "It's..." She goes to the dresser and pulls open the bottom drawer, then shoves aside several folded sweaters. "Here."

She hands me an envelope with my name written across the front.

Just hours ago, I was taking a different envelope, tearing open its flap, unraveling its secrets.

That envelope produced a deed to a house.

What will this one give me?

I look up at Bran and Kelly, both watching me with barely constrained apprehension.

Unlike Bran's envelope, this one isn't sealed, but the flap is tucked inside.

I find a letter folded up and my mother's looping cursive scrawled across the paper.

I read it out loud.

Dear Jessie,

If you're reading this, it means I'm not there to tell you myself and that absolutely breaks my heart. I hope your sister is by your side. If she is, I know she's doing the very best she can under the circumstances. Please go easy on her.

First, I need to tell you, everything I did I did with a mother's love.

After your father died, and after I somehow managed to crawl out of the grief to the extent I could function, I was so grateful to be pregnant with his baby. I could have one more piece of him by my side.

But then the absolute worst thing happened—I started having complications.

After many tests and several visits to the doctor, I found out the baby was dying. I petitioned Julian and asked for his blood, but he refused. Vampire blood while a baby is in gestation can result in Very Bad Things.

Yes, all caps. That's the impression I got when he explained it to me.

I went to Rita next and she performed a healing spell but it didn't take.

I had one last idea. One last ditch effort.

I was so desperate to save a piece of your father.

So I went to the faerie realm and sought out fae magic.

But by the time I found someone willing to help, I was already in labor. I passed out, the pain was so intense, and when I woke, there was a baby in my arms.

You smiled up at me and when you cooed, I swear my heart swelled in size.

I loved you so much.

Instantly. Without question.

When I returned with you to Midnight, I thought we'd been blessed with a miracle.

But then...strange things started happening.

And I started to doubt that the baby I had in my belly when I went to the fae realm was the baby that I returned with.

You were just over a year old when I took you for a walk through the park and we crossed paths with a fae, a brownie.

He immediately came over to us and got down on one knee in front of you and peered at you like he was inspecting a strange creature. He said to me, "Did you steal her?"

"She's my daughter," I told him.

"What you believe and what is true are not the same thing."

And then he walked away like he hadn't just shattered my entire world.

Because deep down, I knew, I *knew* you weren't my flesh and blood.

Right then and there, I had to make a decision.

The fae realm had already been sealed off by this point, so I had nowhere to go, no one to turn to.

I went to Rita begging for help again, but I couldn't tell her what you were. I was too afraid of what others would do if they found out the truth. Like the brownie, I worried they would think I kidnapped you and the fae, while peaceful here, have never exactly been on our side.

I asked for a binding spell and Rita performed it, no questions asked.

I did it to protect you and if I'm honest, to protect me and your sister too.

The things you did, Jessie...you were only a year old and it *terrified* me.

If you're reading this, I'm begging you, burn it and forget about it and go on with your life.

Sometimes, baby girl, secrets are better left buried.

Ten

Terrified.

That was the word my mother used to describe the strange things happening around me before I was bound by Rita's magic.

When I was only a year old.

What. The. Hell.

When I look up at Bran, the expression on his face makes me a little ill.

There's the barest glimpse of fear pinched in the fine lines around his eyes.

Then it's gone, tucked away.

Bran Duval cannot afford to be afraid.

Even of little mice.

Kelly comes over to me and wraps me in a hug. We're nearly the same height, so I get a face full of her hair. It doesn't smell like her expensive shampoo though. It smells like Locke House, like vodka and cigar smoke.

She cries against me. "If I knew…I mean, maybe I did and Julian made me forget. But you're…we'll always be sisters no matter what."

"Of course we will." I squeeze her tightly. Do I feel different knowing she's not my blood sister? Do I even want to believe it's true?

There's a little voice in the back of my head that says subconsciously I always knew.

Maybe that was why I was so desperate to leave Midnight. I didn't feel like I fit in my own skin, let alone the life I thought I was destined for.

"I'm so sorry, Jess," Kelly says to me. "I'm so, so sorry."

"It's okay."

"No, it's not," Bran says.

Kelly pulls away and frowns at him. "Excuse me. I don't need—"

I squeeze my sister's arm. "He's just like that. You'll get used to it."

"Why would I have to?" She frowns at me.

"Because he isn't going anywhere," I say. "You were the one who wanted Duval House to bid on me, anyway."

"I—*right*." She presses at the space between her brows. "I forgot about that. Your Pledge is..."

"Technically tomorrow, now that it's after midnight."

"Tomorrow? Oh fuck. I haven't planned the party! What are we—"

"I think we have more important things to worry about." I give the letter in my hand a shake.

"We still need a party! Your Pledge will happen, letter or not. I need a glass of wine and my planner. I need to start making a to-do list."

"Slow down, Kels."

"We need a party!" she shouts.

"Okay. I know. We'll have a party."

The outburst catches me by surprise and I just stare at her as she stares at me, eyes wide. This is so unlike her. Both of us are the non-confrontational sort. Sometimes to our detriment. We'll often leave things unsaid when really, we should be communicating them, even if it's hard.

Kelly exhales and folds her arms over her middle. "You deserve a celebration."

"While I am positively thrilled about planning a party," Bran says, which gets a scowl out of me because I know he's being sarcastic, "we have an issue we should discuss right now. Julian might have let us leave his house, but he'll be looking for another way to get what he wants. Namely you, mouse."

"Mouse?" Kelly frowns at me.

"Long story."

"Because you like grilled cheese so much." She laughs to herself. "Clever."

"I am a clever boy," Bran says, still dripping with sarcasm.

I had no idea what I was getting into, putting Bran and my sister in the same room. I don't know if I like it.

"What do you propose we do about Julian?" I ask him.

"He'll continue to use Kelly against you. She's pledged to his house, so he'll have some strings he can pull to get her back."

Kelly deflates. I slide my arm over her shoulders. "There must be something we can do."

"We can petition the court to reverse her pledge," Bran says.

"We can?"

Kelly nods. "Yes. Technically that's true, but they're rarely approved."

"That's because they rarely have the backing of a Duval."

Kelly gives him a look. "The arrogance of a Duval is simply astounding."

"It's not arrogance if it's fact."

"We petition the courts. What do we say?"

"*I* petition the court," Bran says. "I will attest to finding Kelly with compulsion fever. On its own, it's not necessarily a reason to reverse a pledge, but if I'm asking for it, it'll go through."

"And then what?" Kelly asks. "I'll be without a house. Without protection. Julian won't let it go that easily."

"That's true. Which is why you'll be adopted by Duval House."

Kelly snorts. "You must be joking."

"He doesn't joke," I say. But also, seriously? "What will Damien say?"

"Damien and Kelly used to fuck before she was Pledged to Locke House. So I doubt he'll object."

"Excuse me!" Kelly shouts.

I cut a look to my sister. "You slept with Damien Duval and didn't tell me?!"

Kelly is still shooting daggers at Bran when she says to me, "It was a very long time ago."

"Was it?" Bran challenges, like he already knows exactly how long ago it was.

"I can't believe you didn't tell me," I say.

"It was...it wasn't something I wanted to go around shouting from the rooftops, okay? I wasn't in a good place."

"Not a good place? If Damien is anything like his brother, I'd say it was probably fucking nirvana."

"Jessie!" She whacks me on the arm.

"What?" I laugh and rub at the sting as it fades. "I'm proud of you, is what I'm saying. You're not usually the scandalous type."

"I'm not!"

"Was it good?" I whisper behind the cup of my hand, like Bran can't hear me. "Is Damien amazing in bed?"

"Mouse," Bran says in his scolding tone of voice.

When I look across the room at him, his eyes are starting to fire. "I suggest you stop asking about how good my brother is in bed."

There's considerable tension in the lines around his mouth. Is he jealous? We've yet to have a discussion about what this actually is between us. Vampires don't put girlfriend/boyfriend labels on their relationships usually, but are we *in* a relationship? Are we exclusive? Am I overthinking this?

When the glow in his irises intensifies, an errant thrill buzzes between my legs. My heart thumps harder. Bran's chest expands as he takes in a deep breath.

"Mouse."

I straighten. "Okay. I hear you."

"Wait." Kelly frowns. "Are you saying you're sleeping with *him*?"

I make an innocent face at her. "Maybe?"

"Jessie!"

"I'm growing less and less fond of this conversation as it goes on," Bran says.

"Is he fond of anything?" Kelly asks.

Mmmmm, yes. Teasing the living daylights out of me with his clever fingers and dirty mouth.

The buzz comes back and Bran scowls at me.

"Okay, so when do we petition the courts?" I ask, trying to shift the night back to the business at hand.

"Now," Bran says.

"Now?" Kelly squeaks.

"Is there a better time? The vampire courts are only open at night." He tilts his head, pinning her with a look. "Or perhaps we give Julian a few days to plot his revenge?"

Kelly plops onto the edge of Mom's bed. The frame creaks. "Will Damien...I mean...have you spoken to him about this?"

"I have, yes," Bran says.

I can't ignore the way Kelly flushes, talking about Damien. I had no idea. How did I miss that? I guess I've always been a little oblivious to my sister's personal life.

"What did he say?" A thread of hope turns her voice thin.

"He agreed to it."

There's a faint smile tugging at the corner of my sister's lips before she brings her hands in front of her face, hiding it.

Maybe like me, my sister saw her life going in an entirely different direction.

Maybe like me, she's spinning, unsure of where she'll land but is hopeful that it'll be better than where she started.

"Until we get an approval from the court, you'll stay at my house," Bran says.

"*My* house," I correct.

The look he gives me is akin to the smack of his hand across my ass. And thinking about it, my clit throbs, new wetness soaking my panties.

I have to stop thinking about Bran doing naughty things to me or we'll never get through the night.

"I'll pack a bag," Kelly says and leaves us.

I go across the hall to my room and Bran follows me. A chill creeps down my spine. If I thought him being in my living room was bad, my bedroom will be far worse.

Did I clean my room last I was here? I mean, I always have a clean room but what if I left something out that I don't want him to see?

I quickly scan the dresser, the desk, the bedside table. My room is neat and uncluttered, but I spot a stupid picture of Sam and me from last summer where we're making funny faces at the camera.

I snatch it from the mirror hanging above my dresser and quickly shove it into my top drawer.

"How long do you think we'll be staying at your house?" I ask as I head into the closet.

Bran doesn't immediately answer me and when I turn around, he's suddenly there. He presses into me and I bang against the door. "If you don't get control of yourself, little mouse," he says, "I'll take you right here, right now. I'll fuck you loudly and without restraint." He takes my wrist in hand and brings my arm up, baring the pale underside. He traces a vein with the tip of his finger, sending a warm jolt down my belly and gooseflesh down to my elbow.

"Maybe *you* should control *yourself*," I argue.

"Oh, should I?" Fangs protrude from his mouth.

"Yes."

"But you're so tempting." His eyes go vampire bright in the dimly lit closet, and then he sinks his fangs into my wrist.

It's unexpected and I gasp, instinct telling me to pull away. But Bran holds fast to me, one hand on my wrist, the other snaking to the back of my neck.

There is an immediate primal need to go still beneath the pressure as he sucks the blood from my veins. Within seconds, I'm drenched.

Behind closed lids, the world sways as the air in my lungs stutters up my throat.

I want him to take me. Right here. Right now. *Loudly and without restraint.*

There's a sudden chill at my wrist when Bran's mouth leaves me.

I whimper at the absence of his warmth.

With the swipe of his thumb, he catches a rogue drop of blood from the corner of his mouth and sucks it back. His eyes are still glowing as he watches me.

"A word of caution, mouse," he says.

I pant against the door, wound up tight. "What?"

"Don't talk about other men in bed." His leans in again and slips his hand inside the waistband of my pants, sending a flash of heat down to my core.

"Or what?"

"Or I'll lose my fucking mind."

His fingers trail along the seam of my panties.

"If talking about other men in bed gets you like this, maybe I don't want to stop."

The rumble of laughter deep in his chest is almost sinister. "You have no idea what you're getting yourself into."

"You're probably right."

On my next breath, he invades my panties and roughly shoves two fingers inside of me. I gasp out as he grabs me around the throat, forcing my chin up, exposing the column of my neck to his fangs.

"I'm going to spend every waking minute making sure everyone knows you're mine." Then he sinks those fangs into my throat.

Eleven

Delirium is a state of mind characterized by restlessness and incoherence.

Pressed against my open closet door, when Bran fucks me with his fingers and drinks the blood from my neck, I think I sink into delirium.

And what a place it is.

Every thrust of his fingers is rough and punishing, and the force of it has the closet door banging against the wall behind me and my heart banging against my ribs.

Being with Bran like this always feels like a leap off a suspension bridge.

Illicit and a little reckless.

When his teeth leave my throat and he towers over me, blood drips from one of his fangs. I'm in a V-neck, so when the blood lands on me, it trails down the valley of my cleavage.

Bran ducks down and runs his tongue from the swell of my breast all the way up the crimson line, sending a full-body shiver straight to my core.

When he straightens again and hangs his head back, eyes heavy, lost in the ecstasy of the taste of my blood, I can't help but marvel at the sight of him.

Like he's walked out of some macabre renaissance painting, all hard lines and pale, sharp beauty.

Some days, I don't know what to do with him and I'm terrified that I can't contain him, his thirst, his violence, the rawness of the power that runs through his veins.

Some days I'm worried that he'll wake up one evening and realize he's too much for me too.

"What is it?" he asks, his voice thick with bloodlust.

"What are we?"

The question is out before I can gnash my teeth to trap it. I thought it, but I didn't mean to ask it.

I don't want to know what he thinks we are in case it's different than what I think it is.

He still has two fingers inside of me and he rubs his thumb over my clit as he slowly withdraws, then slides back in.

I collapse against the door, weak and trembling.

"Labels are just a way to persuade someone to act or be a certain way." He slides in slowly again, presses his thumb against me. The wave is building, a slow, steady build.

"That's a bullshit answer," I say a little breathless.

"You want me to say you're my girlfriend?" He pushes in hard. It catches me off guard and I yip as the door bangs against the wall again. "You want me to tell everyone I'm your boyfriend?" He puts pressure on my clit, holds it there.

I wiggle beneath him but he's unshakeable. The delirium crawls up my throat, the restlessness up my bones. I want to scream.

"Maybe," I say.

"Are you still leaving Midnight?"

His thumb moves, just barely a flicker and the sensation sends a jolt of pleasure through me, goosebumps down my arms.

I'm *this* close. My nerves are clawing for release.

"I don't know." I'm just baiting him now and he catches on easily enough.

His fingers pull out of me and I moan at the loss of him.

"Try that answer again," he says.

I swallow hard. I've never been bold. Not until I got myself entangled with Bran. It's a little liberating, saying and doing whatever the fuck you want.

"I want to stay," I admit. "With you. I want to stay *with* you."

He props his hand above me and leans in, bloody and still a little sharp with hunger and lust.

"And I don't want this"—I grab the considerable bulge between his legs and he groans—"inside anyone else."

He breathes out through his nose. "The little mouse has finally found her voice, has she? What if I say no?"

Now he's baiting me.

And even though I agreed to obey him, I'm not about to roll over and be a doormat.

"If you get to fuck whoever you want, then so do I."

His eyes tighten, fine lines fanning out as the very thought sends him spiraling into prickly rage. "Absolutely not."

I know what I'm asking him is pretty much unprecedented. Even when he was with Sky, he was sleeping with other women. He's never had a blood mate. Or at least not since I've been alive. I also know women throw themselves at him.

How could they not? Look at him.

But I'm not going to be some side piece.

The thought of him with someone else makes me want to smash things.

"Then tell me what we are," I challenge.

He frowns down at me. "I will not be a vampire *boyfriend*." He says *boyfriend* like what he really meant to say was *terrorist* or *hobo*.

"I don't care what you call it so long as we both abide by the same set of rules."

The air grows charged between us. He leans in closer, his mouth just inches away from mine. "I would murder anyone who touched you."

I think he might actually mean it this time.

"Do you know how many men I've murdered over a girl?"

"No."

"None." He brings his hand to my jaw, rubbing his thumb over my bottom lip. "If that's not loyalty, mouse, I don't know what is."

"Say it," I press as he leans closer, my heart raging in my chest. "Tell me."

He rips off my pants, then my panties and lifts me easily. It's hard not to feel small and fragile in the arms of a vampire and I pant out an excited breath.

"I will never"—I hear the familiar rasp of a zipper—"feel another pussy wrapped around my cock for as long as you live. I swear it on my life."

He positions the head of his cock at my opening and I get a buzzy thrill at the thought of him being mine, followed immediately by a seed of doubt. He'll be a twenty-something vampire forever. I can't imagine being sixty years old someday, gray and wrinkly, the promise still lingering between us.

That is until I remember I'm fae.

Fae stay young for a very, very long time.

He pushes in an inch. I'm so wet, so eager for him that he has to hold himself steady so he doesn't slip further.

"Will that suffice, little mouse?" His mouth brushes against mine, featherlight.

I pant out, my breath hot between us. "I think so."

"Try again," he scolds and shoves in further. I sense him straining against me, desperate to fill me up. His patience must be legendary. I don't know how he's holding back.

"Yes." I nod for emphasis, just as desperate to feel the full length of him.

"Good." He thrusts in. The door bangs. I tighten my grip around his neck.

Bran Duval always keeps his promises.

He fucks me loudly and without restraint.

———

Even though I changed into a nice dress and brushed out my hair, when I come downstairs and find my sister on a stool at the kitchen island, I can't help but feel like I'm doing a walk of shame. My face pinks when she gives me a look like I'm being irresponsible and ridiculous.

"Was that really necessary?" she asks me.

"Yes," Bran answers.

Kelly frowns at him. I'm reminded of her calling him a boy when he first moved in next door. Kelly looks a handful of years older than Bran and I think sometimes she fixates on that to make herself feel better.

Damien looks closer to her age in human years.

"I don't know if I like you having your way with my sister," Kelly says.

Bran gives her a blank look. "I don't really care what you like."

"Hey. Both of you. I'm standing right here."

Kelly sighs. There's a glass of wine in her left hand, the glass only half full.

"We should go," Bran says. "Monday mornings at the courts are always busy."

"Oh, you mean the notorious Bran Duval doesn't have a skip-the-line card?" Kelly quips.

"Depends on who's manning the line." Like a magician pulling a tablecloth from beneath a dinner set, Bran snatches the wine glass from my sister's hand. One second, she's tipping it back and the next it's just gone from her grip. She doesn't realize it until she opens her mouth to drink and there's nothing there.

"Hey!"

"You can't petition while drunk. It's against the law."

She huffs out a breath. Kelly works for the human courts. She knows the rules and can't argue with facts.

"We'll pick you up a fresh bottle on the way home," I say, trying to smooth things over and make her feel better. I think I'm realizing she's been dealing with far more than she's let on. The wine was just to numb herself.

This entire time, I've been blaming her. I was the victim, she was the perpetrator hiding things from me, keeping secrets.

But Kelly was just trying to hold us together and doing the very best she could.

"Depending on what the court says, perhaps we could go to Duval House afterward," Bran amends. "You can select a vintage from our wine cellar. I have several bottles of a 1985 red from Château Mouton

Rothschild in France. It's nearing the end of its peak and needs to be uncorked soon."

Bran has wine older than me.

Sensing the olive branch, Kelly softens. "Okay. That sounds amazing, actually."

He nods at her, then makes his way for the door. "Come, MacMahon sisters. Before the night gets away from us."

It's hard to ignore the command of a Duval.

Clearly my sister already knows this because she gets up without question and follows Bran out the door.

———

The drive to the courthouse takes all of six minutes with Bran behind the wheel. I'm full of butterflies the entire way. Not because of the speed, but because Kelly and I are clearly embarking on something that will change both our lives.

The entire town will be talking about this by dinnertime tomorrow.

And I can only imagine how Julian will take the news.

I just hope everything works out for my sister.

I don't want to see her hurting again.

I'm not sure what went on between her and Damien and I have to admit, I'm a little worried about her future in Duval House because of it.

Damien, like Bran, has never had a blood mate, but he's had plenty of women and being Head of House only attracts more. I don't want to see my sister get tangled up with that. In a way, as the head of one of the most influential houses in Midnight, Damien is a king and kings always tend to destroy what they touch.

Maybe he's moved on. Maybe my sister has too.

But when we walk up to the grand front entrance to the vampire court, Damien Duval is there waiting for us.

Twelve

"What is he doing here?" I whisper to Bran.

"*He* can hear you," Damien calls across the parking lot.

I wince. You'd think I'd know better having grown up in a town of vampires.

Bran doesn't say anything, but I get the feeling he doesn't really know either.

The vampire courthouse, situated on the north end of downtown Midnight, sits directly across from Kramwell Park. The park sprawls over several acres of rolling land with a large pond in the center, a paved biking trail that winds around it, and a little café along the edge.

Even though it's well after midnight, the park is full of life. The café, constructed to look like a 19th century conservatory done entirely in glass, glows like a snow globe in the night.

When Mom was alive, we'd pack food in a vintage picnic basket and come to the park in the summertime to sit on one of the gently sloping hills.

Kelly and I haven't done it since Mom died and I feel a pang of sadness at the thought of it now.

We cross the parking lot beneath the soft light of the old-fashioned streetlamps and Damien waits for us, leaning against the stone building like a dark vision.

He's wearing all black just like his brother and from afar, when they're standing next to each other, you could easily mistake them for twins.

But Damien's hair is shorter, his lips thinner, and his gaze a little more penetrating.

"Kelly," Damien says, his eyes sweeping over her, not in a hungry way, more like he's checking her for wounds.

"Hey," my sister answers. "Hi."

They stare at each other for an eternity.

Bran says something in a language I don't speak. I think it's French.

Damien's eyes tighten and he responds the same way.

"You know, it's rude to talk in another language in front of people who don't speak the language."

Damien's tense gaze settles on me, but when he speaks, it's still in French.

Bran grits his teeth and says something low and below his breath.

Kelly, always wanting to unravel confrontation, looks at Damien. "Are you sure you're okay with this?"

"Of course." He acts like he wants to reach out to her but clasps his hands behind his back instead. "Julian has overstepped. He must be held accountable."

And also the Duval brothers hate Julian, so I think this is really a win-win for them.

I remember one of my first conversations with Bran when he told me Kelly promised Damien something he'd been wanting for a very long time if he bid on me.

Now I'm desperate to know what that is. My sister? Power over Julian? Revenge against Julian?

I don't know where their war began. Jimmy insisted most vampire feuds start over lovers and cattle.

Were Julian and Damien fighting over my sister?

"And if it's approved?" I ask Damien. "If the courts allow my sister to leave Locke House, can she be adopted by Duval House? She won't be safe otherwise."

Kelly avoids looking at Damien. I think she's just as worried about her life after this as I am. But maybe for different reasons.

"I don't much care what the court says," Damien answers. "Kelly will come home with me."

My sister's eyes dart to the older Duval brother as her cheeks pink beneath her freckles. I quickly reach over and take her hand in mine and squeeze. Her grip is clammy but tight, like she's holding on for dear life.

I don't blame her.

Since I've become involved with a Duval, every day feels like a hurricane.

"Shall we?" Damien gestures to the front entrance.

Bran shifts in front of me and pulls one of the doors open. They're easily ten feet tall and made of solid wood with windows inlaid with an iron diamond grid. The door creaks and clanks the way I think a door would on a medieval castle.

The vampires like their drama. Even their entrances are dramatic.

Inside, iron lanterns hang from the tall ceiling and intricately carved metal sconces flicker golden on the wood paneled walls.

Bran leads the way, but Damien stays at our back, sandwiching us between two Duvals. I can't help but shiver.

We go down the main hall, then cut left down another where a sign hangs from the wall and reads *Small Claims Court*.

But there's nothing small about this.

I'm aware that something of this magnitude will shake up Midnight Harbor. The Duvals are never involved in this sort of thing. No mortal has ever been important enough to start a potential war.

I look over at Kelly. Her face is blank, but her hand is shaking in mine.

We enter into a clerk office. There are seven people in line ahead of us but Bran clears his throat and the others scatter like dry leaves on pavement.

He goes to the head of the line and the woman sputters. "Good morning, Mr. Duval. What can I do for you?"

"Pledge petition."

"Oh?" Her eyebrows rise. "Oh. Okay. Sure." She rifles through some papers and produces a single application that she sticks beneath the metal arm of a clipboard. "This needs to be filled out and turned in before you can go before the council."

Bran takes the clipboard and a pen and returns to us. There's a bank of waiting room chairs against the wall, so Kelly and I sit. Bran and Damien remain standing and Bran fills out the form, his hand a blur across the paper.

He frowns at a line, looks up at Damien, and asks him something in French.

Damien gives him a quick response.

Within minutes, the form is complete and Bran returns it to the woman.

We don't wait long. I guess whoever is manning the line today is the right person to move us ahead.

I can vaguely recall a study unit in my government class in high school that covered the supernatural courts. Each supernatural— vampire, shifter, and witch—get their own court, but a representative from the other factions serves on each council. The fae don't have a court, unfortunately. They never saw a reason to start one, since they had always gone back and forth between the realms and they had their own system on the fae side.

I wonder if those stuck here are regretting that decision now. They literally have no representation.

When we walk into the courtroom, we're ushered in front of a bench where two vampires sit next to a shifter and...

"Bianca?" I blurt.

I went to school with Bianca, though she was a few years ahead of me. She's one of the witches from the Mulligan family. I had no idea she was a councilwoman now.

She's wearing a tailored black blazer with a high collar that stands around her long, pale neck almost like armor. Her short blond hair is cut in a sharp bob. It's tucked behind her left ear where a diamond encrusted cuff glitters on her lobe.

I shouldn't be surprised she's here. She was always ambitious, incredibly smart, and heavily into politics. She was class president in junior high and high school and often volunteered during local elections. She loves this kind of thing.

"Hi Jessie," she says and then her gaze sweeps over the Duvals and she gives me a frown.

I want to explain to her. I want her to know that I know what I'm doing (do I?) but one of the vampires on the bench starts speaking and I clamp my mouth shut again.

"Case Number 0788358," the vampire says, his voice booming across the room. "Duval vs. Locke. Pledge petition for one—" He scans the form. "Kelly MacMahon?"

"That's correct, *Vasill*," Damien answers.

I remember *vasill* from my class. The title is the vampire equivalent for a judge.

"What's the charge?" the *vasill* asks.

"Willful misconduct," Damien answers. "My brother, Bran, and Miss MacMahon, Kelly's younger sister, found Kelly suffering from compulsion fever earlier in the night. In addition to that, several nights ago, Kelly also returned to her mortal home with a sizeable neck wound." Damien stops and his jaw flexes, teeth gritting.

After a deep breath, he adds, "Ms. MacMahon was healed only by the blood of my brother. I would like to petition for permanent adoption of Ms. MacMahon, as is my right by vampire law."

Bianca's eyes widen.

"We can't approve a legal adoption of a pledge until we've allowed Julian Locke to speak in his defense," the *vasill* points out.

"Yes, but you can approve a temporary removal order for the safety of the pledge as is stated in Section 71.329 of the Pledge Civil Rights Act."

My head is literally spinning with all of the legal speak. I'm suddenly grateful Damien is here. I think he had all of this planned out before he took one step into the courthouse.

He knew he wanted to win today and he knew just how to do it.

"I have a question for the MacMahon sisters," Bianca says.

Kelly and I, hands still linked, step forward.

"First, do you have any objection to the Duvals adopting you into their house?"

Beside me, Kelly shakes her head, then clears her throat. "No, councilwoman."

Bianca folds her hands on the bench and her shoulders scrunch up, causing the collar of her blazer to stand further erect around her face. "And do you know what you're doing? Right now?" She narrows her eyes, assessing. "Do you understand what you're asking for?"

Yes. No. Maybe? *Do we, Kelly?*

Maybe Kelly and I are both in over our heads. It's all fun and games fucking Bran, being with Bran, but what happens after tomorrow? What happens if Kelly is adopted into Duval house?

Where do I go for my pledge?

I look over at my sister, at the exhaustion smudged beneath her eyes, the downturned corners of her mouth, the paleness of her skin.

We have so much left to figure out, but I want her by my side. She may not be blood, but she is my sister and she's the only family I have left.

"We do, councilwoman," I answer. "My sister's safety is my highest priority."

Kelly smiles at me. She pats our linked hands, then kisses me on the cheek. "My answer is the same as my sister's. I'll do anything for her and Julian Locke is..." Her voice catches. I catch the glint of tears welling in her eyes.

"He's what?" Bianca prompts.

"He's—"

The courtroom door slams open.

We all turn to the commotion.

Julian Locke is there, a piece of paper clutched in his hand. "Stop!" he shouts. "Kelly MacMahon cannot be adopted into Duval House."

"Mr. Locke," the *vasill* says, "you'll be given ample opportunity to def—"

"She can't be adopted into Duval House," he says again. "Because she's my blood mate." He waves the piece of paper in his hand. "And I have the signed license right here to prove it."

Thirteen

My sister is Julian Locke's blood mate? That can't be right.

"Approach the bench, Mr. Locke," the *vasill* instructs and Julian walks passed us to the front of the courtroom.

He looks over his shoulder at Damien for the briefest of seconds and I swear I catch a flicker of triumph on his face.

That mother fucker.

The *vasill* takes the blood mate license from Julian and reads it over. "Ms. MacMahon," he says, "did you perform the blood mate ceremony and sign this license?"

My sister sputters beside me. "I...that's not...*no*, your honor. I wouldn't—" She looks at Damien. Her breathing is labored and her eyes wide. "I wouldn't," she says low and beneath her breath.

When he meets her eyes, Damien's expression is blank, but his hands are fists at his side.

The *vasill* hands the license to one of the courtroom guards. "Take that to Ms. MacMahon please."

The guard, another vampire, brings it over and holds it up for all of us to see.

"Is that your signature, Ms. MacMahon?" the *vasill* asks.

"Fuck," Kelly whispers.

It is her signature. My sister has very distinct handwriting. It's half print, half cursive, with tall, skinny letters.

Her K dips down far on the signature line and her Y loops with a curl on its tail.

"As you can see," Julian says, "as my blood mate, Kelly MacMahon should be returned to me and this matter resolved immediately."

"Even a blood mate has rights," I blurt.

The guard hands the license back to Julian. I want that piece of paper so I can burn the damn thing.

"While that may be true," the *vasill* says, "dissolving a blood agreement is much more complex than dissolving a simple pledging."

"Bran!" My voice rises, near hysteria. "They can't do this."

"You can re-petition the court to dissolve the blood agreement," the *vasill* adds, "but that matter needs to be sent to the civil court and they're not open on Mondays."

Bran looks over the top of my head to his brother. He says something in French.

Damien responds the same.

They go back and forth over us ignoring the *vasill* as he drones on.

It's hard to tell what the Duval brothers are discussing. Their voices are even, their expressions distant, almost cold.

Out of the corner of my eye, I catch Bianca standing to her feet. Horror is rising on her face. It's the same expression a man might wear when he watches the ocean pull back right before a tsunami hits.

Bianca speaks French.

My stomach drops.

Oh shit.

"Damien!" she calls across the courtroom, "you can't—"

Damien and Bran are a blur.

The sound of cracking bone reaches my ears like a gunshot, but it isn't until the body hits the floor that I realize it's one of the guards.

I yelp in surprise.

A second guard drops.

The *vasill* drops next.

Julian's eyes burn bright blue, ready for war, but Julian isn't fast enough.

Julian isn't a Duval.

His head twists to an unnatural angle beneath the massive strength of Damien's capable hands.

One second Julian is snarling with rage and the next he's motionless on the marble floor.

"What the fuck?" The other vampire, the second councilman, kicks his chair back and lurches to his feet. "You can't do this."

"Yes, I fucking can." Damien crouches beside Julian's temporarily lifeless body and plucks the blood mate document from his pocket.

"You're going to start a war!"

Bran takes another step behind the bench. There is a hunger burning in his eyes that has nothing to do with blood and everything to do with carnage.

"Come on, man." The vampire backpedals. Bran advances. "Okay!" The man holds up his hands. "All right. Fuck, Duval. All this over some pussy?"

Bran's nostrils flare. His gaze is on the other vampire, but he says something in French.

Damien answers, "*Oui,*" and Bran's hand sinks into the other vampire's chest and tears out his heart. Blood splatters across his face as his fangs turn razor sharp in his mouth.

Adrenaline rushes through my veins, sending a flash of warmth all through my body.

The councilman blinks at his heart in Bran's hand right before he bursts into ash.

The air goes still and silent. I can taste the cinders on the tip of my tongue.

Bran lets the heart drop from his grip and it bursts into ash mid-fall. He gives Bianca a quick tip of his chin and she races out of the room. The wolf shifter is already gone.

"Time to go," Damien says, his voice even and calm like they didn't just decimate an entire vampire court and start a war.

Bran comes over. There's a trail of blood from the bench to us where it dripped from his hand. Blood like bread crumbs. I can't seem to look away from it. I am entranced by it.

The brothers discuss something in French and Damien sweeps Kelly into the wide span of his arms.

"Wait, my sister—"

"Is coming with me," Damien says, barely looking at me, and they disappear from sight.

"Better if we go separately," Bran explains.

I don't move. I can't seem to move.

"What's wrong?" he asks.

"I...we..." Pinpricks of light dance in my eyes. My stomach is full of wings.

"It had to be done," Bran says. "Can you walk? If you can't, tell me now because we need to move."

How is he so calm?

"Mouse."

"Okay." I nod. "I can walk."

"Then go. *Now*."

———

I don't know how we get out of the courthouse. It's all a dark blur.

One minute I'm staring at the blood on the marble floor and the next Bran is racing down a desolate street in the Bimmer.

The radio is off. It's just the silence and the pounding of my heart.

I want to crawl out of my skin.

"All of that was because of me."

"No," he corrects. "That's been meaning to happen for a very long time. Long before you."

"You just killed a vampire. Not like, pretend killed. Killed-*killed*."

He looks over at me briefly, the light of the dashboard liming him in an eerie glow. "Yes. And?"

"And he's dead. You tore out his heart."

He frowns, slightly exasperated with my need to state the obvious. "You wanted your sister, didn't you?"

"Yes, but—"

"No, mouse. You need to realize the gravity of what's happening here. Julian must know what you are and he's willing to use your sister against you to get to you. If we had let him walk out that door with Kelly, you might not have ever gotten her back. That needed to happen. It was unfortunate how it did, but I'm not going to dwell on the death of a vampire when he blatantly disrespected you."

"Who cares what some vampire says about me?" I mutter.

"I do, mouse. I fucking do."

I knew Bran was capable of violence. But up until now, I assumed, for the most part, that he followed the rules. All of this tonight—the court, the death, the blood—proves he doesn't.

His disregard for the rules is both frightening and fucking hot as hell.

Because Bran Duval doesn't give a fuck. He knows there are so few who could stand against him.

The power *is* intoxicating.

He is flesh and blood and walking fucking carnage.

And he's mine.

All fucking mine.

The headlights cut across a sharp turn in the road and Bran pushes the clutch and downshifts, the tendons in his forearm rising, flexing.

There's still blood coating his hand, drying in flakes around his fingernails.

The sight of it makes me yearn for something I have no name for.

Now I'm that man standing in front of a tidal wave.

"Stop the car."

He narrows his eyes. "Why?"

When I don't elaborate, he downshifts again and slows, steering the car onto the dirt shoulder.

I climb out and he meets me at the front and I jump into his arms without warning and he catches me easily, hands hooked around the backs of my thighs. I wrap my legs around his hips.

The wind picks up and the boughs of the hardwoods creak, the leaves rustling against one another.

"Thank you," I say to him, my hair hanging like a curtain around us. "Thank you for helping me save my sister."

"You don't have to thank me." He licks his bottom lip, his gaze going to my mouth. "I fucking enjoyed it."

I shiver beneath his words. "Even though it was terrifying, there was something overwhelmingly hot about it."

I would never admit that to anyone other than Bran, and I'm only just now realizing that the tingling I'd felt in my bones wasn't fear, but exhilaration.

And when I watched the blood drip from his hand, distantly, in some far corner of my subconscious, something dark stirred.

"Wicked little mouse," he says with a growl.

I can feel him growing hard beneath the center of me. He drops me lower on his hips, rocking me against him and a thrill pulses through me.

I sink my mouth to his, claw my hands into his hair, trying to get closer. Never close enough.

Our breathing quickens. I slide my tongue over his and catch the sharp edge of a fang. Blood fills my mouth, coppery and sweet, and Bran whirls me around and slams me against the car door, ravenous for the taste.

"Fuck me," I say, panting against him.

He lowers me to the ground, wraps his hand around my neck. His grip is rough as his eyes burn in the night.

"Bend that ass over the hood then." His voice is raspy and thick. "And be quick about it, mouse."

Fourteen

I don't dawdle. I'm naked and bare for him in seconds. I don't even stop to think about the possibility that someone might drive by at any second and see me looking like a whore on the side of the road for one of the infamous Duval brothers.

I don't care. Because it's true.

I move to bend over the car, but Bran stops me.

"Hold on, little mouse." He hoists me up on the hood and I squeak from the shock of the cold metal on my ass. He hooks his hands around my thighs, yanking me to the edge with his vampire quickness. It happens so fast, my head spins.

"What are you doing?"

I would be lying if I said his promise from so many days ago to bend me over the hood of my car hasn't been ringing through my head like the distant toll of a bell.

He made me a promise.

He always sticks to his promises.

I'm not above pouting at this point.

The hunger in his eyes causes his irises to throb bright orange. "I want to see what murder does to the taste of this pussy."

Before I can respond, he's covering me with his mouth.

Feeling him on me in that way, beneath those words, is a sensation I wasn't prepared for and I arch toward the sky.

Bran's mouth is clever, his tongue a master.

And of course.

Of course he knows how to treat a girl with his mouth.

My hands turn into claws and if I had sheets beneath me, they'd be fisted in my grip. Instead I scrabble at the cool metal and then satisfy my instinctual need to hang on to something by taking a fistful of Bran's hair.

"Oh fuck," I say through a moan as Bran laps me up.

He flicks at my clit, then dips to my opening and fucks me with his tongue.

"Well, well, little mouse," he says, his hot breath sending a new shiver to my core. "Murder makes you sweet."

It doesn't make sense, but the insinuation that I can be vile and wicked makes me fucking hotter than hell. My clit throbs as my nerves, lit like a firecracker, beg for release.

I tighten my hold on him and try to bring his mouth back to me, but he snatches both my wrists and forces me down, pinning me to the hood.

He tsk-tsks at me.

I close my eyes and exhale with frustration at the dark sky.

He's slower to taste me this time, dragging out the tortuous pleasure of his tongue on my wet pussy.

I buck as if that'll get me what I want and he nips at my thigh, causing me to squeal in pain.

There's the telltale sensation of blood welling from a puncture wound, dripping down the curve of my thigh to the swell of my ass.

Bran laps that up too.

"Stop punishing me," I say.

"Stop fighting me," he answers.

"I want you inside of me."

"And I want to hear you scream my name."

My breathing turns labored as my heart races in my ears.

Screaming doesn't come naturally to me.

I've always been afraid of my own voice.

Don't be loud.

Don't draw attention to yourself.

We're in the middle of nowhere. No one would hear me. Would they?

Bran flattens his tongue against me, tastes me long and deep and moans against me like I'm the sweetest thing he's ever put his mouth to.

It makes me feel like I'm made of starlight and honey. I tremble, squirm, and Bran tightens his hold on my wrists.

"Come for me, mouse."

"I want you to fuck me," I say.

"Oh, I will. But I'm fucking that tight little ass tonight and it's not going to be fun for you. Because I'm going to destroy it."

The sudden spike of fear blends with the pleasure in a riotous flutter in my belly.

I have my safe word.

I could use it if it got to be too much.

But...

But...

I want to be wicked and vile with Bran.

I want him to destroy me in all of his wicked and vile ways. Even if it hurts.

He returns to my pussy, works at my clit, and the wave builds at my sternum, and down through my belly.

I writhe on the hood.

Bran holds me down.

I'm just skin and nerves and blinding need.

He hits my swollen clit again and the wave cascades through me.

The stars in the sky blur into bright white smudges and I open my mouth and scream.

"Bran! Fuck. Oh fuck. Bran!"

He takes me through the wave, rides my pussy with his mouth as I buck beneath him, my body trying desperately to curl into itself. But he doesn't let me. He doesn't let up until I'm a puddle on the hood.

When he finally lets me go and straightens, dragging the back of his hand over his soaked chin, he smiles down at me with bright amber eyes. "That's a good girl."

I'm boneless.

Spent.

Satiated in a way that feels both liberating and gluttonous all at the same time.

Bran lifts me off the hood and puts me on my feet. He kisses me, giving me a taste of my own pleasure.

He's right—it does taste sweet.

His mouth travels to the curve of my neck, then up to my ear, his breath sending a warm shiver down my skin.

I can feel the hard press of him against my thigh.

His movements have grown frenzied, hungry.

I reach down between us and undo his pants, pulling him out.

As soon as my hand is wrapped around his cock, he growls deep in his chest, fangs sharpening in his mouth.

"If you only knew what you do to me, mouse..."

"I'd what?"

He licks his lips, looks down at me with heavy, glowing eyes. "You'd run."

My heart kicks up in my ears. "I'm not going anywhere."

"As if I'd let you."

Even though I just rode the biggest high on that orgasm, my inner walls clench up at the reminder that he's claimed me as his.

As I stroke him, I can't help but watch his face, the way his mouth hardens and his jaw flexes, the way his Adam's apple sinks low in his throat. All of these little movements that add up to one thing—Bran Duval wants me.

He wants me as much as I want him and I've never been wanted in my entire life.

Pre-cum coats the head of his dick and I rub my thumb over the slit, then bring it to my mouth, suck it off. He growls again, nostrils flaring as his broad shoulders rise and fall with heightened breaths.

"You're not prepared for this, little mouse," he says.

"Yes, I am."

"No, you're not."

He brings his wrist to his mouth and bites into his own flesh. Blood coats his lips and drips from the wound.

I frown at him, unsure of what he means to do and then—

He holds his bleeding wrist over his cock, coating it in wet crimson. Fisting himself, he strokes long, once, twice.

He's using blood like lube.

Oh shit.

He spins me around, bends me over the hood and grabs my hips, forcing my ass up.

"Fuck, mouse. That tight little hole is just begging to be fucked."

I breathe out quickly.

He positions himself at my ass and I can feel the head swell against me, ready to plunge inside.

I hold my breath.

More blood slides down my seam, wetting our near joining.

If I wanted wicked and vile, I'm getting it.

He pushes in an inch, slow and steady, and I tense up.

Bran tightens his hold on my hips. "Breathe, mouse."

"I am."

"No, you're not."

I exhale, my breath fanning across the hood.

"That's a good girl."

He pushes in further, stretching me, and a squeak escapes me.

It feels like I'm being split in two. Stretched too thin. He's too big.

"Fuck, mouse. You're so fucking tight."

My chest fills with butterflies.

Another inch.

Another.

The wind shifts again and leaves skitter over the pavement and Bran Duval finally seats himself fully in my ass. He holds himself steady, the head of his cock swelling deep inside of me. "Remember your safe word."

"I will." My voice is too high-pitched and thin.

He pulls out, then slides back in and I clench against the sting.

"Mouse," he says on a groan.

I breathe hard, scrabbling at the hood as his pace picks up. He's enjoying it now and being used in this way makes me feel sickly satisfied.

This is the most illicit thing I've ever done and I don't want to like the way it makes me feel—not physically, not yet—*mentally*.

Does that make me wicked and vile?

Oh fuck.

Bran pumps faster, punishing me. His grip is bruising, his thrusts no longer gentle and I'm wetter than I've ever been as those satisfied wings take flight in my belly.

He's getting closer. I can tell by the tempo of his fucking, the rough groans, the hardness of his cock.

The in and out, in and out of his cock.

And I think I could come again.

I don't know how. I've never come twice in one go, but I'm primed, burning, clit throbbing.

I think I could.

I want to come while he fucks me this way.

I want to prove him wrong—this *is* fun for me even if it is painful.

Whatever dark thing stirred inside of me at that courthouse is now ravenous for more.

I reach down between my legs and take command of my own pleasure.

The beat of the orgasm flashes through me like oil in fire—quick and hot and consuming. I cry out and my voice bounces off of the hood of the car and echoes in the forest and Bran pumps deep, spilling hot cum in my ass.

"*Fuck, mouse.*" He slides out, shoves back in, the head of his cock throbbing at my center. He stays buried for several beats and I collapse against the car, legs shaking. And when he finally pulls out of me, I twist and slide down to the ground and hang my head back against the tire.

Bran drops beside me and takes my hand in his.

When I turn to him, there's a noticeable pinch around his eyes.

"What are you thinking?" I ask.

I want to know the intimate details of what's inside his head. I want to know him like no one else does. Because in the end, it won't be the fucking or the violence that makes what we have special, it'll be the quiet moments like this when no one is looking, when he tells me his secrets and I guard them with my heart.

"Sometimes I'm afraid I'll break you," he admits. He reaches over with his other hand and pushes aside a lock of hair that's stuck in the sweat on my cheek. "I will always be a little sadistic and you will always be breakable and so devastatingly beautiful it makes me ache."

Tears immediately well in my eyes. I don't know what to do with this compliment. It feels too big to hold.

He stands up and gently hoists me to stand beside him. He takes my face in his hands. There's firelight in his irises as he says, "I was turned too young to know what it means to love with a mortal heart, but if I had to guess, this must be pretty fucking close."

"Are you saying that you lo—"

He clamps his hand over my mouth, snuffing out the word before it finds air.

"Don't."

I dare not move.

"Don't say it, mouse."

I give him a quick nod. When he pulls his hand back, satisfied that I'll obey, I have to ask.

"Why not?"

He glances away from me, his gaze going to the dark horizon of the back road. "Because it fucking terrifies me." When he meets my eyes again, there's no glow to his irises. Just a hooded darkness. "And it should terrify you too."

He scoops up my clothes and helps me dress even though I'm an absolute fucking mess and desperately need a shower.

Our drive back to Duval House is comfortably silent, but Bran's grip on the stick shift is white-knuckled the whole way there.

Fifteen

Bran is quiet on the drive back to Duval House. Quiet and distant. He parks beneath the *porte cochère* and hands the keys off to a girl who avoids his eyes. He doesn't say a word to her or me as he guides me through the house and toward the back where French doors lead to what looks like a courtyard.

Something is wrong. But I don't know how to help him.

Right now, I can sense his energy literally vibrating through his body. I don't think now is the time to have a conversation, but I'm not going to let us go to bed without tackling it.

Because we have to talk about it. We have to talk about all of it.

"Jimmy," Bran says.

Jimmy appears within seconds. She's wearing the most adorable denim overalls rolled at the ankles. She's barefoot with paint splattered across her toes and smudged across the front pocket of the overalls. Her arrival disrupts the air around us and she brings with her the scent of something woody and floral.

"Hi," she says and looks from me back to Bran. I've noticed Jimmy is always watching Bran when she's near, like a snake charmer might watch a snake, making sure it isn't ready to strike.

I don't know what their relationship is, but Bran did admit that he'd die for Jimmy. I think Jimmy might feel the same way about him.

I would be lying if I said that didn't stir a little bit of envy. Jimmy clearly knows him better than I do and I have a lot of ground to cover to even match her depth of knowing.

"Take my little mouse to the Anneliese," Bran says.

I have no idea what that is.

"Show her to a shower and get her some clean clothes."

"Wait, where are you going?" I grab his arm, feeling him pull away from me. Last time I was left alone in Duval House, Sky sought me out and turned everything upside down.

It's hard to say how she feels about me now.

"I have to see my brother," Bran answers. "The Anneliese will keep you safe. And so will Jimmy."

Jimmy nods.

"Clean up, mouse," he adds with a smug grin.

I'm a mess, covered in blood and cum. I desperately need a shower and the promise of one has me salivating. But...I don't want him to leave either.

"I'll be back soon," he says and slides his hand around my neck, dragging me in. The kiss he plants on my forehead is featherlight, but his grip is firm and I want to melt beneath the pressure.

But then he's pulling away.

Jimmy rushes ahead to stop him and the two exchange words. They're nothing more than a whisper and I can't hear what's said.

When Jimmy turns back to me, Bran is already gone.

"I'm sorry," I say.

"For what?"

"Well, because you're babysitting me again."

She reaches out for one of the handles on the French doors. "Do you think the secret service rolls their eyes every time they're tasked with guarding someone?"

Jimmy gestures for me to head outside and we walk into an open-air courtyard beneath the starlit sky.

"I'm not the president of the United States."

"No, but you're valued by Bran. That makes you important. I have a duty to this house and to Damien and Bran. I don't care what the task is. I'll do it."

She walks ahead of me on the stone-paved path. It's a short walk through well-tended flowering bushes. Soft solar lights illuminate the path and somewhere to my left, a water feature gurgles in the dark.

We stop beneath the overhanging roof of a building separate from Duval House.

"Is this the Anneliese?" I ask.

Jimmy nods and punches a code into a digital panel beside the door. The panel beeps and a deadbolt clanks open.

"It's deeded to a human who doesn't live anywhere near here. Only Bran, Damien, and myself have been invited."

"Why's it called the Anneliese?"

We step inside. The air is cool and smells clean.

"It's named after Damien and Bran's little sister."

"They have a sister?"

"Had," Jimmy corrects.

"Oh god. That's..."

"A long story," she finishes.

"Right. Of course."

The Anneliese is open floor plan in the front. Directly to my left is a dining table nestled in a room done entirely in glass. Even though it's dark, I can tell the room is surrounded in greenery outside so that it must feel like you're dining in the forest.

There's a kitchen to the far left, and a living room to the far right, with a cozy seating area directly to the right of the front door.

A wide hallway runs through the center of the house and appears to break off left and right at the end.

"Come this way," Jimmy says. "Bran's room is down here. There's an attached bathroom."

"Is my sister here?" I ask.

"Yes, but I believe she's already sleeping. She'll be in Damien's room down the hall if you want to check in on her."

I eye the closed door. "No, that's all right. She's been through a lot in the last twenty-four hours. Better to let her rest."

But I'm so damn relieved we're beneath the same roof, protected by the Duvals.

We enter Bran's room. This is...what, the third place of his I've been to in so many days? There are more black and white photographs hung on the wall. The bedding is an exact match to the bedding he has at the house next to ours.

It's so decidedly him that it makes me immediately feel at home.

"Shower is through there." Jimmy points at a closed door to the left of the bed. "I'll get you some clothes and will leave them on the end of the bed."

"Thanks, Jimmy."

She gives my shoulder a squeeze. "Don't mention it."

When she leaves me, I strip off my clothes, toss them in the trash, and immediately jump into the shower. God, the hot water feels amazing. I'm learning to accept that being around Bran will always be bloody, but damn if my germaphobe OCD-self isn't crying a little inside.

As promised, I find folded clothes waiting for me on the end of the bed. There's a pair of sleep shorts made of soft linen and a tank top and panties. Jimmy has found me a lounge bra, but I go without.

Once I'm clean and dressed, I pace the hallway outside the room. I find Jimmy keeping watch in the sitting area, giving her a clear view of Duval House and the courtyard. She's reading a book and gives me a smile when I come out.

"How long do you think Bran will be?" I ask. It's nearing 4 am now. Where the hell is he?

"With Bran and Damien, it's always hard to tell," Jimmy responds. "I haven't heard anything to cause me to worry."

"Okay. Will you let me know if you do?"

"Of course."

What if they went to confront Julian? I'm sure he's up and on his feet now, having healed from the broken neck.

I bet he's burning with rage.

Can Bran and Damien take him and Locke House? I'm sure they can but not if they're ambushed.

Bran better be okay, goddamn it. Just thinking about something happening to him makes my stomach knot up.

I busy myself with a glass of water from the kitchen, then get nosy at the bookshelves in the living room as I wait. I spend a half hour flicking through a book about eighteenth century France until I can't stop yawning and decide to give in.

"Goodnight, Jimmy," I call.

She looks up from her book. "Night. Let me know if you need me."

In the bedroom, I climb in beneath the soft sheets of Bran's bed and am disappointed they don't smell like him. My eyes are burning I'm so tired, but I can't sleep. I toss and turn. The digital clock on the dresser says it's after five now. The sun will be up soon.

Where is he?

Finally, I hear the front door click closed and the air part in the bedroom a second later.

"Bran?" I ask the dark.

"I'm here, little mouse." His voice is hoarse and quiet.

"Where have you been? I've been worried." I slip from the bed and reach over to click on the bedside lamp. "You could have call—"

Light fills the room and I catch sight of him.

He's covered in blood.

So much blood.

"What happened?" I rush over to him, the panic tightening like a band across my chest. "Are you hurt?"

"It's not mine," he says.

"Then who—Julian?"

He ignores me and goes to the bathroom and starts stripping, adding his bloody clothes to the pile of mine in the trash can.

It's been a bloody, violent night.

"The who doesn't matter," he answers once he's standing naked in front of me.

I can't help but drag my eyes over his body. The blood is still splattered on his neck and over his face. It coats his arms and has dried on his hands. But the rest of him is clean.

God, he is so fucking hot.

He's got abs for days and those shadowed lines that arch over his hips and run to a V right down to his cock.

He's not hard, but he's still big and I have the urge to take him in my hand.

He tsk-tsks at me, clearly scenting the stirring of my arousal, and it's becoming my new favorite thing. It makes me feel naughty when he does it.

"Are you okay?" I ask him, echoing Jimmy's earlier question that he so artfully dodged.

"Of course I am."

"You were distant when you left and now this." I gesture at him.

"Damien and I went for a hunt."

I don't even want to ask for the details. It's better if I don't know.

He comes over to me and I backpedal into the tiled wall next to the vanity. A startled little breath escapes me. "I've been thinking," I say. "There's something I want to get out." My heart picks up its tempo. "You keep telling me to find my voice. So I need you to listen."

"I'm listening."

"I'm not afraid of you."

"Your heart rate says otherwise."

I swallow, licking my lips. Bran towers over me, naked and intimidating.

"I'm not afraid that you'll hurt me," I correct. "If I use the safe word, I know you'll listen and I'm not worried about what comes after. I don't think you're going anywhere and I'm not either. I have faith in you. I trust you. And you have to trust me when I say I know what I want. So stop telling me I should be terrified of you and stop telling me I should be afraid of how I feel or how you feel or what we—"

He kisses me, long and slow, his tongue sliding over mine, his bloody hand on my throat.

Butterflies fill my stomach as he breathes out through his nose, almost like a sigh.

When he pulls back, his eyes are glowing. "Now it's time you listen."

I swallow hard. This better not be a rejection or I swear to god—

"I love you, Jessie."

My heart stops beating.

I just blink up at him, on the verge of screaming or sobbing. Not out of fear, but triumph, relief.

He said it.

He said it.

My eyes turn watery and when I blink several tears escape.

Bran reaches over and swipes them away.

"I will never leave your side. Feel safe in using your safe word should you need it." He smirks and tucks a lock of my hair behind my ear. "I can control myself, even around that tight little ass."

I laugh and duck my head. Heat rises in my cheeks.

"I am your knight," he goes on. "Your protector. I'll even be your vampire boyfriend if it pleases you. And while I don't think you fully understand what you've gotten yourself into, I am yours, in all of my bloody glory."

I smile and look down at his glory.

He's semi-hard, growing harder by the second. I instinctively reach down to touch him, but he bats me away. "I will bow at your feet," he says, "but you'll still obey me. And you'll only get this cock when I say you get this cock."

I pout up at him. "Then say I get it."

"Absolutely not. You need to rest. I fucked that ass hard."

"Stop talking about my ass."

"Why?"

"Because it makes me blush."

"I know. It's adorable."

I rake my teeth over my bottom lip, trying not to smile about it. "But I'm fae, remember. Which means I heal quickly, it seems. Which explains why my entire life, I never had to go to the hospital and—"

Bran pulls me back toward the bedroom. "I'm taking a shower and you're going to bed." He tucks me into the sheets.

"Fine. But hurry," I say up to him.

"I'll only be a minute." He flicks off the light. The shower turns on a few seconds later.

I lay there, eyes wide open, waiting for him to come to bed.

So much has changed. So much is yet to come.

The room is dark, but beyond it, I know the sun is rising, which means it's Monday, the day before my birthday and my Pledge.

How will I sleep at all before then?

But as soon as Bran comes to bed and slips in behind me, wraps me in his arms and surrounds me with his scent, I give in to the exhaustion and fall quickly to sleep, warm in the knowledge that Bran Duval loves me.

He fucking loves me.

BOOK THREE

One

The digital clock says it's a little after eleven a.m. when I wake, but blackout blinds have the room feeling like it's the middle of the night.

Even though I can't see him, I sense Bran filling up the bed beside me.

He's mine. All mine. I can't believe it.

There was a time when I thought he hated me.

And now he's confessed he loves me.

I'm not going to dismiss his warning that I don't entirely understand what it means to have the love of a Duval, but I'm not going to waste it either.

Does Kelly know what it is to have the love of a Duval?

Damien attacked in the middle of a vampire court to get her to safety, and while there is inherently some value in keeping her safe—because of who I am and who Kelly is to me—I think he did it mostly for himself.

Is he currently sleeping next to her?

The little sister in me is just nosy enough to want to know.

I ease from the bed. Bran doesn't stir. I'm not entirely sure what it means for a vampire to sleep, since they're technically dead-*ish*. Do they breathe? Are they dead-dead while they sleep?

We're taught a lot about vampires in school, but there are some secrets they've always closely guarded. Like how a vampire becomes a vampire. I still don't know. But I have heard it's a long, drawn-out process and incredibly painful.

I tiptoe from bed, carefully open the door, and slip out.

Diffused daylight fills the Anneliese. What an odd design decision for a vampire. The house is literally a snow globe.

From the kitchen, there's the distinct sound of pans clanging together and the smell of fresh coffee.

Jimmy assured me the Anneliese was the safest place in Midnight, but a clever human could probably break inside.

Clever human, dumb human. You couldn't pay me a million dollars to break into a Duval property.

When I turn the corner into the kitchen, I find my sister at the stove.

"Hey," I say.

She jumps, putting her hand to her chest. "Christ. I didn't hear you get up."

"I'm quiet. Like a mouse."

She looks at me and then bursts into laughter. I can't help it. I laugh too.

"What are you making?" I ask her.

"Eggs and toast. That's all there was in the fridge. I'm guessing they didn't have time to plan ahead for humans to be staying here."

I go over to the cupboards and start opening doors. I find black coffee mugs in the cupboard by the sink and fill one with fresh coffee just as my sister heats up a cast iron pan on the stove.

"How do you feel?" I ask and pull myself up on the counter by the sink, legs dangling over the edge.

"Better." She taps an egg on the pan, cracks it open. The white sizzles when it hits the heat.

"Did Damien stay with you?"

She says nothing, adds a second egg.

"Kels, did he?"

"I slept alone. As it should be."

"But—"

"There is no Damien and I," she says.

"Yes, there clearly is."

She sighs and brings her hand to her forehead, presses at the center as if massaging out an ache. "It's complicated."

"Well, I'm not going anywhere."

She flips the eggs with a spatula. "He's mad at me. Damien isn't as easy to please as your vampire."

I snort. "Easy to please? Bran is like one of those novelty puzzles. You know the ones you impulse buy at gift shops and don't actually have solutions?"

"Yes, they do. And if that's your comparison, then Damien is the creator of the puzzle."

I lift my brows. "Oh? Okay. Well. I'm sorry?"

I recall overhearing a conversation my sister had on the phone with one of her coworkers. Damien had come into the City Clerk Office for what I assumed was business. She told her coworker that Damien was an iceberg. I thought she meant because he was cold. But now I wonder if she meant that with him, you only see what's above the surface, that the real danger lingers beneath in the dark.

"There was a time when I thought Damien sent Bran to live next door," Kelly admits.

"Really?"

She presses the button on the toaster, sinking the bread to the bottom. "I thought he wanted to keep an eye on me, but now—" She looks over at me. "Clearly it was only you."

I frown at her. "Kels. That's not...I mean...I think Damien does care about you. If that's what you want? *Is* it what you want?"

"I don't know what I want," she admits.

The kitchen fills with the smell of toasting bread and fried eggs. She reaches around me for two plates she set aside. Using a towel for the pan handle, she lifts it and slides the eggs onto the plates.

"Want to have breakfast in the belvedere?" she asks me.

I smile over at her. "Nothing would make me happier."

With plates and coffee cups in hand, we go to the dining room surrounded on all sides by windows. I was right in my assumption last night—we're surrounded mostly by greenery but have a clear view on the one side of the courtyard and Duval House. The main house is mostly dark and sleepy right now, considering most who live there are vampires.

"So what do you think happens next?" I push the tines of the fork into the egg yolk and the liquid spills out. I quickly soak it up with the toast.

"I honestly don't know. What happened last night at court won't go unanswered and—" She pulls to a stop.

"What?"

"Tomorrow is your birthday." Her eyes are wide.

"Yes. And?"

"Tomorrow is your birthday! And your Pledge and the party!"

"We've covered this, Kels. Don't you remember? We don't have to do a party."

"But it's your birthday."

"But is it?"

Her mouth drops open as if she means to argue, but the energy behind it quickly wanes when she realizes the truth—we don't actually know when I was born.

We don't know anything about who I am or where I came from. Clearly the fae realm, but why? Who gave me to my mother? Was it my birth parents? What kind of fae were they?

Out of all the supernatural beings in Midnight Harbor, the fae are the kind I'm least familiar with. The gate was already closed by the time I was old enough to pay attention. I know a few fae families—there was the family I babysat for as a teenager—but their numbers are scant compared to the vampires and witches and shifters.

What I do know is that on the fae side, they have legit courts, the *royal* kind, and that they're broken up into Seelie and Unseelie. The light and the dark. The Unseelie rarely frequented our side, so those that live in Midnight are all Seelie.

The fact that I could be either is both frightening and exciting.

"Even if we don't know your true birthday, we'll move ahead as if we do. Besides, you have to Pledge and you'll accept the Duval bid."

"Oh, will I?"

"Jessie." She gives me her mom look, the one with the wide, stern eyes.

"Yes, you will."

Kelly and I both jump at the sound of Bran's voice.

"This is the part I hate about living with vampires," Kelly says. "I'm always on the edge of a heart attack."

Bran's shirtless and his jeans hang low on his hips, revealing that fine-as-hell V that is like an arrow pointing at his cock.

Fucking hell.

Why does everything about him have to be so deliriously sexual?

He walks into a room and I'm wet.

That's literally all he has to do.

He pulls out the chair across the table from me and sits in a slouch. The muscles and tendons running across his shoulders flex with the movements.

I look down at my egg, but the seeping golden liquid just has me thinking of blood and cum and it doesn't help me at all.

"Damien will bid on you," Bran says, "and you will accept."

"Even though none of us know what I am?"

"Even though." He reaches across the table and snatches my coffee cup, taking a long swig even though it's piping hot.

The steam kisses his face as he looks at me over the dark rim.

"I could be a liability," I say.

"We can't protect you if you're not under our House."

"It's the right move, Jess," Kelly says.

"I know you think so. You already went to Damien about it. It's the whole reason Bran came to the coffeeshop to warn me."

Kelly turns to Bran. "You did?"

He's still looking at me. "She deserved to know."

"Was that before or after you seduced her?"

"Kelly. That's not—" I start.

Bran sets the coffee down. He turns to my sister in a way that is decidedly sinister.

"I've risked my life for Jessie. What the fuck have you done? You've just made a mess of—"

The front door opens and suddenly Damien is standing at the end of the table.

"No," he says.

Just one word.

That's all Damien Duval has to say to quiet a room.

Kelly licks her lips and swallows so hard, I can hear it across the table.

"Kelly did what she thought she needed to do," Damien says. "We'll not hold it against her. Understood?"

Bran takes in a long, exasperated breath. "Yes, fine, dear brother. As you wish."

"He didn't seduce me," I say.

They all look at me.

"What? I'm a big girl. My sex life is not up for discussion. All right?"

Bran winks at me, causing me to blush.

"Finish your breakfast," Damien says. "Jessie needs to file her paperwork for her Pledge. Unless you've done so already?"

"I haven't," I answer. I had thought I'd be long gone by now. "After what happened last night, I didn't think we'd want to leave the house."

"The court is powerless against me," Damien admits. There's no bravado in his voice. It's just a fact. "The *vasill* will be too afraid to speak ill, and the shifter and the witch won't defend one dead vampire."

It's a little disconcerting, the fact that Damien and Bran can just walk into a court and start tearing out hearts with very little consequence.

But I'm grateful for the power, nonetheless. Because I need it. I need them on my side unless I want to be a slave to Julian.

I don't know who—or what I am—but my mother's warning keeps ringing in my head.

The things you did, Jessie...you were only a year old and it terrified me.

What did I do?

Why couldn't she tell me in the letter?

I don't feel powerful. I don't feel terrifying.

And yet...

I can't help but feel like my Pledge is only the beginning of the unraveling of my secrets and the beginning of so many terrifying things to come.

Two

In Bran's bedroom in the Anneliese, I find more clothing hanging in the closet from thick wooden hangers. There are several dresses, a few t-shirts, sweaters, jeans, and leggings. Since we're going to the human court to file paperwork for my Pledge, I decide I better act the part of a respectable mortal and go with a deep crimson dress with a pleated skirt and a white Peter Pan collar.

It's as I'm getting dressed that Bran comes into the room and steals the panties I have sitting out on the bed.

I try to snatch them back, but my speed is no match for his.

I put my hands on my hips. "Is this another test of my obedience?"

He tosses the ball of fabric into the bathroom. "This time it's for my pleasure and nothing more."

A buzzy warmth fills my veins. He scents the air, his eyes burning golden, and then bends down to me and plants a chaste kiss on the corner of my mouth.

Then he turns away.

"Wait...is that it?"

"Did you expect more?" he asks from the door.

"Yes. You just took my underwear. That feels like a promise."

I'm wound up tight, waiting for him to touch me, grab me, slip his hand beneath the dress. But he doesn't, and the ache starts immediately.

"Come, Mouse, we really should be going." His face is blank, but I know him well enough by now to sense he's pleased with himself and my wet desire.

I could put the panties on. Pretend I'm not vexed by this at all.

But the promise of him having easier access to me is enough to make me abandon the idea. And I think he knows that.

I follow him out of the room and down the hall. We find my sister filling the dishwasher and Damien on a call on his cell phone.

He cuts it short when he spots us.

"In and out," he tells Bran. "Let's play our cards right. Don't piss anyone off."

"I take offense to that, brother. I'm a goddamn delight."

I snort beside him. He smiles down at me.

"Don't leave her side," Damien adds.

Bran's tone of voice immediately turns biting. "As if I would."

Damien seems satisfied with this and gives his brother a nod. "Call me if you need me. I can be there quickly."

Bran sets his hand on the small of my back. But before we leave, I look back at my sister. "You'll be all right while I'm gone?"

"Of course." She dries her hands on a plush gray towel. She's looking at me, but I think most of her awareness is on Damien.

"I'll look after her," Damien tells me.

I'm not sure if that's a good or bad thing.

———

My mother worked in the human government until she died and my sister has been in the clerk's office since she was old enough to have a job there. I've been to the court a lot, but never on official business.

Our court isn't as fancy as the vampire court, but it feels imposing anyway with its creaking, wide plank floors that gleam beneath old-fashioned pendant lights.

The main floor houses the clerk's office, the Pledge office, and the county surveyor with a maze of waiting rooms and smaller offices throughout. The second floor has one main courtroom and three smaller ones with several large offices for our mortal judges.

Years ago, I overheard one of the receptionists telling another woman that one of the judges asked out my sister only for him to be turned down. I vividly remember them whispering, "If she'd said yes, I would have worried we'd find the judge staked in his bed the next day!"

At the time I thought it was strange that they were insinuating Julian would have staked a mortal judge because of a date, but now I'm wondering if they maybe knew more about my sister's love life than I did and were gossiping about her involvement with Damien.

I vaguely recall seeing him at the mortal court once in a heated conversation with my sister.

There are all of these little memories that I brushed off at the time, thinking they were nothing.

Would Damien go so far as to kill a mortal for touching my sister?

I think Bran would.

I think his brother might be worse.

Sometimes it's weird to think back on all of the forked paths we ignored, and the others we took.

The Pledge office is at the end of a hallway where arched doors open to an annex. There's a high counter that separates the annex from the rest of the admin.

Alice, one of the assistants, stands at the counter stamping paperwork with vigor.

Thunk. Thunk. Thunk-thunk.

Bran and I enter the annex and Alice looks up and sputters on a greeting.

"Hi Alice," I say, trying to stop her flustering.

"Jessie! Hi! Wow. Hey." She looks at Bran with quick interest, her face burning red before turning back to me. "Is it time for your Pledge already?" She trails off in a nervous giggle.

"Yep. Can you help me get started?"

"Of course." She sets the stamp down and grabs a few sheets of paper and a pen. "Come this way. I'll put you in one of the consultation rooms and a Pledge Clerk will be with you shortly."

She leads us down another hall of closed doors and shows us into room #3.

"Go ahead and get started on that paperwork. I'll have a clerk in soon."

"Thanks."

The door clicks shut behind us a little too loudly.

I sit at the table in the center of the room while Bran circles it with interest.

"What are you doing?"

"Looking for cameras or microphones."

"Seriously? I don't think the mortal court has a budget for that."

"Better to be sure."

There are two windows behind me that overlook the nearest side street. Bran stops at one and leans against the casing while I work at the forms.

It's basic information that I've filled out many times before, but now I have to question whether any of it is true. Parents? Not biological. Birthday? Who knows? Ethnicity? No clue.

"Should I even be here?" I ask Bran while marking off several boxes on the form. "I'm technically not human."

"They don't know that. And we're not going to offer it. Not yet, anyway."

"What happens afterward? Like after I'm Pledged? After Rita undoes the binding? There isn't a single fae in Midnight bound to a vampire house. Someone's going to get bent out of shape about it."

"But there's little they can do after the fact."

I finish one form and start on the second.

Bran shifts to the other window.

Fifteen minutes later, I'm finished with the paperwork but the clerk has yet to visit us. "How long is this going to take?" I drop back against the chair. "Do you think they forgot about us?"

Bran's gaze goes distant. "No, they're currently discussing me being here with you."

"Oh, really? Well, if they stopped gossiping, they could speed this up."

Bran comes over, grabs me at the hips and sits me on the edge of the table. "However will we pass the time?"

His hands come to my thighs, fingers slipping in under the hem of my skirt.

"You planned this," I say up to him.

"Not this, exactly, but the ability to touch you whenever I'd like? That I will always be guilty of."

"What are they doing now?" I ask him as he brings his mouth closer to mine.

He listens, then, "Discussing who will take your case." His hand trails higher.

"How long do you think we have?"

Leaning over me, he brings his mouth down on mine, gentle at first, a brush of his lips, a flick of his tongue. It's enough to send a shock of anticipation through me, sinking to a buzz in my clit.

The thought of getting Bran in a waiting room while people are just beyond the door going about their days is exhilarating.

"Sounds like Ed is getting the short stick," Bran says, his mouth still on me, his hands slipping further up my thighs, sending gooseflesh up and down my body. "He's grumbling now."

"Why?" I circle my arms around Bran's neck, urging him closer.

"He's telling the office girls he wants to leave here with his head attached to his neck."

I hook my feet around Bran's legs and my skirt slips up my thighs. I'm so close to being completely bare for him. "You'll behave, won't you?"

He adjusts his grip on me, grabbing my ass and yanking me to the edge of the table. "In what way?"

"No heads will leave their necks."

"Mmm." He kisses me again. "Ed is telling Alice that his wife is making a lasagna and they plan to re-watch *Lord of the Rings*. 'You heard what the Duvals did at the vampire court last night, didn't you? Alice, I can't miss Lord of the Rings! Janet will kill me!'"

I burst out laughing. "I think Ed might be more terrified of his wife than of you."

"Every man knows that to be fact."

"What's that?"

"That if his partner is not happy, then he might as well dig his grave now."

I roll my eyes as his mouth sinks to my neck. "With regular people, maybe, with you? Never. You aren't afraid of me in the slightest."

"On the contrary. I'm terrified of you." And then he nips at my neck, breaking the flesh.

I jolt beneath him from the sharp pain, but he tightens his hold on me and flattens his tongue against the bead of blood.

I breathe a little faster, heart drumming a little harder. "You are not terrified of me."

"I'm terrified of how you make me feel."

"How's that?"

He pulls back, meets my eyes. There's a stain of red on his teeth. "Whole," he answers. "Awake."

"And that scares you?"

"I think I'm more terrified of losing it. And you."

"You won't."

"I won't if I do my job." He runs his tongue over his teeth, swiping away the blood.

"Which is?"

"To protect you. Which circles us back to the original argument. If you are unhappy—or unwell—then I might as well dig my grave."

I reach between us and unbutton his jeans. "We'll be all right." With the zipper down, I slip my hand into his pants and grope him. He growls deep in the base of his chest. "We make a good team."

His eyes close as I put more pressure on his cock. "Indeed we do, Mouse."

"You think you can fuck me in the time we have before Ed comes in?" I pull his cock out, fist him in my hand, and his eyes flare up.

His attention wanders for a split second to the hall beyond our waiting room and then he spins me around and impales me on his cock in one swift motion as he sits in the chair, me on his lap, my back to his chest.

Just as the door clicks open.

I yelp and scramble to climb off him, but he tightens his hold on my hips and says, "Stay put, Mouse."

His cock throbs deep inside of me just as Ed walks in the room.

THREE

A choked sound leaves my throat as Ed stumbles into the room like someone shoved him.

He loosens the knot of his blue tie and says, "Good afternoon, Ms. MacMahon," his voice wobbling on my name.

Ed is a short man with thinning brown hair and black-framed glasses that are threatening to establish dominance over his face.

"Afternoon," I answer, my voice so high-pitched, I'm surprised the windows don't shatter.

Bran's fingers dig into my hips as he buries himself a little deeper inside of me.

"Mr. Duval," Ed says, barely looking at Bran, barely registering that I'm literally sitting on Bran's lap despite the fact there are three other chairs at the table.

"Good afternoon, Edward," Bran says. "How's Janet?"

Ed's face turns red as he pulls out a chair and tumbles into it. "She's fine. Just fine, thank you."

I don't know Ed well, but he's now joining me in the same room where I'm being fucked by a vampire.

My face burns with shame and the shame makes my inner walls

clench. It's dirty and it's wrong and for some reason, it's making me so much wetter.

"I'll try to be brief," Ed says as he shuffles some papers in his hands. "For a Pledge register, it's mostly just perfunctory. Dot the T's, cross the I's." He shakes his head. "I mean...not...cross the T—"

"We knew what you meant, Ed," Bran says as he sits forward a little, jostling me just enough that his shaft drags in and out an inch.

A strangled little cry threatens to spill out so I clamp my teeth over my bottom lip.

"You probably know this," Ed says, "but I'm required to inform you that you are free to choose whichever house you'd like to be bound to, though it is within a House's right to deny you. You, too, are free to deny a bid and forgo being bound to a House altogether." He turns a piece of paper around and slides it across the table to me. "If you understand this, please mark this box and sign here."

I carefully, slowly, reach forward for the pen, but Bran is quicker.

"Here, let me," he says, but he flicks the pen across the table and says, "Apologies. Sometimes my vampire speed gets the better of me. Can you grab that, Jessie?"

"Of course," I say through gritted teeth.

Ed's attention is solely on the paperwork as he shuffles and reshuffles like he lost something.

I lean forward but have to stand a little to reach the pen and Bran's cock slides out of me, inch by inch.

Sweat beads on my temple.

This is so fucking dirty.

I snatch the pen and Bran pulls me back down, seating himself fully inside of me. My clit buzzes, not from the friction or the pressure, but the illicit thrill of fucking Bran out in the open, in public, in front of someone.

The head of his cock throbs at my center as he brings his mouth to the shell of my ear and whispers, "Good girl."

I choke on a breath, flushing all over. Bran rocks his hips again, punishing me. I've never felt so *full* of him. I've never felt every little twitch and swell of his cock as acutely as I do now.

Ed frowns at the papers. "Looks like I forgot something."

"Maybe you should go get it," I suggest a little too quickly.

Bran chuckles. I reach down between us and grab his balls and he groans. I'm soaking wet and my juices are slick across him.

I'm losing all sense of decency. I'm about to fuck him with Ed in the room or not in the room. It doesn't really matter.

"It'll just take a second," Ed says.

"Take your time," I say.

Ed shoves the chair back and the legs groan on the hardwood floor. "Be right back."

"Close the door behind you," Bran tells him.

"Right. Of course."

The door clicks shut.

Bran is suddenly moving.

He lifts me off him and lays me back on the table and bunches my skirt around my waist, baring me to him. He teases my clit with the flick of his tongue. I cry out and he clamps his hand over my mouth, snuffing out the sound of my pleasure.

"Be quiet, little mouse," he warns and laps me up.

I moan around his hand, wrapping my fingers around his wrist, holding on for dear life. He's quick with my clit, bringing me so close I'm squirming on the table.

"Not yet, Mouse. I want to feel you on my dick while you come."

I pull his hand away. "Then you better fuck me now."

He lifts me up again and sits me on his lap facing him. I'm needy for his cock, quick to line myself up, my knees on the seat of the chair.

"Fuck. This is...*fuck*."

He pushes inside of me and his eyes brighten, his mouth coated in my pleasure.

"Bounce on my cock," he orders me, so I do, finding a quick rhythm as his hands slip up my thighs, shoving the skirt of my dress aside.

He watches our joining and a new thrill pounds through me.

"Faster, Mouse."

I increase my speed, his grip going to my ass, spreading me wide for him.

"You have about eight seconds to make me come," he tells me, his eyes bright gold in the fading afternoon light. "You think you can?"

I try to catch my breath. "Yes."

"Seven seconds."

I brace myself on the arms of the chair, bouncing faster as he grows harder.

"Six."

My heart is racing in my head, pounding in my chest as my own pleasure stalks through me.

He feels so good. All of it. Every part of him.

"Five." He grits his teeth, bucks his hips. We're pounding together so loudly now, they have to hear it in the office. And the illicit, shameful rush of it has me racing toward my own orgasm.

I'm so frantic for release. Bran's rock hard.

"Four," he says.

"Fill me up, Bran. *Please.*"

I meet his gaze as his jaw flexes, his fangs sharpening.

He stills me against him with a death grip and then—

He growls loudly, spills inside of me, and I reach between us, rubbing my clit with a swirl of two fingers. It's all I need. I hang my head back, moaning at the ceiling as the release sparks through me like a firecracker, hot and fast.

Bran brings a hand up to my throat, fingers circling my neck, driving me back down on him so he can spill the last of his load.

We collapse against one another, panting.

"How many seconds left?" I say, tired and so lost to the ecstasy, I don't really care.

Bran laughs against my neck.

"What?"

"They heard us."

I curl into him, a little delirious. "I should be embarrassed, shouldn't I?"

"I'm not. I'd fuck you in the town square so everyone could watch and know you were mine."

I lean back so I can look him in the face. "That will never happen."

"As you wish, Mouse." He tucks a lock of hair behind my ear. "How about we go out there and hurry this along? Then I'll take you out for a grilled cheese and French fries as a celebratory lunch."

"For fucking you?"

"For filing your paperwork. But if the dirty girl wants to celebrate my cock, I'll let her."

I laugh and lift myself off of him. I spot a box of tissue on a cabinet, but before I can grab one, Bran is in front of me. "You know better, Mouse," he says, a devilish look in his eye.

His hand slips beneath my skirt and he walks me back, pressing me against the wall. "You know better than to clean my cum from your pussy." He dips his thumb inside of me, then brings it up and rubs it across my bottom lip. My tongue flicks out to meet him so I can taste him, taste me.

Then he kisses me, slow and gentle.

When he pulls back, he's smiling.

"What is it?" I ask.

"They're flipping coins now."

I laugh and thread my hand with his. "Come on. Let's put them out of their misery."

We leave the room together, his cum dripping down my thighs.

Four

I'm aware, on a visceral level, that when I walk out of the waiting room in the Pledge office, I am officially marked as Bran's girl in the eyes of the mortals in Midnight.

If there was any doubt before, it's all gone now.

Jessie MacMahon belongs to Bran Duval.

I knew this before now. I know that he loves me. But there's something inherently thrilling about other people knowing it too.

When we reach the annex, we find everyone in the office in a gossip huddle behind the counter. Bran clears his throat and leans a shoulder casually against the door frame, arms crossed over his chest.

Most of the office people scatter like scraps of paper caught in a gust of wind.

Only three remain. Alice and Ed and a dark-haired girl I don't recognize.

Alice won't look me in the face and I can't tell if it's because she's disgusted by me, Bran's whore, or if she thinks of me as some lucky interloper who stumbled her way to a throne. Because whether we admit to it or not, there is a hierarchy in Midnight and being attached to a Duval is like being attached to a king.

I suppose even royal whores hold power in court.

I decide I don't care what Alice thinks of me. I won't be ashamed. In some twisted way, fucking Bran loudly in a government office has secured me a certain level of power I didn't know I wanted or needed.

So, while his cum drips out of me, I take the crown and act the part.

"I got tired of waiting," I tell Alice. "Will someone please get me the right paperwork?"

I swear it's like watching bumper cars at the state fair.

Alice turns around and runs into the dark-haired girl. Ed trips over Alice's foot and lurches backward to catch himself, but he bumps a tray of paperwork and it spills off the back counter, crashing to the floor.

Good god. Is this what it feels like for Bran when he walks into a room?

As Ed picks up the mess of paperwork on the floor, Alice locates what I need and places the forms neatly on the counter. "Sign here. And here. Initial here."

I mark where indicated and finish the last signature. "Good?"

"Yes. All good." She nods excessively.

"Thank you, Alice."

"Of course. Our pleasure."

The dark-haired girl giggles at the word *pleasure*. My gaze only shifts to her because the sound is a contrast from the silence.

But as soon as my eyes land on her, she stiffens and clamps her mouth shut.

A dark flame at the center of me grows a little brighter.

This is *fun*. I like it more than I should.

"Come, Mouse," Bran says and smiles smugly at me. He slips his hand into mine and pulls me away. Once we're in the hall and moving for the exit, he bends down and says beneath his breath, "My ruthless little mouse."

"I wasn't being ruthless."

He holds the door for me and I slip out ahead of him.

The sun has dipped low enough that I can no longer see it over the rooflines of the surrounding buildings and the descending light has painted the sky in soft pastel shades of pink and lavender and orange.

The air smells of summer and possibilities.

"I like you pulling rank," he tells me. "It's fucking sexy."

Heat rises to my cheeks. "Stop it. You're being ridiculous."

He slips his arm around my waist and spins me around, pressing me against the railing on the stairs. "Don't tell me what to do."

"As if I could ever boss you around."

He plants a chaste kiss on the corner of my mouth. "You were getting pretty bossy in that waiting room. 'Fill me up,'" he says, mimicking me and now I'm really and truly blushing.

I decide to roll with it. "Yeah, and you listened to me. So maybe I was wrong. Maybe I can get what I want from you if I'm clever about it."

"Naughty little mouse." He tightens his hold on me, sending butterflies zinging across my chest. I like his hands on me. I like being so close to him that I can see the gold flecks in his irises, the throb of his pupils.

Being close to him means he trusts me, and somehow having his trust is almost as good as having his heart.

"You made your mouse a promise. Do you remember?"

He kisses me again. I'm aware that we have an audience with a few onlookers across the street. And it finally dawns on me that Bran has never engaged in PDA with me. Not on this level.

"Mmmm," he says against my mouth. "Who makes the best grilled cheese in Midnight?"

"Stanley." I don't have to think about it.

"And where does this virtuoso of the grilled cheese wield his spatula?"

I laugh again. Bran brings his hand up, threading his fingers through my hair. "At The Greasy Spoon."

A rumble starts at the base of his throat. "I always thought that was an atrocious name for a diner."

"Nevertheless..."

"To the Greasy Spoon we go then," he says.

———

The diner is close enough to the courthouse that we walk and Bran keeps my hand in his the entire way.

Every time we pass someone on the sidewalk and their gaze strays to our hands, my stomach fills with more butterflies.

The Greasy Spoon is one of those little 1950's diners crammed into the leftover space between a nail salon and a real estate office. It's only big enough for the kitchen, a counter, and narrow booths along the wall.

A neon sign buzzes in the window while rockabilly music plays through the sound system. The floor is black and white checkered, the walls painted pale blue and pink, the counter covered in chrome, and the booths trimmed to match.

I love it here.

"Where were you in the fifties?" I ask Bran as we slide into one of the booths near the front window.

"On a journey of self-discovery."

I snort. "That sounds like bullshit."

He leans back against the booth, spreading his arm over the seat, his bicep straining against the sleeve of his shirt. "Remember the photo you saw in my bedroom? The self-portrait at the cliff? I mentioned it was taken in the fifties."

"Yes. I remember."

"That was taken in the Porcupine Mountains in Michigan. I had never been to Michigan before then. You can live hundreds of years and still not see every corner of the world." His attention darts to the door as a new customer enters, but seemingly satisfied that the man bears no threat, Bran looks back to me. "By the fifties, Duval House was well established in Midnight and I was growing bored with it all. My brother and I have always gotten along, but sometimes his need to control every-thing is insufferable."

A waitress comes over. She's dressed in a bubblegum pink uniform with a white apron tied around her waist. Her name tag says Gertrude, but I know her name is Judy.

"Evening, sugar," she says to me and then gives Bran a side-eyed look frothing with wariness. "It's been a while since I've seen you in here."

I've been coming here so long, Judy and Stanley are like my surro-gate grandparents, always asking how I've been and what I'm up to. They sometimes feed me more than Kelly does.

"It's been a wild few weeks."

Judy looks at Bran again. "I'll bet."

Bran frowns at her, clearly unaccustomed to humans giving him shit. Especially little old ladies. I can't help but smile. "Can I have my usual?" I ask before Bran can get temperamental.

"Of course." Judy slips her pencil into her bun out of respect for Bran because of the whole stake-thing. "And you?"

"Coffee," he answers.

"Coming right up." She darts away, but not out of fear, out of efficiency. Judy may be in her seventies, but I think she could give me a challenge in a foot race. Bran watches her go.

"So... Damien wanted to control everything," I repeat. "What did you want?"

He sits forward and lowers his voice to a sinister octave. "I wanted to corrupt innocent virgins in the Porcupine Mountains."

"You're lying and deflecting."

He collapses back against the booth. "Yes. I am."

"Tell me."

He picks up the wrapped silverware, unfurls the napkin and takes the knife in hand. The metal glints beneath the fluorescent lighting. "My brother has always believed vampires are the superior race and he's always wanted to be in control. It suits him. He does it well. I won't deny that."

None of this surprises me, but it's still massively insulting to hear Damien thinks Kelly is inferior to him because she's mortal. Or is she an exception?

"The Montenaros," Bran goes on, "the House we were turned by, has always ruled by fear. And their belief was that strength lay in likeness. It's why, when we established Midnight, we segregated into houses." He sets the knife down but separates it from the fork and the fork from the spoon. "That's a Montenaro philosophy."

Judy comes over and I'm frustrated by the interruption. She sets down my glass of cola. Bran gets his black coffee, taking the mug in hand.

"Right back with your food, sugar," Judy says and leaves again.

I'm impatient to hear the rest of what Bran has to say. We've been so wrapped up in me and who I am and my Pledge that I haven't had the chance to peel back his layers.

Now that I am, I'm desperate for more, desperate to get to the center of him and see what lies there.

"What do you believe?" I ask.

Steam from the coffee rises between us.

"I think that there is strength in diversity." He turns the mug, focusing on the swirl of the dark liquid inside.

"Like a mixed house?"

"Exactly."

"Why?"

He pauses, looking around the diner as if to reassure himself there's no one worth worrying over. "Because if you can earn the loyalty of the strongest of each house and they come together under one roof..." He picks up the fork, the knife, the spoon. I know what the symbolism means—you possess all of the tools, all of the talents, all of the skills.

"So do it," I blurt.

His eyes narrow.

I reel back, shocked to hear the words come out of my mouth. I hadn't meant to say it. I hadn't meant to insinuate he should abandon his brother and all of the systems in place in Midnight Harbor. Change centuries of tradition and rock the boat so hard, it might threaten to tip.

But now that it's out, I can't take it back, even if it is a little crazy.

And I have to admit, I'm incredibly curious to hear what he has to say about it.

Five

BRAN

I can hear my little mouse's heart beating over the shit music playing through the diner's meager sound system.

I think she thinks she's excited about the prospect of me starting a new house, but I know better.

She's running.

My little mouse has always been running from something.

It's why she wanted to leave Midnight. She didn't fit in and she didn't want to try and it was just easier to leave.

She doesn't think she has a legitimate place in Duval House. But I'm not letting her get off so easy.

I have too much to lose and so much to gain.

She peers up at me with wide eyes.

I love her when she's like this. When she's just a girl full of raw hope.

It makes crushing her that much harder.

"Maybe we could rescind that deal with Julian," she tries. "We could use your lake house as your house and—"

"Mouse."

She's learned to bend to the sound of my voice and she stops rambling immediately.

"I can't leave my brother."

The line of her brow sinks. "But you already have. You did when you moved in next door to me."

"That was always meant to be temporary."

"Don't you want to be out from under your brother's control? You said—"

"I know what I said." I take a drink of the coffee but it's no longer bitingly hot and the tepidness does nothing to hide the bitter taste of the cheap grind.

Mouse takes a breath and organizes her thoughts again. "I think diversifying a house is a good idea and—"

"I obviously agree, but I can't afford to dilute my power by splitting Duval House. It puts us both at risk."

Her dejection tastes almost as bitter as the coffee.

I would give my life to protect her, but we have a much better chance of surviving if I have Damien by my side.

I need my brutal brother.

But I can't be second in rank any longer.

I do need to lead if I'm to shield her from the worst.

"Finish up," I tell her. "I need to speak to Damien."

"Why? What are you going to say?"

"All of the right things."

———

My little mouse is quiet on the ride back to the house. I sense her trepidation growing. She's stuck on a tidal wave, crashing toward a destiny she doesn't want and isn't ready for.

I want to reassure her, but I need to see my brother first. I take her to the Anneliese and deposit her inside so she's safe beyond the threshold. "Stay here. Do not leave."

She crosses her arms over her chest and her tits swell against her shirt. She screws up her tight little mouth. I like it when she acts like a brat. Makes me hard as fuck, makes me want to punish her.

"For how long?" she asks.

"As long as I tell you."

Damien is mid-conversation with Sky when I enter his office.

"Look what the cat dragged in," she says.

I grab the pack of cigarettes from my brother's desk and steal one, then his lighter. The tobacco crackles when I put the cigarette to flame and inhale, the smoke filling my lungs.

"Did you make that transfer?" Damien asks Sky.

"I did. It's in the account now."

He gives her a nod, taps at something on a tablet, then hands it back to her. "Leave us. Shut the door behind you."

"Sure thing." Sky comes over to me and puts her hand on my shoulder. "Is it ironic that the cat dragged in something that smells distinctly like pussy?"

"Don't be vulgar, Sky. It does not become you."

She smiles at me, fangs sharp against her full lips. "Everyone's talking about her, you know."

I take a deep breath before I lose my fucking shit. "Then clearly you're not doing your fucking job."

"I can't stop all gossip."

"Then try harder."

She smirks. "I'll see what I can do."

Fucking Sky. I almost think I need to worry more about her than I do Julian.

When the door clicks shut, Damien says, "She's not wrong, you know." He stands at the bar pouring us each a drink. "Did you really have to fuck her at the human court?"

"That's what they're talking about? That didn't take long."

I'll admit, it was a moment of weakness, fucking that tight pussy out in the open, making her come loudly while everyone was out in the office listening.

My cock grows hard, recounting it in my head. Everything Mouse does, every second she's on my dick makes me hunger for more of her.

Damien hands me a tumbler and I pour half of the bourbon down my throat. The alcohol is a different burn from the cigarette, but a welcomed one just the same.

As the bourbon warms my gut, I push away the thoughts of Mouse and her wet pussy. There will be plenty of time for that.

"She wants me to start my own house," I tell Damien.

That's my opening move. The first right thing to say.

Damien goes rigid. His reaction doesn't register on his face, but I've known my brother long enough to know when he's weighing his options, half of them bad.

I take a long hit from the cigarette and it burns like a wick between my fingers.

"And?" he finally asks. "Are you considering it?"

"Maybe."

His jaw flexes. "Don't condescend to me."

I take another hit. Smoke curls in the light.

"What do you want?" he asks, resigned, as he goes to the balcony doors and pulls them open. "Name your price."

If I wasn't so desperate to protect Jessie, I might have considered her idea. I might have left my brother for good and established my own house, been the king of my own keep. It does hold a certain appeal. Damien has always been the proverbial older brother, too stubborn for his own good.

"Co-Head of House."

His attention cuts to me like a whip. "Absolutely not."

My brother has always been insufferably predictable.

"Then I guess we're leaving." I start for the door and make it barely three steps.

"Wait."

I bury a smile.

It feels a little unconscionable, using Jessie as a bargaining chip, but I knew before I walked into this office that Damien wouldn't want to let her go. He's just as desperate as I am to control her, for different reasons, in different ways.

The difference is I'd die for her.

And Damien wants to control the shiny new toy, the one that glimmers in the light.

"Is that it?" he asks.

I turn back to him. "I think we should revisit the idea of bringing on a few witches."

He snorts.

"Now who condescends?" I counter.

"Why?" he asks.

"Because we're going to need magic. We're not going to understand all of the intricacies of having a fae in our house. And I don't know if you noticed or not, but we're shit at protecting what's ours in the daylight."

He knows I'm right.

He lights his own cigarette and flicks his wrist, snapping the lighter shut with a resounding clack.

"You really think you can find a witch who would leave their house for ours?"

"Half this town would abandon their post to be a Duval."

"Who would you approach first?"

His gears are turning. The chess player has pulled up a chair.

"Bianca."

"Mulligan? Why?"

"She's ambitious."

"She's young."

"Young enough to mold."

"Mmm." He takes another hit and paces out to the balcony. "The shifters will lose their fucking minds if we take on a witch. So will the other vampire houses."

"The other vampires will begin recruiting the day after the news breaks."

He sighs. "You're probably right." He goes to the balcony railing and leans against it looking back to me. "It could be a dangerous move."

"I don't think we have a choice at this point."

He takes a hit, lets the smoke cloud from his mouth before sucking it in through his nose. "You never wanted to lead with me before."

"I never had a reason to want it."

"You're different with her."

"You want to go down that road? You want to rehash all of the stupid decisions you've made for her sister's pussy?"

Damien darts back into the house and stops just a foot from me.

Rage cuts into the fine lines around his mouth. "Careful, little brother." His voice is sinister and dark.

"Then let us both agree to tread carefully when it comes to our MacMahon sisters."

He rakes his teeth over his bottom lip, annoyance plainly written across his face. Damien doesn't want to admit just how much Kelly gets beneath his skin and it pisses him off when I force him to show it.

"Fine," he says and shifts away again, this time for the door. He stops with his hand on the knob. "We'll make the announcement tonight. From this day forward, Duval House is ours, together. Well played, little brother."

Well played, indeed.

Looks like I said all of the right things.

And as much as I like the fantasy of starting my own house with Jessie, my gut is telling me this is the right decision.

In fact, I think it might be the only one we've got.

Six

I sit in front of the mirror in the bathroom in Kelly's room as she pins up my hair in a neat bun. There's to be a celebration tonight at Duval House and Damien is going to announce that Bran will be Co-Head of House.

I know he did it for me.

Even though Bran has the influence and the self-assurance to be a leader, I get the distinct impression he never wanted to bother with it, almost as if the responsibility was beneath him.

But I guess being a co-leader is better than a sole one, as much as I liked the idea of him having his own house.

Maybe that was my own selfishness, wanting to desperately get away from vampires like Sky. She's going to make my life miserable here. As much as Bran promises to shield me and protect me, he can't be with me at all times.

I guess I better learn to deal with it.

Pins hang from the corner of Kelly's mouth as she works her way around the bun. When she plucks one from between her teeth and sinks it into my hair, I notice a new ring shining on her pointer finger. It's thin with a low profile but it's encrusted with several tiny diamonds.

Kelly has always loved her nice things, but I've never seen this piece of jewelry before.

"Where'd you get the new ring?"

Her face immediately pinks and I think I have my answer.

"Damien?"

She keeps working at my hair. Damien must know my sister well if he's gifting her shiny objects. It's literally the interstate to her heart. "If he's giving you gifts, that must be a good sign."

She snorts and then talks around the pins still hanging in her mouth. "Damien is literally a billionaire. This is like pocket change for him."

"Are you exaggerating?"

She shakes her head. "Bran is too, I'm sure."

"How—"

"They've been around a long time and they are both incredibly smart."

I knew they were rich, but *that* rich? Duval House is elegant and luxurious and huge, but the brothers don't act like billionaires.

"Well, regardless of the cost, it's still a gift."

Kelly sighs. "It's just another way for him to mark me as his. Damien has always been extremely possessive. And I maybe—"

She frowns at my hair, but I think she's lost in thought.

"You what?"

She sets the pins on the vanity and they plink against the marble. "Sometimes I push him too far just so he'll show it. I get a perverse sort of satisfaction when he acts all possessive like that. And then we're both pissed off and obsessive and then when we end up in bed—" She meets my gaze, reading my thirst for more. "No. Stop it," she says.

I pretend to be innocent. "So tell me, how long has it been since you've *ended up in his bed*?"

She whacks me on the arm.

"Hey! I could use a distraction and your screwed up love life is exactly what I need. Please."

Folding her arms over her middle, she leans into the vanity. The color of her cheeks flushes a deeper shade of scarlet.

"Kelly?" I coax.

"Okay, fine. While you were gone." The smile that spreads on her face nearly swallows her up.

"Ohhhh, ohhh, sister. Okay. Okay. I thought you were going to say like a few months ago or something or... You have to tell me. Tell me what it was like." Bran is in the main house with Damien as far as I know, so he can't scold me for asking about our siblings' sex life. And I really want to know.

"Damien and I...when we're..." She winces and trails off.

I think it's adorable that my sister is having a hard time getting the dirty details out. Come to think of it, she's never really divulged this kind of thing to me. For a very long time, she's been more parent than sister.

But maybe that can change now.

"Go on." I lean forward.

"When he lets go, and I let go—

"Yes."

"It's—" Her eyes sink closed and her entire body shivers. "It's consuming. Mind-blowing." She lets out a breathy sigh and then, "Okay, listen. I have to tell you this because I have to tell someone. But promise me you won't freak out."

A secret. YES.

"I promise."

"Sometimes he'll tie me to the bed."

I know the shock must register on my face because Kelly pulls back. "Is that weird? I shouldn't have told you. Am I crazy for letting him do that?"

"Um, no. Not at all. Do you like it?"

"Yes." She tilts her head, looks at the floor, her eyes wide, maybe revisiting their last encounter. "I like it a lot."

I feel like I'm relearning who my sister is. How is it that you can live with someone in the same house and yet barely know them? "Then it's not crazy," I say. "You like what you like. As long as you're safe."

She nods. "Before him, I had never done anything like that. Like my sex life had been so vanilla until Damien and I didn't know it could be that way. Like...I don't even know how to describe it." She shivers again. "Sometimes when I'm with him, it feels like I leave my body. Like all time and space ceases to exist and there's only him and me and the *euphoria*."

"I know that feeling well."

She smiles over at me. "We may have strapped ourselves to a rocket ship."

"Maybe. But it'll be a wild ride. Has he bitten you?"

"Yes, but it's been a while. When I was with Locke House, we were able to cover our scent with witch charms that we got from a Vane witch. But a bite leaves a stronger scent."

I pinch my fingers together and bring it to my mouth. "When Bran bites me—chef's kiss."

She shakes her head and I can tell she's fighting her sister/mom reaction, which is to reprimand me. "I still can't wrap my head around all of this. You being with Bran. Me here at Duval House. How the hell did we get to this place?"

"I don't know but I don't hate it. I just wish Sky didn't hate me so much."

"I heard." Kelly grabs a bottle of hairspray and gestures for me to close my eyes. She blasts my bun with spray. "Damien said if Sky doesn't behave herself, he'll kick her out."

"Seriously? Over me?"

"I don't think you realize how much sway you hold here."

It's hard for me to believe that I'm anything other than the old me. The skin is much harder to shed even though it's peeling off and starting to chaff.

I don't know who I am as this new person and I guess I won't fully know until Rita unbinds me and I find out more about my origins.

"I don't want her to get kicked out," I tell Kelly. "I just wish she'd leave me alone."

"And that is entirely up to her at this point. She'll learn quickly once Damien puts her in her place."

I can't imagine witnessing that.

But not going to lie, I'm kinda looking forward to it.

———

By the time Bran returns to me, I'm a vision of party perfection thanks to Kelly. She finished my hair, then my makeup, and helped me pick out a dress. We decided on an emerald green lacy dress with a silky lining underneath. The scalloped edges of the bodice neckline plunges all the way to my navel and the back is completely bare, making it clear I'm not wearing a bra.

Jimmy let me borrow some jewelry—a set of gold tassel earrings and a tiered gold necklace with a simple star charm on the end. The charm hits at my sternum.

When Bran sees me in our bedroom, he does a double-take and my insides light up like a supernova.

He comes close, slides his hand around to the back of my neck, and draws me into him so he can speak directly at my ear. "You look lovely, Mouse. I'm already fantasizing about all of the things I will do to you in this dress."

I warm beneath him and then pull away so I can look up at him. "First, we celebrate. You deserve that much."

"It's not as special as you're making it out to seem."

"Bullshit."

He tilts his head down, narrows his eyes. "Careful, little mouse. I'm not above making the party wait for me."

I breathe out and grin. "So you can fuck me?"

He drags his thumb over my bottom lip. "So I can punish this smart mouth. Give me an excuse. Any one will do."

His touch turns punishing as his fingers trail down to my chin, forcing me to turn, exposing my neck.

My breath quickens, heart thumping loudly.

And then a knock sounds on the door and Bran groans. "It's Jimmy," he tells me even though the door is closed and there's no way for him to see through it.

He darts over to it and whips it open. "You have impeccable timing, Jimmy."

"If you're going to be Head of House, you'll have to get used to everyone always needing something from you."

The line of Bran's shoulders rises with a deep, exasperated breath. "I detest it when you make points I can't argue."

"I'm glad to be of service." She nods at me. "You look beautiful, Jessie."

My face is probably still flushed. I'm sure she heard us. "Thanks, Jimmy. You too. That dress is amazing."

She's left her hair natural and the curls spring with her movements. Her gauzy gold dress looks gorgeous against her dark skin. Giant emeralds swing from her ears.

"Thank you." She gives us a spin. "It's vintage Chanel."

Bran scowls. "Coco was insufferable."

"You hated her because she was brilliant."

"I hated her because she bought that flat I wanted. Right out from beneath me."

Jimmy rolls her eyes. "Ignore him. He collects real estate and when he loses out on it, he gets grumpy."

"When isn't he grumpy?" I counter.

"Also another excellent point." Jimmy smiles innocently at Bran.

"I can see the two of you together might very well be the death of my last nerve," he says.

"And how we will delight in it." Jimmy waves us on. "Now hurry up. You both are the guests of honor tonight and the party is waiting for you. Chop-chop." She disappears from the doorway.

Bran winds his arm around my waist, drawing me to his hip. "Stay by my side tonight," he tells me. "And if you're a good girl, maybe I'll treat you like a bad one after."

I try to pretend like that doesn't sound like the best night ever.

Seven

The party is being held in the ballroom because *of course* Duval House has a ballroom.

A dozen chandeliers hang from the soaring ceiling, their crystals glittering in the light. Round tables dot the perimeter of the room while a raised dais to the left of the entrance holds a full band. People have coupled off to dance in unison in a way that reminds me of all of the Regency romance movies Mom used to watch when I was a kid.

Over the years, I've attended a few Locke House vampire parties, but nothing like this. Nothing that was planned at the last minute and somehow turned out like an event that was planned by a team for a year.

Bran leads me across the room and the crowd parts for us, the others bowing or bending their heads to him as he passes. He ignores them.

We come to a private table where Damien sits at the head. Jimmy is there too with a few other vampires that I recognize but whose names escape me.

"Late, as usual," Damien says, his tone scolding.

"Sorry, brother. But you know what they say about those who are chronically late."

"No, I don't think I do. Enlighten me."

"They don't give a shit."

Damien scowls. Jimmy curls her hand over her mouth trying to hide a laugh and Damien turns his displeasure on her.

"Oh, don't give me that look," Jimmy says, the laughter still trilling in her voice. "It's funny because it's true."

"Yes, well, if he's going to be Head of House and you're going to be second in line, then you both need to act the part."

Bran and Jimmy share a look like, *can you believe this guy?*

I don't know if I'll ever be able to penetrate the tight-knit relationship the three of them share, but I hope I can find a place on the edge at the very least.

There's something to envy about what they have and it immediately makes me miss Sam.

It feels like a year since I spoke to her last.

"Let's get the fun part over with," Damien says and rises from the table. "Come to the dais."

Bran looks at me. His hand is still at the small of my back, very clearly an act of possession, and it makes me flush inside and out.

"I won't be long," he says to me.

"I'll be okay."

"Behave," he warns me, with a glint in his eyes.

Some distant, dark thought comes to mind that if I don't, he'll punish me for it, and he's been oh-so-clever with his punishments.

"Mouse," he says, nostrils flaring, a rumble in his voice.

He can smell me, smell the first hint of my desire.

"Sorry," I say. But am I?

And then, in the middle of a Duval party with literally everyone in attendance, he kisses me on the forehead.

It's a simple act but it speaks a thousand words.

Together, Bran, Damien, and Jimmy make their way across the ballroom. If the crowd parted for Bran, it practically gets to its knees for the three of them together.

Because I had always been dead set on leaving Midnight, I never paid careful attention to the vampire politics and the hierarchy.

I never realized just how powerful these three are.

Like the sun and the moon and the earth. Everything and everyone has to bend to them.

Julian never commanded a room like this.

When they reach the stage, the band lets their current song fade out and the room quickly falls to silence.

Damien takes the lead while Bran stands on his right and Jimmy on his left.

They are a sight to behold. Damien and Bran look ridiculously handsome standing next to one another in their dark designer suits, and it's easy to see them as brothers. Jimmy radiates power and energy and dazzles in her dress.

And in this moment, I am ridiculously grateful to be where I am. I want to be a part of their group. I want to command a room with them.

I've never hungered for significance...until now.

"Thank you all for gathering here tonight on such short notice," Damien says, his voice booming across the room. "We have an announcement to make."

Excited energy breezes through the crowd.

"As you all know, my brother and I helped found Midnight Harbor and this house wouldn't be what it is today without him. So I'm pleased to announce that Bran and I will now lead Duval House together as Co-Heads of House and Jimena will assume the role as second-in-command."

The crowd comes to life with applause.

When it dies down again, Damien adds, "And as many of you are aware, we've welcomed two new members to our house."

Oh shit.

The crowd's attention starts to wander, half of it landing on me, the other half finding Kelly by the bar.

Now I wish I would have gone to her earlier so I wouldn't be standing here like a butterfly pinned to a board.

I distinctly feel like I'm on display.

"I know many of you have wondered why we have a Locke human within our house. All you need to know as of right now is that Kelly MacMahon is under our protection, and tomorrow, at her Pledging, Duval House will bid on Jessie."

My face warms beneath the attention as the whispers start.

"Like Kelly, Jessie is under our protection. And if I catch any of you trying to haze her, you can expect a private meeting with me. Do we understand one another?"

The crowd quickly murmurs its agreement.

"Now that business is done," Damien says, "carry on with your celebrations and be responsible with your blood drinking."

The vampires hoot and whistle as their Pledged humans prepare for a night of being human juice boxes.

I hover by the abandoned table waiting for Bran to return to me, but as he leaves the dais, he's cornered by Sky.

My insides immediately clench up.

She gets in close to his side and leans in to whisper something to him, her hand on his arm. He laughs at whatever it is.

My chest tightens as a cold sweat prickles down my arms. Has he only been pretending to be indifferent to Sky?

There is a voice in the dark depths of my mind that says: *Get back at him.*

I scan the crowd for a familiar face and spot Lance, the vampire valet who parked the Bimmer the first time I came here with Bran.

"Lance!" I practically shout. "How are you?"

He's mid-drink of a glass of blood and nearly chokes on it when I sidle up to him.

"Me?" He looks behind him.

"Yes, you. Is there another Lance here?"

Lance isn't a bad looking guy. I'm not exactly sure what his story is, but I don't think he's one of the older vampires, otherwise he wouldn't be a valet.

"I needed a friendly, handsome face," I tell him. "Can you be my friendly, handsome face, Lance?"

"Ummm..." He clutches at his glass, hand shaking. "I'm not so sure—"

I bat my eyelashes up at him, smile as brightly as I can, and put my hand on his arm, just like Sky did with Bran. Honestly, coming over here I just wanted to make Bran jealous, but now that Lance is bumbling beneath my attention, there is a bright flare of pride igniting at the center of me.

If I have this kind of power, what else can I do with it?

"How long have you been at Duval House?" I ask him, and sip from my drink, elongating my neck as I tip my head back. His eyes immediately zero in on the pulsing artery in my throat.

"1983," he answers. "I was twenty-six at the time."

"So that makes you..."

"Sixty-five. I'm sixty-five years old."

He could be a grandfather right now if his life had turned out differently.

I look back toward the dais and find Sky still talking to Bran, but he's not looking at her. He's looking at me. And his eyes are bright, burning gold.

The thrill intensifies and my clit pulses.

Oh fuck.

The absolute satisfaction I'm getting out of this is so fucking wrong. But...

Lance follows my line of sight. "Oh shit. Bran," he says, even though we're a football-field apart and the room is full of the cacophony of the party. "I'm sorry. We were just talking."

My heart beats harder.

And in the next blink, Bran is gone.

Lance yelps and darts away.

Goosebumps erupt on my skin as that dark flame burns brighter.

He's going to come for me.

I turn around and run.

———

I'm like a child that's just lit a bomb.

And now I'm running away, both terrified and giddy, waiting for it to go off.

There are three side doors to the ballroom and I take the closest one to me. The hallway is empty beyond and the lighting is low with just a few hanging pendant lights sending a halo of golden glow over the polished hardwood floors.

The sound of the party fades behind me as my heart hammers in my head.

When I turn down the next corner, a hand lashes out, grabs me by the arm, and yanks me into a darkened room.

I know it's Bran the second I inhale. There's no mistaking his scent—the sweetness of amber, the richness of leather.

He has me pressed against the wall in no time at all, and I let out a little moan.

"I told you to be a good girl tonight." His voice is hoarse and edged with a sinister rumble. "It's like you want to be punished."

I clench up, clit throbbing. I'm wearing panties tonight, but the fabric is already soaked.

"Am I not allowed to talk to other guys?" I ask.

"Am I not allowed to talk to other girls?"

"*Touché.*"

He smiles. "Do you know the origins of that word?"

I wiggle beneath him. He tightens his grip on me, pressing closer. "I can't say that I do."

"It's French," he says, "and it means *to touch.*"

My heart kicks up. Bran takes in a deep, satisfying breath.

"Oh, little mouse, you thought you could play me, did you? Manipulate me into punishing that pussy."

I lay my head back against the wall, exposing my throat. The tingling sensation between my legs is so intense now, I squeeze my thighs together trying to hold it at bay.

When is he going to touch me? When will he end the torture?

"Is that so wrong?" I ask him.

He laughs, low and beneath his breath, and then reaches into his pocket and pulls out a black teardrop-shaped object. He holds it up by its flat bottom.

"Open up, Mouse."

"What—"

He shoves it past my lips. It's cool to the touch with layered petals around the head, almost like a rose.

I watch him as he fucks my mouth with it, slow and steady, and then he pulls it out fast, making my lips pop.

"What is that for?"

He kicks my legs apart, reaches beneath my dress, shoves aside my panties, and slides it into my pussy.

I exhale in a rush, surprised by its use and shocked at how much wetter I already am because of it.

In his other hand, he holds up a remote.

I don't think I need an explanation for that.

He presses a button and the plug buzzes deep inside of me.

The moan that escapes my throat is both shrill and lacking oxygen.

"Before the little mouse decided to play games, she should have asked herself what the rules were."

He presses the button again and the vibration shifts rhythm and my clit throbs harder.

"Bran," I say, gulping down air.

He wraps his hand around my throat and kisses me gently, then nips at my bottom lip.

"Okay, I give in," I say. I want more than this. I want his hands on me. I want him inside of me.

My clit is swollen and needy and without thinking, I reach between my legs, desperate to rub myself.

But Bran snags my wrist and tsk-tsks. "Come on, Mouse. We have a party to attend."

"Wait."

"No."

I wanted him to bend me over a desk and fuck me. Or throw me on a fainting couch and punish me with his cock. Not this prolonged torture.

Wrapping his hand around the back of my neck, he steers me like an animal from the room, the plug still buzzing.

I'm finding it more difficult to walk the more the pleasure builds. The layers on the plug cause friction with every step and the vibration pulses from my clit to my ass.

Fuck, I'm about to go rabid.

"Bran, please."

When we reach the ballroom again, Bran stops me at the threshold and says at my ear, "Before the little mouse decided to play games, she should have asked herself if she knew how to win."

Then he pushes me into the ballroom.

Eight

BRAN

Hitting the OFF button for the plug, I give the little mouse a break as she stumbles through the party.

She holds herself up on the back of a chair and sucks in a deep breath.

Her cheeks are flushed.

I'm going to fuck her hard later, make her scream my name.

But not yet.

I am a patient man. I think she forgets that.

My little mouse is always too eager to plot how she'll win.

Once upon a time I warned her not to play games with me, but I think I'm eating my words.

I'm enjoying this far too much.

Taking a deep breath, Mouse straightens, smoothing down the front of her dress. I know she's drenched and thinking about her soaked panties has me so fucking hard, it hurts.

I track her through the party as she nears the bar a little unsteady on her feet.

The band switches music and plays Handel's Water Music Suite No. 2 just as three vampires approach. One of them says, "Bran, can we tell you—"

"No."

I grab a tumbler of scotch from a passing waiter and sling back half of it.

Mouse catches my eye. More blood paints her cheeks and my fangs sharpen.

"Sorry," the vampire says, "but maybe we can—"

"No," I say again and finally look at them.

I don't recognize their faces. Damien has always been more interested in knowing everyone's name. Where they came from, what their story is. Damien is devious like that. He knows he can use even the lower-level vampire to his advantage someday. But I'm not mining coal here.

I just want the gold.

That's why I've focused more of my attention on making the right friends in the right houses.

"Bran," Jimmy says as she sidles up next to me and hooks her arm through mine. "The boys wanted to share something they overheard. Perhaps hear them out?"

I watch Mouse for another second as she orders a whiskey neat, tilting her head so she can hear the bartender over the rise of the music.

Fuck, if everything she does makes me this hard, we're going to spend the rest of our lives in our bed.

Our bed.

The thought catches me off guard.

Our bed?

It's decidedly *my* bed. I bought it.

But I want her in it. Always. It will become her bed too.

It's the little things like this that I am unprepared for, the minute details of loving something that you don't want to break.

I'll buy her a dozen beds. I'll fuck her and love her in all of them.

But first I need to torture her.

"Bran?" Jimmy says.

I finally meet her eyes. She's annoyed with me. Maybe she has a right to be. I just manipulated my brother into giving me Co-Head of House and I'm already bored with its duties.

"Listen," she says, and pinches my arm with a nasty little grit to her teeth. "*Please.*"

I sigh. "What is it?"

The vampire on the far-left bumbles over his words. "I don't know if you know this or not or maybe you do but—"

"If I knew it, then why would you be here telling me?"

"Right. Right. Of course."

"Spit it out. Contrary to what you may think, I have better things to do."

Like fuck my mouse senseless.

Across the ballroom, Mouse gets her drink—in record time too, now that she's princess of the house—and she takes a long pull from it, breasts swelling at the lacy collar of her dress.

I press the remote again and she chokes on the drink, clamping her hand over her mouth to keep from spitting it out.

She glares at me across the room and a sick little flare of pleasure lights in my chest.

It's a reminder that I control her pleasure. Her pussy belongs to me.

The vampire tries again. "I was turned about a decade back so I still have family around here. My dad works at the guard station and he overheard the chief talking to Cal about Jessie's Pledging tomorrow."

That gets my attention.

"In what regard?"

"Cal is planning on coming."

The Alpha of the Midnight Pack is going to attend a routine Pledging?

Even if the pack wanted to bid on Jessie, they wouldn't send the Alpha to do it.

"Did your father say why?"

The boy looks sheepish as his friends fidget by his side.

"I don't have all night, kid."

"It's Julian, I think," the kid says. "It sounded like the chief and Cal were discussing Julian planning something big at Jessie's Pledge."

Of course he is. This part isn't surprising. It's the Alpha caring that is.

"Thank you for telling me," I say.

The kid gulps and nods. "Y-you're welcome."

"Now get the fuck out of here."

They're gone in a second.

When I look back at Jimmy, she's frowning at me.

"What?" I say. "Don't start."

"You can't be Head of House and be an asshole."

"Yes, I can. Damien does it every day."

"Damien isn't obvious about it, though, which is why people respect *and* fear him."

I grumble. "I don't need their respect, Jim. Just the fear."

I hit the remote again and Mouse takes a heavy breath. She's collapsed in a chair now, panting.

I can just imagine how wet her pussy is, how swollen her clit must be.

"So what do you plan to do about it?" Jimmy asks.

"About what?"

"Jessie? Her Pledging? Julian?"

Good question.

"I'll talk to Damien about it later. In the meantime, can you get me a meeting with Bianca Mulligan before tomorrow?"

"The witch?"

"Yes."

Jimmy shrugs. "Maybe? What do I tell her?"

"Ask her if she's open to new opportunities and see what she says."

Taking a step back, Jimmy crosses her arms over her chest and regards me with her cool indifference. "You got Damien to agree to expand the house, didn't you?"

I smile at her. "You know I always get what I want."

"Mmm. Sometimes at the expense of everything else."

"Set it up." I start to walk away.

"I'm not your assistant," she says.

I stop and give her my most innocent smile. "Please, Jimmy? My dearest, oldest, best friend? Will you set up a meeting with Bianca?"

She rolls her eyes and her earrings swing from her ears. "Fine. But we're getting you an assistant. I don't have time to do your errands."

"I don't want an assistant," I call over my shoulder.

"Too bad!"

Mouse has her eyes closed and she's slouched in one of the chairs at an empty table.

I hit the button again and her eyes pop open.

I disappear into the crowd.

She looks for me and when she doesn't find me, she bolts from the room again.

Naughty little mouse.

I'm not sure if she's running from me or trying to provoke me into chasing her again.

Either way, it doesn't really matter.

I love the hunt.

I love the sound of her rapid heartbeat and the blood rushing through her veins.

She won't get far.

Little mice never do.

————

I catch her halfway between the ballroom and the French doors that lead to the courtyard.

It's easy to wind my arm around her waist and haul her into the nearest office.

She's breathless, forehead a little clammy, heart rate accelerated.

I spin her and press her against the closed door.

"Bran," she moans and fuck if I'm not hard all over again.

My name on her lips is a sin I will not repent.

Iron sconces are lit in the office and the soft light burnishes Mouse in gold.

She is a dream.

She's more than I deserve.

Blood pounds through her veins and I salivate at the thought of sinking my fangs in her while I fuck her hard.

The plug is still buzzing and with my cock pressed against her, I can feel the soft vibration of it in my balls.

"Take it out," she begs. "And fuck me."

I had planned on it, but now I have other thoughts.

Darker thoughts.

"No," I tell her.

She mewls beneath me. "Have I not suffered enough?"

I run my thumb down her cheek, dragging it roughly over the corner of her mouth. Her tongue darts out to meet me.

The air is overwhelmed by the scent of her desire and I am overwhelmed by her.

Her thighs rub together as the plug continues to buzz.

There is a sensation in my chest and deep in my gut, something I cannot contain when Mouse is like this, when she's desperate for me to fill her up.

If she knew what she did to me, she would play games with me all day long.

I am powerless against her.

"Bran," she says again.

"Yes, Mouse?" I kiss at the corner of her mouth and she wiggles beneath me, her hands coming to my hips to drag me closer. I grind against her, so fucking hard, I want to pound her pretty pussy until she can't breathe.

"Fuck me. Now." Her words are a whisper against my lips.

I can't take it anymore.

"Try that again," I order.

"Fuck me, please?"

Fucking finally.

I pull her to the desk. It's bare save for a pen holder, an armillary sphere, a few leather-bound books.

"Hands on the desk," I tell her.

She curls her grip around the opposite edge.

"Don't let go."

She pants out an agreement when I relieve her of her panties and shove her dress up around her waist.

Bare for me, I push her head down, pull her ass up.

Fuck if she isn't glorious.

"You've made a mess of that plug, Mouse."

She moans. I hit the remote again and change the tempo of the vibration. She gasps out in delight.

"I thought you were going to fuck me," she says around several gulping breaths.

"I am."

I spit on her ass and it glistens in the light.

"Both holes will be filled up tonight, Mouse."

And then I shove my cock in her ass.

Nine

I THINK THE MOST SUBLIME PART ABOUT BEING A VAMPIRE'S girlfriend is that Bran has been around for centuries and knows all of the devious ways to make me feel vile and wicked.

And oh how vile and wicked I feel being bent over a desk with the plug inside of me and Bran in my ass.

I gasp out as he pushes in and accidentally let go of the desk as the sensation takes me by surprise.

"Mouse," he warns, "what'd I tell you? Hands on the desk."

Goosebumps roll up my arms as I resume my position like a dutiful little mouse.

"Good girl," he says and then shoves back into me.

It hurts at first as my body automatically tenses up, but then when I take a deep breath and settle into the sensation, I realize being filled up, *really* filled up, is fucking nirvana.

And when Bran is fully inside of me, it forces the plug forward so that it buzzes against my clit.

I don't even have to touch myself and I'm already *this close*.

I'm throbbing and so fucking wet and Bran's hands on my hips sends a flare through my belly.

Every time he slides into me, fingers bruising my flesh, it feels like him claiming me all over again.

Mine.

Mine.

Mine.

Fuck, I'm so close.

My clit rubs against the edge of the desk as Bran slows his tempo, savoring the feel of me wrapped around him.

"My little mouse," he says, sliding a hand up to the back of my neck, to the back of my head, pressing my face against the desk. "Taking your punishment like a good girl."

I pant out as the plug buzzing in my pussy meets the buzzing in my clit.

"Oh god," I say, knuckles white as I hold onto the desk.

"Your ass is so fucking tight, Mouse." He leans into me and curls his hand in my hair, pulling on it, forcing my back to arch, my ass to push into him and he claims me harder, faster, the desk sliding over the hardwood floor with each thrust.

The pressure builds in my clit as the plug buzzes against my inner walls.

"I want you to come while I fill up your ass," Bran orders.

I exhale in a rush, words failing me.

"Mouse," Bran says sharply.

"Okay."

He thrusts forward. The desk groans, the legs scraping forward another inch. I keep holding on.

The wave builds. Butterflies fill my stomach and sink to my clit.

Bran pounds into me, forcing the vibrating plug to rub against the front of my inner wall.

The sensation lights me up and suddenly I'm hot all over and moaning loudly against the desk.

Bran picks up his tempo.

The orgasm rushes through me, blinking through every muscle and nerve.

I clench up. Suck in a breath.

The wave rushes out.

The air gets stuck in my throat and then Bran buries himself deep and lets out a guttural groan and the plug rocks against me and a second orgasm comes out of nowhere, pulsing through me.

It's like my body is exploding with pleasure, like my nerves have turned to firecrackers, the blood in my veins to honey.

I can't contain it.

Can't control it.

I hold onto the desk with everything I have as my legs tremble and the wave turns into a tidal wave and I scream out.

"Oh fuck! Oh my god! Bran!"

He wraps his hand around my throat, yanks me back, pulls down the front of my dress and sinks his fangs into the curve of my neck.

Sparks light up behind my eyes. Instinctively I try to pull away, but Bran tightens his grip and pushes his cock in further, spilling more cum as he sucks the blood from my neck.

My body turns into a kaleidoscope. Full of color and wonder and spark.

Bran pulls us upright and his hand sinks between my legs, holding me as if he can feel the pleasure just by touching my clit.

I jolt, still overly sensitive. He pulls more blood from my veins.

The room spins.

Bran rides me as the pleasure ebbs out, his other hand still firmly wrapped around my throat.

He pulls his fangs out first but leaves his cock in my ass.

"You took your punishment well, Mouse," he says, his voice ragged, his breath hot on my bare shoulder.

Several beads of blood well in the puncture wounds and he dips down, lapping them up with a soft swipe of his tongue.

I shiver. "That was amazing. I've never come twice before. I didn't think that was possible."

"When I'm done with you, Mouse, you'll be coming a dozen times." He pulls out and steps back and I immediately lose my footing, I'm shaking so badly.

Bran scoops me up before I hit the floor and cradles me in his arms. "Jessie?" There's blood on his lips, fire in his eyes.

"I'm okay. Set me down."

"I will not." He carries me over to a leather chair and sits with me, cradling me in his arms. He shuts off the plug. "Open your legs."

I pry my knees apart, thighs quivering, body still jolting through the aftershocks, as he reaches down, and gently takes the plug out. It glistens in the golden light. Bran drags his tongue over the petals.

"Fuck, Mouse," he says, his eyes burning again. "You taste so fucking good."

Another tingle rocks through me making my toes curl. Bran sets the plug aside and tucks me closer.

"I'm going to put you to bed," he says, his mouth at my temple. "Clearly that was too much for you."

I laugh against him and snuggle into his chest. "No, it wasn't. It was just enough."

"Did you learn your lesson?"

I tip my head back to look up at him. He's mopped up the blood, but his lips are still stained red. "If you're asking if I've learned my lesson not to provoke you, the answer is absolutely not. That was incredible."

"Mouse." His voice is edged in warning.

"I made my life choices. I'm not going to regret them."

He sighs and runs his fingers through my hair. "You will be my undoing."

"I'm just getting closer to your gooey center."

"Never say that again."

"I know the truth."

"*Mouse.*"

I smile against his chest, close my eyes and drink in the scent of him, knowing damn well that whatever version of Bran I get, it's not the same as what other people get.

He may fuck me into oblivion, but being snuggled in his arms, surrounded by the strength and solidity of his grip, is enough to tell me I get the very best version.

———

We stay there for several minutes before Bran rouses me.

"Let me take you to bed."

"Fine." I *am* sleepy. And my legs are still a little wobbly.

When I get to my feet, I can feel cum leaking out of me, but of course I don't clean up. I know better.

Bran threads his fingers with mine and pulls me into the hallway.

And we run right into Sky.

Almost like she was waiting for us.

"Well," she says, eyebrow arching as she takes in the sight of me a little disheveled, "I think the entire house might have heard that."

My face pinks.

"Didn't know you had it in you, Jessie," she adds.

Bran goes rigid, drops my hand, and closes the gap between him and Sky. She backpedals and slams into the opposite wall, but there's laughter in her voice.

"It must just kill you," he says down to her.

She curls her mouth. "What's that?"

"The fact that you had me for a century, but never had my love. It took Jessie barely any time at all."

Holyyyyy shitttt.

He did not just say that!

I clamp my hand over my mouth to hide the smile that involuntarily spreads across my face.

I don't want to gloat, but...*holy shit.*

What was it Bran said to me earlier?

Before the little mouse decided to play games, she should have asked herself if she knew how to win.

Bran loves me and he's not afraid to tell everyone he does and somehow *that* feels like winning.

Sky glares up at Bran. "You'll break her eventually," she says. "Like you break everything you love."

Bran's shoulders rock back and the air grows charged.

I don't have to be a mind reader to sense his thoughts have gone dark.

I don't know if it's bravery or stupidity, but I step between them. "What do you want, Sky?"

She crosses her arms over her chest. "Damien wants you," she tells Bran.

"For what?"

"The Alpha of the Midnight Pack just showed up on our doorstep asking to see you and Damien."

I glance at Bran over my shoulder. "Were we expecting Cal?"

I know Bran much better than I did a month ago and the look on his face is the look of a secret.

"Bran," I say again. There should be no secrets between us. He promised me.

"We weren't expecting Cal. Not exactly," he admits.

"What does that mean?"

"He knows something about your Pledge tomorrow. Something about Julian."

Sky pushes away from us and starts down the hall. "Apparently, the Alpha has a psychic on his payroll and the psychic had a vision," she says as she walks away. "It's smart, really, if you can find a legit psychic. Most are charlatans."

"Did he say what the vision was?" I ask.

"Just that Kelly is going to die."

TEN

Sky's declaration is like a bomb going off.

"What?" I shout and my voice echoes down the hallway. "Bran? *No*. We can't—"

He grabs me to pull me to a stop. "Look at me."

My heart is racing and my body is numb with panic.

"Mouse."

I meet his eyes.

"Your sister is under the protection of Duval House." His face hardens. "*I* will protect her. Do you hear me?"

I swallow and nod.

"And Damien would sooner light himself on fire than let something happen to Kelly."

"*Really?*"

"Yes," Bran says. "You have me and you have my brother and nothing is going to happen to you or your sister."

That helps calm me down a little. I know that when it comes down to it, Bran and Damien are the ones you'd want at your back.

I know that, but I can't shake the bad feeling in my stomach.

My Pledge is an impending doomsday, apparently. I no longer want to leave Midnight, but I suddenly don't want tomorrow to come either.

"Come on." Bran takes my hand and pulls me down the hall. Sky is already gone. She dropped the bomb and quickly dodged its destruction.

Bran leads me through the maze of Duval House. We don't return to the party. Instead we cross through the foyer, go down another hallway, then another, and enter a large office. It's rich and masculine and smells like tobacco and liquor and dark forests.

Damien is at the bar pouring bourbon.

And the Alpha of the Midnight Pack is sitting in one of the leather club chairs looking sorely out of place.

I've rarely crossed paths with Cal and now I've been in the same room with him twice in a month.

He stands when we come in. He's the tallest in the room and that's saying something because Bran and Damien are tall on their own.

Cal is all muscle and raw power. If the Duvals are a hurricane, then Cal is a landslide.

He could easily bury you before you could take a full breath.

Dark jeans, ripped at the knees, cover his muscular thighs and a black t-shirt skims his body in all of the right ways.

The dark Scandinavian tattoos on the side of his scalp somehow look more menacing in this lighting and without an overshirt, his full sleeve tattoo on his left arm is on display.

I chose Bran and I love Bran, but goddamn, Cal is hot.

I swallow hard and Bran wraps his hand around the back of my neck and brings me close, his mouth at my ear. "Careful, little mouse. I will lock you in a room if I must."

Taking a deep breath, I try to drive away any dirty thoughts of what that might entail and focus on the task at hand. Cal is here for business, not to overwhelm me with his raw sexiness.

I pity the girl that gets his heart. She's going to be in so much trouble.

"Jessie," Cal says. "Are you well?"

His question is clearly an interrogation of the Duvals.

Damien comes over with a glass of bourbon and hands it to the

Alpha and says, "You are in my house. Disrespect me and we'll have a problem."

Cal takes the glass, not at all put out by the threat. "Jessie is just a girl caught in the predator's snare. You'll have to excuse me for caring about her well-being."

They both look at me.

They're all looking at me.

I lick my lips and try not to fidget beneath the overwhelming attention of three alpha men.

"I appreciate your concern, Cal, but I'm good. Really."

And also...why does he care?

Cal isn't a man that just does things out of the goodness of his heart. I have heard he is fair and just, but he's also the Alpha. He's got better things to worry about.

"Why are you here?" Damien asks. He goes to his desk and leans against the front edge of it. He takes a long pull from his bourbon and then sets the glass aside. He's still wearing his party clothes but he's left his jacket off, the sleeves of his white Oxford rolled up to his elbows. There's an expensive watch on his wrist that glitters in the light.

"I told you already." Cal sets the bourbon aside without sipping from it. He has on a watch too, but his is chunky black, more rugged than elegant.

That's the difference between these two men. All you need to know you can know by the timepieces they wear.

"A psychic, yes," Damien says. "How is it I'm just hearing about this now?"

"You think I play all of my cards at once?" Cal shakes his head, amused. "You clearly don't know me, Duval."

Bran crosses the room to stand beside his brother. "How accurate is this psychic?"

I go to one of the club chairs and drop into it. All of the energy has been sapped from my body. Because of that out-of-this-world sex and the immediate panic that came after it.

"Well," Cal says as he eyes Damien, "the psychic knows you're fucking a Locke blood bag."

Damien goes rigid. Bran lashes out and puts his hand on his brother's arm, anchoring him.

"Cal," I say. "That's my sister you're talking about."

His face softens. "Of course. Please accept my apology."

I catch a barely perceptible uptick in Bran's expression.

Something weird is happening here and we're both picking up on it.

The Alpha is giving me considerable leeway.

"Why are you here?" Damien repeats.

"I have information about Jessie's Pledging tomorrow. Specifics about what may go down there."

"Why give us this?" Bran folds his arms over his chest. "What's in it for you?"

Cal's hands are loose fists at his side, but when he looks at me again, his thumb rubs back and forth over the inside of his fingers like he's thinking hard on what to say and how to say it, like maybe he doesn't want to say anything at all, but knows he has to.

"Someday I'm going to need a favor from Jessie," he says.

"Me?"

"What favor?" Bran asks.

"I can't tell you that."

"Bullshit. You can't? You mean you won't."

Damien's gaze cuts to me. Immediately my skin tingles. I don't know how my sister handles his attention. I want to crawl beneath the chair when he looks at me. His dark brow pulls together like he's trying to cut beneath my layers and figure me out.

"If you can't tell us," Bran says, "then we don't know the cost and if we don't know the cost, we don't know if there's equity in the exchange."

God, it's sexy when he talks like that.

I had no idea intelligence could be such an aphrodisiac. I'm coming to the realization that Bran's allure isn't just the vampire strength, the control in the bedroom, or the power of being a Duval.

It's all of those things, and the constant mental chess he plays.

I like being caught in that snare sometimes. I like it very, very much.

Like the plug, the sex, being filled up—

All three of the men take in a deep breath and look at me.

"Jessie," Bran says. His irises light up.

"Sorry." Heat rushes to my cheeks.

Gelatin cake. FUCKING GELATIN CAKE.

Cal trembles.

Bran pushes away from the desk and straightens his spine, leveling his shoulders. "Careful, Alpha."

Cal's jaw clenches. "Contrary to what you may think about shifters, it isn't the full moon that sends us off kilter. It's the absence of the moon. I'm on edge, but I have it handled."

"I don't care if it's the cosmic equivalent of Armageddon," Bran says and points a finger at me. "That one is mine. Not yours."

Cal growls. "I know that."

I want to turn into a puddle and slip from the room.

Good god.

I might have to ask my sister if she has any more of those Vane witch charms, the ones that guarded her scent. I could use about fifty.

Cal settles and some of the tension ebbs from Bran's body. Bran rests against the desk again and says, "Regarding this favor, the answer is no."

"I can appreciate the chivalry. You Duval brothers trying to protect Jessie from the big bad Alpha. But Jessie owes you nothing. She isn't Pledged yet. Which means she can make the decision on her own." The Alpha turns to me. "What is *your* answer, Jessie?"

I lick my lips and then worry at the corner with a drag of my teeth.

There is something I admire and respect about Cal. I don't think he'd screw me over. Maybe Damien and Bran, but not me.

After all, when he witnessed Sasha bite me all those years ago, he went to my mother because it was the fair and respectful thing to do.

But beyond all that, if my sister's safety is on the line, I'll give him pretty much anything he wants.

"Think about this carefully," Damien warns.

"You need this information as much as I do. Unless you're okay with something happening to my sister?"

Damien's jaw flexes, teeth grinding together.

"That's what I thought." I get up, legs still a little wobbly. "You have a deal, Cal." I hold out my hand.

The Duvals don't contradict me, but I can tell neither of them is happy about this.

Cal comes over and slides his hand into mine. His skin is much softer than I'd expect an Alpha's to be. But his grip is strong and my hand is nearly lost in his.

"Now tell us what you know," I say.

———

"Midnight has been ready for a shake up for a very long time," Cal says as he sits in the leather club chair across from me. "Unfortunately, you're caught in the middle. These two know that Julian has been trying to assume more power. And I've made it no secret that I think the vampires hold too much sway all-around."

"We founded this town," Damien says. "We have a right to the power."

Cal glances at him over his shoulder. "Well, times are changing, old man. Best catch up."

"What does this have to do with me and my Pledging?"

"Julian has allied with a witch house," Cal answers.

"Christ," Bran says beneath his breath. "What the fuck did I tell you?" he says to Damien.

"Fine, brother. You were right. Are you happy?"

"Pleased as punch," Bran says, but his voice is cold.

"Which house?" Damien asks.

"Renshaw."

Bran's eyes slip closed and he presses at the bridge of his nose as he takes in a deep breath.

Damien says nothing.

Renshaw witches are the Addams family of Midnight Harbor. They live in an all-black Victorian on the marshy side of Midnight Lake. They're a small house and they mostly keep to themselves. But when they don't, you know about it.

There's a thread of dark magic that runs through the family dating all the way back to Catherine de Medici, the Poison Queen of France.

It wasn't actually poison though; it was magic that was her weapon of choice.

"They plan to make a stand before Jessie's Pledging has been finalized," Cal goes on. "Kelly will be on the north end of the Pledge Hall when she's struck down. The vision wasn't clear which direction the strike would come."

"Okay," I say, trying not to freak out. "It's good that we know this ahead of time. How do we stop it? What do we do?"

"Cancel the Pledging," Bran says.

"We can't," Damien answers. "Besides, that's exactly what Julian is hoping will happen. The longer she's untethered to a house, the more time he has to scheme."

"Kelly will stay here." I sit forward in the chair. "That's the easy solution."

"Of course she will," Damien answers. "But if the Alpha's psychic saw it happening, then just leaving Kelly at home likely won't solve the problem."

Cal nods and winces when he looks at me. "Sorry, Jessie, but he's right. When it comes to visions, the strategy must always be how to react to it, not prevent it. Because you usually can't prevent it."

I lurch upright. "So my sister has to die? Is that what you're all telling me? No. Fuck no."

"There is an obvious solution," Bran says.

"Which is what?"

Damien scowls at him. "Don't even fucking suggest it."

"It solves all of our problems and it fits in the narrative of the vision."

"What?" I say. "Tell me."

Damien turns his hardened expression on me. "He means turn your sister into a vampire."

Eleven

Turn my sister into a vampire? I only have to think about it for two seconds before I know how I feel.

"I'm with Damien on this one," I say.

Never thought that would come out of my mouth.

"Why don't you ask Kelly what she wants?" Bran says to his brother. "Or do you make all of her decisions for her?"

Damien pushes away from his desk to face his brother. "And if it was Jessie?"

Bran looks over at me. "I'd trust my little mouse to make the right decision."

The Alpha of the Midnight Pack scoffs. "All three of us in this room might like to think we'd relent to our women, but let's be honest. When it comes to protecting them, we will not bend. I don't think you should give Kelly a choice."

Damien glares at the Alpha. "You don't have a woman," he points out. "And no one asked you."

The Alpha grumbles.

"Why are we against this idea?" Bran says. "Who cares if Kelly is a vampire? I like being a vampire and I know you fucking love it."

I watch Damien for a reaction because in all honesty, I am a little curious as to why he opposes it. Fine lines appear around his eyes. There is a reason, but he's not willing to say it.

It does make me wonder what my sister would want. Her future is decidedly up in the air right now, what with Julian and the supposed blood mate certificate. Even if it's real, I think he might have compelled her to sign it. But it's still a thorn that needs to be dealt with.

Once it is...what does she want? Does she want to be with Damien for the rest of her life?

I don't want my sister to become a vampire, but I don't want her to die either.

"Maybe Bran is right," I say. "Maybe we should ask Kelly."

Damien's jaw clenches. "Oh, should we?"

"And I think you should be the one to do it. But ultimately, let her decide."

Damien is stoic for several long seconds. I try not to fidget beneath his gaze. "Fine," he says and starts for the door. "I'll give her the choice. If this should go wrong, then the guilt will rest on your shoulders, Jessie. I hope you can live with that."

Bran sighs. "Ignore him."

"I don't want my sister to be a vampire, but I'm not entirely sure why he doesn't want her to be."

"Because it changes us," Bran says. "It always does. And he's probably terrified of what it'll do to her. If she'll wake up a vampire and realize she doesn't need or want him."

I think I'm beginning to accept the fact that Damien Duval legit loves my sister.

"I need to talk to Jimmy," Bran says. "Alpha, I'm sure you can find your way out."

Cal stands. "I'll be at the Pledge tomorrow. Let me know if you need me before then." He goes to leave.

"Wait," I say before I can think better of it.

Both men glance at me. I make an apologetic face at Bran before I make the request because I know he's going to hate this.

"I need to speak to Cal...alone."

"Absolutely not."

"Bran."

"No, Mouse."

"Do you trust me?"

He grits his teeth, inhales through his nose.

Cal waits halfway to the door.

"Fine." Bran's smile is tight. I might catch hell for this later. "Mind your manners, Alpha."

"I have more than you do, Duval."

Bran grumbles. "Come find me later, little mouse. That's an order."

I give him a nod and then he's gone.

Leaving me alone with the big bad wolf.

————

"That was brave," Cal says and folds his massive arms over his chest.

"I need to know what that favor is."

It's not the most important thing going on right now, but that's exactly why I have to know it. I hate loose threads and I especially hate secrets and mysteries.

"Jessie." He sighs and uncrosses his arms. "I can't—"

"Yes, you can."

The Alpha relented with me earlier, which makes me think he might give me what I want now.

And I'm betting that now that the Duvals are gone, Cal might be more willing to share.

"I have a lot going on in my life, Cal. I don't want that unknown thing haunting me in the back of my mind. Please."

He turns away from me, rubs at the back of his head. "It's about my fated mate."

"Really?"

Cal's lack of a mate is gossip fodder for Midnight. The *Midnight Sun* does annual coverage on it, usually around the blood moon.

Midnight's Most Eligible Bachelor – Will this be the year the Alpha takes a mate?

I'm sure he must hate it.

There's a lot about pack politics and fated mates that I don't know and never gave the time to figuring it out. Most of the mates chosen for pack members are chosen based on politics or convenience. There are several mortal families that have been almost universally bound to the pack.

But fated mates...that's something else entirely.

That's magic. There's nothing political or convenient about it.

"What about him or her?" I ask.

"Her," he says and then turns back to me. "I know who she is."

"Okay. And what does that have to do with me?"

His tongue pokes at the inside of his cheek, his nostrils flaring. "We don't like each other."

"Oh. Ohhhh." Okay, I'm really glad I asked about this now because I could stand for some drama that's not mine.

"I know she's my mate, but *she* doesn't know yet and she comes from a family not typically bound to the pack."

"Complicated. I like it."

He growls.

Do I need to be worried about his edginess on the new moon?

I would put a billion dollars on a bet that Bran is actually just down the hall listening in to be sure nothing happens to me.

It does make me a little bolder.

"Go on," I say.

The Alpha sighs. "I'm going to need her to submit to me. Sooner rather than later. My wolf will not wait much longer."

"I still don't know how I factor into this."

He meets my gaze, scrubbing a hand over the blond stubble on his jaw. "You know her."

"I do?"

"She'll listen to you."

"Who—"

Oh god.

Ohhhh god.

"*No*," I say.

"Yes."

"Sam?"

He doesn't deny it.

"Sam is your fated mate?" My voice has turned shrill. "But she's promised to the Mulligan witches. They'll expect her to Pledge to them and—"

"Over my fucking dead body." This time when he growls, it rumbles deep in his chest, almost animalistic.

"Okay. Okay." I hold up my hands. This is the oddest shit I've ever witnessed. He says he doesn't like Sam, but the absolute torture on his face right now at the mere thought she'd Pledge somewhere else...

Oh, Sam. Oh, I can't wait to tell her! Oh, but she is really, really going to hate this. Because she *does* hate the Alpha. Her dad was the pack's handyman until Cal fired him for reasons unknown.

Sam's family is big, tons of kids, and their mom doesn't work. They don't have a lot of money. Her dad had a hard time finding a new job. He'd been the handyman for the Pack House for nearly two decades.

I once heard Sam say if she could castrate the Alpha, she would.

"So you want me to talk my best friend into pledging to your house and becoming your mate? The Alpha's Mate?"

"Yes," Cal says. "Exactly that."

I laugh, bring my hand to my mouth. I laugh again.

"Jessie." His voice rumbles.

"Oh, I am very sorry for you, sir. Because you are going to have your hands full with Sam."

"You think I don't know that? Every time I'm around her, I want to strangle her."

I laugh again. Cal's shoulders rise with a deep, disgruntled breath.

"Sorry. It's just...I needed this."

He glares at me. "I am glad my frustrations amuse you. Now will you do it?"

"I mean...yeah. I'll talk it through with her. When?"

"I can handle waiting until after your Pledge."

"I appreciate that. There's a lot going on."

"I've noticed."

"You'll be at the Pledge tomorrow? On our side?"

"You help me with Sam, you'll get anything you need from me."

"All right. You have my word on that. And thank you for telling me. Really." I come around the leather chairs. "You've actually been really kind to me and I won't forget that."

He softens. I think the Alpha might have a gooey center. If he and Sam can find even ground, she might be the most spoiled girl in all of Midnight by the end of the year.

"I need to get back to the house," Cal says. "But please, don't say anything to Sam before I'm ready. I need to prepare for the firestorm. Promise me that."

"I promise."

He gives me a nod and starts for the door. "And Jessie?" He looks at me over his shoulder. "My psychic was vague on most of the particulars about tomorrow, but one thing was sure—your sister will die one way or another. At least as a vampire, she'll come back."

When the Alpha is gone, I collapse back into one of the chairs.

My head is spinning.

My sister might become a vampire. My best friend is the fated mate of the Alpha.

Just a regular Monday night now.

Twelve

The Alpha of the Midnight Pack shows himself out of Duval House so I go in search of Bran as I promised I would. When I don't find him, I head back to the Anneliese a little annoyed with how big Duval House is and the fact that I still don't feel like I belong here.

Bran finds me just before I reach the courtyard.

"Did the Alpha tell you his favor?" he asks.

"Yes, but it's a secret," I say, pushing the boundaries because now I know what it'll get me.

"Mouse." His gaze turns dark.

"Oh, fine." I go through the French doors to the open courtyard where crickets are chirping in the garden. Low lights send a soft glow over the walkway. "It was about his fated mate."

Bran is in front of me in a second and the expression that comes over his face is filled with horror. "I swear to fucking god, if you say you're his fated mate, I will tear off his cock and balls and serve them to him on a fucking dish."

"Bran!"

"I'm fucking serious, Mouse."

I trail off in laughter as I push past him and follow the paved stone path to the Anneliese. "You are one sneeze away from murder every second of the day, I swear to god."

"Only where you are concerned."

"I'm not his fated mate."

I hear his soft exhale of relief.

"But you know who is," he says.

"I do."

"Tell me."

"Later."

"Mouse—"

As soon as we're inside the safe house, I catch the soft whimpering of my sister from Damien's room down the hall.

Immediately, I'm on high alert.

I race down the hall and push in the bedroom door and come to a halt.

Kelly is swallowed up in Damien's embrace, sobbing into his chest.

He's holding her like he doesn't want to let her go.

Like he wants to take all of her pain away.

When I stumble over the threshold, he turns to me, looking at me over the top of Kelly's head, a deep scowl on his face.

"I'm sorry," I say. "I didn't know you were here."

"It's my bedroom, is it not?" he says. "In fact, this entire house is mine, last I checked."

"Not just yours," Bran reminds him from behind me. "Speak to my mouse like that again and I'll cut off your cock and balls too."

"I'd like to see you try."

Kelly pulls away from Damien and wipes at her face. "It's okay. I'm okay. Everything is okay."

"You told her, I take it?" I ask the older Duval.

"I did."

I take another tentative step. "How do you feel about it, sissy?"

I haven't called her by that nickname since I was ten years old and I didn't exactly mean to use it, but once it's out, it causes fresh tears to well in her eyes.

"How do I feel about being turned into a vampire? I don't know. Confused. Afraid. Really, really unsure. Just...lots to think about."

Damien's jaw tenses.

"Well…maybe we can find some other solution. What about Rita?" I suggest. "She might be able to create a protection charm or—"

"I respect Rita," Bran says, "but she's not powerful enough to stand against the Renshaw witches."

"Okay. So who is?"

Damien crosses his arms over his chest. "Maybe the Mulligans."

"We're setting up a meeting with Bianca," Bran adds.

"Really?"

Damien nods. "It was your boyfriend's idea."

I have to stop a smile from spreading over my face, hearing Damien refer to his brother as my boyfriend. I get the sense in his tone of voice that he might not be happy about the turn of events. Maybe he wanted to use me for whatever magical secrets I might possess, but he probably didn't want his brother to fall in love with me.

Complicates things, I'm sure.

But too bad for him.

"I just talked to Jimmy," Bran says. "We have a meeting with the witch in an hour. So put your piss poor attitude away, brother, so we can make something happen."

"I don't have a piss poor attitude," Damien argues.

Bran cocks his head at an angle, regarding his brother with an amused expression on his face.

Damien growls, exasperated, then looks at my sister. "I'll return to you later. Do not leave the house."

She nods and then he's gone.

"Is he always this churlish?" I ask my sister.

She sighs. "When he doesn't get his way."

"I can attest to that," Bran says.

I look back at him. "What exactly are you hoping will happen with Bianca, anyway?"

Bianca seems like an odd choice for an ally. She's my age. There are plenty of more experienced witches in Midnight Harbor. But she is extremely powerful. And I suppose it'd be harder to get the older witches to agree to work with vampires. They all have formed opinions on the Duval brothers.

"I'm hoping that whatever agreement we come to will help keep your sister alive."

"Bianca will help if she can."

"I'm counting on it." He reaches over, grips the back of my neck and hauls me to him, planting a kiss on my forehead. "Stay in the Anneliese. Both of you." His gaze cuts from me to Kelly, then back at me. "Say you understand, little mouse."

"Yes. Fine. I understand."

Kelly nods. "I'm not going anywhere."

"We'll be back in a few hours. Be good girls while we're out." He gives me a devilish grin and then disappears after his brother with his vampire speed.

———

Kelly lies down on the bed and I hover in the middle of the room unsure of what to do with myself. This is the first time I've been inside Damien's bedroom in the Anneliese and now that I have a chance to look around, I'm surprised by the décor. Bran's room is a reflection of him—dark, masculine, full of hard lines and solid furniture.

Damien's room is very...feminine, and it reminds me of Kelly's condo on the river.

The wall behind the bed is painted dark red, but the giant rug on the floor is thick, white, and furry, almost like sheepskin. The duvet is soft creamy linen, the pillows thick and matching.

The bedside tables are blonde wood with gold handles and matching gold lamps.

Behind me is a sectional couch the same color as the duvet with mismatched throw pillows, all with various patterns done in the same shade of red as the accent wall.

Now that I've been in Damien's office, I know that this isn't his style—this is Kelly's.

Damien designed this room in the safest place in all of Midnight precisely to my sister's taste.

God, how far back do they go?

"Can I join you?" I ask my sister.

"Of course."

I kick off my shoes and climb onto the bed. She opens her arms for me and I snuggle into her side like I used to when I was a kid.

Her hand absently trails along my hair.

"So...a vampire."

She sighs and the breath tickles at the hair along my crown causing me to shiver.

"Once upon a time, I wanted a family," she admits.

"Really?"

I feel her nod against my forehead.

"But..." I coax.

"But then...Mom died and I had you to take care of and Julian..." She sniffs. "I stopped wanting a family a long time ago so it doesn't matter now."

My heart aches for my sister, for all of the things she wanted and never got. All of the paths she wanted to take but couldn't.

And now...

"Do you want to be with Damien? He's rather broody."

She laughs. "He is. More than he was when we first got together, but part of that is my fault."

"Why?"

She sighs. "Because I broke his heart."

I frown, trying to realign everything I thought I knew about my sister and the older Duval.

I guess it's easy to think vampires don't have hearts, and especially not vampires like the Duval brothers. But I know Bran does. Somehow, I managed to wiggle my way through his cold, unaffected exterior. It stands to reason my sister found a way in through Damien's aloofness.

"Has he forgiven you?"

"I think we're getting there."

I immediately go back to the sight of them in a tight embrace and think they might be closer than Kelly realizes.

"So are you going to do it?" I ask. "Are you going to let him give you his blood?"

"I don't think I have a choice."

"You always have a choice."

"I'm not leaving you. And I'm not going to break Damien's heart a second time."

"He doesn't want you to do it though."

"Only because he asked me once before and I told him no."

I lurch upright, propping myself up on my elbow. "He did? When?"

"It was a long time ago."

"When, Kels?"

"Before my Pledge."

"That was...nearly ten years ago."

"I know."

"You guys have been secretly seeing each other for ten years?"

She scrubs at her face and then looks at the ceiling. "Not all of ten years. Off and on."

"Holy shit. How did I not know this?"

"You had your own life."

"Yes, but this is...why did you turn him down?"

She looks over at me, fine lines deepening around her eyes. "I turned him down for you. To protect you."

The guilt is immediate and overwhelming.

"If it wasn't for me, would you have taken him up on his offer?"

She nods. "Back then, absolutely."

"And now?"

"Now...we come with a lot more baggage now." She laughs, but there's nothing funny about it. "I would rather have more time, you know? Time to think about it and consider my options. But—" she pulls me back into her side "—you're fae, Damien is a vampire—I'd be the only one getting old and gray. This is the best option. This way I can be around for you for as long as you need me."

"I can take care of myself. You don't have to do it anymore."

She gives me an affectionate pat on my head like I'm a little kid again. "Let's pretend that's true." When she laughs this time, it's genuine.

"Hey." I sit up again. "I have an idea."

"Okay. What?"

"Remember when we used to curl up together on the couch and eat popcorn and watch cheesy 80s movies?"

The smile that comes to her face is genuine and lights up her eyes. "I do."

"Let's do that while our vampire boyfriends are out playing. What do you say?"

She considers it for just a second and then says, "That sounds amazing, actually. Which movie?"

"Easy." I slide off the bed. "*Footloose.*"

Kelly lets out a quick burst of laughter. "I thought you were going to say *The Goonies*. Remember when you used to hide treasure around the house and then would draw me a map and make me go search for it? Classic Jessie."

"I love treasure hunts."

She follows me to the door and ruffles my hair. "I know you do, you nerd."

We fall in step together as we make our way to the kitchen, joking about what used to be, how we were.

Come tomorrow, the MacMahon sisters will have been irrevocably changed.

For better or for worse.

Thirteen

BRAN

Damien has always hated my driving.

"You know," he says from the passenger seat of my Audi, "these days, car accidents account for nearly 2% of all vampire deaths. When a head gets lopped off, it's hard to come back from that."

"If a vampire were to piss off his brother, he might get his head lopped off anyway."

He barely looks away from his phone in his hand. "I'm just saying— if you're dead, who will protect your little mouse from Julian?"

The leather steering wheel creaks beneath my grip.

"That's what I thought," Damien says because he's a fucking know-it-all.

As the road cuts right, I let off the gas and the speedometer sinks. "Better?"

"Yes," Damien says, his eyes still on his screen.

"I need to tell you something."

He finally looks up.

"It's about Jessie."

"You have my attention."

Red and blue lights flash in my rear-view. "Christ." We're out in the countryside, so it's likely a deputy.

"See," Damien says. "If you'd been obeying traffic laws—"

"Oh, shut the fuck up."

He laughs. "I'll just eat him. I could use a drink." He taps out of whatever he was reading on his phone, darkens the screen, and slides the phone into the inside pocket of his bomber jacket.

"Let's make it a game instead." I slow the car down and pull to the shoulder. The car is fast and nimble and stops with ease.

Turning in the leather bucket seat, Damien's eyes flare with interest. "Which game?"

"How about we play Worth It or Not?"

He considers it, then, "All right. We placing bets?"

"Of course."

The lights get closer as the Sheriff's car catches up to us.

"I call Not," he says.

"Fine. Worth it."

"If I win, I'm sending this ridiculous car to the junkyard."

"I'll just buy another one."

"Yes, but I'll get a great amount of satisfaction watching it get pulverized."

"All right. If I win, I'm kicking Sky out of the House."

He frowns at me. "She's my assistant."

"And she's my pain in the ass."

The way she spoke to Jessie tonight was the last fucking straw. I know my little mouse thinks I was flirting with Sky right after our House announcement. I did laugh at her, but only because she was being fucking ridiculous.

"How long before you dump that mortal and come back to my bed?" Sky had said.

I'd laughed and replied, "When the sun stops rising and the air no longer fills my lungs."

The Sheriff's car pulls up behind us, the lights still flashing. We're on a desolate back road, not a house in sight.

Damien sighs. "I suspect Kelly won't want Sky around anyway. So you have a deal."

"Bowing at her feet already, are you?"

"Fuck off."

In my side mirror, I see the deputy climb out of his car. He's late twenties by the looks of it, stocky, likely works out. I hear the crackle of his radio from inside the car.

"I'll get the deputy," I tell my brother. "You get the dash cam and the radio."

"Count of three," Damien says.

"One."

"Two."

We're out of the car on three.

The deputy sees the blur that is my brother and me, but it takes his stupid mortal brain an extra two seconds to comprehend what that means.

His hand is on his duty belt, unclipping his gun by the time I reach him. I tear off his body cam, drop it and smash it beneath my boot.

Damien rips off the passenger side door of the car, wings it into the field, and tears out all of the comms.

I use compulsion to bring the deputy to a standstill and his hands go limp at his sides.

Damien shuts off the flashing lights and then comes around the front of the car, a cigarette clipped between his lips. He lights the end, curling his finger around the filter as he takes a long hit.

"Evening, Deputy"—I look for his gold nameplate—"Kent. What's your first name?"

He blinks at me. "Mike."

Damien takes another hit from the cigarette, the smoke curling in the light of the deputy's headlights.

"Mike, tell us your biggest secret."

His pupils pulse beneath the compulsion. His face is blank, but his hands are trembling.

Sometimes the big dumb ones can fight against being compelled, but never hard enough to get out of it. Geniuses are the easiest to control. It's the hubris and the naïve belief no one can outwit them.

Mike starts sweating.

"He probably thinks murder is the worst sin," Damien says and hands me the cigarette.

Clipped between two fingers, I take a drag and fill my lungs with burning smoke. "Whatever it is, he doesn't want to give it up."

Mike's lips are trying to form the words and his face is turning red from the effort not to spill them.

"Spit it out, Mike," I say. "Deepest, darkest secret."

"I cheated on my wife!" He immediately dissolves into giant, heaving sobs.

Damien and I share a look. Mike buries his face in his hands.

"Pathetic," I say and hand the cigarette back.

Damien comes around and snaps his fingers. "Mike. Look at me."

The big idiot straightens, fat tears wetting his face.

"You love this wife of yours?"

"Yes. I love her with all my heart."

"Then why the fuck did you cheat on her?" I ask him.

"Temptation."

"Is that all?" Damien asks.

"We've been having problems."

"I didn't know this was going to turn into a marital therapy session," I say. "Should have brought booze."

In the field to my left, an animal rustles the dry grass. We're still alone way out here in the middle of nowhere.

"Problems can be fixed," Damien says. "So why haven't you?"

"I'm scared," Mike admits.

"Of what?"

"Losing her."

"You keep dipping your dick in other pussy, you will, Mike," I say.

He starts sobbing again.

"Hey, Mike. Get your shit together." Damien gives the bigger guy a shove. "Look at me." Mike does as commanded. "Call your wife right now and tell her everything. She'll decide your fate."

"What do you mean?" He drags his cracked knuckles over his face, wiping away the tears.

"Your wife will decide if you're worth it or not," I tell him. "If you're not, we're going to kill you. Now go. Call her."

He returns to his car, retrieves his cell phone, and taps at the screen.

Damien drops the spent cigarette to the pavement and crushes the ember beneath his boot. "What were you going to tell me? About Jessie?"

Mike's wife answers the phone and he launches into a blubbering confession.

I pull Jessie's mom's letter from my pocket. The one that told the story about going to the fae realm with a baby dying in her womb. How she returned with something else. I took the letter when Mouse wasn't looking.

"Read this."

Damien frowns at me as he takes the slip of paper and unfurls it. He starts reading.

"I love you so much, baby. I've just been so overwhelmed at work," Mike says. "I've been trying to distract myself. I don't love her. You're the only woman I've ever loved."

His wife is sobbing on the other end of the phone. I can hear a baby crying in the background.

"Go get the baby," Mike says. "We can talk about all of this when I get home. If you'll let me come back."

There's a long pause on the other end. The wife sniffs and says, "Yes. Please come home."

The wind shifts and the animal in the field catches my scent. It's gone in a flash.

"Why didn't you tell me about this sooner?" Damien says behind me.

"Because I wasn't sure how you'd react."

Mike says his goodbyes in a long, drawn-out pathetic mewl.

"I wish I could say she's just a changeling," Damien says.

I turn to him. He's leaning against my car, his legs crossed at the ankle, the left side of him bright against the glare of the headlights. The letter is hanging from his hand.

"But changelings don't have terrifying abilities," I say.

"Precisely." He thinks for a second. "There are only a few brownies in Midnight. We could track them all down, see what they know."

"Worth a shot."

He folds the letter back up and returns it to me. "If she's more powerful than you or me—"

"Don't."

"What?"

"Don't go there."

"Bran—"

"If she's more powerful than you or me, then we'll be glad she's on our side."

He narrows his eyes.

"We're having Rita undo the binding," I tell him. "And you'll not stop us."

He watches me with that cool indifference. I know my brother unsettles most people, but I will always know him as the brother who held our little sister in his arms, sobbing over her dead body.

Death reveals who we really are, deep down, and my brother has always been the type who loves harder than anyone. And I know he loves me.

We are all we have left of our blood. He'll do what I ask.

"The fae gate closed right around her arrival," he points out.

"I know."

"There are very few reasons someone would close a fae gate."

"I know that too."

"And if the gate were to be opened again, and we find out she's—

"I know, all right? I've thought about all of that."

"Here, we're kings. But standing against one of the princes from the Unseelie Court? We would not measure up."

"I know that. For fuck's sake."

Mike slips his phone in his pocket and stands in the middle of the road, a little shellshocked.

"You could just let it go," Damien says. "I could talk to Rita, tell her to pretend to perform the unbinding. Jessie won't know any different. We could go on with our lives. You would have Jessie and I would have Kelly and everything would be as it should be."

Mike's shoulders are drooping, but his eyes are clearer. Will he be better off having risked his entire life just for the truth?

"Your wife is keeping you?" I call out to the deputy.

Mike nods numbly.

"I guess you were worth it." I dart across the road and stop a foot from him. I zero in on his pupils as I tap open a connection so I can compel him one last time. "You'll go to your wife and you'll treat her like she's a goddess and you'll be faithful to her for as long as the breath fills your lungs. Say you understand, Mike."

"I understand."

"Good. Now get in your car and go."

He quickly slides in behind the wheel and takes off, gravel crunching beneath the bite of the tires.

When it's just my brother and me, I turn back to him. "Jessie deserves the truth."

"You think she's worth it, do you?" he asks, prolonging the game.

"Yes."

He gives me a quick nod. "Then let's hope you're right."

Fourteen

I wake to Bran giving me a gentle nudge. "Mouse." His voice is quiet but raspy like he spent all night shouting. He's crouched beside the couch in front of me, putting him at eye-level.

"Hi," I say, stretching on the couch. "What time is it?"

He reaches over and pushes a stray lock of hair away from my face and instinctively I turn into his touch.

"It's four a.m."

"Really? You've been gone a while."

"Damien and I got hung up."

For the Duval brothers, "hung up" could mean a hundred different things, half of which would be bloody.

I don't ask because I don't want to know.

I look down the length of the massive couch to find Kelly's head in Damien's lap. His fingers are trailing through her hair. Neither of them is speaking, but I still get the impression that what they're saying can be heard loud and clear.

My sister is in love with Damien Duval.

And Damien is in love with her.

Whatever has to happen today for them to be together will be worth it.

And thinking this—*today*—makes me realize it's my birthday.

"I need you to get up," Bran says.

I groan. "Can't you just carry me to bed?"

"It's not that."

I look up at him with clearer focus. "Then what?"

Please tell me it's not some other crisis. Some other secret or war on the horizon. I can't take anymore.

"Bianca is here and she wants to speak to you."

"Oh?" I sit up and look around the living room, but don't spot my witch friend.

"She's in the main house," Bran says. "Come." He straightens and offers me his hand. Before I take it, I give my sister another glance. "Kels?"

"Hmmm?" she mumbles, her eyes still closed.

"I'll be back in a bit. You're okay?"

"I'm fine." Her voice is muzzy and faraway.

I follow Bran out of the Anneliese and smooth down my hair as we walk. I've never gotten the impression that Bianca is the type to judge people, but it's hard not to feel sloppy and inferior next to her. She's always put together. Always looking fierce.

Bran leads the way across the courtyard, then through the halls of Duval House. The hallways are full of vampires either returning to the party or leaving it. There's still a few hours left of darkness and they seem dedicated to taking advantage of it in one way or another.

Everyone we pass nods at Bran then immediately casts their gaze to the floor.

He ignores all of them.

We enter a sitting room with a giant fireplace and an oil painting of a black horse hanging over the mantel in a gilded frame.

I immediately know this is one of Bran's personal spaces. It smells like him. Feels like him. And looks like him.

Except for the horse painting. That's the only thing that sticks out from the décor.

I never took him for a horse enthusiast. Of course, he comes from a time when horses were the only mode of transportation so maybe I'm wrong.

Bianca rises to her feet when we enter. She's wearing a pleated plaid skirt with a navy-blue sweater, the sleeves rolled up to her elbows.

As she rises, two delicate gold chains slide down to her wrist.

Despite the late hour, she looks like she just walked off stage from a mock political campaign at a New England boarding school.

I must look like I just rolled off a couch.

"Jessie, hi," she says and smiles brightly at me.

"Hey, Bee. It's nice to see you."

She nods and then looks at Bran.

He sighs behind me. "I promised Bianca I'd let her speak to you alone. I am a man of my word." But he smiles tightly while he says it, like it gives him no great pleasure. "You have ten minutes," he adds and then leaves, shutting the door behind him.

"He's probably just listening somewhere beyond the room," I warn her.

"I know." She breathes out through her nose with exasperation. "But I suppose it's the show of privacy that's most important. Come here. I feel like it's been forever since we saw each other last." She holds out her arms to me and I give her a quick hug.

"Things have been...wild," I say.

"Yes. That might be an understatement."

"I appreciate you not saying anything about what happened at the trial at the vampire court. This whole thing with my sister and Julian is—"

"Wrong," she says.

I nod. "Yes. That." I sit in one of the leather wingbacks. "So did you agree to help my sister against the Renshaw witches?"

"Not quite yet." She sits down in the chair next to me. "How much did Bran tell you about his plan?"

"Not much. Only that he wanted to ally with you because you might be strong enough to stand against the Renshaws."

She nods. "He also asked me to join Duval House as their personal witch."

"He *what*?"

"I wanted to hear your opinion before I gave him an answer."

"But...he...*hold on.*"

"I know it's unprecedented, but I will admit, I like being a trailblazer."

"So…you would leave your house and join Duval House? Would the Mulligans even let you do that?"

"Witches aren't the same as wolves and vampires. We're not territorial. My dad will hate it. My mom will love it." She rolls her eyes at the mention of her mother. "The coven will really, really hate it. But like I said, they can't force me to stay and they won't want to stand up against the Duval brothers. Not when I came by choice."

"But why would you do that?"

"You have to seize an opportunity when it comes to you even if it sounds potentially foolish." She laughs to herself. "If I'm honest, Bran really sold me on you."

"Me?"

"He told me you're fae."

I go still in the chair.

"So it's true?" she asks.

With a sigh, I give her a nod.

"Then my decision is made."

I snort. "Because I'm fae? There are plenty of fae in Midnight."

"Yes, but why has your identity been hidden? And why is Julian so desperate to possess you and your sister?"

Leave it to Bianca to suss out the details in literally a few hours of possessing just a few pieces of the puzzle. She was always the smartest in school. She graduated Valedictorian of her class. She could have gone on to one of the ivy league schools if she'd wanted.

"Instinct has always been my driver," Bianca goes on. "You have to listen to your gut, but more than that, you have to hone that skill so that when the time comes, you know exactly what decision to make based on nothing more than a feeling." She sits forward and clasps her hands in front of her, elbows on her knees. "And my gut is telling me not only will you and your sister need me, but that whatever type of fae you are, I will want to be on your side because of it."

My throat thickens and I swallow against it. "I'm no one special, Bee."

Her red lips spread into a grin. "I don't believe that, Jessie. And I suspect deep down, neither do you."

A shiver races up my spine.

I don't know what to say to that. Is there anything to say? My brain is telling me I'm no one special, but everything else—*everyone else*—is saying the opposite.

Thankfully, Bran saves me by coming into the office without knocking. "Now that that's settled," he says. "We need you to work your magic on Kelly."

Bianca nods. "Of course. Lead the way."

———

Since Bianca is technically human, the magic of the invitation doesn't apply to her and she walks into the Anneliese between me and Bran with no trouble at all. We find Kelly and Damien sitting silently in the living room.

When Damien sees Bianca, he says, "Do we have a deal?"

"We do," she says. "But we should talk about our options before you decide on the best course of action."

Damien gestures to a chair. "Sit."

Bee sits in one of the two chairs by the window and takes a deep breath before explaining. "Vampire blood is a good plan, but it's permanent, right? So I think it should be our last resort. There are several other spells I could perform, all of which would have varying degrees of protection and success.

"I'm sure you know that spells are like keys and without knowing the corresponding lock, it'll be impossible to give you a hundred percent guarantee that Kelly will be safe."

"We know how magic works," Bran says. He's standing at the edge of the living room, his arms crossed over his chest. "What's the next best line of protection after vampire blood?"

Bee glances at Damien. His gaze is on her, but she doesn't shrink away from him. "You could link Kelly to you. You are immortal. Your life essence is infinite. If she was to die, the spell would activate and your energy would flow her way."

Damien doesn't react. Kelly scoffs. "We're not doing that," she says.

"Yes, we are," Damien answers.

"You should know the risk," Bee says.

"I don't care what the risk is."

"Damien!" Kelly shouts. "You're not doing that."

He finally looks at her. "You don't tell me what I can and can't do, *mon petit chaton.*"

She scowls at him, but clamps her mouth shut.

I arch a brow at Bran, but he just shakes his head at me.

What does *mon petit chaton* mean? I'm definitely going to ask him later.

"What are the risks?" Bran asks.

Bianca clasps her hands together, her arms resting on her thighs. "Whatever happens to Kelly, happens to Damien. That's the way I'd structure the spell. If it's a life we're worried about, Damien has plenty to give. So it wouldn't be an issue. But there can be a sort of backdraft of magic depending on the power behind it or the type of spell the Renshaws use, and the current can shift to the deeper well, that is, *Damien.*"

The brothers talk over us, but this time they speak in a language that is neither English nor French.

"That's not fair," I say. "Bee?"

She shrugs at me. "That sounds like Greek. I don't speak Greek."

"Bran," I say. "Quit cutting us out of the conversation."

Damien glares at me then carries on.

Bran gives him one more answer in Greek and then sighs. "We'll do the linking spell."

"What if I refuse?" Kelly asks.

"I won't allow it." Damien settles his darkened gaze on her. "You will do the spell. I won't tell you again."

I don't know if I should hate Damien for trying to boss my sister around or be a little jealous of Kelly. I know what it's like to be commanded by a Duval.

Damien is even better at it than Bran.

"What do you need?" Damien asks Bee.

"Just blood."

"No herbs or crystals or any of that shit?" Bran asks.

Bianca shakes her head. "Mulligans don't need accoutrements."

Damien stands up. "Then let's get started."

———

Because Bianca doesn't need all of the witchy accessories that Rita does to perform magic, I have to admit, it's not quite as magical.

There's just a knife and a stainless-steel bowl on the kitchen island.

"We draw blood," Bee explains, "and the blood from both of you will go into the bowl. I'll perform the spell and that will link you. It usually lasts a few days before the effects wear off."

"What will it feel like?" Kelly asks.

"I've never been linked myself, but I've been told it's different for different people. Some describe it as nothing more than a phantom sensation. Others have been able to sense what the other is feeling. It really all depends on how close you are."

How close are my sister and Damien? Maybe they love each other, but they've been holding each other at arm's length for a while, I suspect.

"Ready?" Bianca asks.

Damien gives her his hand. "Be quick," he tells her. "The wound will heal fast."

She nods and pulls the blade over the palm of his hand, then turns him toward the bowl. She gets out barely a dribble before the wound is closed.

"Is that enough?" Damien asks.

Bianca winces. "Not quite."

He takes the blade from her, fists it in his other hand, then jams the blade right through his palm.

Kelly yelps and staggers back. Bianca frowns. Seems living with Duvals requires constant exposure to blood and guts. I'm coming to expect it now.

With the blade still stuck in his flesh, Damien holds his hand over the bowl and lets the blood trail down.

"That should be good," Bianca says after a few seconds.

Damien pulls the dagger out, spins it around and hands it to Bianca, hilt first.

She hesitates a second before taking it.

Next, Kelly holds her hand over the bowl and Bianca draws the blade over the fleshy part of her palm.

Kelly hisses from pain as blood wells in the wound, then trails down into the bowl, mixing with Damien's.

When Bianca is satisfied with what they've gathered, Damien bites his wrist and adds his blood to my sister's glass of wine.

"Drink," he orders her.

"I thought the whole reason we were doing this is so I wouldn't turn into a vampire? If I drink that and I die tomorrow, I will be changed."

"It's for the wound in your hand," he tells her.

She frowns at him. "You expect me to believe that?"

He doesn't answer.

With a huff, my sister takes the offering and drinks it back.

"I'll link you now," Bianca says. "If you're ready?"

"Carry on." Damien crosses his arms over his chest as my sister slouches against the edge of the counter.

Beside me, I sense Bran growing agitated and when I look over at him, his brow is sunk in a deep V. It makes me wonder what the conversation in Greek was.

Bee holds her hands over the bowl of mixed blood and whispers Latin beneath her breath.

The hair along my arms rises.

Bran takes a step closer to me.

The bowl ignites with a *WHUMP* and bright green flames dance inside of it, highlighting Bianca's face in a sinister glow.

Kelly lurches and in a blink, Damien is beside her, his arm around her waist. "*Minou?*" he says, worry hardening his eyes.

"I'm okay."

"It's done," Bee says.

"That's it?" I ask.

"Magic, at the root of it, is very, very simple."

"Thank you," Damien says.

I have a feeling Damien doesn't thank people very often.

"You're welcome," Bianca answers.

"Sky," Damien calls.

Bran says something in French.

Damien responds in English. "You'll get what you're owed. Just not today."

Sky appears outside the Anneliese, hands on her hips. "You summoned me?"

"Show Bianca out."

"I can find my own way," Bianca starts, but Damien shoots a warning glance her way and she relents. "When would you like me to move into the house?"

"As soon as you've wrapped up your business with the Mulligans and have packed your things. You tell me how quickly you can make it happen."

"Give me two days."

The brothers exchange a look. "That will suffice," Damien says. "But be at the Pledge today."

She nods and then follows Sky back through the courtyard.

"Do you guys feel any different?" I ask.

Kelly's face is flushed and her chest is heaving, almost like she just ran around the block. Damien meets her gaze. Some silent conversation passes between them and then Damien grabs my sister by the wrist and drags her out of the house.

"Hey! Where are you—"

Bran wraps his hand around my upper arm and swings me around to stop me from chasing after them.

"Let them be," he tells me.

"But where—"

He gives me a look.

"What? What is it?"

"Listen to me."

"I am."

"Let. Them. *Be*."

It finally dawns on me.

"Oh. *Ohhhh*."

"Yes."

I sigh and scrub at my face. "I'm just worried about her."

"I know you are." Bran pulls me into him and wraps me into a hug. "I think she'll be fine."

"So why were you talking in Greek? What were you trying to hide?"

I try to pull away so I can look him in the face, but his embrace is tight. "Bran." I grumble against his chest.

I don't need a magical linking spell to tell me what Bran is thinking and feeling. "You're pretending everything is fine, but you're worried about Damien."

He finally lets me go and heads to our bedroom.

"Talk to me."

In the room, he goes to the bathroom and flicks on the light. Under-cabinet lighting glows against the stone floor. He turns on the tap and splashes cold water on his face.

"Bran."

"If you must know, he was telling me that should something happen to him, I would find the necessary paperwork for the estate in his safe. And I was telling him that nothing would happen to him and if it did, I'd kill him twice."

He hunches over the vanity and inhales deeply, water dripping from his nose.

"You love him a lot, don't you?" It's not really a question.

"He's all I have left, Mouse."

I go to him, placing my hand on his back. "This is all my fault."

"No." He narrows his eyes at me. "Don't you dare say that."

"But it is."

"Mouse."

"If it wasn't for me—"

He straightens. "This is Julian's fault and the Renshaw witches, should they side with him. Not yours. Don't even think that."

The guilt is still there, though.

"Sometimes I wonder what would have happened to all of us if I'd just left Midnight."

He puts his hands on either side of my face and forces me to look at him.

"Say that again and I will bind and gag you until you learn your lesson."

Blood rushes to my cheeks at the thought of being bound and gagged by him.

He clucks his tongue at me. "I have to come up with better punishments, apparently."

With everything that's going on, I want a distraction.

My sister is getting one. Go sissy.

"Do it now," I say, my voice going reedy. "Teach me a lesson."

He presses closer, his hands dipping to my waist. "You should rest."

"I will. *After*."

His tongue runs over the sharp tip of his incisor as amber fire comes to his irises. "Don't tempt me."

I don't just want a distraction. I *need* one. There's no chance I'll sleep now.

"Sometimes I wonder," I say and then lick my lips, drawing out the temptation.

"Mouse." His voice rumbles in the base of his throat.

"—what would have happened to all of us—"

The brightness in his eyes grows.

"—if I'd just left Midnight."

The air goes still.

I have approached the center of the storm and the hair rises along the nape of my neck.

My heart is thudding loudly in my head and heat is settling between my legs.

Without warning, Bran hooks his fingers into my panties, yanks them off, then shoves them into my mouth.

"You asked for it," he says, and spins me around.

Fifteen

I can smell my desire with my damp panties stuffed in my mouth.

I breathe hard through my nose.

Bran's belt buckle clatters as he undoes it. The leather snaps when he yanks it from the loops.

In two seconds, he has it twisted into a figure 8, then yanks my arms behind my back and slips the restraints over my wrists. When he pulls the tail, it tightens, binding me.

The leather is biting.

His hand comes around my throat, his hardness pressing against the back of me.

I huff out another breath as our eyes meet in the mirror.

"Is this what you wanted, little mouse?"

I clench up, buzzing with sudden heat and need.

His pupils are blown wide, fangs sharp in his mouth.

I am nothing but prey now, caught in the predator's snare.

But I chose to be here, to feel the terror of being used by someone more powerful than me.

I'm still wearing my party dress and Bran yanks the plunging neckline off my shoulders, baring me.

He still has one hand wrapped around my throat, veins bulging, running along his knuckles.

His other hand sinks to my breast and pinches at my nipple.

I arch against him, but he presses back, pushing my hips into the edge of the counter. I mewl around the lacy fabric stuffed in my mouth and wiggle against the restraints.

He pinches again and pain and pleasure mingle in my gut.

"If I could keep you like this all night, I would," he says. "Keep you bound and gagged and just on the edge of coming until you can't take it anymore." His fingers trail over my chest, sending goosebumps down my arms. "I would fuck you until you were begging for release."

My clit is buzzing, desperate to be touched. Any friction at all would do, but Bran takes his time teasing over the sensitive flesh of my breasts, then grazing my nipples just enough to force them to peak.

"Do you know all of the wicked things I want to do to your body, Mouse?" he asks.

I breathe hard and close my eyes, just imagining it.

"Ah-ah," he says and tightens his grip on my throat. "Eyes open. You'll watch me punish you."

My pussy clenches and I moan, eyes widening.

Bran's other hand dips lower and drags up the hem of my dress. I'm swollen and wet and buzzing and needy.

Touch me.

For god's sake, touch me.

In the mirror, I watch as his hand disappears beneath the fabric. I breathe hard, anticipating his touch.

I part my thighs for him and he slides his fingers down my slit and I almost lose my mind.

I clamp my teeth over the lace.

"So. Fucking. Wet." Bran's irises are bright gold fire when I meet his gaze. He slips his hand out and brings it to his mouth, then sucks each finger clean.

The groan that comes out of me, watching him taste my desire, is feral.

With my bound hands, I try to reach between us to grope him, but he's faster than me and grabs at the center of the binding and yanks me to a standstill.

"You don't get to touch." He lifts my dress up and smacks me on the ass.

I jolt from the sting and collapse on the counter, only for him to bury his hand in my hair and yank my head back up, forcing me to bend.

"Eyes on me, Mouse. Don't disobey me."

My clit swells, throbbing at his words.

I need him to fill me up.

Now. Right now.

I give him a quick nod.

"Good girl."

He steps back. I keep my gaze on him in the mirror and watch intently as he lifts his shirt off with a quick snap of his wrist. I appreciate the view while I have it, the deep lines between ab muscles, the swell of his biceps, every fiber of muscle that twines across his chest as he unbuttons his pants.

Bran's body is a symphony when it moves. A dark and dangerous symphony and I want to sink into the music of it.

When his cock is free, he fists it in his hand and gives it several pumps until pre-cum glistens at the tip.

I test the strength of the belt, straining against it, but there's no give.

I push out my ass, desperate for his attention.

He keeps stroking his cock, watching me struggle, enjoying it even.

Cool air is stealing beneath the hem of my dress, reminding me of the untouched heat and the unspent desire.

I'm going to break soon if he doesn't do something about it.

He strokes faster, muscles working hard, his breath quickening.

He better not come without me.

Oh god, what if he does?

What if that's the punishment?

I groan around my panties.

"What's wrong, little mouse?" he says.

He knows I can't respond, which makes him grin in the most wicked way.

I grumble again.

"Get over here," he orders.

I lift myself off the counter and hurry to him.

"Get on your knees."

I sink in front of him like I'm worshipping at his altar.

He stops pumping at his dick, pulls the fabric from my mouth, and tosses it aside. "Open up."

I pop my lips open for him, butterflies filling my stomach.

"No," he says, his eyes brightening. "Stick out your tongue."

I heave out a needy breath and do as he asks, flattening my tongue for him.

One hand on the back of my head, the other around his cock, he strokes himself again and again, growing harder as I peer up at him, waiting like a good little mouse.

With a growl, teeth clenched and fangs sharp, he comes on my tongue, pulling on the back of my hair while he goes to angle me up to him.

It's so much cum that I can't hold it all and it drips down my chin and then down my chest and his gaze darkens as he makes a mess of me.

My clit pulses as Bran breathes heavily above me. "Swallow it, Mouse."

I close my mouth and swallow the taste of him down my throat. Being used and commanded sends a flush down my entire body.

"That's my good girl." He lets up his grip on my hair, then yanks me to my feet. Using his vampire speed, he removes the belt, but I'm only free a fraction of a second before he's binding me again, this time with my arms in front.

Before I know what he's doing, I'm pressed against the opposite wall. He lifts my arms above my head and hooks me by the belt on one of the towel hooks.

He covers my body with his and I am lost in the size of him.

"Now that you have a taste of me on the tip of your tongue," he says, his voice raspy at my ear, "perhaps it's my turn to get a taste of you."

I whimper beneath him, trussed up by the hook. I'm at his mercy and I want him to do anything and everything to me.

He trails from my ear down the curve of my throat, then kisses gently at my rapid pulse point.

A shiver rolls up my spine.

His fangs graze my flesh.

Instinctively I curl into myself, curling away from the predator, but Bran grabs me by the jaw and opens me back up.

He bites me. I squeak. He pulls on my blood and all of the fight runs out of me. I melt into him.

"Bran," I say on a breath.

The pressure at my clit is so intense, I think I could go off at the slightest touch. But I need to go off. I need to come.

My pussy is tingling and my body is shivering and I can barely breathe.

"Bran."

When he pulls back and runs his tongue over his fangs, his eyes are burning brightly.

"Yes, little mouse?"

"I need...I need—"

He bends into me, his forearm propped on the wall beside me. "Yes?" he asks and kisses me, just a quick graze of his lips.

"I need—"

He covers my mouth with his and I can taste the tang of my blood. His tongue slides over mine, and fills me with the coppery, sweet taste. He's hard again, digging into my thigh. I go up on tiptoes so I can feel the hot throb of his cock at my wetness.

He rocks his hips forward, sliding between my thighs.

I'm so wet, he finds no resistance and teases me with a slow back and forth motion, hitting my clit with every thrust.

"Just like that," I say, practically begging.

The pressure builds. He grabs my ass and positions me better to find the most leverage between us.

"Oh fuck."

"Maybe I'll make you wait," he says.

"Oh god, no." I focus on him, pleading with my eyes.

"I've only had half my fill of you, little mouse," he says and steals the heat of his cock from me.

"Bran." I whimper and pull at the binding. "Please. Stop teasing me."

He drops to his knees. "Spread your legs for me."

I widen my stance and he lifts one of my legs, draping it over his shoulder.

In the mirror across the bathroom, I watch him as he leans into me and devours me with his mouth.

I exhale with a rush and arch away from the wall, the hook capturing me by the belt.

I am entranced by the reflection, by the sight of the back of Bran's head as he moves against me, lapping me up.

The sight of him, the feel of him, the sensation of the flat of his tongue against me makes the pressure build and build.

"Oh my god," I say as he dips down to my entrance and fucks me with his tongue, then comes back up to my clit, nipping at it, causing me to moan and quiver.

I'm buzzing and burning, chest heaving. If it wasn't for the belt and the hook, I'd be sinking to the floor.

Bran repositions himself, his hand trailing up my thigh, then closer and closer to my wet slit.

"You'll come in my mouth," he tells me. "I want to taste all of you when you let go."

He fills me up with three fingers, stretching me.

"Go on," he orders and sucks at my clit.

"Shit. Oh fuck."

He licks and sucks and fucks me with his fingers and the orgasm slams through me and I buck against the wall.

Bran holds me still with one arm hooked around my thigh.

He leans into me as I cry out, riding the wave through.

"Look at yourself," he says up to me. "Watch how you glow."

As the orgasm spasms through me, I force myself to look at my reflection as I tremble all over.

I'm flush, sweating, shaking.

But he's right.

There's something otherworldly about me in this moment as the pleasure fills my veins and my own juices drip down my thighs.

I've never felt so empowered. Even when I'm strapped down by a belt to the wall.

Bran pulls his fingers from me and stands in front of me, his lips swollen from the effort of eating my pussy.

"Did you learn your lesson, little mouse?"

I sag against the wall and he unhooks me, unlatching the belt. "Yes," I tell him, even though I think it's a lie.

He catches me when my knees buckle once I'm free.

His arm winds around my waist as the other arm hooks behind my knees and he carries me to bed. I'm practically boneless when he lays me on my side.

He disappears in a blur, then returns a few seconds later with a hot, wet cloth. "Open, Mouse," he tells me and I spread my knees apart so he can clean me up.

"I thought I wasn't supposed to clean your cum from my pussy," I say, my voice thick with exhaustion.

"You're not. I'm cleaning you up. There's a clear difference."

I laugh when he hits my still sensitive clit. "A girl could get used to this."

He disappears again to take care of the cloth, then flicks off the bathroom light, lengthening the shadows in the room.

Next, the bedside lamp goes dark and then he's sliding into the bed with me.

"Naughty little mouse," he says against my neck as he pulls my back to his chest.

I sigh contentedly. "I will never learn my lesson."

He snorts. "I can see I have my work cut out for me."

I snuggle into the pillow, my head suddenly heavy. "Bran?"

"Yes, Mouse?"

The air conditioning runs through the vents with a whir. I can hear the ticking of the analog clock that sits on Bran's dresser.

"Will we be okay today? After my Pledging?"

His arms tighten around me. "Whatever happens, I will protect you. You have my word."

I sigh and tangle my legs with his. "I love you."

"I love you too, Mouse."

Sixteen

When I wake, I roll over and reach out for Bran but find the bed empty beside me.

The windows are still shuttered so it's impossible to tell what time it is.

I stretch for the bedside table and pat around in the dark for my phone. When the screen lights up, I read 4:00 p.m.

That's early for Bran. Late for me.

My Pledge is in three hours.

I flop to my back, air rushing out of the thick pillows and surrounding me with Bran's scent.

Today is the day when everything changes.

If all goes according to plan, by the end of the day, I will officially be a member of the Duval Vampire House.

I will be Bran's and there will be no turning back.

My brain is telling me I should be freaking out. It's a lifetime commitment. But my heart and my gut are telling me this is exactly where I should be.

If only there was a better way to guarantee my sister's safety without her having to make the very permanent transition to vampire.

In the dark hush of Bran's bedroom, my mother's words echo in my head.

The things you did, Jessie...you were only a year old and it terrified me.

What could I do at such a young age to terrify my mother enough that she bound me?

And now that I'm twenty-one...

I place my hand over my beating heart and wish someone could just tell me these terrifying things I'm capable of.

Maybe if I knew, I could help protect my sister.

Because the fae gate has been closed since I was born, my knowledge of them and their abilities is minimal.

We are two days away from the new moon Rita said she needed to undo the binding, but...is it possible to weaken it?

I sit upright in bed as a thought comes to me.

Whenever my necklace is off, the taste of fae is much stronger in my blood. Bran said maybe when the necklace is off, the magic thins.

I toss the blanket back and click on the bedside lamp. I don't hear much beyond the bedroom.

I dress quickly in jeans and a t-shirt, then slip on a pair of tennis shoes.

Out in the main part of the Anneliese, I find my sister in the kitchen making a cup of coffee.

"Hey," I say. "How are you?"

She looks tired, but there's a new glow to her cheeks.

"I'm okay," she says. "You?"

I shrug. "Impatient for today to be over."

She brings the mug to her mouth and breathes across it, stirring the steam. "You and me both."

"Where's Bran?"

"He and Damien are in the main house discussing strategy for today."

I worry at my bottom lip, contemplating what I'm about to do. Bran will be pissed. But his anger is worth it if I can help my sister. I suspect I only know the half of what she's done to protect me since Mom died.

"I'm gonna go to the main house," I tell Kelly. "If you see Bran before I do, will you let him know?"

"Sure." Kelly's gaze is distant and glassy as she takes another sip from the coffee.

"Thanks."

She doesn't respond, which is just as well considering what I'm about to do.

———

Somehow, I make it out of Duval House without anyone questioning me. I find the Bimmer in the parking lot and drive off without any trouble at all. I feel a little guilty as Duval House fades in the rear-view mirror.

Since it's mid-afternoon, I know I can probably find Rita at the coffeeshop.

I park outside and head in, the bells chiming above the door when I open it.

Rita looks up. "Jessie, hi. Happy birthday!" She frowns, then adds, "What are you doing here?"

"I need a favor."

The frown deepens and aged lines appear on her forehead. "Why do I have a bad feeling about this favor?"

I scan the coffee shop and spot a few witches, none of them close allies of Rita's house, the Bowens. "Can we talk in the back?"

"Sure." Rita passes by Gwen and gives her a squeeze on the shoulder. "I'll be back out in a bit. Let me know if you need me."

"Will do." Gwen smiles at me.

In Rita's office, my skin crawls when I see the mess on her desk.

Don't look at it. You're here for a very specific reason and that reason is not to organize Rita's office.

"Remember when I came here to ask about the necklace and the binding and you said we needed a new moon to undo it?"

Rita folds her arms over her chest. "Of course."

"Whenever I take off this necklace"—I finger the charm hanging from the chain—"the magic is distant. I know that because Bran can taste fae blood when he bites me."

Rita turns her office chair and plops into it. "What are you asking?"

"Is there any way to undo the binding early?"

"Well, sure, we could try, but a spell that old, I'd much rather err on the side of caution and do it right the first time."

My stomach drops. I pace the small room. "Is there a way for you to take the necklace and help distance the magic? Like some kind of neutralizing spell or something?"

What I don't say is—is there a way for me to tap into my terrifying power *today*?

But I think Rita probably knows that.

Maybe not the terrifying part.

Rita thinks this over, her hands folded on top of a pile of crinkled receipts. "I suppose it's possible, but..." She looks up at me. "Is this because of your Pledge and the rumblings I've been hearing about it?"

I bite at the corner of my lip, considering how much to tell her. I know I can trust Rita, but I'm not sure Cal wants everyone knowing he has a psychic.

"The Renshaw witches are working with Julian and we think they're planning something for my Pledge and I don't want anyone to get hurt in the crossfire."

"You don't even know what your power is," Rita points out. "You wouldn't know the first thing about using it."

"But could I? With whatever spell you do? That's what I need to know."

If I could use the power when I was just a year old, then surely I can use it when I'm twenty-one. I just need to have access to it.

"I mean...theoretically, yes," she says. "A binding is a current just like any other magic. So yes, I think I could dam it temporarily until we can really undo it. But Jessie...what you're asking me is dangerous and extremely reckless."

"All of this is happening because of me. I need to be an active part of this, Rita. *Actively* defending those I love."

She pursues her lips, breathing out heavily through her nose.

"Bran will probably kill me," she says with a weary laugh.

"Let me handle Bran."

She arches a brow. "Well, all right. I suppose you want to do this now?"

"My Pledging is in three hours. It needs to be now."

Out in the shop, the steamer hisses as Rita gets up. She goes to her shelves and slips her reading glasses on, scanning the jars that are haphazardly arranged. She finally selects one that is full of a mixture of dark herbs and what looks like crushed crystals.

"Take off your necklace," she says as she brings the jar down.

I undo the clasp and the chain tickles my skin as it slides off my neck. When I hold it out, the charm spins from the end.

Rita takes it and then pops off the lid of the jar, placing the necklace inside. "I'll need some blood. Not a lot."

"All right."

She sets the jar on her desk and pulls a jeweled dagger from a drawer. I hold out my hand for her and she drags the blade over the palm of my hand, biting into my flesh.

I hiss and instinctively want to pull away but hold my hand steady in her warm grip.

Once blood wells in the wound, she turns my hand over to the mouth of the jar and several drops patter into the herbs and stones and covers the binding charm.

"That should be good," Rita says and nods at a box of tissue on the filing cabinet.

I pull a few out and press them to the wound as Rita whispers to herself, holding the jar in her grip.

A flame immediately ignites inside, tendrils of smoke and fire dancing over the rim.

Rita whispers one final word, then clamps the lid on, snuffing the flame.

My skin tingles.

A shiver creeps across my shoulders.

I lick my lips, still tasting the bite of Rita's magic on the air.

"Is that it?" I ask as blood soaks through the tissue.

"That's it."

"Did it work?"

"I don't know. Only you will."

"I don't feel different."

Though I do feel naked without the necklace. I've rarely taken it off since I was a kid.

"I should go," I say. "Bran will be wondering where I am soon."

Rita nods. "I'll be at your Pledging, just in case. You have me and the support of the entire Bowen house. Just so you know."

"Thank you, Rita."

I hurry to her side and wrap her in a hug. Beyond the magic, she smells like coffee and tea and warmth and familiarity.

"I really, really appreciate you."

When I pull back, her eyes are glistening. "That's very sweet of you. Now go on. Before I have a cantankerous vampire breathing down my neck."

I laugh as I leave. "I'm definitely going to use that someday. Bran's going to love it."

————

I keep checking my phone all the way back to Duval House, half expecting to find a barrage of texts from Bran admonishing me for leaving.

But there are none.

I think he's distracted. I think he and Damien are probably trying to plot for every contingency.

When I get back, I hurry in through a side door and avoid looking any of the vampires in the face as I pick up the pace for the Anneliese.

The house is empty when I walk through the front door.

I decide to shower and get ready. The earlier the better, I suppose. And I need the distraction.

What if Rita's spell didn't work? What if we try the unbinding on the new moon and it fails too? What if I never know who I am and what I'm capable of?

I suppose my mother warned me not to go down this road anyway.

I linger in the shower, soaking up the heat and scrubbing the blood from my hand.

I'm not sure if I should be surprised or relieved when I find the cut on my palm has vanished.

I've always healed quickly, but not *that* quickly.

The tingle returns, racing down my limbs, lifting goosebumps on my arms despite the intense heat of the water.

When I finish, I wrap a towel around myself and step out and find Bran waiting.

"Good morning, little mouse," he says.

"Afternoon," I correct.

"You start living with vampires, you'll realize soon enough that afternoon and morning are interchangeable."

He straightens as I come over to the vanity.

I sense his eyes on me.

"Where is your necklace?" he asks.

Inwardly, I groan. Of course he noticed. Nothing escapes Bran.

"I took it off."

"Mouse."

"Oh, don't Mouse me. I'm allowed to take it off."

"Where is it?"

"Not here."

"Now is not the time for surprises."

I want to help. I need to help.

If only I could figure out how to tap into this well inside of me. The one my mom said terrified her.

What can I do?

I meet my gaze in the mirror and try to dig up my secrets. I can't sense magic inside of myself. I don't even feel fae most of the time.

Who am I?

Who am I?

"Put the necklace back on," Bran orders. "Right fucking now."

I turn to him and clutch at the towel. "No."

"Mouse."

"I don't have the necklace," I say, anger tightening in my chest. "So I can't put it back on."

"I have vampire speed. I can retrieve it in ten minutes, tops."

"I'm not putting it back on."

"This was not part of the plan."

"You didn't let me be part of the plan. So I made my own."

His eyes narrow, jaw flexing. "What do you know of war and strategy, little mouse? Nothing."

"I'm not putting it—"

The bedroom door opens and there's a current of air as Jimmy appears in the bathroom doorway. She sees me in a towel and apologizes.

"It's okay," I say.

"What is it?" Bran asks, his words biting.

"The pack is here."

"Which wolf is it? The Alpha?"

Jimmy cants her head and her chain earrings swing. "You're not listening to me. I said, the pack is here. As in, the *entire pack*."

The surprise on Bran's face is a delight. It takes a lot to catch him off guard.

"For what?" he says.

"The Alpha said he's giving Jessie a personal escort to her Pledging."

Bran scowls and starts for the door. "The fuck he is."

Seventeen

The Alpha showing up with the pack has given me the distraction I need. Bran has all but forgotten about the necklace as he stalks from the room.

"Wait," I call and jog to catch up. "Bran, wait."

He stops at the end of the hallway. Jimmy is already gone.

"Think about this for a second."

"Which part, Mouse?" he challenges. "The Alpha thinking he can insert himself into *my* business or you disobeying me?" There is a pulsing glow in his irises and a clear bite to his words.

Maybe he hasn't forgotten about the necklace after all.

"I'm not your *business*," I correct. "I'm your girlfriend and I would think you'd use any tool at your disposal to protect me. Also you don't have to be territorial all of the damn time."

"Yes. I do."

I roll my eyes. "Okay, fine, but Cal is an asset and not taking advantage of him is a stupid strategy. If you want to be all tactical or whatever."

The angry glow fades from his eyes.

"If Cal wants to risk his life for this, let him."

Some of the tension ebbs out of his shoulders. "Perhaps you have a mind for war after all."

I try not to beam beneath the compliment.

"So the Alpha stays?"

Bran huffs out a disgruntled breath. "Fine. Yes, he stays. Now hurry up and get dressed. If I have to look at you in nothing but a towel for much longer, I will be bending you over the nearest piece of furniture."

A searing heat comes to my clit and Bran gives me one quick shake of his head. "No. We do not have time for that. Now go." He smacks me on the ass.

"Hey!"

"Go on, naughty little mouse."

"Fine. I'm going. You'll wait for me?"

Pulling out his cell phone, he taps at a name and gives me a nod. "I promise," he says.

Bran never breaks his promises.

Back in the bedroom, I pull out my Pledge dress from the closet. Kelly had it finalized for me months ago before all of this went down. Bran had someone return to our house to fetch it and I'm grateful he did.

I'm not one to go gaga over a dress, not like Kelly. But this one is special.

It was Mom's Pledge dress.

Mom had always had a thing for Audrey Hepburn, or really anything from old Hollywood. The dress was an A-line made of green satin with beading along the modest V-neck.

Kelly and I had it taken in at the waist to fit me better and had the sleeves taken off.

When I pull it on and stand in front of the full-length mirror, I'm suddenly overcome with emotion.

I wish Mom were here.

I wish I didn't have to worry about my sister.

I wish Mom would have told me who and what I was before she died, what this power is that might be running through my veins.

There is still no hint of what that power might be.

Why did you keep this secret from me, Mom?

Why?

Before I turn into a blubbering mess, I pull in several breaths and close my eyes, counting to ten.

No sense dwelling on what is and what isn't. I can't go back and Mom isn't coming back so I have to deal with the hand I'm dealt.

"Jess?" Kelly's voice sounds from the hallway.

"I'm in here. You can come in."

She appears behind me in the mirror a few seconds later and when she takes in the sight of me, her eyes get misty.

"No," I say. "No crying."

She bites at the corner of her bottom lip. "Sorry. I'm trying not to get emotional."

"Let's focus on the dress instead. How does it look?" I hold up the skirt and do a half turn.

"Lovely. Mom would have loved seeing you in it."

"I think so too. It turned out so well."

She comes into the bathroom and messes with my hair. "You should have blow-dried this. Now it'll be all messed up."

"Just put it into a bun."

"I suppose I could do that. Sit."

I pull out the stool from beneath the vanity and sit.

Kelly fusses behind me. "I wish I could be there."

"I do too. But promise me you'll stay here? In the Anneliese?"

"Of course I will." With skills that border on magic, Kelly tames my hair into a neat bun, then pulls a few wispy strands out along my face. "Any makeup?"

I grab a tube of mascara and lipstick. "This will do."

Within a few minutes, I'm ready to go."

"You look beautiful."

"Thank you."

"Everything will go according to plan."

A lump forms in my throat. Kelly plants a kiss on my cheek.

"Love you, sissy," I say.

"I love you too."

We leave the bedroom together and find Bran and Damien waiting by the front door, both in tailored black suits.

When Bran sees me, his eyes widen and his body goes rigid.

"What?" I ask.

"You look gorgeous, little mouse."

He rarely compliments me in this way. I think for Bran, physical appearance is not as important as it is for other people. He operates on feeling and gut instinct and what we have is something far deeper than physical attraction.

But even so, hearing him say those words makes me immediately blush and want to bat my eyelashes like an idiot.

What, this old thing?

He'd admonish me for playing *that* game.

"Thank you," I answer.

The look in his eyes tells me that if we survive this day, he will be doing very naughty things to me later. It'll give me something to look forward to.

"If you're done," Damien says wearily, "we should be going. Kelly, you'll stay here with Jimmy. There will be several vampires stationed outside the Anneliese. You are not to leave under any circumstances, understood?"

She nods. "I got it."

"Now come," Bran says and takes me into the wide sweep of his arms. "Let's go see what the Alpha has to say and then we'll be on our way."

———

Jimmy wasn't lying. The entire Midnight Pack is waiting outside Duval House.

"Well, this is unprecedented," Damien says from the wide wraparound porch. The sun has already sunk below the trees, but the night is still light enough to make out the vast size of the pack. There must be sixty men and women here.

Cal stands at the head with Fox at his left. The rest of the shifters are behind.

"Alpha," Bran says, "we didn't discuss this."

"I made a deal with Jessie, not you," Cal calls back, his deep, raspy voice reverberating across the property.

Bran's tongue runs along the inside of his bottom lip.

"Bran," I mutter beside him.

He clamps his mouth shut and takes my hand. He and Damien have me sandwiched between them as we make our way down the steps.

We come to a stop several feet away from the Alpha.

"What does this deal entail?" Bran gives me a sidelong glance before turning to Cal.

"I promised her I'd have her back," Cal answers. "In exchange for her help with my mate."

"And who is this mate?" Damien asks.

Fox steps forward. "That's none of your business."

Cal holds out his arm, stopping his beta from going further.

"I'm just here to lend my support," Cal says. "Imagine what your enemies will think when they see you show up with the pack behind you."

"I imagine they'll wonder if I have enough dog food to feed you all."

"Bran!" I shout.

He crosses his arms over his chest.

"No need to worry, Jessie," Cal says. "I suspect I will be growing on your vampire boyfriend soon enough."

Bran's mouth drops open. "Excuse me? Why do you say that?"

"I have a psychic, remember?"

"Yes, I do. And if you're insinuating that I might come to regard you as a friend or ally, you are very much mistaken, Alpha."

Cal snickers and turns away. The pack parts for him.

"Alpha!" Bran shouts.

"We should be going," Cal calls over his shoulder. "The night is getting away from us. If you'll drive, the pack will run beside you."

I can't help but laugh. This is a gift I didn't know I needed. But is Cal being serious? That seems a silly thing to joke about. I suspect Cal doesn't exactly want to be friends with Bran, but maybe our interests will continue to intersect and the two alpha men will come to an understanding.

I like the thought of it. Especially if Sam is destined to be with Cal.

"Stop smiling, Mouse," Bran mutters.

I clamp my hand over my mouth, but I'm sure he can tell the smile is still in my eyes.

He scowls and starts for his SUV, grumbling the whole way.

———

Bran drives with me tucked in the back, hidden behind dark tinted windows. Damien is in the passenger seat.

We don't speak.

I watch the blur of the pack racing through the woods beside us.

My stomach turns into knots the closer we get to the Harbor.

I can get through this.

It's going to be fine.

Most Pledges are just routine ceremonies. You make your Pledge. You sign some papers. You carry on with your life.

Nothing will be different about mine at all—

Except when we pull into the parking lot outside the Harbor, my heart drops.

It's packed.

More packed than on any other Pledge Day.

Judging by the number of vehicles and people milling around outside, everyone who matters is here.

"Holy shit," I say from the back. "Who are all these people? Is there another Pledge today? Maybe ten?"

"No," Damien answers, "yours was the only one on the schedule."

Christ.

Is this a good thing or a bad thing?

There is always reserved parking for the Pledgees, so Bran parks along the front of the building.

And standing just outside the entrance is none other than Julian, with half the Renshaw coven beside him.

Eighteen

Seeing Julian makes my stomach twist and my blood turn hot.

There was a time when I thought he was on our side, that he was concerned with our safety and well-being. But after what he did to Kelly, I know that was never true.

Julian Locke is only out for himself and he's willing to do whatever it takes to get what he wants.

Once we're out of the car, Bran offers me his arm and I eagerly take it. Damien steps to my other side and behind me are Cal and Fox. I catch sight of Bianca hurrying up the sidewalk. She's not wearing heels but sensible tennis shoes with a pleated plaid skirt.

Tennis shoes are always better for running. Is Bianca worried about getting away?

"An escort from the wolves?" Julian calls over to us as we make our way up the main walk. "Bran, I'd think that was beneath you."

My body goes rigid.

"Do not engage," Bran says beside me.

"I won't," I say beneath my breath, but then grip harder at the crook of his elbow.

"If I wasn't a vampire," he says, "I think you would be piercing my flesh."

"Sorry." I let up a little and exhale.

Everything will be all right.

Bianca falls into step on Bran's other side.

"You're late," he says to her.

"Apologies. My father tried stopping me from coming."

"Don't make that my problem."

"It won't be. I've handled it."

The Renshaw witches line up behind Julian. They're all in varying shades of black, white, and dark gray. The coven leader—Tabitha—watches me from Julian's left. Her gaze is penetrating and it makes me shiver. I've never had the bad luck of crossing paths with Tabitha until now. They've mostly stuck to themselves. The fact that they've aligned with Julian makes me wonder what they're getting out of it.

When we finally enter the Harbor and are out of their prying eyes, I exhale. But the relief is short lived.

I'm used to the Harbor being busy. I mostly only come here when there are parties to attend, so seeing the halls full of people is nothing out of the ordinary. But the two dozen witches and shifters and vampires just lingering in the hall for a routine Pledge is certainly *out* of the ordinary.

And worse, everyone's eyes are on me. "There are so many people here," I whisper to Bran.

"Everyone is ready for a show," he answers.

We go left, bypassing the onlookers.

The Pledge Hall was added to the Harbor sometime in the fifties. It was constructed as a circular amphitheater with sloping seating on tiers so that everyone in the back can see easily down to the front.

When we enter, we go down to the reserved seating.

The Pledge director, Carl Philmore, greets us with a wide smile. "Jessie! Did you see the turnout today? My god, this must be exciting for you."

If only he knew.

"Yes, so exciting," I say as he shakes my hand vigorously.

"We're just about ready to get started if you are."

I swallow hard and Bran watches me.

"I'm ready."

"Great. Excellent." Carl rubs his hands together and the dry skin rasps. He's a nice man with a small family in Midnight. He's not Pledged to anyone, since he's Pledge Director. He's a man of the humans, as I've heard him say on more than one occasion. "Have a seat," he tells me, "and we'll bring the room to order."

I drop into the padded seating and try not to fidget.

I have several powerful, strong allies on my side.

How can any of this go wrong?

Carl disappears into a side room while my heart races and my hands grow clammy. When he returns in a black robe, much like a judge, my knee starts bouncing. Bran reaches over and grips me reassuringly, and I can barely meet his eyes, afraid that if I do, I'll start sobbing with nerves and anxiety.

I have to get through this. There's no way out but through.

"We call to order Pledge number 207 of this year for Jessie MacMahon. Jessie is twenty-one as of today and now eligible to Pledge to a House in Midnight Harbor."

Behind me, I hear chairs squeaking and clothing rustling and bodies shuffling around as everyone finds a seat and gets settled.

I dare to look over my shoulder and catch sight of Julian taking a seat two tiers up. But he's noticeably alone.

My stomach drops.

Carl rubs his hands together again. "Now, I know many of you are familiar with the Pledge Code, and this part will bore you to death, but my boss makes me do it. Of course, my boss is the law." He laughs to himself. There is a weak chorus of laughter behind us.

"As soon as we get through this part, we can move on to the fun stuff!" Carl opens a book in front of him and starts reading from one of the passages. He's not lying—the Pledge Code is boring and dry and if I wasn't so keyed up, I would be sleeping by now.

Bran gives me another squeeze. I lean into him and whisper into his ear. "I'm so glad you're here with me."

"I wouldn't be anywhere else, Mouse."

Carl flips a page and continues.

I catch sight of Bianca on the other side of Bran, her big, wide eyes searching as much of the room as she can from her vantage point in the front.

Beside me, Damien is still as water, but I sense an underlying tension in his body.

Finally, Carl reads the last of the code from his book—blah blah a Pledge agrees to show his or her house the utmost respect and be a stand-up representative of his or her chosen House.

When he shuts the book with a thud, I have a hard time taking in a full breath.

This is happening.

It's really happening.

"Now!" Carl booms. "We'll start with House bids and will conduct opening bids in alphabetical order." He steps back where the wall has been divided into twelve sections, each with a button and an old-fashioned light bulb above it with the House name in bold, block letters.

"Abernathy," Carl calls. Witches. There is silence in the room for a beat and then Carl goes to the next house. "Bowen." Silence again.

We make it through several more houses before finally reaching Duval House and when Carl calls out the name, both Damien and Bran stand up.

"We would like to formally bid on Jessie MacMahon to be a member of our house," Damien says.

"Excellent!" Carl taps at the button for Duval House. The old-fashioned light bulb glows bright gold before Carl calls out the next name. "Locke House."

Fuck.

Behind us, Julian stands up and I hear the shuffle of papers. "Before I formally make my bid," Julian says, "I'd like to submit to the court a promissory note from her mother."

"What?" I shout.

Bran grabs my hand and holds me in my seat.

Carl frowns and makes his way up two tiers to retrieve this supposed promissory note. He squints as he reads. "Interesting. Did you have this authenticated?"

"I did. I had it authenticated by both the human court and by the Renshaw witches." Julian hands over a second piece of paper.

I lurch from my seat. Bran reaches out for me, but for once, I'm able to dodge him. "Fuck you, Julian," I yell.

The crowd takes in a collective breath.

"That's probably a lie just like my sister's blood license. Or did you compel my mother too? Make her your puppet?" Anger and frustration and fear are pounding through my veins. I don't know what else to do other than to lash out. "I'm not Pledging to your house. Fuck you and fuck the Lockes, and you can fuck off!"

The scandal of it all races through the room. People are snickering and openly gaping.

If they wanted a show, they're about to get one.

Julian's teeth grind together. There is a tell-tale twitch at the corner of his mouth and glowing ire in his blue eyes.

"Your mother did make this promise, and she was under no compulsion. She knew what was good for you and Bran Duval was not on that list."

Bran stands up to flank me. "You don't get to decide that, Julian. She's not going to be yours."

Julian sighs. It's not a sigh of defeat, but of exasperation. As if we're petulant children he now has to correct.

Still in his seat, Damien's cell phone buzzes in his pocket. He pulls it out and lights up the screen and I can't help but be distracted by it, by him. Because watching him digest the message is like watching someone learn they've just been diagnosed with a fatal disease.

His shoulders level out, his eyes widening, nostrils flaring.

He looks up at his brother and Bran looks down at him.

"Jimmy just woke up," he mouths.

It doesn't take me long to parse out the meaning of that.

Jimmy just woke up...meaning she was either knocked out or had her neck snapped.

If Jimmy just woke up, then Kelly—

One of the doors in the far back pulls open and a Renshaw witch steps through.

And held in her grip is none other than my sister.

———

We knew this was coming and yet now that it's happening, I think we're all a little shocked by it.

What was it Cal warned us about?

"Kelly will be on the north end of the Pledge Hall when she's struck down."

And where is Kelly now?

On the fucking north end.

I can barely hear the whispering of the room over the rapid thudding of my heart.

Damien is on his feet in a second. "Julian," he says, his voice rumbling with warning. "I don't think you fully understand what it is you're doing."

"On the contrary." Julian steps into the aisle. "You think I would, *what*, just let you take something that was owed to me? Something powerful beyond comprehension?"

"I'm not *something*," I say. "I'm a fucking human being."

He screws up his mouth. "Don't play dumb, Jessie. We all know you're far from human."

The whispers pick up in the room.

"Wait," Carl says. "Jessie isn't human?"

Julian's face falls as he realizes his grave error.

"If she isn't human," Carl starts.

Julian gestures to one of the Locke House vampires and he darts over to the director, compelling him to forget this minor detail—if I'm not human then I can't Pledge.

"This is a stupid plan," Damien yells. "You have two hundred witnesses in here. You can't compel them all."

"I won't need to."

The Renshaw witch drags my sister further into the room and down two steps. Kelly fights against the woman, but judging by my sister's lack of progress, I'd say the witch is using some kind of magic to keep her under control.

"What do you want?" Damien asks.

Quietly, slowly, people start backing out of the room.

"I want what's rightfully mine. Both Jessie and Kelly. Those are my terms."

"Absolutely not," Bran and Damien say in unison.

"Then you leave me no choice," Julian answers.

The witch at my sister's side pivots behind Kelly and places her hands on either side of her head.

For a fraction of a second, I see Damien ready to move, ready to spring and save my sister.

But even he can't beat the speed of magic.

The air around my sister's head undulates like heat rising from an oil fire.

Then her eyes roll back so that all I can see are the whites. Blackness appears beneath the fingertips of the Renshaw witch and the black spreads like wiggling tendrils of ink beneath Kelly's skin.

Beside me, Damien jolts.

Darkness is seeping into his skin too.

And within seconds, Damien and Kelly are consumed by the spell and both hit the floor with a resounding thud.

Nineteen

It can be like a storm cloud, the darkness rising on the horizon, the sky flashing with lightning long before the storm lands. You know when a storm is coming. You can see it and you can feel it.

But war can also be like an earthquake. One minute your life is normal and the next it's falling in around you, the ground cracking beneath your feet.

This is like a storm and an earthquake. Because we felt this coming, but I don't think we were prepared for the ground to shake.

Everything is still and then suddenly everyone is moving.

A Renshaw witch stands from her seat in the back of the room and lifts her arms in my direction. She mutters something to herself.

Bianca whips her hand toward me and there is a clash of air two feet away, followed by the overwhelming scent of magic—like tinder and wild earth.

The hair rises on the back of my neck.

"Mouse!" Bran yells. He is caught between coming to me or going to Damien. He picks me, but a Locke vampire catches him off guard and puts his hands on either side of Bran's head, ready to give his head a swift yank to break his neck.

And that's when the Alpha jumps in.

Cal slams into the Locke vampire and the sound of bones breaking rings in my ears.

Bran looks at Cal and gives him an appreciative nod.

The room erupts in battle.

Witches fighting witches and wolves tearing through vampire flesh. Vampires darting back and forth, tossing people like they're nothing more than dolls.

What do I do?

What about Kelly and Damien and—

Another vampire punches Bran in the chest and his ribs cave in. He gasps for air as blood spills from his mouth.

Those who aren't ready for a fight scatter from the room, screaming and flailing, ducking when a body flies overhead.

This isn't right.

Everyone I love is in this room.

There is the sharp tang of blood in the air and the whiff of defeat.

We don't have enough witches on our side. Julian has the entire Renshaw house.

I'm not cattle. I cannot be bought or bartered for, but if my mother really promised me to Julian...then by law, I have to go with him. It's an old rule left over from the founding days of Midnight Harbor. No one uses it anymore.

I never would have thought my own mother would turn on me. And worse yet, I can't even yell at her.

Bran goes down when a vampire and a witch gang up on him.

He's covered in blood. He's healing just as fast as they're beating him.

If something happens to Kelly and Bran, I will not survive it.

What is the point of being terrifying if I can't do anything to save them?

"Stop," I hear myself saying in a shaky whine, tears blurring in my eyes. "Please stop."

Julian comes up on Bran and takes a fistful of his hair, yanking him to his feet.

"No," I whisper and take a step, goosebumps lifting on my arms, a chill racing up my back.

A witch throws a hit at Cal and the Alpha is tossed into a row of seats.

"*No.*"

Everywhere I look, there is carnage and pain.

"Your problem," Julian says to Bran as Bran sways on his feet, "is your arrogance. You and your brother always assume you'll be the most powerful person in the room. What you don't factor in, is someone who is smarter."

Bran spits in Julian's face, splattering blood across Julian's cheek. "You're the dumbest little shit I've ever met," Bran says. "I've never doubted that."

One of the Renshaw witches flicks her hand at Bran and Bran's body lets out a horrible crunch.

Fire comes to Bran's eyes as he grits against the pain.

Behind him, one of Julian's vamps grabs a chair and snaps the leg in two.

"*No*, please..." My voice rises, hands shaking.

Two witches stand over Cal, hands raised in a spell. The Alpha roars.

Damien and Kelly still aren't moving.

Fox is cornered by two Locke vamps as more shifters are caught in battle.

"I will be glad to be rid of you," Julian says.

The Locke vampire lifts the makeshift stake behind Bran, ready to strike at his heart.

No. *No.*

I can't lose Bran.

I can't lose this battle.

It's too much.

It's all too much.

"*STOP!*" I shout.

And the room goes eerily still.

———

I'm gasping for air. I'm hot all over. My skin is crawling.

What is happening?

No one is moving. Everyone is frozen mid-stride.

They're all breathing, though, blinking through the disbelief.

"Mouse," Bran says. He can't seem to turn his head my way, but he can speak. He's caught in place in front of Julian, the Locke vampire at his back, the stake inches from piercing Bran's flesh. "Mouse."

"I don't know what's happening," I say, voiced edged in panic.

Julian blinks, his teeth gritted, his hand half-raised. "You undid the binding?"

"No," Bran answers, not moving a muscle.

"Wait—" I take a step and Julian's eyes narrow as if he wishes he could dart away. "You're not surprised by this? What is it?"

Julian doesn't answer.

"Tell me right now or I swear to god—"

"You'll what?" Julian challenges. "You don't know the first thing about your power. Not what it is or how to use it."

"Mouse," Bran says again.

"What?"

"Use your voice."

It's an echo of what he's said to me before. Use my voice. Speak my mind. Quit hiding what I want and who I am.

But he means it differently now. Julian was wrong—Bran is always the most powerful and the smartest person in the room.

He's put it together much quicker than I have.

I used my voice. I told the room to stop and they did. All of them. Caught like a bug in a drip of amber.

Use my voice.

The things you did, Jessie...you were only a year old and it terrified me.

A year old, when a child, especially a fae child, might learn to *speak*.

A tingling chill runs through my entire body.

I turn on Julian. His eyes narrow.

"Jessie," he says.

My heart thuds in my ears.

"You know what I can do," I say. He doesn't deny it. I think he's known since Sasha bit me and I think he must have somehow forced my mother into admitting it. "You knew and you kept it from me and everyone else because you wanted to use me for your own gains.

"That's not what it was—"

"You've been conniving and controlling and manipulative from the beginning because you knew that if you possessed a power that no one else did, you would be the most powerful person in the room. You would strip Bran and Damien of that title and you would take over Midnight to be the king of a castle he stole."

"Jessie—"

The heat builds in my chest. The blood pounds through my veins. And that dark thing, that dark feeling I had after Bran and Damien decimated the vampire court swims much closer to the surface.

I can feel it yawning inside of me, no longer tethered.

And the thirst for vengeance takes root.

I want him to die.

I want Julian to burst into ash beneath my hands.

"Jessie," Bran says again.

I go behind him and take the stake from the Locke vampire. The bigger man grunts and groans, but there's nothing he can do to stop me.

"Help me get out of this and I will take care of this for us," Bran says. "Let *me* have blood on my hands."

I stop in front of Julian, the stake held firmly in my grip.

"Mouse."

"You deserve to suffer for what you did to my sister," I tell Julian. "But I'm too impatient."

"Don't do this," Julian begs.

"Fuck you."

"Mouse!"

I drive the stake right through Julian Locke's heart.

———

There is a moment between Julian's life and death where he just blinks at me and then down at the stake protruding from his chest.

His lips move, as if he means to protest.

But before any words can come out, he bursts into ash.

A gasp wends through the room and the last of Julian Locke paints the air in swirls of dust.

"Mouse," Bran says again. "Unfreeze me."

I stagger back.

"Mouse, please."

I bump into him, swallowing hard.

"Jessie," he says, as if my real name might better get my attention.

I turn around to face him, caught between shock and awe.

I just killed a man and froze an entire room.

The tears start running down my face.

The line of Bran's brow sinks over his eyes. He takes a breath. "Unfreeze me."

"I don't know how."

"Just say the words, Mouse."

I take in a breath and nod. "Okay." Closing my eyes, I try to focus on what I want. I don't know exactly how to use this power that burns through my veins, but it *is* mine. It's always been mine. "Um...*Bran...* you can move freely."

When his hands come to my face, I open my eyes and meet his gaze. More tears blur my vision. "Are you okay?" he asks.

I nod and bite at my bottom lip, not entirely sure I can keep it together for much longer. "I'm okay." For now.

Bran blurs away and sinks beside his brother, turning Damien on his back. I go to Kelly's side and check her breathing, putting my ear to her heart. The blackness from the spell has disappeared, leaving her unmarred. It's almost like she's sleeping.

"Kelly?" I give her a shake. "Can you hear me?"

She doesn't respond, so I pinch her arm. Still nothing.

"What did they do to you?" I whisper.

"Jessie, I need you to unfreeze Cal," Bran calls. "Get Fox and Bianca, and anyone else that we consider an ally."

"I...I'm not..."

He looks up at me. "You can do it, Mouse. But hurry."

I go to Cal first. He's closest and the strongest. One of the Locke vampires has a fistful of his shirt in his grip. He's got his teeth gnashed as he watches me, unable to stop me. There's blood spilling from the corner of Cal's mouth, and several splatters painting his blond hair.

I still don't know how this power works, but hopefully it's enough just to believe in the words. Otherwise, we're all in a world of shit.

"Cal," I say and push emphasis into my meaning, *"you can move freely."*

Like a movie suddenly set to PLAY, Cal staggers forward and then pries his shirt from the Locke vamp's hand.

"Thank you, Jessie," he says.

One by one I go around the room and unfreeze those we consider friends. And with every one, my body aches a little more, my vision gets blurrier, and my heart races in my head.

By the time I've done the last one, I feel faint, legs shaking. I nearly crash to the ground before Bran is behind me, catching me.

"Come on, little mouse," he says and scoops me into his arms. My body is boneless in his grip, but I cling to him because I don't know what else to do.

"I've got your brother," Cal calls. Damien is slung over his shoulder.

"Kelly?" I ask.

"Fox has her," Bran tells me.

The rest of the room—the remaining Locke vampires, the Renshaw witches—are still frozen in the grip of whatever power I wield.

"How long do you think they'll be like that?" I ask.

Bran carries me toward the door. "This can become their tomb for all I fucking care."

"You can't just leave us like this!" one of the Renshaws says.

"The fuck we can't," Bran says as he leaves.

"Hey! Please! Don't leave us!"

Someone shuts the door behind us, muffling the sound of their calls for help.

Twenty

I'm numb all the way back to Duval House.

Numb and faraway.

The things you could do, Jessie...

When we reach the house, we pull in beneath the *porte-cochère*. Jimmy is there, waiting with several other vampires. They have pole stretchers for Damien and Kelly.

They still haven't regained consciousness.

I turn in the passenger seat of the SUV to glance back at my sister. Bran settled them into the crook of the SUV's back door with Damien leaning against it and Kelly tucked into his side.

Will they ever wake up? Or are they trapped in a spell like Sleeping Beauty, forever waiting for the other's kiss?

Once we're parked, Jimmy and another vampire slowly open the back door and pull Damien out first and deposit him on a stretcher. Kelly slumps over in his absence, before Bran catches her and lifts her out like she weighs nothing at all.

"Take them to the infirmary," Jimmy orders.

I don't have the energy to be shocked that Duval House has an infirmary.

Bianca races up to us, having driven separately. She's disheveled and there's still a smudge of blood on her cheek.

Is she already regretting joining Duval House?

"I'm here," she says, panting.

It isn't until Bran comes around to the passenger side that I realize I'm still sitting in the SUV. "Come on, Mouse." He offers me his hand. I just blink at it.

"I...I'm not..."

"Can you walk?" he asks.

"I..."

He moves to carry me out, but I push him away. "I can walk."

"Then I need you to do it. Come."

I slip out of the SUV and feel slightly better once my feet are on solid ground, once I drink in a deep breath of fresh air. It's dark beyond the golden glow of the house, and the crickets are chirping in the warm summer night. I wish I was doing anything else other than this.

Bran hooks his arm around my waist and drives me toward the side entrance. He barks orders as we walk. "Michael and Anthony on the east side of the property, Isaac and Danielle on the west side. Jimmy, get the rest of the guard on the north and south ends and then double check that the security system is functioning properly. Bianca."

"Yes?" she says from my right side.

"I need you to tell me what happened to my brother and Kelly."

"Of course. I'll do my best."

"Your best is only good enough if it gets me answers."

Bee nods at him. "I'll figure it out."

"Good. If you need something in the meantime, ask Jimmy. No expense is too large. Whatever it is, you'll get it. Keep me updated."

"I will," she promises before she veers off, chasing after Damien and Kelly.

"I want to see my sister," I say, but my voice sounds far away.

Bran says nothing. He steers me through the house, through the French doors and into the Anneliese. He's silent still as we enter the house and go to the bedroom and finally to the bathroom. He starts up the shower.

"Bran," I say, my voice wobbling. "I want to see my sister."

"After you shower," he says.

"I don't want a shower. I want to—"

"I can smell Julian on you, Mouse. You reek of his death. I need you to shower. Right now. *Please.*"

I finally look at him and meet his eyes. There's no glow to his irises. But there is something else. Some shifting shadow.

Fear.

He's being gentle. When has Bran ever been gentle with me?

I swallow hard and try not to let my own fear consume me.

"I don't know what that was back there," I tell him, the hysteria making my voice shake. "I don't know how I did it. Maybe it was just a fluke or—"

Steam fills the bathroom.

"Please get in the shower."

Every muscle in his body is coiled.

Every fiber of him on the edge of vibrating.

I nod and strip off my clothes and get in the shower.

Once I'm beneath the hot spray, some of the tension eases out of my muscles. That is until I hear the bathroom door click closed.

I can feel the distance widening between us.

I stopped Bran in his tracks with nothing more than a single word.

The things you could do, Jessie...

Something tells me Bran Duval isn't familiar with being powerless.

Everything has changed. Did he expect it to be this way? He knew I had a hidden power. Surely he must have known it was something with some worth, otherwise Julian wouldn't have gone to all the trouble.

But maybe this is worse than he thought.

Maybe I *am* terrifying.

I finish up and get dressed. Hair still dripping and knotty, I make my way to the living room and spot Bran in the courtyard smoking a cigarette. I've yet to see him smoke, but I've smelled it on him.

There's something inherently sexual about the way he inhales, how the curl of his finger is exaggerated as he pulls it away from his mouth.

When he exhales, he paints the night in smoke.

"Are you okay?" I ask him.

He takes another hit, holding the smoke in his lungs a beat. "I don't know," he admits and exhales.

"Anything from Bianca yet?"

"Not yet." He goes over to a stone bench nestled among flowering bushes and sits.

I join him and am horribly aware of how rigid he is beside me. "Bran—"

"You're more powerful than I thought you'd be," he admits, then snorts, bringing the cigarette back to his lips. He takes another long drag, the ember blazing orange. When he pushes the smoke back out, he goes on. "I thought maybe you could wield fae magic like a weapon. Maybe you could cast a really, really deceptive glamour. Controlling an entire room of extremely powerful supernatural creatures?" He shakes his head to himself and looks across the garden. "That...that I never would have imagined."

I lean into him and hook my arm through his, resting my head against his shoulder. "I don't know what to say."

"There's nothing to say."

"But...what does this mean? Are you...I mean, are we...?" I don't know what I'm trying to say. *Are we okay? Will we survive this? Am I terrifying to you?*

He drops the cigarette and crushes the ember beneath his boot, then takes my hand in his. "Make me a promise, Mouse."

"Of course. Anything."

"Give me a safe word."

"What?"

"Something we can both agree on that should *that* happen again, if I use the word, you'll release me immediately."

"Bran—"

"Give me this, Mouse."

I meet his gaze and find a pulsing glow in his irises. There's desperation there.

"Okay. What's the word?"

He squeezes my hand and brings it to his mouth. His breath is warm across my knuckles as he thinks.

"Lavender," he finally says.

"Really?"

"It reminds me of home."

I don't think he means Duval House and it makes me realize I know nothing about where he was born or what life he had before he was turned. The only thing I know about him is who he is in Midnight Harbor at this moment in time.

"Okay. Lavender. You can use it at any time, for any reason," I say. "Not that I plan on using that power on you. I don't know if I'll ever use it again. In fact...what if we just don't undo the binding? I mean...I could put the necklace back on and we could forget about it and—"

"No." He stands and pulls me up beside him. "It's part of you and you should absolutely use it for that reason. But beyond that, everyone who matters was in that Pledge Hall tonight. You'll have to use it. Because if you don't, they'll use you."

Bran's attention wanders away from me and Jimmy appears a second later. "Damien?" he asks her.

"No." There are bags beneath Jimmy's eyes and her lips are chapped. She looks about as great as I feel. I don't know what the Lockes did to get past her and grab Kelly, but I am absolutely sure she did everything in her power to protect my sister.

"If it's not Damien," Bran says, his words turning coarse, "then I don't—"

"There's someone at the front door," she blurts.

Bran's brow furrows. "Who?"

"A brownie." Her gaze darts to me. "Says he knows Jessie. Says it's time they talk."

"The fuck is a brownie doing here?" Bran says.

A tingling numbness rushes down my limbs. "The letter," I say. "The one my mom wrote."

Bran sighs. "Fuck."

"Yes."

My mom mentioned a brownie in her letter, the one she crossed paths with in the park when I was just a year old. The same one who knew instantly what I was and asked my mom if she stole me.

"What do we do?" I ask.

Bran turns a circle, his hands on his hips as he considers it. "If a brownie wants to speak with you, he'll find a way. It's better to do it on our territory, when we know the lay of the land."

I nod. "All right. I'll follow your lead." I don't want Bran to worry about where we stand.

He starts for the French doors. Jimmy and I follow him out and down the hall and to the front door.

"Where is he?" Bran asks.

"He refused to come in," Jimmy answers. "He's on the front porch."

I have to quicken my pace to keep up with Bran's determined gait. At the front door, hand on the knob, he hesitates.

We all know that everything has changed. But a fae showing up on our doorstep is a true marker of it.

Bran pulls the door open.

I immediately recognize the brownie.

It's Stanley from The Greasy Spoon.

The cook who makes the best grilled cheese in all of Midnight Harbor.

Usually I see Stanley in his Greasy Spoon uniform—a pale blue shirt with his name embroidered over a pocket on his chest, The Greasy Spoon logo embroidered on the back. Now he's in a pair of dark trousers and a rough cotton button-up shirt with a tweed cap on his head.

In this setting, he seems different. Less grizzled diner cook, more withered fae. Like he just stepped out of the hollow of a tree and has yet to shake off the magic of the forest.

"Stanley?" I say and come out on the porch. "You're a brownie? How come you didn't—"

He takes a mirroring step back. "You used your magic."

I level my shoulders, feeling defensive of it. "Yes. It is my magic, isn't it?"

"They'll feel you," he says.

"Who?"

His eyes dart to Bran just behind me. "This your idea?"

"Of course not, old man. I tried to stop her."

"Who, Stanley?"

"The Autumn Court," he answers.

"The court isn't here though and the gate is closed."

He licks his lips, nods. "Now that you've used your power, they'll find a way to get through."

"Why?"

He looks at Bran again. "You could take her away from here. Compel her to forget."

"Excuse me—"

"I won't do that to her."

"I'm right here."

Stanley's gaze darts back to me. He removes his hat and clutches the brim in his gnarled hands. "They'll come for you, Jessie, and it's hard saying what they'll do when they find you. Are you ready to become who you are?"

"Do you mean my fae side?"

"That is half."

"What's the other half?"

"Are you prepared?" he asks again. "Once you decide, there's no turning back." His voice is deep and hoarse. I used to think he smoked a lot, but now I wonder if it's just age. Brownies can be ancient. He could very well be older than Bran by a millennium.

"I'm not running, if that's what you're asking me."

"Very well." He turns his hat in his grip and then he sinks to one knee.

My mother's words come back to me in a rush.

He immediately came over to us and got down on one knee in front of you...

I thought she meant he knelt to get down to my eye level.

But this is not that. For one, I'm an inch or two taller than Stanley. And two...his head is bowed.

The panic takes hold quickly, turning into a band across my chest.

"You'll need all the help you can get," he says. "When they come, they will not be merciful."

"*Stanley,*" I whisper-shout, desperate for him to get up.

"The name is actually Grimwall," he says. "And I am at your service, Your Royal Highness."

BOOK FOUR

ONE

YOUR ROYAL HIGHNESS.

I just gape at Stanley bent low on his knees on the wide front porch of Duval House and struggle with the urge not to laugh or cry or vomit.

Your Royal Highness?

What complete and utter bullshit.

It can't be true.

No fucking way.

Right?

Right?

"Get off your knees, old man," Bran says and surges ahead, hooking his hand beneath Stanley's arm. Stanley comes easily and follows Bran into the house. "You." Bran points a finger at me. "Come."

I scurry after him, ever the dutiful little mouse, as he leads Stanley through the foyer, then down the hall and into Damien's office.

When we're all inside, Bran shuts the door and goes to the wet bar. The cork top lets out a loud *fwop* as Bran pulls it out of the crystal decanter and fills a glass with liquor. He slings it back. All of it. All in one gulp.

He bows his head, sets the glass back down.

Stanley and I share a look. It's odd seeing him outside of the diner.

Like a deer that has wandered into the milk aisle at the grocery store. Not that Stanley doesn't deserve to have a life outside of The Greasy Spoon. I've just literally never seen him beyond the four walls of the place.

He spins his hat in his hands, working at the brim with gnarled fingertips.

He seems nervous. I don't blame him. Bran is on edge and Stanley just dropped a bomb.

"This is a mistake," I say, trying to ease the tension from Bran's shoulders.

Stanley takes a deep breath, pushes it back out, and says, "I assure you, Your Royal—"

"Stop that." I shake my head. "You've been making me grilled cheeses for years. Now you're trying to tell me you're a brownie and I'm some...what, royal fae?"

He blinks. "Yes. That's precisely what I'm saying."

"But I'm not a *royal fae*."

"Jessie—"

"Stanley—"

"Enough!" Bran's voice cuts across the room even though his back is still to us.

Stanley clamps his mouth shut, curling the brim of his hat like an ocean wave.

Bran refills his glass and captures it in a white-knuckle grip before coming over to us. His energy is different than mine—less jittery, more raw chaos like a tornado about to touch ground.

He points a finger at Stanley. "You can't just barge into my house and start bowing in front of the whole fucking place!"

Stanley's bushy gray brow furrows over his brown eyes. "It's customary to bow before a—"

"I don't fucking care what's customary! You expose us all and risk far too much by getting on your fucking knees." A vein pulses down Bran's forehead. He turns away again, takes another sip of the alcohol, and paces the length of the room.

"Bran," I try but he holds up his hand, cutting me off.

"I need to think, Mouse."

I thought if we made it through my Pledge, Bran and I would be returning to the house and to our bed to celebrate. Instead, my sister and his brother are in some kind of magical coma and my favorite grilled cheese cook is a brownie who claims I'm royalty.

I'm starting to expect the unexpected, but even this is too much.

Plopping into one of the leather chairs, I prop my elbow on the arm and set my head in my hand. I'm exhausted. Mentally. Emotionally. Physically.

I've barely had time to think about what might be wrong with my sister let alone what any of the rest of this means.

I stopped an entire room with my voice. Dozens of extremely powerful vampires and shifters and witches.

Stopped them in their tracks with nothing more than four letters.

Everything is moving far too fast. I'm strapped to a speeding train and I can't get off.

When Bran has had several minutes of silence, he drains the second glass of liquor and then sets it on Damien's desk. The vein in his forehead has relaxed, but there's still a pinch to his eyes, a hardness to his jaw.

As much as my world is spinning, Bran's is too.

"What is she?" he asks.

Stanley licks his lips, nostrils flaring. "That's a very complicated question and I—"

"Wait." They both cut their gazes to me. "What if I don't want to know?"

I can't get my mom's words out of my head.

The things you did, Jessie...

There is a monster lurking in the shadows and that monster is me.

Do I really want to put a name to it?

Maybe it's better if I don't know.

Bran scowls at me. "You went against me." He takes a step toward me and I sit up straighter in the chair. "You removed your necklace and refused to put it back on." I stand and lurch backward as Bran's eyes bleed to gold. "*You* made this decision. *You* made a show of force. This is not a genie that can be stuffed back into a bottle!"

I back into Damien's desk and a pencil holder rattles on top.

"Okay," I say, and hold up my hands. "Okay."

Bran heaves out a breath, fangs protruding from his mouth. I know he won't hurt me, but I'm worried he'll run away because he's *worried* he will.

I take his hand and bring it to my chest. "Make me a promise."

His face softens. "Now is not the time—"

"Make me a promise, Bran Duval."

He tilts his head and squeezes my hand in his. "Very well. What is it, little mouse?"

"Whatever I am, *whoever* I am, you'll stay by my side no matter what. Even if it terrifies you."

"I'm not afraid of you."

I know he's lying.

I know we're both terrified of the truth.

"Promise me."

"*Fine*. I promise."

There is nothing Bran values more than his word.

The relief that washes through me is nearly palpable.

I give him a nod. "All right then." To Stanley I say, "Tell us. Tell us everything you know."

———

Stanley sets his cap on the arm of the chair and folds his hands in his lap. He clears his throat, then swallows, the sharp line of his Adam's apple sinking like a weight. "War has been brewing on the fae side for a very long time. The Autumn Court and the Winter Court are both of the Unseelie, but the Winter Court had always held more power and had always been a little crueler than the others. They lost that power in the Autumn Revolt many, many years ago. Long before you, vampire." He eyes Bran with a wary look, the same kind of look a grandfather gives to the kids who think they know everything.

"The Autumn Court had the full support of the Summer and Spring Courts, and during the war, they were able to wipe out the entire royal line of the Winter Court."

My heart hammers a little harder beneath my ribs.

"Or at least…that's what we thought," Stanley adds.

I suddenly can't breathe.

"When I crossed paths with your mother in the park," Stanley goes on, "I realized someone must have escaped."

Cold dread spills down my spine.

"You smelled like the Winter Court, but more than that, you spoke like one."

What you could do, Jessie…

"The royal line of the Winter Court had always had one very distinct power—the ability to control anyone—and I mean *anyone*—with nothing more than the sound of their voice."

"Like a siren," Bran says.

Stanley nods. "That's a mortal term that's been combined with mermaid, but yes, it is fitting. They could make men jump to their deaths. Women bow at their feet. Stop armies in their tracks. And worse, they were the only fae that could lie."

Stanley sits forward in his chair. "And you, Jessie…you seem to be the only surviving member of the Royal Winter Court. The only living fae who can command others with nothing but the power of her voice. And now that you've used the power, the fae realm will be looking for a way to get to you."

My chest rises and falls with several deep breaths. "Why, though? Why do they care now?"

"Because…the entire reason they were at war? It was because your family tried to overthrow all of the courts so they could rule the faerie realm under one banner. And they were using their voice to do it."

He levels me with a heavy gaze. "As far as they're concerned, you are the villain of their story."

Two

Do not puke.

You totally got this.

Everything is okay and everything will be okay and—

Shit.

I lurch across the room to a trash can, hit my knees and heave.

Oh god.

Oh god.

Bran is beside me in an instant, his cool hand at the nape of my neck. He says nothing. Just lets me retch and vomit in silence.

When my stomach stops revolting, I suck in several deep breaths.

"Jimmy," Bran calls, but no one comes. Probably she's still busy with Bianca and Damien and Kelly. "Stay here, Mouse," he tells me and then is gone.

I push away from the wastebasket and fall back on the plush rug. Stanley blocks out the ceiling light when he comes to stand over me, several tissues in hand. I take them quickly and wipe at my mouth.

The old man kneels again. I groan but he offers me his hand and says, "Just to help you up."

I suppose I can handle that.

When I'm back on my feet, I amble over to the chair and drop into it and let my head rest against the backside, eyes closed.

There is this overwhelming urge to just sob and sob and sob, but no tears come.

"Do you know why I love The Greasy Spoon so much, Stanley?" I ask.

He's quiet a moment and then says, "Why?"

"Because even when I was having a shitty day, I knew I could go to the diner and order a grilled cheese and as soon as it arrived at my table and I took the first bite, everything would feel all right again."

He chuckles to himself and the chair groans as he sits in it. "Diners and melted cheese are good for that."

I open my eyes. "I think I need that right now, more than anything. I need the comfort. I need something that's—" My voice catches. "I need something that's normal. I need to go somewhere where I'm not feared or loathed. Where I'm not a powerful tool or a villain."

"When Bran returns, we could ask—"

"No." I stand up. "I don't need his permission to go get a grilled cheese."

"With all due respect, Your Royal—"

"Please, for the love of god, stop saying that."

His chin wrinkles up, his mouth pressed firmly together as he considers his options. If he really does believe I'm some fabled royal fae, he'll listen to my commands.

"As you wish," he finally says, and I swear the ground trembles beneath me.

Everything is changing and I am freaking the fuck out.

I swallow several times, taking in a deep breath. "Did you drive here? Or ride in on some magical faerie steed?"

He laughs again. "I drove."

"Then will you drive me to the diner and make me a grilled cheese and super salty french fries?"

He bows his head just slightly and I don't miss the act of reverence. "Of course. I'll call ahead and have Judy get the fryer going. But Bran—"

"Is my problem, Stanley. Don't you worry."

"Very well." He returns his cap to his head and follows me out the door.

———

I'm not sure where Bran disappeared to, but we make it out of Duval House and into Stanley's old sedan without anyone stopping us. I'm aware that I'm taking some risks here, but if Stanley wanted me dead, he could have killed me as an oblivious one-year-old instead of stuffing my face with grilled cheeses for twenty-one years.

And everyone and everything else that might pose a threat to me in Midnight Harbor will learn soon enough what I did at the Pledge Hall.

I won't even have to open my mouth. They'll scatter at the mere suggestion of it.

What's the saying about power? Power corrupts absolutely.

My biological family tried to overthrow an entire kingdom.

What if I turn out just like them?

Don't panic.

Breathe.

The lights are on inside The Greasy Spoon when Stanley parks out front, but the neon sign is dark. I can make out Judy behind the counter, her hair wound up in a claw clip.

"Is Judy fae too?" I ask as Stanley unlocks the front door with his key.

"She's human."

I'm not sure if I'm relieved by that or disappointed. I'm going to need all of the fae guidance I can get.

"Evening, sugar," Judy says after the bell stops jingling overhead. "I take it the old man told you?"

"So you knew?"

She eyes Stanley over the glass donut case. "I did. Told him he should tell you. He said you weren't ready."

"She wasn't," Stanley says, his voice dry and grumbly. "She is now."

"Well, have a seat. We'll get you fixed up with some good old-fashioned comfort food if you'd like. Is that what you'd like?"

"It's what I need. More than anything in the world."

There's that familiar burn in my eyes again, the unsettling in my bones, the world swaying on its axis. My mother is dead. My sister is in a coma. My boyfriend is afraid of me.

I feel utterly alone.

I want to run away. Even more than I did before I became entangled with Bran, back when I thought I was human and leaving would be easy.

If I ran now, there's nowhere Bran couldn't find me. I'm sure of that. Not that I want to leave him. I just...I want things to go back to normal, goddammit.

And I know they won't.

How the hell do we move forward though?

I just want someone to tell me everything is going to be all right. But my support system is dwindling by the second.

Except for Sam.

"Can I use your phone?" I ask. I purposefully left my cell phone at Duval House.

"Of course." Judy hands me an old cordless telephone and I'm extremely grateful I memorized Sam's cell number in case of emergencies just like this.

She answers on the first ring. "Sweet baby Jesus," she says, her voice thin. "Where are you? What is happening? I just heard about your Pledge. The Guard is there now but we can't get any more details on it."

Elbow on the countertop, I scrub at my face and clutch at the phone with the other hand. "Where are you now?"

"I'm at the bookstore. I just finished closing up."

"Come to The Greasy Spoon and I'll tell you everything."

I can hear keys jingling through the phone. "I'll be there in less than ten."

———

Judy keeps the front door locked to avoid walk-ins, so when Sam arrives, Judy turns the deadbolt with a loud thud and then suddenly Sam is rushing me, her arms wrapped around my neck. "I hate hugs but I know you need this," she says.

I squeeze her back. "You have no idea."

"Well, I'll have an idea when you tell me."

"Anything to drink or eat, sugar?" Judy asks, a pencil sticking out of her wound hair. Behind the counter, Stanley drops in a basket of fries and the oil snaps and crackles.

"Diet Coke," Sam says as she slides onto a stool. "And a grilled cheese and fries."

Judy fills a red plastic Coke cup with ice, then soda from the tap. The carbonation fizzes when Judy puts the cup in front of Sam. "Food will be up in a few minutes," she says, then leaves us alone.

"All right." Sam tears off the wrapper on her straw and jabs it through the ice. The chunks plink against the thick plastic. "Tell me what I've missed."

———

A half hour later, after giving Sam the condensed version, she stares off into space, absently eating her fries one by one.

"Say something." I nudge her with my foot.

She chomps on another fry. She hasn't blinked in at least two whole minutes.

"Sam."

Wiping the salt and the grease on a napkin, she turns the stool slowly toward me. "You remember when clogs got really popular in school and we were like, 'Ummm, no.'"

"Yeah?"

"And then we bought a pair because fuck it, whatever, and we realized secretly we loved them? Hideous but easy to slip on and go, super comfortable." She rolls her eyes. "Like so comfortable."

"Yes. And?"

"And maybe this whole thing is like foam clogs."

"You must be joking."

"Maybe you'll realize you like being the villain. Maybe you like being royalty. I mean, have you even asked if there's a crown? A throne? Like what do you get out of this?"

"An entire fae race hunting her down," Judy answers from behind the counter.

"War, surely," Stanley calls.

Sam waves it away. "If you're a siren, then use your voice."

It's an echo of what Bran keeps telling me. Something I've always been afraid to do. And now, looking back, I realize it was a learned behavior. My mother was always telling me to be careful what I said and how I said it. *Keep your voice down. Don't be bossy.*

I just thought she was doing what mothers do and now I think she was trying to teach me not to use my powers, even though she'd already bound them.

My stomach clenches and a flare of anger sends warmth across my chest.

Mom robbed me of a lot, most of all choice.

And there's nothing I can do about it now. I can't scream at her. I can't give her the cold shoulder. I can't tell her all of the ways she hurt me.

Somehow that makes me even more mad.

Use my voice?

What's the first thing I do with it?

Where do I even begin?

I think the first thing I need to do is make sure my relationship with Bran is unshakeable. I know he's on unsteady ground. I know he's uncertain of how much to fear me. But I need to reassure him that I will never go against him. Well, my secret trip to The Greasy Spoon notwithstanding.

I'll ask for forgiveness. That's always better than permission, right?

"Thank you, Sam." I lean over and rest my head on her shoulder as she drags another fry through her pool of ketchup. "I'm so grateful for you."

"Same, Your Royal Highness."

I lurch upright. "Don't even start."

She laughs, salt glittering on the corner of her lip.

"Let's stop talking about me for a second," I say and my stomach fills with butterflies just thinking about my best friend being the Alpha's fated mate.

Is now the time to tell her? I don't know if there's a perfect time for that bomb to drop. But I like distracting from my own problems.

"Are you insisting we talk about me?" Sam asks. "You will be left wanting. The most exciting thing that happened to me in the last week is that I accidentally put on my little sister's underwear when I was running late for work and then spent the rest of the night picking fabric out of my ass crack."

I hang my head back and laugh and I swear some of the weight leaves my shoulders. Sam makes everything feel lighter.

Once I've sobered, I try again. "In all seriousness, there's something I need to tell you—"

Sam leans in. "Okay."

"And you're not going to—"

Just then, the front door of The Greasy Spoon pulls open and the locked deadbolt tears through the door frame as one very strong arm rips it back.

And, as if summoned by mere thought, the Midnight Pack Alpha walks through the door of the diner, his eyes brilliant wolf gold, and says, "What the fuck do you two think you're doing here alone?"

Three

When the Alpha's name flashes across the screen of my cell phone just five minutes after I've called him, I'm not sure if I should be annoyed or impressed.

I tap to answer. "Yeah?"

"Is that how you answer all of your phone calls?" he says.

"Did you find her or not?"

The Alpha laughs. It's a rumble through the phone, more animal than man. "Yeah, I found her."

"Where?"

I'm already moving toward the nearest exit in Duval House. Several lower ranking vampires duck out of my way as I stalk down the hall.

When I put eyes on her, she's going to regret running away.

Did I not tell her to stay put? Five minutes was all I needed to find her a wet cloth, something to clean the vomit from her mouth.

And she took those five minutes to run off like a naughty little mouse.

"She's at The Greasy Spoon with Sam," the Alpha says.

I turn the next corner and one of the newer vampires practically keels over at the sight of me.

"Sorry, sorry!" He dodges right, bumps into a marble pedestal and the priceless vase on top teeters. He spins, grabs it, holds it still. Looks like he's about to piss his pants.

The vase means nothing. Jessie means everything.

Is she indestructible? A villain with a voice that can command a room, but if a knife were to pierce her flesh...

I can't fucking think about it without losing my fucking mind.

"She safe?" I ask.

"Safe enough." The Alpha's voice levels out again. He's as annoyed as I am.

"What is it?"

I hit the night air. It smells like rain again and the wind is crisp.

"Sam must have heard by now that there was trouble at Jessie's Pledge," he says, "and yet she's here at the diner with a complete disregard for her safety."

"Why the fuck do you care about one of the witches' mortals?"

The Alpha is silent.

"Ahhh," I say and follow the stone path to the garage I share with my brother. "Sam's your fated mate." It's not much of a leap of logic.

The Alpha sighs. I hear the defeat and the frustration in the sound.

I can relate.

"Sam safe too?" I ask.

"Safe enough," he repeats.

"Try not to strangle her before I get there."

His grumble turns into a warning. "I don't need you to protect my woman."

"Does she know she's your woman?"

"Not yet."

I hit the remote on my key ring and the nearest bay door in the garage lurches upright. I duck beneath it before it's opened all the way. My Audi is backed inside. I reach for the door handle, but Jimmy is suddenly there, that look on her face. It's equal parts annoyed and worried.

I like annoying her. I hate when she worries.

She is much like my little sister in that regard. Too big of a heart, too intuitive for her own fucking good.

"Gotta go," I tell the Alpha.

"I'll be here until you arrive."

I disconnect, sliding the phone into the pocket of my jacket. "What?" I say to Jimmy.

"Since when do you voluntarily involve the Alpha in our business?"

"His nose is better than mine. Might as well use it to our advantage."

"Mmhmm." She folds her arms over her middle and leans a hip into the side of my car. "You're starting to like him."

"I like him the same way I like a can opener. He performs a function that I happen to need."

"As if you've ever opened a can in your life."

"That is entirely beside the point. Now move so I can leave."

She doesn't budge.

"Jimmy, I swear to fucking god—"

"She's safe. Take a breath and give her a minute to catch hers."

I scowl at her. "Absolutely not. Running off puts us all at risk and she needs to obey me if—"

"Obey you?" She laughs out loud and the hoop earrings hanging from her ears swing beneath her curls. "Are you that oblivious?"

I let my eyes close as I summon a deep, disgruntled breath. "I don't have time for this, Jimmy."

"You can take two seconds to talk to me and reorient yourself now that literally everything has changed. Because I know inside you're losing your fucking mind and it terrifies you. I know that, because I know you better than anyone and I would not be a very good friend if I didn't help you when you needed it the most."

Before I can argue, she takes my hand. Hers is warm. She's always run a little hotter than I do, despite us all being undead vampires.

I've always taken that to mean her heart isn't as cold as mine.

Despite the undeniable tug to get to Jessie, I let Jimmy pull me away from the car and out into the night.

———

"Sit."

I look between my best friend and the fallen log that rests on the shore of the large pond on the back of the Duval property. Even when Damien and I were living in 18th century France, I would never lower myself to sitting on logs.

Jimmy is the kind of girl who can find comfort and light in anything, even me.

I sit. She sits next to me and threads her arm through mine.

The pond ripples as the wind shifts direction. There is barely a sliver of moon left. Once it's gone, Rita will unbind Jessie and then there will be no turning back.

It's what I want for her. More than anything, I want her to be who she is and to hold the power that she was born with.

But I would be lying if I said it didn't change things.

Jimmy is right—everything is different and I don't like it.

"Let's talk about Anna," Jimmy says and I immediately tense up beside her. "Do you remember when she asked for your and Damien's permission to marry the shipbuilder and you both denied her?"

A duck swims out of the cattails along the eastern shore of the pond. I watch it coast along the surface.

I do not love women often. All of the women I've ever loved are dead.

Except for Jimmy. I think the only reason I allowed her in is because she is a vampire.

Now I have to add Jessie to that list.

There is a thread of anxiety at seeing the list grow.

"Bran," she says.

I look away from the duck and to her. "I can't do this right now."

"You and Damien both held on to Anna with too firm of a grip and she ran away because of it. Don't make the same mistake with Jessie."

I hang my head and turn my ears to the lapping of the water against the shore, the sound of the wind in Jimmy's hair. If I focus on something else, maybe I can forget how hard it is to let go when all I want to do is hold on tightly.

I know I have control issues. For fuck's sake, I know I do and for good fucking reason.

I can still see the blood dried on Anna's neck. I can still see the stillness in her body and the dead stare in her eyes.

Rage is a close cousin of heartbreak. I have disowned heartbreak. I will only let the rage remain.

"Like it or not," Jimmy goes on, "Jessie is not so little anymore. And the more overbearing you are, the further away she'll pull. I know you admire a woman in power. You always have."

I snort and look over at her. She gives me one of her smug ass smiles.

"Shut up," I say.

She leans into me, rests her head on the rise of my shoulder. She still smells like lavender, like home.

I do not like to give away any part of myself. I am fortified, just as Damien is. We gave everything we had to our sister and somedays I think we both thought there was nothing left to give after her death.

I don't want to think about it.

I hate thinking about Anna.

And now Damien...

Fuck.

Fucking hell.

I can't think about Damien either. Not right now.

If I must relent to Jessie in order to keep her, then I will relent.

"Stand *beside* Jessie," Jimmy says. "Not in front. And you both will be unstoppable."

The duck quacks loudly.

"Do you know what I hate above all else?"

"Oh, I can only imagine," Jimmy says.

"When you bring up irrefutable truths."

She laughs out loud again, head hung back, and the duck flaps its wings and flies away.

"That's why you keep me around, I suspect. Because I am the only one who will tell you the truth."

"I keep you around because you're the only person I can stand for more than ten minutes." I get up from the log and start back toward the house.

"Be gentle with her."

"Fine. Yes. I will be gentle and kind. Not at all an asshole."

"Promise me." She jogs to catch up.

"Fine. I promise."

"Thank you." She gives my arm a squeeze. "Wanna race back?"

"As if you'll ever beat me."

We both take off at a run.

And I win.

Four

My first thought, seeing the Alpha of the Midnight Pack standing in the now torn doorway of The Greasy Spoon is:

Damn, the Alpha is hot when he's pissed.

My second thought is:

Oh shit, the Alpha is pissed.

Cal stalks into the diner and I think the narrow building shrinks in size because he looks like he takes up at least half the room.

His wolf eyes flash bright yellow with a pulsing ring of black around his irises.

"Heyyyyy, Cal," I start, but Sam slips off the stool at the diner counter and squares her shoulders and says, "What we do is none of your business."

Cal's eyes widen with rage as his hands clench into fists. "You put yourself at risk by being out here and—"

"You don't get to boss me around!" Sam jams her finger in his direction. "I'm not promised to you or the pack!"

All of the tendons and veins in Cal's forearms bulge beneath his skin. "We're at war and you could get hurt."

"Like you care."

"I fucking care more than I—"

I step between them and face my best friend. "There's something I need to tell you."

"No need," Sam says as she narrows her eyes at him. "I already know he's a gigantic egotistical asshole."

"Okay, but listen. Sam. Look at me."

She finally focuses her gaze on my face, a pinch of confusion between her blonde brows.

"It's about you and Cal, and—"

"Maybe now isn't the time, Jess," Cal says behind me.

"Jess?" Sam's frown sharpens to a scowl. "Jess?! She's Your Royal Highness to you, jerk-face."

"Sam!"

She snaps back to me.

"You're Cal's fated mate."

I see the moment Sam's brain stops working. There's a dead look in her eyes. She's staring right at me but I don't think she's seeing me.

Cal takes a step closer.

And then Sam hangs her head back and laughs out loud.

She laughs and laughs until tears stream down her face.

"Tell Jessie that's bullshit," she says through the unhinged tears.

Cal sighs.

"Tell her."

I'm not sure where Stanley and Judy disappeared to, but they are noticeably absent, the fryer quiet, the grill cold.

"Sam," Cal says.

"Tell her!"

"I can't!" he shouts back. "I won't."

Sam clenches her teeth so hard I hear her molars grit together. She reaches across the counter and grabs a canister of sugar and lobs it at Cal.

"Sam!" I yell, but the sugar never lands.

Instead, it's caught mid-air by someone's outstretched hand.

Bran.

My heart thuds against the back of my tongue.

The diner goes eerily silent.

It's Bran that breaks it.

"Violence is a tool," he says in that cool, calm, detached tone of voice. "It should never be a reaction. That's a lesson the Alpha's mate needs to learn sooner rather than later."

"I'm not his mate," Sam argues, but some of the heat has left her voice.

"I'm quite sure the word 'fated' is not one you can fight," Bran points out.

Sam huffs and then crosses her arms over her chest.

"I'm sorry, Sam," I say. "I just found out. I thought you should know."

"It doesn't matter." She narrows her eyes at Cal again. "I'll never agree to it."

Cal growls. Literally *growls*.

Bran edges closer to Sam and me and faces the Alpha. "You need to get control of that."

"I am!" Cal says as his teeth sharpen, not unlike Bran's fangs.

"Why don't you return to the Pack," Bran says. "I'll make sure Sam gets to where she's going."

Cal's nostrils flare as he looks over top of us to Sam. Pain etches itself into the fine lines around his golden eyes. Not physical pain. This is an ache that does not bleed.

He doesn't want to let Sam out of his sight.

"Let me take you home," he says to her, now with more control. His gaze is locked on Sam and only Sam. "*Please.*"

I watch several emotions pass over my best friend's face. Regret. Heartbreak. Worry. Fear. Hunger.

I think Sam has been keeping some things from me, namely how she *really* feels about the Alpha.

I mean, I totally believe she believes she hates him and maybe in some ways she does, but the hate is not complete. There are cracks in that hardened exterior and they are starting to show.

"Fine." She makes her way for the door. "But don't talk to me."

"As if I have anything to say to you," Cal says.

"Jerk," Sam says.

"Brat," Cal says and follows her through the wreckage of the front door.

"That's either going to be a match made in Heaven or a train wreck," I say as I watch them leave.

Bran sets the canister of sugar on the counter and comes over to me. "You—"

"Oh, don't start with me too."

"I owe you an apology," he finishes.

That pulls me to a stop.

"Umm...really? You owe *me* an apology?"

"Don't get cocky about it," he says.

"Me? Cocky? Never."

He takes my hand in his and brings my wrist to his nose. He inhales, his eyes slipping closed. "I'm sorry if I gave you the impression you should be worried about me or about us." He opens his eyes again and there is the hint of sharp fangs in his mouth. "We have a lot to figure out and much to discuss, but I don't want you worried about us.

"We stand side by side," he adds. "Partners. We will not hide from one another. Promise me, Mouse."

I lick my lips as his mouth drags closer to the thumping pulse point in my wrist. "Tell me the truth."

"About what?"

"Are you afraid of me?"

Dropping my arm, he takes another step closer, closing the final gap between us. His thumb drags over my bottom lip. "I trust that this mouth will do only what it needs to do. No more and no less."

My tongue darts out to meet him and his eyes flare to life.

"But I need you to trust me, Mouse."

"I do."

"No. I mean it. You may have more power than either of us expected, but I have centuries worth of experience."

I roll my eyes at him. "That feels very close to mansplaining to me."

His expression doesn't change. If anything, he grows more serious. "I need you to trust me."

I tip my head to look up at him, his eyes starting to bleed to that bright gold. "Okay. But I need you to let me make mistakes."

I hear his teeth clench. *Loudly.*

"That's the promise I need from you."

"Mouse—"

"I can't become who I'm supposed to become by being coddled."

His eyes close again and the breath he takes is long and deep.

"Please, Bran."

When he meets my gaze again, there's defeat in his eyes. He knows I'm right.

I'm not sure where any of this is going to take us. I'm not even sure what comes after we walk out that door. But I do want us on the same side, on even ground. But I don't want to be afraid of acting and I sure as hell don't want to ask for permission.

Bran's grip on my wrist slides up my arm, and then he takes my hand in his again and brings my knuckles to his lips. He plants a soft kiss there. "You have my promise that I will try very hard to allow you to make stupid mistakes."

I laugh. "That's not a promise!"

"It's all you'll get from me."

"Fine. Then I promise to *mostly* trust you."

He yanks me into him and wraps his arms around my waist. "I love you, and you are a menace."

"I love you too, you asshole."

He brings his mouth down on mine and breathes out, almost a sigh.

Now when we kiss, it's an act that feels like home.

"Oh, little mouse," he says when he pulls away just enough to speak, "I think I need to take you home and to our bed."

I grind against him as his hands sink to my hips. "I agree."

Someone clears their throat behind us.

I jolt away from Bran, embarrassed. I totally forgot we were in the diner with Stanley and Judy.

"What is it, old man?" Bran asks, an edge of warning in his voice.

"We have a problem."

"For fuck's sake," Bran says. "When don't we have a problem?"

"What is it?" I ask quickly.

Stanley nods toward the front of the diner and the street beyond. I can just make out the shape of a crowd in the dark.

Maybe it's the Guard come to haul me away.

Or maybe the Lockes have reorganized and want their revenge...

But when Bran and I step out onto the sidewalk, we find almost every single fae that resides in Midnight Harbor.

And they're all on their knees.

Five

The fae on this side of the gate have always kept to themselves. Most of the time, I could go days without running into one of them. Now there's a crowd of fae in the streets of Midnight Harbor and worse...they're kneeling for me.

I immediately recognize a few of them. In the front holding a baby in her arms is the woman Sam and I ran into not that long ago on the river walk. The baby had been fussing in her stroller while the mom cleaned chocolate off the face of her toddler.

The baby had quieted as soon as I lifted her into my arms.

Fae babies have always taken to me.

I swallow hard, realizing there were clues dotted in my past about who I was and how I was different.

Fae babies are notoriously fussy now that they've been sealed off from the fae realm and all of its power and magic.

My mom complained more than once that I was just as bad.

"Get up," I say to them, but my voice is weak and too quiet.

I'm lacking conviction, overwrought with fear.

Why the hell are they kneeling? Didn't Stanley say I was the villain? Shouldn't these people be afraid of me or outright hate me?

Of course, Stanley did tell me that kneeling is customary, if not compulsory.

But I don't want this. I don't want any of it.

"Get up," I try again, this time louder.

The crowd stands to their feet just as Bran steps off the curb, putting himself between me and them. With the waning moon, it's hard to make out all of their faces, but the crowd is spread out all the way to the opposite side of the street. There must be close to fifty of them.

"Why are you here?" Bran asks them, keeping his voice level because Bran knows how to act when in the face of something unexpected.

I wish I had his spine of steel. I wish I had his confidence.

Someone in the center of the crowd starts forward and the others go quiet.

The hair lifts on my arms and along the back of my neck.

I can't be sure if it's the night or some baser instinct, if it's my fae side taking notice of this man as he steps forward into the pool of light cast from The Greasy Spoon's windows.

My first thought is: *I've never seen this man before.* I would remember him if I had. And my second thought is: *how odd that I've never seen this man before.*

His dark hair is shorn practically to the scalp on the sides, maybe to make it easier to see the intricately knotted tattoos on the side of his head. The top is left long, and several strands hang in his face.

His ears are pointed, meaning he's full blood fae.

I *should* have seen him before.

How have I never seen him?

And why aren't my ears pointed?

Instinctively, my hand trails up to the soft shell of my ear where it rounds like a mortal's should.

There are so many questions still, too many unearthed answers.

When the fae comes to a stop just a few feet from Bran, he clasps his hands behind his back and the metal rivets in his leather clothing glimmer like gold. More metallic threads shine in his highly decorated tunic.

Now that he's much closer and in the light I can tell his hair isn't black but midnight blue, like a pool of expensive ink spilled across a desk.

He looks like he stepped out of a child's fairytale book. Even in a place like Midnight Harbor, he looks like he doesn't quite belong.

"What's your purpose for being here?" Bran asks, bypassing any kind of introduction.

"My purpose," the man says, "is no concern of yours."

Bran's shoulders rise slowly with a deep breath. "Excuse me?"

"Bran—" I thread my hand with his and give him a squeeze. He shifts, tipping his chin so he can look at me over his shoulder. "Be nice."

"Be nice, Mouse? Be nice? This is a blatant display of *something* and until we know what it is, I will not *be* nice."

With a grumble, I turn back to the fae. "Can you help us out? He's a man that likes to know what he's dealing with."

The fae turns his bright blue eyes on Bran. "Not quite a man, is he?"

"Vampire. Close enough. Why are you kneeling outside of a diner?"

He cants his head and his tunic glimmers again with the movement. "It is our duty to show respect. But beyond that, you used your power, which means everything is about to change."

I said it, didn't I?

The fae looks back toward the diner where Stanley and Judy are now standing outside.

"You kept this from us, brownie."

Stanley doesn't balk. "There was a reason she was hidden and bound, and it wasn't my place to decide to undo it. Nor was it yours."

"Stanley, do you know this man?" I ask him.

"The name is Arion," the fae answers. "And I am a Lord of the Summer Court."

Though I'm trying my hardest not to appear overwhelmed, hearing his title makes my eyes pop open with awe.

"I didn't know any of the high born were on this side," Bran says.

"You wouldn't." Arion narrows his eyes when he looks over at Bran. "As I said, it's none of your concern."

Oh, well, shit. This isn't going well.

Bran practically vibrates with rage.

I take a step, inserting myself between them before Bran has a fae heart dripping blood from his hand.

"It's really nice to meet you, Arion," I say, trying for diplomacy and kindness. After all, if I'm regarded as the villain, I need to do everything in my power to prove to them that I'm not.

"Can you at least tell us if you're friend or foe?"

Arion shrugs, but it's a calculated shrug with no ounce of casualness to it. "I think the answer to that question is entirely up to you." He unclasps his hands from behind his back and offers up a thick card captured between his middle and pointer finger.

Before Bran can tell me otherwise, I snatch the card from the fae.

It's thick, the paper creamy, but textured like linen. The text on the front is an elegant, looping handwriting and the note says: *Moonlit side of Bramwell Pond. Tomorrow night at midnight.*

I look up at Arion.

"Come if you wish. Or don't. I don't care." He turns away and the fae crowd parts for him. He clearly rules what few fae remain on this side and my fear and anxiety turn into a knot.

I don't like that I've literally never met this man, and I definitely don't like that he immediately knew how and where to find me. It means he knows more about being fae than I do, which isn't much at all.

He has the upper hand no matter how powerful I'm supposed to be.

I take a step to follow him when Bran hooks me by the elbow and whirls me around. "Where the hell do you think you're going?"

I lean into him and lower my voice. "We need to find out what's going on here."

He takes the card from me and reads it over, then curses beneath his breath. "Waiting will be better, little mouse. Trust me." He yanks me down the street away from the fae where they're dispersing fast and following after Arion, the darkness of the night swallowing them up.

"Aren't you curious about him? I hate waiting and I don't want to run away," I argue.

"There's a difference between running away and knowing when you're at a disadvantage, and following some random fae lord into his territory is an error in strategy and intelligence."

"Are you calling me dumb?"

He makes a tsk sound. "No, Mouse. Inexperienced is the better word."

I pull out of his grip and cross my arms over my chest. I hate that he's right. And we did just establish some new rules within our relationship and here we're already testing the limits.

I want to make perhaps unwise decisions and Bran wants to keep me from doing it.

We stand off against one another. His eyes glimmer with golden anger.

"No," he says, reading my stubbornness.

"Yes."

"Mouse, I will not hesitate to throw you over my shoulder and cart you back to the house and chain you to a fucking bed."

I narrow my eyes at him. "You wouldn't."

He takes another step toward me, nostrils flaring. "Try me."

Do I hate this idea? I feel like either way, I'm winning here. If he lets me chase after Arion and the other fae, I'm getting my way. If I disobey him, he'll chain me to the bed and maybe do *other* things to me.

I take two steps backward. Bran's jaw flexes.

"*Mouse.*"

I can't help it—a tease of a smile spreads over my face. I need this. *We* need this.

I step off the sidewalk, but before my foot hits the street, Bran has me in his arms and thrown over his shoulder.

It happens so fast, the world spins.

"Hey! Come on!" I say, but my fight is full of laughter.

Bran pulls out his cell phone and makes a connection.

Someone answers on the other end. "Yes, Mr. Duval?"

"Get me a length of chain. Have it in my bedroom in ten minutes."

"Yes, sir."

Bran hangs up and then smacks my ass. A high-pitched yelp escapes me.

"Naughty little mouse," he says and then carts me off into the night.

Six

In no time at all, we're back at Duval House and in the Anneliese with me chained to our bed.

The chain clanks against the frame when Bran clamps a metal cuff around my wrist. I don't even ask where he got a metal cuff with a perfect eye ring welded into the side on such short notice.

Once the cuff lets out a loud *ting* as the teeth lock into each other, Bran darts away.

"Where are you going?" I ask, not even bothering to hide the eagerness or flare of disappointment in my voice.

He drops into the wingback chair in the corner of the room and slouches into the curve of the wing, watching me with a cool, distant interest.

"Bran."

"Now what, little mouse?" he challenges.

"I thought..." I pull myself up into a sitting position and lean my back against the headboard.

"You thought what? That you'd disobey me and reap some kind of benefit from it?"

Oh, the devil is here, ladies and gentlemen, and he's taunting me. It causes a flare of joy to light in my chest. This is the Bran I know and love and it gives me hope that we'll be all right, no matter how much things are changing.

"It was certainly *implied*," I say.

His long legs are bent at the knee but splayed open, giving me a clear view of his crotch where a bulge is showing.

"Why torture us both?" I ask.

"You must know by now, little mouse, that I can be a very patient man." His voice is husky, his eyes glinting with a hint of the vampire gold I've come to love.

But he's right—I do know just how patient he can be.

"So you're just going to sit there with a hard-on and watch me suffer?"

"Yes."

I try to cross my arms over my chest in an act of annoyance, but the chain isn't long enough and I'm too far to the center of the bed. The chain snaps and rattles. I scoot closer to the edge.

Bran props his elbow on the chair's arm and brings his long, elegant fingers to the curve of his jaw.

It's hard not to stare at him when he's at rest, when I can appreciate every sharp edge, every masculine curve, every dark shadow that makes up the whole of Bran Duval.

My heart beats a little harder and I get a flash of when he had me on my knees in the bathroom, ordering me to stick my tongue out for him.

I feel new slickness between my legs and close my eyes, trying to draw the thoughts away and somehow overrule biology and instinct.

But it's useless.

I can feel the weight of his gaze on me. His hunger. I can smell him everywhere in this room and everywhere on my skin.

I may be, apparently, an extremely powerful being, but I am powerless against Bran.

If I were a drug addict, my drug of choice would be the very hot-as-hell vampire sitting just out of my reach.

I want to fuck him.

I want to fuck him all of the time.

And he knows it.

I arch my back purposefully, letting my legs drop open so that the skirt of my dress slips up my thighs, revealing the now damp triangle of fabric at my center.

His gaze immediately sinks to my panties and his nostrils flare, taking in my scent. But his body is held impossibly still.

I grab the hem of my dress and pull it even higher until it's bunched around my hips.

Still, he hasn't moved, but the hard ridge of his cock is clearly straining against the front of his pants.

With a wiggle of my hips, I shimmy out of my panties, taking my time slipping them down the length of my calves, then over my feet. When they're off, I sink back against the pillows, ball the fabric in my free hand, and toss them.

Bran blurs out of the chair and catches them before they hit the floor.

His eyes are bright gold now, and when he brings the bunched fabric to his nose and inhales, his irises flare like flames.

I shiver beneath the heat of his stare.

"Naughty little mouse," he says, his voice scraping over a raw throat.

"Your turn," I suggest.

He takes another breath of my damp panties and then straightens his spine, looking down the sharp line of his nose at me. "Make me."

I frown. "What?"

"Use your talents, Mouse. Make me do as you please."

A lump immediately forms in my throat and I swallow it back. "You're serious?"

He says nothing as his eyes pulse with hunger.

"You made me promise not to use it."

"This is under controlled circumstances, when I've given you permission." He tosses the panties to the floor and comes closer to the end of the bed. The under-cabinet lighting in the bathroom sends a soft glow into the room and it skims the left side of his body in a hazy white light.

"Besides," he adds, "you have to learn how to use it if we're going to infiltrate the fae house. Best start now."

"Infiltrate? This isn't a covert mission."

"Everything is a covert mission, Mouse." He leans over and lets his fingertips trail up my bare leg. "The sooner you accept that, the better off you'll be."

I lick my lips, goosebumps lifting on my arms and legs. "Are there any rules to this exercise?"

His fingers come to the sensitive flesh of my inner thigh and I grow wetter.

"No."

My eyes pop open. "None?"

"I've done a lot of dirty things in my lifetime." He smirks. "There isn't much that will turn me off."

I narrow my eyes. "I don't like thinking about you doing those dirty things with other women."

"Then think about me doing them with you and make it so."

His hand is now just a few inches from my pussy, and I spread my legs for him, thinking he'll give me a tease at the very least.

But no.

He darts away, back to the chair.

"Bran!"

"I'm waiting," he says and looks ridiculously smug and patient as he stretches out his legs.

I sit up again. The chain rattles. For some reason I feel like I need some leverage to get this right, so I curl my legs beneath me and sit on my knees.

The chain settles.

At my Pledge, there was no thinking about my power. I just used it. It was almost involuntary. And I still have yet to be unbound. Will I even have access to it now? Rita still has my necklace captured in her magical jar, so that's something at least.

Clearing my throat, splaying my hands on my thighs, I say, "Take off your clothes."

Bran doesn't move an inch and I grumble with frustration.

"Try again."

I shake out my hands like I'm getting ready to throw a pitch at a softball game. The chain complains more loudly.

Expanding my chest, filling up my lungs with oxygen, I say, "Bran, take off your clothes."

Still nothing.

"Goddammit." I fall back on my butt. "This isn't working."

"You're barely trying."

"I just want to fuck you," I say with a pout.

"Then try harder."

With a grumble, I close my eyes and try to put myself back at my Pledge. I was afraid then. Terrified of losing Bran and my sister. The fear made the blood pump fast through my veins.

I can't replicate that same feeling, but maybe if I latch onto that memory, if I let all of the muscles and tendons in my body tense up, maybe I can get close.

I imagine the smell of the Pledge Hall. The floor polish on the pine floors. The fresh water of the river nearby. The smell of all those shifters and vampires and witches. A mix of spice and musk and sweetness.

In my mind, I see Kelly go down again and Bran under attack, and my heart skips.

I take in another long breath as heat races up my arms, then down my torso and into my core.

"*Bran*," I say and open my eyes, "*take off your clothes*."

I know I've found it by the uptick in his face, the fine lines around his eyes creasing with frustration as he loses control of his own body.

He stands up, kicks off his boots.

My heart races a little faster.

He never takes his eyes off of me as his belt comes out of the loops with a snap of leather. He tosses it next to my panties, and the metal clasp clanks loudly.

His pants are off in a second and then he yanks off his shirt, exposing all of those hard packed ab muscles.

The breath in my lungs rushes out in a moan of delight.

Just two seconds after that, his black boxer briefs are gone and his thick cock stands erect in the open air.

I lick my lips. I can't help it.

This is too much power for one person to have, but goddamn, am I enjoying it.

"Now what, Mouse?" he says on a husky rasp.

"Stroke yourself."

He tilts his head. "Try again."

"Take yourself in your hand."

"Again."

A frustrated grumble rumbles in my chest. "Stroke your cock."

He stands in the middle of the bedroom, his hands at his side.

"You're killing me," I say.

"You have until the count of five and then I'm putting my clothes back on."

"Wait—"

"One."

"That's not fair!"

"Two."

I crawl down the length of the bed, but the chain yanks me back. I forgot about it already.

"Three."

The urgency takes root in my gut.

"Four."

"*Get over here,*" I say.

He's suddenly beside me on the bed.

"Better," he says and wraps his hand in a length of my hair and gives it a sharp yank, forcing me to bend to his control. "Keep going."

I reach between us for his cock, but he smacks my hand away.

I take another deep breath, focus on the beating of my heart, and then, "*Grab your cock.*"

With my hair still wound around his left hand, he uses his right to take control of his shaft. Excitement burns in my belly.

"*Stroke yourself from base to tip.*"

He does as I command and I can hear the soft rasp of his hand on his cock.

"*Faster,*" I say, and he picks up the pace.

Our eyes are locked on one another as he pumps himself harder, muscle and bone twining in his shoulder as he works himself. His irises burn brightly, and pleasure makes his lids heavy, his fangs sharp against his puffy lips.

"*Don't stop,*" I say.

He keeps going, racing close to the finish line.

"Mouse," he warns.

"*Don't stop until you come*," I say again.

He pushes me back against the bed and the chain clanks loudly on the headboard. He bats my knees open with his free hand, but keeps pumping himself with his other.

His breathing is ragged now, his teeth clenched tight.

He lines himself up at my center so that every stroke of his cock brings the backside of his knuckles against my clit.

The first graze of him makes me jolt, but he quickly wraps his free hand around my throat, driving me into place beneath him.

"You said faster, didn't you, Mouse?" His assault on my clit is bringing me too close too quickly.

"Yes, but...*Bran*—"

He clamps his hand over my mouth.

"My turn, Mouse."

The head of his shaft swells in the cup of his hand and rubs against my clit.

He keeps up the pace until he growls above me, body tensing, the tendons in his neck straining as he clenches his teeth.

"Come for me, Mouse," he says as he pumps against me.

Oh fuck.

Fuck.

I wrap my hand around his wrist, his own hand still clamped on my mouth as I come hard and fast.

The pleasure is sharp, more a bolt of lightning than a growing crash of thunder, and heat races through my body.

I squeeze my eyes shut, my breath heaving out around Bran's fingers.

And then he shoots his load all over my pussy, turning me into a slick mess as he growls above me and then slides his length up my wet slit. Another bolt of pleasure shoots through my core.

I clench up and moan into his hand.

"That's my good girl," he says at my ear and then kisses the sensitive flesh just beneath my lobe, his fangs grazing over my pulse point.

Oh god.

Oh fucking hell.

Eyes closed, I sink into the sated heaviness that makes me feel like I'm floating.

Bran curls up beside me and then rubs his wet, sticky fingers over my bottom lip. "You did well, Mouse. Taste it."

I dart my tongue out to clean off his cum.

"You may have the power to command me," he says, "but I will always control your pleasure."

"Yes," I say on a breath, still lost to the calmness that has washed over me.

He turns me, then wraps his arms around me, pulling me into him.

"Take off the chain," I tell him.

"No," he says. "Go to sleep."

I want to argue, but I'm suddenly too tired. That took a lot out of me and I'm not entirely sure if it was using my power or coming.

I guess it doesn't matter.

Both felt ridiculously good.

Maybe too good.

I might like using my voice more than I want to admit.

I drift off quickly, held safely in Bran's arms. But it doesn't feel like I'm asleep for long.

A pounding at the bedroom door forces me to lurch awake. Bran is out of bed before I can orient myself in the sleepy haze.

"This better be good," he says when he whips the door open.

Jimmy is on the other side. "Get dressed," she says. "And hurry."

"Why?" he asks on a growl.

"Because Damien is awake. And something is wrong."

Seven

BRAN

In 1737, a strain of flu found its way through Aquitaine, and Damien was the only one to fall ill to it in our household.

There is something unsettling about seeing your older brother slowly dying in his bed, a certain helplessness at not knowing how to fix it.

As much as Damien and I war against each other, we have always stood solidly at each other's backs when it mattered most.

He is my best friend, and he is the only true thing that remains of who I was when I was human.

Damien is awake and something is wrong.

I will burn the Renshaw House to the ground for what they've done, just as soon as I know what it is they did.

When I burst into Damien's bedroom, the door slams against the wall. Bianca is at his bedside, her hands hovering over his prone body. Jimmy is at the foot watching carefully, her arms crossed over her chest.

Sky is there too and I have to bury the urge to snap her neck and toss her out with the trash. I suspect Sky might be the new weak link in

Duval House. How else did the Renshaw witches get through our defenses and take Kelly captive?

But I'll deal with her later.

"Get her out of here," I say to no one in particular.

"Me?" Sky says. "I'm Damien's assistant. Why wouldn't I be here?"

I snap my fingers at the two vampires who've been put on guard and the big guy takes Sky by the arm.

"Bran!" She tries to yank out of the big guy's grip, but his fingers are like a vise and I can hear Sky's bones crack. "What the fuck, Bran?"

I go to Bianca's side. "I thought he was awake?"

"He was," Jimmy says.

"So?" I'm impatient for answers.

I was the only one who visited Damien when he was sick all those years ago, the only one willing to risk their life to see him.

I remember the smell, the burn of the tallow candles and incense to drive away the scent of death.

But I remember the rattle of his chest the most.

"You shouldn't be here," he'd said to me when I brought him a fresh bottle of brandy.

"And you shouldn't be in this fucking bed."

He'd snorted, then dissolved into a coughing fit. I'd poured him some brandy and helped him drink.

"You need to keep yourself healthy," he'd said. "Someone will need to care for mother and sister when I'm gone."

"You will when you live."

Damien hadn't believed me then and if I'm honest, I hadn't believed me either.

There'd been dark circles around his watery, bloodshot eyes. His lips had been cracked and bleeding. He'd looked so pale, so weak.

But somehow, he'd pulled through.

I was convinced then that my brother was invincible.

Except right now, I am reminded all over again of those long nights in our house in France. I am reminded of feeling helpless.

Bianca pulls her hands away. "He seems to be going from consciousness to unconsciousness, and when he's awake he—"

Suddenly Damien lurches upright, and Bianca yelps and steps back.

Now I see what they mean.

Something *is* wrong.

Damien's eyes are open but they're pure white.

"Brother?" I say.

He's sitting rigidly, hands limp at his sides. Though he has no pupils, it looks like he's gazing straight ahead.

I snap my fingers in front of his face. He fucking hates that.

"Damien."

Nothing.

"Has he responded to anything yet?" I ask.

"No," Jimmy says. "It's just this." She nods at him in bed. "He'll sit up. Do nothing. Saying nothing. Then he'll collapse again."

"What does this mean?"

Bianca rakes her teeth over her bottom lip. "I'll be honest, this is new to me. No witch I've worked with has ever mentioned anything like this."

Damien hasn't moved yet, nor has he blinked. I've seen a lot of fucked up weird shit in my day, but this has even my skin crawling. "Okay. So, how do we figure out what it means?"

"You should tell him what you felt," Jimmy says to Bianca. "He needs to know everything."

The scowl I turn on Bianca could singe hair. "Do not make me ask questions, witch. I need details. *Now.*"

"Sorry." She swallows audibly. "When I hold my hands out like this" —she repositions over Damien— "I feel something I've only felt once before, when I played with magic I wasn't supposed to play with."

There is a sinking weight in my gut. "Go on."

"Dark magic."

This isn't unexpected. "Which means—"

"It means..." She gnaws at her lip again and then yanks her hands back as if something bit her. "We all know and can agree that the fae realm exists, right?"

"Yes," I answer, growing more impatient by the second.

"Witches are always taught that magic—all magic, including witches and vampires and shifters—originated in the fae realm, that over the millennium, we've evolved to become what we are, which means…if this is magic not from this realm, it's…"

"From the fae realm," I guess and she nods.

I turn away and scrub at my face as my heart races in my ears. I need a drink.

No, I need my fucking brother.

Damien was always the one who solved problems. I was just along for the joy ride.

With my back to them, I ask, "How would the Renshaw witches tap into fae magic if the gate is closed?"

"The gate may be closed," Bianca says, "but there are currents to tap. It's not an impossibility."

"And how would a person undo that magic?"

There is silence and it hangs heavy.

I turn to them just as my brother drops to the bed and a puff of air escapes his pillow as the feathers resettle beneath his head. Damien refuses to use anything other than feathered pillows. It reminds him of home. I know it does even though he won't admit it.

Bianca licks her lips and takes a deep breath. "The Renshaw witches could undo it, but if they won't or are unwilling…you'd…I mean…the *origin*…"

"Spit it out, witch."

"You'd have to open the gate and get Damien to the fae realm."

———

The Alpha answers on the second ring. "I'm busy," he says.

"And yet you answered."

He growls through the phone. "What do you want now, Duval? I'm not your personal errand boy."

"No, but everything we do from here on out affects us both."

I'm moving through the house, the phone clutched to my ear. I can hear Jimmy not far off, telling Mouse the abbreviated version of what's transpired and the news that I'm leaving. The sun will be up within the hour.

"What did the Guard do with those who were trapped inside the Pledge Hall?" I ask.

The Alpha is silent for a beat. I can hear the sound of clothing rasping against skin on the other end, then a door creaking open. "Why do you think I know anything about it?"

"Stop fucking around. Everyone in Midnight knows you control the Guard."

He grumbles again. "It's in moments like these that I hope my psychic misread her prediction."

I rush down the front steps of Duval House and down the driveway. "Hurry, shifter."

"The spell broke eventually. Whatever Jessie did, the effects faded. The Renshaws were already gone by the time the Guard got there. The humans took longer to come out of it. They were the only ones left by then and all of their memories were wiped."

"Thanks." I pull the phone away to disconnect, but the Alpha stops me.

"Wait. What stupid shit are you planning now? You going to murder the entire Renshaw House?"

"Don't be silly. Torture first. Answers second. Then murder."

"By yourself?"

"Careful, Alpha," I say as I near the end of the driveway. "Keep talking like that and someone will think you care what happens to a leader of a rival house."

"Put eight on the perimeter," he says to someone beyond the phone. "Two on each entrance."

"Where are you going?" Fox asks.

"Trying to prevent a massacre," the Alpha says as I hear the shift of the wind in the phone.

"I don't need your help," I tell him.

"What do you think your brother will say when he wakes up and realizes you're dead because of some stupid revenge mission?"

Beyond the pines, the sky is starting to brighten. Really, it's the perfect time to infiltrate a witch house. They'll never expect a vampire to be out this late.

"I'm meeting you there," the Alpha says.

"To stop me or to help me?"

"Aren't those the same thing?"

"Don't make me fight you too."

"Fine. To help you, you fucking idiot."

"You flatter me, Alpha."

He laughs.

"How long will it take you?" I ask him.

"Less than ten."

"Make it five."

"I can't run that fa—" I hang up, slide the phone into my pocket, and start running.

Eight

Damien has no love for the Alpha, and yet I suspect he would agree with the wolf—I'm perhaps being a bit reckless going to the Renshaw witch house with an imperfect plan and an overwhelming desire for revenge.

I want to fucking kill something.

Something being witches.

But I need answers first in order to save my brother.

And I suppose, in a way, Kelly too.

We are all connected now. The MacMahon sisters. The Duval brothers.

When I reach the Renshaw property, the vibration in the air tells me there is a border spell. Not surprising, not insurmountable, but fucking annoying.

I pace away from the property and tap at a name on my cell phone. Bianca answers on the first ring. I'm glad she already knows not to keep me waiting.

She begins with a greeting, but I cut her off before she can get the words out.

"How do I get past a barrier spell?"

I'm in the thickness of the woods where the night is still clinging to the shadows. The boughs of the hardwoods creak above me as the wind shifts. We're not far off from autumn now and the air already smells crisper as the leaves start their change and the ground grows colder night by night.

And thinking of autumn has me thinking of the Autumn Court.

My little mouse will be hunted by them before too long, if they get their way.

I am reminded of Damien's warning on that desolate country road just a few days ago.

If the gate were to be opened again... Here, we're kings. But standing against one of the princes from the Unseelie Court? We would not measure up.

I wanted to help Mouse identify her origins. There is no way to embrace your power when you don't even know who you are.

But this...this was never on the list of possibilities. How the fuck am I to protect Mouse from the entire Unseelie Court?

Before the fear takes over, I push it away. Another problem for another time.

"Renshaw border spell?" Bianca guesses, pulling me from my reverie.

I pace in a circle beneath the canopy of an oak tree. "Yes."

"They'll have perimeter markers holding the spell in place. Trees or rocks. Look for carvings or paintings of symbols. Renshaws tend to grip the darker side of magic so you'll likely see primitive runes."

I dart back to the property line where the air shifts again, sensing an intrusion, and I start a path along the perimeter. When I find a carving in an old maple, I relay the rune to Bianca—intertwined V's with a circle in the center.

"Okay..."

I hear her hesitation. "What is it?"

"Well...that's an easy one to undo, is all. How old is the cut?"

I can smell the tang of fresh wood on the air. "Hours maybe."

"Hmmm."

"Spit it out, witch."

"This might be a trap."

"And?"

"And I wouldn't be doing my job if I didn't warn you of it."

"Just tell me how to undo it."

"You'll need to break it. Anything will do, but you'll not want to touch it."

I scan the forest floor and find a stone about the size of a grapefruit. Picking it up, I pace back several yards and set the phone on a fallen log.

"You'll want to be sure the entire symbol is destroyed," Bianca goes on.

I toss the rock up and catch it again, testing its weight.

"I wouldn't try a knife," Bianca says, "because you'll still be connected to it through metal—"

I cock my arm back and throw the rock like a baseball.

It's flying so fast, the air whistles and when it hits the mark, a loud crack echoes through the forest as the tree trunk explodes.

The canopy shudders overhead and the tree wavers, no longer able to support its weight with half the trunk missing.

Thick roots lift from the dirt and the tree sways again.

"There you are," the Alpha says as he comes up beside me a little breathless, sweat coating his forehead. "Where should we—"

The tree cracks several yards away as the last of its trunk gives. And when it hits the ground, the reverberation sings across the earth.

Bright violet light flashes through the forest as the air takes on the scent of burnt wood and magic.

"What the fuck are you doing?" the Alpha asks. "Everyone in a five-mile radius probably heard that. Is that...fucking hell. *Witch magic.*" He says the latter like it tastes bitter, and then he wrinkles his nose and waves his hand through the air as if that will help drive the scent away.

I only smell what reminds me of anise and maybe a thread of sulphur. Nothing to gripe about. But wolves hate magic.

"Is that Callum?" Bianca asks.

The Alpha notices the phone.

"Thanks, Bianca," I say, ending the call.

"I see your witch is already coming in handy," the wolf says. "Might have been a good idea after all, bringing in someone not of your ilk."

I smile at him. "I only have good ideas, wolf."

He snorts and crosses his arms over his chest. "So full of hot air. I'm shocked you don't float away."

Now he's the one smiling.

"You can come or you can go," I tell him and head off in the direction of the Renshaw house. "No one forced you to join this adventure."

He decides to come.

Even someone like the Alpha can't say no to putting a rogue witch house in their place.

———

The Renshaw house really fits the brand of the witch.

It's a hulking Victorian with black siding and black-framed windows with trim work that looks like spiderwebs.

When we reach the wraparound porch and start up the front steps, we find no resistance from magic.

The Alpha and I walk right in through the front door.

Of course, that's just one more sign that we've walked into a trap, but I'm going to pretend it's just the hubris of a witch.

Voices filter out through closed pocket doors to our left.

The conversation is about the Pledging and the Guard.

I count four heartbeats in the room.

The Alpha and I share a look. There are no overhead lights on in the house, only lamps, and the low lighting casts thick shadows. He doesn't look worried, only eager, and I'm glad of it.

The Alpha nods at the pocket doors and I nod in agreement.

He puts his fingers into the recessed handles on the doors and gives them an outward push. The pocket doors slide open and bang against the stoppers embedded in the tracks.

The room turns to us.

There's Tabitha, the matriarch of the Renshaw House, and three other Renshaw witches. Two men, one woman. I recognize the woman as being Tabitha's Irish cousin. She moved to Midnight several years ago and is now second-in-command of the Renshaw House.

The men are lower in the hierarchy, and I don't recall their names.

None of them are suffering any visible wounds despite the fighting at the Pledge Hall. Witches are good at healing themselves, but not as good as vampires and wolves.

"Bran," Tabitha says in a tone of voice that is not surprised and, dare I say, expecting? "It's nice to see you out so close to dawn. It changes your sunny disposition." She smiles with closed lips.

The Alpha and I break away from one another and circle the room, boxing the witches in. It's a dangerous move, but one of strategy if we play our cards right.

Tabitha clasps her hands in front of her. She's wearing all black to match the mood of her House. All black save for a bright yellow garnet that hangs from a silver chain around her neck.

"Won't you have a seat?" Tabitha gestures at the sitting area around a cold fireplace.

"Were you expecting us?" I ask.

I don't like beating around bushes. Or threats.

"Of course."

I catch the Alpha scenting the air, looking for traps. He gives me a quick shake of his head.

Nothing.

"We prefer to stand," I tell her.

"Very well."

"You know why I've come," I say.

Tabitha takes a breath, lifting her chin just slightly so she can regard me from the broad slant of her nose. "Julian Locke was blinded by greed and desperation. Our goals were a bit loftier, but there was some overlap."

This isn't going the way I thought it would and I'm not sure if I like it.

"And you decided to use my brother as a pawn?"

"Wouldn't you do the same if you saw the opportunity?"

"Would I use Damien as a pawn? Only a fool would."

"Fair enough. But the ship has already left the harbor and now we need to find a solution if you want to get it back."

"Is my brother the ship in this analogy?"

Tabitha smirks. "I suppose he is."

"He'd hate that."

"I know."

"Go on."

"When Julian came to me, all he wanted was Jessie. He didn't think beyond that. He knew that Jessie equaled power, and power was what he wanted. He thought that was what I wanted too. He never bothered to ask though."

I come around a wingback chair, keeping my eyes on the other witches flanking Tabitha like guards. All of them have their hands clasped in front of them—a clear sign of respect for those in the room who are not witches.

What an odd morning this is turning out to be.

"I knew that when Julian decided to use Kelly in his revenge plot, that Damien would do everything in his power to protect her. And I knew you would do everything in your power to protect him."

She's right, of course. But I'm not going to admit to my weaknesses, even if everyone knows of them.

"So it stood to reason that I could use both Kelly and Damien as leverage," Tabitha goes on. "It's no mistake that they are alive but unconscious. Dead men hold no value."

The anger that ignites in my chest has my heart thumping hard against my ears.

She'll pay for that. One day.

"What was the end goal, witch?" I ask.

She takes a deep breath. "I want the fae gate opened. You need it open to save your brother. And I can help you do it."

I meet her eyes, looking for the catch, the lie, or the misdirection. Tabitha has always been a straightforward person. When she wants to speak.

"Why would you want the fae gate opened?" I ask.

"I had a brother too," she answers, and the waver in her voice does not go unnoticed. "Until one of the fae took him from me."

Nine

It's Jimmy who undoes the chain from around my wrist. I want to be annoyed that Bran just left me here, fucked and wet and sticky, but I guess I can't blame him when it comes to his brother.

"Thank you, Jimmy," I tell her and rub my sore wrist, trying not to blush. "We were...I was..."

"No need to explain. We all have our kinks." She winks at me and then turns to leave.

"Is Damien better? Is Kelly—"

"Not yet." She pauses at the door, her hand curled around the wood. "We're still trying to figure it out. Bran is going to the Renshaw witches to get answers."

"He what?" I bolt upright, forget that I'm still half naked and a mess and then grab the bedsheet to wrap around myself. "I should go with him and use my power and—"

"He's taking the Alpha," Jimmy says. "And I would highly suggest you don't go chasing after him. He'll never let you or me forget it."

With a grumble, I take a fold of the sheet in hand and cross the room. "I'm tired of just sitting on the sidelines. I was the one who saved us all at my Pledge."

"Do you want my advice? Or do you just need to vent?"

"Umm...well...no one has ever asked me that." I think for a second. "Your advice."

"Okay." She straightens and her hoop earrings swing with the movement. "Almost no one is an expert at something when they first begin, and power is always easier to access without training when under duress. But reaching for it might not always be that simple. You need to figure out more about your abilities before you can rely on them."

She takes a step into the room. "Bran has been in hundreds of dangerous scenarios. He's an expert at navigating them. And even better, he's not so easily killed." She tilts her head and a rogue curl of hair slides over her forehead. "You may be fae and immortal, but fae can die a lot easier than vampires."

A shiver makes my skin crawl across my bare shoulders. She's right, of course. And I can't help my sister if I'm dead.

"Okay, fine." I exhale loudly. "I won't go running after Bran."

She nods. "I need to get to bed before I shrivel into dust. If you need anything, there are always several of our bound mortals on duty during the day. You'll find them in the main house."

"Thanks."

She gives me a quick wave of her fingers and then she's gone.

———

I take a shower and dress in jeans and a tee. The house is still quiet as I leave the bedroom while running a brush through my wet hair. Beyond the Anneliese, the sky is already showing daybreak.

Where the hell is Bran—

"Mouse."

I yelp and jolt back.

Bran is standing behind me in the hallway.

"Goddammit! Don't do that."

He laughs even though he looks like he's about to pass out on his feet. There are dark circles beneath his eyes, and bags are starting to form in the shadows. His lips are dry, the whites of his eyes bloodshot.

"Are you okay?" I ask. "Did the Renshaw witches hurt you?" I search him for injuries and find none.

"It's past my bedtime." He laughs again and then rests his shoulder against the corner where the hallway spills into the living room. He's slouched, as if being upright is starting to wear on him.

"Did you get your answers? You just *left* me."

His head lolls against the wall. "Would you forgive me if I apologized?"

"No."

"Then I won't."

"Such an asshole." I roll my eyes and set the brush aside. When I reach him at the hallway, I slide my hands over his stomach, feeling the tautness of his abs beneath the thin material of his shirt. "You left me chained to the bed."

"That's my favorite way to leave you."

I gaze up at him and find his eyelids heavy. It's hard to say if it's exhaustion or lust. Maybe a little of both.

"Don't ever do that again," I warn him halfheartedly.

"I absolutely will." In a flash, he grabs me, presses me against the wall, and wraps his hand around my throat. A little breath escapes me as he tilts my chin up, his lips hovering just an inch above mine.

"You did good, using your voice on me," he says, "but I still prefer you at my mercy."

Our breath mingles. My heart races faster, thudding against my ribs.

I may have told him never to do it again, but he and I both know I also prefer being at his mercy.

Bran picks up on it and says, "My naughty little mouse."

Then he kisses me. It's a slow meeting of lips first, then his tongue invades my mouth as his hips press into mine, driving me into the wall. I moan into him and he grinds his cock against me and then—

He's gone.

I stumble away from the wall, a little drunk with need. "You're teasing me."

"That's all you get for now, little mouse." He walks backward, disappearing into the shadows. "Come to bed with me."

I follow the sound of his voice down the hallway, skin erupting in goosebumps as my base instinct senses the predator watching me from the darkness.

I know Bran and I have new ground to cover and our relationship has to transform as we uncover more and more about who I am and what I'm capable of, but we operate at our best when Bran has the upper hand and I submit to him.

He likes it and I like it.

We just have to figure out how to exist on equal ground outside of our relationship.

Maybe that's the key.

Submit in the bedroom.

Assume my power outside of it and give Bran the grace he needs to find his place in that new balance.

His hand grabs mine in the dark and his touch is gentle as he guides me into the bedroom, then over to the bed. I slip off the jeans but leave the tee on. I'm not entirely sure I'm going to sleep yet.

A second later, the bed shifts beneath Bran's weight and he slides over the thick, plush mattress to curl into me.

I notice he hasn't said a word about the Renshaw witches or what answers he may have gotten, and I can't help but worry it has something to do with me.

"Good night, little mouse," he says.

"Good night."

———

I wait until he's fast asleep.

It's hard to wake a vampire, especially in the first few hours so I don't worry about slipping out from his embrace.

At the door, I pull it open, careful with the slant of light, and then slip out and close it softly behind me.

I'm not tired.

I don't think I've ever been this keyed up, so ready to *do* something.

We're supposed to meet Arion, Lord of the Summer Court, tonight. I'm excited and a little terrified. What can he possibly have to say about me? Stanley warned about the fae courts coming for me, but I don't know how they'll get through if the gate is still closed.

Before I leave the Anneliese, I check Kelly's room only to find it empty. I'm not surprised, but the small flame of hope I was nurturing quickly extinguishes.

I make my way across the courtyard and into the main house. The place is much quieter in the daylight. While quieter means safer, because all of the vampires are in bed, I don't think I like the emptiness or the silence. Duval House is supposed to be full of noise. Hearing the absence of it feels wrong.

I head to the library where a few of the pledged humans are dotted around the room, their attention on their phones or tablets or books. Soft jazz music plays through the sound system.

I go to the café counter where a guy is washing dishes in the sink.

"Excuse me," I call.

He turns to me, then drops the dish in his hand when he realizes who I am. The dish hits the water with force, splashing it across his black apron.

"Oh shit," he says and steps away from the sink, assessing the damage. "Sorry. Hi."

"Hi." I fold my arms over the counter. "Need help?"

"No. Absolutely not. Bran would kill me."

I frown at him.

The guy ducks down and tosses a dirty towel over the mess on the floor.

"Why would he kill you?"

"You're Jessie MacMahon," he says. "Practically Duval House royalty now." He straightens and slides the towel around on the floor with the toe of his black Converse sneakers. "And royalty does not do menial chores."

I scoff and come around the counter. "You can't be serious."

"I'm extremely serious."

I pick up a second towel.

"Ahh-ahh," he says, like he's a parent scolding a child. Except we're practically the same age.

Slowly, deliberately, I reach around him and mop up the mess on the counter. He doesn't try to stop me. I guess royalty can do as they please.

"See." I toss the towel into a nearby bucket. "No murdering or maiming."

The guy crosses his arms over his chest and his biceps swell against the sleeves of his gray t-shirt.

He's thick and muscular, but just a few inches taller than I am with messy blond hair that hangs in his face. There's a hoop earring in his left nostril and a full tattoo sleeve on his right arm. The tattoo is of a gorgeous shieldmaiden with a dark, stormy sky behind her and blackbirds in flight.

"You know my name," I say to him, "but I don't know yours."

He smirks.

"What?"

"It's King, actually."

"Wait...seriously?"

Ducking his head, he tries to hide his embarrassment. "Kingston is my full name. Everyone calls me King."

"I thought royalty didn't do menial chores?"

He laughs to himself, a quick shot of air through his nose. "The name is ridiculous. I will give you that."

"No, I like it." I offer him my hand. "It's nice to meet you, King."

There is a second of hesitation, like he actually believes the lie he's telling, that I'm somehow above him and shouldn't be engaged with. But he finally shakes.

"Nice to meet you too, Jessie. *Formerly*."

"Now that we got that out of the way...could I use your phone?"

I left my phone at Duval House when I went with Stanley to the diner, but I keep forgetting to charge it. At home, I had a routine—set my phone on the cordless charger on my desk right before I went to bed. Now my routine is all screwed up and my charger is still at the house.

It might be time I admit to myself that I've officially moved into Duval House, and if that's the case, I need to move some of my things here too.

King pulls his cell from the back pocket of his jeans and unlocks the screen. "Here you go."

"Thanks."

He returns to the sink and picks up another dish to wash.

Because I was smart enough to memorize Sam's number in case of emergency, I easily tap it out and connect. She answers groggily on the fifth ring. "Who is this and what do you want?"

"It's me. My phone is dead. I know it's early—"

"How early?"

"Like nine?" I lie. It's actually closer to eight, but I don't want Sam to veto this idea before I get it out.

With a grumble, she readjusts the phone and says, "Speak."

"Right after you left the diner last night, I was visited by a fae lord."

There's another rustle of fabric through the phone. "I'm sorry...did you say, 'fae lord?'"

"My mom used to be in charge of the mortal census, do you remember?"

"Yeah," Sam says.

"And do you remember what she used to complain about every year?"

"Trying to track down all of the fae and getting them to cooperate."

"Right. Because it was decided that the mortal court system would take on the responsibility of managing the fae records."

Sam sounds like she's moving now. "So you want to go to the mortal court and see if you can find records on this fae lord?"

"You know me so well," I answer.

Keys jingle in Sam's hand. "Mom, I'm leaving!" she yells through her house. To me she says, "This is the only time I will ever get out of bed early."

"What better reason than to go dig up dirt on a fae lord?"

"You have a good point."

"I'll meet you there in ten minutes?"

"Already walking out the door."

We hang up and I hand the phone back to King. "Thanks. I'll see you around?"

"Of course, Your Majesty." He bows with a laugh.

———

Sam and I meet outside the mortal court. Her strawberry blonde hair is braided into two messy braids that hang over her shoulders. Several wispy strands flutter in the warm morning breeze.

There is an oversized vintage movie t-shirt tied into a loose knot at her hips so that the material hugs her waist. She's wearing cut-off denim shorts, white tennis shoes, and sunglasses with a horn-rimmed flare to the frame.

Despite clearly throwing together this outfit as she stumbled from bed, she looks effortless. Neither of us has ever been particularly fashion focused, not like Kelly. But somehow Sam has always pulled off a look that feels intentional and rebellious at the same time.

"Good morning," I tell her.

"You lied about the time." She follows me up the cement steps.

"I rounded up."

She scoffs and when we enter into the darker hallway of the courthouse, Sam slides the sunglasses atop her head. She may be tired, but I'd recognize that glint of excitement anywhere.

Sam's big family may be chaotic, but they love their game nights, and Sam is always on the hunt for a win. This is just another game to play and she loves it, even if she's complaining about getting out of bed.

In the clerk's office, we find Alice behind the counter stapling packets of paper. When she spots me, her eyes get big. In the cubicle beside her, the dark-haired girl, who I recall was here when Bran and I fucked in the waiting room, stops clicking on her keyboard.

Alice yanks nervously at the hem of her blouse. "Jessie! Hi! What can I do for you?"

I lean over, as if I'm sharing a secret. "I need help finding some information on one of the fae. Is it possible you could help with that?"

She runs her tongue over her lips. "Um...okay. What fae are you looking for?"

"Arion?" I wince just hearing his name out loud, knowing that I'm technically breaking the rules and getting a little bit too nosy for my own good. I'm sure Bran has a much subtler way of getting this info, but the curiosity is getting the best of me and I'm not entirely sure Bran wants to dig up this information.

The dark-haired girl pushes away from her desk and disappears through a side door. I spot her name plate on the corner of her desk. Hailey. I can't seem to place her at a House. Is she vampire, shifter, witch pledged? She doesn't strike me as someone who would choose to be a virgin her entire life.

But can she be trusted?

"If you want to have a seat in the waiting room, I'll see what I can dig up," Alice says.

"Perfect. Thank you."

The waiting room smells like it looks—like it's a time capsule from another era.

"If your mom was still working here, she'd just let us go digging into the archives," Sam says and pops some change into a soda machine.

"Not if we wanted to know about the fae." I sit in one of the chairs next to the window that overlooks the parking lot. "Looking back, I realize she tried to keep me from interacting with the fae. Even when I babysat for the Leaf family, she would try talking me out of it."

Sam ducks down to grab her can of cola. "Knowing what you know now, clearly she was trying to keep you from finding answers."

"Yep." I slouch in the chair and fold my arms over my chest. I'm not tired, exactly. Just worn out and afraid.

I'm worried for my sister. I have yet to check in on her. I'm terrified of what I might find or how it'll make me feel to see her helpless in bed yet again, all because of me.

If I push it down deep and focus on this instead—*go, go, go*—maybe the wait for answers about my sister won't be so hard to endure.

Sam sits beside me and her can clangs open when she flicks the tab. She takes a long gulp and then hands it off to me. I could use the caffeine.

"So you want to tell me how last night went with the Alpha?" I ask.

Speaking of ways to distract myself from my own problems…

Sam takes the can back after I've had a long drink. "We barely spoke in his truck. There isn't much to report."

"What are you going to do about it?"

"Nothing. I'm just going to ignore him until he goes away."

I laugh. "I have a suspicion that someone like Cal does not just *go away*."

Sam rolls her eyes.

"Maybe he—" My words are cut off by a shadow in the waiting room doorway. I look up to see Arion, Lord of the Summer Court, leaning casually against the door frame.

"Hello, faeling," he says. "I hear you're trying to unearth my secrets. Let me save you the trouble." He moves with an ethereal quickness that catches me off guard. And suddenly he's standing in front of me, hauling me to my feet.

TEN

Arion, Lord of the Summer Court, spins me around and slams me against the nearest wall. He towers over me, his scent everywhere. Like thistle and honeysuckle and something richer, darker, like rainwater soaking stone.

"You don't get to know my secrets," he says. "You don't get to ask questions. You don't—" He cuts himself off with a hiss of air between his teeth.

The smell of iron and burning flesh drives away the heady scent of fae lord.

"Put her down," Sam says.

Sam has a tool in her hand that looks like a Swiss Army Knife. But this one is built for supernatural weapons. The tool flipped open is a small iron knife and Sam has it pressed to Arion's throat.

Arion turns to her slowly. The blade pierces flesh and blood beads from the cut. "Careful, mortal," he says.

Sam narrows her eyes. "I said, '*Put her down.*'"

Arion's fingers exert more pressure on my throat, breaking off my supply of air. My lungs burn. My ears are ringing. I may be fae, but I still have to breathe.

Sam turns the point of the blade against Arion's jugular. "Try me."

Smoke curls in the air between us before the fae lord finally relents and drops me. I sputter, sucking in air. He stands back and folds his hands behind him like this was all a minor misunderstanding.

When I'm able to fill my lungs with a full breath, I straighten and smooth over my shirt. When Bran finds out about this, and there's no doubt he will, I will never hear the end of it.

But I'm determined to navigate this new terrain with some measure of autonomy. I love Bran and I know he'll do everything in his power to protect me. I just need to prove to myself that I don't always need him to save me.

"I am not your enemy," I say.

"Does that make you an ally, faeling?" Arion tilts his head in consideration. "Allies do not dig for secrets they have not earned."

Well, he has me there.

I rub at the sore spot of flesh beneath my jawline. "I needed to know what I was dealing with. You can't blame me for that."

He says nothing.

"So are you? An enemy or ally?" I ask.

"Once upon a time, you were an enemy," he answers. "Now, it's up for debate."

It doesn't escape me that he's chosen his words carefully. Unlike me, the fae lord can't lie.

"So tell me what you want."

"I want to go home," he admits, with little to no emotion on his face.

"And you think I can help you with that?"

"You were quite possibly the last fae to come through the gate before it was sealed. So yes, I do think you can."

"And if I say no?"

The first hint of emotion filters into his eyes, making them glint. But I can't tell what it means.

He takes a step closer and I take a step back, bumping into Sam. She still has her supernatural Swiss Army Knife open, the iron pointed at Arion. But he ignores it.

"I'm sorry," he says. "Did I ask for permission?"

My stomach knots. "Are you insinuating you'd force me to help you?"

"I'm insinuating that I can take your blood with very little effort."

Is that what will unlock the gate? Arion doesn't seem like an idiot. If he thinks I'm the answer, he probably won't give up so easily in testing out the theory.

"Have you forgotten I can literally use my voice to make you do whatever I want?" I counter.

His nostrils flare. His hands are still clasped behind his back, but his body has taken on a new level of alertness, as if he could snap my neck in the next second before I even notice he's moved.

"Try it," he challenges.

I snort and then open my mouth to say, *"Bark like a dog,"* except the second I take a breath to utter the words, a gale force wind shoots into the room. My eyes burn from the shift in pressure and several papers pull free of a bulletin board and fly around the room. I throw my arm up to shield my eyes.

Arion is standing in the center of the whirlwind, his hair lightly fluttering in the breeze. He's watching me blankly, a little bored.

I try again to reach for my voice and give a command, but the wind kicks up, stealing all the oxygen from my lungs.

I turn around and Sam and I huddle together, shielding our eyes, trying to catch our breath.

When the wind dies down, paper flutters to the floor.

Arion hasn't moved, but his point has been made.

My family might once have been considered an all-powerful enemy of the other fae courts, but I barely know anything at all about being powerful. He's probably had several hundred years' jump on me.

"Cooperate or don't," he says. "I don't really care. If you accept our invitation for tonight, I'll assume you chose our side and in that case, we'll celebrate. If you don't show up..." He tilts his head again and a lock of his dark hair falls over his forehead as he narrows his eyes at me. "Well, I know where to find you, now don't I?"

And then he turns around and leaves.

———

I can't go back to Duval House. Not yet. Bran probably isn't up, but by the time he's had his first drop of coffee later today, he'll know what happened at the courthouse.

And because sometimes avoiding confrontation is better than, *well*, *confronting*, I decide to go back to my house.

Sam insists on coming with me.

"I'll be fine," I tell her as I pull open the driver's side door on the Bimmer.

She goes around to the passenger side and is in the seat before I'm behind the wheel. "I'm sure you will." She buckles her seat belt. "But on the off chance you're threatened again by a fae lord, it might behoove you to have me and my supernatural widget to save you."

I sigh and settle into the driver's seat. "Where did you get that thing, anyway?"

Sam props her elbow on the door rest and wrinkles her nose. "Cal."

"Well, props to the Alpha," I say and turn the engine over. "That little widget came in handy."

"No props to him," Sam practically snarls. "*Zero* props."

I let her have that one. She's going to get enough push back from practically everyone when they find out she's the Alpha's fated mate.

When the news breaks, she'll practically be a Midnight Harbor celebrity and everyone will be watching what she does, what she says, how she dresses and where she eats. They'll be pressuring her to dish on the Alpha and hounding her to reveal her own private thoughts about him and their relationship.

As her best friend, I just need to let her hate him—for now.

We park in the driveway outside my house. I find the front door still locked, and when I turn the key in the deadbolt and the lock thunks open, I breathe out with a sigh.

It's familiar, even if it's silly, and it makes me suddenly miss everything that was before.

I kick off my shoes and trudge over to the couch and dramatically throw myself into the cushions. Sam sits at the other end, snagging the TV remote from the end table.

I yawn and let my eyes slip closed.

"Do you have to work today?" I ask sleepily.

"No." Sam clicks on the TV and the room brightens with the glow. She scrolls through apps, landing on a streaming service.

"Will you stay with me all day?" I ask, feeling the exhaustion catch up to me.

"As long as I can," she says.

I curl into my side and Sam grabs the throw blanket draped over the back of the sofa and tosses it over me.

"Bran will show up around dusk," I warn her.

"My widget has a stake too."

I laugh and try to find a comfy spot on one of Kelly's throw pillows.

"Don't kill him," I tell her.

"Just give him a warning poke, got it."

The sleep tugs me down instantly.

When I wake hours later, the sun has set and Sam is no longer sitting at the other end of the sofa.

Bran Duval is.

Eleven

We watch each other in the half-darkness for several long beats. There is a stillness to Bran that is unsettling and hot as fuck. I may be able to control him with just the sound of my voice, but I think his vampire speed could beat the words on my lips.

And the thought of him clamping his hand over my mouth and having his way with me has my insides churning and my thighs aching to wrap around him.

His nostrils flare as he scents the air.

"Where's Sam?" I ask.

The house is dark and silent.

"I sent her home."

"Did she stake you?"

He ignores me and says, "You were a naughty mouse today." His voice vibrates with annoyance.

"I want to say I'm surprised you found out so quickly, but I'm not."

"There is nothing you can hide from me, Mouse."

"I know. But don't forget your promise."

He narrows his eyes. "Which one?"

"The one where you said you'd let me make mistakes."

There is a tsk of air between his teeth and he looks away. The light of one of the street posts outside spills into the room and across his face and pools over the broad line of his shoulder. His smell is everywhere even though it's my house. Wherever Bran is, he overwhelms. In scent and presence and fucking power.

His chest rises with a deep breath and then he says, "Once upon a time, if someone were to disobey me, I would do very terrible things to them."

I don't dare move.

"The urge to bend you over this couch and smack your ass is hard to ignore."

Heat surges to my pussy.

Is he trying to get me riled? Because it's working.

He leans over and snatches me by the wrist and hauls me onto his lap. My thighs straddle him and his hands come to my waist, fingers just *this side* of bruising as he seats me on his groin. My hair spills forward as the air quickens in my throat.

I want to rock against him so fucking badly, but I'm not about to give in to him.

"Do you feel satisfied with yourself, little mouse?" His eyes glow amber in the shadow cast by my body, and it causes a shiver to race up my spine.

I wiggle a little and he increases the pressure on my hips, forcing me still.

"I wanted information," I say, my pussy suddenly buzzing. "And I got some."

"Did you?" His voice vibrates in his chest. He rocks his hips, pressing the bulge of his pants into the heat between my legs. "Tell me."

"Why, when you're clearly mad I went after it?"

He drives me down on him and pleasure builds in my clit.

I can't help but moan. I try to grind into him, but he lifts me again, creating an aching distance between us.

His irises glint like twin flames. "Tell me, little mouse, and tell me now."

Fuck. I may have the power to command with my voice, but I lack the authority that Bran can tap into so damn easily. And if I'm honest, I don't want to give this up, this dance of obedience and defiance between us. The give and take of power.

We will find our new ground, and if I give in to the journey instead of stressing about the destination, maybe I'll even enjoy it.

I suck in a deep breath when he finally sits me back down on him, teasing me more. "Arion wants my blood," I answer.

"Why?"

"He thinks I can help unseal the gate to the fae realm."

Bran goes still.

I refocus my eyes on him and find his gaze suddenly distant and his brow furrowed.

"What is it?"

His frown deepens. "The witches want to unseal the gate too."

"The Renshaw witches?" He nods. "Why?"

"Apparently they were using Julian as a means to an end. Tabitha lost a brother to the fae realm when it was sealed off."

"So she wants us to open the gate to rescue her brother? Why would we care enough to do that? We already won against them."

Bran looks up at me. His jaw flexes. Not with anger, but anguish. "She linked the spell she used on my brother to the fae side. It cannot be undone without opening the gate."

Numbness runs through my limbs, and the flame at my core immediately extinguishes.

"So Kelly…"

"Same spell," he confirms. "Same solution."

I climb off of him and sit on the cushion beside him. A car drives past on the street outside the front windows. One of the neighbors calls for their dog.

I want to scream.

If I were playing a game of chess, I have already lost, backed into a corner with no escape in sight.

I feel so fucking stupid.

And helpless.

Bran threads his fingers through mine and gives me a squeeze.

"If I *can* open that gate," I start, "and more fae come through and they realize I exist…"

"I know," Bran says.

"What if they want me dead?" My voice pitches with panic.

"They'll have all of Duval House and the Pack to get through."

I snort. "You really think the Alpha would put his pack on the line for me? There's no way—"

"Yes," he interrupts. "I do think he would."

"Why?"

"Because you're his fated mate's best friend. If Sam didn't hate him enough already, she'd murder him if he let anything happen to you."

Okay, he may have a point.

"Even if you're right, will that be enough? What if the entire Autumn Court comes through the gate?"

His grip on me tightens, pulling my attention to him. "I am not afraid, Mouse."

My chest heaves at the assurance in his words. He is so confident it almost takes the fear away.

Almost.

I run my teeth over my bottom lip and try to keep the anxiety at bay. "But I am, Bran."

He winds his arm around me and pulls me into him and I deflate, resting my head against his shoulder. We haven't made it to the point of our relationship where we're so familiar with one another that cuddling comes naturally. We were built on annoyance first. Annoyance and frustration that turned into blazing heat.

I need his assurance now, I realize. Because his confidence in making it through this might just be the only thing holding me together.

"Let me tell you a secret, Mouse."

I hold my breath, wondering what other things he might be keeping from me.

But it's something better than all of that. It's a truth straight from his heart.

"When Damien and I were mortal, he nearly died from a strain of flu. He had always protected me, my wise older brother. It made me feel invincible and I was terrified of losing him." His shoulders rise with a deep breath. "I know I can tell you all day long that I will protect you. That I will do everything in my power to shield you from pain, both physical and mental, but ultimately your own strength will protect you even better than I can. And I know that it's difficult to believe in your power when it's still so new, but someday you'll realize that with or without me, you can do extraordinary things."

Tears bite at my eyes as I tilt my chin to look up at him. A wave of emotion stings at my sinuses and clogs in my throat. I don't feel strong, even though I know I hold a great deal of power. I still can't seem to believe it. Or believe in myself.

"I have trouble seeing it," I admit to him.

"I know." He kisses my forehead gently. "And until then, I will see it for you."

We sit in the silence for several long minutes as the darkness descends outside the front windows. Bran doesn't move. He keeps his arm firmly around me, what little body heat he radiates enveloping me.

I don't want to get up, but I know I have to. There's still so much to do.

"I had a thought earlier," I say.

"Tell me."

"I should probably officially move into Duval House."

"I agree."

There is a little bit of relief at hearing him say it. I mean, all of the evidence points to him wanting me near, but I'm still keyed up, looking for signs of his flight or dismay at being with a fae princess with the power to command with her voice who also happens to be a hot fucking mess.

"So I should pack my things and—"

He shifts beside me, untangling us. "Gather the necessities. I'll have someone pack the rest."

"But—"

"You and I have better things to do, Mouse. We pay people for this." He gets up and offers me his hand.

"Fine." I take it and he lifts me easily off the couch then steers me toward the staircase. "Just the necessities then. Give me—"

I falter on the first step, suddenly lightheaded, and the room sways. "Mouse!"

Bran catches me as I tilt backward. He has me pressed against the nearest wall a second later, his hands firmly on my body to keep me upright. "What is it?" His eyes are dark, his brow furrowed as he examines me. "What's wrong?"

"I don't know...I'm kinda dizzy all of a sudden and—"

A cell phone pings.

Bran's teeth grind together as he pulls his phone from his pants pocket. But as soon as he reads the name on the screen, his expression softens. "It's Bianca."

He opens the screen and reads the text, his scowl deepening. "Damien is muttering in his sleep."

That must be a good sign, right?

"What did he say?"

Bran turns the phone around and shows me the screen and I scan the words quickly.

He's coming, the text reads.

The fae prince is coming.

Twelve

I'M PRESSED AGAINST THE BACK OF THE PASSENGER SEAT AS Bran shifts the Bimmer into third gear and propels us through the night.

He's silent, his attention on the road, but his body is tight, the tendons and muscles in his forearms flexing beneath his pale skin as he works the transmission and the speedy engine to his advantage.

The urgency is nearly palpable even if he won't speak of it.

Damien was talking in his sleep, and if he was talking in his sleep, does that mean he is closer to consciousness?

I tried talking Bran into running home, that it would be faster and I'd meet him there, but he wasn't having it.

"You've been out of my sight once today," he'd said. "And look at the trouble you got yourself into. Once is enough."

I would have rolled my eyes at him and stood my ground, damn the consequences, if not for the news about Damien.

It doesn't take Bran long to turn down the winding driveway of Duval House. The windows are lit up and all of the landscaping lights are on, washing the green manicured grounds in golden pools of light.

As Bran pulls the car beneath the *porte cochère*, I can't help but wonder if my sister might also be clawing her way back to consciousness.

I don't want to hope, because I don't want to be disappointed, but it's really fucking hard not to cling to any glimmer of possible good news.

Please come back to me, Kelly.

Bran slams the car to a stop and yanks up on the emergency brake. He's out of the car a second later and tossing my key ring into the air. He doesn't check to see if anyone is there to catch them, because of course there is.

The girl at the double doors fumbles the keys but catches them before they hit the ground. She quickly darts in behind the wheel. Bran is already through the wide double doors as I scurry around the car's front bumper. "Catch up, Mouse," he calls, already halfway to the main staircase.

I run after him.

Somehow his fast walk is twice as fast as my run, but I catch up, practically breathless, as he takes the stairs two at a time and then turns down a hallway, then another, until we come up to a closed door far into the depths of the second floor. I've never been to this side of Duval House so I can only guess this is Damien's bedroom. The door is large and ornate, clearly hand carved, with laurel leaves and baroque filigree.

It's regal but not garish, just like the Duvals.

Without knocking, Bran pushes through and steps into the dim. I slow my pace and edge in just behind him, unsure if I should be here.

There's only one lamp on in the large space and the light skims a huge, heavy wooden bed pushed against the far wall. There is a sweet but masculine smell hanging in the air, like musk and lavender.

"Damien," Bran says. But when he gets to the bed, he stops, his eyes going wide.

Something slams into me from behind and shoves me to the floor.

I let out a yelp as a knee is pressed into the center of my back, driving me into the rug. A cold hand grabs my chin while the other comes to the back of my head, bracing me.

"Damien!" Bran yells.

Damien is awake.

And he's on my back, just one wrist-flick away from snapping my neck.

My heart thuds in my ears.

"If she dies, they have no reason to come," Damien says, his voice wet and raspy.

The heady scent of lavender overwhelms me.

"If she dies, so will you," Bran answers.

I huff out as the pressure increases between my shoulder blades, squeezing my lungs.

"You would kill your own brother over a girl?" Damien sniffs. "I thought we were immune to chivalry, brother."

"Immune to chivalry, perhaps," Bran answers, "but not MacMahon sisters. Remember? Remember the lengths you went to, to protect Kelly? Kelly is the reason you can't think straight now. Because you wanted to protect her."

Damien's grip on me shifts.

Bran comes closer. "What do you think Kelly will say when she finds out you killed her little sister?"

Would I survive my neck being snapped? I race through all of the facts I know about the fae, their anatomy, and their immortality. They can live practically forever, heal easily, but survive a snapped neck? Probably not.

Can Bran reach Damien in time?

How far away is he?

"I can smell her fear," Damien says.

"Do you blame her?"

"Please, Da—"

He shifts his grip, putting the palm of his hand over my mouth.

"How do you trust a girl who can command you with her voice?"

When Bran speaks, he's just a few feet away from us now, getting closer by the second. "You always taught me that trust was fickle and fickle things hold no value. It was always loyalty we wanted."

Some of the weight of Damien's knee lifts. "You must think yourself clever, using my own lessons against me."

"Let her go, Damien."

"Where is Kelly?" he asks.

"In the room across the hall," Bran answers. "I haven't checked on her yet today, but we can go over there together if you'd like."

"Very well. Perhaps you've won after—"

Damien gasps out, his chest rattling, and then he grunts and tilts to the side, slipping off of me.

Even though I'm lying on the floor, my head swims. I'm light-headed, my vision tunneling.

Bran is suddenly between us.

"Something is wrong," I say. Pins and needles run up my arms and legs. I try to sit up now that I'm free, but my vision sways.

"Do you feel it too?" Damien asks. He's on all fours beside me, looking directly at me, his eyes burning bright blue in the murky light.

"Feel what?"

He takes in another deep breath. "They're trying to get through. The fae. They're trying to get through the gate."

———

Bran gets Damien's arm slung around his shoulders and then pulls him to his feet. "Can you stand, Mouse?" Bran asks.

I give him a nod, even though I'm still dizzy. His brother should take priority right now. I'm going to pretend I'm okay as long as I need to.

I slowly climb to my feet and take in a deep breath to steady myself.

Damien lists in Bran's grip.

"Hey," Bran says and slaps Damien on the face. "Look at me."

Damien's eyes refocus and he looks over at his brother. "We should kill her," he says again.

"Shut up," Bran says as he carts Damien back to the bed and helps him onto the thick mattress. "Jessie is off-limits, even to you. You touch her again, I stake you. First in the ass. Then in the heart. End of story."

Damien lays his head against the pile of pillows, his eyes heavy. "Do you remember the bread Ma used to make?"

Bran goes still, his brow sinking low over his hooded eyes. "Yes."

"Do you remember the smell of the yeast baking on a winter after-noon?" Damien's head lolls on the pillows, his eyes closed now. "Do you remember the way it would taste when she cut off a fresh slice for us?"

"Of course." Bran's voice is thick with the memory.

"Why did we outlive them? Do you ever wonder?"

Bran pulls the blanket up around Damien. "Because we are cursed."

Damien swallows loudly. "Perhaps dying wouldn't be so bad after all."

"Don't talk like that."

I slink back into the shadows, my heart squeezing, suddenly uncomfortable with witnessing the intimacy between the Duval brothers. I'm not sure if Bran wants me to see them at their most vulnerable, when they are more brothers than immortal vampires. Brothers with mothers and sisters and memories of fresh baked bread on cold afternoons.

"I can't help you fight them," Damien says as he slumps into the bed. "Not like this."

"I'll fix you. I just need you to rest and not kill my little mouse."

Damien's mouth lifts in an attempted laugh. "That's a horrible pet name for her." He's quiet for another beat, his chest rattling with his breaths. "The mouse has become the monster."

A shiver races down my arms, lifting goosebumps.

Bran looks over at me and even though I'm shrouded in darkness, I know with his vampire eyes he can see me the same as if I were standing in the light.

His eyes burn bright gold.

"We're all monsters," Bran says, his gaze still on me.

———

Within seconds, Damien is unconscious again and Bran ushers me into the hallway. As soon as we're alone, he puts his hands on either side of my face and examines me with a furrowed brow and bright golden eyes.

"Are you okay?"

"I'm fine."

"Did he hurt you?" He checks my skin for bruises.

"He was gentle like a cat."

Bran scowls at me. "This is no time for jokes."

The door across from Damien's catches my eye. "Is she really in there?"

"Yes." Bran pulls away, satisfied with the state of my face, neck, and body.

"Can I..." I huff out a breath, trying to keep the emotion at bay. I will be practical about this. Kelly is unconscious because of witch magic. This is fixable. We'll find the solution and we'll fix her.

"Go see her," Bran says. "I'll come with you."

I give him a nod and reach out for the handle. The door clicks open and I peer inside.

There is a small figure in the giant bed across the room. There are more lights on in here—small lamps glowing on several end tables.

My steps are slow as I approach the bed.

I'm not sure what I expected to find—Kelly looking like a corpse? Like a sleeping Snow White?

Her eyes are shut and her breathing even. Her skin is pale, yes, but there's still a healthy glow to her cheeks. When the witch spell hit Kelly and Damien at the Pledge Hall, blackness spread beneath their skin. But it's gone now. Like it never was.

"What are we going to do?" I muse.

"Did you feel it?" he asks.

I cut my attention to him.

"Was Damien right? Were you both feeling the fae trying to get through?"

Pressure builds at the bridge of my nose. "I don't know. I felt...something."

Arion thinks my blood can open the gate. And the spell used against Damien and Kelly is linked to magic on the fae side. It would make sense that we would feel any attempt to break the seal on the gate.

Bran leans a shoulder against the thick wooden post at the bed's footboard. "We need allies, Mouse. Fae ones."

"Arion," I say and he nods. "Does that worry you?"

"Nothing worries me. There is only strategy and outcome."

"You're lying."

His mouth is pursed, the glow gone from his eyes, but I can tell he *is* worried. Maybe even a little afraid.

I turn back to my sister, the odd stillness to her body. I reach out for her hand and the second our skin touches, I'm crying.

Not giant heaving sobs. But slow, painful tears.

I can't ignore the hope that I can save her.

I think it might be the only thing I have left.

I'm not afraid.

I'm hungry to prove myself.

"I'm going to Arion tonight," I say and wipe the tears away with the pad of my thumb. "And you're coming with me and we're going to make a bold statement."

The corner of Bran's mouth lifts. "You're sexy when you're determined."

"I'm serious, Bran."

"So am I, Mouse."

I check on Kelly one last time before surging to the door. "Who do I call to help make me a fae princess in just a few hours?"

"A princess will always be lacking. In her position, she is inherently vulnerable and weak." Bran takes my hand in his and pulls me down the hall. "Fuck a fae princess. We're making you a queen and I have just the thing for it."

Thirteen

When we leave the wing of the house where Damien and Kelly's rooms are, Bran doesn't take me downstairs. Instead we go to the opposite wing, and deep, deep into the recess, down several more hallways until I'm well and truly lost again.

I guess this is another reason why he put me in the Anneliese when I first came to Duval House. I don't think I would have lasted a day in the main house. I would be lost in some distant corner like a mouse in a maze.

I snort at my own joke and Bran casts a sidelong glance my way.

"Why are you laughing?"

I wipe the smile from my face. He's disgruntled, tense, and clearly on some mission he has yet to share with me.

I told him I wanted to make a bold statement tonight with Arion and the rest of the fae community in Midnight. Bran said he had just the thing for it, but he has yet to tell me what the *thing* is.

"I was just thinking about mice in mazes looking for cheese," I tell him.

He comes to a sudden stop and I have to backtrack several steps to meet up with him again. There is no hint of emotion on his face, but I can still read the rigidity of his body, catching the barest of annoyance in the fine lines around his eyes.

He's so fucking hot when he's annoyed. Sometimes I want to annoy him on purpose to watch him scowl and brood at me.

"What?" I ask.

"My brother nearly snapped your neck just now and you're making jokes about cheese?"

I shrug. "Damien isn't the first person to try to do me harm."

To be honest, I haven't quite processed how close I was to death just a few minutes ago. I mean, when you live around vampires and were-wolves, you're always close to it. We may have created a treaty of peace between us all, but if the vampires and wolves wanted to take an innocent life, who is to stop them?

Maybe that's why death doesn't seem as frightening. Maybe we've all been desensitized to it living in Midnight.

"It was a funny joke," I tell Bran.

He grumbles. "Maybe a little funny."

"Hah! I knew it."

"Come on, little mouse. Let me lead you to the cheese." He beckons me deeper into the house.

I jog to catch up. "You still haven't told me where we're going."

He takes another corner and a long hallway opens up before us. At the end are two large doors, arched at the top, with giant curved handles. There is a golden plaque above the door that reads ARCHIVE.

"You're so fancy you have an archive." I gape at it, then look over at him. "The closest thing we had to an archive was stale corn chips in the couch cushions."

I smile innocently at him.

The next second he has his arm around my waist and yanks me into his side. I let out a gasp, my mouth dropping open.

His fingers apply the barest hint of pressure. "No more jokes, Mouse. And if you don't stop gaping at everything, I'll find something to put in that tight little mouth."

The breath hitches out of me as my pussy buzzes with his meaning.

"You're teasing me." I reach between us and grope him. He groans.

"No, I'm telling you what your punishment will be if you don't behave."

I demur. "Or my reward."

"Mouse."

I apply more pressure to his cock. It doesn't take him long to thicken beneath the attention of my hand. His eyes still on my mouth, he brings his thumb to my bottom lip and presses down, opening me wider for him.

I dart my tongue out to meet him and his fangs lengthen into two pointed tines.

"Maybe we could slip into a closet somewhere," I suggest.

"Oh little Mouse, I would destroy that pussy and we've no time for rest."

I squeeze him harder and he leans into me just as the latch on the Archive clanks open.

I lurch away from Bran.

The doors swing open to reveal a woman in a dress straight out of the twenties, with fringe and pearls and glinting sequins.

"I can hear you, you know!" she says. "This isn't a whorehouse!"

"Ramona," Bran says. "If you're here, it's automatically a whorehouse."

She hangs her head back and laughs at the ceiling and the pearls hanging from her ears swing back and forth.

I have no idea what I'm supposed to think of this exchange.

"Ramona was a whore in the twenties," Bran explains.

"I was a successful one too." She winks at him. "That's where I found this asshole."

"I think you mean, *I* found *you*."

Oh god. Did they...did he...

"No," Bran answers before I can even get the thought out. "Ramona tried. She failed."

She frowns at him. "Too good for whorehouses. He and his brother both. Not too good to pay me for my time though, were you?"

"I needed information. Whores always had good information back then."

"That we did." Ramona beams at him. In appearance, she doesn't look much older than I am. Maybe late twenties. She must be a vampire. She's shorter than I am, maybe five feet. Next to Bran she looks like a sprite.

Her dark, thick hair is pinned back in a chignon, not a lock out of place. Her makeup is flawless—black winged eyeliner, smoky shadow, and deep purple lipstick.

She is exactly the type of woman who should be in charge of a vampire archive. I bet she loves every single piece in here.

Speaking of which...

I try to peek around her—the doors are just barely cracked—but I can't really spot a clue.

"Jessie!" Ramona pulls my attention away from the doors by taking my hand in her cold ones. "What a pleasure to finally meet you."

It still catches me off guard when people of Duval House know me and I don't know them.

Up until recently, I thought I was a nobody in Midnight. Or maybe I was and it was Bran who changed that and pulled me from obscurity.

Or maybe there were always whispers. Julian marked me as off limits. The vampires must have known there was something different about me for him to go to that much trouble.

"Pleasure to meet you too," I tell Ramona. "I love your dress."

She does a twirl and the fringe on the skirt twirls. "It belonged to Norma Shearer. She wore it to the premiere of The Mummy in 1932. As an aside, The Mummy was not a hit with the critics but was considered a modest box office success. I do believe we have a prop from the set around here somewhere. Oh, where did I—"

"Ramona," Bran says. "We're here for a dress. Not a movie prop."

She pouts at him, but quickly recovers and twirls away. "Very well! What sort of dress?"

"One from the fae collection."

She pauses at the Archive doors, hands on the curved handles. "It must be a special night?"

"Jessie needs to look like a fae queen."

"Say no more."

She gives the doors a wider push, revealing what's inside.

———

When I step over the threshold and into the Archive, I look around and gasp.

I'm not sure what I expected. A department store dressing room? A closet crammed with old garments?

It's none of that.

It's a fucking ballroom with glass-topped cabinets like in a museum, and racks of clothing, and printer's cabinets with thin drawers for documents.

More cabinets line the walls with drawers on the bottom and glass doors on the top, revealing a wide array of treasures beneath soft inset lighting. Feathered hats and giant jeweled necklaces and carved stone objects.

"Holy shit," I breathe out.

"Holy shit yes!" Ramona claps her hands again and her short legs cart her off down an aisle, and the archives quickly swallow her up. "This way!"

Bran gives me a nudge. I head in the direction Ramona disappeared, weaving through the clothing racks. There are sequined dresses and pantsuits and dresses with pearls sewn into the bodice.

Does Kelly know about this place? She would lose her mind.

We finally come up on another door in the recess of the archive. It's also arched like the main doors, but smaller in scale. A shaft of light pools at the threshold, warm and inviting.

I enter to find a room done in rich wood paneling. There are built-in cabinets and drawers in a circle around the space, with a sitting area directly to the right of the door.

In the center of the room are five dress forms displaying the most dazzling garments I've ever laid eyes on.

"It just keeps getting better," I say like a huge dork, even though I'm not the least bit enamored with fashion.

Bran sits on the velvet settee the color of dawn and props his elbow on the gilded gold arm, curling his hand around his face.

If we were anywhere else, in any other clothing store, he would look like a bored boyfriend waiting for his girlfriend to finish shopping. But even bored, I know he's watching, calculating, *waiting*.

Bran is always playing a game.

I can only imagine what card he has up his sleeve now.

Ramona goes to the third dress on the left and pulls delicately at the skirt. A rainbow of gemstones glimmer beneath the light. "This would fit her beautifully and—"

"No," Bran says, cutting her off.

"No? Okay. We have this purple one with the emeralds in the–"

"No," Bran says again.

Ramona clucks her tongue. "Then which one?"

"Get her the Winter Court dress."

Ramona goes still.

"Now," Bran orders.

"Absolutely not," she says.

"Ramona." His tone leaves no room for negotiation.

My insides spin and dammit, my pussy clenches when he uses that commanding voice.

I cannot fucking wait to have him alone.

Ramona levels her shoulders, bracing for an argument. "Forgive me, but...the Winter Court dress...the message it would send–"

"I know what fucking message I want to send, Ramona," he says.

She licks her lips, diverts her eyes, and nods as she turns away. "Very well."

What the hell is the Winter Court dress anyway?

And what message do we want to send?

Ramona opens a cabinet and soft light turns on, activated by the doors opening.

And nestled inside is a dress made of the finest white fabric with a high collar that curves away from the form's neck, making the collar look like the pointed curves of fairy wings. The skirt is scalloped around the hem, but long enough that it would trail behind me like a train. A heavy belt is secured around the waist, with more jewels and ribbons woven into it.

The dress is beautiful, but it's damaged. And more than that, it appears to be bloody.

There is a tear above the left breast. Dark red has stained the white fabric and the color spills down the front of the skirt where it pooled at the wearer's feet.

"She can't wear that dress," Ramona says.

"She can and she will."

I take a tentative step toward it, a cold sweat beading at my spine. "What happened to it? What's the story?"

"We don't know the story," Bran answers, suddenly behind me. "But I bet Arion will."

My stomach turns sour.

The cold sweat races over my shoulders.

Just because this dress belonged to someone from the Winter Court doesn't mean I was related to them. I do know that fae courts are just as diverse as the Houses of Midnight. There is some family, yes, but primarily the courts are made up of unrelated fae that came together because of magic, power, and similar beliefs.

But even knowing that, and even though my brain wants to say I am far removed from this macabre dress, something in my gut says otherwise.

Bran reaches around me and lifts a bloody length of fabric to his nose.

I swallow hard as a lump forms in my throat.

Without warning, Bran grabs my wrist and pierces my flesh with his fangs. "Hey!"

There's no pain though, just surprise as he takes a shallow pull of blood.

"This isn't time for a snack," I tell him beneath my breath.

His eyes are bright gold when he retreats.

His frown deepens.

"What is it?" I ask.

"This blood..." He nods at the dress. "Your blood...it smells the same."

The cold sweat turns to a cold chill as it races over my shoulders.

"Like fae?"

He grits his teeth. "Like family."

Fourteen

There is only the loud thumping of my heart in my ears.

Family.

That's what Bran said.

The bloody Winter Court dress smells like *my* family.

Up until this point, having a fae family was just an idea, a story. Now it's real. And worse than that, it's carnage right before my eyes. Proof that the fae courts really will do whatever it takes to destroy my line.

Bran snaps his fingers at Ramona and she scurries out of the room, shutting the door behind her.

I'm breathing faster now, my vision blurring on the edges.

They're going to kill me.

And then they'll all rejoice over my corpse.

"Sit down, Mouse," Bran orders, his hand on my arm, guiding me away from the dress. The backs of my legs bump into the settee, and I drop hard to the cushions.

"Mouse," he says.

I blink over to him.

"Tell me what you're thinking."

I swallow, trying to fill my lungs with oxygen.

He crouches in front of me and takes my face in his hands. "You don't have to go. We don't have to go." There's concern between his brows. A flicker of worry in his amber eyes.

"Arion already said..." I trail off and suck in another breath.

"He said what?"

If I tell Bran Arion's exact words, he'll lose his fucking mind.

I'm insinuating that I can take your blood with very little effort.

"We have to go," I tell Bran. "We have no choice."

"There's always a choice."

I look past him to the dress, to the dark crimson stain down the front, the tear of fabric at the chest.

Stabbed in the heart.

Someone who shared my blood.

"What would you do?" I ask him.

He rises so he can sit next to me on the cushion. He puts his elbows on his knees and folds his hands in front of him while he thinks. I give him all the time he needs because I want his honest answer, I want him to work his strategic magic.

"If it were me," he says, and looks over at me, a lock of his dark hair falling over his forehead. "I would go and I would wear the dress."

"Why?"

My heart rate slows and I can finally take a full breath.

"Arion wants to intimidate you," Bran says. "The dress symbolizes the carnage that's already been wrought. If you wear it, you tell him you are not afraid of more spilled blood. If he can't intimidate you, he can't control you."

I link my arm through his and lean my head against his shoulder. His scent soothes me, that amber and musk. Even the coolness of his body helps ground me.

"And if Arion asks me to help him unseal the gate?"

Bran looks over at me. He takes my hand in his. "Better he ask than coerce."

"True. But I'd rather not do it at all."

He sighs and closes his eyes. "I wish that was our best option, but Damien..."

"I know." I unlink our arms and cross the room to stand in front of the dress. It really is gorgeous. Like starlight trapped in a dress form. And in some macabre way, the blood adds to its beauty. Violence with beauty, trapped in time.

"I'll wear it," I say.

Bran is suddenly behind me. "If at any moment, you feel uncomfortable, we'll take it off."

"You'd like that, wouldn't you?" I glance at him over my shoulder.

"I was being serious. But yes." He smirks.

"Devil."

His arms wind around my waist, and he pulls me into him. His nose nuzzles at the crook of my neck, drinking in my scent and the pulsing heat of my veins. "When this is all over, little mouse, I will take you to some faraway castle and chain you to my bed and delight in your body again and again. And I will show you just how devilish I can be."

———

It takes Bran no time at all to assemble an entire team to get me and him ready. Ramona selects a fae-made suit jacket for him. It's black, with silver embroidery along the collar and down the lapel, and buttons shaped like orbs that when they catch the light, they almost seem to churn like an ocean.

Once Ramona is finished with him, she returns to me with blue metallic thread and needle and sews delicate knot-work around the stab wound in the chest of my dress, closing up the tear.

Next, my hair is curled, braided, and then pinned into a crown. While my vampire hair stylist finishes up, a tall, lanky woman who introduces herself as Charlie swipes bright red lipstick on my lips, finishing off my makeup.

When Bran and I finally come back together in front of a gilded floor-to-ceiling mirror, we match so well, it's hard not to think it was planned weeks ago.

"You are gorgeous," he says with hungry eyes.

"And you are ridiculously handsome," I say back.

"How do you feel?"

I turn to my left, then my right, checking the dress on all its angles. If a person didn't know the story of the dress, it would almost look like a fairytale avant-garde dress with a giant paint splatter.

But no, just dripping with blood.

I finger the stain. The fabric is thicker there, still a little stiff with a life drained from flesh.

My stomach swims. I take a breath.

I will not be disgusted by this dress. I will wear it with honor.

I may know absolutely nothing about my family, but I won't believe I was born from something evil. My family must have had a story, a reason to do what they did, even if it wasn't the right one.

"I feel ready," I finally tell Bran.

His gaze meets my reflection in the mirror, and he gives me a nod. "Then let's not keep them waiting any longer."

———

As Bran and I make our way through Bramwell Park, my heart starts thumping against the back of my throat.

I don't want to be nervous.

"Can't you compel the anxiety out of me?" I ask him, my arm tightly woven through the crook of his. He can see much better in the dark than I can. Even though Arion's invitation said to meet him on the moonlit side of Bramwell Pond, there is barely a moon in sight.

Which means if I survive tonight, tomorrow Rita will finally undo my binding spell on the new moon.

Arion couldn't have better timing.

"I'm not compelling you," Bran answers.

"Why not?"

"Because you need every instinct you possess."

I wrinkle my nose at him. "I could do without the anxiety."

He pulls me down one of the paved bike paths that eventually hugs close to the shore of Bramwell Pond. I don't know which side is the moonlit side, but Bran seems to have a destination in mind.

Crickets and frogs chirp and croak in the darkness. The air is warm, with a slight breeze that makes the dry leaves of the underbrush scrape and rattle.

Bran finally comes to a stop where the bike path curves back toward the opposite park entrance.

"Is this it?" I ask.

He looks around. "This is it."

The night is still. There's no one around.

"Is it a trap?" My stomach spins and I look down at my dress again, and at the long skirt pooled around my slippered feet. I couldn't run in this thing if I tried.

Bran's dark brow furrows, eyes narrowing.

"What?" I ask.

"The air is different. Do you feel it?"

"Different? How—"

I cut myself off when a faint break of light wavers off to my left. There are two birch trees with trunks that curve away from one another but canopies that curve back, forming what almost looks like a doorway.

I let go of Bran and take a step. He mirrors me, keeping less than a foot between us.

His nearness makes me bold and I reach out, waving my hand through the air.

And suddenly a doorway appears...

...and Arion, Lord of the Summer Court, steps through.

Fifteen

I stumble back.

I knew the birch trees were hiding a magical fairy door, but I didn't expect the fae lord to be waiting for us.

Bran immediately steps in front of me.

"No need for caution," Arion says. "You were invited here, after all."

Some of the light pouring around Arion dissipates and I can finally take in the full sight of the doorway.

The birch trees are the frame, with several branches that bend and curve over one another, forming the archway. Star jasmine and honey-suckle grow around the branches, the white and red flowers seemingly glowing in the dark night.

It takes my breath away, how gorgeous it is. But it's more than that. It feels...familiar almost.

"A fairy grotto hidden right in the middle of Bramwell Park," Bran says. "Clever."

"*Necessary*," Arion corrects.

He glances over at me and then his gaze catches on my dress.

There is a moment where his eyes are wide, his mouth slightly agape, and I realize I've surprised him, and the realization fuels my confidence.

But then he catches himself and he quickly corrects, teeth gritted, jaw flexing. "What is this?" His voice rumbles and the air, I swear to god, crackles around him, "Is this some kind of joke to you?"

"It's an homage," I answer, folding my hands in front of me, trying not to betray the fact that every move I make tonight, I've already doubted it twice over. Including wearing this dress.

"An homage?" He scowls at me. Just like Bran, he's more beautiful when he broods. "An homage to death and betrayal?"

The way he speaks about it leads me to believe he does know the story behind it. He knows exactly what dress this is, and who wore it, and what happened to them.

"Perhaps if I knew the full story," I say, "I would know the full score of wearing the dress."

"If I didn't know any better," Arion lowers his voice as he steps toward me, still half blocked by Bran, "I truly would think you mortal. Only a mortal would make such a bold move without knowing the full breadth of the consequences." He glances at Bran. "But you, vampire, I'd expect more restraint from you."

Bran's eyes flash gold, but he says nothing.

Did we make a mistake?

My stomach spins.

Arion turns away and steps into the doorway and says, "Come, faeling. The party is waiting and you're clearly ready to make an entrance." The way he says it is disparaging, not admiring.

I look over at Bran. His face is blank, his gaze unreadable.

He gives me a subtle shake of his head, so I take a deep breath and follow Arion through the doorway.

———

I'm immediately dazzled by light.

The hidden fairy grotto really is like a fairy tale. Not the Cinderella kind, with castles and mice and sewing birds. The kind you find in books written by Grimm brothers. A little dark, a little magical, a little wondrous, a little eerie.

We enter into an earthen hallway, the walls covered in blooming vines. And at the end of the hallway, a large arched doorway opens to a great hall.

The lyrical notes of a lute greet us as we enter the main room, followed by the high tinkling sound of a woman singing along. A violin jumps in next, filling the hall with music that raises the hair along my arms.

Dozens of fae are dancing in the center of the room, some linked arm and arm, others twirling in and around each other.

And there are so *many*. More than I ever knew resided in Midnight. Possibly more than were reported on their census.

There are fae with deer horns and fae with ram horns. Fae with red eyes and pink hair and pointed ears. Fae that look human save for a slight upturn of their nose or a dusting of bright blue freckles along their cheeks. Everyone here is an adult though, not a kid in sight. I don't see the Leaf family or the mother I helped on the riverside not that long ago, and I don't see Stanley either. It's unfortunate, because I really could have used a friendly, familiar face.

My slippered feet are just a soft whisper on the stone floor as I crane my neck, trying to take it all in. The sheer size of the great hall is astounding, like a football field, if a football field were enclosed by earth and tangled, blooming vines.

Hanging from the ceiling are pendants fashioned from thick vines with glowing orbs at the ends, the lights various shades of pink and gold.

Arion precedes us into the great room, his hands clasped behind his back.

I notice there are faded black tattoos along two of his fingers. Shapes and symbols I can't decipher.

He's wearing a dagger at his left hip, and if I didn't know any better, I'd say he's hiding another sheath beneath the sleeve of his royal blue tunic. I can just make out the faint line of the leather through the material.

Attention starts to wander to us. First because of Arion and then because of me.

Their eyes lock on the dull red stain covering my dress from chest to toe.

I swallow, sweat breaking out along my hairline.

When we reach the center of the room, the music fades out. The shuffling of the assembled fae echoes around us until they all bend to their knees.

Are they bowing for me or for Arion?

I suppose it doesn't matter, because *he* isn't bowing.

Bran comes up beside me. His shoulders are loose, his hands hanging by his sides, but I can read the tension in his body. Bran only likes supplication when it's aimed at him. I don't think it's envy or jealousy. It's worry and fear. Power means a target and at any moment, any one of these people could turn on me to test that power.

"We welcome the princess to our great hall," Arion says, his voice booming across the domed space. He steps in front of me and walks the perimeter of the circle of bowed fae around us. "The princess has been apart from her people for too long and we are honored she would join us in our hollowed halls. Let us drink and rejoice tonight, the eve of the new moon."

He turns back to me, a knowing glint in his eyes. "Let us show the princess what it truly means to be fae."

A servant appears with a silver tray and three golden goblets set on top. Arion takes two and offers them to me and Bran. Bran takes the drink and sniffs it and I wait for his approval.

"We grew up with warnings not to drink or eat anything of the fae," I say.

Arion grabs the third goblet and the servant scurries off. "I assure you, princess, the wine is safe for both fae and vampire."

Bran eyes Arion over the rim of his goblet before taking a long gulp.

My heart thumps a little harder in my chest as I wait for any reaction. But Bran seems fine.

The assembled fae are still on their knees, but they're heads are craned, watching, *waiting*.

I can't very well snub them and the offering of their fae lord.

I take a drink.

The moment the fairy wine hits my tongue, I know I've made my first mistake.

The taste is delectable. Like the plumpest, juiciest, ripest strawberry, mixed with spices, mixed with a sharp tang of something that should be citrusy but is far more complex.

The wine goes straight to my head and then floods my body with warmth and ease.

I'm no longer worried and the fear fades away like the silhouette of someone I should be following but can't.

Arion smiles at me.

In the far, dark, deep trenches of my mind, my conscious brain thinks, oh shit.

But my fairy-bombed brain thinks, yes. Yes. Yes. Yes.

Arion gulps down his entire goblet then lifts the cup. "To the princess!"

The fae rise, and hoist up their own goblets if they have them and shout, "To the princess!"

"Now," Arion says, "drink and be merry."

The music picks up again, this time a punchier tune clearly meant for lively dance.

I take another drink of wine. Then another. And another.

Arion waggles his fingers at a passing servant with a glass decanter of the bright red drink and orders the man to refill our glasses.

This is bad, my conscious brain says.

This is good, my primal brain says.

Bran upends his second goblet.

"Another!" Arion shouts, gesturing to the servant. Bran's glass is refilled again.

"You said this was safe," Bran says, his mouth curved in a devilish smile, his eyes bleeding to that bright gold. "Why am I drunk? Are you trying to get me drunk?"

"It is safe," Arion answers. "You are standing on two feet, are you not?"

"Fae tricks," Bran says, but he's laughing now and I'm laughing right next to him.

"Enjoy yourselves tonight." Arion tips his drink at my dress. "It's a nice touch."

"Wait." I grab him by the arm and pull him to a stop. He looks down where our bodies meet. "We should talk. Right? Isn't that why you asked us here?"

Arion smiles at me. I'm taken aback by how dazzling he is when the lighting is better and there's a little fizz and pop in my veins.

Are all the court fae this gorgeous? And how come I didn't get this gene?

"Slow down, princess," he says. "There will be plenty of time for talking. Enjoy the party for now. Get to know your people. We'll meet up later."

"Okay, but—" I say, but the crowd quickly swallows him up.

I turn back to Bran. He's on his fourth (fifth?) glass of wine. His fangs are protruding from his mouth, which tells me he's in a very, very good place.

The dancers twirl in and around us and the great hall glitters with light and merriment.

"Dance with me," Bran says.

"What, now?"

He gives his glass to a servant scuttling past, then takes mine too.

"I don't want to dance. This dress is too long."

"I'll catch you if you trip." His pupils are blown wide, his smile wider. It's hard to tell him no when he's like this. Bran very rarely gives in to indulgence. Unless it's my body.

I place my hand in his outstretched one and as soon as he has hold of me, we're spinning through the crowd. It's like I'm a child again on a carnival ride, the world blurring beyond my nose.

Bran wraps his arm around my waist, keeping me upright and close to his body as he guides us through the music and the crowd.

I can't stop the laughter from spilling from my mouth and Bran's eyes glow brighter as my pleasure grows.

"You're really good at this!" I shout as we spin nearer the band.

"I've had hundreds of years of practice," he answers and twirls us back to the center of the room.

Never once does my dress get tangled. I don't know how Bran manages it.

And when the tune ends and the crowd stops to applaud, my head keeps spinning, that fizzy warmth spreading through my limbs, then up, up to my belly and chest.

Beside me, a short woman with pink hair lowers her voice to her friend and says, "I just heard the decorating party started."

The friend, a woman with dark skin and emerald green hair, waggles her eyebrows. "Ohhh, let's go watch."

"What's the decorating party?" I ask Bran. He snatches another glass from a passing tray and drinks half of it before handing it off to me.

"Sounds like an orgy," he answers.

"What?!" I giggle around the goblet. Several beads of wine dribble down my mouth and Bran reaches over with his thumb, swiping them away before sucking them off.

I am bright with need for something...anything that feels pleasing. More wine. Food. Sex.

"It can't be an orgy," I say, hoping I'm wrong. What a way to begin this night.

I track the women as they navigate through the crowd and then down the next hallway.

Bran gets in close to me. "If 'decorating party' isn't an orgy, I'll eat my hand."

"Okay. If the decorating thing is not an orgy, you'll eat your hand."

"Okay." He smiles at me with a closed-mouth smile, all eyes and bravado. "And if it is an orgy, we fuck in it."

I giggle and then clamp my hand over my mouth to stop the high-pitched glee from filling the air around us.

Bran has pushed me outside of my safe bubble, but to partake in a fae orgy? No way. But he seems so sure and quite honestly, I'm not.

I don't know why a fae party would include decorating. That seems odd. But a fae orgy? Far more likely.

I grab Bran's hand and pull him through the crowd in the direction the women disappeared.

The music fades and when we reach the hallway, different music fills the empty spaces. This is softer though, more sensual, more languid.

Oh shit.

There's a smaller arched door at the end of the hall. It's cracked just enough to see flickering blue and pink and golden light inside. I can smell the debauchery, even from a distance. Sweat and musk and the earthy scent of oil.

When we reach the door, I stop. This entire night is starting to feel like one giant carnival ride.

Bran puts his hand on the back of my neck and leans in, his mouth at my ear, his breath tickling down my exposed neck. "Go on, little mouse. What's inside?"

I can hear the moaning, the pumping, the reedy whines.

I give the door a push and reveal dozens of naked fae fucking and sucking and locked in ecstasy inside.

Sixteen

I get why it's called a decorating party now.

Half of the people in the room are covered in cum.

It drips down naked chests and glistens on swollen lips. It's on faces and running down bare thighs.

I shiver, despite the heat. I feel like I've stumbled into a naughty secret.

Bran winds his arm around my shoulders, pulling me in to him. He empties whatever glass he's on. His arm is heavy on me, as if he's having trouble keeping himself upright.

"This place is magnificent," he answers. "Also, I told you so."

"You're drunk," I say, swaying.

"So are you," he counters and laughs through his nose.

"I feel like I shouldn't be watching this, I can't seem to take my eyes off of it."

There's so much to see, so much movement, too many limbs, bare cocks and bouncing tits. It reminds me of a computer screensaver, all of those curves moving in and around each other.

"The whole point of an orgy is to watch, Mouse." Bran's arm comes around me, his hand wrapping around my throat, his fingers on my jaw guiding me to watch.

It's art come to life. Depraved, debauched art.

I'm enthralled by a couple closest to us. The man is sitting on a circular velvet couch. There's a woman straddling him, fucking him. His hands are on her ass, bouncing her on him. Swirls of metallic paint cover the woman's back while black ink covers the man's hands. Again with the symbols I can't decipher, though his are softer, rounder symbols than Arion's.

Speaking of the fae lord...

I scan the room, hoping not to spot him. For some reason, the energy I get off Arion is an energy that reminds me of the whole concept of elders. Like one misstep and they'll be giving you a disconcerting look.

I don't want him to know that I'm drunk and enjoying this orgy. I don't want him to think I'm a spicy little faeling. Even though I am, let's be honest.

Bran's hand sinks to my midsection. Butterflies fill my belly and then dip down between my legs as he presses me against his chest. I can feel him growing hard at my ass. And how could he not? We're watching live porn and we're drunk.

Another server appears at my side. "More wine for m'lady?"

Of course. Don't mind if I do.

I down the glass. Bran downs his.

We're staring at one another, laughter bubbling up our throats.

Everything beyond this room fades away. My heart warms beneath the wine as Bran's pupils blow out, a thin sliver of his irises glowing gold.

He takes my hand and yanks me to the back of the room where a half-moon couch is tucked beneath hanging lights and tangled vines. The air back here smells sweet of honeysuckle and my head goes swimmy with excitement.

Are we doing this?

Bran tears the dress from my body, leaving me in nothing but a black lace corset and matching panties. "The dress didn't make the impact we wanted anyway," he says, tossing the scraps to the floor. He spins me around and sits me on his lap so I'm facing the room. A flush of heat rises to my cheeks as he hooks my legs over his knees and spreads me open.

Excitement spins in my belly and my clit pulses with anticipation.

His hands come to my thighs and trail up, and the air catches in my throat making me squeak. I'm kinda nervous, a little shaky.

In front of us, a woman sits on a plush settee with cushions that look as though they're stuffed with feathers. A man goes to his knees in front of her and she upends her glass of wine, giggling to herself. There are thick horns protruding from her bright red hair and sharp fangs that peek through her parted lips.

The man slips his hand inside her skirt and watching them burns a fire in my veins.

This must be part of the allure of an orgy—getting to watch someone else indulge in pleasure while you do too. It's a double dose of sensory fire.

I can't say I've ever watched porn and had sex at the same time, but I imagine even that pales in comparison to this.

As the man teases at the woman's pussy, Bran slips inside my panties and finds me already wet.

"You like watching others, little mouse," he says at my ear, his voice practically a purr.

"I guess I do."

Bran's touch is light at first, priming me, making me wiggle.

Across from us, the man leans forward and nips at the wet panties of the woman on the settee and her body jolts.

Bran sinks his middle finger inside of me and my hips shift, wanting more of him, to be filled up despite the whisper of doubt in the far trenches of my mind.

I'm drunk on fairy wine and swept up in a fairy orgy.

Surely there's something wrong with this scenario?

But I can't seem to care. I can't seem to tell Bran to stop.

The man on his knees hooks his fingers around the woman's panties and stretches them to the side, baring her. Then his mouth is on her, eating her out like she's a delicacy.

The woman hangs her head back, her mouth popped open in ecstasy.

An answering thrill pulses in my pussy and Bran presses his thumb against my clit.

"Oh fuck, yeah, yes," I tell him, but my words pull him to a stop. He slips out of me and flattens his hand against me, holding still.

"Bran," I whine and tremble in his grip. He's hard beneath me, digging into my back. How is he showing restraint when sex is everywhere and I'm ready and willing?

I grab his wrist, push his arm back, and spin around so I can straddle him face-to-face.

His eyes are hooded, irises glowing. "Naughty little mouse."

I kiss him. His tongue darts out to meet mine and the kiss deepens. His hands go to my ass, grabbing me possessively as our lips crash together.

I can't get enough of him. He's just as addictive as the fairy wine.

His cock presses against the dark material of his pants, so I reach between us, and fumble with the button before tearing it off and yanking the zipper down. He's in my hand in just a few seconds and his groan of pleasure fills my mouth.

"Fuck, Mouse," he says. "I need the heat of that pussy wrapped around my cock."

"Then hurry up," I tell him between kisses.

He tears off my panties, not bothering with the delicacies of the man behind us.

Bran lifts me up so he can get beneath me and then seats himself inside my pussy with a hot, wet rush.

I yelp in surprise. He lifts me again and slams me down on him.

The sound of our fucking joins the chorus of fucking in the room.

"Keep bouncing on my cock, Mouse." I find my momentum and fuck him fast. "Just like that. Don't stop."

I find the right spot so that my clit rocks against him every time I go down. The tide wells up, higher and higher.

Bran's fangs protrude from his swollen mouth and he bites me on the breast. I feel nothing but the heat of his mouth. He drags his tongue over the well of blood before covering the wound entirely, drinking me back.

"Oh fuck," I say and keep the rhythm going, fast, fast, don't stop.

Blood runs from his mouth, drips between us, down my pussy, making us wetter.

We're a mess, but we don't care.

There is only the carnal pleasure of sex and blood and the pressing energy of ecstasy behind us.

Bran growls, pulling in a long draw of crimson as he buries himself deeply. "I'm filling up that fucking pussy," he tells me. "Come on my cock, Mouse."

I close my eyes, feeling the thickness of his cock grow the closer he gets to coming.

His hands go to my hips, taking control of me with a hungry possessiveness that makes me fucking lose my mind.

The pressure explodes, burning through me, and Bran slams me down hard on him, filling me up.

I push all my weight forward, rocking my clit against him as the orgasm takes over my entire body, bones and all.

I'm shaking, trembling, breathless. Sweat beads at the back of my neck.

I ride the wave, Bran's grip on me tight and sure, his tongue lapping up the last of my blood.

Gravity pulls me down as the pleasure blinks through my nerves. Bran takes on my weight as I sink forward against him and my hair tangles around his face.

"That was fucking amazing," he says around heavy breathes. "You did good, Mouse." He chuckles to himself, his breath smelling of wine and blood.

With what little energy I have left, I slip off of him, sticky and sweaty, and collapse onto the couch on my back. He finds a blanket at the end of the couch, the yarn coarse like wool. He drapes it over me and then sinks to the couch behind me, pulling me into him.

"We should get up," I tell him, snuggling into the warm glow.

"Let us bask in this a moment longer."

My eyes sink closed.

Bran's breathing evens out beside me.

Everything is beautiful, especially this man and the way he makes me feel.

Before I know it, I'm out.

Seventeen

I wake to the warmth of sunlight on my skin and the prickle of dry grass beneath me.

It takes my brain several seconds to catch up and realize that this is wrong.

When did I fall asleep? And better yet, where?

Then I remember the fairy grotto, the sharp, bright taste of fairy wine, the orgy...

Bran.

I lurch upright, head foggy, my vision swimming.

Through squinted eyes, I make out a meadow in front of me and rolling hills that eventually meet a line of hardwood trees where a clear path disappears into the forest.

I've been here before, but only once.

Every human kid in Midnight Harbor grows up hearing the warnings about the fairy glen and the sealed gateway to the fae realm.

You never know when it may open again and the faeries will steal you away.

You get too close, the door may crack open and a monster may come through.

I came to the fairy glen with Sam when we were twelve years old.

Like most kids, we were equal parts terrified and curious about it. There were no photographs of it, no paintings or sketches. It was as if Midnight Harbor wanted to forget it existed, like a skeleton tucked behind shoe boxes in the far corner of a closet. The fae were stuck in Midnight Harbor as reluctant refugees, and there was nothing any of us could do about it, so there was no sense talking about it either.

When Sam and I snuck into the glen, it was late and the moon was new and it was so terrifying, we barely lasted a full minute before we ran back down the dirt path.

Still, I'd remember this glen. It's not just the circular meadow or the blooming flowers that somehow seem more vibrant than anywhere else. It's the energy too. Like the pulsing, electric feel of a storm just minutes before it lands.

It's an energy that whispers down your spine.

I feel that energy now.

I look over my shoulder at the gate and am not surprised to see Arion there, draped over a large boulder at the foot of the archway. His back is leaning against the gate's thick wall, one knee up. His eyes are closed, head lolled back, basking in the sunlight.

"Why are we here?" I ask him.

Is this a dream?

The light is hazy and golden enough to almost be fake. I fell asleep practically naked and now I'm wearing a thin, gauzy tunic with golden embroidery along the sleeves and hem.

It does not escape me that the color of the material is the same shade of thick ice in the middle of winter.

Without opening his eyes, Arion says, "It was a mistake, wearing that dress."

I climb to my feet. A singing robin flutters past and lands in a nearby tree.

The gate is a freestanding stone feature with an archway made of thin, rectangular stones, and the base of thick boulders. There's a door embedded in the archway, the rivets, straps, and handles made of bronze that's long since turned green from weather and age.

Moss and vines climb up the archway with bright yellow and pink flowers blooming between the crevices.

I lean against one of the boulders on the opposite side of the gate, facing Arion.

I'm not sure if I'm in danger yet, but there's now full sun in the sky, which means no vampire is going to swoop in and save me.

I have to solve this one on my own.

It's not time to panic *yet*.

"You know the story of the dress?" I ask, even though I think that's been made clear.

He opens one eye and glances over at me. "I was there when it happened."

"It" being the violent stabbing of my relative.

"Tell me."

"I was the one with the blade."

With both of his eyes open now, I'm rendered still by the intensity in his gaze.

Is this some kind of revenge? I threw his past in his face and now he's kidnapped me from a fairy orgy?

I guess it could be worse.

I adjust on the boulder, positioning myself better so that I can run if I need to. "Who wore the dress?"

He stands and goes to a thick raspberry bush growing just down the wall of the gate. He plucks a ripe berry from the stem and pops it in his mouth. "Your mother."

I take a deep breath.

Arion can't lie. He's not like me. And there's no way to misinterpret that. Two words that can only mean one thing.

"You killed my mother?"

He plucks several more berries and piles them up in the cup of his hand. He's changed clothing since last night and is now wearing leather armor on his shoulders and across his chest. A sword at his hip. The outfit of a warrior.

There's a dull ache in my left arm that begins to throb, so I hold it against my torso.

"Why would you do that?" I ask him. "Because she was from the Winter Court?"

A berry disappears in his mouth, then another. He shakes his head. "She was Summer Court."

"What?" I slip off the boulder. "But...I'm from the Winter Court. That's what everyone said."

"Your father was from the Winter Court. Your mother betrayed her people and joined your father in the revolt."

I might still be hungover because it takes me several long seconds to digest his words and for them to make sense.

I'm not entirely Winter Court? I'm half Summer? I know any fae can leave their court of birth and join another, so there's no such thing as purity in most of their blood lines. Except, *usually*, in the royal lines. I always assumed both my mother and father were from the Winter Court.

I look at Arion with new understanding. "If my mother was from the Summer Court, you must have known her?"

He tosses a berry into the air and catches it in his mouth. His teeth are stained bright red and a shiver rolls over my shoulders.

"She was my mother as well."

The numbness that settles over me rolls in slowly, then all at once, until it seems like I've left my body entirely because I can't feel a thing.

She was his mother?

Which would mean...

"You're my family. You're my...brother?"

He nods.

Heat flames across my face when I realize... "Oh god," I squeak out. "The orgy. I was...*you*..." I look down at the new clothing that someone must have put me in.

"Have some decency," he scolds. "I had another fae fetch you."

I collapse back against the gate wall. "Thank fucking god."

He clucks his tongue. "You always speak with such foul syllables?"

"Yes, when my modesty is on the line!"

"Modesty." He bites into another berry. "As if you know what that is."

"Hey, listen here—"

"Shut up," he says.

The shock of his words makes the argument dry up. I clamp my mouth closed.

It might be time to panic.

"I don't want to be part of this fight," I tell him.

"Then you shouldn't have worn the dress. You made a move on the chessboard, and you didn't even know the pieces."

Goddammit, Bran.

I should have listened to my own gut. What was it trying to tell me? Not to ruffle feathers. I'm pretty sure that's what it was saying, right? But I'm so damn obsessed with pleasing Bran that sometimes I don't listen to my own instincts.

"A year ago, I had no idea I was even fae..." I tell Arion, trying to think on my feet. "I don't want to make trouble. But I don't want you all to think me weak either. I spent the first several decades of my life thinking I was mortal, destined to be a blood bag..."

He takes a step toward me.

A breeze shifts across the glen and some of his midnight black hair flutters across his face.

"Arion, please...I'm not my mother. *Our* mother. Or my father, for that matter. I'm not even very fae. I'm like dollar-store fae." I laugh nervously at my own stupid joke. "Maybe if we talk about this, we can figure out how to open the gate for you so you can go home and—"

The ground rumbles and I spread out my arms instinctively to catch my balance.

A loud clank sounds behind the gate.

My ears start ringing.

Oh shit.

"What's happening?" I ask.

Arion goes still, his eyes trained on me, but his face blank.

The ground shakes again and dirt rains down from the archway, taking pieces of vine and flower petals with it.

A flock of birds lift from the nearby oak tree and fly away squawking.

"Arion?"

I look down at my arm again, at the blooming bruise in the crook of my elbow. The perfect spot to draw blood.

"Oh gods," I breathe out. "Tell me you didn't."

"I can't," he answers.

A loud boom thunders across the glen, raising the hair along the nape of my neck.

More dirt falls from the stones.

Arion and I both turn to look at the fae gate...

...Just as it cracks open.

BOOK FIVE

One

The fae gate cracks open and light spills out.

Arion, Lord of the Summer Court, has betrayed me, and worse, he's my brother?

I stumble back, but Arion is behind me, cutting off my escape.

I pivot at the last second, stumble over a rock, and pitch forward... and someone catches me.

I look up into the face of the most dazzlingly handsome man I've ever laid eyes on.

"Hello, princess," he says in a voice that sounds like silk brushing over stone.

"Who—" I start, but the question is cut off by the loud clank of metal.

Something heavy and cold settles around my neck. I reach for it instinctively and try to pull it away, but there is no give. The metal is thick and strong, the fastening solid.

"What is this?" I yank at it again. It feels like a collar, but I can't see it to know for sure. Beneath my fingertips, I can feel sharp etchings in the metal.

"Ah-ah," the man says and bats my hands away. "It's for your protection as much as ours."

I turn around to face Arion. "What is this?"

His eyes sweep over the collar, his dark brow furrowing, before he looks past me to the newcomer. "Was this necessary?"

"Queen's orders," the man answers.

"What queen?" I say, looking between them. "What the hell is going on? Who are you?"

"Allow me to introduce myself." The man spreads out his arms like he's a performer on stage. His hair is the color of saturated daybreak and it's long and straight with several small braids throughout. The tops of his pointed ears stick out through the braids.

There is something vaguely familiar about him. The sharp slant of his nose, the cut of his jaw, and the bright, flecked blue of his eyes. But I can't place it.

"I am Maven," he says. "Prince of the Summer Court, and this one's smarter, better-looking older brother."

I glance back at Arion, looking for confirmation, because if he's Arion's brother, then that means...

"Different mothers," Arion answers. "No blood is shared between you."

When I turn back to Maven, he's grinning again. "Fear not, princess. You can pine for me freely and openly."

"Good god. Is he always this egotistical?"

"Yes. I had forgotten just how much, though." Arion frowns. "Time has weathered my memories, it would seem."

Maven chuckles. "I missed you too, baby brother." He turns back to me. "I'm very pleased to make your acquaintance, princess." He sweeps his arm across his flat stomach and gives me a shallow, courtly bow. "And how pretty you are." When he straightens, he wrinkles his perfect nose and adds, "Though I had hoped you'd look less, *well*, mortal."

Embarrassment flames through my face. I don't care what he thinks and yet...

I am fae. That fact is established. But I don't feel fae and having someone else point it out makes me want to crawl beneath a rock.

"Come." Maven turns back to the gate. "The queen is expecting you."

Arion steps beside me. "Will Jessie be assured her safety?"

"As if you care," I tell him. "You did drug me, kidnap me, and steal my blood."

He tilts his chin down so he can appraise me from the sharp tip of his nose. "If I wanted you dead, faeling, you'd be dead."

"True!" Maven stops in the slant of light pouring through the open gate. "He did kill your mother in cold blood after all!"

My stomach twists, being reminded of that fact. But when I glance up at Arion again, there is sorrow on his face that he quickly tries to hide beneath a scowl.

"We have no time to waste!" Maven claps his hands and disappears through the gate, the bright light swallowing him up.

I turn to my brother. "Did you notice he didn't answer your question?"

He furrows his brow. "I did."

"If I turn around and run...if I run back to Midnight and to Bran... what will happen?"

Arion considers it, his gaze trained on the doorway. "They will come for you," he finally says. "And they will turn everything you love into ash." His voice catches on the word *love* and then he blinks, as if catching the emotion. His teeth grind together so loudly, it makes my own molars ache.

There is something he's not telling me.

I know there are always two sides to a story. I could easily blame my current predicament on my mom for hiding who I was, not only from others in Midnight, but from me too. But I know she had a good reason for doing what she did.

So how did Arion find himself here? His mother's—*our mother's*—blood on his hands? How did he become trapped on our side? Did he know I was under his nose the entire time? Or did Mom's actions hide me so well, not even my own flesh and blood knew who I was?

My head is still reeling from all of this, and I might still be a little drunk. So many questions. So many revelations to digest and sort out into their neat little boxes so I can make sense of them. I'm desperate to reorder my world, but there's no time for that.

"What is this thing he put around my neck?" I finger the metal. It's still cool to the touch.

Arion barely looks at it, as if the sight of it pains him. "It's called a Prisoner's Quell."

"That already doesn't sound good."

"That's because it's not."

"What does it do?"

"First, it subdues the magic of the wearer. They're likely trying to steal your voice from you."

"And second?"

"*Second*," he repeats and sighs. "If you go outside of the bounds they've deemed acceptable, it will kill you."

I take a deep breath, then another, but it doesn't help. My lungs don't want to expand fully. They're squeezed tight by panic.

Bran isn't going to be able to save me from this one. It's still early morning and he may not even be awake yet. I don't know how fairy wine affects vampires. I don't even think that was normal fairy wine.

But more than that...I don't want him endangering himself. Not until I know what we're dealing with. This is my problem. *Not his.* If something were to happen to him because of me and my fae family drama, I would never forgive myself.

"Bran will come eventually," I say, more a statement than a threat.

"I know he will." Arion glances at the gate again. The door is still cracked open, hazy light shining through. Maven is nowhere in sight. I could almost pretend he was a fever dream. A mirage. "If your vampire boyfriend is wise, he will stay away."

"He is wise," I answer. "But not always rational."

Arion laughs, but it almost sounds sad. "Love and rationality are two different sides of the same coin. One will always be face down."

I glance up at him again and find the line of his dark brow furrowed, his gaze distant. "What aren't you telling me?"

He scowls at me. "I've told you before, faeling, you are asking for secrets you have not earned."

"So tell me how to earn them."

He pulls back. "Excuse me?"

"Tell me how to earn your secrets."

I may not have known Arion long, and he may have betrayed me in order to get this gate opened, but I feel like we can come to trust one another.

He is my blood, after all.

I just hope it's not my mind playing tricks on me, my intuition clouded by the desire to know my fae sibling.

But I have to hold on to something, even if it's the scant hope that he and I could be on the same side.

"You earn my secrets by earning my trust," he answers. There is no hint of gruffness to his voice. No abrasiveness in his answer.

"Where do I start?"

He turns to me, arms clasped behind his back. "Just like that?"

"Yes, just like that."

His frown deepens. "Fine. Walk through that doorway and go to the queen and help me fix this mess that our mother began."

Schooling my features, I try really fucking hard to hide the fact that he's just given me his first secret. I thought he just wanted to use me to open the gate to go home, but now I realize it's much more than that.

He was betrayed by our mother. Or at least that's what he believes. And he wants to make amends for what she did.

I can see the guilt in the fine lines around his eyes, the shame buried in the sharp, rigid way he carries himself.

He does not want her legacy and now he wants me to help prove it.

By using me to open the gate, he's taken the first step in his own redemption tour.

"Okay," I tell him. "Let's go see this Queen of the Summer Court." I follow the overgrown path to the open doorway. "Is there anything else I should know?"

Just as I'm about to step through to the light, Arion adds, "Yes. If the same woman is still sitting on the Summer Throne, it's probably best you should know…"

I glance at him over my shoulder, ready to walk through.

"…she was our mother's greatest rival. And it was she who commanded my hand in killing our mother."

Two

BRAN

Everything aches. Every joint and bone and muscle.

That's my first clue that something is profoundly wrong.

The second is that it feels like my skin is melting from my bones.

Opening my eyes, I'm greeted by the blazing light of the sun. There is no time to comprehend why. There is only time to act.

I'm beneath the dark canopy of a mature hardwood tree in no time at all.

The burning subsides and my skin regenerates. As the smoke clears, I take in my surroundings.

I'm still in Bramwell Park, but the fairy grotto is gone and so is Mouse.

The rising tide of panic starts in my gut and crawls its way up my sternum, squeezing my heart until it hurts.

Where is she?

I scent the air, scanning the horizon. The light burns my eyes, and tears well beneath my lids, but I look harder, look farther, trying to spot her. Anything. Any clue at all.

But she isn't there.

She is gone and it's my fucking fault.

"A little toasty, is it?" a voice calls from slightly behind, to my left.

I glance over my shoulder to find a fae standing in dappled sunlight beneath a much younger red maple. He is pale and ethereal. There is a pack at his feet.

He's not one I'm familiar with.

Over the years, since the gate closed, the fae have dwindled in number and power here in Midnight. There are greater populations in Europe and a lot of them left here for there. I've heard stories of other gates, ones that open and close on a whim so that you must be vigilant and nearby in order to catch them.

I've never laid eyes on one. Some say they are myths.

Only the gate in Midnight was a permanently open and accessible doorway. It's why Damien wanted to establish Midnight just outside the gate. "Greater access to power," he'd told me.

"For whom? Us or them?" I'd countered.

"Controlling the land directly beside their gate puts us at greater advantage."

I could see his strategy. I could even agree with it. But it didn't mean I liked it.

I've always been wary of the fae.

Until Mouse.

"This your doing?" I ask the fae. He's leaning against the trunk of the tree, one leg crossed over the other at the ankle. He's chewing on what looks like a piece of licorice.

"Depends on what you mean by 'this.'"

Typical fae, dancing around a straight answer.

"I'm a vampire."

"Yes," he says.

"And I'm in the sunlight."

"Yes, indeed."

"Which is bad. Did you put me in the sunlight?"

"Yes," he finally answers. "But ask me why."

"Why?"

"Arion ordered me to."

This isn't unexpected. He wanted Mouse to help open the gate. And I delivered her directly into his trap like a stupid little shit. I should have taken the reins. I should have stood in front of Mouse instead of letting her lead.

The panic is still beating at the back of my head, but I can't let it take control. Panic is only good for one thing—*flight*. And I will not run.

I will, however, maim.

But not until I have answers.

"You follow all of Arion's orders?" I take a step to the left, so I can face the fae.

"Only the orders I cannot deny."

I'm starting to catch on to what he's not saying—he was ordered to dump me, but he's not necessarily loyal to Arion.

Could be another trap. But at least I'm not drunk this time, though that throbbing in the back of my head might also be from a hangover.

"Where is she?" I ask.

"Do you feel it?" he answers instead, his gaze going to the sky. But I don't think he means the fucking clouds.

I turn my senses inward and find a vibrating energy at the back of my neck.

A feeling I haven't had in a very long time, one I never put thought to until it was absent.

Fae magic.

The gate is already open.

"Where is she?" I repeat and test the boundary of the sun only to get a searing shot of pain up my arm. It's bright today. Blinding. And the hangover might be making me more vulnerable.

I'm trapped in the fucking sunlight with no way to get to Mouse.

Do not come undone. I can practically hear Damien's voice in my ears. *There is time to fall apart later. Now, you must act.*

"Arion wanted the gate opened and your girl was his key," the fae answers. He grabs the pack and steps out of the canopy of leaves and into a pool of light. His blond hair glitters. He's even more pale in direct UV, like pure ice held to the sun. Is he Winter Court? Not high ranking.

If he was, he'd already be dead. But perhaps just close enough that he may still hold some allegiance to the idea of the court.

"If your only job was to drop me here," I say, "then why stay?"

"We might be able to help one another." He tosses me the pack. It drops at my feet. It's light and lumpy like it's full of something soft.

I don't smell gunpowder or metal, so likely not a bomb or some other explosive that would send wooden shrapnel through my body. And the fae may be lacking in power these days, but they aren't dumb. If they wanted me dead, they could have staked me already instead of making a spectacle in the park in the middle of the day.

Crouching beside the bag, careful of the sunlight just beyond, I pull the zipper back and find a thick black tarp folded inside. I quickly yank it out, unfurl it, pulling it over my head to block out some of the UV light stealing through the tree branches.

Some of the stinging eases.

The fae holds up my cell phone. "Catch," he says and tosses it to me.

I snatch it from the air and when I activate the screen, I find everything as it should be.

"I'd call someone to come get you. The noon sun fast approaches." He goes back to his tree and waits.

My options are limited on who to call for help. Can't call Jimmy. I'm tired of calling the Alpha. I decide on the witch. Bianca picks up on the third ring.

"Where are you?" she asks.

Excellent question.

"Long story. The fae have Jessie and they dumped me in Bramwell Park."

There's a beat of silence.

"Witch," I say. "Did you hear me? I need a ride. *Now.*"

"Bran?"

Hearing the deeper voice come through the line nearly makes my knees buckle.

"Damien?" I clutch to the phone harder and pace a circle around the tree trunk. "Is that really you?"

"It's me," he answers.

"Are you...okay?" I wince at the catch in my voice. I am a boy again, desperate for his older brother.

"I woke up an hour ago," Damien answers.

"The gate," I say.

"Yes. The witch says when the gate opened, the Renshaw spell broke." There's a rustle of something on the other end, and then Damien adds, "Stay where you are. We're coming to get you."

When I hang up the phone, I slump against the hardwood. The tarp crinkles loudly.

The fae clears his throat. "You're welcome."

I do not say thank you.

"My number is programmed in your phone under *Baspin*. When the sun gets low enough for your safety, call me and we can talk." He turns and starts off.

"Why can't we talk now? Jessie has already been missing at least an hour and—"

"They won't kill her. *Yet*." He starts for the park entrance. "Arion knew as well as any of us that wiping out the Winter Court was not in their best interest. They were reckless, and I suspect they've been reaping what they sowed."

"So what will *they* do with her?" I'm not sure who he's referring to – Autumn Court? All of the Seelie? The war started with Autumn, but the way Baspin is talking, it feels like more. Like a collective.

Shit.

The fae keeps walking, but says over his shoulder, "Force her obedience."

And then he's gone.

Three

As a child, I often daydreamed about what the fae realm would look like. There was art that survived on our side, of course. Sketches and paintings done by some of the mortals that had visited the fae realm and documented what they saw.

There's a famous painting called "Dream in a Fae Meadow" that hangs in the lobby of Midnight Harbor's Public Library. It was done by Monroe Holstead in the early 1900s and depicts a meadow with a vibrant array of wildflowers in every shade of the rainbow with a fae woman in the center twirling in the sunlight, her white dress billowing around her.

The art practically glitters with light and magic even though it's only paint and canvas.

When I push through the doorway into the fae realm, I have that painting stuck in my head. It's the consolation prize, I tell myself. If I'm marching to my death, at least I'll get to see the beauty of the fae realm before my last breath.

But it's nothing like the painting or the fantasy.

The light is too bright, almost blinding. I throw my arm up to shield my eyes thinking maybe it's just my deficient eyesight that's been tainted by the mortal side and the mortal sun. Then I notice Arion do the same beside me.

He groans loudly. "What is that godawful smell?"

The air is musty, like an old wet basement.

I blink into the light, desperate for a pair of sunglasses. Shapes and colors start to come into focus, and I see an overgrown forest just behind Maven. Moss hangs from the velvety green branches. Ferns are tangled around one another on the forest floor, almost like they're matted. There's a worn dirt path down the center, but it's fighting for relevance against the encroaching woods.

The air is too hot, too wet, and it clings to my skin and makes my shirt stick to my spine.

"What the fuck?" Arion looks around. "What happened here?"

Maven laughs it off. "Just a bit of overgrowth, is all."

But the look on Arion's face tells me this isn't normal, that it's not the home he remembers.

I take in a breath, and the wetness of the air weighs down my lungs. It's like breathing in soup.

I immediately hate it.

This is nothing like the dazzling Holstead painting.

It's not bright and gorgeous and glittering.

It's heavy and oppressive.

I can literally feel the energy of the place buzzing up my legs, like something is off, like the energy is looking for anything else to cling to because there's too much of it, too much *wrong* energy.

"Come," Maven says and starts down the overgrown path. "The queen is expecting us to be prompt."

I glance at Arion. "You look worried." I keep my voice low.

He starts to say something and then clamps his mouth shut, jaw flexing. "I remember it differently."

"Better?"

"Hurry along, faeling," he answers, dodging my question. "My brother is right; we can't keep the queen waiting."

With a huff, I follow him down the path, unsure of what I'll find at the end.

The thick, green woods carry on for far too long. Sweat soaks my back. My hair is plastered to my forehead.

Somehow Maven and Arion don't look the least bit affected by the heavy air. They clearly have something I don't. Do fae not sweat? And if not, how come I'm like a drenched rat right now? Or rather, *mouse*.

I blame it on the binding. I'm still not fully tapped into my fae power.

The woods finally break for rolling hills where a serpentine river cuts into the land. The moving water helps dispel some of the heat, but just barely. I get close to the edge and look down to find muddy, dark water.

The buzzing in my legs is more noticeable.

The river cuts away from the path, and we trudge up the hills.

"Almost there, princess!" Maven yells over his shoulder, the bright sun glaring off the metal detailing on his tunic.

"Just over the next hill," Arion adds, probably sensing my struggle.

I'm not out of shape, but I'm not athletic either. It's been a while since I've gone on a hike. And never in hot, sticky summer air.

Arion and Maven stop together where the hill, from my vantage point, meets the blue sky.

"Just look at it," Maven says, his hands on his hips.

Arion catches his breath, frowning into the distance.

One foot in front of the other.

Come on, Jessie, you can do it.

The sooner I get this over with, the sooner I can get back to Midnight and Bran.

Well, *maybe*.

No, no maybes!

I *will* make it back home.

I *will* get through this.

I had nothing to do with this rebellion. They must know that.

I reach the top of the hill and come up alongside Arion. Hands on my knees, I bend over, taking in several deep breaths.

"Did the mortals break our princess?" Maven asks with a chuckle.

"She's been living as a mortal for twenty years. Give her a moment." Arion crouches in front of me. "Are you all right, faeling?"

My lungs are tight, my body drenched. The buzzing in my legs isn't helping the weakness in my muscles. And my head is spinning.

"I don't feel so good," I huff out.

"You need water. We're almost there. Stand up and take in several deep breaths." He hooks his hand around my inner elbow and coaxes me up. I suck in another breath, thinking it's more woods or hills in front of us, dreading it already. But then, in the distance, sitting in a smoggy valley is a giant castle with a dozen spires stretching toward the sky.

"Holy shit," I say.

Maven smiles at me. "The Summer Court. Isn't it lovely?"

"It's...something."

The air from here reminds me of the smog I've seen in pictures of polluted cities. It's thick and almost yellow.

Something is definitely, definitely wrong with the fae realm.

"It's all downhill from here." Maven follows the path, heading for the palace.

Arion waits beside me, his jaw set in a grim line.

There's no going back at this point. He knows it and I know it.

"If she commanded it," I ask him, "would you kill me too?"

He cuts his gaze to me, eyes narrowed. "Why would you ask me that?"

"Would you?"

"I don't know yet."

"Well, it could be worse. You could have said yes."

He grumbles.

I start ahead of him on the path.

I should be afraid. I *am* a little worried.

But something in my gut tells me there's more going on here than just my parents' rebellion.

Like Arion said, if they wanted me dead, I'd already be dead.

———

The hike down the hill isn't as bad as it was up the hill and I'm able to catch my breath. Some of the path is steep and rocky though and I have to watch my footing. Whoever dressed me after I passed out in the fairy grotto didn't think to equip me with hiking boots.

When the earth levels out, the castle looms larger, and cottages start to dot the countryside. As we pass, some of the fae come out of their houses to watch. A man with big purple eyes glares at me from his front stoop. At the next house, two children with tined horns like that of a deer point and whisper.

Do they know who I am?

The closer we get to the castle, the more fae we pass as if word is spreading before us.

They bow for Maven. They gawk at me.

The worn dirt path soon meets a cobblestone road. Mature hardwood trees line the road, equal distance between them creating symmetry I absolutely love.

Maybe this place won't be so bad after all.

Arion is beside me suddenly causing me to jump. His scowl has deepened, and his eyes are darting this way and that.

"What is it?" I ask.

The crowd has thinned out.

"Something is wrong," he answers.

"Like what?" I keep walking and it takes me several steps to realize he's stopped. "What are you—"

"Down, faeling!" He barrels toward me just as an arrow is shot from the nearest tree...directly at my neck.

Four

I pace beneath the hardwood tree, the black tarp clutched tightly around my body. I'm trying not to let the fury sweep me away.

How fucking long does it take to drive to Bramwell from Duval House?

My phone says it's only been nine minutes.

It feels like a fucking eternity.

Force her obedience, Baspin said.

I'm the only one who gets to force Mouse to do anything.

No one else.

The anger rises again and my teeth grind together, fangs sharpening in my mouth. I need blood. I need sleep. But I want none of it.

Not until I have Mouse back.

I'm going to kill them.

Kill them all.

Maybe not Baspin.

Definitely Arion.

Maybe the fucking brownie, depending on when I see him next and what kind of mood I'm in.

I hear the distant churn of an engine. There are no roads into the park, only pedestrian pathways, but I spot Damien's SUV making quick work of the turf anyway.

I start toward the vehicle, and it pulls up alongside me.

The back driver's side door opens, and I climb inside, tarp and all.

Once the door is shut behind me, the cooler darkness of the tinted windows allows me to breathe more easily.

I fight with the tarp, shoving it into the back with a loud, angry rustling. "Bran."

I glance over to find my brother in the opposite seat.

It really is him. He's really alive and awake and speaking.

"You're okay," I say, even though he already assured me he was.

"Yes," he answers. "Well...*okay enough*."

I settle into the seat as the driver takes off. I know it's King behind the wheel without checking. Beyond working in the house, he also maintains mine and Damien's car collection, and King always smells like oranges, like the gritty hand soap made for mechanics to scrub the grease from their hands.

He says nothing as he tears through the grass of the park and gets us back on the road.

That's my favorite thing about King—he knows when to keep his fucking mouth shut.

"How did this happen?" Damien asks and I have to be mindful not to wince. My brother's tone is not accusatory, but I've known him long enough to know he will judge me for my errors. And why not? I got cocky. Reckless. And while I'm grateful to have my brother back, it was not something I wanted at the expense of Jessie.

"We were tricked," I tell him instead, because it's the truth. "I think they drugged the wine."

"You drank fairy wine?"

Now he sounds like the judgy older brother I know.

"Don't start." I rest my head against the back of the seat. "Let me return Jessie to Duval House and then you can give me a lecture."

He laughs through his nose. "Fair enough. I will spare you for now."

I roll my head along the back of the seat so I can face him. It's dark back here, but it takes nothing for my vampire eyes to examine him.

There are still dark circles beneath his eyes, but I would expect nothing less after lying unconscious from a witch's spell. He's as pale as ever, his eyes a little duller and bloodshot.

I'm reminded again of seeing him lying on his death bed all those years ago, and the hopelessness, the fear, and the desperation I felt.

Sometimes I forget that we are not entirely invincible. That there are still things to lose that would break me.

"I'm glad you're awake," I tell him.

"I am too."

King turns through one of the main intersections in Midnight, taking us home. I don't want to go home, but I have no choice.

"You have a plan?" Damien asks me. "To rescue your little mouse?"

I sigh and rub at my burning eyes with thumb and forefinger. I can barely think straight through the exhaustion and the hangover and the fury. The sunlight is my greatest weakness and there is literally no way to fight it. Not only will it burn me alive, but the light saps all of the energy from my bones. My arms are leaden. My head is foggy.

And yet time is ticking by in my head, reminding me that every second Mouse is in the fae realm, she is more and more at risk.

What did Baspin mean when he said they'd demand her obedience?

If any one of those fae touches my mouse, I will rip their ribs out of their chest cavity, one by fucking one, and pick my teeth with them.

"I can hear your anger," Damien says.

I grumble and only now realize my eyes have slipped closed. I open them again, fighting the heaviness. "I'm going to kill them."

"I know you are, and I will help you."

"You sure you're up for it?"

His eyes glow vampiric blue. "Of course, I am. Just as soon as we sleep."

I don't think I could possibly rest until Mouse is home, but even though I'm a supernatural creature with untenable power, there is one thing I cannot fight: the exhaustion of a vampire.

I wake hours later in the backseat of the SUV, the vehicle parked securely in the Duval House garage.

It's dark.

The seat beside me is empty.

I pop the door open and climb out and smell, over the grease and gasoline of the garage, the faint scent of cigarette smoke and freshly poured bourbon.

I find Damien in the open doorway of the garage, shoulder leaning into the frame. There is a cigarette between his knuckles, a glass clutched in his hand. He looks better than he did this morning. The rest did us both well.

He hands me the cigarette and drains his glass.

I take a hit, smoke burning in my lungs and everything, *almost*, feels all right.

On an exhale, I ask him, "Did Kelly wake with you?"

His gaze is on the forest behind the garage, but his attention is elsewhere. "No. The witch theorizes because Kelly is human, she may need more time to recover."

I can hear the tenor of hope in his voice, underlined by fear that perhaps the witch is wrong.

"She'll come around," I say.

He nods and waggles his fingers for the last of the cigarette, so I pass it off. He finishes it, exhales, then crushes the embers beneath his boot. "Tell me the rest of your story," he says, changing the subject. "How did you come to have a tarp and a phone in the park?"

I tell him about Baspin and his offer to help, and my theory that he's a member of the Winter Court.

"Could be a trap," Damien points out.

"Aren't they all potential traps?"

"Yes. Do you want to call him?"

I look past my brother over the dewy grounds of Duval property. The house is to our left, and I can hear the din of conversation as the vampires wake.

"We could have an army assembled in less than twenty minutes. Do we really need to waste time playing verbal judo with a cast-off fae? He's given us all we need—they'll keep Jessie alive as long as she serves their purpose, and I intend to get her back before then."

Damien considers me. "You don't want to rush into this."

"What I want, dear brother, is to cut out hearts and tear out tongues."

He tosses the empty bourbon glass in the air, catches it, tosses it again. A few dribbles of liquor slide down his arm. He starts pacing as he plays catch with the glass.

"You really want to go in blind?" he asks.

"Is it blind if we have a goal?"

"It is if we have no strategy."

He's right but I don't care. Though to be honest, I'm surprised he's even entertaining the idea. Maybe he hasn't fully returned to himself. Maybe I'm getting us both into deep shit.

But I want my little mouse back. Right fucking now.

Thinking about her not with me makes my stomach knot up and my blood fucking boil.

"I don't want to wait. I'm going with or without you."

He stops pacing to scrutinize me, then tosses the glass up again, but this time abandons it and lets it shatter on the pavement. The sound is loud between us, the forest still beyond us.

"Very well." He turns for the house. "Let us assemble an army and storm the fae and rescue your pretty little princess."

"You don't have to tell me twice."

If I have it my way, I will be bathing in fae blood within the hour.

FIVE

Like a big, dumb mortal, I freeze up and just stare at the sharp, pointy tine of the arrow as it sails right for my jugular.

But then a hand snaps out and catches the weapon mid-air.

THWAP.

I blink and let out a hiccuping gasp.

Arion has caught the arrow literally an inch away from piercing my flesh.

We both stare at it in his hand.

"Seize the would-be assassin!" Maven shouts.

A half dozen fae soldiers rush the tree, and two make quick work of its branches disappearing into the canopy.

There's a rustling, a grunt, then a body drops from the tree and hits the ground with a thud.

The two fae soldiers hop out of the tree, landing with far more grace.

Within seconds, the culprit is surrounded.

"Christ," Arion mutters, which seems like a very mortal thing to say.

Hand on my neck, knees wobblier than I'd like to admit, I ask him, "Who is it?"

"Autumn Court." He snaps the arrow in two in one hand and walks over. "Who sent you?"

"Yes, who sent you?" Maven puts his hands on his hips. "Are you working alone?"

The assassin rolls onto all fours and hoists himself up.

Or rather, *she*.

A long red braid falls from the hood of her leather jacket. She scowls at me, then pretends to spit on my shoes.

"Hey!" I hop back at the same time Arion pushes forward and grabs the girl by the throat.

"You dare enter Summer territory and threaten the life of the Winter princess? Then insult her?"

"She's a traitor of the realm," the girl says. "She's the reason everything smells like shit!"

What the hell?!

"Are you working alone?" Maven repeats as the fae soldiers take hold of the girl, her arms pinned behind her.

"Wouldn't you like to know?" She tests the hold of the soldiers and the metal plates along their shoulders clank as they adjust their weight, pulling her back.

Not a yes. Not a no. Clever.

I want to hate her—she just tried to kill me—but I don't think I can. There's something about the girl that makes me want to know more. She's shorter than I am, barely five feet. I can see the sharp points of her ears in the shadow of her hood. There's a roughness to her that I admire, and I immediately think of Sam never backing down from a fight.

"Take her to the tower," Maven instructs. "Two guards at her cell at all times until I say otherwise."

"Yes, Your Royal Highness," the man at the front says and gives a deep bow before turning with the others, carting the girl off.

"Well, that was exciting!" Maven says, smiling wide.

"That's not the word I'd use," Arion counters, still clutching the broken arrow in hand.

"I see you still have excellent reflexes." Maven pats Arion on the back roughly. "Let's report our heroism to the queen. She'll love it!"

He starts off with a bit of swagger in his step, as if he was the one who stopped the attempt on my life.

"Thank you."

Arion frowns down at me. "Never thank a fae."

"Even when they save your life?"

"Even then."

"What about a brother?"

His frown deepens.

"Especially brothers," he answers and follows Maven.

I watch the assassin disappear around a gate on the other side of the palace. She doesn't fight the soldiers, almost as if she isn't worried about being locked in a tower.

Almost as if she's sure she'll escape.

She'll probably try to kill me again if she gets away. If this stupid collar wasn't attached to my neck...

I yank on it again, but it's useless. I'm just as much a prisoner here as the Autumn Court assassin.

———

Up close, it's much easier to see what must have once been a grand palace.

There are still hints of it hidden somewhere beneath the dense overgrowth.

Tangled vines cover the entire left side of the palace, deep roots caught in the white stone, clawing their way up and around columns, hanging from archways that line a portico. More greenery covers the palace spires that soar up toward the sky.

There's more color here than in the forest where we entered the fae realm. Pink and purple and blue flowers find purchase amongst the vines and moss, but it's easy to see they're suffering. Some of the stems are wilting, the leaves brown-spotted and laced with holes.

We enter into a courtyard where a cobblestone path forks in front of us, circling a reflection pool. Except the water is too mucky and thick with lily pads to see much of anything.

Maven takes the walkway to the left and several fae step aside, letting him pass as they bow and call out a greeting.

"Did you grow up here?" I ask Arion once I've caught up to him.

"I did," he answers.

"Did you like it?"

The path curves back in toward the center of the courtyard where steps lead up to a half-moon terrace that looks over the reflection pond.

"I did."

"Can you say more than, 'I did?'"

"I can."

I catch the barest hint of a smirk on his face.

Is my brother amused by me?

I want us to get along. I want to joke with him and confide in him and...

Don't get ahead of yourself, Jessie.

The sadness I feel now knowing I missed out on having a brother for the first twenty-plus years of my life will pale in comparison to being outright rejected by him in the future.

When we come up on the landing, I spot a large, arched doorway hidden in the shadows of another upper terrace. The doors are thrown open and inside, banners hang from the vaulted ceiling, but the fabric is limp in the still air.

We go in, everyone bowing and gaping and whispering as we pass.

I want to gape and gawk at all the sights—I'm in the fae realm! In the Summer Court!—but I pretend I'm indifferent. I don't want to be the stupid fae girl raised by mortals, shocked by the very sight of a palace.

The hallway leads us deeper inside, but domes of glass above us cast hazy light throughout the space, making it feel warm and cozy and bright.

When the hallway ends, we're deposited into a large circular room with a high ceiling with hand-carved arched beams that remind me of European abbeys. There's a gurgling fountain in the middle of the room and hanging above it, a giant chandelier with crystals that wink in the light.

And directly across from us, past the fountain, is a raised dais where the queen sits on her throne.

There is a crowd here. They've clearly been expecting us. There's no mistaking the buzzing energy here is different than the buzzing I felt in my legs. This is excitement, apprehension, a hunger for drama.

"Bring her here." The queen's voice rings out, echoing around the room.

"Of course, Mother." Maven takes my hand, and I can't help but look back at Arion, begging him to help me.

But he's powerless here. I'm seeing that now. His mother betrayed the courts. His mother was a traitor.

He's no prince.

Maven drags me across the room, skirting around the fountain, then up the three marble steps to the expansive dais.

The air is cooler here, thank god, and the wet basement smell is gone, but I can tell they've had to work hard at that, overwhelming the throne room with florals. It's like a perfume counter in a department store after a someone sampled every scent under the sun.

My nose itches.

The queen rises from her throne. I try not to look directly at her, but it's hard not to gape at a queen. Even one who probably wants you dead.

Her steps are silent as she comes nearer, the long, silky train of her dress dragging behind her.

She's flanked by two other women—one with bright blue eyes and milky skin, the other with dark green hair and darker skin. Both are wearing swords at their hips and armor that reflects the light.

Silence descends over the room, but it's hard to hear it over the loud thumping of my heart in my ears.

What happens now? Am I supposed to bow? Curtsy?

The queen just stands there several feet in front of me and I keep my eyes trained on the marble floor, trying not to overthink this thing.

Just act normal.

Just act normal? How?

"Well?" the queen says. "Did you ask her?"

Maven laughs. "I forgot in all the excitement!"

"Ask me what?"

I look up and catch the queen's eyes. Her irises are a deep shade of amethyst, almost black. I can't read anything there. She gives nothing away other than distant distaste.

My heart thuds harder and my hands tingle with new energy. I can't feel my toes. My stomach churns.

Don't barf on the Queen's dress.

"Apologies, Mother," Maven says and then he gets down on one knee. "Jessie MacMahon, Princess of the Winter Court, will you take my hand in marriage and be my wife?"

Six

BRAN

The first text from Baspin comes within minutes of me entering Duval House. The asshole programmed his number to have a unique chime, and the unfamiliar sound immediately pulls my attention.

His name is in bold over the notification, and then, *Your silence is concerning, vampire.*

I darken the screen and slide the phone in the back pocket of my pants.

Damien starts barking out orders to the room as we enter through the side door, as if he didn't just wake from a magically-induced coma, as if nothing has changed. "I need at least fifty vampires ready for battle," he says. "No one under a hundred. Feed before we leave. You have twenty minutes."

"Where are we going?" That from a vampire draped over one of the wingbacks in the far corner. There's a human in his lap, head resting against his shoulder, a bead of blood running down the slim column of her neck.

"Fae realm," Damien answers.

Damien and I leave them to discuss this revelation. It won't be long before word spreads through the entire house. Can they feel the fae magic like I can? That discordant buzz along the neck?

In our private wing, Damien and I break at the hallway. "I'm changing," I tell him. "Meet me downstairs in ten."

He nods as he turns, headed for his private quarters. "I'm stopping by the armory first."

"Grab me an iron dagger. Or two."

When I push through the closed door of my rooms, I find Jimmy at the dark fireplace, arms crossed over her chest.

"Christ," I mutter and bypass her for my closet.

My phone dings in my pocket. I pull it out and set it on the island in my closet. "Don't start, Jimmy."

Her hair is wound up in a neat bun on top of her head. She's wearing no makeup, but there's fresh color in her cheeks, indicating she must have just recently fed.

I need blood too. I need it soon.

"You can't just go running after her like this." Jimmy pulls herself up on the island. It's topped with a slab of solid marble I had shipped over from an abandoned palace in France. There are thick black veins running through it.

"That's where you're wrong, Jimmy," I say, tearing my shirt away and tossing it into the corner. "I can and I will."

My phone pings again. Then again.

"Who is that?" She reaches over and snatches the phone before I can grab it. "Who is Baspin?"

"No one." I yank off my pants and add them to the pile.

"Bran."

I cross the room and pull a black t-shirt from one of the velvet hangers. The hanger swings on the rod, then clunks against the wall.

"Bran."

"He's the fae who dumped me in the park." I pull the shirt over my head, then rake my hand through my hair, straightening it.

"Why is he texting you?" She reads one of the notifications. "'*You need my help, vampire. Here's a fact: fae can't lie even over text. So if I say you need my help, you know that's the truth.*'"

I can feel Jimmy's eyes on me, even though I've given her my back as I flip through several pairs of jeans.

"If a fae is offering to help you, why are you ignoring him?"

I pull down a pair of dark jeans. "Did you miss the part where I said he dumped me in the park? In the daylight?"

I can practically sense Jimmy frowning at me. "You're leaving out one important detail. He gave you a tarp. And your phone."

I scoff. "Can no one keep a secret in this fucking house?"

Deftly, she hops off the counter and comes to my side, my phone still in her grip. "If the fae are offering to help, you should take the offering."

Pants buttoned, I reach for my phone but she holds it out of reach like we're two little shits playing a game of finders keepers.

"Jimmy."

"Take the home advantage."

"This isn't a game of baseball."

"No, it's a game for Jessie's life."

I grit my teeth. The reminder is like ice in my veins. My stomach sinks.

"I know what the fucking stakes are."

"Do you?"

The phone dings.

I reach for it. Jimmy stretches further away.

"Careful, Jim," I tell her, my voice even, but my eyes bleeding to gold.

Even though I am implying I will hurt her if she gets in my way, she and I both know I won't.

She steps back from me and types in my phone's password. I grumble and yank on boots. "You're fucking intolerable."

"There. Fixed it. He's on his way," she tells me. "And you'll hear him out."

"Or what?"

The smile she gives me could melt iron. "Or I will burn down your French chateau."

I narrow my eyes. "You wouldn't."

"It's for your own good."

She knows how I feel about my real estate. It's not nearly as important as Mouse, but certainly ranking nearly as high.

And the French chateau is my favorite. It's the first estate I purchased after I was turned into a vampire.

It's symbolic.

She hands me the phone and looks up, meeting my glowing gaze. "I'll get you someone to bite. Then you'll meet me on the front steps and you'll utilize all of the tools you have at your disposal, even if it's a fae who dumped you in the park."

I close my eyes and suck in a long breath, trying to keep it all in control.

I am impatient. And I don't like being told what to do. And I sure as hell don't like being coerced.

But Jimmy will always be the exception.

Always.

"Fine," I tell her. "No women," I add. I refuse to drink from the veins of any woman other than my mouse.

———

Fifteen minutes later, I'm satiated and feeling much better when Baspin emerges from the shadows surrounding Duval House. He's wearing a simple blue tunic and black pants.

"Were you going to ignore me?" he asks, arms clasped behind his back as he comes to a stop in a pool of light from the lamp post.

"It's been decades since you've been to the fae realm," I answer. "What good would you do me now?"

Jimmy nudges me on the left. "Be nice."

"No," I tell her.

Behind us, the front door of Duval House opens and I recognize the cadence of my brother's steps. I left him to feed on his second donor just a few minutes ago. His hunger seems to have no bottom. But I suppose I can't blame him, having just woken up from a coma.

Baspin's gaze tracks Damien as he crosses the front porch and comes down the steps to stand on my right.

"Damien Duval," the fae says and smiles, giving a shallow bow. He knows what he's doing. Even though the fae hold no allegiance to the vampires on this side, everyone in Midnight knows to show at least some respect to Damien Duval.

"You changed your mind?" Damien asks me, ignoring the fae.

"I made him," Jimmy says from my left.

"She convinced me," I correct, avoiding both of their gazes.

"What's in it for you?" I ask Baspin. "Surely you have a price."

"Of course I do." He takes another step. All three of us are acutely aware of his every move, the outline of every one of his pockets, and the shadows that surround Duval House.

There are no other heartbeats hiding in the dark. It appears he's come alone after all.

"I can help you get into the fae realm. I can help you locate Jessie. I can even help you infiltrate the Summer Court if need be, and I suspect the need *will be*. And in exchange for my help, I would like a title."

Damien and I share a sidelong glance.

"What kind of title?" I ask.

"Lord of Winter Court."

I snort. "Is this some kind of trick? The court no longer exists. How do you suggest we pay that price?"

"It will be easy," he answers with confidence. "Just as soon as you help your *little mouse* reclaim her throne."

Seven

When Baspin suggests Jessie reclaim her throne as heir apparent to the Winter Court, it's painfully obvious just how distracted I've been.

Not for one second did I entertain the idea that Jessie might take back her court.

I was more focused on keeping her alive and saving my brother.

And keeping my little mouse all to myself.

How fucking oblivious I've been.

And maybe a little bit of a selfish prick, too.

I know how war works and there are always two sides, always people who rally around whoever they think can win so they can suck off whatever power they can in the war or the victory after.

Baspin is no different.

Hell, Damien and I have done the same over the centuries, aligning ourselves with this house or that, elevating ourselves until we no longer had to worry about our own sovereignty.

I can't really blame Baspin, but I am suspicious of him.

"You're suggesting that once we rescue Jessie, we fight."

It's not a question. And he doesn't deny the truth of it. He can't.

"She's not ready," I admit.

"She can be," he answers. "With the right teacher."

"Are you suggesting you're the teacher?" Damien asks. "You beg for a title and yet think you're capable enough to teach a Winter Court princess how to use the power of her birthright?"

Baspin smiles at my brother, like he's been waiting for this challenge for hours, days, maybe months.

"I have no title, true, but I did serve in the Winter Court."

"In what capacity?" I ask.

"I was the king's personal servant, and when he needed to practice using his power, he used it on me. I know what it feels like. I can guide Jessie."

I glance at my brother. We immediately know what the other is thinking. We are no match for an Unseelie prince, or worse, a Seelie queen. There is no way to go back to how things were before. The gate has been opened and the fae have Jessie. The only way out of this is through.

"You must know we can't pay the price you're asking for," I tell Baspin. "I don't have the power to hand out fae titles."

He nods. "But you have the power to persuade the one who does."

It would be for her own good, I tell myself. If the cost of saving Jessie is a title to some low ranking fae, then the price is right.

"Fine." I come down the steps and offer Baspin my hand. "You take us to the fae realm. You help us rescue Jessie. Then and only then will we revisit the discussion of you getting a title of lord."

He considers this for a moment, then slips his hand into mine. I am far colder than he is, and I catch the faint tremor of his shoulders from the chill.

Just a little reminder that I too am powerful, that I am not one to fuck over.

I let my eyes bleed to gold as a final warning.

He tips his head in acknowledgment.

"Shall we leave now?" he asks. "We've no more time to waste."

———

Jimmy stays back to watch over Duval House with the witch by her side. Damien and I follow Baspin to the fae gate.

It's been a very long time since I've been to the field where the gate stands. There was never a point with it being sealed.

The door is now ajar with a trickle of light spilling out. Being that it's another realm, time moves differently there than it does here, and sometimes night is day and day is night in the fae realm. Luckily for vampires, sunlight in the fae realm doesn't have the same potency as the mortal.

When we walk through the doorway, however, it's immediately clear that something is *different*.

The air is thick and hot, almost insufferable, and the light is too. Baspin pauses on the other side of the threshold, a deep frown on his face.

"It's as I expected," he tells me over his shoulder. "With the Winter Court gone, the seasons are out of balance and Summer has taken over. They were always just too pompous to admit they needed the Unseelie, and the Winter."

Damien pulls a fern from the ground, examining the roots. Dirt cakes his fingers. He takes in a deep breath of the dark brown root system. "It's rotting." He tosses it aside. "And how do you suppose the Summer Court feels about it now?"

Baspin doesn't speculate. Instead, he says, "We should hurry. Before the night grows older."

I can remember from past visits that fae palaces are always buzzing with activity. But when we approach the Summer Palace, its exterior grounds are noticeably quiet. All sound can be traced to the interior, to the heart of the palace.

There are whispers between fae.

That's the Winter Princess.

The daughter of the traitor.

Shorter than I expected.

Prettier than I expected.

What an ugly princess. Rounded ears!
Why has the Summer Prince brought the likes of her here?
She should be put to death.

That last one has me pushing past Baspin down the domed hallway of the palace.

She's close. My little mouse is close and I won't stop until she's back in my arms and—

There is a crowd gathered in the throne room. And over the assembled, I can just make out Jessie on a dais, a woman in front of her and another fae...on a knee?

The crowd is thicker the closer I get to the dais and I shove them back, knocking many to their asses, panic driving heat through my veins.

"Bran, wait!" Damien calls.

But I'm already through. I'm already at the steps up to the dais where Jessie is standing, stunned, with the fae on one knee and his words tumbling out with excitement and glee. *"Jessie MacMahon, Princess of the Winter Court, will you take my hand in marriage and be my wife?"*

The fuck?

I take the stairs two at a time and yank the dagger Damien retrieved for me from the hidden sheath at my hip.

The dagger is made of iron and it will kill any fae.

And I plan to kill this one. No questions asked.

I'm across the dais in half of a second, blade poised to plunge, my vision tunneling, my blood lust pounding in my chest, when a tiny hand catches me, fingers wrapped around my wrist, sending a jolt of warmth through my body.

"Don't," Mouse says, her voice low but insistent.

The rage is barely repressed. They thought they could steal my mouse and then arrange a marriage for her, to steal her throne too?

The pieces are starting to fit together. I may not be fae and I may give two fucking shits about this godawful place, but I can see the strategy in this.

Without the Winter Court, with the seasons out of balance, the magic of their land is choking on itself.

They need to unite the courts in order to restore the balance and they think a marriage between the Summer and Winter Court will solve the problem.

I can see the logic in the plan. I can even respect the tactic.

But it'll happen over my dead fucking body.

I'll gut every single fae in this room.

I'll tear off their fucking heads if—

"No, Bran," Mouse says and gives me a shake of her head.

Trust me, she mouths, so only I can see the words, the way her full lips form the plea, the way her eyes squint, begging me for restraint.

Trust her? Giving her the lead is what got us here.

Does she know they need her? Does she know she has bargaining power? Does she know they're using her because of their own fucking mistakes?

Trust her?

Does she even know what the fuck she's doing?

"Mouse," I start, but she turns away from me and says to the queen and the fae on one knee, "I accept your proposal of marriage."

Eight

I'm so relieved to see Bran that I forget for a second that he's a killer and that he's probably here to *kill*.

But if he unleashes the full power of his wrath, I'm not so sure he'll make his way back out.

Adrenaline shoots through my veins, and I'm shocked at how quickly I can move in this place. I have my hand wrapped around Bran's wrist, coaxing him to a stop with little effort, all within seconds.

"Don't," I tell him.

I need him alive.

His immediate anger and agitation thrums over my body.

Can the rest of the fae sense it too?

Bran is barely holding it together and saying yes to the marriage proposal has only made it worse.

Over his shoulder, I catch sight of Damien, awake and on his feet. And beside him a blond fae I'm not familiar with.

If Damien is conscious, does that mean my sister is awake too?

I scan the crowd for her, but of course Damien wouldn't bring her to the fae realm.

I want to go home and see her.

I need to get us through whatever song and dance the fae would like us to perform so we can return home and reconvene and come up with a plan.

Maven's proposal caught me off guard, but honestly, it's the best possible outcome of all this. They aren't killing me—yet. Instead, they're trying to marry me off, and every single history book knows that an arranged marriage always has a benefit, some kind of leverage.

The queen points her nose at Bran and says, "Who is this?"

"He's a vampire," Arion answers. "From Midnight."

"Kill him," the queen says easily, no different than if she'd asked someone to smush a fly.

Two soldiers surge forward but I throw myself in front of Bran, arms spread wide like a shield.

"Little mouse," his voice rumbles in a whisper behind me. "You're playing a very dangerous game."

I ignore him and say, "The vampire is mine. There is no marriage without him."

I'll probably get a swatting for that later, and you know what? I'll enjoy it. In this new level of our relationship, Bran might have to stand down in public, and I might have to stand up, but in the bedroom...I will gladly submit to him.

"This vampire," the queen says and looks at us from the deep, dark pools of her dark amethyst eyes, "just tried to murder a crowned prince of the Summer Court. That's grounds for immediate beheading."

"He was just trying to protect me," I argue.

"Why?" The queen furrows her brow. "Who is he to you?"

I take quick stock of who in this room knows who Bran is—Arion and Damien. Maybe the blond fae? Those are small numbers. Great odds.

"He's my bodyguard," I answer.

Bran snorts.

The queen turns her gaze to Arion. "Is this true?"

Oh shit. He can't lie to her! He's going to tell her—

"Bran Duval is of no concern of mine," Arion answers. "But I can assure you, Your Majesty, that he has guarded Jessie with his body."

Oh thank god.

That was clever and honestly, a little unexpected. Tears nearly burn in my eyes at his sudden show of loyalty.

"I can award you an entire army of guards," the queen tells me, folding her hands in front of her. "I have many accomplished and skilled fae. Vampires cannot be trusted. They lust for our blood. They are too animalistic in nature to control their urges."

Bran bristles beside me. I put myself between him and the queen. "He would never hurt me. And he's nonnegotiable."

I can practically feel his bright golden gaze on me now, the sinking of his dark brow. Is he annoyed I have to protect him? Is he shocked I am? I'm desperate to know what he's thinking. I want to prove myself. I want him to be proud of me. I want him to have confidence in me.

I want him to know that here, in my land, I can handle myself.

Maybe.

Probably.

The queen takes several more calculated steps, the long train of her dress twisting behind her making her servants scurry forward to straighten it.

She stops just a few feet from us.

This is the woman who demanded my brother kill my mother.

There is nothing remarkable about her up close. She is beautiful, but there is something about her that is making it all seem wrong. Like a gorgeous daffodil with its stem bent and tattered.

From afar, it might be hard to see the brokenness of the flower, especially when it's surrounded by many other pretty things.

But if you get close enough...

"I'm not sure you're in the position to be negotiating," the queen counters.

I vaguely remember an old neighbor giving my mom haggling tips over the bleached concrete of our driveway way back when I was a kid. My dad always handled negotiations, but Dad was dead and Mom needed a new car—she wasn't ready to turn Dad's Bimmer into an everyday ride.

"When they counter," the neighbor had said, "and if it's something you don't agree with, just stay silent. Just keep looking at them."

Mom managed to talk the car salesman down by a thousand dollars and also got three free oil changes out of it. She was so proud of herself that day.

I just stare at the queen now and say nothing.

The woman on her left, the one with the green hair, gives the queen a side-eyed glance.

The other woman on her right adjusts her grip on the hilt of her sword as if preparing to draw the weapon.

Bran could have me out of here before the entire blade was unsheathed. Couldn't he?

"We can see how he does," the queen finally answers, raising her nose even higher. "But the iron blade must be destroyed." She snaps her fingers. There's a rustling to the left and two fae clatter over, a large black pot suspended on two poles between them.

They stop beside Bran.

"Into the pot," the queen says.

One of the fae—the man with sharp teeth and wide-set green eyes— uses a hook to pull off the lid on the pot. Steam hisses out and heat blooms in the air. Whatever concoction is inside is bright blue and the consistency of taffy.

Bran gives me a look. I give him a look right back. *Toss the damn dagger*, I tell him with my eyes. *It's my only fucking weapon, Mouse*, he says back with his glowing amber gaze.

We can find you another weapon.

With a grit of his teeth, he tosses the blade in and the thick liquid bubbles up around it, burning the metal into nothing but silver glitter.

The queen turns away and walks the perimeter of the dais, her hands now clasped behind her back. "I am a very happy mother this day. My eldest son is betrothed, and what was once our greatest enemy will soon be our kindred. Tonight, we will celebrate this union and in five nights, their betrothal will be consummated beneath the glow of the smiling moon."

The queen turns for an arched doorway.

"Wait!" I shout and my voice echoes around the large, domed room.

I sense a collective intake of breath.

It's probably not a good idea to speak out of turn to a fae queen, but a girl's gotta do what a girl's gotta do to get shit done.

The queen turns. A wave of her dark hair falls over her shoulder and sparkles in the diffused sunlight pouring through the glass overhead.

"I should return home to prepare," I tell her. "I'd like my sister to attend. And...there are things...things I need to wrap up."

"Wrap up?" she repeats, like these are the two stupidest words she's ever heard.

"Yes. I can take Arion with me if that helps. And you already have this collar on me to stop me from using my power."

Just gotta pretend to be the good girl, the innocent one, the harmless one.

The queen snaps her fingers again and six guards step forward.

"Take them with you instead. I have much to discuss with the Lord of the Summer Court."

Arion makes eye contact with me as the queen disappears through the doorway.

I really wanted him by my side. But he gives me the barest shake of his head before turning and following in the queen's footsteps.

———

The six guards break off into pairs. Two lead us from the palace. Two split off and hedge us in on the left and right, while the last two bring up the rear.

It's me, Bran, Damien, and the blond fae in the middle.

"Who's he?" I ask and nod at the newcomer.

"Your boyfriend's savior," the fae answers.

Bran snorts. "That's being generous."

"I am very generous, yes."

"He's Winter Court," Bran fills in as we leave the palace's main gate and follow the path back through the trees. I can't help but scan the branches looking for a flash of an Autumn Court girl. But there's nothing.

"He wants a title, by the way," Bran answers. "In exchange for helping us locate you."

"A small price to pay," the fae answers.

"What's your name?" I ask.

"Baspin, Your Highness."

I will never get used to hearing that.

"Nice to meet you. But can I trust you?"

His attention goes to the guards marching us along the path. I think I sense what he's thinking. He has to be careful what he says. The first chance I get to shake these guards, I will.

"You can trust that I will always have your best interest at heart," Baspin answers. His eyes twinkle with the promise, but I know those words can mean a lot of things. My best interest is his best interest, so his motivations could be selfish in nature.

The guards are silent as we leave the palace grounds behind and make our way back up the hill toward home.

I'm relieved to have made it this far, but I think so much has happened in such a short amount of time that I'm starting to become desensitized to people trying to kill me or use me.

Is that a good thing or bad thing?

"So where to first, little mouse?" Bran asks. His voice is even and devoid of emotion. He's testing me.

"We need to visit my boss," I tell him. "Let her know I can no longer work at the coffee shop as I will soon be married."

His chest rumbles at the mention of marriage. "Right," he says, course correcting. He has to pretend he doesn't care and I can tell he very much wants to paint the day in blood because of this whole thing. "Smart choice, Mouse."

He knows what I really mean—we visit Rita as soon as possible and see if she can help get this collar off. And then, finally, once and for all, unbind me and unlock my full fae powers.

Nine

When we reemerge on the mortal side of the gate into the meadow just outside Midnight Harbor, the sun is gone and the sky is clear and filled with stars.

The air smells crisp, promising rain, and I'm relieved by it. The fae realm was too hot, too sticky. I hated every part of it.

Baspin says to the guards, "Do you even know where we're going?"

They pause when we reach the forest where crickets and frogs make a song in the night.

"I've never been to this side," the guard on the right admits.

"Neither have I," the other one in front adds.

"Then let me take the lead." Baspin pushes through me and Bran, but Bran stops him.

"Best you stay behind us." Bran gives the blond fae a leveled look. "I can lead so that on the off chance we run into anyone, or *anything*, in the forest, I can easily and quickly vouch for you all."

It sounds logical when he explains it that way, but I know Bran well enough by now to know something else is afoot.

"Careful, vampire," the burly fae beside me warns. "If we don't return to the fae realm, there will be war."

"Of course." Bran gives a shallow bow. It's all for show. Bran doesn't bow to anyone. "I would never risk such a thing."

Yes, he would.

He turns and heads down the dirt path.

Goosebumps rise on my forearms the deeper we get into the woods. The trees are so thick with leaves, it's hard to see the stars above.

The path curves around a cluster of pine trees and for a moment, Bran disappears from my sight.

I hear his voice though, whispering from the dark...in *Greek*.

A chill slithers down my spine.

I glance at Damien, just a pace behind me. His eyes are glowing blue in the dark.

Oh shit.

Damien replies in Greek.

And then it's chaos.

Vampires dart across the path, their movements a blur.

A fae cries out. Another grunts and hits his knees. A third tries to pull his sword out, but there's already a long gash in his throat, blood spilling out in a curtain.

The burly fae grabs for me, putting me in front of him like a shield.

Something slams into him from behind. I hear the familiar sound of a bone breaking.

The fae howls.

Bran is suddenly in front of me, blood splattered across his face, dripping from his mouth, his fangs sharp in his mouth.

"Your first mistake," he tells the burly man, "was existing."

The wind kicks up and the buzzing of fae magic starts down my back. But it's too late. Bran sinks an iron blade into the fae's chest and my back is immediately coated in the hot geyser of his blood.

The man takes me down with him, but I quickly roll onto all fours, then scramble to my feet. He coughs up blood, his big body trembling. The wind dies and the fae magic dissipates.

It's over within minutes.

That's all it took for Bran, Damien, and several vampires strategically hiding in the woods with iron weapons to take out six highly trained fae guards.

I stand in the middle of the carnage trying to decide how I feel about it while their blood drips from my fingertips.

"Why the fuck would you do that?" I finally ask, my body trembling from the shock and the chill in the air.

Bran crouches beside the burly fae and checks the man's pockets pulling out a medallion, a dagger, and several gold coins. He thieves all of it.

The vampires who ambushed gather round. The only one I recognize is Jimmy.

"Well done, Jim," Bran says. "Right on time."

"Jimmy was always the most punctual out of all of us." Damien swipes the messy blade of his dagger across his leg, cleaning off the blood.

"How are we going to answer for this, though?" I turn a circle, pointing at the damage with flailing arms. "The queen is going to wonder where her guards are! She's going to want to know what we did to them, and she'll find out and then—"

"Let me worry about that," Bran says, dragging a fae off the path and into the underbrush.

"*Let you*—you must be joking! This is insane. We're going to be in so much trouble and—"

He stalks over to me, still bloodied, eyes still glowing from the rush of the kill. He wraps his hand around my throat and pushes me into the thick trunk of a nearby tree. "You are mine. Do you understand what that means, Mouse? That means that if someone threatens you, even if it's wrapped up under the guise of protecting you, I will destroy them. It might be one stone at a time, like this, disposing of guards so I can get us to the next stage of fucking their shit up. Because that's what I intend to do. I will fuck their shit up for thinking they have any fucking right to take you from me." He leans in closer, his pupils contracting, allowing more of the golden glow of his irises to show against the night. "No one will ever have you. No one but me. That is my vow to you. My promise. And that promise will always be steeped in blood and destruction. Maybe even war. I would start a dozen if it meant keeping you."

My pulse is thrumming hard beneath his grip. Even though we're surrounded by death and several other vampires, I'm feeling a carnal response to his authority in the space between my legs.

He notices right away, nostrils flaring, pulling in my heated scent.

"Dear brother," Bran says, his eyes still on me, searching me.

"Yes?" Damien replies.

"Can you handle the rest of this mess?"

"Of course."

"Good." Bran grabs me by the hand and yanks me away.

———

We find Bran's Audi parked at the side of the road waiting. He says nothing. Just coaxes me inside, clips me into the seat belt, and then climbs in behind the wheel.

His speed is death-defying, and I hold on, white-knuckled, to the door handle as he guides the nimble sports car through Midnight Harbor. But he doesn't return to Duval House. He takes me, instead, to his old house, the one right next door to mine.

It wasn't that long ago that I was standing on his front porch, debating knocking on his door. But it feels like another life, another girl.

The porch light is on, casting a soft glow over the railings as Bran pulls me up the stairs. He kicks the door in with his boot, then slams it shut behind us once we're inside.

"Bran, do you—" I start, but he has no patience for my words. He slams me against the door and kisses me.

His mouth is frenzied, angry and terrified.

I am his and he will do whatever he must to keep me, but everything is threatening us right now. Everything, at every turn.

His tongue meets mine as his hand holds my face to him.

I can smell the blood clinging to us, the crispness of night, and the leftover muskiness of the fae realm.

"I missed you, Mouse," he says when he pulls back enough to let me take a heavy breath.

"I wasn't gone that long."

"Any time is too long."

There is a light on in the kitchen, just beneath the stove hood. It's enough to see Bran, the outline of his body, the desire on his face, the wetness of his lips.

"You will not be his," he says, his voice haunted and raspy.

"I know."

"Never. In any world. In any scenario."

"I know, Bran." I take his hand and bring it to my mouth, kissing the ridge of his knuckle. "It was just to buy us time to get us back here so we can do the unbinding."

His other hand comes up taking a chunk of my hair. He puts just enough pressure on his grip to prove to me who is in command.

"Over to the couch, Mouse."

I dutifully follow the order and he keeps his hand in my hair, pushing me down so my belly is resting on the arm of the couch.

The cushions sink beneath me as he lines up behind me. We're still fully dressed, but I can feel the thick ridge of him through his pants pressing against my ass.

He yanks on my hair, forcing my spine to S-curve, my head to come back. His voice is a tantalizing whisper at the shell of my ear.

My pussy is throbbing now, primed for his touch. But he's not ready to give in yet.

"I will not share you either," he warns.

"I know."

"No other man, human, vampire, or fae, is allowed to touch what's mine."

His fingertips press hard against my right hip, and I wiggle my ass against him, causing him to growl.

"But I'm not above showing you what it'd be like."

"What?" I gasp out and try to look at him over my shoulder. But he puts pressure on my head again, forcing me down, my ass in the air.

"Don't move," he warns.

I sense the air shift as he darts away. I can't tell which direction. I stay firmly in place, following his rules, because I want whatever wild punishment he's come up with. I want to get lost in him for just a few minutes longer. He's always been the best distraction for when my life gets shitty and complicated and scary.

A door shuts and locks a second later and when I dare to peek at

Bran, rimmed in the soft, diffused light of the kitchen, I find him holding one of my toys — a giant, hot pink dildo.

Ten

Excitement spikes in my chest as soon as I see Bran holding the dildo in the rim of light spilling from the kitchen. I know what he intends to do with my toy—he's going to fill me up, in both holes, and while I don't ever want either of us inviting another into our relationship or our bedroom, I do like the idea of Bran making me feel just a little bit naughty by pretending we have.

He comes over to the couch, his footsteps slow and deliberate, and every step makes my heart beat a little harder.

There's fire in his eyes, the same kind of heady anticipation that is bubbling up in my lower belly.

"This is an awfully big cock, Mouse," he says, holding the toy up at his crotch.

"Not as big as yours," I tell him, and I would know.

His smile is smug. He already knew that.

When he reaches the couch where I'm still draped over the arm, he shoves the end table aside so he can place himself right in front of me. "Open up."

I pop my lips open for him and he guides the dildo into my mouth. The silicone is cold, slippery, but it's ridged like a real cock, with a hard, round head.

My enthusiasm gets the best of me and I swirl my tongue over the head as Bran slides it in and out, his hand gripping it by the shaft.

He sinks down, crouching in front of me. "I've never watched you suck a cock from this angle, this close. It's fucking hot, Mouse. Don't stop."

I pick up the rhythm, closing my eyes so I can pretend it's him in my mouth, while it somehow feels sexier knowing how intensely he's watching me, almost as if I am fucking someone else.

My pussy throbs, so fucking ready, and I can feel the dampness coating my panties.

Suddenly the dildo is gone, making my lips pop at the loss, and when I look up, Bran is gone too.

A second later, he rips off my pants, the fae tunic, and every last shred of fabric on my body. When my nipples hit the air, they harden to peaks and Bran reaches around from behind me, pinching one between his fingers as he teases my opening with the soaking wet dildo.

I whimper, pushing back into him, wanting him to fill me up, either with himself or the toy. But he does neither because he likes to torture me.

Taking my breast in the palm of his hand, he traps my nipple between two knuckles while holding to me tightly.

He sinks the toy an inch inside of me and I wiggle my hips, looking for more.

"Be patient, Mouse," he warns.

"I don't want to," I tell him.

His hand leaves my breast and smacks me across the ass, causing me to yelp.

"Be patient," he repeats.

"Okay," I say, a little breathy, my clit throbbing with anticipation.

There is no sound in Bran's house other than the distant ticking of a clock. It's so quiet that I can hear the raggedness of my breath and the wetness of my pussy. I sound so damn needy, but I don't care.

I am.

When Bran and I are fucking, nothing can touch us. Not even war.

"Which hole should I fill, Mouse?" he asks as he slips the dildo inside of me another inch, eliciting a long groan from my throat.

"Any," I breathe out.

He smacks me again on the ass and my body tenses up from the sudden sting.

"When I tell you to choose, you choose."

It's been a while since he's been in my ass and I don't know if I can take him. The dildo is smaller.

"Fuck my pussy," I tell him.

"Good girl. Hold still."

Elbows planted on the arm of the couch, I dare not move.

Something cold and wet hits my ass and I realize it's lube he's produced from somewhere. Maybe my bedroom or his.

I let out a little yelp until he rubs the head of the dildo against my hole. I'm so sensitive there, the pleasure is immediate, and my face flushes.

He's slow and deliberate, careful not to overdo it. The head of the toy opens me up, stretching me for more.

Pressure and pleasure and pain all mix together as he sinks the toy further inside of me. My hands curl over the arm of the couch as my clit throbs for any kind of friction or touch.

When will he stop torturing me?

He gets another inch inside of me and then slowly pulls out, then slowly pushes back in.

Reaching up, he takes a chunk of my hair and yanks my head back. "How does that feel?"

"I want more," I whine. "I want you inside of me too."

He sinks the dildo deeper and I moan at the pressure. Now that he has me stretched for him, he chooses a slow rhythm with the toy, fucking my ass with it and the naughtiness of it has my belly soaring.

Letting my hair go, Bran unzips himself and though he's a vampire, and cold most of the time, I immediately sense the throbbing heat of his cock near my pussy.

I'm blazing with need, every nerve firing for more.

When he lines himself up, I sink back on my knees, risking another smack for getting impatient.

But he doesn't punish me this time.

Instead, he gives me exactly what I want.

I'm so slick with desire, he slips in with no resistance, and with both him and the dildo inside of me, he matches the pace, fucking me in both holes.

I've never been so filled up.

It's the dirtiest, sluttiest thing I've ever done and giddy heat builds in my chest and in my belly, sending butterflies through every hollow of my body.

"Who do you belong to, little mouse?" he says, fucking me harder, faster, pounding into me.

"You."

"Say it again."

"I belong to Bran Duval and no one else."

"That's my good girl."

His pace is relentless now, as if the frenzy of our fucking is the only way to drive home the point—I am his, and only his.

He reaches around me, caressing my clit, and a shockwave of pleasure pours through me.

I arch into him, starving for an orgasm from him.

"Come for me," he finally orders. "Let me hear your pleasure as I fill you up in both holes."

My swollen clit needs only the barest of touches before I'm sailing over the edge.

"Oh god," I scream out, my body jolting as the pleasure pounds through me, melting away the tension of war and blood and carnage.

Bran fucks me harder and faster, grunting with his own pleasure as he keeps the dildo in my ass.

He slams into me, growling loudly as he fills up my pussy with his cum, and before he's finished spilling his load, he slips out of me, coming all over my ass and the hot pink toy.

"I like seeing your ass glistening with my cum," he says. "And now it'll be dripping from both holes."

I shiver beneath his words.

I like it too, if I'm honest.

I take in several deep breaths, letting the last of the pleasure fade out.

We disentangle and I turn around, collapsing into the crook of the couch. Bran takes the far cushion, pulling my legs over his lap.

"I missed you," he says.

"You already said that," I point out.

"I don't miss many things." He takes my bare foot in hand and kneads at the soft flesh of my arch. A new, different kind of pleasure washes through me and another groan comes out of my throat.

I close my eyes and lay my head back against the arm of the couch. Bran hits all the sensitive spots on the bottom of my foot.

"I have an idea," he tells me.

I barely open my eyes. "About what?"

"How to thwart the marriage proposal of the fae prince."

I'll talk about anything if it means keeping him on the foot massage.

"Okay. Tell me," I say.

"Marry me instead."

Eleven

BRAN

Mouse's eyes fly open and she bolts upright. "Are you proposing to me?"

"Yes. Was I not clear enough?"

She huffs and yanks her foot from my grip and folds her legs beneath her. She's still naked and her tits bounce as she gets herself upright. I can still smell my cum leaking out of her, just the way I like her.

"Are you insane?" Her nose wrinkles up in that adorable little angry way I love.

"Marrying you before the prince is not illogical, it's not foolish. So no, not insane."

"Okay, *reckless.*"

I won't argue that point. It is reckless. But I've never loved anything enough to want to keep it for eternity. At least not anyone beyond my family.

And the thought of losing Mouse causes me physical pain.

I will stand in front of fire or arrow or stake for her.

I will face down an entire fae court to defend what is mine.

I love her. My little mouse.

And I will do whatever it takes to keep her by my side.

"The fae are ridiculously traditional," I explain. "They have to respect a marriage contract, regardless of whether or not they agree with it. It's practically written in their codex."

"Contract? I'm not an acre of land!"

"Mouse," I say.

A car drives past the house, the headlights sweeping through my front window, sending a block of sharp light across Mouse. There is frustration pinched between her dark brows.

"No," she says, and then swallows hard. "I want to do this my way."

Panic festers in my chest, but I push it down deep.

I know she doesn't want to marry the fae prince. But her wants will mean nothing if they sweep her into their fold and drag her to the altar before I can stop them.

I don't like variables I cannot control.

"And what is your way, little mouse?" I ask her, keeping my voice even. I can't be angry with her. I can't even be disappointed. I know how badly she wants full agency in her own life.

Even if I fucking hate it.

"We go to Rita, we do the unbinding and see if she can get this collar off my neck." She gives the metal a yank, but it's held fast by some kind of fae magic. "And maybe she can help us gain an edge over the fae. If she can, we can return to the fae realm with a weapon and a plan."

"We should take Baspin too," I add.

Mouse frowns at me, then grabs her clothes, pulling them back on, much to my disappointment. I could stare at her naked body all day long.

"Do you really think we can trust him?" she asks.

"He has followed through on his promises so far."

She stands up and shimmies into her pants. "I don't want to take him to Rita's."

"Fair enough."

"But when we return to the fae realm, maybe it would be good to have someone who's familiar with the place. I'm not sure which side Arion is on. I don't know if I can trust him yet."

"Why is that even a question?" I stand beside her, towering over her and she has to crane her neck to meet my eyes.

"Because he's my brother."

The reveal takes me by surprise. "Really? Did he tell you that?"

"He did." She smooths over her just-fucked hair. "And apparently he was the one who killed our mother."

"Wow. Have to give the prick points for style."

Mouse scowls. "It's disgusting." She thinks for a second. "But it's probably more complicated than I'm giving him credit for. The Summer Queen ordered it and I don't think Arion felt he had a choice."

"We always have a choice."

She nods. "Yeah, I guess you're right." Then, "Speaking of choices. What do you plan to do about the fae guards you killed? That's a huge barrier to our return to the fae realm."

"Witches," I answer. "At least one of them must know a good illusion spell. We can mask several vampires as the guards for as long as we need."

Mouse cocks her head. "I guess that sounds like a good plan."

"What do you mean? It's a brilliant fucking plan."

She rolls her eyes. "Come on. I'm going to stop at my house before we head into town. As beautiful as fae clothing is, it's not the least bit comfortable. I need some leggings if I'm going to save myself."

———

Twenty minutes later, we're parking outside of Rita's house. It's too late for the coffee shop and what we need her for isn't exactly for public spaces.

I text Damien our plan so he knows where to find me if he needs me. I don't get a reply from him.

At the front door of Rita's bungalow, her husband Francis is the one to greet us. He peers out at me before seeing Mouse by my side and once he does, the line of his shoulders relaxes a bit.

Francis and I have no trouble. He's mortal, easygoing, keeps to himself, but he's extremely intelligent, which means he's immediately, always on guard around me.

For the better part of his adult life, he was a civil engineer for the township south of Midnight. He'd always known about Midnight and the magic but kept his distance until he started seeing Rita. They were married in their late thirties and when Francis moved to Midnight, he became our lead civil engineer.

"I need to see Rita," Mouse says.

"She's been expecting you." Francis's gaze slides from Mouse back to me. "Vampires don't get invitations into our house. I hope you understand."

"I'm not leaving Jessie's side," I tell him. "So if you can make accommodations, I won't be an asshole about it."

Francis lifts his chin once. "Around back then. Rita will meet you in the garden."

"Thank you," Mouse says and then follows the brick pavers around the side of the house and through a gate painted black. The latch clangs loudly when Mouse lets it drop closed behind us.

Rita's garden is hidden behind a six-foot privacy fence. There is a wide range of flowers in bloom and the air is sickly sweet with their scent. In the back corner, water trickles from a fountain installed in a koi pond. String lights make an X above us. With the new moon, the lights fill the night with a golden glow.

"This is beautiful." Mouse makes a full turn.

"Jessie!" Rita calls as she exits the house through a screen door. She comes over, wrapping Mouse in a hug. "I had heard you were kidnapped to the fae realm." She pulls back and puts her hands on either side of Mouse's face. "I'm so glad you're all right."

I snort. "She's not all right. They're trying to force her to marry a fae prince and they've put a collar on her."

Mouse pulls her hair aside and Rita's gaze falls to the metal hanging from her neck.

"I see." Rita frowns. "A Prisoner's Quell?"

"You're familiar?" Mouse asks.

"I am. I removed one from a brownie many years back."

"You think you can remove this one?"

She examines it with a sweep of her fingertips. "This one looks a bit more complex, but I can try."

"Please." Mouse yanks on the metal. "This thing is already chafing and I can't use my powers with it on."

"And I can't unbind you with it on either." Rita gestures to a circle of Adirondack chairs situated around a stone fire pit. "Sit. I'll get my bag and we'll get to work."

Mouse gets comfortable, but I hate Adirondack chairs so I pace with my arms crossed.

"Will you relax?" Mouse says.

"No," I answer.

Beyond Rita's privacy fence, I hear a car pull up. From the sound of the deep tread on the tires and the churn of the engine, it's a Jeep Wrangler.

Damien?

I go to the gate and pull it back to find my brother headed my way with Kelly MacMahon right behind him.

Twelve

Bran opens the gate at the back of Rita's house and I peek around the broad line of his shoulder, adrenaline shooting through my body, muscles tensed for a fight.

But it's no enemy approaching.

It's my sister.

"Oh my god. Kelly!"

I rush at her and wrap her in a hug. She smells like soap, her breath like coffee, and it's the most Kelly thing I can think of in this moment that it immediately makes me teary-eyed.

She lets out an *umph*, and staggers back a step before returning the hug.

"Hey," she says against my hair.

I won't cry. I don't want to cry.

"I'm so glad you're awake," I say, my voice wavering as the tears spill over.

"We came straight here," she tells me and pulls back, smoothing over my hair. "I've tried to get caught up—it sounds like you've had a wild ride while I've been..." She pauses and frowns. "Asleep."

Asleep?! She was in a coma! But I don't want to cause her more stress, so I take a deep breath and nod and say, "There's time to catch up. But yeah, it's been a lot. I'm just so happy to see you."

There are dark shadows beneath her eyes and she looks paler than normal, even in the darkness of a new moon night. But at least she's awake.

"You didn't have to come see me," I tell her. "You should rest."

"That's what I told her," Damien says, sounding disgruntled that he wasn't obeyed.

Kelly rolls her eyes at him. At least they're right back where they started. "I can rest when my little sister is safe." She squeezes my hand. "What's first?" She glances at Rita who now stands just behind me with a large canvas bag looped over her shoulder. "It's nice to see you, Rita."

"Nice to see you too, sweetie. I heard you were knocked on pretty good by a Renshaw spell. Glad you're on your feet again."

"Me too." Kelly smiles, but the light doesn't reach her eyes. In fact, for a brief second, it's almost like she checks out, like her gaze is empty.

I try not to dwell on it. It's probably because she's tired.

Rita goes to the picnic table set in the center of a brick patio. The table is covered in a black and white checkered tablecloth with a bouquet of freshly cut flowers in the center and a flickering lantern beside it with what looks like a solar light but might actually be magic.

Rita plops the bag on the table and digs inside, pulling out three jars. Inside the first is what looks like sand, and in the other two, a dead beetle and a mottled feather.

"All items from the fae realm," she explains. "Witch magic, on its own, cannot undo fae magic. So I'll channel what I can from the items to help remove the collar. And once we remove it, we can perform the unbinding."

Bran steps beside me. His energy is putting off serious bodyguard vibes even though he knows damn well Rita would never hurt me.

I suppose getting kidnapped is reason enough for him to be on edge, so I say nothing and let him do what he needs to do to feel comfortable.

Rita unscrews the jar with sand and spreads it out on the picnic table. Next comes the feather. She holds it in her hand like a quill and writes several symbols in the sand. A few of them look vaguely familiar and I wonder if they're a match to some of the tattoos on Arion's fingers or if I saw them while in the fae realm.

When she finishes, Rita looks up, the string lights highlighting her cheekbones in gold. "I'm ready if you are."

Kelly takes the place on my other side, with Damien flanking her.

I give Rita a nod. "Will it hurt?"

"Probably like hell," she admits. "I'll try to make it quick."

"Do what you have to do." I glance up at Bran. "Don't stop her. Whatever happens."

He narrows his eyes at me and says nothing.

"Do it," I tell Rita.

She unscrews the jar with the beetle, and reaches inside, capturing the dead insect in the curl of her fingers. She brings her hand to her mouth and whispers several words into it, before slamming her hand to the sand, crushing the beetle, then smashing it in with a hard twist of her palm.

I have no idea how this works, so I watch raptly, wondering when the pain will start, braced for it.

Rita keeps mumbling.

A breeze shifts through the backyard and the leaves on a large magnolia tree rasp against one another.

Rita pulls up a handful of sand and as she does, the grains start to glow bright green, the same shade as the beetle. She flattens her palm, brings it level with the collar, then sucks in a deep breath.

On her exhale, the sand lifts, swirling in the air around me and settling on the collar.

The metal heats up.

Still no pain.

Bran shifts his weight beside me.

Kelly sways on my other side.

The warmth from the metal seeps into my skin, flowing outward down my shoulders, down my arms.

It's nothing I can't tolerate. Maybe Rita was wrong and—

Blinding, searing pain shoots along my collarbone like a thousand tiny needles breaking my skin open, tearing the flesh nerve by nerve.

I cry out, knees buckling. Bran catches me around the waist, holding me upright, his own mental anguish etched into the fine lines between his dark brows.

He promised me he wouldn't stop the spell.

But right now, I almost wish he would.

The pain sinks deeper, tearing through my ribs. I squirm in Bran's grip.

The throbbing ache knots in my stomach and I have to clamp my teeth together to stop vomit from coming up.

"How much longer?" Bran asks.

Rita ignores him and takes up another handful of sand, blowing it my direction.

The pain intensifies.

I'm sobbing now, face soaked with tears.

I can't stand on my own two feet. I can't think. I can't escape. I can't do anything and—

Kelly steps into my line of sight.

She's blurry through the tears, but I immediately know something is wrong.

Her eyes are the same deep shade of amethyst as the Queen of the Summer Court.

"Guards!" she shouts. "Guards!"

"What the fuck," Bran says.

"I should have known you'd betray my trust," Kelly says, her voice hollow and raspy. "Winter Court has no honor. Guards!"

"Fuck," Bran says. "Damien."

"I know," Damien says and swoops Kelly into his arms.

"Get off of me!" she shouts and fights him. But Kelly is no match for Damien.

"What is happening?" I manage to choke out just as another fresh wave of pain takes over, making my toes curl.

"I think the Summer Queen is using Kelly as a conduit," Bran says, tightening his arm around me.

"The Renshaw spell," Damien says, bear-hugging Kelly into submission. "The link may still be open."

"Get her somewhere she can't get free," Bran orders.

"Is she..." I grit my teeth as a sharp poke starts in my ribs and blooms down to my hips. "Will she be all right?"

"One problem at a time, Mouse." Bran lifts me up. "How much longer, witch?"

Rita looks worried. "It should have come off by now. I need more fae magic."

"Baspin," Bran says quickly.

"No," I tell him, my knees buckling again.

"Yes. We're running out of time. The Summer Queen knows we've betrayed her. We need to move. Right fucking now." He drops my hand but keeps his arm locked around my waist, holding me up. He pulls his cell from his pocket and taps in a command.

The fae answers on the second ring. "Took you long enough."

"I need you here now."

"Send me the address and I will be there without delay," Baspin says and asks no questions.

Maybe we can trust him.

Maybe I have more allies than I first thought.

———

I think it takes Baspin less than ten minutes to reach Rita's house, but it feels like an eternity. I clutch to Bran with everything I have, his cool skin being the only comfort as wave after wave of pain fills my bones.

The fae magic Rita had on hand wasn't enough, but the spell is deadlocked, trying to finalize itself without enough juice to do it.

By the time Baspin comes into the back garden, I'm on my knees clutching at my stomach, sweat pouring down my temples, my body trembling.

"What have you done to her?" Baspin says, anger turning his ethereal beauty even more lethal.

"Shut the fuck up and get over here," Bran orders, and Baspin scoffs but does as commanded.

Rita produces an iron blade. Baspin scowls deeper at it.

"I need your blood," she says.

With a sigh, he offers his pale hand.

The blood comes rushing to the surface the second his skin is split with the blade. He hisses but doesn't flinch.

Rita catches the blood with the last of her fae sand and blue flames ignite in her hand as she whispers several more words to the magic.

"This should do it," she says, but she sounds anxious and that makes the pain harder to bear.

I shake in Bran's grip.

The last bit of sand, now heavy and wet with Baspin's blood, is smeared over the collar.

The metal burns, sizzling my skin.

I have no control over my body anymore and I tilt my head back, screaming at the sky.

Bran sinks to the earth beside me, holding me fast to him as I flail in his arms.

"How much longer?" he asks.

"Almost done," Rita says.

The throbbing fills my joints, thrumming along every muscle and tendon.

And just when I think I couldn't possibly bear it a second longer, the collar clanks open and drops to the ground.

Thirteen

The relief is immediate.

I take in a deep breath as Bran wraps his cool hand around the back of my neck, driving the sticky sweat from my skin.

The collar is off. I can relax and—

"Hurry with the unbinding," Bran says.

"Maybe give her a minute," Baspin suggests.

"No." Bran's fingers press harder at my skin. "We have no time to coddle her. We do this now."

"Bran. I can't," I sob, body trembling as I hunch forward on my knees, arms wrapped around my chest. "Not yet."

"We can't wait, Mouse." He looks over at Rita. "Do it now."

With a frown, she swivels on her heels and digs into her bag again, producing the jar with my pendant inside. The same one Mom gave me all those years ago.

"Bran. *Please.*" Tears spill over my lids.

Even though this is what I've wanted all along, ever since I learned that Rita bound my powers at my mother's request, I can't think beyond the pain.

"You said not to stop, Mouse," he reminds me. "So we don't stop. Okay? You have more to give."

"I can channel some of the pain." Baspin crouches in front of me. "Give me your hand, Your Highness."

I don't balk at the title. I don't care what he calls me if he can help.

With one hand in Bran's grip, I give the other to Baspin. His hand is still bleeding, and his hold is hot and slippery, but as soon as our skin touches, warmth floods through me and the pain fades out.

I sway, leaning my weight into Bran's side.

The relief is sudden and damn near intoxicating, almost like a drug.

"Better, princess?" Baspin asks.

I nod. "Thank you."

"Go on," Bran says to Rita.

She sets the jar in front of me and pops off the top. The smell of the magic immediately permeates the air. This magic is different than the magic of the collar. It's crisper, cleaner, like a sharp winter breeze.

The scent of it stirs something old and forgotten inside of me.

Rita whispers a few foreign words and the nighttime breeze shifts across the garden, rattling the big leaves of an evergreen shrub behind me.

Next, Rita drops the pendant back into the jar, lights a match she pulls from a small box from her pocket, and drops that in too. The jar's interior ignites with a WHUMP as if it were full of gas. Blue flame licks along the glass, dancing over the rim.

Tingling starts in my fingers like my nerves have fallen asleep. The tingling spreads up my arms, then across my shoulders, down my chest.

Rita slams the jar's lid closed, hoists it over her head, then brings it down swiftly, smashing it into a thousand pieces on the cobblestone patio.

My body jerks back as if I have no control over it.

Bran locks his arms around me and Baspin grips my hand tighter.

The tingling morphs into a burn so bad, I feel like I've touched the sun.

Every nerve is fried. Every muscle locked up, cramping. I flail in Bran's hold. He brings my back to his chest and holds me tightly.

"Almost done, Mouse," he says to me.

I lose myself to the pain.

I think my eyes are squeezed shut, but I can still see the flickering twilight behind my closed lids, and the twilight turns to frost until it edges my awareness.

Teeth chattering together, the heat turns cold, but the painful burn of it remains as the magic works its way through my veins, through every hollow of my body.

I know I must endure this to get to the other side, but in this moment, there is only the rawness of my body, and the persistent pain flooding every joint.

How much longer?

How long do I have to endure this torture to become who I was always meant to be?

A voice deep down at the far recess of my mind whispers: *You were always you.*

Like a snap of the fingers, the cold vanishes, the tingling fades, and power rushes through my body.

I suck in a deep breath, filling my lungs with fresh, crisp air.

"Mouse?" Bran says over top of me.

"*Let me go,*" I order and both Bran and Baspin drop me immediately.

I tip forward onto all fours, hands planted firmly on the cobblestone.

Frost spreads out from my fingertips.

My breath puffs out white on the air despite the warmth of late summer.

"Get back," Baspin commands.

"What's happening?" I ask, but my voice is hoarse and raw and the words are unintelligible even to my ears.

"Gods forgive me," Rita breathes out and when I look up, I see frost channeling up her legs, up and up toward her torso.

"Get out of here, witch!" Bran shouts. "Go, now!"

All around us, fully bloomed flowers glitter with frost, then burst like broken ice.

"It's too much power," Baspin tells Bran. "She can't control it."

"No shit." Bran reaches out for me, but hisses when our skin touches. His fingertips come away black with frostbite.

"How should she channel it?"

Baspin frowns and steps back as the frost spreads. "I don't know. This is a first for me."

"Christ." Bran scoops me up in his arms. His skin pinks, then blisters, then turns black. "Hang on to me, Mouse."

"Put me—"

"Do not command me." His eyes are glowing like fire, the space between his brows pulled taut with annoyance and worry. "Don't even fucking think about it."

"Where are you taking her?" Baspin asks.

"Somewhere far away. You figure out how to help her control it while I figure out how to neutralize it for now."

"Got it. Call me when you can."

Bran nods, pulls me in tight to his chest, and takes off at a run.

———

The world is a blur as Bran races through the night and it's hard to mark the landscape to know where he's taking us.

It isn't until he slows to a jog that I recognize the Pack House up on the hill.

Bran takes the stairs up to the front door two at a time, then drops me on the porch, his skin blackened with frostbite. He curses beneath his breath as he rings the doorbell with a jab of his elbow.

It's Fox who answers after several minutes. He sees Bran first and crosses his arms over his chest. "What the fuck do you—"

He spots me next, huddled on the porch.

"I need the Alpha," Bran says, holding his left arm close to his body as if he's trying to warm it up. "Hurry. We don't have a lot of time."

Frost licks up the porch columns. I'm shivering now, power radiating through my bones.

Why can't I stop this? Why can't I control it? It feels too big and I feel too small.

I thought unbinding my power just meant I'd have better access to my voice. No one told me about *this*. About ice and frost and the piercing cold.

Is this normal?

Am I broken?

The Alpha of the Midnight Pack fills up the doorway of the Pack House. Several lamps are glowing in the house beyond him, rimming his broad shoulders in golden light.

He looks from Bran to me.

"Heat," Bran says. "We need to counteract the magic and I run too cold. I just make it worse."

Cal thinks this over, then pulls out his cell phone and taps in a few commands. "I think I have an idea," he says and comes over to me, slipping his phone back into his pants pocket.

"Just be careful," Bran warns.

Cal frowns at me and I can see the sympathy in his eyes.

"Jessie?"

My teeth clack loudly together. Snow starts to fall in the summer air.

"I'm going to pick you up," Cal says. "All right?"

I can barely nod.

The Alpha ducks down and threads one arm beneath my knees, the other around my waist. He growls from the sudden chill, then the bite of frost, but his wolf's heat radiates through his skin, burning off the cold.

"I've got her," Cal tells Bran. "Go drink so you can heal."

Bran shakes out his blackened fingers. "I'm not leaving her."

Steam fills the air between me and Cal.

"You're no good to her missing fingers. Go."

Bran looks like he wants to argue but knows better. The Alpha is right.

"Don't leave her side," he says.

"I won't," Cal promises.

"The Summer Queen will be coming for her."

"Then I guess you should hurry up."

Bran grumbles as Cal turns away, carrying me off down a darkened path into the woods.

"I mean it, wolf," Bran calls. "Don't leave her side."

The light from the Pack House fades the further into the woods we go. Cal says nothing, but I can hear the steady drum of his heart through his shirt.

When the trees thin out to a clearing, I spot a little outbuilding shaped like a large barrel with a door and a long, rectangular window beside it.

Cal wrestles the door open, trying to keep me firmly in his grip, and when we walk inside, I catch the faint scent of cedar. The air is already warm.

"It's a sauna," he tells me and gingerly sets me on a bench along the far wall. "I started it up ahead of time with my phone so it's already nice and toasty. I use it for contrast therapy. It helps me regulate my wolf's aggression."

The chattering in my teeth lessens. "What's contrast therapy?"

"Hot and cold." He pulls off my boots, then my socks. They're stiff and ice flakes off the toes. "There's a deep spring nearby. I go into the cold water, then come into the hot sauna. Some days I have to go back and forth for hours. It seems to be worse since..." He trails off, his gaze going distant.

"Worse since what?"

"Sam," he says, with almost a growl. "But that's another conversation for another time. Let's get as many layers off as you can. I'll turn around."

"I can't feel my hands."

With a grumble, he grabs the hem of my shirt and pulls it off slowly, then helps me wiggle out of my leggings leaving me in just my bra and panties. Within seconds, his back is to me and he's handing off a clean, dry towel to wrap around my body.

"Thank you." I tuck the thick cotton around my chest and then lay back on the bench, soaking in the heat.

The overwhelming rush of power dissipates, taking the chill and the frost with it.

"That was bad," I tell him. "I didn't know..."

He drops onto the bench across from me, the steam of the sauna making him look more dream-like.

"You'll get it figured out."

I snort and close my eyes. "I'm not so sure. Every time I think I'm on a path to become more of who I'm supposed to be, something bad happens."

"Well did you think it would be easy?"

I glance at him with heavy eyes. "I guess I did, yeah."

"That was your first mistake."

"You sound just like Bran."

Cal laughs. "I'd ask you kindly to keep that to yourself."

I lay my arm over my forehead feeling infinitely better now that the hot air of the sauna is driving out the cold.

"You two are more alike than you'd like to admit."

"Probably true."

"Definitely true." I peek at him again from around the shadow of my arm. "So...Sam."

Cal sighs and looks down at his hands. He absently rubs his thumb over the opposite knuckle like he's trying to ease some of the tension in his joints. "I'm confident we'll work through our stuff."

I laugh through my nose. "Have you met Sam?"

He laughs too and leans back against the wall, hands now folded over his midsection.

My eyes start to droop.

"Get some rest, Jessie," Cal says. "I'll stay by your side until Duval returns."

With that promise, I'm immediately out.

Fourteen

When I wake, I'm still shrouded in steam, but soft rose gold light fills the sauna. It's coming from a half ring light installed in the arch on the back wall of the barrel. It reminds me of the Himalayan salt lamp Kelly bought several years back that she plugged into the front room. At night, it would instantly make the place feel cozier. But when Kelly got a little too tipsy on wine and accidentally knocked it over, cracking it, she never replaced it.

As everything of the last twenty-four hours comes rushing back, I'm overwhelmed with longing for the life I had. It was boring and lacking, and when I was in the middle of it, I hated it, but now it seems so blissfully simple.

Why did I ever take it for granted?

The Alpha caught me in one of my own stupid mistakes—I thought shedding the old me and embracing the fae-me would be easy. Even though everyone on the face of the planet knows that anything worth doing is going to be hard.

I never fit in that old, boring life. That's why it was lacking.

Or rather, why I felt that void yawning at my core.

Every day I would wake up and feel like something was missing, never having the language or the capacity to put my finger on what. It's why I always thought about leaving. I was searching for something to fill that void.

I can't go back.

And if I could, would I choose to?

Simple isn't always better.

I don't think I would choose to go back.

"You're awake."

Bran's voice startles me upright and I clutch at my racing heart and the towel drooping over my chest. I find him sitting in the front end of the barrel, hidden partially in mist and shadows.

"You scared me. I forgot how eerily still and silent vampires can be."

He leans forward into the light, bracing his elbows to his knees. He's fully clothed even though it's bordering on stifling hot in here. "How are you, little mouse?"

To anyone who did not know Bran well, it would almost sound like he was indifferent to the answer. But I think I've come to know Bran better than most people at this point. He's pulled back his protective layers and allowed me to see his vulnerabilities.

And I can detect the fragile lace of fear in his voice.

He is afraid of the answer. He's afraid of things getting worse and being unable to save me.

It makes me want to immediately reassure him.

I take stock of my body.

I'm not shivering anymore, so that's a good sign. I see no frost, no ice on the large rectangular window.

My mouth is a little dry, but no big deal. I feel a little woozy, but that's probably because I've been in a sauna for...how many hours?

The buzzing in my legs is completely gone and when I give my shoulders a roll, testing the joints, I'm surprised to find no ache, no tension, no pain.

Everything feels lighter, looser, *less human*.

Had I always been achy and never noticed it? Did the binding make me *feel* human? Prone to muscle soreness, joint pain, just the regular ache of existing in this world?

Or was it my fae side always trying to push to the surface? The power struggling against the binding?

That flame of anger aimed at my mother returns for a second before I remind myself of what she sacrificed to protect me.

I can't be mad at a dead woman who raised a child that was not her own. Mom could have easily tossed me to another fae family, and who knows what they would have done with me if they found out my origins.

The anger at my mother will always be fruitless. And worse, not entirely warranted.

I glance over at Bran, still hunched forward. He's watching me with an intensity that scalds, his eyes flaring amber orange in a cloud of thick steam.

My heart kicks up and there's an answering pull at my core.

"You're hot when you look at me like that."

The line of his dark brow sinks in annoyance. "Don't make me ask a second time." His voice is vibrating with warning now, and when he's like this, I know I'm either going to get fucked or scolded. Or option three: *both*.

"I'm fine."

"*Fine*? Don't lie to me."

I heave out a sigh and rub at my forehead. "I feel better than ever. I feel...*not human anymore*."

The admission comes out in a rush, like the words have been dying to get out.

"You were never human, Mouse." Bran's voice softens as a tear spills over the edge of my eye.

I nod. "I know." My teeth rake over my bottom lip. "I know that, obviously. But...I *could pretend*."

Steam hisses into the air and I lurch away from the bench, feeling the instant chill on my skin.

I turn around to find frost on the wooden bench.

"Shit. Shit. Get out, Bran. I can't control it!"

More tears spill over. I don't know why I'm freaking out, but I suddenly am and my heart races in my chest, making it hard to breathe.

Snow forms in the air.

"Get out! Before I hurt you!"

He's on his feet in a blur, across the sauna in less than a second, and then he grabs me by the throat, driving me back against the flat side of the barrel.

I lose the towel and it puddles at my feet.

Bran towers over me. "Look at me, Mouse."

Frost climbs up his arm.

"Bran, please."

"Look at me!"

I crane my neck to meet his glowing gaze.

"I'm not leaving you."

The wood groans from the change in temperature. I can no longer see past the broad line of Bran's shoulders, the steam is so thick.

I start to shiver.

Ice crackles along the domed roof above us.

The light bar flickers.

"I can't control it."

"Do you trust me?" Bran asks.

"What? I—"

He drops to his knees, tears my panties from my body and hooks one knee over his shoulder.

He tastes me in one long stroke of his tongue and my mind immediately goes to the sensation and the primal pleasure of my vampire boyfriend being between my legs.

Bran hooks one hand around my thigh, spreading me wider as he sinks two fingers inside of me. "I'm not...leaving you," he says between licks. "There will always be this." He nips at my clit, causing me to jolt, and my body relaxes. "There will always be the distraction of pleasure." He pulls out of me, then sucks my juices from his fingers, eyes glowing up at me. "I will never abandon you." He fingers me deeper, tongue swirling over my swollen clit. "If I must get on my knees to help you through power flares, I will." He sucks at my clit again, then explores my center with the slide of his tongue. "I will do anything to help you balance your power." He nips at my clit and my hips rock back.

Bran tightens his grip around my thigh, pulling me back into him, back to his mouth.

"I will be here"—he tastes me deeply—"until the end of fucking time."

The steam thins out and the chill around me dissipates until there is only the burning need in my body.

I focus on the feel of Bran between my thighs, his mouth on my pussy.

Fuck, he knows how to bring me to the peak in no time at all. I try to push him away—I don't want to come without him. Not yet. But he is relentless, and unmovable. Bran Duval takes orders from no one. Not even me.

"Give in to me, Mouse," he says with a growl, his tongue swirling over my clit, tasting me deeply. "Come for me and let me taste the sweetness of it."

He takes me flying to the edge.

I brace myself with a hand on the wall behind me, the other buried in his hair as I rock my hips forward, chasing the pleasure of his mouth on me.

"Fuck, Mouse," he groans into me. "You taste so fucking good."

The bloom of pleasure spills over and I cry out.

Bran's fingers press into my inner thigh, keeping me open for him as my body instinctively wants to close.

I squirm beneath him as he chases the last of my orgasm, as if he wants to memorize the taste of it.

When I come down on the other side of it, he scoops up the towel and in one fluid motion, wraps it around me.

"You can come in, Alpha," he says.

My mouth drops open. "Wait. Was he there the entire time?"

"Not the entire time," Cal says as he pushes the door in and steam billows out into the darkness around him. "Get dressed and meet me in the Pack House. One of my scouts just came back with a report."

Bran scowls. "And?"

"And..." Cal sighs. "Arion just came through the gate. And he brought an army of fae with him."

Fifteen

I'm still buzzing from the orgasm Bran gave me in the sauna when I'm ushered into a closed room in the heart of the Pack House.

Everyone is talking at once.

But Bran is silent beside me.

It's not that he doesn't have something to say, it's that he wants to hear all the things that are said.

We are at war with the fae because of me and while the very thought terrifies me, I can't imagine facing this without Bran. *He* can be terrifying. And I know he's more than capable of death and destruction. The only thing that might hold him back is his need to protect me.

He glances over at me as if he can sense where my thoughts have gone. The considerable height difference between us means he has to look down, then down some more. His arms are crossed over his chest, making his biceps bulge against the sleeves of his black t-shirt.

"What are you thinking?" he asks me.

Across the room, Fox, Cal, and three other shifters are in a heated discussion about what they should do about this latest development. A woman on Cal's left shakes her head at something Fox said. Fox frowns at her. Beside him, a lean man with a big beard and short brown hair scoffs and then gestures to the woman sitting in front of him.

"I'm thinking that it's too soon," I tell Bran. "I'm not ready to fight my own brother and I'm sure as hell not ready to fight the queen."

"Let me tell you a secret, little mouse." Bran turns to face me, arms still crossed. He dominates my line of sight and overwhelms me with his presence. Will that feeling ever ebb? Will I ever get used to having Bran Duval all to myself? Every taut muscle, every hard edge?

I'm not sure that I'd even want to.

"Okay, tell me," I say.

"No one is ever ready for war."

I sigh and roll my eyes because it's such a Bran thing to say.

"I'm serious." His arms drop to his sides. "It's easy to think everyone else knows what they're doing. But they don't."

"But I bet my brother can control his power."

Fox grumbles at something the bearded man says, and they dissolve into an argument.

"Every ounce of power you possess right now, in this moment, is power you've always possessed. Which means you've always been capable of controlling it. It's not a skill you must learn, like writing or stabbing.

"Power is no different than the blood that pumps in your veins and you never have to think about your heart beating for it to work."

I sigh and scrub at my face. "It's not that easy."

"It is. You're just making it hard."

"Cal told me that it was *supposed* to be hard."

Bran looks across the room at the Alpha currently in discussion with a dark-haired woman half his size. He's listening intently like what she says matters to him despite him being the one in charge.

"What does a beast know about wielding fae powers?" Bran asks.

"I heard that," Cal says before turning back to the woman.

Bran ignores the Alpha. "The point is," he starts, but I cut him off.

"The point is no one here knows what it is to wield fae power. I get it. But there's something else we're lacking."

Bran frowns. "Go on."

"We don't understand court politics. Or fae motivations. And while

Baspin might be able to help in some ways, it's Arion who knows the queen better." I pace to the left, thinking through the situation. "The queen wanted me to marry the prince, which means she needs me, but how far is she willing to bend to get me? I bet Arion knows."

"Yes, and he is currently on his way to murder us."

"Arion wants redemption." I pace back. "Not revenge."

"Get to the point, little mouse," Bran says.

"I need to speak to the queen," I blurt out.

The discussion between the shifters has stalled and they're all looking at me now like I've gone absolutely mad. And maybe I have.

I glance back up at Bran. "Where did Damien take my sister?"

"Fuck no," Bran says, seeing where I'm going with this.

I give him a gentle poke in the chest and smile innocently at him. "Fuck yes."

———

Thirty minutes later, we're in the basement of Duval House, deep in the recesses of it where the air is cold and wet. I shiver and rub my hands over my arms using friction to warm up.

Do I have to worry about my power if I get too cold? Guess we'll find out.

Bran leads me down an uneven hallway that's constructed of old stone. He has to duck to navigate it.

Cal is behind me, with his third-in-command, Keiko, behind him. Keiko is the dark-haired woman who, I later learned, was trying to talk him out of joining this fight. He took her concerns and decided to ignore them. Despite all that, she volunteered to join us, leaving Fox in charge at the Pack House.

"If you're going to be an idiot," she'd said, "I'm going to make sure I have your back while you're doing it."

I think she's annoyed with me simply because I'm at the center of his stupidity, but I'm secretly in awe of her.

Who talks to the Midnight Alpha that way and lives to tell the tale? Keiko, that's who.

When we reach the end of the hallway, there is a single naked bulb hanging from the stone ceiling and it sends sharp light and sharper shadows around the space.

Two vampires greet us and unlock a thick wooden door, allowing us inside.

Damien is there with my sister. Kelly is sitting in a wooden chair, her legs chained to the floor, her left wrist chained to the wall.

"Jessie!" She lurches upright to give me a hug, like she's relieved to see me, but the chain is too short and the force of it going taut yanks her back down.

"She's just pretending," Damien says. He's leaning against the wall, legs crossed at the ankles, arms crossed over his chest.

"It was worth a shot." My sister's face goes blank, all of the emotion gone from her voice.

"Summer Queen?" I ask.

"Where are we, princess?" She looks beyond me to Bran, then the Alpha and Keiko. "I didn't know the vampires worked with the shifters. Much has changed since the gate was sealed."

"I have a question for you." I go to the center of the room where the floor dips down, the stone worn over time.

"Ask it then," she says.

I try not to get distracted by the fact that my sister is being possessed by a fae queen.

When will Kelly catch a break? Hasn't she suffered enough because of me?

"Why did you really want me to marry the prince?"

She takes in a deep breath, hands resting on her knees. She considers me for several long moments, and I realize even through Kelly, she can't lie. It's why she's taking her time answering, choosing her words carefully.

"I wish to restore the balance to the fae realms."

Obviously true if she said it, but it's too easy, too obvious. There has to be more to it.

And then another truth dawns on me.

If the Summer Queen must speak the truth through Kelly, then perhaps she can also be commanded through Kelly.

"Tell me why you really want me to marry Maven."

It's easy to tap into my voice. Bran has been drilling the lesson into me for weeks.

It's not the same power as the frost or the cold, and not nearly so new to me.

And I see the moment the queen realizes her mistake.

Her eyes get wide as the power latches on to her and she's compelled to answer.

"Maven is a Winter bastard." She clamps her free hand over her mouth.

"*Tell me more*," I command. The power radiates at the center of me, warming my chest.

"Arion is next in line for the Summer Throne," she blurts out. "Which is why I plan to have him killed in this war. And once Maven is married to you, legitimizing his standing, I plan to kill you too."

"So you can rule both Summer and Winter," I finish. "*Tell me if I'm right.*"

She knows answering is inevitable, but she still fights forming the letters even as she says them.

"Yes." Her eyes narrow. "I want to rule it all."

I pull my cell phone from my pocket and stop the recording. "I'm sure Arion will love to hear this."

The Summer Queen, through my sister's body, grits her teeth and lunges for me.

Sixteen

The Summer Queen, possessing my sister, and determined to destroy me, doesn't make it any farther than a foot from her chair before Damien is between us, his back to me.

"Don't even consider it." His voice is quiet and even.

But a quiet, controlled Damien Duval is no less terrifying than a violent one.

I think that's where his violence resides: in the silence.

"Or you'll what?" The Summer Queen challenges using my sister's mouth, my sister's voice. "You'll do nothing to put your precious mortal girl at risk."

"It's not the mortal girl you have to worry about."

The queen's smile is tight for a beat before a laugh interrupts it. It's a little trill in the back of her throat, meant to sound sinister but instead betrays her fear.

Even with the gate sealed all these years, she must know of Damien's reputation. He's been around a long time.

The queen sits down again and the chair legs rock back and forth on the uneven stone floor.

"I guess that's it then?" Kelly—*the queen*—leans to the side so she can see me around the hard line of Damien's body. "We've drawn our lines, princess. So I will be going."

Kelly slumps suddenly, eyes closed, and then a second later, she's awake and screaming.

The chain rattles and grows taut as she lurches for the door. Damien catches her. "Stop. Look at me, Kelly."

Big, fat tears are streaming down her pale face. Her hands are practically claws on his bicep, like she's holding on with every ounce she has left.

She finally looks up. "Damien?"

"I'm here," he tells her, his tone soothing and filled with worry.

I know Kelly is strong—she had to be in order to take over my care when our mother died—but this is different.

The queen may be gone, but I'm not stupid. She can come back whenever she likes until we figure out how to sever that open magical link between Kelly and the fae realm, the one left over from the spell cast by the Renshaw witches.

With that connection still open, if the queen wanted to, could she make my sister jump off a bridge? Light herself on fire? I shudder at the possibilities. I don't want to contemplate all of the horrible things that woman could do to my sister if given the freedom to do it.

I'm grateful we caught the connection early enough so we could put Kelly in a safe location. The queen revealing it so soon was a reckless mistake.

She's clearly no strategist. Not like Bran and Damien.

And I'm going to use that to my advantage.

I turn away from Damien and my sister. "Please keep her safe," I tell him before I leave and he barely acknowledges me, as if to say, *How dare you question my dedication to her.*

At the door, I find the Alpha and his third-in-command waiting. "Well played," Cal says, nodding at the cell phone in my hand. "But how do you plan to get that recording in front of Arion?"

Bran comes up behind me. "He's lived here on the mortal side for decades. He must have a cell phone."

"Yeah, and do you have his number?" Cal asks.

"I'm sure someone does."

"No." I shake my head and make my way back down the stone hall-way. "I want to see his face when he hears the queen's words. I want to make sure he doesn't dismiss it as some kind of ploy."

They follow me out of the basement, and I realize, once we reach the first floor of Duval House, that they've all been waiting for me to give my final thoughts.

In the side hall, where the door to the basement is tucked into an alcove, I turn to the three of them. Bran, tall, dark, and scorchingly handsome, equal parts dangerous and terrifying, and Cal, hard-edged with muscle, raw with power, and Keiko, fierce, loyal, but willing to speak her mind, and all of them are staring at me waiting, willing to hear me out.

Not that long ago, I thought I was just a mortal girl who was destined to pledge her life to a vampire house and let her veins become a 24-hour buffet unless I escaped.

And now some of the most powerful figures in Midnight Harbor are watching me with interest, waiting to see what my plan is. As if my ideas might also hold value.

A flare of pride rushes through my body and because I'm a dork about this stuff, tears burn in my eyes until I sniff them back and turn away.

"Let's put together a team," I say over my shoulder, making my way back through the house to the library and the coffee bar. I need some caffeine first.

"A team for what?" Bran asks.

"A team to help separate my brother from his fae army."

Bran doesn't argue my plan. And neither does Cal. In fact, I think they like the plan way too much because they've assembled several vampires and three more shifters in a gallery hall in the back of Duval House in record time, much to Keiko's dismay.

I approach her as the vampires and Cal talk about possibilities and concerns.

"I'm really sorry he's dragged you into this," I tell her, lifting my chin in the Alpha's direction.

She uncorks a bottle of whiskey she's pulled from the small bar along the wall and pours a shot into a glass. "He didn't drag me into it. You did."

I wince. "The Alpha is his own man. He can make his own decisions."

Glass in hand, she takes a sip, but if the alcohol burns, she doesn't show it. "That's where you're wrong." She curls her arm inward, holding the glass up by her shoulder as she considers me. "A shifter is always fighting for balance with their animal. It's a give-and-take relationship. And what Cal and Cal's wolf want is their mate. And both of them think you have influence over that mating. So they're going to do whatever they can to protect you too."

I really can't argue with any of that. Cal said as much when he revealed the secret to me. But I would never force him to follow me into battle just to manipulate the situation with my best friend.

Keiko doesn't look much older than I am. Maybe in human years, she'd be about thirty. But as a shifter, I know she could easily be a hundred. Probably she has lots and lots of wisdom from experiences that I don't have.

"Okay," I say and pour myself a glass too, downing the shot for courage. I, unlike the dark-haired shifter, do wince at the burn. "If you were me, what would you do?"

She narrows her eyes, assessing me. She takes another tentative sip, letting the alcohol roll around on her tongue before swallowing it. "In your position, I would do the same thing." She knocks back the rest of the whiskey and sets the glass down with a loud thud. "Doesn't mean I have to like it."

"Fair enough."

"Just know that when it comes down to it, I'm protecting him, no matter what. Even if it leaves you in the lurch. Even if you end up dead. Even if he'll hate me for it later."

"I understand."

She crosses her arms over her chest. She's wearing a black crop top that's boxy on her lithe frame. There's an Art Deco dagger tattooed on the underside of her left arm with the initials MXP etched on the hilt.

"I would regret not trying one last effort to save him though," she says to me.

"What do you mean?"

She pulls her cell phone from the back pocket of her jeans and types out a message. It takes me a second to put it together—she's typing me a message so Cal won't hear it, whatever it is. In fact, I can feel his eyes on us, watching, waiting for some detail to slip.

Keiko shows me the screen.

Use your voice power on him. Turn him away from this.

I look over at Cal again. In the overhead lighting, his blond hair almost looks white. It's a sharp contrast from the black ink that swirls in an arch over each side of his scalp.

Our gazes lock and he gives me a barely perceptible shake of his head.

It doesn't matter what the request was, he doesn't want to ditch this fight.

And I think this might be where Keiko is wrong. I don't think Cal is here solely to protect me because I'm Sam's best friend. I think it's more complicated than that.

I think he's a good man who wants to do the right thing.

But I also think he and Bran are becoming friends, and men like Cal and Bran do not turn their backs on the people they care about.

It makes my chest a little warm and fuzzy with how adorable it is, but I don't want to get distracted by it. Not yet anyway. Someday when this is over I will properly admire their growing bromance.

For now, I need to focus on one thing: kidnapping my fae brother.

Seventeen

When I accidentally faced my fae brother in the mortal courthouse not that long ago, he overpowered me easily. I'm not so foolish now. I know better than to go toe-to-toe with him without a plan. Which means I need something else, an edge over him, even if I have been unbound and now have an unwieldy winter power that seems to have no qualms about harming anyone in its path.

I find myself, yet again, with a power I don't know how to use properly or control when I need it. So it's not a viable weapon.

I have the vampires and the shifters on my side, but they're the muscle. My best bet is witch or fae magic.

Which is why Bianca and Baspin are now sitting in the Duval House library at my invitation. Bran and Cal are with me. Cal is sitting in one of the leather chairs on my left enjoying a beer someone fetched for him. Bran is on my right, arms crossed over his chest. He already drank two glasses of bourbon, and he doesn't seem any less settled. If given the chance, I think he would tear Arion's head from his shoulders just for having the audacity to come after me.

"I need something that will help me kidnap Arion," I tell Bianca and Baspin.

Bianca's eyes get big. "Arion, as in the Lord of the Summer Court?"

"You know him?" I ask her.

"Of course. I did an exchange term with the fae in eleventh grade. I worked beneath him for months. He is extremely powerful."

"He's my brother," I tell her. "Half, actually."

"No fucking way." Her eyes get bigger and her mouth drops open. She looks at Baspin for confirmation.

"The girl tells the truth." Baspin has his legs crossed, one hand curled around the side of his face with his elbow propped on the arm of the chair. He seems bored, but I think that's just the way he is.

"How do I best him?" I ask them both.

"It won't be easy," Baspin says.

"I need everyone to stop telling me things will be easy or hard." I give Bran and Cal a pointed look.

Cal laughs through his nose and shakes his head. Bran just scowls at me.

"What would either stop Arion or subdue him?" I ask.

"I wish I could tell you I could help you with witch magic." Bianca frowns, her perfectly shaped brows sinking over her green eyes. "But if I'm being totally honest, witch magic is beneath fae magic. We usually need something to draw from. Blood, plants, elements. Fae magic can function on its own. It needs no source. It *is* the source."

I had no idea. And having no idea how the different magics even work is an embarrassing underscore on just how much I don't know about who and what I am. Or what I'm capable of.

"Okay." I glance at Baspin. "You got anything?"

"Well." He pulls his hand away from his face and straightens in the chair. "Weapons used against other fae are crafted with fae magic. There are lots of fae weapons in our realm and in yours. Obviously retrieving one from your side would be easier than journeying into the fae realm. So my question would be, do you know of anyone in Midnight who possesses objects crafted by the fae?"

My mind goes to Stanley first. Maybe he has weapons hiding in the diner? But no, I don't think so. It's not like he crafted a magical spatula in his spare time. And what would I do with that anyway? Tempt Arion out of hiding with a magical grilled cheese?

So Stanley is out.

And then I remember something I spotted on Rita's shelves in her office in the back of the coffee shop when I confronted her about the amulet.

"What about a red flower called fae quarrel?" I ask.

Baspin sits upright. "Are you sure it wasn't Qua rrel?"

When he pronounces it, it sounds like two words, not one, with a roll of his tongue on the R.

"Maybe?" I admit. The label on Rita's jar was peeling and faded, the handwriting hasty. "Why?"

He narrows his eyes. "Where do you have a Qua rrel?"

"Tell me what it is first."

With a sigh, he says, "The fae Qua rrel is typically crafted from *faerie botanica rubrum,* and if the one you have is red, then it sounds authentic. But the rubrum were destroyed in the Autumn Revolt."

"Why?" I ask.

"The Royal line from the Winter Court have the ability to control with their voice. But many years ago, they learned that if they put their magic into the rubrum flower, they could cast their control."

"So the flower is like a speaker or something?"

Baspin shakes his head. "It emits no sound. It's nearly undetectable. You merely speak into it what you want done and then place it wherever needed. In this case, you'd want it in the same room with Arion for it to work."

Despite the fact that I haven't set eyes on this flower in weeks, and don't even know if Rita would give it to me, or if I have the ability needed to put my magic into it, I ask Baspin, "Would you be willing to take it to Arion?"

He grins a smug, crooked grin. "Of course, Your Highness."

———

I still have keys to the coffee shop so when I call Rita to ask her if I can have the flower, she says, "I was wondering when you'd ask," and then tells me to go ahead and let myself in.

Bran and Cal and Keiko and Baspin all come to the coffee shop with me. It's late now and most of the shops on the street are closed, so we don't look too out of place, a merry band of vampire, shifter, and fae entering a witch's coffee shop.

The others wait in the front while Bran and I make our way to the back. I find the jar right where I spotted it before, tucked in between books and other jars full of various witchy goodies.

Gingerly, I bring the jar down and inspect the flower inside. The petals look just as velvety as I remember them, but the stamen has a slight glow to it that I didn't notice before.

"You haven't said much about this plan." I look up at Bran, hovering by the doorway.

"All of it is a risk to you and so I am worried about every part of it."

There's no emotion in his voice, but his words are telling enough. Bran has gotten really good over the years at hiding his emotions, but I like that he doesn't mince words with me anymore.

He tells me like it is, even if it shows his vulnerabilities.

"Just think of how amazing our lives will be if we can get over this hump."

He snorts. "You say that like it's a flat tire or an unwanted bill."

"I'm optimistic."

"I've never had patience for optimism."

"I know." I go to him, clutching the flower jar close to my chest, almost like it's a baby. "You're more pragmatic. Just stab people who don't agree with you."

He tries to pretend like that doesn't amuse him, but it does. I can see the glint in his eye.

"Tell me I'm wrong."

"Yes, fine, little mouse. I like killing people who get in my way. If that makes me pragmatic, then so be it."

I grow serious. "I don't want to kill Arion. He's the only real family I have left."

Bran tilts his head, examining me. "You do know that blood means nothing when one is trying to kill you."

"You can't tell me you and Damien haven't tried to kill each other once or twice."

"Of course we have. The difference is, he and I are immortal, and we are very hard to kill for real. You age slowly and heal quicker than mortals. But you are not invincible. Not like a vampire."

"Thanks for pointing out my deficiencies."

"I'm serious, Mouse. One must always know their limitations. You can't win a war by pretending you have none."

For a second I fall into his trap, and I believe him. After all, I've spent most of my life believing I had many, many limitations in a town full of supernatural beings that had none.

But I'm not that girl anymore.

Like Bran already told me, I never was her.

I was always a fae princess, always careening toward war, whether I knew it or not.

"Do you believe in me?" I ask him.

He uncrosses his arms. "I believe in your determination," he admits. "I worry about your recklessness." His gaze goes distant, like he's trapped by a thought.

"And?" I prompt.

"And—" His eyes dart back to me, irises just beginning to glow amber. "And if I lost you, I would come undone. So I worry about your recklessness, about you getting hurt. And most of all, I worry about who I would become if I lost you."

My heart squeezes in my chest, hearing his admission.

I set the jar down on Rita's desk and then lunge at Bran, wrapping my arms around his neck, kissing him fiercely.

He sinks into the kiss easily with a welcoming ferocity, his hands gripping the backs of my thighs, hoisting me up into his arms.

When we break the kiss, I tell him, "You've taught me how to be calculated."

He kisses me again, slipping me his tongue.

I pull back. "And you've taught me how to be brave."

He grumbles. "Should have never done that."

"And most importantly, you've taught me how to be fierce."

He spins me around and presses me against the doorframe, planting another kiss on my mouth. And all of his love and worry and fear for us makes me fizzy with happiness, but it also makes me bold.

"I want to take my rightful place in the court," I confess.

Our mouths linger, just an inch apart. My hair spills forward as I press my forehead against his.

"Whatever will come of me, I need to do it, Bran."

He closes his eyes, stealing the amber glow for a split second. His shoulders rise with a deep breath and then he expels it, ruffling my hair.

When he opens his eyes again, he nods against me. "You must do what you must do. No one knows better than me that regret will haunt you like a ghost."

I don't need him to tell me he's referring to his little sister and I don't want to press him for more of it.

"Thank you." I kiss him with a quick peck and then he lets me down to retrieve the flower.

Is it reckless to put so much faith in a flower trapped in a jar?

Maybe. But this is about more than defeating the Summer Queen.

It's as much about her as it is about saving my brother.

And I'm willing to do whatever it takes to get him on my side.

Eighteen

The flower is innocuous on its own. Faintly tropical with its long, curling petals and vibrant red color. But when Mouse opens the jar and plucks the flower from inside, the petals unfurl for her and the stamen glows brighter.

If there was any question of its magical nature before now, it's quashed.

Mouse looks up at me and smiles, the glow of the flower glancing off her cheeks.

Watching her become the fae princess she's always been is fucking sexy as hell. Even if I object to her chasing power and waging war. Even if I dislike her endangering herself. Perhaps there was always some deep, dark part of me that wanted a partner who could fuck shit up beside me.

Because watching that powerful, magical flower react to Mouse like she's the sun has me slightly aroused.

"So now what?" Mouse asks Baspin. Long curling vines grow from the cut stem. Several of them curl around her index finger, but gently, I notice. As if they don't want to hurt her.

Behind me, the Alpha and his third-in-command are whispering to one another. I can hear every word—she's still worried about the risk, and the Alpha is being far too nice about being questioned.

Of course, Jimmy questions me all the time. I suppose I can understand where the Alpha is coming from.

"The power is already open to you," Baspin tells Mouse, nodding at the glowing flower in her hand. "Now use your voice and tell it what you want. But be careful with the words. You have to be extremely direct and concise."

Mouse nods. We've already discussed what we'd like the flower to do, what commands we'd like it to issue to Arion. That's not the hard part. The hard part will be getting it to him, and then getting him out, separate from his army.

We've discussed that too, but it's a bit of a risky plan.

Mouse bends forward and whispers to the flower. There is a hint of a blush to her cheeks, as if she feels silly speaking to a plant.

"*Arion*," she says, using the power of her voice, "*come to me directly, without question, without harming anyone, without speaking a word of it to anyone. You'll find me at my home. Bran will take you there.*"

I'm not one to be physically moved by words, but when Mouse uses her voice, it's fucking nirvana. Even though the words aren't directed at me or the Alpha or his shifter, we're all a little dazzled by it.

It's like a cool drink of water on a hot summer day.

The flower pulses once, then twice, and then the glow fades until the flower looks like any flower.

"Is that it?" Mouse asks.

Baspin gives her a nod of encouragement. "That should suffice. Well done, Your Highness."

She smiles at the title now instead of cringing.

She's well on her way to being a queen.

———

Because I'm still an asshole who wants to shield Mouse at all costs, we split up. Jimmy takes her to her former house in Midnight suburbia, while the Alpha, Baspin, Bianca, and I go to Bramwell Park.

Our latest intel on the fae lord is that he's preparing for our battle in the fae grotto. So we need to get inside and get to him. I suspect he doesn't want to fight his sibling and so offering him some kind of truce will get us an audience with him. After that, things get a little shaky and I'm putting all of my faith in Baspin and Bianca.

"Everyone know what to do?" I ask them on the edge of Bramwell, far from the grotto's entrance.

The Alpha strips off his clothes without hesitation. Shifters care not for modesty.

Though most shifters have a hard time using their animal form outside of a full moon, most Alphas I've met can use their animal at will. It comes with the power. And Cal is no different.

Within seconds, a few pops of his joints, a contortion of his back, the Alpha is a wolf.

His animal form is a large black wolf with bright yellow eyes. It's plain to anyone that he's a shifter and not a wolf, considering his shoulders reach as high as my torso. But we're not trying to hide that fact.

"Ready?" I ask them and they all give me a nod. Cal growls deep in his throat. "Let's go kidnap a fae lord, then, shall we?"

———

The hidden door into the fae grotto appears as soon as we near it, almost like they were waiting. Two guards come out to greet us and Baspin, as planned, speaks for us. "Friends of the princess would like to speak to our esteemed lord to discuss a truce."

The guards stand back, giving us entrance and we move forward with Baspin in the lead, the Alpha at our rear. His hearing is better than all of ours combined in wolf form, and we all agreed if an attack were to come from behind, he'd be the one to hear it first.

The grotto is quiet as we're led across the main gathering room. It's a far cry from the party atmosphere when I was here last.

In fact, I don't see a single soldier. Baspin already warned us that the soldiers are likely hiding in the level below the main hall, so this isn't unexpected.

I'm not nervous, *yet*.

We're led to a hallway tucked behind a half-wall of entangled vines. Yellow and purple flowers bloom along the vines and the air smells sickly sweet with their scent.

At the end of the hallway, two large, arched doors pull open, revealing a suite of rooms beyond. "Our Summer Lord will see you here," one of the guards says and gestures for us to enter.

I glance at Baspin, and he gives me a nod. I don't yet know if I trust the lower ranking fae, but he's all I have, so I go with it.

Beside me, Bianca's fists are curled at her side and her teeth worry at her bottom lip. Before the fae lord comes in, I grab her hand and give her a squeeze. She glances up at me. I need her relaxed. I need her in control. Not afraid. Not anxious.

She swallows and gives me a nod and I let go.

The anteroom has a domed ceiling with more vines. Tendrils of moss grow along the thicker branches. Lanterns are fastened to the wall every six feet, giving the hollowed room a bright golden glow.

The furniture is elegant and gilded, the furniture of royalty.

If only Arion knew he had more of a right to the throne than Maven does.

If all goes as planned, he'll know by sunrise.

At the far corner of the room, the wall pops open, revealing a door.

The fae lord steps through.

He's in full battle gear. I know this for the tactic it is. He wants us to know he means to follow through.

I have no doubts about him or his intentions.

He scans us. "Where is she?" he asks. "And why bring a dog?"

The *dog* growls.

"This is the Midnight Alpha," I tell him. "Have some respect."

Now he's on guard. His shoulders rock back, his fingers twitching at his side. "Last I knew, the vampires and the shifters were not cooperative."

"We've had a change of heart," I answer.

"That change of heart have anything to do with a fae princess and impending war?"

"Don't all changes of heart start with war?"

He tilts his head, regarding me. I can tell he wants to reach for his sword but won't risk war right here in his pretty little grotto.

"And the witch?"

"I don't trust your fae," I say and nod at Baspin. "I needed some kind of magical intervention just in case."

"She's no match for me," he says.

"I have no doubt."

"So, you come to speak of a truce. Speak."

It's ironic, really. Speak we shall.

"Baspin?" I say.

He smiles at his superior. Even I can tell the smile is loaded. Is Arion really so oblivious that he never noticed Baspin's ambitions?

"My lord," Baspin says and bows ever so slightly. And as he does, he reaches inside the pocket of his pants and produces the flower with a flourish.

Everything hinges on this moment, this magical flower. And for a brief second, I worry that Baspin has tricked us all. That somehow this plant will do nothing but earn us a laugh from both fae, but the look on Arion's face tells me all there is to know. It's a look of horror.

He tries to bring his hands to his ears, boxing out the sound, but he's not quick enough.

Mouse's voice slithers from the petals. The stamen glows, the anther pulsing, the filaments stretching.

The command comes in a whisper, a ribbon of words curling in the air.

Arion's back goes rigid as Mouse's voice takes over like she is the puppeteer, and Arion her man on strings.

The fae lord grits his teeth, his arms locked at his sides. "Clever," he says. "But you'll never get me past my guards."

"Let us worry about that," I tell him. "Witch?"

She goes over to the fae lord, her gaze downcast as if she's afraid to meet his eyes. "Bianca, isn't it?" Arion says. "I remember you working for me a few years ago. This isn't like you."

She licks her lips. "I've made my loyalties, and I am a woman of her word."

"Hurry, witch," I tell her.

Cal trots up beside her and Bianca buries her hand in his thick ruff. She whispers several foreign words and magic glitters in the air.

"You'll pay for this," Arion says right before he turns into a wolf, an exact copy of Cal.

The Alpha shifts back to his human form and gives his shoulders a roll.

Bianca's face turns bright red at the sight of the fully nude Alpha. She turns away, a hand over her mouth.

Baspin points at the door Arion entered from. "Through there," he tells the Alpha, "then the second door on the left. Follow the hall all the way down. Take another left. That's where the hall will turn into a tunnel. There will be other fae coming and going. Make sure you use your nose to avoid them. If you need concealment, you'll find lots of alcoves dark enough for you in your wolf form to hide. Keep going straight and you'll eventually come to a door. That'll get you out the other side of Bramwell Park."

"Be careful," I tell the Alpha.

"I'm more careful than you," he counters.

"I'm just saying, I would hate for you to get your dick cut off in a faerie grotto on my account."

He laughs. "I'm glad you care, Duval. I'll meet you at Jessie's house in thirty minutes."

"Make it twenty," I tell him, and he grumbles before shifting back into his wolf and slipping through the door.

"Here we go," I tell the rest of them and snap my fingers at the newly transformed fae lord. "Come, doggie."

He growls, but come he does.

Nineteen

I pace the front room of my house, hands balled into fists.

Every now and then, frost spiderwebs across the living room windows and I have to stop and take in several deep breaths so the power doesn't get away from me.

"It's going to be all right, Jessie," Jimmy says, but I know she can't know that, and she's just trying to keep me from turning the house into an igloo.

"Arion is powerful," I say and swivel back around once I've reached the dining table. "And he's not on my side."

"*Yet*," she reminds me. She's leaning against the casing on the front window, arms crossed casually over her chest. She's wearing a black t-shirt and black leggings that, on anyone else, would look like a yoga outfit. But I know better—those are the clothes of a warrior ready for battle.

"What if he turns on Bran before Bianca can work her magic? Or worse, what if the Summer Queen ambushes him and—"

Jimmy's line of sight pivots to the street.

My heart hammers in my ears as I skirt around the couch and join her side.

Bran is standing in the front yard with the Alpha, Keiko, Bianca, and Baspin. And on Bran's left is a large wolf with watching eyes.

"I smell blood," Jimmy says and hurries to the front door.

We cross the porch together, but she's down the steps in a blur of movement and in front of Bran a half second later, examining him with a sweep of her hands.

"It's not mine, Jim," Bran tells her.

When I come up behind her, and the light from the streetlights hits him just right, I can see what she was worried about. There's blood splattered across his face, dribbling down his neck, smeared across his shirt.

"What happened?" I ask.

"Ran into a bit of trouble on our exit," Baspin answers.

"Bran took care of it," Bianca fills in.

Jimmy steps back, giving me room. "Are you okay?" I ask him.

There's still a faint pulsing glow to his irises, but I don't see any wounds. "I'm fine," he tells me. "But it's hard to say how he'll feel about it all when we make him fae again." He tips his head at Arion still in wolf form. "Were they friends of yours, fae?"

Arion growls at us.

"How long will the Qua rrel's command last?" I ask Baspin.

"We have at least a few more hours."

"Good. Bianca, turn him back?"

"Of course." She steps forward and whispers two sharp words. There's a soft WHUMP, then a flash of light.

When the air clears, Arion is crouched in front of me on all fours. He stands to his full height, rolling his shoulders, stretching out his joints. There's anger etched into the space between his dark brows. "Never do that again," he warns me.

"We did what we had to do," I tell him, squaring myself against him. "You never would have come otherwise."

"Well, I'm here. Now what?" He grits his teeth. "I'm still at your command, *Your Highness*."

He says the latter with enough venom to sting, as if the title is a sham. Maybe it is.

But I'm not going to let him get beneath my skin.

"We need to talk." I turn back for the house. "Come inside, listen to what I have to say, and then you'll be free to go."

He frowns. "Just like that?"

I pause halfway up the stairs to glance at him over my shoulder. "Just like that. No one will hurt you. You have my word."

———

Arion, Lord of the Summer Court, paces around my living room, eyeing the forgotten stack of magazines, the framed family portraits. I pour us each a glass of wine.

Bran agreed to give me and Arion privacy, but I can see his shadow on the porch, and I know he's hanging on every word just waiting for an excuse to barge in. I'm glad for his protection.

"You really did live an entirely different life, didn't you?" Arion's squinting at a framed picture of me and Kelly at the aquarium several years back.

I hand him the glass of wine, then take a sip from mine. "It seems like someone else's life, if I'm honest."

"Do you wish you could go back?"

"No. Never." I tip my head at the photo. "That was a lie and I felt it every day in my bones, even if I didn't know what it meant."

I watch him for recognition.

Does he know?

Does he know he's being used, that the Summer throne will be his if the Summer Queen is deposed?

His frown deepens. He sets the wine glass down without drinking. Smart. Smarter than I am, apparently. "What do you want to say to me? Say it so we can be done."

"Do you want to be fighting this war?"

"Why?"

"Just answer the question."

"You're not going to make me?" The last part, bitten out.

"No."

He huffs out a breath. "I didn't want any of this."

"And by *this*, you mean killing our mother?"

His nostrils flare. "You know nothing about our mother. Careful what you speak of her."

"You're right." My anger flares up to match his. "I know nothing about her because she's dead. And I will never have a chance to know her unless you tell me."

"What is this about, Jessie? What do you want from me?"

I pull my cell phone from my pocket, tapping at the screen. His confusion doubles. I bring up the recording and hit play.

It's clear the voice is Kelly's, but the tenor is off and there's a slight echo as if she's speaking through a microphone.

I watch Arion's face for his reaction as Kelly—the Summer Queen—makes her plan known.

She'll kill Arion. She'll install her illegitimate son on both thrones.

Arion staggers back. His eyes are wide, but his focus far away.

"Is this some kind of trick?" he asks. There's pain in his voice, an almost desperate plea. He wants it to be a trick. If it's a trick, then it's a lie, and if it's a lie, he can continue on with his life.

I shake my head. "I don't want to fight you, Arion. I want to fight *with* you."

He turns away, shoulders a rigid line.

"She's using you," I go on. "She's been using you to get what she wants."

He whirls on me. "And what are you doing right now? Are you not also using me to get what you want?"

"How dare you!" I surge forward, pointing a finger at him. "I didn't ask for any of this. I didn't ask to be born into this family. I didn't ask to be switched out a birth. Smuggled away. I just want to be left alone! I barely know what it is to be fae—"

"Jessie."

"—I want to stay in Midnight Harbor with my vampire boyfriend and live my fucking life!"

"Jessie!"

I find Bran's hands on me, frost turning his pale skin a paler blue. Ice grows from the pendant light hanging over the dining table and snow falls from the ceiling.

When I breathe out, it's a puff of white air.

"I'm sorry," I say. "I didn't...I don't know how to control it yet."

Arion swallows, nods. "It's all right."

"I just want—"

"I have to go." He turns for the door.

"Wait, Arion—"

Bran pulls me back. "Let him go."

"What? Why?"

"You just shattered his worldview, Mouse. Let the man digest it."

Arion disappears out the front door and down the front steps. Everything in me says to stop him from going. But I know Bran's right. If I want my brother to join me, I can't rush him into it, even if the clock is ticking.

Twenty

Bran drives the Bimmer back to Duval House, blood still splattered across his face. I don't want to look at him and have dirty thoughts about him being bloody and savage, but I do. Bran unhinged is sexy as hell and I've come to miss that side of him. I think he's pulled back a lot lately, trying to let me stand on my own, let me take the spotlight.

And as much as I want my independence and autonomy, I also want Bran in all his bossy, bloody glory. Basically I want my cake and to eat it too.

It takes Bran no time at all to reach the house and after parking beneath the porte-cochere, he hands the Bimmer's keys over to the attendant at the side entrance. With sunrise fast approaching, I expect his energy to be waning, but I have to jog to keep up with him. He doesn't take me to the Anneliese. Instead, we head further into the mansion to a bedroom I've yet to visit.

It's dark and elegant like Bran, but with a bit more frill to it, with a gilded, tufted headboard and velvet upholstered furniture the color of dark moss.

Bran flicks on a light switch, but the giant crystal chandelier hanging from a hand carved medallion in the center of the ceiling stays dark, while several lamps and crystal sconces light up around the room keeping it cozy and semi-dark.

There's a large, flat screen TV hanging on the wall directly across from the bed and on the opposite wall, with two wingback chairs in front of it, is a giant fireplace, the mantel and surround carved from marble.

"Is this your room?" I ask him.

"It's *a* room," he tells me and strips off his t-shirt. "This is still the safest place for you, but the Anneliese will do nothing to keep a fae out. It's best to stay in an unassigned room in the bowels of Duval House."

I crane my neck at the high ceilings, the delicate crown molding. "I wouldn't necessarily call this the bowels."

The zipper on his jeans comes down and he tears them off quickly, tossing them into a nearby bin.

Now he's standing in the soft golden light in nothing but black boxer briefs with blood dried and flaking on his pale skin and a hungry glow to his eyes.

I can make out every hard-edge of muscle, every tendon, bone, and vein swelling beneath his skin. He looks like he's lost weight—not much, but enough to notice.

"Have you been eating?" I ask him. "Drinking," I correct.

Nothing about his expression changes, but I still sense his gnawing hunger. It's the way he holds himself rigid, as if he's afraid that one sudden movement might result in violence.

I'm not worried about him losing control around me, but I am worried about him being satiated.

I reach up and pull a length of my hair aside, exposing my neck to him.

Just the thought of him biting me has my heart jumping in my chest.

I see the moment he decides to take my offering.

His irises flare amber and he zeros in on the echoing pulse point in my neck.

One second he's standing still across the room, and the next he's a blur as he crosses it, grabbing me roughly, and driving me back against the wall. He sinks his teeth into my neck with all the delicacy of a hammer and a startled cry comes out of my throat.

But Bran doesn't stop.

Fangs sunk into my flesh, he draws on me. There is heat and pain, but pleasure too and my body is confused by which to give in to. Instinctively I try to draw away from him, but his grip is rough and firm at the back of my neck, keeping me against him as he pulls on my blood. And his command of me has a buzzing pleasure slithering down my belly, down between my legs.

Bran takes another long drink of my blood, groaning against me as his hard cock grinds into my thigh.

He pulls back just long enough to tell me, "You make me lose my fucking mind, Mouse." He drags his tongue over the puncture wound and a shiver races down my spine as the soft golden light catches the dark wetness before his eyes slip closed and he swallows it back.

"You have to drink," I tell him. "You can't hold off like that."

He smiles at me, eyes burning orange in the dim lighting. "Don't tell me what to do, little mouse." His grin turns dangerous. "That's my job." His hand comes to my shoulder and drives me down to my knees in front of him.

My clit buzzes with excitement. Sometimes, with Bran, the way he controls me and teases me with his words is more potent than any touch.

He's straining against his underwear as he takes a fistful of my hair and wrenches my head back. With his other hand, he drags his thumb over my bottom lip, parting my mouth for him.

"Be a good girl for me, Mouse," he says.

He doesn't give me further instruction, but I know what he means.

I grope him first, provoking him, and a growl rumbles in his chest.

Wrapping my hair around his knuckles, he pulls hard, angling me up to him. "Don't tease me, Mouse. Not tonight. Open up." He pulls down the waistband of his underwear, freeing his cock. He prods my mouth with the head and when I open for him, he plunges inside, immediately filling me up.

"Fuck," he says on a growl, pumping his hips into me. "That's what

I need. I needed your tight fucking mouth wrapped around my cock, the taste of your blood on my tongue."

I suck in a breath through my nose as he holds me in place, using me for his pleasure.

I'm buzzing all over, feeling dirty and so fucking needy for him.

I'm dripping wet, burning with desire, but in no rush for him to be done with me.

I love it when he can't think of anything but me, anything but the pleasure I give him.

His pace picks up and he wraps his hand around my throat as he spills in my mouth. It's a hot spurt of cum, too much almost, and I have to quickly swallow it back, tears burning in my eyes.

He pulls out, lets me take a deep breath, before saying, "Clean it up, Mouse. All of it."

Another drop of cum leaks out of him and I swipe my tongue over the slit, following his command.

Gods, I want him to touch me.

I'm practically a writhing ball of wicks needing desperately to ignite.

Lips swollen, eyes still teary from being fucked brutally in the mouth, I look up at him. "Fuck me or touch me or do whatever you want with me," I tell him. "But I need you."

In a blur of movement, he hoists me up over his shoulder and carries me to the bed, tossing me down. Using his vampire speed and strength, he has me fully naked within seconds.

"Hands on the headboard," he orders and I scurry over the thick duvet, doing as he commands.

As he lines himself up at my entrance, he reaches around, capturing my breast in his hand, teasing my nipple.

I push back against him, wanting him inside of me, and he gives me a smack across the ass for it.

"Be patient, Mouse."

I practically whimper beneath him.

He plays with my nipple, pinching it, causing me to jolt beneath him and I feel the answering swell of his cock against me.

"Please, Bran," I say on a moan.

His hand sinks between my legs, two fingers swirling around my clit. "Hear how wet you are, Mouse?"

"Yes," I breathe out.

"You want to come?"

"Yes."

"Beg me for it."

"Please Bran. Please let me come." I rock against him again and the head of his cock sinks in an inch. I push back, but he shifts his hold to my hips, keeping me firmly in place.

"You keep pushing that ass into me," he says, "and I might have to fuck it."

I don't care where he fucks me, so long as he does.

I push back again, tempting him, and then fall all the way back when he disappears in a gust of air.

He returns with a bottle of lube a second later.

"Get back up there," he tells me, so I resume my position, hands on the carved headboard. A shot of cool gel hits my ass and Bran uses the head of his cock to spread it around.

It's not that cheap department store shit — the lube is slick, but not sticky, and his cock slides over me easily, waking up all of those sensitive nerves.

Fisting himself, he pushes in slowly and the pressure is immediate as he stretches me out, filling me up.

He goes in another inch and groans. "Your ass is so tight, Mouse, you might make me come again."

I hold onto the headboard, knuckles almost white as my pussy tingles, needing his touch, needing release.

The lube helps him go in slowly, but without resistance and when he's nearly all the way inside, he starts pumping into me.

"God, I love fucking your ass," he says. "So fucking tight, Mouse."

When he finds a good rhythm, his hand comes around, his fingers still slick with lube as he teases at my clit. His fingers slide over me so easily.

I'm buzzing so much that his touch feels electric and a gasp comes out of me as the wave swells up, unbidden.

"I'm not going to last long," I warn him.

"Neither will I in that ass." He fucks me faster and our fucking is loud and untamed.

"Come for me, Mouse. I want to feel your ass tighten around my cock."

He plays with my clit again and finds the most mind-blowing tempo, slow but persistent, that I come fast and hard for him.

And as my cries fill the room, he pushes his hips forward, sinking his cock deep into my backside, spurting another load inside of me.

Oh my fucking god.

My body trembles. Jolts. Shivers again as the pleasure races through my veins.

I feel like I'm floating. Like I've left this plane and am just flying through a deliciously warm ether.

Arms shaking, thighs trembling, I sink forward and Bran slips out of me, dropping onto the bed beside me.

His hand comes to rest on my ass.

"You are fucking divine," he says.

I laugh into the pillow. "I could say the same for you. I love it when you boss me around."

"I know."

I look over at him and find his eyes glowing bright orange. "I needed that," I confess.

"We need each other," he admits. "Especially in times of chaos."

"I love you," I tell him and shift over so I can snuggle into the crook of his arm.

"I love you too, Mouse."

I reach up to kiss him and unlike our fucking, our kiss is slow, gentle, soft.

It almost makes me want to cry how grateful I am for him, how lucky I feel to have him.

"I should clean up," I tell him and move to get up.

"Five more minutes." He tucks me back into his side. "Just five more minutes and then I'll clean you myself."

"Deal," I tell him and return to his side, but it doesn't take long before we're both out.

Twenty-One

I wake with a start and look around the unfamiliar room.

For a second I think I must be dreaming, or worse, kidnapped again, and then I see the long line of Bran's body next to me in bed. His eyes are open and he's staring right at me. He's still got speckles of blood on his skin.

I sigh and drop back to the bed. "How long have you been awake?"

The heavy drapes have been pulled closed, but there's a sliver of daylight stealing through a part in the curtains. He should be sleeping.

"A while," he answers.

"Can't sleep?"

"Something like that."

I suppose I can't blame him, considering what we're about to face.

I roll into his side and he tucks me into the crook of his arm. I inhale his scent. The familiarity warms my belly. That heady vampire scent of his, a little coppery with blood but with an edge of something masculine, that leather and amber I love so much.

"I have an idea."

He absently plays with my hair. "Go on."

"Let's shower and get dressed and go to Stanley's for a grilled cheese."

He laughs lightly, the rock of his shoulders jostling me. "Of course you would pick a grilled cheese as your last supper."

I rise up, propping myself on my elbow. "Excuse me. I plan to win this thing. Last supper, my ass."

He laughs again. "All right, little mouse. Ask and you shall receive." He climbs from bed and holds out his hand for me. We're both still naked and I ogle his backside as he leads me into the attached bathroom. He really does have the finest ass.

———

I'm half expecting to find Stanley's closed, what with the impending war. Thankfully, Stanley is nothing if not consistent. The Greasy Spoon is open seven days a week, come rain, hail, snow, or war.

"Well, look what the cat dragged in!" Judy shouts from behind the counter. "Our favorite customer."

The others seated inside the diner look up at me and frown, clearly annoyed that the server has decided to pick favorites.

I recognize a group of people I went to school with at the big U-shaped booth in back. Their gazes dart between me and Bran. I know we are an unlikely pair. And there's no way in hell anyone I went to school with would have ever considered me up to the standard of the Duvals.

Well, look at me now, side by side with *Thee Duval*, still full of his cum.

I start to slide into the booth where the seat faces the door but Bran gives me a shake of his head.

"I need to watch the front," he tells me.

I roll my eyes. "If someone wanted to ambush us, they could just as easily come through the back door."

"Yes, but the backdoor is metal. I'll hear it clank open. They have twice as much ground to cover to reach you from the back door as they do the front. So, I sit here." He points at the bench seat facing the front. "You sit there."

Well, his logic is sound, but I'm not about to tell him that. "Fine."

We slide into the booth. Judy comes over, her order pad tucked into her apron pocket. "Do I even need to ask?" she says to me.

"Nope. Give me the usual."

She nods and then glances at Bran. "And for you?"

"Coffee. Black."

"Coming right up." She disappears behind the counter.

"So," I say.

"So," Bran says.

"What now?"

He spreads one arm over the back of the booth. Freshly showered, the blood scrubbed from his skin, he could easily pass as human, but he would never blend into a crowd. There is something extremely bold about Bran Duval. Like a fast sports car with sharp edges and a roaring engine.

That's what he is here, or anywhere. Unmistakable. I can feel the eyes of my former classmates watching us. And I'm so glad I'm here, on the other side of the booth with Bran instead of across the diner speculating what it's like to have a Duval.

What a lucky girl I am.

Other than the brother that wants to kill me, of course. And the sister possessed by a fae queen. And a bastard fae prince that I'm sorta still betrothed to.

"*What now?*" Bran repeats, his gaze casually scanning the diner and the street beyond. "Well, your brother didn't show up at Duval House to gut us, so I think that's a good sign."

"Is it?"

Judy reappears at our table with a black coffee and a Diet Coke for me. "Stanley's making that grilled cheese for ya, sugar. Be just a few more minutes."

"Thanks, Judy."

Bran sits forward and lets the steam from the coffee curtain between us. "Have you thought about what happens when you win this war?"

A cold chill runs down my spine. "No, why?"

That's a lie. I have thought about it. Quietly. In the deep, dark recesses of my mind. Even if I didn't want it, even if most of the fae realm wants me dead, I still feel a sense of responsibility to the throne. The fae realm is in chaos, the seasons out of sync. They're in trouble and they need me to help fix it.

But even if everything worked out perfectly in my favor, what does that future look like? And how will Bran fit into it?

Bran levels me with an intense stare. I squirm beneath his gaze.

"You have thought about it," he says, more statement than accusation. "And you and I both know that if you win, you'll have to return to the fae realm, claim your throne, and then guard it every day for the rest of your life."

I swallow hard.

I know he's right.

"If I do that," I start, feeling suddenly sick to my stomach, "will you come with me?"

He opens his mouth to answer but then quickly clamps it shut again as his gaze darts up to the door. He lurches out of the booth. I spin around on the bench, following his alertness and find Arion walking up to the diner.

Oh shit.

I hurry out of the booth, wanting to be on my feet. Bran steps in front of me, shielding me from my brother as he pulls the door open, the bell chiming to ring out his entrance.

Stanley is suddenly beside me, a plate in hand, a crispy grilled cheese steaming beside a pile of fresh fries. "Not here," he warns Arion.

Arion, Lord of the Summer Court, looks down at Stanley. "I have no intention of fighting."

"Then what *is* your intention?" Bran asks.

Arion takes one step to the left so he can look at me over the broad line of Bran's shoulder. He swallows hard, tension showing in the fine lines around his eyes right before he sinks to one knee on the grimy black and white checkered floor of The Greasy Spoon.

He bows his head, and I think I might cry at this display of deference. "I've come to pledge my allegiance to you, my sister, heir apparent to the Winter Court."

There's an audible gasp from the crowd that has formed behind us.

My heart is racing in my chest.

Arion looks up, new fire in his eyes. "On one condition."

I lick my lips, take a deep breath. "What is it?"

"When it comes to the Summer Queen, it will be me and my blade that kills her."

Twenty-Two

I thought Arion wanted redemption, but now, looking down on him bending one knee to me in The Greasy Spoon, I see only the sharp want of revenge.

Maybe there's space for both for him. Maybe, in his position, there is not one without the other.

"You want to kill the Summer Queen?" I ask him. I want to be sure I'm not mishearing. Misunderstanding. I want to be extra clear that what he wants is also what I want so we can move forward.

"Yes." He gives me a curt nod to emphasize the answer.

"What changed your mind?"

The rest of the customers at The Greasy Spoon are watching, completely riveted. I can hear something bubbling in the fryer in back, but the air is taking on the scent of burning potatoes. Stanley is beside me, plate in hand, the white ceramic overwhelmed by a thick grilled cheese and a giant pile of fresh fries.

"You gave me compelling evidence," Arion answers. His nostrils flare, shoulders leveling in a tense straight line. "And if I'm completely honest, I always had my suspicions about Maven. The fact that the queen circumvented the truth about his lineage in order to skip me in the royal line of ascension is"—his teeth clench—"unforgivable."

"I agree," Bran says.

Arion's gaze shifts to Bran standing beside me. I don't think my brother likes Bran much, but there is a softening in the hard lines around his eyes.

"Get up," I say. "There's no need for you to be on the floor when we're both destined for thrones."

Making this bold statement sends butterflies skittering through my stomach.

Sometimes it still catches me off guard. All of it really. That I have a brother. That he's fae. That I'm supposed to inherit a fae throne of my own.

I can almost see it, he and I coming together in the fae realm, restoring the balance. Becoming friends even.

I want that.

I don't want to disappoint him.

He slowly climbs to his feet and dusts off his knee with a swipe of the back of his hand. He straightens out his jacket. It's royal blue with threading in gold and delicate stitching along the lapel showing swirls and four-petal flowers that sorta remind me of four-leaf clovers.

His blue-black hair is swiped back from his forehead and the sides are buzzed short as if he's just come from a fresh haircut.

"If you're serious," I say, "you and your blade can have the Summer Queen if you'll join me in fighting back against her. I sure as hell don't want to marry Maven."

Bran snorts.

"It won't come to that," Arion answers. "The betrothal was just a shroud meant to obscure the truth about Maven and the queen's ultimate plans to steal more power for herself. Once she realizes the ruse is up—"

"Once she realizes you are no longer her puppet, you mean?" I raise a brow.

"Yes." Arion nods. "Once she realizes she's lost both of her best avenues, she'll go to outright violence. It will not be pretty. She may be blinded by her hunger for control, but she isn't dumb, and she is powerful. She'll use all of her assets against us."

I can sense my grilled cheese growing colder by the second. Stanley is still standing there, waiting patiently to serve me. Though I think a little part of him wants to know the details too, and has stuck around so he could have them, regardless of whether or not he plans to fight. I don't think brownies ever do. They've been neutral as long as I've been alive, both here in Midnight, and in the history books we read in school.

"Sit down with us," I tell Arion. "Let me eat that delicious grilled cheese and you can fill us in on everything you know that might help us win this war."

While I swipe crispy, salty fries through a puddle of ketchup, Bran and Arion are discussing ways into the Summer Queen's palace using salt and pepper shakers and hot sauce bottles as entry points.

We have all of The Greasy Spoon to ourselves. Arion's arrival sent a few people running out the back door, and those that remained Stanley shooed out, claiming it was a fae holiday and the Spoon was closing early.

The people I went to school with nodded at me and called out hello as they passed my booth where I now sit beside Bran and across the table from a Summer fae lord.

I was never super popular in school. I had Sam and she was all I needed. Bianca was always friendly, though we were never close. Now I think I'm all anyone can gossip about in Midnight Harbor.

"What about this entry?" Bran asks.

Arion clucks his tongue and shakes his head. "This door and the hallway beyond it leads directly to the dance hall. There's no place to hide here." He lifts the lid on the straw dispenser, pulling out wrapped straws to make a rudimentary perimeter for the palace, then shifts the saltshaker to the back corner. "This is for deliveries. It tends to be busier during the day, but it's a great way inside, regardless of if we try to sneak in or waltz in, blending into the crowd."

I bite off a corner of my grilled cheese. "Which do you recommend?"

He hands me a napkin when cheese catches on the corner of my mouth.

"Thank you."

"It will be hard for us to blend in," Bran points out.

"Why can't you use the same magic you used to kidnap me?" Arion asks, just a hint of accusation in his voice.

I look over at Bran. "It's a good idea."

"We'd have to bring Bianca with us," he answers. "And I'm not so sure I'm willing to risk our witch in the fae realm."

"She'd say yes if you asked her." I take a sip of my Diet Coke, then lick my lips. "She made a choice to join Duval House to be an *asset* to Duval House. If you ask her, she'll want to help, and you should let her continue to make her own choices."

Both men are silent, staring at me.

"What?"

Bran blinks.

Arion says, "Sounding like a fair and honest queen already."

I blush because for some stupid reason, his compliments make me proud of myself.

I want my older brother to not only like me but respect me.

And more than anything, I want to live up to this title I was born with.

"All right, little mouse," Bran says. "We'll let the witch decide."

Arion steals one of my fries. "I'll be honest, Duval, I assumed your arrogance would get in your way and you'd constantly be at odds with Jessie as the power shifts. You're surprising me."

"Jessie and I are on the same page," Bran answers, indifferent.

"No, you're not." Arion bites off the end of the fry. "You're not even in the same book."

"We are," I assure Arion. "We will always be on the same page."

My brother arches a brow. "Well, if that turns out to be true, even hell should watch its back. You two will be unstoppable."

I rest my hand on Bran's thigh and give him a squeeze. I meant what I said. We are on the same page, regardless of whether or not I wear a crown. And I want to be unstoppable with him. I want us to be a force to be reckoned with.

———

We leave The Greasy Spoon once my plate is clean and my stomach full. We head straight for Duval House to ask Bianca if she'd like to venture into the fae realm to help us deceive the Summer Queen.

"Absolutely," she says too quickly. "I wouldn't miss it for the world."

With that part settled, Bianca leaves to prep the spellwork. Lance reports to us that Damien is with Kelly and because we don't want to risk the Summer Queen learning that Arion is working with us, we keep our distance and head out of town to the Alpha's Pack House. If we're fighting a war, we're going to need more than the vampires on our side.

Because the Bimmer is a super obvious car and literally the only vintage BMW in all of Midnight, we leave it safely tucked away at Duval House and take one of the nondescript black SUVs. And because I want Bran and Arion to like each other, or at the very least get to know one another enough to tolerate the other, I give Arion the front seat and climb in back.

The leather seats are so plush, the SUV such a smooth ride, that it's easy to slink down and let my eyes slip closed.

"Christ," Bran says and I lurch upright, having dozed off.

"What? What is it?"

He pulls the SUV around the Pack House driveway and nods at the large front porch.

A chill floods my veins.

Sam is there next to one of the grand porch columns and she's pointing a very angry finger at the Alpha while talking to him. And he's got his arms crossed tightly over his chest, jaw flexing.

"What are they saying?" I ask Bran.

He grins.

"Bran!"

"Apparently, she heard about you going to the fae realm to defend your throne and she plans to go with you and the Alpha forbade her and so now she's telling him where he can stick his head. Would you like me to repeat what she said?"

"No, I think I got it." I scrub the sleepiness from my face. "Sam can't go. She's mortal. It's too dangerous and—"

Bran parks the SUV and talks to me through the reflection in the rearview mirror. "I swear someone was just saying something about female empowerment and letting women make their own choices? Arion, do you remember someone saying something like that?"

"Yes, I do remember," Arion says with a smirk.

Well, shit.

Twenty-Three

As soon as Bran puts the SUV into park, I leap out and hurry up the steps to the Pack House porch. Before all this, the very thought of jumping in front of the Midnight Alpha would have made me break out in a cold sweat.

Now it's like I'm trying to protect him from Sam.

Her finger is directed at him, her voice raised. "You will not dictate what I do with my life!" she's saying, when I step between them.

"Sam. Hey. Hi."

She blinks and looks over at me. There's still tension in her face and she's just on the edge of grinding her teeth, something she does when she's really, really mad.

"Jess." She steps back and crosses her arms over her chest. Her stance nearly mirrors that of the Alpha behind me.

"What's going on?" I ask even though I already know. Sometimes vampire hearing really does come in handy. Bran's already told me all the details of this argument. If only I wasn't on the Alpha's side.

Cal doesn't want Sam to risk her life and march into the fae realm with us on my behalf, and I definitely don't disagree with him.

But how hypocritical could I be? Considering I just argued with Bran about letting Bianca come with us to aid in our plan.

I can't be all female empowerment yay and then deny my best friend the right to join the fight.

If only I wasn't so worried about her very mortal body getting crushed in the middle of the fight.

"He's trying to control my life," Sam says. "And I told him to fuck off. No one tells me what to do."

"Can we talk?" I ask her and then glance at Cal over my shoulder. "Alone?"

The Alpha sucks in a deep breath through his nose and gives me a quick nod of his head. "You'll find the most privacy at my cabin."

I hook my arm through Sam's, steering her away, down the steps, across the yard. I sense Bran trailing us but don't bother to tell him to buzz off.

He won't listen to me anyway and I can't really blame him, what with a fae queen trying to kidnap me or off me, depending on the day of the week.

Sam and I follow the trail around the Pack's property and back through the woods to Cal's cabin. The door is unlocked and inside, a few table lamps are flicked on. The place is clean and cozy.

She sits down at the table and lets out a sigh.

"Hi," she says. "You look like shit."

I snort. "I could say the same about you."

It's not really true though. Sam's always been gorgeous in an effortless sort of way. She's wearing her favorite jeans, the vintage Guess, threadbare and tearing at the knees, along with chunky white sneakers and an oversized plain black t-shirt.

She doesn't look dressed ready for war. She looks like she should be lounged back, reading Kerouac in Rita's coffee shop.

"Cal just wants to protect you," I tell Sam.

She rolls her eyes. "Not you too."

"Well, yeah, I also want to protect you, but he's got a better chance of making it happen. Those big Alpha biceps and all."

She gives me a blank look. How the hell is she immune to the gorgeousness of the Midnight Alpha? She must have some kind of blind spot where he's concerned because everyone in Midnight Harbor would kill to have the undying devotion of the Alpha.

"Your vampire boyfriend must have told you what we were arguing about?"

"He gave me the highlights."

She sits forward, propping her elbows on the table. When I look down, I realize there are claw marks in the wood. Old rivets of splintered pine.

"I feel like I barely see you anymore," she admits, her voice low, almost like this admission is a secret.

"I know."

"I miss you, Jess." She looks away when her eyes get glassy. "And if something happens to you, I...well, this place would get real shitty really quickly. So I might as well fight by your side. I have a great left hook. You know that."

I laugh. "I remember you taking out Jonathan Lowman when he got too handsy with you at that graveyard party and wouldn't take no for an answer."

"See!" She laughs with me. "I know what I'm doing."

I can't tell her no. Even if I want to.

And truth be told, I want her by my side and maybe that's selfish in a way, considering what it is we're up against.

"All right," I say and Sam gives me a wink.

"I knew you'd see my way."

"But you have to make me a promise."

Now she's regarding me with suspicion. "What is it?"

"When this is over, consider giving the Alpha a chance."

She huffs out her indignation. "That man is an asshole and I hate him."

"Oh really? Tell that to your face."

"What about my face?"

I laugh and push away from the table.

"Jessie. What about my face?!"

There is a blush spreading over her cheeks, turning into a flush that runs down her neck. Sam may want to resist the Alpha, she may want to pretend that the fated mate bond between them is Cal's problem to deal with, not hers. But I know my best friend. She's fighting her attraction to him with everything she has and she's losing.

"Fine," she says, following me out the door. "I'll give him a chance just to prove him, and you, wrong."

———

I expected Cal to push back when we returned to the Pack House and announced Sam was coming with us, but he kept himself cool and collected and told Sam, "If you insist on being reckless, fine. But you'll stay by my side and if things go awry, you'll let me get you to safety."

"Let you? I don't need you to —"

The Alpha had ducked down, putting his face level with hers. The height difference between them is so large that he practically had to bend in half. "I'll chain you to my bed if I have to."

She rolled her eyes. "Fine. Whatever."

And knowing that that was about all he'd get from her, he left it at that.

Now, with the vampires and the shifters assembled, we make our way to the fae gate.

The air is cool and crisp with the first sign of autumn and as we walk through the woods, my breath puffs out white in front of me.

I'm sandwiched between Bran, Cal, and Arion with Sam beside me. Bianca is ahead of us with Baspin, both of them leaning into one another discussing the spells Bianca plans to use and the fae magic Baspin might lend to make the spells even stronger.

The closer we get to the gate, the more my body buzzes with the connection to the magic.

The hair lifts along the back of my neck.

Bran takes my hand and gives me a squeeze, but the coldness of his skin only makes me shiver.

We have so many strong allies on our side. Practically titans of their Houses. So why am I nervous?

The path curves around a briar patch and when we come around to the meadow, Bran grabs me roughly by the arm, yanking me back.

Standing in front of the gate, is none other than Maven with an army on his flanks.

"There she is," he calls, his voice ringing out calm and assured. "My bride to be."

Twenty-Four

Maven's words ring across the meadow.

Bran tenses beside me.

It means nothing to me—I never had any plan to follow through with my betrothal—but I know Bran is terrified that somehow, some-way, the marriage will go through and he'll lose me to the fae.

Baspin and Bianca are still ahead of us, standing between me and Maven with several vampires and shifters hovering on the edge, waiting for a command to attack.

Bran's grip on me tightens. "Mouse," he says, his voice low and throaty. I know he wants me to stand back and stand down, but there's no way in hell I'm letting anyone else fight my battles now.

Bianca snaps her fingers and blue flame ignites in her hand. Beside her, in his opposite hand, Baspin holds a matching flame.

"Lending your power out to witches now, are you?" Maven says. "I know it's been a while since I've seen you, dear Baspin, but I never would have expected you to have stooped so low."

The flame blooms wider in Baspin's hand. He doesn't strike me as the kind of person to be ruffled by a little bit of goading, but clearly there's something between him and Maven to stoke his irritation.

"And I never would have taken you for a man who would have to force a girl to marry him."

Maven sniffs at the insult.

Cal and his shifters spread out in a formation that reminds me of predators corralling prey. The fae echo the movements and when Arion gets a good look at them as they step further into the ethereal fairy light pouring from the open gate, his brow furrows into a deep V. He turns to me and Bran.

Voice low, he says to Bran, "I think you should take her away from here."

"Are you insane? I'm not leaving."

He gestures with a thumb over his shoulder. "The fae warriors you see over there? Those aren't just any soldiers. Look at them. Look at their clothing, their markings."

I scan the people standing beside Maven.

They aren't wearing the bright, shiny clothing of the Summer Court, all sequins and pastels. Instead, they're dressed in dark fabric and black leather armor with blades strapped to their backs and their hips.

Several of them have black markings on their hands and on their necks, symbols and swirls that are distinct enough they must have specific meanings. But whatever they are, I'm not familiar with them.

There is a man standing on Maven's left who has the kind of pride in his shoulders that makes me think he's the one in charge of this army.

A dark mark, like a swirl of black smoke, covers half his face, the bottom of it starting at his collarbone, splashing across his face to the opposite side at his temple. His eyes are gold like Bran's.

Just looking at him makes me shiver.

"Who are they?" Bran asks.

Arion is quick to answer. "They're known as the Fairies of Suffering. They belong to no court. The darkest of the dark fae. I'm shocked the queen was able to bring them to her side." He glances back across the clearing. "She must have offered them something they couldn't refuse."

"I've never heard of them," Bran admits.

"They don't usually make themselves known. They reside on the far edges of the fae realm. It's been a long time since I've laid eyes on one. They keep to themselves but—"

"But what?" I coax when he trails off.

"They do tend to show up at times of war and, well, *suffering*."

Great.

"Jessie," Maven calls out. "Can we speak privately? This really is a matter meant for royalty, not the peasants."

Arion grits his teeth and whirls around. "You're one to talk, brother."

Maven smiles that dazzling smile. Even in the darkness, across the meadow, I can see the bright white of his teeth. "Whatever do you mean?" He has no idea he's walked right into Arion's trap.

"Didn't your mother tell you?"

"Arion," I warn, because I'm not sure this is the time or place for big family revelations.

But he ignores me.

"Your mother had an affair with a lowly winter courtesan. Which makes you, dear brother, a bastard, and me the heir apparent."

Maven's smile grows taut against his teeth.

"Her plan was to marry you to Jessie, legitimizing your lowly blood," Arion goes on.

Maven's nostrils flare. I can sense his desire to accuse Arion of lying, but of course, as a Summer fae, Arion can't lie. Not like I can.

Everything he's said is the truth.

"Deep down I think you always knew you didn't belong," Arion adds. "I know I felt it."

"Maybe you believe it to be true," Maven says. "Doesn't make it so."

Arion shakes his head. "Your mother admitted as much to Jessie. I heard a recording of her confession."

Maven's just digging a deeper hole, every word Arion says cementing the truth a little more.

The Fairies of Suffering are spreading wider as the brothers talk. The way they move is not unlike that of the shifters. Nearly silent, hard to detect without staring right at them.

"Mouse," Bran says again, the warning clear in his voice.

The air is charged with impending carnage. I can feel it. I know Bran does too.

I put myself in front of Sam. "Please promise me you'll run if things go south?"

She snorts. "You're funny."

Dammit, Sam.

If only I didn't have such a stubborn, badass best friend.

Before we left, Cal gave her a blade that she has strapped at her hip. It's a fine weapon, crafted by some infamous weapons master that Cal has on speed dial apparently. The blade has a stout handle but with a delicate filigree along its side. It's hard not to think he had the blade specifically made for Sam because when she took it in hand, it fit her perfectly, all of it balanced for her grip and size.

But will it be enough to fight fae known as the Fairies of Suffering? Highly doubt it.

"I came here to retrieve my future wife," Maven calls out. "Regardless of what stories you've been fed, brother, that fact will not change. Jessie and I will be married, and we will unite the courts and restore the balance to the fae realm."

"Think again," Bran says, his voice ringing out, and then he shoots across the clearing, headed straight for Maven.

———

Now that I've been in the middle of several fights and battles, I have to wonder if all war starts the same: quietly at first, and then all at once.

Unseen one moment, absolute carnage the next.

The shifters and vampires go after the Fairies of Suffering and my stomach drops when I see how they fight.

Their violence is like physical poetry. Elegant. Concise. Every movement short but punctuated with pain. They cut through the vampires and shifters with barely any effort at all.

Goosebumps race up my arms.

We are in trouble.

Going straight for Maven, Bran lands a punch to the prince's stomach and the fae doubles over. Arion charges too, his blade drawn. But Maven dances away, sucking in air.

Bran moves faster than the fae prince, but not by much. And Maven recovers quickly, pulling his own sword from the sheath at his hip.

Now it's Maven against Bran and Arion. They circle one another.

On my left, Baspin and Bianca fight two Fairies of Suffering with their blue-flamed magic and manage to bring one to their knees.

On my right, Cal steps between Sam and another fairy, his face already covered in splatters of blood.

Maven swipes his blade in an arch, catching Arion across the arm. The fabric of his shirt splits open and blood pours from the wound.

A chill spreads over my shoulders and my breath puffs out white in front of me, then crystalizes into snowflakes.

The crackle of power dances down the nape of my neck.

I know Maven is a victim of circumstance, and he's been lied to his entire life by a mother who wanted only power, but he is not, and will not be allowed, to harm my brother or my boyfriend.

I won't let it happen.

Instinct takes over.

I may not fully understand my own powers, but I have faith my body does. The power has always been there. And now I'm going to use it.

The darkened sky grows darker as thick clouds roll in. Snow swirls in the air, the wind picking up. Soon the snow is ice, cutting across my skin, swirling around me like a tornado.

Maven charges after Bran as Arion tries to stop the flow of blood pouring from his arm.

I raise my hands, pulling from whatever deep well of power I have. Ice spreads out from my fingers and power snaps through the air.

"Maven!" I shout, distracting him before he hurts Bran.

I yank on that power, feeling the buzz of it, the connection between me and the earth and the air.

Maven looks up just as giant icicles fall from the sky aimed right for him.

Twenty-Five

BRAN

The fae prince, or rather, the *bastard* prince, charges toward me.

I'm prepared for a hit. Prepared to take the blow in order to distract him in the seconds that come after.

It's always best to strike a man when he thinks he's winning a fight. Pride gets in the way. Excitement steals focus.

I have none of those weaknesses.

Except…Maven never reaches me.

Lightning crackles through the darkened sky and thunder rumbles, chasing it.

I run cold, but even I can tell there's been a precipitous drop in temperature.

Snow swirls in the air.

"Maven!" Mouse shouts.

I dare to look away from Maven and over at my little mouse, but one second turns into two, then three.

She is extraordinary.

Snow and electricity ribbon around her, tossing her hair around her shoulders.

She is the Winter Court Queen finally come to life.

I can't look away. I am mesmerized by her beauty and her power. And I'm not alone.

At least half of those fighting in the meadow go still.

Until giant icicles start falling from the sky.

They sail through the air with a loud whistle, then hit the ground with a THWAP and CRACKLE.

The earth shakes and splits open. They're at least twice as tall as me, twice as wide.

Maven has to stagger back when one slices into the ground between us.

"Fall back!" one of the Fairies of Suffering calls. I suspect he's the one in charge. He commands that kind of attention.

The fairies change their formation, falling back toward the gate into a semi-circle. The icicles are only hitting the meadow.

Mouse is using her power to target Maven.

That kind of control, that kind of precision...

She is more powerful than even she realizes.

That bastard clearly has no hope of making it out of this clearing.

And the second he realizes it, the second he turns his attention toward Mouse.

Maven starts running toward her.

More icicles fall between us.

The icicles create a fence between me and him.

"Mouse!" I shout. "Stop!"

But she either can't hear me or is ignoring me.

The air crackles around her.

"Jessie!"

Her gaze skitters to me.

Her eyes have gone icy blue.

The fuck. That's new.

"Pull back!" I yell at her.

She drops her hands, but the ice has already formed, and three more icicles pierce the earth between me and her.

Maven barrels into her.

"Mouse!"

Maven takes her down. I have to sprint fifty feet in the opposite direction to make it around the icy fence and by the time I reach the other side, Maven has Mouse by the throat, hoisted off the ground. Her feet pedal at the air.

"I know you're fast, vampire," Maven calls. "But are you fast enough?"

Jessie wraps her hands around his wrist, trying to get some relief from the pressure. Her power has retreated and I know in this moment she's beating herself up, talking herself down in her own head.

I can practically hear her thoughts.

I'm not strong enough. He's going to win.

Fuck that.

"How do you plan to legitimize your spot in the Winter Court if you have no queen?" I ask him. "Put her down."

"I'm sure we can find another way."

Mouse gasps for air. She's turning blue in his grip.

I ease forward.

"Stop," Maven commands. "Don't come any closer."

"All right." I raise my hands. "You have my attention. Whatever you want from me. Just put her down. She can't breathe."

"She nearly killed me. I'm not putting her down."

"Then what do you want to do?"

The bastard prince looks at me. There's desperation in his eyes. Fear. Dread. Uncertainty. He came here to prove a point and to win and now he's realizing he night not accomplish either.

There is nowhere for him to go.

"I never wanted the power," he admits, his voice low and hoarse.

"Then walk away."

"I can't."

"Why not?"

He frowns. "Mother would never allow me."

Mouse gasps for air. How much longer can she hold on?

"The only thing I can do," he says, "is prove my worth to the

Summer Queen and the rest of the realm." He turns to Mouse. "And I can do that by killing our greatest enemy."

Fuck.

"No!"

Maven tightens his grip. Mouse chokes. I calculate the distance between us and it's too far. He could snap her neck before I reach her and—

I catch movement out of the corner of my eye. Movement behind Maven.

The lithe silhouette of a soon-to-be fairy prince.

Arion appears out of the darkness, takes three long steps forward, raises his blade, and plunges it into Maven's back.

Maven immediately drops Mouse and she lands with a thud on the grass, choking back air. I rush to her side, take her in my arms, and the relief to have her safe is immediate.

"Are you okay?" I ask her. A bruise has already appeared around her throat and if Maven didn't already have a blade in his back, he would soon have my foot in his ass.

He coughs. Blood sputters from his mouth and pours from his chest where Arion's blade has sliced straight through muscle and bone.

Maven staggers around and when he sees his brother, when he realizes the person he thought was his greatest ally has just stabbed him in the back, his knees buckle.

He gasps for air, the sound wet and raspy.

"You don't deserve the throne," Arion says through gritted teeth. "And you sure as hell aren't going to be responsible for the death of my sister."

Mouse sits up, her body weight leaning into my side. I hear her slight intake of breath and when I glance over at her, there is wetness welling in her eyes.

Her brother came through for her.

He chose her over Maven.

Even though he had more history with Maven, and perhaps because of that, more loyalty, he still chose Mouse, not because of their shared blood, but because it was the right thing to do.

Because her heart is probably the purest out of all of us.

Maven shivers and gasps out another wet breath. "How...could...you?" he says and then falls over face first into the grass.

Arion stares at his brother for several long seconds. I can hear the sharp grit of his molars against one another.

"Help me up," Mouse says, her voice compromised because of the pressure Maven exerted on her. I try not to let the anger about it take control. Maven is dead and there's no revenge to have.

My arm around her waist, I help her stand upright. We shuffle over to Arion together.

"I'm sorry," Mouse says when she comes up alongside him.

"Me too," he tells her. "But he never would have relented."

Behind us, the icicles crackle as they melt.

And further out, near the fae gate, the Fairies of Suffering are in formation, watching us.

"Arion?" I say.

He turns slightly toward me but keeps one eye on Maven as if he's afraid he might come back to life. "What?"

"If we were to appeal to the Fairies of Suffering, what might they want? What do you think the Summer Queen offered them?"

He thinks. The seconds tick by, growing heavier by the moment. The leader of the fairies puts his hand on the hilt of his sword, eyeing us through the melting ice.

"They get their power from suffering," Arion explains. "It's where they got their name. If I had to guess, the queen has promised them the suffering of lesser fae. Likely a certain number on every solstice to sustain them for a while."

I know immediately what I have to do.

"Take her," I tell Arion and shift Mouse's weight.

"What are you doing?" She scowls up at me. "Bran? What the fuck are you doing?"

"We have plenty of people on our side, but we need a wild card, Mouse. And stealing the queen's mercenaries? That's exactly my kind of move."

Arion winds his arm around her waist, holding her upright. She tries to pull away from him, but he tightens his grip. "Let him do his bidding," he says.

"No fucking way." She looks over at me. "If they feast on suffering, Bran, they'll—" She catches the look in my eye. "*Bran.*"

"Stay put, Mouse."

I cross the meadow. Our friends have held back, giving the fairies a wide berth.

I stop when twenty feet lies between me and their leader. His eyes are so bright, they're almost glowing, almost like mine when I'm in predator mode. Any other circumstance, he and I might become fast friends.

"Would you be open to negotiating a new price?" I ask him.

He looks over his shoulder at the rest of his soldiers. "Perhaps," he says to me.

"The suffering of lesser fae might be enticing, but how about the suffering of an immortal vampire? I heal quickly. I cannot die. Unless you stake me, of course. I offer you myself in exchange for joining our side and forsaking your agreement with the Summer Queen."

He tilts his head, appraising me. It's obvious what I am. There's no doubt about that. But perhaps he's uncertain just how strong my fortitude is.

"Come forward," he says.

I don't fear very much. But the sound of his voice is like the sound of an ancient monster whispering to you from the dark shadows of a bottomless cave.

I once spent thirty-seven days being tortured in the French dungeon of a rival vampire family. Surely, I can withstand some fairies.

I step forward.

"Closer," he says.

Another foot. Two. Five.

When I am within reaching distance of him, I sense his power. It's a ripple on the air. Like a magnetic field that raises the hair along your arms, it sends a shiver down your spine.

His dark mark splashing across his face makes his golden eye even brighter.

"Close enough?" I ask.

"Close enough," he agrees and then plunges a blade into my gut.

The pain is immediate and intense. If you ask me, a gut wound is the worst kind. Like tearing out the roots of your soul through your fucking nostrils.

I'm on my knees before I can gasp out in pain. Blood pours down the front of me.

The Fairy of Suffering sinks to his knees in front of me and hangs his head back. Several tendons stick out from his neck like he's drinking down the air.

I yank the blade out and list sideways, clutching at my stomach trying to keep my insides from spilling out as my skin stitches itself up. The pain remains for several more heart beats, spreading out like a spiderweb.

When the fairy tilts his head back up, his black mark is moving.

Several tendrils swirl and bend across the bridge of his nose like it's a living thing just below his skin.

He drags his tongue over his puffy upper lip.

"Delicious," he says and smiles. "You have a deal."

Twenty-Six

I race across the meadow and grab Bran by the arms to give him a hard shake. "What the hell do you think you're doing?!"

His face is blank, unemotional. "I am doing what needs to be done, Mouse."

"He just stabbed you! For fun!" There's still blood covering the front of him even though the wound has already healed itself. "You don't know how far he'll take it. What if he keeps you forever? What if he hurts you so badly, you can't recover?"

The leader of the Fairies of Suffering runs his tongue over his lips, like he's lapping up the last of Bran's suffering.

Arion is suddenly beside me and slowly pries my hands from Bran's shirt. "Jessie," he says, forcing me to look at him. The sky is rolling with dark clouds again, thunder rumbling in the distance. I've lost control again.

"Allow me to serve as negotiator," Arion says to me, then to Bran.

"I will agree to that," Bran says.

Arion turns to the fairy leader. "Draggun?"

"Oh for fuck's sake. His name is Dragon?"

"It's Draggun," he corrects me, even though it sounds exactly the same. The fairy leader has barely glanced at me, as if I don't matter.

"Well, Dragon," I say, "you can't have him."

"I'd say you're too late," Draggun answers.

His voice makes my teeth wrinkle.

"Will you agree to a proper negotiation?" Arion asks him.

"Of course."

Arion puts himself between Bran and Draggun. "The deal expires a year from today."

Draggun counters, "A year and a day. And I get him on the last day."

Arion glances at Bran and Bran gives a quick nod. "Any form of suffering cannot be fatal," Arion adds.

The thunder rumbles closer as the panic rises in my throat. I could use my voice, make this stop. But then what? I know logically Bran's right — we need every edge we can get. But at what cost?

I catch his eye as Arion and Draggun iron out the terms of the suffering. Bran says nothing, but the look in his gaze says enough.

You'd do the same for me, is his unspoken response. *And you'd demand I respect it.*

I swallow, tears stinging in my sinuses. I *would* do the same. And he'd hate it. Just like he's hated every other time I've risked my life for this.

Fuck.

"You get him and his suffering for twenty-four mortal hours and only on the solstices," Arion says.

Draggun shakes his head. "Not enough."

Arion glances at Bran and Bran breaks our gaze. "Solstices and equinoxes."

"Still not enough."

Bran sighs. "Every full moon?"

Draggun smiles. "Well enough."

"Great," Arion answers. "One year and one day from now, you will release Bran Duval of any and all further suffering, provided he's fulfilled his end of the bargain."

Draggun pulls a dagger from a sheath on his forearm, spins it in his hand, then catches it by the hilt. He drags the blade over the fleshy part of his palm, blood chasing the sharp tine as his skin parts.

He holds out his hand, then the dagger. Bran takes the weapon, repeating the wound and then they shake on it, blood dripping from their clasped hands.

"I think that settles it then," Draggun says. "Now, if you'll allow me and mine to do what we do best, we'll move ahead of you and get into position outside the Summer Palace. Once we join the fight, we will feast on the suffering and none of you will stop us. Is that understood?"

"So long as it's none of ours," I say.

Draggun finally turns to me and finding his feral eyes directed toward me is a lot to bear. My heart quickens in my chest.

"You are bold, Winter Princess," he says. "I like that." His expression is hard to read.

But despite myself, I blush beneath the compliment.

He's not just a creature of the darkness. He's a master manipulator, I suspect.

And for a split second, I almost tell him thanks before I remember who and what he is.

"I appreciate you noticing," I tell him instead.

His smirk is unmistakable. He did know what he was doing.

"We will see you when the mayhem runs high and not a moment sooner." He nods to Bran, Arion, and lastly, me. And then he's gone, taking his soldiers with him through the gate.

———

"That was really stupid!" I yell at Bran.

"It got us what we needed." He's walking through the meadow, assessing the damage. We only lost a few vampires, now just piles of ash in the grass. Cal instructs two of his shifters to carry the dead back to the Pack House. They lost four.

Thankfully, Sam is untouched, but Cal is sticking close to her like he's worried anything could take her out, even a rut in the ground.

Arion cuts across the meadow after conversing with Baspin and Bianca. "We should hurry through the gate. It won't be long before the queen catches wind of Maven's death. If I had to make a prediction, she has him marked with some kind of charm to track him or alert her to his death. She's done it before. Being on the mortal side, it might take a while for the magic to link up, but it won't be long enough."

"Will we encounter trouble on the way to the palace?" Bran asks him.

"Probably." Arion scans the meadow. "We could split up, use one of our groups as a decoy."

Bran crosses his arms over his chest, thinking it over. "That might work."

Cal and Sam come over to our huddle. Cal says, "I'll volunteer for the decoy group. I could take some of the shifters and the vampires."

"You're sure?" Bran asks him.

"Shifters fight better in the woods anyway. And I'm assuming that's where the ambush might happen?"

Arion gives a nod. "Probably on the trail somewhere about halfway from the gate to the palace."

Several strands of his blond hair hang in his face, so Cal unties it, then rakes it all back again with his bloody fingers leaving several streaks of red amongst the blond. How could Sam possibly resist this man?

"Which way should I take them?" Cal asks, winding the rubber band over the messy bun at the back of his head.

"Follow the main trail," Arion instructs. "It'll take you where you need to go. There are no forks in that path, so you just need to stick to the one."

Sam wraps me in a hug. "I'm so glad I'm doing this. This is the most fun I've had in a long time."

She smells like autumn air and the sharp tang of blood. "I'm not. I wish you were home right now safe and sound."

She laughs against me, then gives me a big smacking wet kiss on the cheek. "I'll see you on the other side of your victory, princess. Then we'll have a slumber party to celebrate, and we'll get super drunk."

"She absolutely will not," Bran says.

I wink at Sam, letting her know I'm totally game.

Bran and Cal split the group, but leave us with Arion, Baspin, and Bianca. Once Cal has the numbers he needs, they wave goodbye and slip through the gate.

"We'll give them about a twenty-minute lead," Arion explains.

"Then we'll go through and head further east. It's an old trader's route and it'll be overgrown, but it should suffice for getting us around any ambushes and to the palace."

As we wait for time to pass, I pace back and forth in front of the gate.

This is it.

This is really it.

Looking back, everything about my life was leading to this moment, starting with my mom making the decision to keep me even when she knew I wasn't hers. Then Julian learning I was something special and shielding me from the other Houses. Rita binding me. Stanley protecting me.

And finally, Bran. Bran who helped me pull back the layers of myself, who stood by my side as I uncovered all of my dark secrets.

Secrets drenched in blood.

But mine nevertheless.

How can anyone embrace who they are without knowing their dark parts? Without knowing their truth, no matter how painful or hard it may be?

"If you have to," Bran says, watching me pace back and forth, lost in thought, "use your voice. Command with it."

I come to a stop. "That's easier said than done. I still feel like my power is like water in my hands. It's hard to hold on to."

"Practice on me now," he says.

I scoff. "I should have used it to stop you from making that deal with Dragon."

"Draggun," he corrects with a smirk.

I narrow my eyes at him. *"Stop smirking at me."*

The smile disappears from his face. "See?" he says. "Easy."

"Get on your knees for me," I tell him.

He tilts his head, jaw flexing with a grit of his teeth as his knees bend and he sinks to the ground. "As much as I don't enjoy this," he tells me. "I'm proud of you."

"Declare your undying love for me. Loudly."

He sucks in a breath. "Everyone! Listen up! I love Jessie MacMahon more than I've ever loved another. She is smart, brave, cunning, and bold. And sexy as hell. And when she's in the bedroom with my c—"

I rush over to him, clamping my hand over his mouth. I can see the glint of a naughty smile in his eyes. "You're an asshole," I tell him.

"You started it," he says, the words muffled behind my hand.

When I pull away, he rises to his feet and scoops me into his arms. "You'll do fine, princess. That barely took any effort at all."

Using my power on Bran when not under pressure is one thing. But I don't say that. I'm tired of defeating myself before I've even begun.

Because I think my voice, my power, might be our best weapon to use against the Summer Queen. And if I fail...

I can't even fathom what will become of me and Bran if I do.

Twenty-Seven

I say a silent prayer for Sam and Cal as they disappear through the portal.

Please keep my best friend safe.

We give them the twenty-minute lead they need to make their way to the Summer Palace as our decoy. Once we cross over to the fae realm, the night is still, the forest quiet, but it's easy to see the freshly trampled ferns on the path indicating they moved forward as planned.

Arion takes us further north, then cuts east on the old trader's route he mentioned. With time moving differently here than it does back home, it's darker in the fae realm and nowhere near dawn. It's so dark that I find it impossible to navigate the path as silently as Bran does behind me. It feels like I hit every single fallen twig on the path and every crack makes me wince.

When we've been walking for at least a half hour, Arion makes us stop in a small clearing that's surrounded by wispy cedar trees that perfume the air with their earthy scent. My brother instructs Baspin to throw up a protective barrier so anyone outside of it won't hear or see us if they happen past.

"Let's send two ahead to scout the path," Arion orders once the barrier is in place. "We're within Summer territory now so I want to be extra cautious." He glances at Bran. "One fae and one vampire feel fair to you?"

"Yes," Bran says. He breaks off from me to discuss with Arion the best vampire for the job. As we wait, Baspin takes his spot by my side.

"How are you doing, princess?" he asks me.

I notice he doesn't use the royal styling of 'your highness' and I'm grateful for it.

With an exhale, I lean against a skinny birch tree and give him a half-hearted shrug. "I'm okay. All things considered."

He nods and turns to me, his shoulder pressed into the birch next to mine. There is always a laziness to Baspin that I think is part of his mask, the way he hides who he really is. I think a lot of fae find ways to hide their truth, since they always have to speak it. Did the royal Winter Court ever feel that way? Or because they could lie with their words, they could be truthful with everything else?

Maybe that's what drew my mother in. Maybe in the Winter Court she felt like she could finally be free.

"What are you thinking about?" Baspin asks me and the way he's looking at me makes me think my thoughts have bled through. I never learned how to be anything but truthful. There was a time when hiding what I thought, who I was, what I might do, meant very little to anyone.

I'll have to change that if I'm to become queen of an entire fae court. Not that there's much left of it.

"Why do you want to join my court?" I ask him, dodging answering his inquiry.

"Because it's home."

"But what if I fail? Aren't you worried about that? If you love your home so much, why not let someone else who actually knows what they're doing take over? You owe me no allegiance."

He pushes away from the tree. "And who would that be, princess? No one else has royal blood in their veins. No one else can wield the power of the Winter Court like you can."

I huff. "I can barely hold on to my power."

"Then let me teach you."

I frown at him. "What, now?"

"Did you have something better to do?"

Of course not. But—

"What do you know about Winter Court powers?"

"I served under your father."

I straighten. "You what?" The words come out a strangled whisper. I know what I heard him say. I don't need him to repeat it and yet I can't quite grab hold of the full truth of it.

"You knew him?" I ask, swallowing, trying to quell the rapid thumping of my heart. I sense Bran's attention on me, checking to make sure I'm all right.

Since I learned I was fae, I've barely thought of my father. I was always focused on my mother. It was the same way with my mortal mother. I loved my dad, but it was my mom who really raised me. I guess the same feelings transferred to my fae parents.

"Your father was powerful," Baspin answers. "One of the most powerful fae kings I've ever met. But he was also greedy for more. It was his undoing, if I may speak boldly."

"Always."

He gives me a nod. "I was his servant in title, but in truth I was his practice dummy, his plaything."

My stomach knots. "Did he...did he hurt you?"

He laughs desperately. "Every day."

I take a breath, holding the emotion back as much as I can. "I'm so sorry."

I don't want to believe that I came from a man who could use his power on another living thing just for practice. And how did my mother fall for him if he was so cruel? She left her court for him. But even I know matters of the heart are not so cut and dried. And that sometimes even cruel men can be kind and compassionate.

Baspin goes on. "When I served under your father, I saw it as an honor. I won't pretend otherwise. He promised to bestow me the title of Lord of Winter for my loyalty and dedication to the court. But when war broke out, he abandoned me and so I fled to Midnight." He turns his attention back to me. "The fae realm needs all its courts. It was always meant to have four. No more and no less. Someone has to rule it. Why not you? There is no one better."

"You barely know me."

"Don't I? You don't think Arion and I have been watching you for years?"

I snort. "Arion didn't know who I was. He said as much to Stanley when he came to the diner that first night after I used my power."

"Didn't he?" Baspin gives me a roguish smile. "I believe what Arion said was, 'You kept this from us, brownie.'"

Shit. He's right. Hearing it again, I can see the clever twist of words. Arion wasn't admitting he was ignorant of my identity or accusing Stanley of keeping the secret. He simply made a statement *about* Stanley keeping secrets.

"Why didn't he say anything?" The shock quickly morphs into frustration. "He could have saved me a lot of trouble. And if I'd known I had a brother—"

"It was never the right time. Even you can see that."

I roll my eyes and cross my arms over my chest, leaning back into the tree. Okay, well maybe I can see the logic. Arion keeping quiet about my identity kept me safe all those years. And if I could go back and change it, would I? Every moment, every part of my life has led to this. To exactly who I am.

"So if you watched me all those years, what conclusion did you come to?"

Baspin says, "Our opinions differed."

"How?"

"He thought you were too mortal, too bratty." He laughs to himself. "He wasn't wrong. But I saw your potential. Heart and bravery and compassion. Those are the things the Winter Court needs. It's why I was willing to defy Arion after he kidnapped you. It's why I helped your vampire boyfriend."

"And now? That opinion change?"

He shakes his head. "I believe it even more now."

I walk into the center of the clearing where an opening in the trees has let the night sky peek through. Stars glow in the dark, their light blocked out every now and then as bats fly over chasing bugs.

"So let's say you help me learn to wield my powers. Let's say you have fifteen minutes, if that. What's the one thing I need to know?"

"Never let your guard down," he says and then darts toward me.

Twenty-Eight

Baspin crashes into me and while he's nowhere near as big as Bran or Arion, he still manages to lift me off my feet, then slam me into the ground.

From my left, I hear Arion tell Bran, "Hold back. Let her do this."

Pain radiates out from my spine, through my ribs, squeezing my lungs. I gasp for air.

Snowflakes start falling from the sky.

I'm angry at first. Angry that I *was* caught off guard even though I know that Baspin's warning, to never let my guard down, should be something I do instinctively, without having to be reminded.

I'm angry that I can't defend myself even though I'm supposed to be this big bad fearsome queen that everyone wants dead because she poses too much of a threat.

The anger is unthinking and before I know it, power is soaring through my body. I clamp my hands on Baspin and push the power through me.

Frost burns up his arms. First, a delicate lace of ice, shimmery in the night, but it quickly turns dangerous, blistering his skin, then turning it a sickly shade of green and black.

Baspin trembles from the pain, but manages to get out, "There you go, princess. Good. Now...where's...the...magic...coming from?"

His question distracts me and I quickly lose hold of the power. The frost retreats, but the bruising remains.

Teeth still chattering, Baspin disentangles himself from me and steps back, shaking out his arms like he's trying to get feeling back in his fingers. He asks again, "Where was the magic coming from?"

I climb to my feet. "I don't know."

"I can tell you that when I worked with your father, his power always started in my chest." He taps over his heart. "It was an icy burn that over several minutes would turn prickly and course through my entire body, slowing me down until I was nearly frozen. When you think about it, the power of your voice is similar. It takes control of the body, freezes the nervous system, in a way."

I take in several more breaths, replenishing the oxygen in my lungs. "So you think he targeted the heart and the power would just follow the bloodstream?"

"It makes sense," Bran says behind me. "People want to believe they make decisions with their brain, but the brain loves to be on autopilot. It's the heart that often guides us." He gives me a pointed look as if to say he's fallen victim to his own heart when it comes to me. I'm not sure if I should take that as a compliment or an insult.

"Okay," I say and turn to Baspin again. "So...target your heart?"

"That's only part of it." He smooths back his rumpled white blond hair. "Your power is activated by fear or adrenaline or sometimes both. It's a common trigger. You can target the heart for the fastest result, but you have to ignite the power somehow without relying only on anger."

Baspin raises his hand where blue flames flicker to life.

"What's this?" I ask him, suddenly weary.

"You have to figure out how to access your power, princess."

"Obviously."

He twirls his hand and the blue flames crack like a whip, hitting my arm with a sharp snap.

"Ouch!" The pain is immediate and intense and courses up my arm and across my shoulders before fading at the base of my neck. A big, red welt blooms on my skin.

"How is that supposed to—"

He hits again, this time on my leg.

"Christ!" I turn away, cringing as pain throbs in my foot.

Again, he snaps out with his blue-flamed magic, whipping me across the back.

The sting is so bad, the anger is immediate. I turn and charge at him. He dances to the left, and I miss him entirely. I'm annoyed, and embarrassed. Everyone is watching me fail at this.

I spin around, run at him, but he pulls his hand back, then gestures wildly with it and a deep burn blooms across my midsection.

I'm losing spectacularly.

"Come on, princess," he says.

I grit my teeth. My instinct is to use my voice to render him unmoving, but I'm much better at wielding it than I am the winter power, and I can't miss this opportunity to get a handle on it.

Everything is resting on my shoulders and my ability to control my power. Not only so I can use it against the Summer Queen, but so I can stop accidentally using it on the people I love and care about.

I concentrate on my own heart, thinking that if my father targeted that area of the body maybe it was where his power originated.

But before I can get any focus, Baspin hits me again and I fall to my knees as the shock reverberates through my hips.

Blue flames flicker around the clearing and my fear and anxiety at being hit again and feeling another well-spring of pain has me lurching to my feet, hands balled into fists.

The snow falls harder, swirling around us.

"What do you feel?" Baspin asks again.

I'm breathing heavy, a coiled heat in my belly.

At the front is the anger still, the frustration, the embarrassment.

And shame.

Shame at being the daughter of a king who tortured Baspin. The daughter of a woman who betrayed her own court and joined her new husband in trying to overthrow the entire fae realm.

I'm their flesh and blood.

A symbol of their love.

What if I'm destined to become them?

What if everyone's worst fears about me come true?

What if I'm also destined to hurt those I love?

"There it is," Baspin says.

The snow goes sideways and then turns to sleet.

"Whatever you're thinking about right now," he says. "Tell me what it is."

I can feel my chin wobbling as the realization takes over. "I...I'm afraid."

"Of what?"

"What if I really am the villain? What if it's impossible to fight it? What if I'm no better than my father, who hurt you again and again?"

Baspin goes still, his blue flame sizzling out. "But Jessie...what if you aren't? You'll never know until you try. Stop getting in your own way. Stop being afraid of your own power."

The sleet blows harder, pelting us in the clearing.

I squint as the wind picks up, whipping my hair in my face.

I spot Bran across the clearing, watching me intently, his eyes bright gold, ready to come to my rescue if I need it.

But I don't want to be rescued anymore.

I don't want to fall victim to the anger or the power or the greed for more.

I want to be exactly as I am.

So be her, a voice whispers in my head.

You are a girl first, who deserves the freedom to decide exactly who she is.

You are a princess second, who deserves the chance to prove she is good.

But most importantly, you are a powerful fae, not because you were born to a cruel king, but because you were raised by a family who loved you unconditionally, with everything they had.

You are not your father. You are not your mother.

You are a MacMahon.

And you are a force to be reckoned with.

The wind and the sleet stop abruptly and the clearing is silent.

It's snowing again, but only in one spot. Only around me like I'm my own personal snow globe.

I raise my hand and the snow follows the movement, dancing around my fingers.

I'm controlling it, even though there's no anger, no fear.

Baspin's mouth drops open before curling into a wide grin. But his eyes aren't on me, exactly. His gaze his trained just above my head.

"What is it?" I ask.

Bran appears, phone out. He taps at the screen, then turns it around.

The camera is on and I immediately fill up the screen.

And there, sitting atop my head, is a crown made of ice, glittering in the night.

Twenty-Nine

I turn my head this way and that, examining the crown made of ice sitting atop my head.

If I didn't know any better, I would think it was some kind of photo filter, that's how perfect it is, how well it fits on my head, nestled in my hair.

But when I lift my hand to press my fingers against the big center tine, *I can feel it.*

The ice is cold but not wet, even though resting on my head, it has a neutral temperature against my scalp. Neither hot nor cold. And there's strength in it even though each tine looks delicate, fragile.

I take a step closer to Bran's phone so I can make out the finer details in the light.

The sharp ridges of each tine are made to look like the arms of snowflakes, but below them, sweeping down toward my eyebrows, are several tines that remind me of antlers or spindly leaves.

It fits me perfectly. And it's light as snow. I can barely feel it.

"How is this happening?" I whisper, following the curve of the crown with my fingers all the way around my head.

Baspin falls to his knees in front of me.

"Don't do that," I tell him, and I can hear the sheepishness in my own voice.

Bran gives me a quick shake of his head.

No, the gesture says, *they bow and you let them.*

Bran may not be royalty, but the Duvals have always operated as if they are. Bran knows that kneeling and bowing is a sign of respect I must endure if I'm to assume the power that's rightfully mine.

I turn to the clearing where the rest of the fae are now on their knees. All of them except for Arion.

My older brother crosses the clearing. I swallow hard, my mouth suddenly dry. Could I look any more nervous and awkward?

Technically he's a Lord and the rightful heir to the Summer Throne, but he doesn't outrank me...*yet*. He didn't bow for me when he and the Midnight fae first appeared at The Greasy Spoon. Will he now? Do I want him to? Maybe I don't. Maybe I make him? Shit, I don't know what I'm supposed to do.

But thankfully, my brother takes the pressure off and sinks to one knee in the short grass.

"Just until I claim my throne," he tells me with a smile and a wink.

"Of course," I answer quickly.

"You look beautiful, little sister," he says and bows his head as the final show of respect.

My eyes well up and I press my lips together, trying to keep the tears at bay. But it doesn't work. One spills out and I swipe at it, feeling a rush of emotions.

Excitement. Relief. Joy. Hope. Pride.

It's finally sinking in, really and truly, that I'm a fae princess and I have a duty to this realm and to all of the fae here to reclaim my throne and reunite the courts.

I'm a fae princess.

Soon to be a queen.

———

The fae rise to their feet but only after Arion does.

"Shall we march on to the Summer Queen?" my brother asks. "Do you feel up to the task now?" As if we are only discussing a quick jaunt to the store and not murder.

"I think so," I answer.

"Think?" Arion arches a brow.

"Yes," I correct. "Yes, I'm ready."

He gives me a nod, then glances at Bran. The scouts have returned—one fae and one vampire—to report that the path is clear ahead.

"Jessie and I in the middle of the procession," Bran says. "Insulate her on all sides."

Arion nods. "I'll be in front of her a few paces. Baspin and Bianca should be behind her with the rest clustered throughout. Fair?"

"Fair," Bran answers.

I don't want to get giddy about my fae brother and my vampire boyfriend making war plans together, *civilly*, but dammit, I am. Arion said that if Bran and I always remain on the same page, we'll be a force to be reckoned with, but I'd have to add that if Arion is with us, we'll be truly unstoppable. He and Bran think a lot alike and there are things to admire in both of them.

With everyone in their places, and me at the center of the line, we move forward outside the protective bubble Baspin had created for us. But just a few steps on, and I start to feel off.

It's a little unease in my gut at first. Anxiety or trepidation, I tell myself and push forward.

We walk another ten, maybe fifteen minutes, and a cold sweat breaks out along my hairline.

Maybe it's the humidity?

The climate in the fae realm hasn't changed since my first visit. It's still muggy, still insufferably thick and warm. Summer is in full force, but there's a different energy in the air that I can't quite put my finger on.

In the distance, the sky is starting to turn soft blue with the rising sun and mist swirls at the horizon.

"How close are we?" I ask Arion.

He glances at me over his shoulder as he answers. "We'll be upon the Summer Palace grounds within twenty minutes."

That's so close.

Shit.

My stomach cramps.

It's definitely anxiety.

I'm about to face the woman who had my mother killed, who tried to marry me off to her illegitimate son in order to steal the Winter Court for herself.

My court, my family, fought the Autumn Court in the Autumn Revolt, and in doing so, they left a void that the Summer Queen sought to fill even though it's clear that the courts being out of balance is no good for the realm.

It makes me angry that anyone would think they deserved more power than the other.

Someday I'll have to reckon with the fact that my family thought the same thing as the Summer Queen.

Right now, I need to break the cycle. With Arion's help.

We make our way up a rolling hill and at the very top, from the higher vantage point, it's easier to see the spires of the Summer Palace in the distance.

My legs begin to buzz and the buzzing slowly rises through my entire body until my head is practically vibrating.

I drag my fingers through my hair, massaging the dull ache in my scalp and my fingers come away wet.

I panic at first, thinking it's blood. "Bran." I pull him to a stop, holding out my hand. But it's just water.

"Your crown—" Bran starts right before I drop to my knees.

The knotting in my stomach intensifies and I double over in the grass.

The air is thick, soupier than last time. Like the humidity is at 100%.

"What's happening?" Bran asks Arion as he kneels down beside me.

"Summer is happening," Arion theorizes. "The queen must know we're here."

All around me, flowers sprout from the hillside. Buttercups and tulips and pansies and roses and foxgloves. It's beautiful, but ahead of me, I hear Arion say, "Fuck. *Everyone run!*"

Without questioning, Bran hoists me up into his arms, cradling me against him. To my left, a bloom of foxglove swings around and nabs the closest fae, tying itself around him like a rope. With the bell-shaped flowers, it almost looks like the tentacle of an octopus.

The flower tightens around him and then drags him below ground.

Oh my god.

Diagonal from us, the thorny vines of a rose bush takes hold of a vampire and within seconds, the woman is just gone.

"Run!" Arion yells. "Run toward the river!"

Bran cuts right and using his vampire speed, makes quick work of the hillside.

But just as the forest edge comes into view, just as I make out the first rushing of the river, a length of ivy lunges for us.

And before I know it, we're tied up tightly, the rising sun blotted out by dark leaves.

Thirty

Bran and I struggle against the ivy tied tightly around us, entombing us in a coffin of green. I'm mashed against his chest, the hard ridge of muscle like stone. Everything is hot and buzzing, and even though I can barely see beyond the foliage, my head is still spinning.

I don't feel so well.

"Can't you break it?" I ask Bran, but the words jumble together — I'm finding it hard to move at all, even to speak.

The ivy tightens like a coiled snake. My bones practically creak from the pressure.

Bran twists his body, then tries to lift his arms.

"It must be magic," he says. "I can't get them to budge."

"What do we do?"

"If this is Summer magic, you can counteract it."

"In theory," I answer. But I have to try.

I reach for the Winter magic that Baspin helped me tap into, but find too much resistance, like I'm swimming against a strong current.

"I think whatever magic the Summer Queen is using is blocking me," I tell Bran. "It feels like I have the flu."

"Keep trying." His hand is at the small of my back and he presses against me, encouraging me.

I close my eyes and dig deep.

The buzzing intensifies. My stomach rolls, like I'm going to throw up.

That would be the worst possible scenario, being tied up like this *and* covered in puke.

"I can't," I tell Bran and then clamp my mouth shut as the urge to vomit races up my throat.

"It's okay, Mouse." His voice is a whisper at my ear. "We'll get out one way or—"

The leaves overhead shrivel up and turn brown.

"What the—" Bran says as more leaves shrink, turn brittle, then flake off. "Is that you?"

"I don't think so?" I mutter against him.

The ivy loses its purchase on us and Bran is able to lift his elbows, finally breaking through.

As daylight spills in, a dark figure appears overhead, the face shrouded in the shadows of a drawn hood.

"We don't have much time," the figure says.

It's a woman, voice a little hoarse. It sounds vaguely familiar.

"Come on," she coaxes, waggling her fingers at us.

Bran sits up, bringing me with him, and then we're on our feet.

"Who are you?" I ask the figure.

She gives me a shove toward the woods. "Questions later. Running, now."

We take off.

There are more figures in hooded jackets helping the rest of our group, but we've clearly lost far too many numbers of an already too small army.

Bran and I, trailing behind the hooded figure, make our way through the sun dappled woods, then burst out the other side where the river splits the forest in two. I slide down the bank and hit the water with a loud, clumsy splash.

Bran is beside me in an instant, barely splashing at all.

"Okay," I say, sucking in a deep breath. "Now, who are you?"

The girl pulls her hood back and a long red braid spills out.

It's the Autumn Court assassin. The one who tried killing me with an arrow.

"What the fuck?" I say. "What are you doing here?"

Bran steps between us. He wasn't there when she attempted to kill me, but he doesn't need to ask questions.

The river quickly fills with our group and several other members of the Autumn Court. They're all wearing the same jackets with delicate leaves embroidered in gold around the sleeves.

No one has tried to kill us yet. So I guess that's a good sign?

"What am I doing here?" the girl asks. "Saving your ass."

"You tried to assassinate me," I point out.

The line of Bran's shoulders goes rigid. "You *what*?" There is a telling growl in his voice.

The girl's hand inches toward the dagger strapped to her hip. "Can a girl not change her mind?"

Behind her, Arion approaches us. His hand is already on the hilt of his sword, ready to unsheathe it. "Lethea," he calls. "Explain yourself."

"Well, if you must know, I came to the Summer Court upon the princess's return without the authority of the Autumn Court. My sister and I have differing opinions on the Winter Court." Lethea turns to me. Her eyes are somehow the color of autumn — a shifting brown and red and orange depending on the lighting. "No offense, but your family and mine have a long history of hating one another and you did try to kill us once."

"Well, I'm a *little* offended," I answer. "You don't even know me and you're making assumptions based on people I didn't even know."

Bran glances at me over the broad line of his shoulder. The look he gives me says he's pleased with my sass. Just as long as it's not aimed at him.

His look emboldens me, and I step around him, squaring off with Lethea.

"If I acted as recklessly as you did, I'd be killing you right now for the same reasons. And would I be justified in that?"

The line of her mouth goes thin as she grits her teeth. "No," she finally answers. "I suppose you wouldn't."

"Then can we agree not to try to kill one another in the future based solely off of what we know of our family?" I extend my hand.

Some of the buzzing and the churning of my gut has lessened.

Lethea glances at my hand, considering.

She says, "We can agree on that."

We shake.

Her hand is calloused and cracked. She's apparently not afraid to get her hands dirty.

Arion comes up alongside us, his grip on his sword easing off. "Now tell us why you're here."

"The queen of the Autumn Court would like to ally with the Winter Court."

My mouth drops open. I can't help it. "Really?"

"Yes, really." Lethea crosses her arms over her chest. "The Autumn Queen would like you to know that she recognizes the need for the balance of power. And the Summer Queen clearly does not want balance. She wants it all for herself. We're here to help stop her."

"And to put the past behind us?" I add.

Lethea nods. "A fresh start for all four courts. And hopefully the healing of the realm."

"So what did you have in mind?"

"I'm so glad you asked." She smiles at me, then turns to the woods on the opposite side of the river and lets out a shrill whistle.

The ground trembles. Once. Twice. Three times. I recognize the pattern as footsteps, but whatever is behind it must be massive.

The trees rattle, then part, finally revealing a V formation of six creatures I've never seen before.

"Holy shit," I breathe out.

"Autumn beasts?" Arion says unable to keep the surprise from his voice.

Each beast is the size of an adult elephant, but they look more like a lion with a ruff of amber hair around a face that reminds me of a fox.

On the backs of each beast is another member of the Autumn Court holding the leather reins attached to a headpiece that fits snuggly against the animals' forehead.

One of them, the beast at the forefront, runs its tongue over its lips, revealing sharp incisors.

Lethea glances back at me. "You have all of us, and six Autumn beasts at your disposal. All we ask is that once you're reinstated on the Winter Throne, you sign a treaty, one that will be signed by all four courts declaring our dedication to the balance of power and season."

Over Lethea's shoulder, I meet my brother's eyes. He should be part of this just as much as I am. After all, if the plan goes accordingly, he'll be signing that treaty too.

Arion nods at me.

To Lethea, I say, "I agree to this condition."

"Starting fresh then," she repeats. "Shall we get started?"

"I'd love nothing better. I hope your beasts are starving."

She grins at me. "They could always go for a bite."

Thirty-One

With Lethea, her Autumn Court soldiers, and the six Autumn Court beasts joining our group, we stick to the river as we head toward the Summer Palace. As we walk, we talk about the plan.

"We needed to take the Summer Queen by surprise," I say, stepping over a large rock jutting out from the river's current. "But I don't know that surprise is on our side now."

"We stick to the original plan," Arion says ahead of me.

The sun has risen above the treeline and the air has grown hotter and more humid. Sweat beads at the back of my neck. Fighting against the river's current is making the journey a bit slower, but I'm thankful for the cool water to balance out some of the day's heat.

Arion steps up on a boulder half submerged in the river, then jumps off it, splashing water.

One thing I've noticed about a lot of the fae here, or the higher ranking fae, is that they move with such grace and surety. Like they've been balancing on high wires and leaping off cliff edges since birth.

Will I ever possess that kind of grace?

Bran holds out his hand for me as we come upon a fallen branch that crosses the river from bank to bank. I frown at his hand and decide to clamber over on my own. I slip on a wet rock underfoot, then get my shirt caught on a broken branch.

Bran watches me with amusement.

"Quit smiling," I say with a grumble.

Lethea plants her hand on the branch and then practically vaults herself, clearing it easily.

Dammit.

Bran continues the conversation once I'm over the branch. "I agree with you," he says to Arion. "Sticking to the original plan is our best option. But in reverse," he adds.

Arion waits for us to catch up and thinks over the new tactic. "I think I see where you're headed with this."

Bran nods.

"I don't," I say. "Someone clue me in."

"What was your original plan?" Lethea asks.

"Use magic to cast illusions," I explain. "So we'd sneak in through a back door looking like someone else."

"What do you mean by reverse?" She looks over at Arion. Arion's face is blank, but so is hers. They are both very good at pretending to feel nothing.

Do they have history? Have they ever worked together? I never thought to ask. But there is clearly some tension there.

Lethea's expression finally changes and it's one of instant understanding. "Oh. I see." She gives Arion a tight smile. "You want to use me as the bait."

"Who better?" he challenges. "You know how to fight when your back is against the wall."

Should I be offended that he's indirectly suggesting I don't?

"Fine." She huffs out a breath. "I promised my sister I'd do whatever it took to secure peace. If playing the bait is our best option, then I guess I'm the bait."

———

We move forward with our plan, and Baspin and Bianca perform the magic they had preconceived before crossing over to the fae realm.

Originally, we'd planned to make myself, Bran, and Arion look like someone else so we could enter the Summer Palace undetected and find and locate the Summer Queen so we could put a sword in her back.

Now that she knows we're here, we have to adjust.

As Baspin and Bianca work their magic with the morning sun at their backs, I close my eyes and let the heat of daylight and the warmth of their magic envelop me.

There's a tingling along my spine and down across my arms, but it's not the same as the buzzing I've felt whenever I cross over to the fae realm. The buzzing feels wrong. The tingling feels right, like magic working the way it's supposed to work. And I realize this is one more clue as to how to zero in on my own magic. Look for that easy feeling of rightness. That's how I'll know when I'm on the correct path.

Despite having my eyes closed, there's the sensation of flashing light, then a rush of air.

I stagger back into Bran's waiting arms.

"I got you, Mouse." His voice is husky but reassuring at the soft shell of my ear.

"Wow," Bianca utters. "I wasn't sure if that would work but..."

I open my eyes and when I look over at Lethea, I see myself. She looks just like me in every way. The dark hair. The smattering of freckles. But her stance is different, her shoulders more rigid.

I glance down to see I'm wearing Lethea's Autumn Court hooded tunic. My hands are crisscrossed with scars.

"This is so weird." I look at Bran. "Is it weird for you?"

"Your scent is still the same," he tells me. "I would know you in total darkness."

His words catch me off guard and butterflies create a whirlwind in my belly. He gives me a naughty grin.

God, he knows how to get to me.

"Everyone know their places?" Arion asks.

The group nods. The six Autumn beasts go into hiding in the woods, waiting for their cue.

Lethea heads to the Summer Palace with several fae and vampire at her back.

My mission is much different and it's one that Arion and Bran fought me over.

Too risky, they said.

Too dangerous, they said.

But there's too much at stake to play it safe. I need to throw it all on the line.

I'm going to walk right in the front door.

Thirty-Two

Okay, so it may be a little risky. And while my brain is trying to tell my heart that it'll all work out in the end, the message isn't translating to the rest of my body because my hands are shaking and my legs feel weak.

We're in an alcove of evergreen trees on the edge of the Summer Palace. Arion knows most of the guards' stations and foot paths, and he assured us this was the best hiding place.

I can just make out the tall spires of the palace through the waxy tree leaves.

Bran grabs me by the wrist and yanks me into him. "Be careful, little mouse."

"As careful as I can be," I tell him.

He gives me a kiss. Quick and to the point but bites at my bottom lip, reminding me who's in charge. Being careful is an order and I'm expected to follow it.

I grin up at him.

When he's sure we've had our moment, Arion comes over. "Just make me one promise, little sister of mine. Don't kill the queen before I reach you."

"You have my word."

He gives me a quick nod and then I turn and walk toward the palace.

———

The guards stationed at the front gate are so fooled by my magical illusion that they bow their heads deeply as I pass beneath the stone archway.

I ignore them the way Arion and Lethea instructed me. Members of royal courts do not look at, speak to, or acknowledge guards.

It takes everything in me to follow this rule. Are they not worthy of a hello or a simple wave? That's the first thing I'll change at my court. Just as soon as I destroy my enemies and reclaim my throne.

Once inside the palace, I go left and then take a right and then enter a receiving room. There are several fae here, some in the middle of a game of dice, others feasting on what looks like roasted meat and sweet tarts.

At the end of the red carpet that runs from the entrance to the closed door at the back, a woman cuts me off.

She's got a long braid of red hair and perfect brown skin. Her pointed ears are capped with gold jewelry and red gems hang from piercings in her lobes.

"Greetings, Princess Lethea," she says. "State your reason for visiting. Last you were here, you were a prisoner, were you not?"

The woman arches a knowing brow.

My first instinct is to laugh like it's a big joke, and then my second instinct is to lie about it. It's not until my third instinct kicks in that I remember I'm supposed to be Lethea—cold, calculating, fearless Lethea, a fae assassin princess who also cannot lie. I keep my face blank and say, "May I please see the queen? I've been sent here with an urgent matter from the Autumn Queen."

The woman's gaze turns suspicious, and it takes everything in me not to fidget beneath her scrutiny.

Lethea probably never fidgets.

"What matter?" the woman asks.

"Confidential," I answer.

"Hmmm," she says.

The seconds grow taut. I keep my hands hanging limply by my sides.

How long will this illusion last? Is it already starting to break and she's scanning my face, seeing the shimmer of magic, the hint of my real features shining beneath?

Oh gods.

Hold it together, Jessie!

"Very well," she finally says and turns to the door. "Wait here. The queen will be right with you."

———

As I wait to be greeted by the queen, I clasp my hands behind my back and try to look bored, not anxious.

The seconds tick by. The urgency to get this over before the magic wanes builds anticipation in my gut.

I clamp my mouth shut to drive off the nausea. It doesn't work.

The group of fae playing dice at the round table behind me finishes their game and leaves.

The other smaller group whisper to one another, then shove aside their empty plates and disappear through an unmarked side door.

Now I'm all alone in the room.

I guess that's a good thing because I can let out a breath, suck in another and wait without scrutiny.

I pace.

There are several round tables in the room with bookshelves lining one wall and a giant woven tapestry on the other.

The tapestry depicts a war scene. The art is detailed and intricate and as I scan its breadth, I realize it must be the Autumn Revolt. On the one side, the fae are wearing blue and silver-blue with snowflakes embroidered around them. On the other, at the forefront, is the Summer Court surrounded by green vines and vibrant flowers. They're shown as the saviors, helping the Autumn Court at the last second when it looks like all is lost.

Would Lethea see it that way?

From the other side of the closed door, I hear a thump, then a grunt.

My instincts raise the hair along the nape of my neck.

Something is amiss.

I take a few tentative steps toward the closed door, keeping my breathing shallow so I can hear what's going on, on the other side.

I'm just about to put my ear to the door when it's yanked open and Sam appears.

"Sam?" I whisper and then check over my shoulder to make sure no one has arrived. "What are you doing here? You weren't supposed to come all the way to the palace!"

She takes me by the arm and yanks me inside, shutting the door behind us.

"Doing my part," she answers and nods at a figure kneeling on the floor.

It's the Summer Queen. And she's tied up, mouth gagged.

Sam smiles at me.

"How did you..."

"Time for details later!" Her eyes are big and bright, her hair a little mussed. "Kill her now and then let's party!"

I frown at Sam. "This wasn't the plan!"

"Who cares about plans? Here is your enemy, bound and gagged."

The Summer Queen shakes her head and tries to talk around the cloth shoved in her mouth. Only grunts make their way out.

Lethea gave me one of her blades to help round out the costume. I hold my fingers over the hilt now, itching to pull it.

This could all be over.

I could reclaim my throne.

But I promised Arion I'd wait for his arrival so he could have his revenge.

But we never talked about this scenario.

What if they're still far off? What if we miss our chance because I sat back and waited?

I will never forgive myself if I fuck up the opportunity to end this war and reclaim my throne. I'll just have to ask my brother for forgiveness.

"Be quick about it," Sam says.

I pull the blade from its sheath.

The queen fights against her bindings, her eyes watery with tears. I imagine her beginning me for mercy but the words are unintelligible.

"You destroy everything you touch," I tell her. "I can't let you keep hunting me down. I can't let you hurt the people I love."

I sink the blade into the queen's chest.

She gives a lurch and tears spill from her eyes.

I feel sorry for her, for just a minute.

But I have to harden myself to it.

She doesn't deserve my empathy.

Blood seeps from the wound and soaks through her shirt.

She fights against the bindings, groans around the gag.

The air around her shimmers bright gold.

Is she trying to use magic on me? I don't feel anything.

Her face is obscured by the shining light and when it breaks, horror washes through me.

Because the queen is no longer the queen.

She's Sam.

Thirty-Three

"It's ironic, isn't it?"

Her voice sounds behind me and I whirl around.

Where Sam stood a second ago, now stands the queen.

"Did you think you were the only one clever enough to use a decoy? To use illusion magic?"

"*No,*" I say, but it's a desperate cry. I don't want to believe my eyes.

I turn back to Sam kneeling on the floor and she lists to the side, her eyes growing heavy as the blood pours out of her body, from the wound I inflicted.

"Oh god no." I sink beside her and catch her as she spills forward. "Sam!" I hurry to untie the gag, freeing her voice. She was trying to tell me all along. She was trying to stop me. But I was too distracted by my own need for revenge.

If I'd kept my promise to Arion...

"I'm so sorry, Sam!"

In the depths of the palace, a ferocious roar echoes through the halls.

Cal.

Sam's head lulls against my shoulder. Her eyes are just slits now.

"Sam. Stay with me." I give her a shake, but she barely responds.

The horror of what I've done sends a cold rush through my veins. My vision grows watery.

"I can save her," the queen says.

I blink and several tears spill out. "How?"

"She's mortal. I'm a fae queen. My magic could easily heal her."

As the seconds tick by, Sam grows heavier in my arms as if all the life is slipping from her body.

"In exchange for what?" I ask.

"Denounce your claim to the Winter Court throne."

"And give it to you?"

She says nothing.

I don't know if that's even possible, or if the rest of the fae realm would allow it, but I don't care. All I care about is saving my best friend.

Bran will probably kill me. Arion will too.

But none of that matters if Sam isn't alive.

I suck in a breath and wipe the tears from my face with the sleeve of Lethea's tunic.

I'm just about to agree to it when a voice, barely there, nothing more than a whisper, says, "Don't."

I look down at Sam. Her eyes are barely open, her breath a raspy wheeze.

But her voice is unmistakable.

"Don't. You. Dare."

"I can't lose you too," I tell her.

The roar grows closer.

"You won't," she says. "I...promise."

I laugh through the tears. It's such a Sam thing to do. Sam always had more courage, more determination. It was the thing I admired about her most. How fearless she was. How she never cared what other people thought, and consequences were always damned.

"Okay, Sam," I say. "Okay."

Her lip quirks as if trying to smile. It's enough.

I set her down and rise to my feet.

The queen's expression has changed from one of confident victory to one of distant apprehension.

A cold draft swirls in the air. The queen shivers.

She steps back as a gust of wind sends the skirt of her dress billowing in the air.

Ice crystallizes on the wall, blooming toward the ceiling.

"You've harmed the last of my loved ones," I tell her. "And now you're going to pay for it."

Thirty-Four

The queen's hands scramble at the wall behind her. A second later, a door pops open, obscured by a mural of a summer garden. Frost covers the mural and the ice crackles when the door breaks away from its inset door jamb.

She runs.

I give chase.

I am going to end this. Today. Now.

There will be no more pain and suffering. No more tricks. No more lies.

I may have only just learned I'm fae and part of the fae realm, but I'm already tired of the battle.

Do we not all deserve peace and safety and balance?

The Summer Queen wants none of that. She is only grasping for power.

The hallway beyond the receiving room is dimly lit with softly glowing lanterns staked into the stone. But I don't need light to guide me—there is only one direction to go and I follow it, chasing the queen's shadow as it stretches over the stone, as the hall curves back and forth on itself like the body of snake.

When I finally emerge, we're in a garden and the sky is dark.

Thick clouds roll in, blotting out the sun. The air is charged and crisp.

I spot the queen's dress disappearing around a hedge row.

I run after her but come to a sudden stop.

The queen is now safely tucked behind the front lines of her army.

"Kill her!" she orders.

The fae soldiers charge toward me.

———

This is definitely not how I intended this fight to go down.

Shit.

Shit.

I got myself into this mess though, didn't I? I didn't follow the plan. I can already hear Bran in my head, chastising me for not thinking strategically, instead allowing my emotion to get the best of me.

He wouldn't be wrong.

A clap of thunder sounds in the sky and reverberates through the ground as I backtrack through the garden.

Where the hell do I go?

The army is an echo of the thunder behind me.

How many were there? A few dozen? A few hundred?

I didn't stick around long enough to find out but I'm no match for ten of them let alone ten dozen.

But I do have one trick up my sleeve.

It's questionable whether or not I can pull it off, but I have to try.

I come up against the palace wall and turn around to face the approaching army.

You are a queen, Mouse.

Now when I hear Bran's voice in my head, it's encouraging.

You are a fae queen with power beyond anyone's comprehension and this fae army doesn't stand a fucking chance.

Adrenaline surges through my body. The heat of excitement drowns out the anxiety, and the overwhelming feeling of rightness undoes the knot of tension in my gut.

"*Stop!*" I call, digging deep to find my voice.

The army comes to a sudden, jolting stop.

Their armor clanks. Their swords are frozen, some raised in the air, some held by their side.

Unease shows on their faces.

A tall woman wearing a full suit of shining golden armor grits her teeth and struggles against the command. She's at the front of the line and if I had to guess, she's the commander of this troop.

Her sword hand moves an inch.

I can feel them all fighting me.

It's like a thousand rubber bands are connected to me and they're pulling and pulling and pulling.

I stumble forward and nearly lose my balance.

The commander takes a step.

She takes another, then another. Her pace picks up.

If she makes it across this garden, I'm dead.

I press my back against the palace wall, bracing myself. "*Stop!*" I call again, but the woman somehow ignores the command and advances closer.

I feel the first sensation of a rubber band snapping.

I'm losing my grip on them.

I don't have any more weapons. I used my knife on Sam and there was no way I was going to pull it out. I learned that in first aid in the seventh grade.

And thinking about that, about Sam dying or lying dead in the Summer Palace gives me another push, helps me summon all the courage and power that I can.

But this time, I try another tactic.

I raise my hands. Pressure builds at my sternum. It feels like a war drum. A constant thump, thump of synergy and power.

The air crackles.

The commander slowly closes the distance between us, but I don't let her distract me.

Goosebumps ripple up my arms and the hair stands up along the back of my neck.

I breathe out and the breath condenses in a puff of white.

The commander raises her sword. The movement is like a movie in slow motion.

There is only five, maybe six feet between us and I'd bet her sword could easily close three of those feet.

Snowflakes swirl in the air and another rumble of thunder sounds in the distance.

"Summer Army!" the commander yells. "Hold back. I've got this one." Her dark brows sink over her eyes with menacing glee.

With the commander giving them an order to hold off, I no longer have to worry about the army. I let go of all the rubber bands, and doing so focuses my magic on one spot—on the commander.

Bran would tell me to be patient, even in war.

Not yet, Jessie.

Not yet.

The snow falls thicker.

The commander swings with her sword, but her movements are faster, picking up in speed.

I won't panic. I will not fear.

Her arrogance will be her undoing.

The sword is just inches from me.

Energy surges up from the ground and a cold wash of power comes over me. It races up my legs and pools in my belly before surging up my chest and then down my arm...where a bolt of ice forms sharp as a blade in my hand.

I sink to my knees. The commander's blade cuts the air above me, just inches from where I was. And she's made one vital mistake: she's left herself completely open.

I heave upward with the ice and it pierces her side. She gives a loud grunt.

I rock back, planting one foot in the ground, using the other knee to brace myself. I shove with more force.

The blade breaks bone. Blood gushes from the wound, down the crystal-clear ice, down my arm.

The commander coughs and blood splatters over her open mouth.

Her eyes get big and she quickly turns pale.

Her sword drops to the ground.

"Looks like you didn't have this one after all," I tell her right before she drops to her knees.

Thirty-Five

There is a moment of silence while the commander hangs on my blade, the life draining out of her.

Her army stands behind, stunned.

As her weight sags forward, I rein the power back in and the blade melts. The water runs down my arm, sinking into my skin. A cool rightness floods my veins.

I duck out from beneath the dead commander as she finally tips over, her body thudding to the ground.

There is a clatter from the army as some of the soldiers whisper amongst each other, looking for orders or direction.

Thunder still rumbles in the distance.

What now?

The queen is still out there. She is still the supreme commander of these soldiers. If she wants them to attack, they will.

The fae at the front line share a look.

A stocky man with a thick golden beard steps forward, sword already drawn.

"Summer Army," he says, his voice reverberating across the garden. He hoists his sword into the air like a banner of war. "On me."

With a roaring cry, he races toward me and the soldiers form up behind him.

How long can I hold them off?

Where are Bran and Arion?

"Wait," I call and hold up my hands. As if I can talk my way out of this one.

The ground trembles with their approach.

I can't summon enough ice swords to take them all on.

My ears grow hot and my head rings.

This is it.

This is how I die.

And the Summer Queen will win. She will dance over my corpse.

I dip back down into that well of power, because if I'm going down, I'm going down swinging.

But right before the bearded fae reaches me, an arrow pierces his back.

He staggers forward.

More arrows slice through the air, lodging themselves into the attacking fae with dangerous precision.

Several go down immediately, dead on impact.

Many others collapse, howling in pain.

Appearing, almost out of the shadows, are the Faeries of Suffering.

———

Even though I know Draggun struck a deal with us, that he's supposedly on our side, goosebumps still run down my arms at the sight of him.

The bearded soldier is on one knee just ten paces away from me, struggling to break off the arrow sticking out of his back.

But the moment he sees Draggun, any color that remains in his face drains away immediately.

"What are you—" he starts, but Draggun clamps a gloved hand over the man's mouth, silencing him.

"Let me tell you a tale, lieutenant," Draggun says. "Your queen made me a bargain. I know you know that part."

The man's brow furrows over his eyes.

"What you don't know is what she bartered with."

The man's shoulders go rigid.

"She promised me your suffering. All of your brethren. One night a year for the rest of your immortal lives."

The man tries to get up but Draggun shoves him back down and then tsk-tsks like the soldier is a misbehaving child.

"The problem is, of course, that you wouldn't survive a night with me." He smiles, sharp teeth gleaming. "So I took the vampire's offer instead because—*and here's the best part.*" He leans in and lowers his voice to a menacingly wicked tenor. "I still get your suffering."

He shoves the arrow deeper, then twists.

The soldier screams into Draggun's gloved hand, thrashing beneath the pain and the pressure. But Draggun holds steady even though on appearances, he's at least half as small as the lieutenant.

It's hard to watch.

It's not at all what I wanted.

But Draggun must be telling the truth. No other fae can lie. Which means the Summer Queen was bartering with some of her most loyal soldiers in order to win this fight.

I almost feel bad for the man.

Draggun twists the arrow deeper and the man's eyes finally roll back in his head and he falls sideways into a cluster of white flowers.

The Fairy of Suffering hangs his head back and tastes the last of the lieutenant's pain, his black mark swirling over his face.

When he refocuses, he looks over at me. "Winter Princess. We'll handle the rest of this." He gestures with a flourish at the mayhem in the garden. The Fairies of Suffering are destroying what remains of the queen's army. And everywhere I look, the dark fae are feasting on the pain and suffering.

"You'll find your enemy deep in the Summer labyrinth," Draggun goes on. "If you want her dead, I suggest you hurry."

"Why?"

"Because there was a second part of my deal with her. She wanted an escape plan, so I showed her the way into the Forbidden Garden—my domain. It's on the other side of the labyrinth. If she reaches it, you will likely lose her. The Forbidden Garden is no place for a princess like yourself."

"And is it a place for queens?"

He smiles, flashing me sharp incisors. "Oh no. If she steps into our realm, we will pick the meat from her bones."

One way or another, she'd be dead. But there would be no justice in that.

And I wouldn't discount her so quickly. If she found a way to survive this Forbidden Garden, she'd return and we'd be fighting this battle all over again.

"Which way?" I ask.

Draggun points over his shoulder, where the soldiers had lined up, where the Summer Queen disappeared deeper into the garden.

"Follow the cobblestone path. Keep to the left. You'll find the labyrinth soon enough."

"Tha—" I catch myself before I can say thanks. Draggun's smile deepens. "You've been most helpful," I correct.

Behind him, his soldiers are a blur of movement as they fight what little remains of the army.

"Go on then," he says. "And leave us to our prize."

Careful not to get caught in the fighting, I skirt my way around the battle and slip into the garden.

———

Once I'm behind a hedge row, it's like the garden swallows up all noise beyond it.

The sound of fighting and suffering is immediately gone.

I take quiet steps on the pale cobblestone path through the main garden, sticking to the left as Draggun instructed.

I only hope Bran and Arion will find me. Bran can usually smell me anywhere. I have faith he'll catch up considering this was never our plan. He and Arion were supposed to meet me in the palace.

It seems stupid now, to have fallen for the queen's illusion of Sam. It was an amateur mistake.

It takes everything in me not to turn around and run back to my best friend, or look for my vampire boyfriend, or my fae brother.

I've never been spiritual or religious, but I have faith that *this* is the right path.

I just have to keep going.

I have to trust myself and my instincts and—

A hand clamps over my mouth. Bran's whisper is at my ear a second later. "It's me, Mouse."

There is a moment of dread and fear that I've been tricked again, that the queen has used illusion magic. But then I inhale and I know that scent. I know the smell of Bran. That amber and leather and musk.

Happy tears spring in my eyes and I twist around, latching on to him. I'm so grateful for him, I could scream.

When I pull back, I spot Arion behind him.

"You aren't supposed to be out here," Arion says.

Bran's jaw flexes as if he too is annoyed by this deviation but he says nothing.

"I'm sorry. Everything happened so quickly."

My brother nods and looks beyond us. "She's out here. I can sense it."

"Draggun said she's running for his realm. He said it's on the other side of the labyrinth."

Arion snaps his attention back to me. "Truly? She must be desperate."

"I don't want to lose her."

His mouth sets in a grim line and he nods. "Neither do I. So we won't. Come on."

———

Arion knows the way to the labyrinth so there is no more guessing on direction. We find the entrance soon enough, but before we slip inside, my brother stops us.

"There is something you should know about this place."

"Go on," Bran says.

"It can sometimes change, depending on its mood. Stay close by my side. Do not split up. Or you may never find your way out."

I glance at Bran. His pale, handsome face is unreadable.

"Should we be worried?" I ask Arion.

"Not if you listen to me."

That's not exactly soothing.

"All right." I tuck several loose strands of hair behind my ear. "Let's do this then?"

"Is that a question, little mouse?" Bran's eyes are glowing amber in the dim lighting. "Or an order?"

His words are dark and husky, but there is a playful edge to them too.

"An order."

"Good girl."

"For fuck's sake." Arion rolls his eyes and walks into the labyrinth. "Save that shit for later."

I smile up at Bran and he steals a quick, deep kiss. When he breaks it, he says, "We will end this enemy and when we are finished, I will tie you to my bed and have my way with you until you beg for mercy."

"I can still hear you!" Arion says.

On my tiptoes, I whisper into Bran's ear. "I dare you."

His eyes flare and I know he will take that dare any day of the week.

Thirty-Six

Arion takes the lead. He turns right, then left, then right again. We turn so many times, deeper and deeper into the labyrinth, that I quickly lose track of any sense of direction. Thank god he's leading the way. We'd be lost immediately without him.

"Do you know how to get to the Forbidden Garden?" I ask him.

I'm sandwiched between him and Bran.

"Most of us know the general direction, but the garden will only reveal itself to those who have been invited or to those whom it covets."

We keep walking. I strain my hearing for any movement beyond the tall hedge rows. Here they must be at least seven feet high. They tower over even Bran.

"Do you hear or smell anything?" I ask him.

He gives me a nod. "We're close."

My heart spikes in my chest.

"Is it just her? Is she with another army?"

"She has only the one army," Arion explains as he peeks around a corner in the hedges and as he does, a vine as thick as a jungle snake leaps out of the hedge, twinning itself around him, locking his arms at his sides.

Bran grabs Arion's leg as the vine tries to yank him back.

"Don't let go!" Arion says with a growl.

"I won't if you fight your way out!" Bran plants his feet.

"That's rather difficult when I have no use of my arms!"

"Will you two quit bickering?"

I get around Bran and hold up my arms.

"Jessie," Bran warns, teeth gritted as he fights at the plant.

The more I do this, the easier it is to identify my magic and grab hold of it, harnessing it. It's almost embarrassing how hard it was at one point, how I thought I would never control it.

The air immediately takes on a cold snap and the leaves of the vine circling Arion's body first turn brown, then frost over.

The chill seeps into my bones but it's the kind of cold that feels like home.

The vine cracks like split ice, then shatters.

Arion falls to the ground, sucking in a deep breath.

"She's near," Bran says, his eyes moving over the hedges.

"How near?" I ask.

There is a crack to our left.

Arion hurries to his feet, sword drawn.

Another crack. A rustle of leaves.

The hedge row beside us gives a giant, heaving tremble.

And then it uproots itself, branches twisting and curling until it takes the shape of a man.

"That can't be good," I mutter.

"Run!" Arion yells as, down the line, a dozen more hedge people emerge.

———

Arion takes the lead again, racing through what remains of the labyrinth. My breath huffs out, lungs burning. I'm no Summer Court soldier, no immortal vampire. I'm no runner.

A vine snaps out. Arion lances it off with the swing of his sword. We keep going, the hedge men close behind.

"What's the plan?" Bran shouts.

"Get away!" Arion yells back.

That's no plan.

We stumble into the center of the labyrinth and the hedge men line up behind us.

And there, standing in front of a giant, gurgling fountain is the Summer Queen.

———

Flowers are blooming chaotically at her feet. A daisy rising up, petals unfurling, then shriveling up a second later, only to be replaced with a buttercup, then an iris.

All around her, Summer is blooming and dying.

The queen is standing with her hands clasped in front of her, her back straight. She appears powerful and regal, but it's impossible to ignore the sheen of sweat on her forehead, the wild tangle of her hair.

I know how much effort it took me to control her army with my voice. How much effort is it taking her to control her hedge men?

"We could have found common ground, Jessie." Her voice carries above the gurgling water.

"That wasn't possible. Not when you wanted to steal power for yourself."

Bran and Arion break apart, forming a half circle with me at the head.

The queen snaps her fingers and the hedge men march forward. They're taller than all of us, wider too, and they quickly have us scooped up in the wide span of their arms.

Two take Bran. Two more take Arion. One wraps its arms around me like a bear hug, locking me in place. A vine whips out, clamping over my mouth, stealing any chance I may have to use my voice.

Bran struggles. Arion tries to hack with his blade.

The queen stalks forward.

The closer she gets, the easier her struggle is to see. Eyes bloodshot, bags beneath. Her skin has a sickly pallor to it.

She starts to speak, to tell me all the reasons she deserves power and I don't. She tells me how I've made a terrible mistake. That I should have married Maven and bowed before her.

And I realize as the hedge man's grip slackens, as the queen takes a raspy breath, that while she holds the title of queen, she is just a girl, just like me, desperate for power over her own life.

But she holds no power over me.

The queen cuts herself off and her eyes dart to my forehead.

The ice crown is light but I sense its presence just the same.

When I wear it, I feel whole.

Hope spreads through my body.

Crystal blue light softens the darkness around me.

The leaves of the hedge man curl up on themselves, then glisten with frost, before pulling free of the branches, flitting away.

When he is barren, when he wears the coat of winter, the hedge man opens his arms and lets me walk right out.

The queen's mouth drops open.

Thundering footsteps sound through the labyrinth.

The ground trembles.

"No," the queen says, sensing the inevitability of it all. She stumbles back as the branches around the labyrinth's center part for the herd of Autumn beasts.

"No!" she shouts. "No!"

The beasts barrel through what remains of the hedge men, shredding them limb from limb.

Soon Bran is free. Then Arion.

The queen motions with her arm, lashing out at me with the thorny vines of a rose bush.

My barren hedge man steps in front of me, taking the brunt of the rose's wrath.

"*Surrender*," I say.

The queen immediately sinks to her knees. Her shoulders shake as she fights it.

I see her resolve crumbling.

She was so desperate to restrain me with her power, to show her might, that she forgot one important thing: all of the seasons exist here, in the same space, present in some way at all times. The seed buried in the frozen earth of winter. Sprouting green in the spring. Blooming bright in the summer. Casting its seeds again in the autumn.

The hedge man, too, is all seasons.

The whole point is to find that balance in all, for all of us to hold equal power.

"*Do not fight*," I order.

Ice crystals form along my arm.

Snow falls softly between us.

Arion comes over carrying his sword in his hand.

"Arion," the queen begins. "This is not who you are."

"You ordered me to kill my own mother." His voice shakes on the word *mother*, and I can't help but think he has years left of healing and grieving.

"She betrayed us!" the queen goes on. "She birthed a bastard! Then tried to start a war!"

Arion hoists his sword up.

"Don't do this," she says.

"You could have had anyone do your dirty work. But you made me do it. You created this monster, did you not? And the dirty work isn't quite finished."

"Arion, no—"

He jabs forward with his blade, sinking it into her heart.

Her eyes get big and her body gives a violent shake as blood gushes from the wound.

Her gaze loses focus, but she tries finding me just past Arion.

"You...remind me...of her," she says and smiles, blood splattering from her mouth. "I don't...know...if that's...a good...or bad—" And then she falls back into the earth, her eyes slipping closed.

Thirty-Seven

I'm not sure how long we stand there, staring at the lifeless body of the Summer Queen.

It feels like a lifetime.

The air is still around us save for the occasional snuffling of the Autumn Beasts.

Is it really over?

I'm not quite sure I believe it.

I glance over at my brother, his sword still in hand, blood dripping from the blade. His face is unreadable, but his nostrils flare with a deep breath and he barely blinks, his gaze trained on the queen.

It's like we're all waiting for the next trick, the next con, the next shoe to drop.

It doesn't.

The queen is dead and we are victorious.

But I think we all know that there is more work to be done.

Behind us, there is a shuffling of feet, a rustling of branches.

What remains of the Summer Court assembles in a circle around the center of the maze. Men in decorated tunics and women in bright gauzy dresses. Others with vibrant makeup and golden thread woven into their hair, dressed in fine linen and embroidered summer cloaks.

A man steps forward. He wears a jacket made of dark green suede with leaves embroidered in gold across the shoulders. It's clear he's someone of importance. It's in the way he stands, shoulders back, hands clasped in front of him, that gives it away.

The man tilts his chin, regarding my brother with distant interest.

"Who is that?" I ask Arion in a whisper.

"Ozaron," he answers. "He is High Lord of the Summer Court."

Great.

"Does he rank higher than you?"

"Not technically," Arion says below his breath.

"But?"

"But he could challenge me for the throne and he may very well win, given the support he has in court."

I square my shoulders, ready for another fight.

But then Ozaron turns to address the court and says, "All hail, the Summer King."

And then the crowd sinks to their knees for my brother.

———

I leave Arion to handle his new court and his new position.

I need to find Sam. I don't want to think about what I may find, but I have to see her.

As we hurry back to the palace, I tell Bran what happened, my voice shaking with remorse.

When we reach the palace wall, Bran stops me, his hand on my shoulder pulling me around. "You don't have to worry, little mouse."

"But I stabbed her and then I left her and—"

"Jessie!"

I look up at the balcony that overhangs the garden. Sam is there at the railing.

My throat tightens, my eyes burning. "Oh my god," I say. "Is this real? This isn't another trick?"

Behind Sam, Cal saunters out. He's covered in blood, even though he doesn't appear wounded. I think it might be Sam's.

Sam races down the stairs and I run over to her, wrapping her in a hug. She feels solid and warm and *real*.

"How did this happen?" My voice is muffled by her tangle of hair. She's a complete mess, but she's *alive*.

Sam groans and pulls away. She eyes Cal over her shoulder where he's literally leaping over the balcony to join Bran at the edge of the garden.

"It's a long story," Sam says. "But Cal..." Some color flashes in her cheeks.

"He what?"

"The only way to save me," she says, "was to bond me to him."

My eyes get big. "*Shut. Up.*"

"Don't make a big deal out of it."

I clamp my mouth shut, eyes still big and round. "Mmmhmm."

She tilts her head, frowning. "I'm serious."

"Of course."

"Jessie."

I'm practically vibrating with excitement.

"Don't," she warns.

But I can't help myself.

"Oh. My. God Sam! You're bonded to the Midnight Alpha! Holy shit!" I hug her again, squeezing her tight, and she lets out a huff of air.

"Stop it. I don't want Cal thinking this is a thing."

"It IS a thing," he says from afar.

"Whatever." Sam lowers her voice. "It's not."

"It is," he says again.

"Stop listening in on my conversations!" she shouts back at him.

Bran laughs. I try to hide my grin.

"You both are adorable," I tell Sam.

"Oh, shut up," she says and then hooks her arm around my shoulders. "So did you defeat that bitch of a queen?"

I lick my lips and look out over the garden where the Summer Court is slowly trickling back toward the palace.

"Yes," I answer.

Sam holds up her hand, waiting.

We high-five and then laugh.

"Good job."

I snort. "I just helped take out a fae queen and you act like I got an A on an essay."

Sam shrugs. "I mean, pretty much the same thing, right?"

I look over at my best friend, alive and breathing, and I hang my head back and laugh.

Thirty-Eight

Arion demands a fae funeral fit for the former queen. The fae don't like to prolong these things, I learn, and by the following night, we're in an opulent gathering room where the queen is laid out on a stone altar, candles lit all around her, lanterns glittering above us. There are flowers everywhere.

Arion stands behind the altar, a new crown sitting atop his head.

He looks every bit a king in a fresh outfit of emerald green and gold.

"We say our final farewell to our former queen of the Summer Court. May she rest in eternal peace," he says, his voice booming around the room.

One by one, the fae approach the altar and leave a rose on the queen's body. Because I don't think it's right that I take part, I stay in the back with Bran beside me.

"He'll make a good king," Bran says.

I watch Arion as he nods to each and every member of the Summer Court who leaves a rose behind.

"I think so too."

Bran takes my hand in his, his cold fingers threading with mine. "And you will make a great queen."

I snort. "Well, that remains to be seen, doesn't it?"

"Mouse," he warns in that growly, demanding voice of his. "Don't."

My cheeks warm. "I can't help it."

"Try that again," he says and even though we're having a conversation far from sex, I still react as if we are, that slow heat rising up between my legs.

"I will make a great queen," I tell him, head held high, a smile playing on my lips.

His amber eyes flare bright gold. "Good girl."

———

There is a celebration of life and a feast after the queen's funeral, which I find hilarious considering she took so many lives just to hold on to her power. But this is Arion's court, and I suppose he knows the fae much better than I do. Or maybe the fae use any excuse to throw a party. I'm just not in the mood. And I'm especially not in the mood after I helped end the queen's life. I can't exactly celebrate it.

Arion finds Bran and me as we slip out of the palace's grand front entrance. Cal and Sam and the rest of the Midnight vampires have already returned home.

"Little sister," Arion says and hearing him call me that makes me want to burst into happy tears.

I don't want to look like a sappy dork, so I suck it up and turn to him hoping the glow of the hanging lanterns outside the palace door don't catch the tears in my eyes.

Arion stops in front of me, hands folded behind his back. "Thank you," he says. "I know you had your own agenda, and with good reason, but I am here now because of you."

"Don't you know you're not supposed to thank a fae?"

He smiles. "I'm willing to risk it." And then he comes forward and embraces me.

It catches me off guard and I go stiff in his arms for a second before finally sinking into him.

Warmth blooms in my chest. I think out of all of this, gaining a brother is the best part.

"We did this together," I remind him.

He plants a brotherly kiss on my forehead. "So we did."

When we pull away, Arion glances at one of his guards and snaps his fingers. The guard comes to attention. "Ready a horse for the Winter Princess and her consort."

I laugh nervously as I check Bran's expression for a reaction. I guess consort really is the best way to describe him in this context, but he probably thinks it's meant to be an insult. Doesn't he?

But his face betrays none of that. If anything, he looks like he wears it well.

"What's the horse for?" I ask. "We can walk back to Midnight."

The guard darts away to fulfill his order.

"There's one place you should visit before you go," Arion says.

"Where?"

"The Winter Palace."

———

The horse given to us is a giant black mare with a dark mane braided and twisted in intricate knots and decorated with jewels of emerald and sapphire. She's standoffish toward Bran until he approaches her slowly from the front, hand extended. She gives him a sniff and Bran murmurs to her so softly I can barely hear.

Finally, she lifts her head and chuffs at him and he runs his hand down her snout.

"I've never ridden a horse before," I say.

"Don't worry, little mouse." He offers me his hand to help hoist me up. "I spent over a century riding them."

As soon as we're in the saddle, the reins in Bran's hands, the mare takes off.

She seems to know the way and Bran doesn't fight her. He keeps the reins in one hand, his other arm wrapped tightly around my middle, holding me in the saddle and against his chest.

The ride is exhilarating and slightly terrifying. I don't know how fast a normal horse runs, but it feels like the fae mare could outrun the Bimmer. Or maybe it's just the illusion of speed, with the forest hugging closely, the darkness closer still.

When the forest breaks, we emerge on an overgrown field, and there, in the distance, is a many-spired palace, and rising up, sharp behind it, is a mountain edged in snow and moonlight.

Even though the heat is still present, summer still retreating, goosebumps rise on my arms and down my neck.

I don't want to cry, but...

"It's beautiful," I say on a breath.

Bran coaxes the mare forward and she navigates the overgrown field nimbly until her horseshoes clomp on cobblestones that poke through the moss.

We pass a dry fountain, a figure of stone in the center. And just past the fountain is what remains of a wide road lined with tall, overgrown evergreen trees. There are more stone statues here, some covered in moss and ivy.

"It's so quiet." Even my voice sounds loud in the liminal space.

Bran slips down from the mare and then helps me off. "Stay," he tells her and she turns to the overgrowth, finding herself a snack.

"This is...weird." I take a few tentative steps toward the palace. It's more of a castle in contrast to the Summer Palace. The Winter Palace is made of solid dark stone, with sharp spires and large rectangular windows.

Bran goes up the front steps and stops with his hand on the curved iron handle of the giant front door. The dark wood is strapped in iron and dotted with iron tacks. "Are you ready, *princess*?"

I swallow.

I'm not sure I am, but when will I ever be? Probably never. I don't think a girl can ever be ready to become a queen when just a year ago she was a barista trying to escape a life she never felt like she fit.

"I like Mouse better," I tell him.

"Very well." He presses the handle and the latch clanks open. "Are you ready, little mouse?"

And then he gives the door a nudge and the Winter Palace beckons me in.

———

I can't believe this is the end!

I started writing Hot Vampire in the summer of 2021. The beginnings of Jessie's story had been sitting on a computer file for months and months. I loved Jessie. I loved the world she lived in. But I never could have imagined her story would carry through the next three years of my life. That I would not only witness her growth, but my own through her.

Now it's 2024 and her story has come to an end.
cue the happy tears

If you've made it this far, thank you so much for reading. Thank you for rooting for Jessie (and loving on Bran!). I appreciate every single one of you.

If you want just a little bit more of Jessie and Bran, and are wondering what they're up to now that she's reclaimed her birthright, I've written a bonus epilogue for you!

You can download it at the QR code below, or visit here: https://BookHip.com/CBMRKXH

ALSO BY NIKKI ST. CROWE

VICIOUS LOST BOYS

The Never King

The Dark One

Their Vicious Darling

The Fae Princes

The Vicious Lost Boys Omnibus

DEVOUR DUOLOGY

Devourer of Men

WRATH & RAIN TRILOGY

Ruthless Demon King

Sinful Demon King

Vengeful Demon King

Wrath & Reign Omnibus

CURSED VAMPIRES

A Dark Vampire Curse

MIDNIGHT HARBOR

Hot Vampire Next Door: Book One

Hot Vampire Next Door: Book Two

Hot Vampire Next Door: Book Three

Hot Vampire Next Door: Book Four

Hot Vampire Next Door: Book Five

Secrets Drenched in Blood: The Complete Midnight Harbor Series

ABOUT THE AUTHOR

Nikki St. Crowe is a USA Today and No. 1 Amazon Bestselling Author specializing in dark, spicy romantasy where the villain gets the girl and the girl gets the power.

As a teen mom, Nikki found solace in books and started writing when she was just sixteen. Back then she wrote (*very bad*) vampire romance and now, many, many years later, not much has changed (other than the quality).

These days, when Nikki isn't writing or daydreaming about villains and anti-heroes, she can either be found in the woods or at home with her husband and daughter.

NIKKI'S NEWSLETTER:
www.subscribepage.com/nikkistcrowe

JOIN NIKKI'S SUBSTACK
https://nikkistcrowe.substack.com/

VISIT NIKKI ON THE WEB AT:
www.nikkistcrowe.com

instagram.com/nikkistcrowe

facebook.com/authornikkistcrowe

amazon.com/Nikki-St-Crowe/e/B098PJW25Y

threads.net/@nikkistcrowe

bsky.app/profile/nikkistcrowe.bsky.social

bookbub.com/profile/nikki-st-crowe

tiktok.com/@nikkistcrowe

www.ingramcontent.com/pod-product-compliance
Lightning Source LLC
Chambersburg PA
CBHW061102310726
48974CB00002B/359